Chateau Ella

Also by Hilary Norman:

IN LOVE AND FRIENDSHIP

HILARY NORMAN

Chateau Ella

**Delacorte
Press**

Published by
Delacorte Press
The Bantam Doubleday Dell Publishing Group, Inc.
666 Fifth Avenue
New York, New York 10103

Library of Congress Cataloging in Publication Data

Norman, Hilary.
    Château Ella: a novel / by Hilary Norman.
        p.   cm.
    ISBN 0-440-50018-4
    I. Title.
PR6064.0743C44   1988
823'.914—dc19   88-16146
                                                              CIP

Manufactured in the United States of America

October 1988

10   9   8   7   6   5   4   3   2   1

BG

For my mother

For my mother

ACKNOWLEDGMENTS

I owe thanks to numerous people and organizations for their assistance during the research and writing of this novel, but I would especially like to mention the following (in alphabetical order): Estelle and David Amsellem; Dr. Herman Ash; Barbara and Jon Ash; Howard Barmad; Carolyn Caughey; George Derbyshire; Howard D. Deutsch; Jackie Farber; John Hawkins; Maggie and Mike of Maggie's Krooked Cafe, Tannersville, New York; Susan Reid; Nicholas Shulman; Imre Szilagyi; Dr. Jonathan Tarlow; Michael Thomas; Rae White.

Pine Orchard,
New York
June 11, 1986

Using every ounce of her flagging strength, Ella Bogarde half dragged, half shoved the massive wrought-iron gates in a supreme effort to close them. They had stood open to all visitors, an impressive twelve-foot salute, for ten years, day and night, spring, summer, autumn, and winter. Now they grated, scraped, and stuck on the gravel driveway and, at the last, no matter how hard she toiled, they refused with maddening, inanimate obstinacy to shut completely.

Ella stood back, hands on hips, gasping from exertion and on the verge of tears. She stared up at the lovely gilded logo and rubbed fiercely at her eyes, smearing the mascara.

Château Bogarde

"You're *closed,* damn you," she said through gritted teeth, "whether you like it or not!"

Turning around, she saw the four dogs, sitting in a straggly line at the side of the road that led up to the hotel. Eight eyes gazed adoringly at her, four amiable tongues panted steadily.

"And you can all stop staring at me like that," she told them darkly. "All good things come to an end—it's a well-known fact."

The animals, all Irish wolfhounds—two of them full-grown, the other two six-month-old puppies already the height of mature

German shepherds—continued to regard her. The smallest of the adult dogs, a brindle bitch with bushy brows and captivating cinnamon eyes, stood up, trotted over to Ella's side, and pushed her elbow with her nose, whining softly.

"*Je comprends bien,* Aphrodite," Ella said more gently. "You're missing her, aren't you?" She bent to embrace her. "Believe me, sweetheart, I know just how you feel."

Three nights ago, there had been five of them, but then the dark, bloody mayhem had destroyed it all, ending all normality.

Ella shivered in spite of the sun's warmth, and straightened. Aphrodite leaned heavily against her, shedding rough fur all over Ella's old, battered Calvin Klein jeans.

"All right," she said to the dogs, fighting to be decisive, "what do we always do when we have a crisis?"

Aphrodite wagged her tail, and three more canine bottoms bounced eagerly into life.

"That's right, my clever ones," she praised them. "We walk!" Her mouth trembled. "Only this time, *mes petites,* I think we'd have to walk every single mile of this whole state to get even close to solving our problems."

With an apathy totally alien to her, Ella began to trudge down the steep mountain road, surrounded by boisterous, snuffling animals. Normally, when she walked, she stayed up inside the boundaries of Bogarde land, but this morning, of all mornings, she needed, with a desperation that was all-consuming, to get as far away as possible, to escape.

She was assailed by contradictory feelings. Half of her longed to be with the people she loved and who loved her; but the other half—the stronger half—was horribly, miserably aware that there was no one alive who could help her today.

Plodding unhappily down the road, Ella looked back at the walls and hedgerows that bordered the land, there to protect the guests who paid so willingly, so eagerly for their days and nights of pampered semiprivacy inside the estate's two hundred acres. And yet, freedom had always been part of the hotel's appeal, freedom to roam at will anywhere and everywhere, through the immaculate flower gardens and tangled woods, over the sweeping lawns and into the vegetable patches that she and Harry and Krisztina had created so lovingly at the edge of this stark mountain, nearly three thousand feet above the Hudson River.

How safe they had all blithely assumed they were, she reflected bitterly, how shielded by the security guards and electronic alarm systems, and by the elemental stability of the mountain itself. And how wrong, how appallingly wrong they had all been!

She heard a sound—a new sound, inconsistent with the heartaching joyfulness of the songbirds; a familiar sound that was not unpleasant, but that this morning raised the hackles on Ella's neck.

A car.

"Merde," she said, and called the dogs to heel. "Why can't they leave us alone?" More policemen, or worse, a fresh TV crew, come to intrude on a little highly commercial grief. She gritted her teeth and clenched her fists.

The car appeared, gleaming white with dark-tinted windows. A Rolls-Royce convertible.

Ella managed a wry smile. Neither the State Police nor the TV stations, nor even *The New York Times,* would send their employees in a car like this one.

The car passed her, slowing to avoid her and the dogs, then accelerating again toward the hotel.

Ella hesitated. So someone had slipped through Louis Dettlinger's efficient net, had they?

"Tough," she said, with unaccustomed harshness, and carried on walking.

Less than ten minutes later the car reappeared and drew up at her right shoulder. The driver's window slid noiselessly down, and the chauffeur, in gray uniform, looked impassively out at her.

"Pardon me, ma'am," he said, "but we're looking for the entrance to the hotel."

"Oh?"

"Château Bogarde," he said. "Gate's back there, but it's all shut up."

"Maybe it needs opening."

"Wouldn't shift—must have been closed for years."

"Oh." She resisted a wan smile.

The rear window whirred gracefully down, and a woman, porcelain-skinned and around seventy, peered out. "You may know it by another name, my dear," she said pleasantly. "They call it Château Ella."

"They do," Ella said.

"Oh, good, you do know it." She paused. "Do you by any chance know where the main entrance is?"

"There isn't one," Ella replied.

"Are you sure?"

"Perfectly."

The woman eyed Ella curiously, wondering how a kennel maid —albeit a kennel maid with the most unusual flame-gold hair, remarkable violet eyes, and a face that was enviably lovely without even a scrap of makeup—came to be wearing a pair of hundred-dollar designer jeans and a Dior original blouse.

"We followed all the signs," she said plaintively. "We were sure we were on the right road."

"You are."

"Really?" she said, surprised. "But then why is it all shut up like that? Perhaps there was a bell that we missed?"

"No," Ella said, "there's no bell. The hotel is closed."

"Closed!" The third occupant of the car, a dark-suited man with thick white hair and a red face, leaned past the woman. "It can't be closed!"

"I'm afraid it is," Ella told him mildly. Where on earth had these people *been* for the last five days?

"But we have reservations!"

"Now then, honey," the woman soothed him. "It's nothing to do with this young lady."

Ella backed away from the car and called the dogs. Her head was beginning to throb, and she wished these poor people would just disappear and leave her alone. This was exactly why she'd made the unprecedented decision to shut down her beloved hotel—she simply could not cope, could not even contemplate being able to cope ever again.

"If she knows that it's closed, she must know *why*. God damn it, ask her!"

"I'm sorry," the woman apologized to Ella, "but we're both terribly disappointed. This is the first chance we've had for a vacation in over a year—my husband's such a busy man, you know . . ."

"Yes, of course," Ella said vaguely, trying to sidle away and beginning to feel horribly guilty.

"And normally," the other woman swept on, "we'd go to Europe, but so many of our friends have recommended Château Bogarde, they all say it's simply the best in America and—"

"Oh, for Christ's sake," the man interrupted irritably. "If she doesn't know anything, okay—but let's get the hell off this godforsaken mountain and go someplace civilized where they have some Scotch and a telephone!"

"All right, dear," the woman said peaceably, still looking at Ella. "Perhaps you know of a suitable place in the area?"

Ella took a moment.

"I'd go for the Beekman Arms up in Rhinebeck," she said, and flushed crimson.

It was a good twenty seconds after the last purring note of the car's engine had faded before the full impact of what had just happened hit Ella. Her arms began to tremble, her stomach churned, her knees buckled, and she sank onto the grass verge, oblivious to the damp morning dew that sank into her jeans and chilled her.

For a decade, Ella had run Château Bogarde, had nurtured it, driven it, loved it with a passion. She had become a consummate hotelkeeper over the years, and her house had come to be known as one of the greats. An American great, even though its roots had drawn their life juices from the fertile soils of Europe, even though the rich, colorful threads of Hungary, France, and England were all woven into the cloth that embraced the estate. It was American breath that had blown vitality and soul into her hotel—if Europe had been the mother, America had been the father, impregnating the European bricks and mortar with the American spirit of warmth, hospitality, and courage. And the result had been more than just a first-rate luxury hotel nestling in the bosom of New York State; it was a magical, elegant American *legend*, a place that had become known as Château Ella.

And now the legend was destroyed, and Ella felt as if she had witnessed the soft underbelly of some lovely, mythical creature being ripped cruelly apart by a rampaging monster. Suddenly she knew she could not bear to look on the face of her creation, could not imagine the raw wounds ever healing. And as if the whole, tragic affair had needed a final, ironic underscoring, Ella had just been faced with that most precious of all things to a hotelkeeper—guests—and with a final, crushing swish of her sword, she had done the unthinkable and sent them away.

She buried her face in her hands, and almost instantly felt a cold nose against her cheek and heard a soft breath in her ear. She knew that it was Aphrodite, and the dog's gentle love was almost more than she could bear.

She heard moaning, and realized it came from herself. She

seldom openly cried; it was hard to surrender to emotion when one was a mother, when there was always someone around to care, when one was in the public eye. Even in the midst of horror, she had been too numb, too angry, too *afraid* to give way, but this morning, as she sat hunched over in the June sunshine with the big dog pressing comfortingly against her side, a vast wave of grief and weakness overwhelmed her. Slowly, painfully, the tears welled up in her eyes, her mouth trembled, and she gave a great, shuddering sigh.

At last, Ella wept.

Hungary
October 13, 1919

The woman stumbled along the empty road, a great white dog at her heels, a small, sleeping bundle clasped tightly in her arms. Exhausted from running, worn down by hiding, she fought to contain her despair in silence, yet still it escaped from her in soft, anguished moans, tearing at the cool night air. This, she knew now, was the fiercest, most hideous pain of all—it sapped her strength, drained her soul, ripped through her like a monstrous tidal wave. Even death itself, death which would soon follow as surely as the next Sabbath, would be easier to bear than this.

Dawn, soft and luminous, was breaking over the small town as she reached the church steps. Before long, people would be on the streets, scurrying out to work and provide, but now, mercifully, there was still no one to see or to question her.

Mercifully.

Carefully, she wrapped her bloodstained shawl about the already swaddled baby and put her down on the broad top step.

"Janka, sit," she said to the dog.

Her eyes were dry and burning and her body trembled, but her mind was numb as she took the gold Star of David from her own neck and looped it twice, gently, around her daughter's throat. Then she knelt on the cold, unforgiving stone, rested her head on the plump little hands, and began, for the last time, to pray.

"May the Lord bless you and keep you. May the Lord make His face to shine upon you and be gracious unto you . . ."

Janka, the dog, whined softly and licked her bare leg.

"Amen."

The mother kissed her child twice—two brief brushes of her lips on the small forehead and rosebud mouth. Then she stood and spoke again to the dog in a soft but commanding voice:

"Janka, guard her."

The animal's ears pricked and again she whined, but she moved closer to the baby.

The sun climbed higher in the sky, and for a moment the mother closed her eyes and remembered the good things; her husband's smile and strong arms, the many nights in the bed he had carved for them with his own hands; their little house with the bright geranium window boxes and the big chestnut tree outside; the golden wheat and vivid poppies of the countryside and the great *puszta* itself.

And when she opened her eyes again, they were wet with tears, but her heart had already withered inside her. And the mother turned her back on her daughter and walked down the steps and along the road, toward the sound of horses, and men, and death.

The dog, Janka, was a Great Pyrenees. Heavy-boned and powerful, covered from head to toe in a thick, long white coat that was now smeared with the blood of human slaughter, Janka had been brought into the house five years ago from the meadows where she had served her time guarding flocks of sheep.

Guard her, the woman had commanded, and Janka had understood.

The town began to stir.

Strangers.

With an effort, Janka clamped the ends of the shawl tightly in her strong jaws and gathered up the bundle, padding swiftly down the steps and off toward the safety of the forest.

For two days and nights the trees groaned, the branches cracked, the grasses and leaves rustled, the creatures of the forest whispered and howled and slithered and crouched, and all the time Janka warmed the child with her body, washed its soft pink face with her tongue, and snarled warnings at everything that approached. The child whimpered and wailed and began to weaken. Janka, having tried in vain to suckle her, killed two plump rabbits and a stoat and tore them to pieces, but the baby lay still and did not eat.

On the third evening, desperation drew Janka, with the child, back to the church. The woman might return. The loyal dog settled down to wait.

"Jesszus-Maria, look!"

The voice, shrill and female, woke Janka from her doze. Two women stood at the foot of the church steps, bags of provisions in their arms.

"It has a child!"

Janka sat rigid, the aroma of salami from their bags driving her nearly mad with hunger, but not daring to move lest the strangers came closer.

"Sweet Lord, there's blood on them!"

They put down their bags, and the taller of the two women set her foot on the lowest step. Janka barked. The woman backed away and straightened her hat.

"Fetch the *pandur.*"

"They'll be having dinner."

"The dog may be mad—fetch the *pandur.*"

The shorter woman hurried off, and the three that remained waited tensely, like figures in a strange tableau: the child pale and still, Janka sitting taut and erect, the woman shifting unhappily from one leg to the other, her eyes fixed on the bundle.

The *pandur* came, his pistol holstered at his side.

"See!" they told him. "See the blood."

"I see," the policeman said, and reached for his weapon.

The church door opened and the priest, young and dark, stepped out.

"Father Jozsef, be careful!" the first woman cried. "The dog is dangerous!"

Jozsef Szabo looked down. The baby wriggled slightly. Janka watched him.

"Hello," the priest said softly. "Are you caring for the little one?"

Janka's ears pricked.

"I don't think the dog's dangerous," the priest called to the *pandur* in a calm voice. "She's just in need of food and time to rest."

"The dog may have time," the policeman said sourly, thinking of his supper, "but the law has more important matters to deal with. I'll shoot the beast and we can all be on our way."

"Surely, my friend," Father Jozsef said evenly, though his face grew red, "there's been enough shooting in this town." He moved a pace back toward the door. "Allow me to fetch a little milk and—"

"Jezus." The pandur grew impatient and made a sudden movement up the first few steps. Janka, alarmed, ducked her head, picked up the bundle, and stood stock-still. The policeman took out his pistol.

"No, please!" pleaded the priest.

The heightened tension and raised voices spurred Janka into action. Taking a firmer grip on the shawl, she bolted swiftly down the steps, neatly evading the small crowd that had gathered to watch. The *pandur* raised the pistol and took aim, but people blocked his target. He lowered the weapon, and spat.

"Rajta!" he shouted. "Come on, Father! It can't get far carrying that weight."

The chase began—first the policeman, followed closely by the gasping priest, chest heaving, soutane flying, the two women trying to keep up but handicapped by their bags. Passersby watched in fascination as the hunt proceeded along Rakoczi Street, over Matyas Square toward the river and onto the wooden bridge. Halfway across, Janka, hampered by the child, stopped. She laid down the bundle and turned, panting, to face her pursuers, still protecting the infant with her body.

"We have them!" The policeman brandished his pistol again.

"Wait, for the love of God!" Father Jozsef shouted breathlessly, coming to a halt beside him. "Let me try again—just one more time!"

The *pandur* spat again. "No more time, Father. Look at the brute, a menace to everyone in the town." He took careful aim, squinting.

"Vigyaz!" shrieked one of the women, just arriving behind them. "Mind the baby!"

Gentle Janka, teeth bared and panting, looked ferocious as she hunched low and snarled at the strangers. She heard the child's sudden high-pitched cry, saw the man in dark robes lift his hands high, watched the two shrill women clutch each other, observed the glint of something dark raised in the air, heard the ripple of the river below, smelled the freshness of nearby grass and flowers, and she crouched lower still, feeling the warmth of the small body beneath her own.

Guard her.

The crack was deafening. Janka, struck cleanly between her beautiful dark eyes, dropped limply to the ground, her great bloodied head almost covering the small human she had, in the end, guarded with her life.

And the child screamed.

PART ONE

Krisztina: Hungary, 1919–1938

Chapter 1

I am in a quandary, Father Jozsef wrote in the brown leather diary that had so often been his comfort in times of stress. *During the past few days, for the first time in my life, my faith and my courage have been called into question, and I am deeply disturbed because of it.*

He leaned back and stretched, feeling the strain in his back and thinking of his bed, though it was only nine in the evening. Oh, how he yearned for a glass of tea, but since it was against his principles—not to mention the law—to pay black market prices, he would just have to tolerate another cup of filthy ersatz coffee.

Together with most of the population, Father Jozsef continued to long desperately for peace and normality to return to Hungary. Since the war, it had become virtually impossible for an ordinary person to keep up with the political turmoil.

He looked around him, surveying his favorite room of the little domain behind the church: his study, where no one but his housekeeper ever entered. He sat here whenever he could, working or rereading the novels of Jokai and translations of Twain and Dickens. The room was simple—plain, whitewashed walls hung with just two pictures, one original painting of the Madonna and Child by his late father, the other a framed print of one of Meszoly's *plein air* studies of Lake Balaton. However, it was his home, the place where he could discard his black soutane, lay down his crucifix, and be himself, plain Jozsef Szabo, dispatched eleven

years ago to this little town near the Tisza River to do God's work
as well as he could manage.

What next? he wrote in the diary, and then tossed down his
pen, his face contorted with frustration. Was there to be no end to
Hungary's misery? First the "red" terror, now the "white."
Gangs of former Austro-Hungarian officers were rampaging
through the south of the country taking their revenge on the
Communists, executing anyone suspected of being even loosely
implicated, radicals, liberals, Jews—*always the Jews,* he thought
miserably, always the scapegoats. And now the madness had
come to his own town. . . .

Just one single afternoon and evening, he mused. *A few monstrous hours, and everything is changed forever.* His face darkened. Not forever, of course not, it was naive of him to think it. In
a few months, when the charred skeletons of the burned-out
homes had been flattened, the memories would be buried forever.

Not for him.

Four days ago, he, a priest, a man of God, had stood on the
sidelines feeling utterly helpless as the Awakening Magyars had
torn through the town, in the name of pure Christian morality,
trampling victims as if they were defenseless insects, looting,
raping, and murdering. And he had done nothing to stop them,
had told himself there was nothing to be done. But that was
wrong. His courage had failed—that was his unpardonable sin.
There was *always* something to be done in the face of evil.

The priest was an unlikely-looking Catholic, dark-haired,
black-eyed, with a round, warm face, curved nose, and full, sensual mouth. In truth, he realized, he strongly resembled a Jew,
and who could say, but for his cassock he, too, might easily have
been murdered four evenings past just for his appearance.

The child was another matter entirely, with her white-gold
hair and extraordinary, vivid violet-blue eyes. As he was picking
her up from the bridge, he had seen the Star of David gleaming
around her neck and realized its implications—she must be a
victim of the pogrom. Instinct had warned him to conceal the
star from the *pandur* and the others. He removed it and slipped
it quickly into his pocket, bitterly aware that in the present neurotic climate, when innocents were being blamed for the tiny
percentage among them who had been prominent in the Bolshe-

vik movement, an abandoned Jewish baby would be cast on the scrap heap without a single moment's compassion.

What to do with her now? That was the question that had plagued his every waking moment, disturbing his sleep and his work ever since he and the policeman had taken the child to Dr. Regos that first evening.

"You must find her a home, Father," the *pandur* had said. "If we go through official channels, you know she'll only end up in some miserable institution."

"And her parents?"

The policeman had shaken his head. "Dead, or miles away. They won't be back, believe me."

"I think we should wait to hear what the doctor says," Father Jozsef had said.

"You think she may die?"

"I pray not, poor little innocent."

The *pandur* had shrugged, thinking glumly of the reams of paperwork that the baby's burial would necessitate.

"We'll talk again, Father," he had said, going to the door. "If the child survives."

Father Jozsef had nodded.

"If she survives."

She survived.

The doctor was emphatic: If not for the protection of the dog, the baby would certainly be dead, but thanks to the animal's body heat, there was little wrong with the infant except dehydration and hunger, which milk would soon cure. A few days later the little girl was home with Father Jozsef, tucked warmly into a makeshift crib fashioned from a wooden drawer lined with a blanket and a sheet.

She seemed content, a good baby who cried only when wet or hungry, and who seemed to find pleasure in gazing into the dark eyes of the priest and playing with the rosary beads he gave her in lieu of a rattle.

A Jewish child, cared for by a priest and playing with a rosary . . . the ironies of life, Father Jozsef mused, staring into the crib and asking himself for the hundredth time if what he was now contemplating was sinful or morally justifiable under the circumstances.

He had, the previous day, been struck by an idea, but he was

not certain if he had been blessed with an inspiration or cursed
with an abomination. He did have a potential home for the baby,
did know a young woman who would willingly cut off her right
arm for the joy of motherhood, who would consider this beautiful
infant a direct benediction from God—his second cousin, Ilona
Florian, who lived in Budapest and had, for many years, longed
for children without reward. She and her husband, Gabor, were
Catholics however, and Ilona was particularly devout. How could
he possibly reconcile his conscience to offering them a Jewish
child?

For hours on end he sat in his rocking chair, tilting back and
forth, agonizing over the rights and wrongs of the matter, finally
ending up on his knees before the altar in the church, asking for a
ruling from God.

He could not say if it was divine guidance, simple logic, or the
child herself who assisted his final verdict—perhaps it was a combination of all three. On the eighth morning, however, the baby
sat on his knee, regarding him solemnly as he spoke to her of his
predicament until, at last, he put the fundamental question to
her:

"So, *baba,* what is it to be? An institution?"

The child stared at him, her blond curls framing her face like a
halo, her tiny mouth gravely compressed.

"Or is it to be Budapest, and a warm and loving home?"

She smiled, a brilliant, captivating baby smile that dimpled her
cheeks and brought a sparkle to her extraordinary eyes. Father
Jozsef's heart melted, and he knew that the decision, for better or
for worse, had been made.

"Holy Mary," Ilona Florian whispered, crossing herself rapidly,
her natural pallor flushed with color. "I knew—last night I believe I actually *knew!* I had such a strange, strong premonition!"
Her eyes were full of tears. "You are really offering us this child,
Jozsef?" Her face was incredulous. "Does no one else want her?"

Jozsef touched his cousin's shoulder gently. "There is the
chance that her mother may return for her, Ilona, and of course I
must pray that she will." He shook his head. "But in all truth, it's
unlikely."

"Mother of God," she murmured in wonder.

The priest was deeply moved. He had never witnessed such
absolute joy on anyone's face, not even the new mothers he had

visited in his parish. Ilona Florian was by no means a beautiful woman, but now she glowed like a pretty girl. She was of medium height with good posture, her brown hair had no curl but gleamed, and she had soft, nut-brown eyes with finely arched brows that endowed her face with a gentle, intelligent expression. Her clothes might be old and lacking fashion, but a special neatness and grace about her transformed potential mediocrity into style. Ten years of marriage to Gabor Florian, a struggling and, these days, often bad-tempered leather goods manufacturer, had etched a scattering of fine lines of strain onto Ilona's face, as had her three miscarriages and years of longing for children. But despite the intolerant streak in Gabor's nature, she was loyal to her husband, and her unflagging faith in God and all His works had thus far carried her through every storm, great or small.

"Ilona," Jozsef said gently, "have you considered Gabor?"

Ilona's flush heightened, and unconsciously her hands clenched into fists. "Gabor will feel as I do, Jozsef, I promise you." She hardly recognized her own voice—it seemed to ring with new confidence. "When I explain it to him, when he realizes that she is a gift from God, he will know that we have no choice but to accept her and to love her."

"All the same," Jozsef pointed out, "no final decision can be taken until he has agreed."

Ilona nodded, but she was barely listening. She had known for so long that she could never again carry a child in her own womb. Now suddenly a miracle was unfolding, and she wanted only to run into the bedroom to kneel before the saints to give thanks.

All through the long afternoon after Jozsef left, Ilona sat in an agony of suspense waiting for Gabor to return from work, praying that business today had gone a little better than usual. He was not a bad husband, and his moodiness tended to manifest itself in general surliness rather than in explosions of rage. However, he was often tetchy for no apparent reason, finding fault with everything that Ilona did or said; too many questions about his day— not enough questions—too much paprika in the *gulyas*—not enough garlic in the *tokany*.

Her prayers were answered. Gabor came home in an ebullient mood, having received the first substantial order in many months from Kaufmann's, the largest leather goods store on Vaci Utca, for two hundred hand-stitched pigskin wallets.

"And the buyer said they'll want briefcases very soon!" he added, rubbing his hands together.

Ilona smiled warmly and kissed his cheek.

"If this continues," Gabor said genially, "I may even have to take on staff again." He sank into an armchair in their modest-sized, but meticulously cared-for salon. It was an eclectic room in which the Blüthner piano and mahogany sideboard brought by Ilona to their marriage gleamed nobly beside the worn sofa, chairs, and table they shared space with. "And more good news," he continued, cutting the end off a cigar and lighting it. "There are strong rumors that a new government is being formed at Szeged."

"Another government," Ilona murmured.

"But this one apparently has the sanction of the French and the English. Many people believe there may soon be an end to the chaos."

"There have been so many rumors."

Gabor puffed on the cigar. "Take my word for it, *edesem*, things are on the move. I'm a businessman, I have a sense of these things. Budapest is stirring herself."

Ilona patted his hand. "I'm glad for you, Gabor."

"Be glad for yourself too," he said with rare generosity. "Life should begin to get a little easier before too long."

Gabor Florian, at thirty-two, was just three years his wife's senior, yet he looked ten years older. When they had met, in the first decade of the new century, Gabor had been a handsome young hussar officer with a fine figure, sleek fair hair, a silky moustache, and soft gray eyes. Time had been unkind; eleven years later he had developed a tendency to stoop, the attractive hair had receded badly, revealing a shiny but otherwise unimposing dome, and the eyes, half hidden by spectacles, had lost their spark and their softness.

But it was Florian's disposition more than his physical appearance that created the overall impression of middle age. He had grown up in the lower reaches of the middle class, and for as long as he could remember, the worm of envy had churned in his belly. He had always been jealous of the gentry—not the justifiable resentment of the peasantry, but the frustrated ambition of a social climber. More than anything in life, Gabor wanted to make money, thereby gaining the power that would never be his by any other route. His life plan had begun well enough; he had married well—Ilona had come to him with a substantial dowry, enabling him to start his own business—but where once he had employed seventeen women in his Pest workroom, he was now reduced to eight, barely scraping together enough orders to pay their wages and his overhead, let alone maintain their house on Kalvaria Street in Buda.

When Ilona broke the news to him, Gabor's high spirits vanished in a swirl of cigar smoke.

"Are you mad?" he snarled. "What in God's name do we want with a cast-off bastard? Is this what you think we've come to—taking in strays?"

But two hours later, after an excellent dinner of *porkolt,* his favorite dish, eaten in almost total silence, Florian looked more closely than usual at his wife and observed a change in her. Beneath the depressed, almost subservient, exterior, a curious exultation simmered, and with it a glint in her eyes that he had not seen before. Gabor lit another cigar and poured himself a glass of *barack-palinka,* and suddenly three thoughts occurred to him.

First, though they no longer discussed such matters, he knew how intensely Ilona still yearned for a child, and he missed the contented and far more sensual young wife to whom he had been married before the string of miscarriages. Second, he had to admit that although he would certainly have preferred a son, a daughter, especially if she turned out to be pretty, was a prospect that he found quite agreeable. And third, if he did agree to take this child, it would be regarded as an act of great beneficence by all their acquaintances, and he would surely grow in the esteem of the church. After all, many of the largest stores with which he aspired to do business were Catholic-owned. . . . Perhaps the price of another mouth to feed might not be too much to pay for such a general upturn in his fortunes.

Two days later, in Jozsef Szabo's town, the savagely beaten and raped body of a young woman with white-blond hair and violet-blue eyes was dragged from the river.

Father Jozsef visited the small, devastated Jewish district, but learned only the barest and grimmest of facts. Virtually every man and boy had been shot, clubbed, or stabbed to death during the pogrom. Most of the women and many of the girls had been marched to the edge of the forest and raped, and those who had struggled too fiercely had also been murdered. The survivors were haggard, with haunted, bitter eyes, silently rebuilding their shattered lives and unwilling to speak to strangers, particularly one wearing a soutane. Jozsef was left to guess what might have happened to the baby's family, and every scenario he pictured was more heartbreaking than the one before. Just one thing was certain: This woman had left her precious child in the only safe place she could think of—outside his church. Jozsef Szabo felt that a sacred trust had been placed in him. He would not betray it.

When Ilona learned that Jozsef and the child would soon arrive, she plunged into a frenzy of activity, determined to have the nursery ready in time. There was a room in the house already set aside for the purpose. It had been left that way for five years, a sad, lonely monument to her third and final pregnancy, which had ended in its sixth month. Now, suddenly, the empty white wooden cradle and every surface in the room gleamed from her joyful scrubbing, and the prettily patterned cotton curtains fluttered in the autumn breeze as the windows were flung open wide, letting new life and hope into the room.

Linen for the cradle, feeding bottles and milk, she needed those immediately, and plenty of muslin and toweling for napkins, and clothes too. Ilona flew from store to store in Buda, her cheeks rosy with scarcely controlled excitement as she spent the extra allowance that Gabor had permitted her for the occasion.

The very first moment she laid eyes on the child, she thought that her heart would explode with love and joy, so that she might not even live to hold her.

If the child had been ugly or misshapen, Ilona knew that she would have loved her all the same, and been grateful beyond belief for the gift. But this was almost too much to believe—this exquisite, ethereal little creature of soft, translucent skin and golden gossamer hair.

But then Ilona touched her, first with nervous, hesitant fingers, and then in an embrace, and the child was anything but ethereal —she was real flesh and blood, warm and solid and wriggling, and unutterably, undeniably human.

Before Jozsef left, they sat together at the pine table in the kitchen and he, without a word, withdrew the leather pouch from his pocket and placed it on the table between them.

Ilona glanced down. "What is it?"

He unfastened the neck of the pouch and tilted it. The Star of David spilled out onto the wooden surface. Ilona touched it and looked up at him. "Jozsef?"

"It was around the baby's neck when we found her."

The skin between Ilona's eyebrows puckered. "But this is a Jewish star."

"Yes."

"What does it mean?"

"What can it mean, Ilona?"

Ilona hardly breathed. "But she can't be . . ." she said quietly. "Her hair . . . those eyes . . ."

"Not all Jews have dark hair and eyes." Jozsef smiled. "And look at me—I look more like a rabbi than a priest."

They paused.

"Why didn't you tell me this earlier, Jozsef?"

He looked at her steadily. "Because an abandoned Jewish baby stands little chance these days. Because I knew you would love her the moment you saw her." He flushed darkly. "Because I am a coward."

Ilona stared at the star. Her heartbeat was very slow. "Have you—considered everything?"

"I think so."

"Then you have asked yourself if it would be right, in the eyes of God, to bring up a Jewish child in our faith?"

Jozsef raised his hands helplessly. "Over and over again, and I have found no clear answer, except that I can find no better alternative." He shook his head. "I thought of tossing the star into the river and severing her last link with her true identity, but that, I'm sure, would be wrong. I decided, since you are to become her mother, that you should know, but I am afraid all I have done is transfer the burden from my shoulders to yours."

"You were right," Ilona said absently, her thoughts whirling.

"Perhaps one day," Jozsef continued awkwardly, "when Hungary is sane again, you may feel the time has come to explain to her. That was my main motive for bringing you the star."

Ilona was stroking the gold with her fingers. "Gabor must not know," she said abruptly.

"Surely that isn't right?"

"Not for him, perhaps," she said steadily, "but for her. He is not a bad man, Jozsef, but Gabor often speaks against the Jews. He believes they are to blame for many of our troubles."

Jozsef's eyes were pained. "I'm sorry, Ilona."

"For what?" She smiled. "For bringing me the most glorious gift of my life?"

"I should have told you the whole truth."

"You have."

"Not until now. It was deceitful."

"You were afraid for the baby."

"I should have given you the chance to reject her before seeing her."

"I would not have rejected her."

"You might have."

"Never." She was calm now. "I could never reject any child."

They sat for a few moments more in mutual silence, and gradually the agitation in the atmosphere seemed to waft out of the open window into the little garden beyond, leaving peace in its place.

Jozsef picked up the star, returned it to the pouch, and handed it to his cousin. "For better or worse," he said.

"Thank you." She took it from him and held it in her hands.

He pushed back his chair and stood up. "You are determined to keep it from Gabor?"

"I am."

"And how do you feel about that, Ilona?"

A shadow crossed her face. "It's only fitting that there should be a price to pay for such a gift. Mine will be the knowledge that I am betraying my husband's trust."

"No small price," he said softly, aware that the sin would cost her dearly.

She smiled again. "But worthwhile, dear Jozsef, infinitely worthwhile."

They went back upstairs to the room that had been empty and lonely and was now a real nursery housing a child. They stood over the cradle and gazed down into it.

"She's sleeping," Ilona breathed.

"She's a sweet, good child." Jozsef's eyes moistened. "She will need a name."

"Gabor and I will speak of that later."

"Of course." Jozsef stooped and gently brushed the baby's curls with his big hand.

"She will need a birthday too," Ilona mused. "I know that the doctor said she's about five months, but she must have a day to remember and to celebrate."

"In many ways, today is the day of her rebirth."

Her lips curved softly. "Today, then—the twenty-eighth of October, nineteen hundred and nineteen." She clenched her fists suddenly, and beat them impatiently against her sides. "Oh, I wish that Gabor would come home soon. I want it to begin!"

"What, Ilona?"

"Our parenthood!"

Joszef smiled gently. "It has begun."

Chapter 2

They named her Krisztina.

She was a will-o'-the-wisp, moonshine child, yet to her new parents, accustomed to an exclusively adult household, she was devastatingly tangible, a melee of napkins, feeding bottles, spattered bibs, scattered toys, tears and dimples. To Ilona and Gabor, little Krisztina was an enigma, a mystery package wrapped inside multiple layers of newly discovered characteristics, idiosyncrasies, moods, and behavior patterns. For the Florians, unlike other mothers and fathers who had some frame of reference—a family tree to consult—it was not possible to watch Krisztina gurgling or frowning or experimenting with new words and to exclaim: "She has your mother's smile!" or "Now she looks just like your Aunt Maria!" There could be no predictions or obvious expectations where Krisztina was concerned, but there were plentiful hopes and lavish aspirations. As the first months and then years of her life in the six-room house on Kalvaria Street passed, most of these were amply realized.

If she ever lacked sibling companionship, her relationship with Miksa, the amiable mongrel dog Ilona had saved from starvation some years before, compensated. From her first day in Buda, Krisztina displayed an extraordinary rapport with the rough-haired, tawny-eyed animal. As soon as she could crawl, the Florians regularly found her early in the mornings curled up with Miksa on his bed in the scullery; when they closed the nursery door in order to discourage these unhygienic nocturnal visits, Miksa simply stationed himself outside the child's room, unshakable from his vigil.

"She must remember the dog that protected her as a baby," Ilona remarked one evening to Gabor.

"Nonsense," he dismissed, irritated as he often was by the dog. "Babies have no memory."

Ilona simply smiled.

The love affair with dogs and other animals continued right through Krisztina's childhood. She was forever rescuing creatures from disaster, whether it was a kitten stranded up a tree, a fledgling fallen from its nest, or even just a common housefly trapped in a spider's web. On a visit to the country, when she was just seven, Gabor and Ilona made the error of taking her to a *tanya* on which geese were being raised for the production of *liba maj*. Young Krisztina caught one glimpse of the geese being force-fed, and was so distraught and outraged at their plight that she sobbed wretchedly all the way back to the city and all through the next night. She then went on an all-out hunger strike until Ilona managed to entice her back, first to vegetables and finally to meat, though reassurances had to be offered at the start of every meal for many months.

"Mama, what is this meat?"

"It's pork, *kis szivem*."

"That's pig, isn't it?"

"Yes, *kis szivem*."

"Who killed the pig?"

"A farmer."

"Why?"

"So that people would have food to eat," Ilona answered patiently.

Krisztina studied her plate of aromatic *szekelygulyas* with gnawing hunger. "Otherwise people would die, wouldn't they, Mama?"

"If all farmers stopped killing animals, then yes, darling, people would soon have little to eat."

"And then they would die."

Ilona smiled. "Probably, yes."

Krisztina picked up her fork. "He didn't hurt the pig, did he?" Her violet eyes impaled her mother. "Not like the geese."

"No, *szivem*, not like the geese."

Two days after her eleventh "birthday," Krisztina woke as usual at half past six, and waited for Miksa to plant his front paws on the bed and to lick her face as he did every morning.

"Miksa?" She sat up abruptly, gripped by foreboding. And then she saw him, lying at the foot of the bed in his accustomed place.

Mama had warned her, had explained that Miksa was old, that some day his time would come . . .

"Miksa?" she said again, her voice strange and high-pitched. Miksa did not move.

"She's heartbroken," Ilona told her husband three days later, "but she's adamant that she doesn't want another dog."

"Foolishness." Gabor shook his head. "A new puppy would soon take away the pain."

"I think we have to respect her wishes at the moment, dear," Ilona replied. "With another child you might be right, but Kriszti and Miksa were more like brother and sister than a girl and her dog. I think we should wait until she's ready."

"But I can't bear to watch her like this," Gabor said emotionally. The sight of his beloved daughter's red eyes and sorrowing expression wracked him.

He had, all through Krisztina's infancy and early childhood, been markedly indifferent to his unbargained-for daughter. She had, admittedly, been little trouble, and she had kept his wife happy, which in turn made his own existence easier, but still she had contributed nothing to his life. As she had approached her tenth year, however, he had found himself increasingly captivated by her. Suddenly she had seemed to him a tiny woman, a fellow human being with the potential for companionship and intelligent conversation. He became intensely proud of her, called her his "princess," was virtually enslaved by her. For Krisztina, his heart's new treasure, almost every trace of parsimony vanished and he became actively generous, regularly bringing gifts home for her. His wholehearted adoration had happily coincided with a continuing uptrend in his general prosperity. He had recently transferred his enlarged staff to a bigger workroom on the outskirts of Pest, and whereas in the past if Ilona had suggested buying new shoes or a dress for their growing daughter, Gabor had grumbled, nowadays he even accompanied them to the stores to help choose the prettiest merchandise for the apple of his eye. If Krisztina was sad for any reason, Gabor was heartsick; when she was, as was more usual, merry and contented, his life, too, passed more pleasurably.

Ilona gave thanks to God each day for the warmth that now encircled her little family. She had not believed Gabor capable of such love, and even if his passion for their child meant an increasing tendency to ignore his wife, she was prepared to tolerate that for the sheer happiness of watching him with Krisztina.

Seven months after Miksa's death, Ilona and Krisztina were shopping for new season's clothes on Kigyo Street in Pest, when, out of nowhere, a large black dog, its coat drenched, muddied, and stranded with reeds, came hurtling down the street toward them and flung itself at Krisztina, knocking off her beret and smearing her blazer with filthy paw prints.

"Get away!" Ilona shrieked, wielding her handbag as a makeshift truncheon to protect her daughter. "Get down!"

"No, Mama, don't!" Krisztina protested. "He's only being friendly. Look."

Ilona lowered her handbag. The animal was certainly not displaying any sign of aggression; far from it, it was actually standing with its front paws on the girl's shoulders busily licking her cheeks in what seemed to be rapturous greeting.

"Kriszti, tell it to get down immediately," Ilona insisted, though more gently. "It's filthy—you don't know where it's been."

"It's a 'he,' Mama, not an 'it,' " Krisztina said delightedly, "and I don't think he's got any germs, he's just very wet." Tenderly, she pushed the dog down on the pavement and plucked one or two of the reeds from his saturated black fur. "He must have been in the river." She fondled him. "Isn't he beautiful!"

"He's very nice," Ilona agreed, "but who does he belong to?"

They looked around, scanning the lunchtime crowds for a possible owner.

"No collar," Krisztina said, inspecting him more closely. "Perhaps he's lost." She stared into the animal's brown eyes. "Are you lost, darling?"

He wagged his tail eagerly and licked Ilona's leg.

"What shall we do with him, Mama?"

"Do? Nothing."

"We can't just leave him all alone."

"He'll be perfectly all right." Ilona glanced at her watch. "Kriszti, it's after one, and we must get something to eat before the shops open again."

"But Mama—"

"Krisztina, you can't go around picking up stray dogs. He's covered in mud, he may be diseased. In any case, I'm sure he has an owner." She tucked her arm through her daughter's. "Come on."

Firmly, Ilona drew Krisztina along the street and into Café Molnar, where they sat at a window table and ordered. Five minutes later, Krisztina gave a small squeal.

"Mama, look!"

The dog was sitting on the pavement outside.

"He's waiting for us!"

"He's probably just resting."

"You *know* he's waiting."

Ilona sighed. "He'll soon get tired of it."

When they went outside an hour later, he was still there, his tail thumping furiously. Determinedly, Ilona pulled Krisztina from store to store, but each time when they emerged the dog was there, a mud-caked, patient statue.

"Let's find a taxi," Ilona said wearily. "I can't walk another step."

Krisztina gazed down. "What are we going to do with him, Mama?"

Ilona fingered her hat nervously. "I suppose we should find a policeman."

"No! He'll be locked up if we do that."

"He's obviously lost, Kriszti. Someone, somewhere, is probably searching for him."

"They can't be very good at owning a dog if they let him wander off without even a collar," Krisztina said with strong disapproval.

"True," Ilona agreed.

"So can we?"

"Can we what?"

"Take him home."

"No, we can't."

"But you and Papa are always saying I should get another dog."

"And you said no dog could replace Miksa."

"That was before I met Mozes."

"Who?"

Krisztina crouched down, hugged the dog, and pulled a reed from his fur. "See? A bulrush."

"She wants to call him *what?*"

"Mozes," Ilona said meekly.

"But that's a Jewish name."

"The dog isn't Jewish, Gabor, just the name."

"It's sacrilegious!"

"I don't think so," Ilona said gently. "After all, she's only a child, and he *was* covered in reeds."

"He fell in the Danube, not the Nile."

"You know Kriszti's imagination."

Gabor softened. "She really wants the creature?"

"You saw her face—she's besotted."

As always when faced with one of his daughter's desires, Gabor's resistance collapsed. "Very well," he scowled. "If the veterinarian says he's healthy, she can keep him, but she'd better make sure he stays out of my way."

Gabor loved, more than anything in life, to cuddle Krisztina, to squeeze her tightly and stroke her wonderful silky hair. He had never known any human being so utterly, perfectly lovely as she was rapidly becoming, with her almost Scandinavian features, her nose straight as an arrow, her mouth soft and sensual, her eyes that astounding violet shade, her coltish legs, lusciously sunburned all summer long, and her fascinating tiny, budding breasts. The absolute purity of the child caught Gabor by the throat, choking him with pride and love and still another, less definable and far less worthy, sensation. Sometimes, when he hugged her tightly, he would involuntarily find himself fantasizing about other young girls he had seen during his working day— girls with pert, bright faces, uptilted breasts, and narrow, seductive waists. Then, guiltily, he would remember Ilona, so many years removed from the enticing freshness that those young girls had and that their own little Krisztina was unmistakably beginning to exude.

Krisztina, too, adored her father, loved to perch on his knee and have him jog her up and down, to snuggle up close and breathe in his masculine smell, so completely different from her mother's fragrance.

Mozes, however, had become a constant trial to Gabor. Father had only to put one arm around daughter and the dog would approach. If he squeezed her, Mozes would bark; if he took her on his lap and bounced her, the animal would growl and then Krisztina would laugh and scold Mozes fondly, embracing Gabor even more fervently just to tease him.

One afternoon, in Krisztina's thirteenth year, coming home from school and finding her father home early from business, she rushed into his study and gave him a happy, welcoming hug. Gabor, delighted as always, swept her up in his arms and then, suddenly, the warmth and pressure of her sweet, firm body, and the delicious scent of her utterly overwhelmed him. The fantasies he often indulged in, those sweet, guilty images of other girls, merged abruptly, shockingly, into an unbidden, forbidden picture of Krisztina, nude and beckoning—and the thought that Gabor had for more than a dozen years pushed strongly to the back of his mind sprang forward.

She is not my child.

He had not noticed Mozes padding into the room, hardly heard the low, menacing growl, but suddenly the dog darted forward and bit Gabor on the ankle, sharp teeth sinking into flesh and crunching on bone. Gabor screamed in agony and Krisztina, thrust from his arms, cried out in alarm.

"Papa, what happened?"

Gabor clutched his wounded leg with both hands and sank to the floor, his face puce with rage and pain. "The brute bit me!" he gasped. Gingerly, he raised his trouser leg and examined the torn, already darkening skin. Then, his rage freshly fueled, he staggered back to his feet and seized a poker from the copper bucket containing the fire irons.

"Papa, *no!*" Krisztina shrieked. "Don't hurt him!"

Gabor turned on her, maddened. "Don't hurt *him?*" Furiously he brandished the poker, and Mozes, hackles raised, began to bark.

"Mozes, stop it!" Krisztina beseeched the dog, her voice trembling with fright. "Papa, please!"

"What on earth is going on here?" Ilona appeared in the doorway, wiping her hands on her apron. "Gabor, what in God's name are you doing? Put that down at once."

"The brute nearly took off my ankle!" Gabor yelled, still wielding his weapon. "Give me one good reason why I shouldn't give it a thrashing!"

His daughter planted herself firmly between him and Mozes. Tears of shock had welled up in her eyes and now began to stream down her face, but she stuck out her quivering lower lip mutinously. "Because I love him," she said passionately.

"The creature's mad!" Gabor roared. "It should be put down! Look at my leg!"

"Jesszus-Maria!" Ilona gasped in shock. "Gabor, we must call the doctor."

"Of course we must call the doctor," he snarled sarcastically. "And the veterinarian, too, to get rid of the beast."

"No!" Krisztina screamed. "He won't do it again. He's never done it before!" She flung herself upon Mozes, who promptly wagged his tail. "Oh, Mama, please don't let him hurt Mozes! *Please!*" She began to sob desperately, burying her face in her pet's black fur.

"I could die," Gabor moaned. "I could die of lockjaw!"

"I'm sure you won't die of anything, my dear," Ilona soothed, and took his arm. "Now come upstairs and lie down, while I telephone the doctor."

Krisztina stopped sobbing. "You won't let Papa have Mozes killed, will you, Mama?"

"If I were you," Ilona said gently, "I would keep him out of your papa's way for a while."

Gabor, his face turning from its dark, angry red to a stricken pallor, glared at Krisztina.

"If he comes anywhere near me again, I'll kick him," he said with quieter vehemence. "And if he ever so much as snaps at me again, I'll go out and buy a gun and shoot him myself."

The doctor disinfected and dressed Gabor's ankle, gave him an injection, and pronounced that all would be well. Ilona tended her disgruntled husband with diplomatic gentleness, brought him all his favorite meals on a tray, put up with his bad temper, and generally spoiled him back to reasonable calmness. Krisztina ensured that Mozes remained outside the house while she was at school and stayed firmly by her side when she was home. She picked bunches of flowers from their little garden to bring to her papa, who grudgingly began to forgive his darling daughter and, finally, to relent.

Mozes, for the moment reprieved, was, however, indisputably on probation. By nature a relaxed child, Krisztina became uncomfortably accustomed to steering her beloved Mozes away from her father, always conscious of tension when Gabor laid eyes on her dearest friend.

Try as they might to overcome the situation, a first wedge had been driven between father and daughter.

Chapter 3

When Krisztina was five years old, Gabor and Ilona had enrolled her at a ballet school. By her tenth birthday, with the same zest she displayed for most things in life, Krisztina was spending hours on end every week poised before the full-length mirror in her parents' bedroom, practicing pas de chat, arabesques, and pirouettes while first Miksa and then Mozes sat patiently nearby on the rug, watching her.

By age twelve, however, Krisztina had grown dramatically taller, shooting up into a slender, willowy teenager. Most girls would have been overjoyed with the blessing of breathtakingly long legs, but to Krisztina it was a blow, for it was one of the pitiless rules of classical dance that excessive height inevitably curtailed the career of any would-be ballerina.

She might easily have remained a student, but deprived of the future she had already begun to dream about, Krisztina cast about for a new avenue of adventure, and by her thirteenth birthday she had found it. Ballroom dancing—less demanding than ballet, infinitely freer, and just as joyous. And there was another valid reason for its appeal. One needed a partner in order to dance—in particular, a male partner.

Until quite recently, like most of her friends, Krisztina had seen boys as less interesting and intelligent than girls, and nothing much short of a nuisance. Suddenly, though, those same boys seemed to have grown taller, with broadening shoulders, strong chins that required daily shaving, and capable, exciting hands. Krisztina's closest friend, Suzanna Kerpel, had been on two dates already with Georg Molnar, a distant cousin. Suzanna reported that they had sat for an hour and a half on both occasions in Gerbeaud, drinking *eszpresszo* and eating delicious slices of rich *Rigo Jancsi*, and not for a single moment had she been bored by him! Krisztina had not yet come across a boy who excited her as much as Georg thrilled Suzanna, but she lived in almost permanent anticipation of its happening. The dance school she now attended offered genuine potential. Though the weekly classes consisted only of girls, who had to take turns at "leading," at the end of each month a party was held at the Hotel Hungaria at which real boys, carefully selected by the head of the school, were invited to attend.

Swiftly, Krisztina mastered the basic steps of the waltz, quickstep, fox trot, polka, and, of course, the sweeping, romantic courtship dance of her own country, the *csardas*. As her confidence grew, her strong feet, released from the imprisonment of their iron ballet shoes, stepped out lightly and firmly across the polished parquet floor, while the rest of her—body, legs, arms, head, even her hair—spun and swayed in perfect rhythm.

At parties, she was everyone's favorite partner. At home, when her parents were not about, Krisztina played records on their gramophone in the salon and, with Mozes standing guard, concentrated on the dances that gave her the greatest pleasure, namely, the Charleston and the Black Bottom. From the magazines she borrowed from Suzanna, she learned that these dances, which had been sparked off back in 1923 by something called the "shimmy", were practically old-hat in Vienna, Berlin and Paris. In Budapest, in 1932, however, they still seemed wonderfully outrageous to Krisztina and her peers, and were frowned upon by their teachers.

On the twenty-eighth day of October, 1933, Krisztina's fourteenth birthday, Gabor and Ilona took her to the Gellert Hotel for a celebration dinner. They dined on stuffed cabbage with sour cream, Balaton *fogas* and chocolate-filled *palacsintas*, and drank champagne. Krisztina danced happily with her father and two boys who came to their table to request the pleasure.

It was almost ten o'clock when a newcomer presented himself to Gabor.

"Vegtelenul orvendek, uram." His voice was mellow, his Hungarian stilted. "David Kaufmann, from Berlin. I believe you are acquainted with my father, Nathan Kaufmann."

Gabor rose quickly, hand extended, expression cordial. "But of course. A great pleasure, Herr Kaufman. May I introduce my wife and daughter."

Krisztina tried, desperately, not to stare. It was vulgar to stare —vulgar and gauche—but when one was confronted, out of the blue, by the most striking, most handsome boy one has ever seen . . .

"Delighted." David Kaufmann smiled at her.

He was tall and slim-hipped, with dark brown, gleaming hair, stylishly shaped into the nape of his neck. His eyes were a twinkling electric blue.

"Won't you join us for a glass of champagne, Herr Kaufmann?" Gabor was still on his feet. Krisztina wondered exactly who the young man was to exact such courtesy.

"Thank you, yes."

A waiter, hovering nearby, drew up an extra chair and both men sat.

Now it was easier to steal glances at him. Krisztina studied the dark, arched eyebrows, the nose that was not quite straight and the firm, even mouth. Half-consciously she straightened her shoulders and patted her hair, which her mother had, for the occasion, waved with a hot curling iron.

"Herr Kaufmann's father, Krisztina," Gabor was explaining to her, speaking German now out of deference to their guest, "is one of my most valued customers."

"You know Kaufmann's, Kriszti," Ilona added. "On Vaci Utca."

"Of course, Mama." *Oh, how* jealous *Suzanna will be when I tell her,* she thought.

"Some day," Gabor said expansively, "I shall take you with me to Berlin, *dragam.* There's a much larger branch of Kaufmann's there, on Kurfürstendamm."

"How is your father?" Ilona asked Kaufmann. "I haven't seen him since last summer."

"In good health, thank you."

Gabor signaled a waiter to bring more champagne. "Are you working with him now, Herr Kaufmann?"

He nodded. "I joined him in our head office last November. And please, *uram,* won't you call me David."

"So this is a business trip for you, David?"

"Indeed." Kaufmann looked swiftly at Krisztina, and she thought she sensed some undercurrent beneath his smile. Oh, he was intriguing as well as handsome! More than anything, she yearned abruptly to waltz with him. It was almost impossible to sit demurely with her hands in her lap.

David Kaufmann was a mind reader.

He rose. "May I have this dance with your daughter, *uram?*"

"Of course," Gabor replied, patting Krisztina's arm fondly.

The orchestra was playing a quickstep to the music of Gershwin's " 'SWonderful." David Kaufmann and Krisztina walked to the edge of the dance floor. The instant he laid his right hand in the small of her back and drew her toward him, she was breathlessly, exquisitely aware that she was in the hands of an expert.

For the first time in her life, she was being truly *led* by a dance partner. Most of the boys she had danced with, and even her father—especially her father—just steered a course around the floor, too busy concentrating on the steps and on avoiding her toes to give themselves up to the music and rhythm. It was patently clear that David Kaufmann was born to dance—the angles of his body seemed molded to the melody, his feet to the tempo. Together, they rose gently and dipped subtly, their bodies maintaining near-perfect symmetry, so that they appeared to skim the floor effortlessly. When the dance ended, the extra ripple of applause was for them, not for the orchestra.

In the brief moments of silence before the music began again, they stood very still and watched each other intently. Kaufmann looked into her eyes and his mouth was smiling.

"Not bad," he said softly.

Krisztina felt so overwhelmed that she could hardly speak. "You're . . ." She hesitated. "You're very good," she said weakly.

"Thank you."

A tango began, splitting the dancers into two groups, those who danced with a sense of awkwardness and those who attacked the steps with a flourish, sometimes at the expense of skill. Again, Krisztina was transported, as her partner seemed to develop a South American flair, tempered with understatement and subtlety. The dance was over almost before it had begun.

"We have to practice," David Kaufmann said, showing no sign of wanting to leave the floor.

"Yes indeed," Krisztina breathed, not at all certain what he meant, but determined not to disagree with anything he said.

"I'm only in Budapest for another week, but we can fit in at least three sessions before I leave. I'll be back again two weeks later."

"Sessions?"

"Practice sessions. Rehearsals."

Krisztina looked up, confused. "What would we be rehearsing for?"

The orchestra struck up a gentle waltz, and she relaxed back into his arms. Again she felt that marvelous guiding hand at her back, felt first her feet and then her entire body respond to him and to the music as they glided across the floor.

"There's an international competition in Vienna in one month's time," Kaufmann said. "With work, we could be ready."

Krisztina almost stumbled, then laughed. "For a moment, I thought you were serious."

He stopped dancing. His bright eyes bored into hers. "I am. Absolutely serious." Abruptly he took her arm and drew her off the floor, but instead of returning to the Florians' table, he led her the other way.

"Where are we going?"

"Onto the terrace."

It was chilly outside, but Kaufmann seemed impervious to the cold. "All right," he said. "What do you want to ask me?"

Krisztina's mind whirled. "I'm not sure," she whispered. "Everything."

"You dance well, Krisztina." He pronounced the soft Hungarian sound of her name perfectly.

"Thank you."

"But you need training."

She stood still, dazed and inarticulate.

"Are you willing to work hard, Krisztina?"

She blinked.

"Well, are you?"

"Yes," she said.

"Good."

"Have—have you danced in competitions before?" she ventured.

"A few."

"Did you win any of them?"

He smiled. "I had the wrong partners."

"And now—" Krisztina stopped, too shy again to go on.

"Now I'm asking you to become my partner."

An intense blush colored her cheeks. She began to tremble.

"Well?" he said.

She could not speak—her brain still reeled wildly.

"Because I think, Krisztina," he continued, more gently, "that with practice we might do very well together. Perhaps even become champions."

Champions! Her thoughts spun on. He was mad! But what a glorious dream! How proud her parents would be, especially her papa! To be able to dance all the time—well, most of the time; she supposed she would still have to go to school—and to travel! And with David Kaufmann!

Another couple came out onto the terrace, leaving the doors open, and the sound of the orchestra playing "Oh, Lady, Be Good" to a fox-trot rhythm filtered out into the night air.

Without another word, David Kaufmann took Krisztina into his arms again and led her in a gentle whirl under the starry sky. Her heart beat faster and her pulses pounded to the music, the pressure of his hands and the overwhelming awareness of his warm, lean body only a hair's breadth away from her own. . . .

Gabor was distraught.

As soon as Krisztina had flown back to their table, radiant and brimming over with news, he had brought the celebration quickly to an end, refusing to be drawn into a discussion of their proposed partnership. He bade Kaufmann a pleasant but distinctly cool good-night.

Now, at midnight, he faced his wife in their bedroom, his face purpling with outrage.

"Who the hell does he think he is? Asking our daughter to go cavorting all over Europe like a common dancing girl!"

"I'm sure he meant it as a compliment," Ilona offered mildly.

"Compliment be damned! Bloody young Jew! How dare he insult us!"

Ilona looked anxious. "It wasn't intended as an insult, Gabor." She tried to smile. "He seems a very pleasant young man, and you must admit they danced beautifully together. They had quite an audience."

"Audience!" Gabor exploded. "Next you'll be suggesting she become an actress!"

"There's no similarity at all," Ilona soothed. "Ballroom dancing is an elegant, graceful pastime."

"The fellow wants her to enter competitions, Ilona, not accompany him to a tea dance."

"Because he sees that she has talent. Kriszti adores dancing, you know that." She paused. "The cream of European society enter these championships, Gabor."

He scowled. "How do you know so much about them?"

"Kriszti showed me a copy of a German magazine once—"

"She reads those scandal sheets?"

"Of course not. This was a very respectable magazine, *Der Tanz*. The competitors come from many walks of life—doctors, lawyers, even the aristocracy," she finished quietly.

Gabor stalked over to the window. He was still wearing his dinner jacket, and he ripped angrily at his black tie. He was in a real turmoil. He detested having to deny his daughter anything, but this was too much.

"He wants her to *travel* with him. It's indecent!"

Ilona sat on the bed and smoothed the creases out of her chiffon skirt. "They would have to be accompanied, of course."

"By whom?"

"I suppose I could go." She waited a moment. "I think he's a fine young man, and the son of your most important customer."

"*Jesszus-Maria*, don't remind me." Gabor flung his jacket over a chair. "Isn't it bad enough that I have to pretend to venerate these people for the sake of business, without having to hand over my daughter to one of them?"

"You wouldn't be handing her over," Ilona placated him. "If you agreed, you'd just be giving her a chance to do what she loves most. Kriszti told me she's never danced with a better partner."

The atmosphere in the bedroom was taut with Gabor's pent-up frustration.

"Adolf Hitler has the right idea," he grumbled, tying the belt of his dressing gown around his waist. "The Jews are the cause of all the troubles in the world."

Ilona hung her dress carefully away in the wardrobe, her flesh crawling as it always did when her husband expressed his anti-Semitic feelings. As always, too, her thoughts turned to the little Star of David, tucked secretly in its leather pouch between her most personal possessions in the bottom drawer of her dresser. Involuntarily, she shivered.

In bed, Gabor lay silent and angry, aware that the two most vulnerable points in his character were under attack—his desire to please Krisztina and his sense of ambition. For years he had sought ways to reach Nathan Kaufmann on a social level in order to improve the lines of communication between them, but the store owner had always remained irritatingly aloof. Here, undeniably, was his chance—he could issue a valid invitation to the Kaufmanns, perhaps even suggest a rendezvous in Vienna to watch their children in this idiotic contest . . .

His acid stomach twinged. Was there no justice in this world? Chancellor Hitler had made some significant advances in his battle against the German Jews, had given his storm troopers real jaws to clamp down on them, had even organized a national boycott of their stores. Yet in spite of all that, despite the new Aryan laws, here was Gabor Florian, still forced to bend the knee to Kaufmann.

He grunted, and turned on his side.

"Gabor?" Ilona's soft voice broke in on his disagreeable thoughts.

"Now what?"

"What shall we tell Kriszti?"

Gabor rubbed his chest. "Can't we put her off?"

"I don't think so. She wants it too much, I saw it in her eyes."

He belched. "Damn Kaufmann."

Ilona touched his arm. "We have to tell her something, Gabor."

He scowled darkly, and switched off his bedside lamp.

"Tell her yes," he said.

Chapter 4

To Krisztina, the end of 1933 and the first months of 1934 were a brilliant kaleidoscope of bewitching color and joy. She was just a teenager, but while her friends were restricted to a diet of dull schoolwork and a traditional Hungarian social life, Krisztina Florian was spending almost every weekend waltzing with a young man she increasingly idolized, through a Europe that seemed to her to glitter with excitement.

When David told her that new laws in Germany barred him from participating in all events held in his own country solely on the grounds of his race, she was horrified. But David, easygoing, warmhearted David, had tried to reassure her that it was just a temporary setback.

"Certainly that's what my father believes," he said with a small grimace.

"Don't you agree with him?"

David shook his head. "Not really. He says we are assimilated. He thinks the German people are too cultured a nation to tolerate a prolonged attack on the race who have contributed so much to German science, art, and industry."

"Surely he's right."

He shrugged. "Perhaps. In the meantime, our actors and musicians are forbidden to perform, our teachers are banned from teaching, and I'm no longer welcome on the dance floor, though there are no laws to stop me from representing Germany abroad."

Krisztina reflected. "Maybe if you refuse to represent them, they'll reconsider."

David grinned wryly. "They wouldn't give a damn, Kriszti. And besides, I want to dance."

She was still outraged. "If my country tried to treat me that way," she flung childishly, "I wouldn't put up with it!"

"Germany is still my country in spite of Hitler," David said. "If I abandon her, then in a way the Nazis are winning." He chucked her gently under the chin. "And as for not putting up with it, *Liebling,* believe me, there isn't the slightest choice."

It was true that David had changed her life, but Krisztina felt that he had also transformed her. In an ecstasy of excitement she bubbled to Suzanna that she felt like an enchanted butterfly, fluttering from one glamorous setting to another. It was not, of course, all brilliance and sparkle; it was the hardest, most grueling work she had ever endured. When they practiced together, David pushed Krisztina until sweat poured from her and every muscle in her body begged for respite. But if she did sometimes object to the punishing physical assault, the competitions themselves were her reward—glorious afternoons and evenings when they were surrounded by scores of kindred spirits all spinning and gliding over the polished dance floors of more than a dozen cities, with orchestras playing music that set Krisztina's pulses racing, with hundreds of eyes seeming to follow their every movement.

Each Friday afternoon before a weekend competition, Ilona helped Krisztina with her packing, checked over every seam of her three dance dresses, and then meticulously pressed each layer of tulle and chiffon, aware that she would have to go through the entire process again once they arrived at their destination.

And the destinations! Between November of 1933 and March of 1934, Krisztina and David, happily chaperoned by Ilona, who had never known such fun, twirled their way through Europe, from Vienna, Prague, Graz, and Marienbad to St. Moritz and Davos, on to Karlsbad and Evian-les-Bains for the French international, and then back again to Switzerland to Adelboden, all culminating in the World Championship competition in Paris at the beginning of March.

They were entered in the B category—the intermediate class. There were no official titles to be won in that category, but David and Krisztina danced with verve and ambition all the same. Then they sat with Ilona through the *Sonderklasse* rounds, carefully studying every step, every line, twist, turn, and pivot of the Championship-class dancers who, without exception, now danced what had become known as the "English" style.

"Next season," David vowed in Paris, after they had won first prize in their category, "we'll dance in A class."

Krisztina's eyes shone. "And the year after that, *Sonderklasse!*"

At the Swiss championships held at the Baur au Lac Hotel in Zurich that April, however, their dreams and aspirations suffered a mortal blow.

David and Krisztina had danced their first round—English waltz, slow fox-trot, and quickstep—and had just breathlessly returned to their table when they were approached by the chairman of the German Ballroom Dancing Association, Otto Kranzler.

"A few words, please, Herr Kaufmann," Kranzler said, politely acknowledging Ilona and Krisztina.

David rose and drew out a free chair. "Won't you join us, Herr Kranzler. A glass of *Sekt,* perhaps?" He indicated their own drinks. "We prefer mineral water during competitions."

Kranzler shook his head. "Nothing, thank you." He sat down. "Just a few moments of your time."

"Of course." David sank back in his chair, mopping his brow.

Kranzler, a slight, white-haired man, himself a former dancer, looked embarrassed. "This is not a pleasant matter for me, Herr Kaufmann." He paused.

"Go on."

Kranzler cleared his throat. "It has been brought to the attention of the Association that you are a non-Aryan."

David, Krisztina, and Ilona stiffened.

"That's correct," David said.

"Unfortunately," Kranzler went on, "we find ourselves unable to permit you, as a non-Aryan, to compete on behalf of Germany."

There was a stunned silence.

"Are you saying, Herr Kranzler," David said slowly, "that I cannot dance for my country because I am Jewish?"

Kranzler's pale eyes were remote. "It is very regrettable, Herr Kaufmann, but that is the case."

"But we've already started!" Krisztina broke in, distressed. "Why didn't you tell us before?"

"An oversight, *gnädiges Fräulein*, and most unfortunate, I agree."

"If we do continue," David said, his voice brittle, "what then?"

"I would strongly advise against such a response," Kranzler replied softly, "since the authorities would have no option but to arrest you on your reentry into Germany." He made a small, conciliatory gesture with his hands. "I repeat, I find it most regrettable, but these are the facts." He looked at Krisztina, and his expression mellowed. "Perhaps I may offer you one suggestion, Herr Kaufmann?"

"By all means," David said tersely.

"Herr Doktor Goebbels is, as you are aware, most concerned for the well-being of the arts in the Reich." He paused. "I am empowered to suggest that if you can identify a non-Jewish blood relation—an Aryan grandparent, perhaps—we might be able to overlook the situation for the time being."

David's face was pale, but his voice was hard and clear. "My grandparents and great-grandparents on both sides have all been pure-blooded Jews, Herr Kranzler."

The air between the two men became even icier.

"A pity." Kranzler glanced at Krisztina. "Then the only remaining possibility is that you enter on behalf of your charming partner's country."

Krisztina gripped the arms of her chair, her eyes glued to David. She was experiencing a tremendous longing to fling her arms around him and to hold him until the frozen, shocked expression on his face melted away. It was at that precise moment that she realized what she felt for David Kaufmann was infinitely more powerful than friendship, or even teenage infatuation. It was a wholly new and unfamiliar feeling, intuitive and prescient, belonging more to adulthood than childhood.

Her cheeks burning, she tore her eyes from him and looked at her mother, wondering if her emotions were as glaringly transparent as they felt, but Ilona was not looking at her. She was motionless and ashen-faced, and there was a glazed expression of horror in her eyes that her daughter had never seen before. Krisztina shivered and returned her gaze to David.

"So, Herr Kaufmann," Kranzler pressed, "what is your decision?" He sounded impatient.

"I need a few minutes to consult with my partner," David answered tightly.

"You have ten minutes," Kranzler said. "The second round will begin soon, and I must have an answer." He rose to leave, nodded swiftly to the ladies, bowing and greeting other couples as he went.

David sat very still. "Well," he said, his voice husky.

"Can they really do this to us?" Krisztina asked.

He reached for her hand. "To me, yes, *Liebling,* it seems they can."

"Mama? What do you say? Do they have the right to treat us so shamefully?"

Ilona sat, taut as a bowstring. "It would appear that they feel they can treat David much as they choose."

"But aren't you shocked?"

"Yes, *dragam,*" Ilona said quietly. "I am shocked."

David withdrew his hand. "I think your mother is all too conscious of the facts of life, Kriszti, as I am."

Krisztina's eyes rounded. "You don't mean you expected this?"

"Of course not." David was still pale. "It's the last thing I imagined, at least at this time—" He broke off, staring into space.

"David?" Krisztina watched him anxiously.

"Leave him, darling," Ilona said softly.

"But we only have a few minutes, Mama. What are we going to say?"

David remained silent and remote. The orchestra began to play a popular quickstep and the audience packed the floor.

Ilona's mind flashed back nearly fifteen years to the day when she had sat with her cousin Jozsef in her kitchen, talking about the baby. The world had been mad then, she reflected, and it seemed to her that another terrible downward slide was gathering momentum. She shivered, and waited for David to speak.

"What do you think, Kriszti?" he asked at last.

Krisztina was startled. "Me?"

"You must know how you feel about Kranzler's suggestions."

"About dancing for Hungary, you mean?"

"In part, yes."

She stared at him in unhappy confusion. She had never felt so torn—between her loyalty to him and her intense desire to dance. She observed his simmering rage, felt his pain, knew that if they reregistered for her homeland, David would regard it as a victory for the Nazis. Yet a great part of her, guilty and sick, wanted to dance.

"I'm not sure," she said miserably. She took a deep gulp of air. "I'll do whatever you decide."

David's jaw clenched in determination. "If they won't let me dance for Germany, then I won't dance at all."

Krisztina looked down at her hands. "All right," she whispered.

Aware of the blow he was dealing her, he leaned gently forward. "Do you understand, Kriszti?" he asked. "Truly?"

"Of course," she said, trying not to cry. "If you danced for Hungary, it would seem as if they were pushing you out of your own country."

"I can't play into their hands, *Liebling*."

"I know."

He rose. "I'm going to find Kranzler." He vanished through the crowd.

Ilona said nothing, while Krisztina gnawed at her bottom lip, ashamed of the bitter frustration churning inside her. *Not to be able to dance anymore!* It was too much to bear! And worse—even worse—if she and David weren't to be allowed to dance together anymore, she would never see him!

He returned, his face whiter than ever. Ilona rose and drew out his chair for him. "David, my dear," she said steadily, "with your permission, I should like to order a bottle of champagne."

"Good idea." David sat down.

Krisztina stared. They were both mad! "I don't know what we have to celebrate," she said, appalled.

Ilona reached over and patted her arm. "Something very important, Kriszti." She looked warmly at David. "Self-respect."

Her legs trembling, her mouth quivering, Krisztina picked up her clutch bag and rose unsteadily.

"Kriszti? Are you all right?" David asked.

She forced a watery smile. "Yes." Avoiding her mother's eyes, she escaped from the table, from the crowds and the music. Outside, she leaned for a moment against a wall, feeling quite dizzy. The powder room was located on the other side of the main hall. Taking a deep breath, Krisztina made for the cloakroom, then suddenly changed direction. Fresh air might do her more good than its exposing mirrors. She made a swift detour to the front door, her full skirts rustling as she stepped past the doorman.

The day had been unusually warm for April, but now the late afternoon was fresh and cool, and even her aching heart found a little pleasure in the sight of the hotel garden, with its lovely lawn, blossoming trees, and beautifully regimented rows and borders of tulips, a welter of crimson, yellow, and white.

Krisztina stepped across the driveway, picking her way carefully, mindful of her pale silk dance shoes. Perhaps the poignancy of the birdsong and the distant, lulling hum of cars and trams might help to calm her, but for the moment a hard lump of unhappiness lodged unyieldingly in her throat.

She watched a solitary blackbird pecking at a worm, reached out to touch the petals of a perfect tulip, and a single tear rolled down her right cheek.

"*Florian kisasszonyt?*"

She spun around, startled. "*Igen?*"

A young man dressed in white tie and tails, with a white carnation in his buttonhole, stood a few yards away, smiling. "That, I'm afraid," he said in accented German, "was more or less the sum total of my knowledge of your language." Again he grinned. "But all Hungarians speak German, don't they?"

Despite her preoccupation, something inside Krisztina crackled to attention. She stepped back two paces, brushing the tear from her face, aware that they were entirely alone.

"Have we met?" she asked. He seemed familiar.

"Never," he said charmingly.

"Then you have me at a disadvantage." She regarded him with curiosity. There was an unusual, tightly coiled air about him, rather like that of a snake about to strike, yet paradoxically his stance was casual, almost cavalier, his head cocked at a jaunty angle.

Clearly teasing her, he pivoted suddenly on one heel, so that she saw the number 32 pinned to his tailcoat.

"You're a competitor," she said foolishly.

"Correct."

She fought even harder to identify him. He was so familiar, and absurdly handsome. Narrow golden-brown eyes dancing, rather sardonically, in a face that, with the single exception of a long, thin scar on his right cheek, could only be described as perfectly constructed—cheekbones high, nose long and straight with flared nostrils—crowned by a head of thick, wavy blond hair.

"Who *are* you?" she asked exasperatedly.

He clicked his heels sharply together. "Laurent de Trouvère, *à votre service,* mademoiselle."

Krisztina blinked with recognition. Of course! *Sonderklasse!* De Trouvère—one of the top dancers in the championship class, one of those she had watched from afar with admiration and concentration. That was why she hadn't realized who he was— she'd spent hours studying him from his shoulders down! Her mind clicked details into place. De Trouvère, a French aristocrat, twice European championship runner-up, partnered by Alice Gébhard.

"I should have realized," she said, looking up at him with new respect.

"There was no reason," he said affably.

"But I've watched you so often, monsieur."

"And I you," he said. "You dance well."

"You've seen us?"

"Many times."

She flushed, wishing David were beside her.

De Trouvère seemed to be studying her closely. "I know," he said slowly, "of your troubles."

"Troubles?" Krisztina echoed, startled.

"Of today. The ruling about your partner."

Her eyes widened. "How?"

A tiny muscle beneath his left eye twitched. "Herr Kaufmann is not the first German competitor to have been affected, nor, I suspect, will he be the last." His tone was matter-of-fact.

Krisztina's anger resurfaced. "It's monstrous, don't you think?"

"It's very unfortunate, I agree."

"That hardly describes it," she said tartly.

"I gather you were offered an option."

Krisztina lifted her chin. "Not one that we found acceptable."

"A pity," de Trouvère said lightly. "But not, perhaps, such a terrible catastrophe for you, Mademoiselle Florian."

"Whatever do you mean?" she asked, taken aback. "I must say I regard it as a disaster for us both equally."

"For your partnership, *bien sûr,*" the Frenchman countered, "but at least you are now at liberty to choose another partner."

"I don't want another partner!"

"Do you have a choice?"

"Of course!"

His mouth quirked. "Not, I should say, if you wish to continue to dance."

Krisztina's unhappiness surged anew inside her. How dare this man—this *stranger*—remind her of her horrible misery! She plucked angrily at her tulle skirt and prepared to turn back.

"Please don't be so furious, mademoiselle," de Trouvère said more gently. "I'm only pointing out what you must already realize. The partnership of Kaufmann and Florian, *B Klasse*, is regrettably at an end." He smiled. "But the partnership of de Trouvère and Florian, *Sonderklasse*, could quite easily be on the verge of beginning."

"I beg your pardon?" She hardly believed her ears.

"I think you heard me."

"But—" She floundered, then recovered. "Aside from anything else, monsieur, you already have a partner!"

"Yes."

"You can't have two partners."

"No."

"Then what are you talking about?" she demanded impatiently.

"Just that I, too, am free to change my partner."

Krisztina was outraged. "Don't be absurd!" She wondered where Alice Gébhard was at this moment, and what she would have to say if she could hear this ludicrous conversation.

Without warning, Laurent de Trouvère seized her hand, so that she gasped in surprise. "If you become my partner, Krisztina Florian," he said intensely, "I promise to make you a champion."

She resisted the impulse to laugh aloud. It was such terrible irony—she remembered as if it were yesterday David's words on the Gellert terrace. That had been magic—David's magic, David, who had become her dearest friend, and much, much more. But what this man offered, couched in almost the same words, reeked of enticement and danger. . . .

Roughly she pulled away her hand.

"Well?" de Trouvère said.

"Well what?" she answered defiantly.

"What do you say to my suggestion?"

She drew herself to full height. "I say that you might first of all consider Mademoiselle Gébhard."

He was unperturbed. "And second?"

She shook her head. "I don't believe you're serious."

"You may be certain I am."

Krisztina faltered a little. It was too much to take in. One moment she had been inside the glittering, unhappy ballroom, all her hopes dashed to pieces—and a few minutes later here she was, standing in this fragrant garden with an arrogant, handsome aristocrat, having what was almost certain success offered to her as simply as a bouquet.

"You were saying, mademoiselle," de Trouvère pressed her.

"Your idea," she said weakly, "is out of the question."

"It's more than an idea. It is a proposition, and I think you owe it to yourself to give it at least some thought before rejecting it."

"I told you—I already have a partner."

He smiled. "So do I."

She had never met anyone so abominably thick-skinned. "I really cannot believe you are serious," she repeated incredulously.

"And I can only reassure you that I am." He looked down at her, one eyebrow raised. "Don't you feel just the smallest bit flattered? You are, after all, only *B Klasse*, and little more than a child." He saw her angry expression, but gave her no opportunity to retort, glancing at his wristwatch. "I must leave you now, with great regret. Alice will be wondering where I am, and I daresay your *maman* and Herr Kaufmann will be growing concerned about you too."

Krisztina frowned. "You seem to know a great deal about me, monsieur."

"I do."

"How, may I ask?"

"As I said, I've watched you." He stepped back and gave a small bow. "And now I really must go, but first there is one more tiny morsel of Hungarian that I have practiced for this moment." Swiftly he seized her right hand again, this time raising it to his lips. *"Kezeit Csokolom,"* he said, and gently kissed the top of her hand.

Another maddening flush flooded through Krisztina, rising from the tips of the fingers that he still held, to the roots of her hair. She cursed herself for her display of weakness.

His eyes never left hers, but he released her hand. "With your father's permission," he said softly, "I shall call on you."

"Please don't trouble yourself," she said, more flustered than ever. Surely he would not come to Budapest?

"*Au contraire*, mademoiselle." He clicked his heels together again. "It will be a distinct pleasure."

Chapter 5

Laurent de Trouvère, son of Armand, the twenty-fifth Baron de Trouvère, lived with his family, as had the five preceding generations, in a ravishing, medium-sized château in the lush foothills of the Vosges Mountains in the Alsace region of France.

The de Trouvère family was proud of its traditions and history, which had begun in the Loire when the first baron, a favored poet at the court of Philippe-Auguste, had been granted his title and estate by the king early in the thirteenth century. It was not until after the original Château de Trouvère was burned to the ground during the Revolution that the twentieth baron, his spirit unvanquished, decided to move his family and entourage lock, stock, and wine barrel to Alsace. It was a part of his beloved France that he had often visited and admired for its physical beauty, excellent hunting, and distinctive native wines. The château into which they moved, originally a seventeenth-century hunting lodge, completely rebuilt in the late eighteenth century by a follower of Guêpière, was situated between Ribeauvillé and Riquewihr in the Haut-Rhin *département*. In 1817, once the baron had finished refurbishing it to a luxurious degree, he changed its name to de Trouvère, thus making it one of the very few châteaux in the district to bear a true French appellation, since Alsace had been absorbed into France quite late in the seventeenth century. As it turned out, twenty-five years later, the region was annexed to the Second Reich of the Hohenzollerns, and was not, in fact, returned to France until after the Great War. Laurent's great-grandfather, the twenty-third baron, was so appalled by the events of 1870 that he collapsed and died, brokenhearted, leaving the newly German estate to his heir.

Laurent was an only child, consequently, Baron Armand's only heir, and he had grown up with a perfect conviction that his life would follow the pattern formulated for him by seven centuries of forebears. The land, the title, and the family were sacrosanct, to be preserved at all costs—but Laurent was in no hurry to inherit. He loved his father as he loved his mother, Geneviève, and he never doubted that de Trouvère would be his in due course. When that time came, without brothers or sisters with whom to share either the advantages or burdens, Laurent realized he would be weighed down with responsibilities.

In the meantime, he had some years of liberty in which to sow his wild oats. Many young men in his position spent their lives traveling, intent on being in the right places at the right time— St. Moritz or Gstaad in February, the Côte d'Azur in April, London in June, Deauville in August. Those noble playboys spent their days riding, backing or simply owning racehorses or polo ponies, playing tennis, and driving fast cars, and their nights playing baccarat or roulette and seducing as many girls as possible. Laurent liked riding horses well enough—de Trouvère horses on de Trouvère land; he enjoyed driving his Mercedes and his father's Rolls-Royce Phantom and even harbored vague desires to own a Duesenberg; but he found gambling wasteful and boring, and while he had, from the age of fourteen, found sex a most pleasurable release, it did not rule his life.

He had been taught to dance on his tenth birthday by his *maman*, whose natural elegance and joie de vivre he had always greatly admired, and she had shown him more than the rudimentary steps, had impressed upon her handsome, limber young son that dance could be much more than a mere social grace and a passport to pleasure—it could be an art in itself. By his thirteenth birthday, the ladies who attended the balls and parties at the château found it no penance at all to be led in a waltz by the golden-haired future baron, who was tall and self-possessed for his age.

Though he had no especially competitive streak, Laurent admired excellence in others and liked to excel himself. When Alice Gébhard, a pretty young Alsacienne from Colmar, invited him to partner her at a gala contest over the frontier in Baden-Baden, he found the idea challenging and amusing. They won first prize, and danced on, but even after one success led to another, Laurent never considered his dancing much more than a charming *divertissement* to occupy and motivate him until the day that de Trouvère, his true mistress, would beckon and command him.

Until the afternoon in Marienbad in 1933 when he first saw Krisztina Florian dance a Charleston at a *thé dansant* at the Esplanade—feet, legs, arms, hands, and hair flying, and her lovely head shaking with such mad, all-consuming effervescence that he feared it might spin from her perfect shoulders. When the music stopped and he heard her bubbling, breathless laughter, and watched her walking back to her table on her partner's arm, Laurent stood quite still, momentarily helpless with a strange mixture of jealousy and exhilaration. In that instant he recognized that the single element that had, until then, been absent from his preordained future, had just fallen from the sky. He had been struck by a *coup de foudre*—had simply, absurdly, completely fallen in love at first sight.

It was a fundamental characteristic of all de Trouvère men to pursue relentlessly whatever was dear to their hearts, and so it was with twenty-year-old Laurent. As he told her when they finally met in Zurich, Krisztina was still little more than a child, but she showed all the promise of a *grande beauté* with her exquisite skin, pale golden hair, and those remarkable violet-blue eyes. Laurent wondered from whom she had inherited such looks —neither from her mother, pleasant enough but mouselike, and certainly not from her unattractive merchant papa, whom he had seen twice at competitions in Vienna and Budapest. On both occasions, Laurent had observed the object of his desire from a distance, his heart captivated, his mind marking every move, every quality. Any shortcomings could be blamed on her drab, bourgeois background, and Kaufmann, her partner, with whom she was clearly infatuated.

He was certain that he had found the woman of his future. She was a little headstrong, that much he had seen in Zurich, but she was still naive enough and sufficiently without artifice to be trained in the ways of his world. She was not of the blood, but she was the kind of human creature to absorb it, as plants absorb light. The only real question, until Zurich, had been how best to tempt her from Kaufmann's side. Now the Nazis had all but done it for him. She might not realize it, but Krisztina needed him. Dance was vital to her—without it she would thirst, would wilt. And he had the notion that to have her as his partner would infuse fresh life into his own dancing. Alice seemed so lackluster beside Krisztina, and had definitely caused him to underestimate his own talent. With Krisztina in his arms, he was almost certain to achieve a world ranking, and that, before anything, he felt, would be the path to her heart.

"But why not just dance with her?" his mother, La Baronne, asked Laurent after he had shared his feelings with her. "I've never had reason to question your good taste, *chéri*, and I'm sure the girl is gifted and very lovely, but you don't know her and already you have her earmarked as a suitable wife. It's folly!"

"Just wait till you see her, Maman—then you'll understand."

"But she's a child, Laurent, you said so yourself, and from a completely different background." Geneviève de Trouvère was not, for a woman of her position, a natural snob, but she loved her husband and son and their traditional values, and wished to protect them.

"She's perfect, Maman," he said helplessly. "You say I have good taste—you know de Trouvère means everything to me and that I would never do anything to harm our name or the estate. Just promise me that when the time is right, you'll persuade Papa to see her."

"I never make promises I can't fulfill, Laurent."

Her son grasped her hands feverishly. "How often have I asked you for something, Maman? When have I ever begged you, as I'm begging now?"

Geneviève smiled wryly. "Perhaps, *mon fils,* that's because you have always had everything."

Laurent had not counted on the swiftly growing maturity and strong streak of independence that travel and increasing adversity had developed in Krisztina, nor had he considered the depth of her feelings for David, which grew stronger with every passing day as the Jewish crisis in Germany intensified.

He had decided to base his campaign—for that was how he now regarded it—on what he felt sure was the virtually foolproof process of wooing. And he wooed magnificently—scarcely a week passed when a massive bouquet of pink roses, orchids, or lilies failed to arrive at Kalvaria Street. On nearly every occasion the flowers were accompanied by a gift of some kind, ranging from a giant-size bottle of Chanel No. 5 perfume to a pair of delicate pearl-and-diamond earrings.

Gabor and Ilona were as impressed as they were intended to be by such a tangible display of admiration for their daughter, but the person Laurent most wanted to overwhelm remained almost impervious to the long-distance courtship. What he simply failed to grasp was that the single-mindedness of Krisztina's first love was just as intense as his own. For every dozen gifts Laurent might shower on Krisztina, a single carnation or a few caring lines from her beloved David meant infinitely more.

"You must write immediately to thank him," Gabor beamed, after Krisztina had unpacked yet another offering, a superb tiny lapis-and-gold Fabergé rabbit purloined from the de Trouvère family collection.

Krisztina fingered the lovely piece thoughtfully. "I think I should return this."

"Whatever for?"

She flushed. "It's too valuable a gift for a casual friendship."

Ilona, who sat sewing in the corner of the room, spoke gently. "It's becoming rather obvious, Kriszti, that Monsieur de Trouvère doesn't consider this to be just a casual friendship."

"But I've given him no encouragement."

"Then it's high time you did," Gabor interjected vigorously, lighting a cigar.

"Anyway, I have to write to David tonight," Krisztina added stubbornly. "I'll write to Laurent tomorrow."

Gabor sighed. His precious daughter was causing him more frustration than ever. He had hoped that when they had been deprived of the chance to dance together, Krisztina and Kaufmann's relationship might have faded, but instead his obstinate child seemed to exist mainly for the correspondence between them. Gabor was terribly torn. The last thing he wanted was for Krisztina to be unhappy, but he detested the very idea of her being besotted by the Jew, let alone running the risk of losing such a prize as the young future baron.

"What I simply cannot understand," he said as patiently as he could, "is why you won't dance with him. It's clear that he's far more accomplished than Kaufmann."

"If I can't dance with David," Krisztina replied, as she always did, "I don't want to dance with anyone."

"But you do miss it all, *dragam*, don't you," Ilona said in support of her husband. "I'm sure David would encourage you to find another partner if he knew."

"He does know."

"And what does he say?"

Krisztina's eyes were misty. "He agrees with you."

"Well then!" Gabor jumped in.

"But he doesn't mean it," she added miserably. "He only says it for my sake. I know it would hurt him terribly if I danced with Laurent." She forced a smile. "In any case, it's only a matter of time before David is allowed to compete again."

"I doubt that," said Gabor.

Increasingly, Gabor used his nightly prayers to beseech God to strengthen Hitler's grip on Germany. Since the issuance of the ban that had affected Kaufmann's competition, Gabor's admiration for the Reich had grown by leaps and bounds. Nowadays Gabor followed events in Germany with even greater interest than before.

Ilona, too, knelt each day to commune with God, but her prayers were different. She felt a wealth of pity for David, whom she had grown to like and respect during their tours of Europe, but for Krisztina's sake she hoped that the relationship would end before the girl became drawn even farther into the problems that seemed repeatedly to beset the unfortunate Jewish people. And as for Laurent de Trouvère, she had to admit that Gabor was right when he told Krisztina that a chance like this came only once in a lifetime.

On two occasions since the Swiss championships, Laurent had made the long journey from de Trouvère to Budapest to visit Krisztina. In the beginning, he had believed it would be a relatively simple matter to seduce the teenager into accepting him, at least as a dance partner, but he had now come to realize that she could not be rushed. Arriving in grand style at Kalvaria Street in his Mercedes Kompressor, he found it easy enough to win over Gabor and Ilona; his status, his Gallic charm, and the evident strength of his affection for their daughter made it almost impossible for the Florians to resist him. But Krisztina sat demurely beside him on the ottoman while Ilona poured tea from her best

Herend porcelain service, spoke politely when she was spoken to but remained maddeningly reticent the rest of the visit.

In mid-September of 1935, the Nuremberg Laws were passed in Germany; Jews were deprived of all civil rights, were forbidden to marry Aryans, were, to all intents and purposes, legally segregated. A month later, Nathan Kaufmann's store on Kurfürstendamm was Aryanized, leaving him in a dilemma over the future of the Budapest branch. Under other circumstances, this would logically have been the moment to scoop up his family and possessions and move to Hungary to resume at least a semblance of normality. But since anti-Semitism was rife there, too, there was no sense leaping from the frying pan into the fire, and besides, Hungary could never be home. By remaining on native soil and making the best of things, Nathan rationalized, one might more easily recoup one's losses. He evaluated his financial situation and then dispatched David to Budapest on a reconnaissance mission, to ascertain how easily and profitably they might sell the Vaci Utca store.

David seized the opportunity to see Krisztina, and found Gabor Florian more welcoming than usual. He was unaware, of course, that earlier the same month Gabor had received a long-distance call from Laurent de Trouvère.

"Forgive this presumption, monsieur," Laurent had begun respectfully, "but I have an idea that the imminent sale of Kaufmann's branch in Pest might be of interest to you."

"How so?"

"I imagine it might be something of a coup for you, monsieur, if you were ready to add the store to your other interests." Laurent paused. "I have learned that Kaufmann is seeking a swift outcome above all other considerations. Have you heard that the Berlin store has been Aryanized?"

"I have." Gabor had heard that news with mixed feelings, since there was no guarantee that the new proprietors would continue to buy from old suppliers. It was so often that way—principles at loggerheads with financial good sense. Now, listening to Laurent, he reddened with excitement. If only he could afford it, how he would relish the chance to win ascendancy over Nathan Kaufmann!

"It would, of course," he ventured carefully, "be interesting to know what price Kaufmann intends to ask."

"My father uses a firm of lawyers in Vienna," Laurent responded helpfully. "I shall ask them to make inquiries on our behalf."

The call over, Gabor had preened smugly. *On our behalf.* This was surely proof-positive that de Trouvère was determined to win his daughter. Gabor rubbed his hands together in delight. Life really was turning around! With help from Laurent and cooperation from his bank, ownership of one of Budapest's smartest stores could become a genuine prospect, and he would never again have to crawl to either Nathan Kaufmann or his son. And who could say? If only Krisztina would see sense, the Florian family might even in time be bound to the French aristocracy by marriage!

By the time David arrived in Budapest, Gabor had formulated an acceptable offer. The bank had been unhelpful to begin with; since the financial panics of 1931, life had become difficult for the small businessman bent on growth. However, Gabor's new connection with Laurent, and the fact that Jewish businesses were going cheap, had brought him the promise of the funds he needed.

David came to Kalvaria Street on a Sunday evening, intending to take Krisztina out, only to find dinner prepared for them by Ilona.

"Kriszti, *Liebling*," he whispered to her in the hall after a swiftly snatched kiss, "we must have some time alone."

She smiled at him through eyes hazy with longing. "Later, I hope. Papa insisted that we eat together first."

He hugged her quickly. "I've missed you."

Gladness surged in her. "Truly?"

"Of course." He ruffled her hair.

"Not just the dancing?"

"No, not just the dancing," he said. "Haven't you read my letters?"

"Over and over," she breathed joyously. It was miraculous the way their love had burgeoned through their correspondence. They had not been able to meet for months, but although she was still only sixteen, she felt as if she had really begun to grow up during their separation. Even David, who had previously seemed to consider her too young for romance, had clearly begun to acknowledge the strength of his own feelings for her.

"Your father seems uncommonly pleased to see me," he said.

"I know," Krisztina replied happily. "He was quite excited when I said you were coming. I think he wants to talk to you."

"About what?"

"I'm not sure." She blushed. "Perhaps about us."

David kept silent, perfectly aware that Gabor Florian had only tolerated his partnership with Krisztina for the sake of business courtesy.

"What's wrong?" Krisztina asked.

"Nothing, *Liebling.*" He kissed the top of her head.

"You look troubled."

"I'm just hungry."

The deal was accomplished within three weeks. Two other prospective buyers entered the bidding and retired—Gabor had never felt such vigor and determination in his life. Ilona was amazed by the general transformation in him while negotiations were in progress.

On the eleventh day of February, 1936, the store on Vaci Utca changed hands. The Kaufmann logo on all signs, bills of sale, bags, and boxes remained, for Gabor realized he had bought sizable goodwill along with the property, but the staff were left in no possible doubt as to who was now the boss, for Gabor was reeling with excitement and flushed with power.

That night, Gabor held a celebratory party at the Gellert Hotel, partying with all the enthusiasm and charm he could muster.

At one o'clock in the morning, he summoned Krisztina and David into the hall, a small, regretful smile on his lips.

"From this night," he told them quietly, "you will not see each other again."

For a long moment, Krisztina stared uncomprehendingly at her father. Then, as the words sank in, she gasped with dismay and disbelief. "Papa, you can't possibly mean that!"

Gabor genuinely suffered for the pain he caused her, but one day he knew she would thank him for it, once she was safely married to the baron. *"Abszolute,"* he said calmly. "I mean it."

"But we love each other!"

"You're too young to know what real love is, Krisztina, and you will do as I tell you." Gabor was not a tall man, but now he seemed to tower over his daughter.

She clutched wildly at David's arm. "Tell him! Tell him what he says is impossible!"

David was shaken, but his face was impassive. "Since you're only sixteen, Kriszti," he said slowly, not looking at her, "I suspect there's little point in my saying anything to your father. He seems quite resolute."

Gabor gave a small bow. "Most perceptive."

Tears began to stream down Krisztina's cheeks. She wanted to kick and scream and tear at her father and at David, too, to remind them that she was an individual with a mind and spirit of her own—that she had a right to happiness and that they could not steal it from her. But instead, she just stood there dumbly, hating her father more than she had ever hated anyone.

"Where's Mama?" she managed, at last.

"Your mother cannot alter what I've said." Gabor turned to David. "It's late, Kaufmann. The party's finished."

David's mouth twisted with anguish and disdain. "Since I'm staying at the Gellert tonight, I'm afraid you'll have to be the first to leave." He looked away from Florian and gently touched Krisztina's cheek with a hand that trembled slightly. "Be brave, my lovely Kriszti," he said softly. "I'll write to you."

"I forbid it," Gabor flared angrily.

David met the older man's eyes again. "I haven't asked your permission." Quickly, he kissed Krisztina's forehead. "Don't give up," he said boldly. "I never shall."

"Don't go!" she pleaded frantically, terrified that she might never see him again. "Don't leave me, David!"

Gabor took hold of her arm. "This is neither the time nor the place to create a scene, Krisztina."

"How can you be so cruel?" she demanded, weeping.

"I hope you will not think me cruel for too long," Gabor said quietly, maintaining a firm grip on her arm. He looked at David. "Good night, Kaufmann." He paused. "And farewell."

David was white-faced. "I deeply regret that I advised my father to turn Kaufmann's over to you, Florian," he said, and now his voice shook. "It was the worst mistake I have ever made."

For a long moment the two men stood very still, their stares locked, like mortal enemies. Then Gabor moved, his hand clenched around Krisztina's wrist, forcing her to leave David's side.

"Where are you taking me?" she sobbed, twisting her head so that she could still see David.

Gabor hurried off, dragging her with him. "I am taking you to the ladies' cloakroom, where I expect you to clean your face and make yourself presentable. And then," he continued relentlessly, "we are going to drink a glass of champagne with Laurent de Trouvère, who is waiting for us in the bar."

"I don't want to see him!"

"You will see him," Gabor countered grimly, "and you will behave charmingly and courteously to him."

They were nearing the corner, and Krisztina craned her neck for one last, desperate glimpse of David. As he disappeared from sight, she slumped in physical submission against the wall. "I will never forgive you for this, Father," she said, her voice grown suddenly dull. "Never."

He pulled her more gently the last few feet to the cloakroom, put one hand on the door handle, and pushed her forward. "You will, child, in time."

Krisztina stepped away from him with a great effort at dignity. She looked hard into his eyes.

"Not in a thousand years."

During the three weeks that followed, three letters arrived for Krisztina from Berlin; all were confiscated, read, and burned in the fireplace by Gabor. Krisztina pleaded with her mother for help, but Ilona felt powerless. She was of a generation of women who considered themselves morally obligated to support their husbands, and she was secretly relieved that Krisztina had been diverted from the Jewish predicament, though her warm mother's heart ached as she observed her daughter's suffering.

Laurent de Trouvère stayed on in Budapest for two weeks after the party. Learning that Krisztina liked venturing out of the city, he took her on long excursions in the Mercedes to Balaton and even over the Hortobagy, seeking, but never finding the fata morgana, the legendary mirage of the Great Plain, where distant images were said to appear to float upside down, and then dining at the Nagy Csarda, but in spite of his efforts Krisztina remained aloof to Laurent's charms, behaving with the good manners demanded of her, but giving nothing more.

The evening before Laurent was due to leave for Alsace, he came to the Florian house to speak to Gabor.

"It's too early," he said, over a glass of *barack* in Gabor's study. "She must have time."

"She is being foolish," Gabor said awkwardly.

"She is simply very young," Laurent consoled him, biting back his own disappointment and channeling all his energies instead into his determination. "And I have a great amount of patience."

"I fear you may need it."

Laurent smiled. "I am also armed with an alternative strategy, in the event that all else fails."

Gabor sat up. "What kind of strategy?"

Laurent shrugged enigmatically. "Let us give her the time she needs first, and then, if that proves insufficient, we can talk again."

A few months later, in mid-July, the two men sat again in the same room. This time they were sipping from the bottle of *prunelle,* the eau-de-vie made from wild plums that was a speciality of Alsace, and which Laurent had brought as a gift along with two cases of excellent de Trouvère Riesling.

"No change," Gabor said morosely, lighting a cigar.

"No, *malheureusement,*" Laurent agreed.

"If she would only give you a chance. She's wasting her life pining for that boy."

"She does not understand what I can offer her."

Gabor scratched his head. "Not even for the sake of dancing, that's what I find so hard to comprehend. For so long, she gave the impression she couldn't live without it."

"I think I have considerably more than dancing to offer her," Laurent said stiffly.

"Of course you have," Gabor amended hastily. "Don't think I don't realize that. The girl is a fool, and I'm ashamed of her."

Increasingly, the eventual fusion of the de Trouvère family with the Florians figured in Gabor's fantasies. Gabor Florian was in the heady business of empire-building, and no one, not even his daughter, was going to stand in his way.

"Perhaps," Laurent said slowly, "the first step is to get her to regard me as her friend, instead of as an interloper, an intruder into her privacy."

Gabor sighed and rolled the tip of his cigar around the ashtray on his desk. "But how to accomplish a change of heart? These days, I must confess, she seems to regard even her own father as her enemy."

"She will get over that, *uram,* given time," Laurent said with a soothing note of respect. "No," he went on, "I think it's time to trace a different route."

Light dawned on Gabor's face. "The strategy you spoke of before?"

"Exactement," Laurent replied. "But I shall need your cooperation."

"Anything," Gabor said heartily.

Laurent raised a cautionary hand. "Better hear my proposition first—you may not care for it."

At five o'clock the following afternoon, Laurent and Krisztina sat at a corner table in Gerbeaud. He ordered coffee and pastries for them both and a cognac for himself, before claiming her attention.

"It was good of you to come."

Krisztina inclined her head. "It was kind of you to invite me."

Laurent smiled. "That completes the courtesies."

Krisztina gazed glumly into her napkin.

"I'm perfectly aware," he continued drily, "that you find me dislikable."

Krisztina was startled. "That's not true."

Again, Laurent's lips twitched. "It would make me happy to believe that, *chère* Krisztina, but it is certainly true to say that, though you are always scrupulously polite, you would rather not be here with me this afternoon."

Krisztina took refuge in silence. She hated having to tell lies of any sort, even those told out of kindness. It was *not* true to say that she actively disliked Laurent de Trouvère—after all, it was not Laurent's fault that her father had turned against David—but she still found him arrogant and presumptuous.

"Why did you invite me here today?" she asked finally.

"You must know how I enjoy your company."

She lowered her eyes. "I'm not much of a companion."

"Because you are unhappy."

"Yes."

"I asked you to come today because I wanted to speak to you."

"About what?"

"About the source of your unhappiness."

Outside, on Vorosmarty Ter, traffic hummed and people scurried by the window of the café. The coffee arrived at their table in a silver pot with a lavish helping of whipped cream, and Laurent and Krisztina dug their forks halfheartedly into their pastries.

"What did you mean?" Krisztina asked after a few minutes. "About my unhappiness."

Laurent laid down his fork. "You are sad, Krisztina, because of the friend you may no longer see."

Krisztina dabbed her lips with her napkin and said nothing. The merest reference to David always brought her close to tears, and she refused to cry in front of Laurent.

"Do you miss him so very much?"

"Yes," she answered softly.

"But your father refuses to allow him to visit you." His tone was gentle.

A strong wave of self-pity washed over her. "He is adamant." Her voice cracked with emotion.

"I wonder."

She glanced at him in surprise. "What do you mean?"

"I mean that I wonder if your papa could be persuaded to relent, at least a little."

Surprise turned to astonishment. "I don't understand, Laurent. Who on earth could persuade him if I can't?"

He paused. "I would be willing to try."

"You!" she cried, amazed.

"Why not?"

"Because you have made it clear that you wish me to become your partner."

"That's right, I do."

"And you have repeatedly sent me gifts and flowers, and—" She broke off, too embarrassed to continue.

"And I have tried my hardest to court you." The golden eyes were warm and appraising.

"Well, yes." She felt the heat rush to her cheeks.

"That does not rule out all sympathy and compassion," he said chasteningly.

"I still don't understand." She leaned forward, trying to fathom his real motivation. "You say you would be willing to intercede with my father on our behalf."

"That is correct."

"But *why?*"

Laurent gave another small, sad smile. "Because, though I would dearly love to have you for myself, *chère* Krisztina, I would sooner have your friendship than no relationship at all."

Taken aback by his candor, she sank back into her chair and gazed at him with growing excitement. "Do you think he might listen to you?"

He shrugged. "It's not possible to be sure, of course, but"—he grinned disarmingly— "he and I have lately developed a certain respect for one another."

A slight suspicion prodded her. "Are you perhaps hoping for my gratitude—my obligation—rather than my friendship?"

Laurent raised his cognac glass in a salute. "Your friendship, I assure you, my dear, suspicious Krisztina. And your happiness."

"Well?" A frown of tension marked Gabor's forehead.

Laurent smiled. "According to plan."

"Her reaction?"

"Astonishment, naturally. A little wariness. But also the first glimmers of warmth."

"What does she expect now?"

"That I shall try to persuade you to relent."

"Which of course you cannot do."

"Of course not, but at least in relation to the letters."

"Ah, yes, the letters." The furrow between Gabor's eyebrows deepened. "I must say I am far from happy with this idea, Laurent. I fear we may achieve nothing but her continued obsession with Kaufmann."

"A few letters, *uram,* nothing more."

"Letters will be just the beginning, you mark my words. They will want more than letters."

"Don't despair, monsieur. This is only the first step of my plan. There is more to follow."

"How much more?"

"You must trust me if we are to succeed."

"I do trust you, my boy." Gabor removed his spectacles and passed a weary hand over his eyes. "But it worries me nonetheless. She is my only child—I have such hopes for her."

"I'm honored to think they include me, *uram.*"

Gabor regarded him with pleasure. "It's time we ended such

formality, don't you think, Laurent? Won't you call me Gabor from now on?"

Laurent gave a small bow of acknowledgment, and his eyes glinted. "And what may I tell Krisztina on the subject of letters?"

"You really believe this is the right way?" Gabor pressed him anxiously.

Laurent placed his right hand over his heart. "The only way," he said, and hesitated for a second before adding: "Gabor."

The older man smiled. "Tell her they may exchange letters."

Chapter 6

The next evening, a hot, stifling night, Laurent escorted Krisztina to a Strauss concert at the Vigado. The venerable building, constructed in the late 1860s in the Romantic style, stood on the Danube promenade and held within it a number of halls. On that particular evening when Laurent and Krisztina arrived, visitors were already thronging the main hall, some waiting to file into a Liszt recital, others to watch a performance of *Swan Lake* and the rest warmly anticipating Strauss. Most were formally dressed, many in the latest evening gowns and stylish dinner suits, and a musky cloud of perfume and cigar smoke wafted about their heads.

Krisztina sat through the concert hardly able to listen to the music. She was in an agony of suspense, having agreed to come this evening for only one reason: Laurent had said he had news for her! A luscious string of waltzes floated around the hall, and Krisztina was conscious of Laurent swaying to the rhythm, but for her increasingly the event became a tortured longing for David.

The concert over, applause still ringing in their ears, Laurent whisked her to a small, elegant restaurant in a Buda side street.

"The food here is first class," he said as they were seated. "And an excellent appetizer for what I have to tell you."

"What is it?"

"First we order."

She wilted back against her chair. "I can't," she said. "I'm much too excited to think about food."

He relented. "Let's at least have some champagne."

Krisztina was burning with anticipation. The news must be spectacular if he insisted on champagne! Her mind began weaving fantasies . . . David on his way to Budapest? . . . Perhaps already here! . . .

The champagne was poured and the froth settling before Laurent raised his glass.

"To you, *ma belle* Krisztina."

She took a sip, hardly tasting it.

"I have spoken with your father," he began.

"Yes," she breathed.

"He is not so rigid as you would believe, Krisztina."

"No?" she said, a little harshness impinging on her eagerness.

Laurent smiled and spoke slowly, relishing every word. "He has given his consent that you and David may exchange letters."

A wonderful warmth washed through her. "And?" she asked.

"And what?"

"Surely there's more?"

He shook his head. "No more." He paused. "Isn't that enough?"

"How can it be enough?" she burst out wretchedly, all the joy draining away. "I love David and he loves me! We want to be together, not just to be correspondents!"

"Of course you do," Laurent soothed her, "but as a beginning, surely you must see it is something of a victory."

Krisztina swallowed hard, trying not to weep, forcing herself to remember how hard Laurent must have worked to get even this far. "I should be thanking you," she said with difficulty.

"I thought you would be overjoyed."

Krisztina bit her lip. "I'm very grateful to you," she said. "It's just that . . . I had hoped for more."

Laurent leaned forward, picked up her glass and handed it to her. "Drink a little," he said kindly. "And consider—it may only be a prelude, but it is still a triumph."

She sipped a little more champagne and managed a weak smile. "You're right, of course." She felt ashamed. "You've been such a fine friend to us, Laurent. I only wish there were some way to thank you."

"Only acknowledge that friendship," he said quietly. "And I

promise you I will try to find a way to persuade your father to let you see David."

"You think there's a chance?" she whispered.

"There is always a chance," he said firmly. "And remember this, *ma chère*, when a de Trouvère makes up his mind to achieve something, he never accepts defeat."

Two months later, Laurent returned to Budapest and invited Krisztina to dine with him at Gundel in Ligetten. Over *szekelygulyas* and paprika chicken, he told her that although he had made no more headway with her father, he had been in touch with David.

"I know," she said, and blushed. "He wrote to me."

"About our partnership?"

"Yes."

"Then you know he has no objection?"

"Yes," she said again, softly.

Laurent paused. "I've been keeping a watchful eye on David, Krisztina."

"How? What do you mean?"

"I mean that life in Berlin is increasingly risky for people like David, and it's always good for a man to have friends."

Fear stabbed her. "What's happened?"

He patted her hand soothingly. "Don't fret, dear Krisztina, nothing has happened to him. Not yet, at least."

Her eyes widened. "Is he in danger?"

Laurent glanced around quickly, and spoke even more quietly. "All Jews in Germany are in danger. Thousands have already left —thousands more are leaving."

Krisztina gripped her napkin. "David will never leave without his parents, and they won't go."

"Then at least warn him to be cautious, to do nothing that might bring him to the attention of the Gestapo. And meanwhile . . ." He hesitated.

"Yes?" she prodded anxiously.

"Meanwhile, I shall speak to my father. He has useful contacts in Germany, especially a cousin in the French Embassy in Berlin. We may perhaps be able to pass on a few good words about the Kaufmann family."

"Oh, Laurent, please!" She took his hand imploringly. "If your father can help, please, *please* ask him to try!"

He squeezed her fingers lightly. "Of course I will, have no fear."

Krisztina's eyes filled with tears. "How can I thank you for your kindness, Laurent? You're being so very good to me, so much better than I deserve."

Laurent sat back in his chair, his expression impenetrable. "There is assuredly one thing you could do that would make me the happiest of men."

"Name it!" she cried impulsively.

"Dance with me."

Her enthusiasm crumbled. "Oh, Laurent, how can I even think of dancing at a time like this?"

"How can you *not* think of it?"

"I don't understand."

Laurent shrugged. "It's easy. You have deprived yourself of *la danse* for much too long, Krisztina. Without it you're only half a person, like a sailor deprived of salt water." His eyes glittered. "If you dance again—*when* you dance again—everything in your life will seem a thousand times brighter than it does now, believe me."

"But David—"

"David approves," he reminded her gently. "You said as much yourself."

Krisztina paused. "He thinks you could turn me into a champion."

"He is right," Laurent said. "With a great deal of work."

There was a long silence. She stared at him pensively. "Will you really try to help the Kaufmanns, Laurent?"

He returned her gaze soberly. "I swear it."

Krisztina had believed that she had grown up through her separation from David, that love and suffering had smoothed out the joyous edges of childhood and turned her into a woman. Now, suddenly, she was aware of a sharp pricking in her soul, as if something deep inside her was being destroyed forever. Was this, then, the death of her youth? And yet there was no sense of mourning, just a calm acceptance of what had to follow.

Her lips curved wistfully.

"Then how can I refuse?" she said.

They began to dance.

Krisztina had almost forgotten the joy of it, the pure sensation

of near flight that overwhelmed her whenever she took to a
dance floor. The thrill of love that had accompanied that sensation when she had danced with David was gone, perhaps forever,
but now there were new and almost equally exciting realizations,
for while David had been a wonderful natural dancer, Laurent
de Trouvère was a dance wizard. Even among the elegant
denizens of *Sonderklasse,* he was incomparably stylish; each time
Laurent stepped out, he gave such a consummate performance
that every man and woman in the audience, and even the most
formidable of the judges, was riveted. And although Laurent
pressured her to work far more intensively than even practice-
conscious David had, there could be no denying that within just a
few weeks of her taking Alice Gébhard's place, Krisztina felt
stronger, happier, and more complete than she had in many
months.

If only she were sure that David was out of danger, all would be
right with her world, she told herself. She had written to him as
Laurent had suggested, and David had sent back pages of loving
reassurance, stressing that he would do nothing to endanger either himself or his family. Still, she was constantly afraid for him.
Even if they were never to be allowed to dance together again, if
he would only leave Germany and come to Hungary, she fanta-
sized, perhaps Laurent would use his powers of persuasion to talk
Papa into granting his blessing, and then they could be married.
. . . In the meantime, every letter grew increasingly precious.

During the winter of 1936–37, dancing for France, the new
partnership of de Trouvère and Florian swiftly captured the attention of audiences and judges alike. Still sheltered under
Ilona's proud, chaperoning wing, Krisztina traveled with Laurent to Paris, Geneva, and Marienbad, winning all three championship competitions. All through the spring they practiced like
demons for the second European championship of the year, to be
held in Berlin.

It was all so different now, Ilona reflected happily as she helped
Krisztina to pack for the journey. Even the dresses told the tale—
glorious flowing dresses by Nils Prien and Hobe, flowing, se-
quined, multilayered creations that played a part in the transformation of her daughter. At last, thanks to Laurent, Krisztina was
up in the exalted *Sonderklasse* ranks. At last, the ballroom spot-
lights followed *her.* And even more importantly, she could no

longer be exposed to the ugliness of anti-Semitism, and for that alone, Ilona would always be grateful to Laurent. Just one lingering shadow cast a pall over the excitement. Gabor had issued dire instructions that on no account was David to be allowed to see or even speak to Krisztina while they were in Berlin, and he had charged Ilona with the responsibility of keeping them apart. It was almost more than her tender heart could bear.

It was certainly more than Krisztina intended to put up with. She *would* see David, and it was absurd of her father to believe that she would be fobbed off. Her mother, she was convinced, would be willing to turn a blind eye, though of course she would not ask her to deceive her father openly. As for Laurent—well, surely he would help her as he always did.

Arriving in Berlin, they checked into the Adlon with two full days to spare before the start of the competition. The three of them spent the first afternoon gazing into store windows on Unter den Linden before Ilona pronounced that it was time for a nap before dinner.

Krisztina waited until Ilona's breathing was even, and judged her to be sound asleep. Noiselessly, she folded back her own quilt, slipped on her blue silk robe, picked up the room key firmly to prevent it from jangling, and crept stealthily out of the bedroom.

Laurent's room was down the corridor on the opposite side. Krisztina tapped on the door and waited impatiently.

He was fully dressed, but had removed his tie and had undone the top three buttons of his shirt to reveal several inches of tanned, hairless chest.

"*Bonsoir,*" he said, showing no particular surprise at finding her, half dressed, at his door.

"Laurent," she said without preamble, "will you let me use your telephone?"

His expression was impassive. "To call David." It was a statement, not a question.

"Yes." She paused. "Please."

"You'd better come in." He stood back to let her pass, closed the door, and indicated the telephone on the walnut writing desk. "You have his number?"

"Of course." It was engraved on her heart.

"Then by all means."

She hesitated.

He smiled slightly. "You would prefer me to leave?"

Krisztina flushed. "I'm sorry. It's just that it's been so long since we spoke." She wavered uncomfortably.

Laurent gave a small, stiff bow. *"Bien sûr."* He walked to the door. "Will ten minutes be sufficient?"

She ran to him and kissed him on the cheek. "Wonderful, thank you."

His mouth twitched. "And then, I imagine, you will need some help to arrange a meeting?"

She flung her arms around him. "Oh, Laurent," she exclaimed, "you really are the finest friend in all the world!"

He returned, exactly twelve minutes later, to find her still seated at the desk, her cheeks hot.

"I gather you reached him."

She nodded.

"How are things with him?"

"Dreadful, I think," she said uncertainly. "He seemed reluctant to tell me, but things sound so strange. Normal, yet at the same time terribly abnormal." She shook her head. "And when you think how ordinary everything appears to us—except for the signs and the swastikas—how civil and complacent the people seem to be, while for them—" She broke off, too upset to continue.

"Perhaps we shouldn't have come to Berlin."

"Oh, no!" she protested.

"Did you speak of a meeting?"

Tears pricked her eyes. "At first, he didn't even seem to want to see me, and then I realized he was trying to protect me. It's inadvisable, he told me," she said bitterly, "for a gentile to associate with a Jew."

"That's quite true," Laurent said quietly.

Krisztina turned her face pleadingly up to him. "Will you help us, Laurent? Please?"

He turned away and stared out the window for a long time. Finally, he turned back.

"I will help you," he said. "On one condition."

"Anything."

"This . . . meeting . . . must not interfere with our dancing. This is the *Europa Meisterschaft,* Krisztina—it's what we've worked so hard for. If I feel that your performance is affected, then I shall never help you or Kaufmann again."

Relief flooding her, Krisztina stood up and put her arms around him again. "I won't let you down, Laurent, I swear it."

He paused. "Then I suggest that you use this room for the meeting." His voice was matter-of-fact. "It's the safest, most private place you could find."

Again, Krisztina blushed. This was more than she'd ever permitted herself to dream of—a chance to be alone, *truly* alone, with David. She had imagined a secret stroll, hand in hand, in the Grunewald, a few snatched moments, a kiss, perhaps, under cover of trees—but the prospect of a real tryst took her breath away.

"It will need to be at a time," Laurent went on, "when I can arrange to safely occupy your mother for an hour or two."

Krisztina looked worried. "How will you do that? I'm sure Papa has told her never to leave me alone."

"I planned to buy you a gift tomorrow afternoon," he said. "A good-luck token for the competition. I shall simply ask her to accompany me and give me her invaluable advice. She will not refuse."

Anticipation began to bubble up inside her, and she clapped her hands delightedly. "You always think of everything!"

Laurent was expressionless, remote. "I gave my word that I would help you, Krisztina," he said, "and help you I will."

Chapter 7

At three o'clock the next afternoon, Krisztina flew to the door of Laurent's room and flung it open. David stood there, daylight from the window striking his face. He looked remarkable, more handsome than ever. He was a little suntanned, for the weather in Berlin had been fine lately, but thinner than she remembered him. His blue eyes still sparkled as they scanned her face, but the strain of the past months was clearly visible.

She held out her arms, and he came into the room, closing the door softly behind him. His body felt lean and hard against hers, his face smooth and cool. She recognized the familiar smell of him, the faintly pine-scented cologne he'd always used, and now, as she inhaled, memories came rushing in, pricking her senses, to be replaced almost instantly by the shock of new experience as he held her briefly at arm's length and then drew her close to kiss her. His mouth felt astonishingly warm and alive, and his tongue tasted sweet and firm as it traced the inside of her lips tentatively, and then flashed lightly to touch hers.

Krisztina shut her eyes, her lashes fluttering as he kissed her left ear and nibbled fleetingly on the lobe before transferring his lips to her neck and then burying his face in her hair. She thought, with a mixture of joy and alarm, that if he let go of her now, she might fall down—her heart was pounding rapidly and she could scarcely catch her breath.

"Oh, Kriszti," he murmured.

She clung to him fiercely, and tears of passion, love, and confusion began to rain down her cheeks.

"Don't, Kriszti," he implored her, brushing her wet face with tender fingers. "I hate it when you cry."

"I can't help it," she sobbed weakly, her hands gripping his arms tightly, urgently. "I've waited so long . . ."

"I know, *Liebling,* I know how you feel," he comforted her. "I feel the same way."

They pulled apart, both realizing suddenly that more than desire and emotion was needed to bridge the distance that had inevitably formed between them, that their thoughts must be translated into words before the sweetness could continue. The ragged wound of enforced separation could not simply be stitched together with a few kisses; it required communication and commitment to draw the edges closer, to bond them so tightly that they could not easily be pulled apart again.

They walked arm in arm to the sofa and sat down, suddenly shy and formal with each other.

"We have only two hours," Krisztina said in a hushed voice.

"At most," David agreed. He reached for her hand and held it tightly.

She looked into his eyes. "How have you been, *edesem?*"

"Not so bad. I told you on the telephone."

"I didn't believe you. Tell me the truth now."

He smiled ruefully. "It is the truth. I've been fortunate. Much more so than some of my friends."

"What's happened to them?"

"Brushes with the Gestapo. Some have disappeared." He shrugged. "People do that these days."

"Where do they go?" Krisztina asked fearfully. "What happens to them?"

"Prison, perhaps," he said, deliberately vague. "I don't know. No one really knows."

She shivered. "David, I've thought and thought. I'm sure you must leave Germany. Can't you come to Budapest? You could stay with us."

"I'm sure your father would be delighted," he said ironically.

"Mama would be on our side."

"I expect she would," David said gently, "but it's quite impossible."

She bit her lip. "What about France?"

"What about it?"

"Laurent says that his father has a cousin at the French embassy in Berlin who could help you. Laurent says there is an invisible, natural chain that links aristocrats everywhere."

"Laurent says a great deal," David said drily.

"Yes, he does," Krisztina agreed, missing the irony. "If you went to France, I could join you—Laurent would help us."

David smiled, touched by her naiveté. "Even if any of that were possible, Kriszti, which it probably isn't, you're forgetting my parents. My father has taken his reversal of fortunes rather badly, and my mother is far from strong."

"They must leave too!"

"They don't want to leave their home, sweetheart. It's all they have left."

Krisztina sighed heavily and nestled against him. Outside in the corridor came the sound of trundling wheels and clinking crockery. David jumped to his feet.

"I'll lock the door." He crossed the room and turned the key.

"Come back," Krisztina said softly. "I want you near me."

He sat down again and put his arm around her. "So tell me," he said, his expression unreadable, "about the dancing. How is it with Laurent?"

She stared at him. "It's—fine," she answered lamely.

"I've read the reports, of course. I know how brilliantly you're doing."

"It's not the same as it was with you," she said staunchly.

"The results are better."

"You and I would have done the same if we'd been allowed the time," she said decisively, her cheeks hot with guilt.

"I know." He watched her. "Tell me how it feels, Kriszti," he probed. "Share it with me, at least in words."

She bit her lip. "It's different," she began shyly. "More . . . professional. Less magical." She met his gaze. "With you, it always felt the most natural thing in the world, as if we were dancing just for ourselves."

"First experiences," he said quietly, "are often the most memorable." He paused. "In anything." The pressure of his arm tightened around her waist, and Krisztina felt a surge of new excitement.

"Kiss me again, please," she whispered, and raised her face eagerly to his, closing her eyes in readiness. The kiss came, softly at first, followed by a series of tiny kisses that covered her face, her eyelids, her forehead, her hair, her cheeks, then flew back to her lips. Then suddenly his mouth crushed hers with a new passion that had her responding breathlessly, shooting quivering jolts of desire throughout her body, concentrating in a pulsating, throbbing heat between her thighs that seemed to radiate right down to her toes.

She drew back, gasping for breath, and her gaze swiveled from his face and came to rest, with a mixture of appalling embarrassment and desperate anticipation, on the big double bed that seemed suddenly to be the focal point of the whole room. She stared at it for a moment, then back at him.

"David?"

He followed her gaze, and a new expression entered his eyes. "I don't think so," he said.

"Why not?"

"It's not the right thing for us."

"We could just lie down together," she whispered, amazed by her own shamelessness.

"Impossible." He smiled, and his lips brushed the soft skin of her neck.

"Please, darling," she begged, half choked with fresh tears. "I want to." She stared at him. "More than anything in the world."

He pulled away. "We don't know when we'll see each other again after today, Kriszti," he said a little harshly. "The last thing I want to do is cause you more pain."

"You won't."

"You can't know that, *Liebling*."

"I swear you won't. And anyway, not being able to see each other is surely all the more reason to use what little time we do have." Deliberately, and with a wild abandon she would never have dreamed possible, she began to plant small, passionate kisses on his lips and eyes, and then down over his neck. She tugged at his tie to loosen it, and with trembling fingers unbuttoned the first two buttons of his shirt, bending her head to kiss the dark hairs at the top of his chest.

"Kriszti, please," David protested weakly, "if you do that, how can I possibly resist you?"

"You're not supposed to resist me," she said, growing stronger by the minute, kissing his ear the way he had her own. "I don't want this to stop . . . ever . . ."

With a low groan, David struggled to his feet and clasped her wrists, tugging her up with him. His expression was a mixture of love and anger as he looked accusingly into her face. "Are you sure, Kriszti?" he demanded.

"Yes, oh, yes!"

"Absolutely positive?" His gaze was unwavering. "I know I want you more than I've ever wanted anyone or anything in my life." His voice was vibrant. "But you have to understand just how important this really is."

The earnestness in his voice brought a smile to her lips. *Important?* This was surely the most breathtaking, earth-shattering, momentous thing that would ever happen to her! She raised her chin and looked deeply into his eyes, only the slight trembling of her mouth betraying her nervousness. "I have never been so sure of anything," she said clearly. "I want you to love me, David, and I want to love you."

Slowly, without another word, they moved toward the bed, gliding like sleepwalkers. Unsure of what to do next, but feeling that one more gesture of resolve was needed to convince David, Krisztina kicked off her shoes and felt the thick pile of the hotel carpet beneath her toes.

They stood in awkward silence, minds racing as each contemplated the next move. David yearned to undress her, to slip the straps of her cotton dress from her shoulders and to kiss her bare skin, but he was afraid to embarrass her by going too fast. He glanced at the windows—it was too bright in the room. *I should draw the curtains,* he thought, but stayed motionless, loath to leave her side and destroy the atmosphere.

Krisztina, now that the moment had arrived, was overcome by a great desire to flee into the bathroom, but she sensed that if she gave the least hint of alarm, David might refuse to go on. Instead she, too, stood her ground and waited for his lead.

After what was little more than a minute, but seemed to them both like an hour, David found a compromise. Quickly, he kissed her again, so intensely that their bodies seemed to liquefy, then he turned her gently around until her back was to him, tugged the zipper of her dress down and left the rest to her while he rapidly undressed himself and slipped into bed to wait for her.

Krisztina heard the rustle of sheets and the creak of springs and closed her eyes, as if her own private darkness might grant her invisibility. Then, summoning all her courage, she let her dress fall to the floor and reached behind to unfasten her brassiere. She opened her eyes, glanced quickly down at her breasts, balked at removing her panties, turned and dived under the covers.

She had dreamed of someday holding David close, but in her daydreams their lovemaking had been securely wrapped in a romantic haze of innocence, had taken place on a grassy meadow or a beach or even sheltered by waving yellow wheat and crimson poppies. . . . What she had never successfully conjured up was this remarkable feeling of flesh on flesh. She had occasionally lain in the bathtub and touched herself experimentally, learning the feel of her own skin, but she was surprised at how different David's felt—it was a little rougher than her own, and it felt strong and immensely supple; muscles and sinews seemed literally to ripple just beneath the surface, ready to hold her, to envelop her, perhaps even to crush her. . . .

David moved closer, still tentative, and put his arms gently around her so that their bodies were very close, touching all the way from shoulders to toes. With a slow, patient movement he reached down and tugged at her panties, grinning boyishly as Krisztina blushingly assisted him. He felt his own desire and strength mounting rapidly, noticed that Krisztina trembled at his every touch, and rejoiced that she didn't attempt to draw away but instead insinuated herself even closer to him, as if his physical nearness infused her with vitality and delight.

Slowly, he began to stroke her, first her back, caressing her softly with even, tender movements of his whole hand, then the tips of his fingers traced the line of her spine down toward her buttocks. He felt her wriggle with a sensation that was wholly unfamiliar to her, both unbearable and unbelievably delectable at the same time. He moved away then, put a little space between them, and Krisztina lay very still on her back, her eyes open and watchful but trusting, waiting for him to show her what to do next, still too uncertain of herself to let instinct take over.

For the first time, David cupped her breasts, first one, then the other, holding them gently, then stroking them and brushing their hard, small nipples, feeling her shiver. His fingers moved down over her smooth belly and farther down into the soft mound of tangled golden fur. Krisztina made a small mewing sound, half moan, half whisper, and her thighs, till then tightly clenched, parted slightly, allowing his gentle fingers to touch and tickle and explore, making her gasp and close her eyes, shocked and yet at the same time overjoyed at the intensity of physical pleasure his hands seemed able to give her.

"Hold me," David instructed, his voice husky. "Put your arms around me."

Eyes still shut, she obeyed, turning on her side to face him, and was mortally disappointed when his fingers vanished from between her legs to clasp behind her back. And then she felt his erect penis for the first time, and experienced another explosive mixture of fear and shuddering excitement as she realized what was about to happen. . . .

"Kriszti," David said urgently, his mouth close to her ear, "are you sure? Really sure?"

For just an instant she had a new longing to run away, to hide in the bathroom and to cover herself again with childhood. But then she opened her eyes and looked into his face, and there was so much love and warmth and concern in his expression that all she wanted was to hold him close to her forever.

"I swear it," she said, and touched his lips with her finger.

"I'll try not to hurt you," he said, terrified in case he did, daunted by the naked adoration in her face, worried that he might disappoint her but driven almost beyond endurance by the sight and feel and scent of her.

"I shan't mind," she whispered, her heart bursting with love.

Tenderly, he turned her over onto her back, kissed her thoroughly on her mouth, and then parted her thighs with his right hand. Again he sought the curling blond hair, heard her moan with welcoming pleasure, and then, with such anticipation that his impatient fingers shook, he stroked her vulva and found her, to his delight, moist and open. Quickly, he slid down the bed and buried his face in her thighs, feeling her go momentarily rigid with astonishment and then relax again as she felt his tongue begin its probing inside her. She began to move her hips in a spontaneous, rocking motion, and to murmur softly, wildly, in Hungarian. He knew the moment had come, and prayed that he was right.

Krisztina had not believed that it would hurt so much. It was like having a spear thrust into her, and she gave a low, involuntary scream of pain. Instantly, David withdrew, his face contorted with desire and worry.

"No!" she cried. "Don't stop!"

"I'm hurting you—"

"It doesn't matter." She flung her arms about him, drawing him back. "I want you too much!"

As gently as he could, he guided himself into her again, and this time, mercifully, it was easier, and the agony became little more than a memory. Then he was moving back and forth, and what had been pain metamorphosed into all-consuming sexual pleasure, and the greatest bursting of sheer emotion she had ever known. They began to move together in almost perfect unison, and Krisztina was scarcely conscious of what she was doing, crying out soft words of love and passion—and then abruptly, David was gone from her body, leaving her desolate, empty, and unbearably frustrated, and it was the greatest disappointment she had ever known, and she cried out loud, begging him to come back. But David gave a great groan, and Krisztina felt the wetness on her belly, and was confused for a moment before she understood, and frustration turned to even greater love.

"I'm sorry, Kriszti, darling," he gasped. "I had to protect you."

"I know, *edesem,*" she said softly, and realized that her own voice was filled with pride.

They lay together again, face-to-face, and she inhaled his new muskiness, first with purest joy, then with a terrible surge of sorrow as reality returned.

David glanced at his watch, hating to do so and yet compelled. "We haven't long," he said quietly. Holding her close, he laid his head on her shoulder, more keenly aware than ever of her vulnerability, her youth, and her beauty, and he knew—was suddenly, unquestioningly certain—that she would soon be lost to him, and the knowledge was so monstrously wounding that he longed to weep.

Krisztina felt his warm, hard body tremble, and heard him sigh. A sob rose in her throat, but she forced herself to swallow it, her bones aching with raw misery and the effort of controlling herself. She lay very still, holding him, utterly resolved to hold back her tears until later, when she would be alone, for she knew that once she began, she might never stop.

Laurent returned to his room just before six o'clock and found it empty. The bed was as tidy as he had left it, the windows open, but a new scent of perfume, cologne, and sex lingered in the air. He tossed the gift-wrapped jeweler's box onto the desk, picked up the telephone and ordered coffee and a bottle of Johnnie

Walker from room service. They arrived several minutes later. Laurent tipped the waiter, locked the door, filled the coffee cup, and poured the black liquid over the sheets, his mouth tight with distaste. Then he buzzed the maid.

"Please remake the bed."

When she had gone, he poured a shot of whisky, drank it in one searing gulp, lay down on the bed, and shut his eyes. The new sheets were cool and clean, but the smell, strong and sickening, persisted in his nostrils, and an image of the two of them, naked and coupling, scorched his brain. He tore open his eyes and stared up at the white ceiling. *Anything,* he thought bitterly. Anything *to have her, whatever the cost.* Still he stared, unblinking, until his eyes burned with unshed tears.

Tomorrow, he thought desperately, *we'll dance and we'll win, and she will forget Kaufmann.* He closed his eyes again and tried to conjure up a vision of the ballroom and the sounds of music and applause, but all that came into his mind were more pictures of Krisztina with David. He sat up, his face contorted with agony, and looked longingly at the whisky bottle. Folly, in view of the next day, but without it he would never rest tonight.

Damn Kaufmann, he thought violently, and then, for a brief, consoling moment, the knowledge of what would soon follow brought a bleak smile to his lips.

Standing, he poured himself another glassful and raised it high in the air.

"Damn him to hell and beyond," he said, and after drinking it down, he hurled the glass at the wall, where it smashed into a hundred pieces that glittered like diamonds on the carpet.

Krisztina woke next morning anticipating a heavy heart, but instead she found herself in a strange, almost euphoric state, her body and mind still warmed by the memory of the previous afternoon. She felt astonishingly positive and vital; somehow, she vowed silently while she waited for her mother to finish her bath, she would see David again. She knew that their first ecstatic encounter could not possibly be their last, no matter how vast the opposition or how daunting the obstacles.

Ilona emerged from the bathroom, wrapped in a big white towel. "Your water is running." She smiled at her daughter. "How do you feel? Very anxious?"

"More excited than anxious, Mama," Krisztina replied honestly.

Today, she promised herself, she would repay Laurent for some of his generosity by dancing better than she had ever danced in her life. With the same conviction that she felt about her love for David, she knew that they could, and would, win.

By eleven o'clock that night, Laurent and Krisztina were the new European champions. For a heady, intoxicating two and a half hours after that, they toasted each other and their victory with Taittinger champagne, danced wild, exuberant tangos and Charlestons, chattered confidently to journalists and radio interviewers, were photographed for local, national, and international newspapers, and were filmed for the *Wochenschau*.

When Krisztina finally went to bed, her soul seemed alight with pleasure. Life was suddenly so good, God was bountiful, fortune was at last smiling on her. Before very long, her thoughts bubbled excitedly, they would soar to the World Championship. And, more important, she and her beloved David, with the aid of dear Laurent, would conquer Gabor and finally be together!

At a quarter past nine the following morning, on a day when Ilona and Krisztina had expected to sleep until at least eleven to restore their strength for the winners' luncheon and gala performance, they were woken by the harsh jangling of the bedside telephone.

Krisztina reached for it first.

Laurent wasted no words.

"Brace yourself, Krisztina." He paused briefly. "David has been arrested."

The room began to spin, and nausea filled her throat.

"Krisztina, did you hear me?"

She could not speak. In the other bed, Ilona, alerted by her daughter's sudden pallor, sat up anxiously.

"Krisztina," Laurent's voice rapped sharply, "you must listen. You are deeply involved in this mess, and you have to pay attention."

"What—?" Krisztina scarcely recognized her own voice as it rasped out the single word. "What happened? In God's name, what's happened?"

"Meet me downstairs in the Marmorsaal."

"What *happened*, Laurent?"

"Not now," he said adamantly. "Come as fast as you can."

Downstairs, in a quiet corner of the marble salon, Laurent took Krisztina's hand. "Did you tell your mother?"

She nodded, white-faced.

"They came to my room last night, very late," he told her, his expression deadpan. "It seems that you and David were"—he paused—"observed the day before yesterday."

Krisztina gasped. "By whom?"

"I don't know. A party member, probably. When they came to me, it was too late—they had already arrested David."

"But for *what*?"

Laurent's mouth was tight. "They call it *Rassenschande*. Race defilement." He still held her hand firmly. "They only came to me so discreetly, they said, out of courtesy to my family. In most cases, where it might be reasonably suspected that I, a visitor to Germany, had conspired with a Jew to—"

"Laurent, stop it!" She was ashen with horror.

"I'm only giving you their viewpoint of such an affair, *ma chère*."

"You sound as if you agree with them!"

"You know I don't," he said, "but as I was saying, in other circumstances they might have been much less considerate."

"*Considerate?* They've arrested David!"

Laurent raised a warning finger to his lips. "Please keep your voice down, Krisztina. They were actually quite generous, at least where I was concerned. They said they were sure I had been unaware of what happened."

"And what did you say?" she asked anxiously. "They must realize you helped us, if we were seen in your room."

"There were other possibilities. I was out of the hotel, after all, and my room was empty. Keys can sometimes be made available for a consideration."

Krisztina tore at her hair. "But that implies David bribed someone—"

Laurent took her arm and pushed her gently but firmly down into an armchair, sitting opposite her. "Krisztina, the first thing you have to do is forget your outrage and listen to me."

"But I—"

"No," he said sharply.

She bit her lip. "All right. Go on."

He continued. "I chose not to enlighten them about my own contribution to the matter. I could see no point, other than to deprive you and David of one of your only allies." He watched her. "They wanted, naturally, to know about you."

"What about me?" She sounded far more controlled than she felt.

Laurent leaned closer, his face kind. "Dear Krisztina, you must realize that this scandal, were it to emerge, would be the finish of you, of our career, of your family's good name . . ."

"I don't care about any of that!" she cried passionately. "I only care about David—about helping him!"

"You cannot help him."

"Of course I can! If I go to them and say it was all my idea, that I talked him into it, that he was against it—and he was, Laurent, he really was, I swear it!" Her eyes were wet with tears of frustration. "If I tell them all that, they'll have to let him go."

"They wouldn't dream of letting him go," he said quietly. "You have evidently not absorbed the gravity of the situation here in Germany for the Jewish people. They have only to step an inch out of line nowadays to be arrested and put away. And believe me, Krisztina, in the eyes of the Nazis, *Rassenschande* is the most deeply offensive of all crimes."

"But it's monstrous!"

Laurent glanced uncomfortably around the salon. They were almost alone, but at the far end of the room two other couples sat drinking coffee. "Please try to be discreet," he remonstrated. "This is not the moment to draw attention to yourself. You're something of a minor celebrity in Berlin. Think what a field day the newspapers would have with a story like this. Consider the effect on your parents."

Krisztina raised a clenched fist and gnawed at her knuckles.

"The first step," Laurent went on, "is to get you away from here as quickly as possible."

She looked at him, startled. "Surely the first step is to help David. Even if I accept that I can't simply go rushing in to save him, there must still be some action we can take to get him released. A lawyer, at least."

"I promise I will do all I can in that direction. I made every effort during the night to persuade them to let him go, but there was no hope. My primary consideration must be to protect you."

"I won't leave Berlin while David's in prison," she said stubbornly. "No one can make me."

The note of rebuke returned to Laurent's voice. "Of course they can make you. You're still a child, legally, at least, and when your father hears of this, you can be sure he will drag you back to Budapest."

"Does Papa have to know?"

"Now you are behaving like a child. One minute you're prepared to do battle with the whole Nazi regime, and the next you want to escape from the consequences of your adulthood by hiding from your father."

As if to underscore the ominous nature of their situation, four SS officers strode through the hall outside the Marmorsaal, and could be seen speaking to the concierge, sinister and threatening. Krisztina thought of David, all alone somewhere—God only knew where. . . .

"Krisztina." Laurent's voice jarred her.

"Yes?"

"Do you, or do you not, trust me?"

"Oh, yes!" she said fervently. "After all you've done for me? Of course I trust you—you're my best friend!"

Laurent smiled again. "*Très bien.* Then please do as I tell you now."

She spread her hands helplessly. "I wouldn't really know what else to do."

"Good. Then you will go upstairs, and you and your *maman* will pack your things right away, leaving out only your clothes for the luncheon, the dress for the gala, and, of course, your traveling suit."

"You expect me to eat?" she asked incredulously. "To chatter with people as if nothing had happened? To *dance*?"

"Certainly," he said decisively. "You forget, we are the new European champions."

"I can't!"

"You can and you must. And we can count ourselves lucky they gave their consent. I thought they might forbid you to appear, but they have assured me that your name will be kept out of the case provided you go home directly after the gala, and take time to reflect on your folly."

Krisztina wanted to scream, but instead she said tautly, "I still feel that David needs me to stay in Berlin."

"Stop being naive, Krisztina," Laurent said heatedly. "I tell you for the last time, there is nothing—not a damned thing—you can do for him." He went on. "While you're packing, I shall make the necessary travel arrangements."

She grew calmer again. "And what will you do for David," she asked quietly, "since I, apparently, can do nothing."

"For David," he replied gravely, "I shall begin by attending to your safe return home, and to the preservation of your good, and as yet unblemished, reputation." With a sudden renewed gesture of warmth and reassurance, he leaned over and squeezed her cold hand. "Then I shall go home and speak to my father, to see how we may best use our family's influence on David's behalf." He regarded her intensely. "Whatever you do, Krisztina, say as little as possible to your father, and don't implicate me. If he stops you from seeing me, too, it may destroy any chances for me to help you." He paused. "David's release will not be easy to achieve, *ma chère.*"

Her eyes were still wet. "I believe you can do anything you set your mind to, Laurent."

He shrugged. *"Peut-être."*

Krisztina rose, bent, and kissed his cheek warmly. "Try your hardest," she urged in a choked voice, "for me."

For an instant, Laurent closed his eyes. "If only you knew," he replied softly, opening them again, "how much I would do for you, Krisztina."

Chapter 8

On their return to Budapest, Gabor invited Laurent to stay for dinner, banishing Krisztina to her bedroom with a bowl of soup and a slice of bread. Gabor ate and drank silently, ignoring Ilona and never once alluding to the episode that had brought them home in such unseemly haste.

Later, when the two men sat in his study, Gabor's cheeks and nose were scarlet from a surfeit of Bulls' Blood and emotion. He hardly trusted himself to speak, so vast was his sense of disappointment and failure. Yes, he had longed for Kaufmann to be removed from Krisztina's life, but he had wanted more for her, specifically the de Trouvère name and all that would have come with it. Now, with this disgrace, this revolting shame, those aspirations were dashed, for surely the baron and his family would spurn the stigmatized Florians from now on.

When Laurent confessed to him that David and Krisztina had met in *his* room, Gabor was incredulous and appalled, humility giving way to outrage. "In God's name, how could you allow such an abomination?"

Laurent looked ill at ease. "I was away from the hotel for a few hours. Krisztina knew my room would be empty." He gestured vaguely. "An inexperienced man at the concierge, perhaps—"

"But her mother . . ." Gabor's wrath mounted steadily. "I gave her absolute instructions that Krisztina was never to be left alone on this trip."

"Madame Florian is a most thorough chaperone," Laurent said. "She rarely leaves Krisztina's side, but on this occasion . . ." He flushed. "I wanted to do a little shopping on Kurfürstendamm, and I'm afraid I asked Madame to accompany me."

"In *Berlin*?" Gabor bellowed, jumping to his feet, then quickly shaking his head. "I can't blame you—you're not my daughter's keeper—but Ilona knew that given the slightest chance, Krisztina would sneak off to meet Kaufmann!"

Laurent rose too. "You mustn't blame your wife. I'm sure if she had guessed the truth, she would never have come with me."

Gabor stubbed out his cigar. "You are too generous."

Fifteen minutes later, Gabor faced Ilona across their bed. His face was still scarlet, hers pale.

"How could you?"

"What?"

"Don't act innocent, Ilona," he snarled. "How could you be so stupid as to let her meet that filthy swine at all, let alone—" He stopped, too choked to continue.

"Gabor," Ilona faltered, "I wasn't even in the hotel at the time."

"I'm quite aware of that, you stupid bitch! If you had been, if you'd stayed with her as I ordered, none of this would have happened."

She tried to remain calm. "I know I was careless, Gabor—"

"*Careless?* Idiotic and treacherous!" He tore at his sparse hair. "All I know is that because of you, Ilona, our daughter's good name has been sullied, and she has lost her only chance at making a fine marriage, a magnificent marriage."

"To Laurent?" Ilona sighed. "Gabor, you know that she loves David, and nothing—"

"*My daughter could not love a Jew!*" he roared suddenly. With a swift, savage movement he ripped the spread from the bed and hurled it to the floor. "She could have been a baroness, you fool!" He rounded the bed toward her and Ilona shrank back.

"Abusing me won't help Krisztina," she said shakily.

"But it will help me!" He grabbed her by the hair, and she shrieked with pain. "Keep your mouth shut!" he hissed, his eyes glittering. "If you wake the house, I'll make you sorry you were ever born."

Ilona struck out at him with both hands to protect herself, and with a low roar he let go of her hair and, with all his force, shoved her onto the bed. He untied the belt of his pajama pants, his face purpling, seeming to swell with a mixture of fury and excitement. "You're such a pious woman, Ilona, but you're no better than a stupid whore. That's how you deserve to be treated."

Ilona stared up at him, at the menacing red face bobbing over her, and the realization that she was about to be raped flooded through her. A host of feelings pierced her mind like hot arrows —the memory of the love she had felt for this man over the years; the unwelcome edges of dislike that had insidiously tarnished that love too many times, and that had sent her directly to her knees to pray for forgiveness; she remembered what her cousin Jozsef had told her about Krisztina's real mother, and how he believed she had been raped before abandoning her baby, and a sudden flash of kinship and empathy seared through her. . . .

She dragged her mind back to the present and looked up at her husband. Gabor had stripped naked and stood before her, erect as a rampant bull, his eyes filled with contempt and lust. Ilona wondered with a strange heaviness whether it was a pardonable sin to fight one's own husband, but she knew at the same time that she could never stop him, that she was weaker than he.

A new, unfamiliar feeling of pure hatred rose up in her soul and threatened to choke her, and a curious, destructive impulse, born out of that hatred, tore from her lips the words she had thought she would never, never utter.

"One thing makes this bearable for me, Gabor Florian," she said, her voice hushed but shockingly clear. "For Krisztina's sake, I am grateful to God that she is not your child."

The words echoed in the bedroom. As if in slow motion, she observed the fury on her husband's face grow to monumental proportions.

Ilona shut her eyes, and made the sign of the cross.

At four o'clock in the morning, Krisztina was asleep, starlight washing over her, illuminating the shallow rise and fall of her breasts beneath the white cotton of her nightdress.

Gabor stood just inside the doorway, watching her, his own breathing harsh in his throat.

Ignoring Mozes, who sat on his haunches, eyeing him balefully, he walked barefoot over to the bed and looked down on the young woman he loved more than anyone else in the world.

Not your child. Ilona's words twisted in his head. Sweat trickled down his back.

She stirred slightly, and a soft murmur escaped her lips. She was dreaming, he thought, and his mouth tightened. Dreaming of Kaufmann, he guessed bitterly. *She still looks like an angel,* he thought, *yet she, too, is little better than a whore.* He stared at the gentle curves of her body, at the silken flow of her hair on the pillow, at the tender lips, slightly parted, and he experienced such a violent heat in his groin that he had to stop himself from groaning out loud.

She had always been so heartachingly lovely; when she was a little girl, he had savored nothing more than holding her fragrant young body in his arms, caressing her smooth skin . . .

Not your child.

He shook the poisonous words from his mind, and gazed down at her with the adoration of fatherhood, then stooped and kissed her very gently on the brow. It felt smooth and cool beneath his lips. With one careful hand he stroked her hair.

And then, as if it had an independent will, the hand, quivering a little, hovered in the air and came softly to rest on her right breast, felt its swell and warmth.

From his post by the door, Mozes growled. Again, Krisztina stirred, and Gabor straightened up quickly, the perspiration wet on his forehead. Unaccountably, his eyes pricked with hot tears, and swiftly, fearful in case she woke, he made his way back out into the cool hall, closing the door silently behind him.

A cloud, passing rapidly through the night sky, propelled by the breeze, briefly obscured the moon, and a shadow fell over Krisztina's face.

She waited a moment more, to be certain, and then she opened her eyes.

The three weeks that followed were wretchedly unhappy ones in the Florian house. The invisible ropes that bind families together, linking mothers to fathers to daughters to brothers, whether they be physically close or spread afar, seemed to have been severed. Ilona spoke courteously to Gabor and continued her role as dutiful wife, but it was no longer the same. Gabor spent longer hours than before in his office and at the store, and when he was at home, he felt the iciness of his wife and the mistrust of his daughter, and it was not the same. Krisztina, fran-

tic for good news about David, felt only disgust for her father and
pity for her mother. It would never be the same again.

Weeks stretched into months. Laurent traveled between de
Trouvère, Berlin, and Budapest, but brought no joy for Krisztina,
only continued hope for Gabor. Krisztina continued to write
long, loving letters to David, knowing he would never receive
them, and still tugged Laurent into huddled, clandestine meetings to hang on his every ounce of news. As 1937 faded into 1938,
bringing with it the new season of championships, she made a
conscious decision to fling herself back into dance, aware that it
was the one remaining aspect of her life that brought her solace.
And, after all, it would be grossly unfair to make Laurent the
loser, especially when he continued to try to win David's release.
That winter they retained their European title but could only
manage second place in the World Championship. The next summer, they won both titles.

At two o'clock in the morning following the *Championnat du
Monde* in Paris, Laurent and Krisztina hugged each other in a
victory embrace and then, for the first time, Laurent kissed
Krisztina on the mouth and she returned the kiss. He felt giddy
with triumph, and drew her into another embrace, but she
pulled away. For Krisztina it had been nothing more than a warm
kiss of friendship, given in the tumult of the moment. Her rejec-
tion was flustered but tender; Laurent looked as if he had been
turned to stone.

Time was running out for Laurent. Baron Armand was in poor
health; a mood of general disquiet had descended on Alsace
because of its potentially front-line position in the event of any
conflict with Germany; and both his parents had recently begun
to pressure him to spend more time in Alsace to concentrate on
the wine business and management of the estate. Laurent had
hoped that with Kaufmann out of her life, Krisztina might forget
him, but it was now clear that this was a vain hope. Her emotions
ran too deep, her loyalty was too intense. Laurent was a man
obsessed. He thought about little else but Krisztina; every morning he woke and imagined her in his bed; every day that he was
not with her, he replayed shining moments of their partnership,
saw her long legs flashing rhythm, hair flying, eyes sparkling;
every night he dreamed of Krisztina. In those dreams she was

always a statue, exquisite and remote, tantalizing him with the marbled gleam of her naked breasts. . . .

The Nazi disease was spreading. In March 1938, the German army had entered Vienna, Austria was absorbed into the Reich, and immediately all-out persecution of the Jews began. Inside Germany, the horror escalated. Many hundreds were dispatched to concentration camps at Dachau and Buchenwald, synagogues in Munich and Nuremberg were burned down, and refugees flooded out of the country trying to escape. On November 6 in Paris, a young Jewish man named Grynszpan, outraged beyond reason by the stories coming out of Germany, went to the German embassy and shot an official, Ernst vom Rath. Two days later, vom Rath died, the Nazis declared the deed as part of a Jewish plot, and that night *Kristallnacht* erupted all over Germany; millions of fragments of glass from blazing synagogues, Jewish shops and homes, glittered in the flames. Hundreds of people were beaten and kicked senseless. Tens of thousands were arrested. Scores simply disappeared, plucked from the streets and out of their houses. Among them were the remaining members of the Kaufmann family.

"They've vanished," Laurent told Krisztina over coffee and cream in Gerbeaud. Lately it had become impossible for them to discuss David in the Florian home.

She stared at him. "But where to? People don't just disappear —it's impossible."

"Not anymore," he said grimly. "At least, not in Germany."

"Someone must know where they are," she insisted.

Laurent stirred his coffee. "They're probably in a concentration camp."

"Oh, my God," she said quietly.

"I think it's possible that David is too."

She blinked. "But you said he was in prison."

"That was what I believed, but I think now that they probably transferred him to Dachau or Buchenwald some time ago."

"Are you sure?" Krisztina whispered.

"It's hard to be sure of anything," he replied, watching her carefully. "*Ma chère*, you must understand by now that Germany is getting rid of the Jews."

"But that's just talk," she protested. "You can't simply get rid of millions of people."

"Not simply, no," he said ironically. "But that is what is happening, nonetheless. It's hard to tell what lengths they'll go to. First it was civil rights, then confiscation of property, now basic freedom. Even here in Hungary it's beginning."

The last vestiges of color drained from her face.

"I wish I could tell you a different story, Krisztina, but I owe you the truth."

She nodded, then suddenly leaned across the table and said in a low, urgent voice, "We have to get them out."

He smiled sadly. "If only it were that easy."

"Not easy," she said fiercely, "but not impossible, surely."

"No," he agreed quietly, "nothing is impossible, but some things are more difficult than others to achieve."

"Laurent, please, help me." Her eyes stunned him with their intensity.

"You know I'll always help you if it's possible."

"Nothing is impossible," she repeated.

His voice dropped to an even lower level. "Finding David will be hard enough, let alone freeing him," he said soberly. "If we couldn't get him out of prison, it's far less likely that we'll be able to extricate him from the confusion of a concentration camp."

"Have you tried everything?"

He raised a hand. *"Attend."* He spotted a waitress, paid the bill, and stood up. "Come on, let's go for a walk. We're less likely to be overheard."

She frowned. "You make it sound as if there are Nazis at every corner in Budapest."

"I just prefer to be careful." Outside he tucked her arm through his, looked around Vorosmarty Ter and began to stroll companionably.

"I was asking," she said, "if you had really tried everything to free David."

"I should say," he answered slowly, "that our lawyers have tried every legal approach."

"Could there be another way?"

"Outside the law, you mean?" He smiled at her innocence. "I don't think so." He paused, and his face became serious again. "I should say there was perhaps one remaining chance."

"What?" She pulled her arm away from his, desperately anxious. "Oh, Laurent, please tell me!"

He took her arm firmly back again. "Money," he said, glancing casually into a store window.

"Bribery, you mean?" She was wide-eyed.

"An ugly word."

"Call it anything," she begged, "but please, oh, please do it!" She crumpled suddenly. "I'm being naive again, aren't I?" she said dully. "It would take a great deal of money, and I don't have it to give."

"But I do."

She shook her head miserably. "I could never ask that of you."

He stopped walking, put his right hand under her chin and tilted her face up to his. "I've told you before, Krisztina, I would do almost anything for you."

"But why, Laurent? Why are you so good to me?"

"Because I love you," he said simply.

She flushed. "You shouldn't."

"You can't stop me." He took his hand from her chin and flashed her a boyish grin. In spite of her anxiety, she smiled back at him.

"Well then?" he said.

"I might never be able to repay you."

"You will," he said. "Believe me."

She stared at him, saying nothing.

"I have a proposition for you," he said.

"Yes." She waited.

"I want very much to be able to help you, Krisztina," he went on, "but there is one major obstacle."

"What is it?"

"If I were able to free David, maybe even help him to escape from Germany, there is very little doubt in my mind that you would want to be with him."

"Of course I would."

"In which case," he continued, "that presents me with a strong motive for not freeing him." He began walking again steadily, with calm, even steps, as if he had said nothing of the least importance.

A sense of dread crept up Krisztina's spine, wrapping itself tightly around her. "What—" She reached out and pulled at his arm to stop him. "What are you saying, Laurent?"

"Only what I've said before," he said, his voice quiet and reasonable. "I love you, Krisztina. I want you more than anything else in the world."

"But we're friends . . ." She fumbled for the words. "And partners. Isn't that enough?"

"Not for me, not nearly enough." He paused. "Will you marry me, Krisztina?"

"No!" she said sharply, shocked.

His expression was gentle. "I'm fully aware that it is David you love, *ma chère*, but you must know by now that you can never have him."

"If he is freed—"

"He will not be freed."

Her legs started to tremble, then her arms, then her mouth. She clamped her lips together hard, determined not to give way in the street.

"He will not be freed," Laurent said, "unless you agree to marry me. You have the power to try to help him. I could make no guarantees, because I am an honorable man, but I would vow to do my best." He paused. "It's your choice."

She tried to speak, but no words came out. She licked her dry lips and tried again. "If I refuse to marry you," she said huskily, "then you're saying that David is lost."

"Exactement."

"That's blackmail, Laurent."

"Another ugly word."

"But accurate." Her voice was harsh.

He gave a small shrug. "I love you."

"And I love David."

"I know. But I also know that you have, at least until this moment, loved me as a friend—"

"But that's not enough!" she cried, outrage swamping her. A group of students passing by them turned to stare.

"Not now, perhaps," Laurent agreed, "not for you, at least."

"But surely it isn't enough for you either, Laurent! You must want a wife who loves you deeply!"

"I want you," he said simply. "And if I can't have your passion, I'll accept your caring and your respect. . . ."

"How can you possibly imagine I could respect you after this?"

He walked on. For a moment, Krisztina stood still, too shocked to move, then she hurried forward to catch up to him.

"When you take a little time to reflect," he said, "you will see that what I propose is not so very terrible. I have been patient—more than patient. But I am not a saint. I am only a man."

Krisztina's thoughts jumbled wildly. *Marriage in exchange for David's freedom, perhaps even his life?* But if she agreed, could she trust Laurent to keep his part of the bargain? Why should he? She shook her head painfully and marched faster. He *was* an honorable man, wasn't he? Was he realistically in a position to help David at all? Might the Kaufmanns not be released anyway, without his help? Perhaps Laurent was exaggerating the drama of the situation for his own gain. Did she have a real choice? Did she love David so completely that she could become the wife of a man she did not love . . . ?

"Would you like to go home?" Laurent interrupted her thoughts.

She stopped walking and stared at him. "Yes," she whispered.

"I'll find a taxi." He flagged down a free car.

Krisztina stepped to the curb, and climbed into the back of the taxi.

Gabor, half drunk from a surfeit of cognac, met Laurent in his study three days later.

"Has she chosen?"

"Not yet."

Gabor banged his fist on the table. "Idiotic child! Has she no sense at all?"

"She needs a little more time," Laurent said softly.

"And you're still willing to wait?"

"For four more days."

"I never cease to marvel at your patience, Laurent, and your devotion," Gabor said fervently. "And when I think how abominably she has behaved . . ."

"The errors of a young girl," Laurent said generously, "should be forgiven."

Gabor reflected. "Perhaps she doesn't believe you can help Kaufmann."

"I think she believes I can."

Gabor snorted. "How naive she is."

"She is just nineteen," Laurent reminded him, "and very much in love." His expression grew bleaker. "But if she does refuse me, Gabor, then I'm afraid I shall, at last, have to accept defeat, and that prospect saddens me greatly." He paused, and then went on, "Not least because it will mean the end of our friendship."

Gabor drained the cognac from his glass. It slid down his throat and stoked the anger already burning inside him. His eyes narrowed. "I could order her to accept you."

"No," Laurent said emphatically. "I must have a willing bride or no bride at all."

She'll be willing, Gabor thought darkly, pouring more cognac and downing it even more rapidly. *She'll be damned willing even if I have to beat her black-and-blue!*

"Persze," he agreed aloud. "Of course."

It was after two when he opened the door to her bedroom, grabbed Mozes by the collar and slung him out into the corridor. Krisztina woke with a start and sat up. "Father, what is it?"

"Get up." His voice was slurred.

"Why? What's happened? Is something wrong with Mama?"

"Just get up!" he ordered sharply.

She scrambled out of bed and reached for her robe. Gabor strode forward and snatched it roughly from her hand. She gasped in surprise, then took a step back when she saw the expression on his face.

"What's happened?" she repeated anxiously. "Why do you look like that?"

"Just who do you think you are?" he cut her short so ferociously that she jumped nervously. He jabbed a finger at her, prodding her hard on her shoulder. *"What* do you think you are? Some great young lady with scores of eligible suitors standing in line?"

Understanding began to dawn. "Of course not," she said defensively, backed right up against the wall.

"Do you imagine that the daughter of a tradesman is offered marriage to the aristocracy every day?" He loomed closer, digging his finger again into her flesh.

"You don't understand, Father—"

"Damned right I don't," he growled. "You have a chance to be a baroness, you little fool."

"I don't want to be a baroness," she said reasonably.

"No, you prefer to marry your great love," he sneered. "Your Jewish jailbird."

"You know David has done nothing wrong!" she protested.

"How *dare* you!" he hissed. "How dare you be so ungrateful to Laurent after all he's done for you!"

"I am grateful," she whispered, "but that doesn't mean I want to marry him . . ."

"It's a miracle that he still wants you, after what you did to him —to me!" He was trembling with fury. "Acting like a common tramp, and not even sorry for it."

Krisztina drew herself up to her full height. "I will never be sorry that David and I took our chance to make love—"

Gabor's hand whipped through the air and struck her before she had even finished speaking. Her head bounced hard against the wall, stunning her.

"Kurva!" he bellowed, maddened. "Whore!"

Krisztina's hands flew instinctively up to her face to protect herself, and she squeezed her eyes shut, waiting for a second blow. Nothing happened. She opened her eyes. To her astonishment, her father stood before her openly shaking, his face contorted with pain.

"Father?"

Gabor's eyes filled with tears, and he shook his head despairingly from side to side. Krisztina watched in confusion. She had never seen her father weep before.

"Oh, God," he moaned hopelessly. "God in heaven, what have I done?"

"Father, don't," Krisztina faltered, torn between anger, fear, and unexpected pity. "It's all right."

"No!" Without warning, he flung his arms around her and held her close. She stood like a stone in the circle of his arms, unsure how to react. Gabor began to sob, wretched, heaving sobs that shook his whole body, and Krisztina relented. Letting instinct take over, she moved closer and let him huddle against her, wanting, in spite of everything, to help him. . . .

"Papa," she soothed. "Papa, don't cry."

Gradually the awful, raucous sobbing quietened, but still she held him, comforting him. And then slowly, at first with total incredulity and then with swiftly mounting horror, she became shockingly aware that a change was taking place. Her father seemed to be pressing himself closer to her, pushing his hips against her. She tried to pull away, but his arms were like iron around her. Still hoping desperately that she was mistaken, she remained frozen, hardly daring to breathe. But there was no mistake. Gabor's erection was growing, pressing through his trousers and her thin nightdress against her belly. A wave of nausea rose in her. A soft groan escaped his lips.

With an enormous effort, she brought up both her hands against his chest and thrust him away, her face white with disgust.

"Get out!" she hissed tremulously. "Get out of my room!" Fear and revulsion rooted her to the spot; she prayed he would leave, not knowing what to do if he stayed.

Gabor was immobile except for the trembling of his hands and arms. His breathing was shallow and rasping.

"Get—out!" she said again, separating the words like pistol cracks. "Before I scream."

"You won't do that," he blustered.

"I will do *anything*," she threatened, "to get you away from me."

The power of her loathing brought Gabor at least partially to his senses. For a brief moment he closed his eyes, took a deep, shuddering breath, and turned toward the door. Then he looked back. She had never looked so resolute, so full of hatred—so adult. There was no point trying to pretend that nothing had happened; it was abundantly clear that she had fully understood what he wanted.

"Don't tell your mother, Krisztina," he begged falteringly. "For her sake, if not for mine."

Her jaw was set rigidly and her eyes blazed with contempt. "I assure you that if I don't, it will *only* be for her sake."

He opened the door, and Mozes, quivering with suppressed excitement, bounded past him as he went out.

Krisztina sank to her knees and buried her face in her hands. Several minutes passed; the big dog lay patiently at her side, occasionally pressing his damp nose against her cheek. Still shaking violently, alternately ice-cold and burning hot, Krisztina controlled her urge to vomit, too afraid to leave her room for the bathroom. She reached up and pulled the quilt from her bed, wrapping it round herself, and after a while she found the strength to rise to her feet.

There was no key in her lock, so she took a chair and pushed it against the door, aware that he was unlikely to return tonight, but needing the fragile security it lent her.

Slowly, she walked over to the dressing table and switched on the lamp. She sat on the padded stool and stared into the mirror. Her reflection looked back, terrified and ghostly.

"I cannot stay here any longer," she said aloud, and Mozes whined softly. Krisztina picked up the small, silver-framed photograph of her parents that stood on the dresser top; her father with one arm round her mother's waist, both of them smiling formally at the camera. Krisztina looked at her mother's dear face.

How can I desert her? she asked herself wretchedly. The photograph fell from her nerveless fingers onto the rug, landing with a dull thud. She shook her head miserably. *I have no real choice left.*

She bent and pulled out the bottom drawer of the dresser, slipped her right hand between the brassieres and panties that lay folded within, and pulled out an envelope.

Opening it, she withdrew another photograph. She laid it on the polished surface, and gazed down at it. It was a picture of David and herself in the ballroom of the Kulm Hotel in St. Moritz almost five years before. Her favorite photograph in all the world. She remembered that they had swept to a halt in mid-quickstep, skidding slightly, to pose, and their faces were open and rapt with joy and vitality. She looked so incredibly young, as indeed she had been—just a child, really—and David looked so wonderful, so heart-stoppingly handsome and proud. . . .

The pent-up tears began to tumble onto her hands and onto the corner of the fragile photograph. With a deep, shuddering sob, she wiped them away with her fingers, smearing the glossy paper.

"I cannot stay here," she said again.

Reality, brutal and remorseless, slammed through her, tearing at her wounds even more savagely. The reality of leaving her mother and her home, of not knowing if she would ever again see the great bridges across the Danube, the fig groves and molten sunsets of Balaton or the great *puszta;* the lacerating reality of ripping up her roots, of losing forever the succor of family life, of being forced to kick away the whole underpinning of her being; the reality of rejecting blessed familiarity and becoming a stranger in a foreign land in a mad, crumbling world. The reality of losing David. . . .

She picked up the picture, rose, and turned out the lamp.

"Oh, David," she cried softly in the darkness, "David, my love."

She held the scrap of paper, all that was left of him and their togetherness, close to her heart. "I know what I have to do," she said, "for your sake and for my own."

Another wild, agonizing sob wracked her, her insides felt torn and violated. "But will you ever be able to forgive me?" she whispered. "For I doubt I will ever forgive myself."

PART TWO

Krisztina: Alsace, 1938–1944

Chapter 9

The silver-haired *adjoint au maire* closed the leather-bound register.

"Au nom de Monsieur le Maire," he said formally, *"meilleurs félicitations."* He bowed solemnly from the waist, his business suit made resplendent by the tricolor sash of office.

Laurent returned the bow, shook hands with the two witnesses, and bent his head to kiss his bride, just as Krisztina turned her face to one side so that his lips brushed her cheek instead of her mouth.

The *fonctionnaire* smiled awkwardly. "This has been a profound pleasure, Monsieur le Baron. As you know, the mayor was most regretful that he was unable to perform the *mariage civil* in person."

"Please reassure Monsieur le Maire that we have been most excellently looked after," Laurent said graciously. "And I must say it is to be expected that the mayor of Strasbourg should have more important matters to attend to in these difficult times."

"Malheureusement, oui," the other man sighed. "So many contingency arrangements." He smiled at Krisztina and addressed her in German. "Though we do fervently hope, Madame la Baronne, that all this planning will prove completely unnecessary." He returned his attention to Laurent. "Shall you and Madame stay in Strasbourg another night?"

"No," Laurent answered, "we are going directly to de Trou-vère. My mother has been alone long enough."

The *adjoint au maire* looked grave. "Madame la Baronne will be grateful to have you back." He paused. "Baron Armand was truly a great man."

There was a moment's respectful silence, and then Laurent glanced at the ormolu clock over the fireplace. "We must be leaving." He turned and picked up the silver fox coat he had bought Krisztina two days earlier on Maximilianstrasse in Munich, and against which she had protested vehemently but lost. *"Viens, chérie."*

They walked past the painting of Premier Daladier into the main hall, and while Laurent thanked the witnesses, the *fonctionnaire* kissed Krisztina's hand. "I wish you much joy, madame, in your new life," he said. "I know you will be happy at Château de Trouvère; I have only visited it once, but I have never forgotten its charms."

"I look forward to seeing it." She smiled at him, and added in slow, careful French, "And I, too, thank you for everything, monsieur." She remembered the date. *"Et bonne année."*

They stood at the top of the stone steps and looked down at Laurent's car. Mozes, his black nose pushed anxiously against the window, was puffing small streams of condensation over the glass, his tail thumping furiously at the joy of seeing his mistress again.

"Madame la Baronne," Laurent pronounced, and grinned. "How does it feel?"

"I don't know yet," she said honestly. "I think I shall need some time to grow accustomed to it."

"Of course." He opened the door for her and stood well back as Mozes thrust his front part over the top of the passenger seat in a passionate attempt to reach Krisztina.

"I hope he's going to get along with the others," Laurent said when he was sitting behind the steering wheel.

She looked at him in surprise. "Others?"

"The other dogs at de Trouvère."

"You never mentioned dogs."

"Three," he said, starting the engine. "Irish wolfhounds. Known as 'gentle giants.' Kept by our family for generations."

For the first time since leaving Budapest, Krisztina found the prospect of the new life to come almost bearable.

*

After Krisztina accepted his proposal in November, Laurent had returned to Alsace for his parents' blessing and to publish the banns, arranging the marriage in the private chapel at de Trouvère as soon as the statutory forty-day waiting period was over. News of Armand de Trouvère's death, however, reached Laurent just three days after his return to Budapest, forcing him to rush home again for the funeral and dashing his hopes for a lavish wedding. Unwilling to wait until family mourning was at an end, and considering that, in any case, it might now be wiser to present his mother with a fait accompli, the new Baron de Trouvère insisted on a civil ceremony in Strasbourg, the first major Alsatian town they would come to en route to de Trouvère.

On December 29, Laurent, Krisztina, and Mozes boarded the Vienna express at Keleti Station while her parents stood on the snowy platform waving, Ilona fighting back tears as her daughter's seven trunks were loaded into the luggage compartment. They traveled under bleak gray skies to the Austrian capital, then on, via Linz and Salzburg, to Munich, where they spent a night before going on to Stuttgart and over the Rhine into France. Laurent had booked rooms at the Carlton Hotel in Strasbourg so that they could be fresh for the *mariage civil* at ten o'clock the following morning, New Year's Eve.

The trains were plush and smooth, but the journey was long and tedious, giving them too many hours in which to contemplate past and future. Laurent was in a strange mood, strung somewhere between jubilation and grief, and Krisztina's only real comfort was in going back and forth to reassure poor Mozes, who had been locked up in the back of the train, that he had not been abandoned.

Over lunch in the restaurant car the first day, Krisztina asked Laurent if, having missed the winter season of championships, they would be able to compete in the spring.

"Of course not," he replied, looking surprised.

"Oh," she said, more depressed than ever, but aware that the proprieties of mourning might prevent them from dancing for a time. "Oh, well," she said, "if we work hard next year, we'll soon make up for lost time."

"You don't understand," he said quietly.

"Understand what?"

"That our dancing days are over."

She stared at him, shocked.

"I am now the twenty-sixth Baron de Trouvère, *ma chère*," he went on, "and after tomorrow you will be La Baronne. We will have many responsibilities—lands to care for, the château to run, the vineyards and fields and orchards, not to mention the children I hope we shall have before long." He smiled at her, his expression tender.

Krisztina sat very still. "Do you mean to tell me that we can never dance again?"

He laughed. "Of course we can dance. There will be parties and balls—"

"I meant competitively," she interrupted, her fists clenched in her lap.

He sat back, quite calmly. "No, Krisztina, there will be no more competitions."

"But you said nothing."

"I thought it was understood."

She shook her head.

"I'm sorry, *chérie*," he said gently, "but that episode in our lives is at an end. *C'est terminé.*"

Terminé. Vege. Finished. Like everything else in her life that had ever mattered to her. She turned her face to the window and gazed out over the stark December landscape, and neither remembered nor cared if she looked at Hungary or Austria or Germany . . .

As they drove out of Strasbourg after the wedding, snow was falling and settling silently on the fields all around them.

"We have plenty of time," Laurent said placidly, "so we shall take the Route du Vin—it's by far the best way for you to learn the character of Alsace. Though at this rate," he added wryly, "there'll be little left for you to see."

"In summer," he told her a little while later, "along this road all you can see for miles on the left are sunflowers, faces tilted to the sky, with the Vosges, soft as velvet, on the right."

"It sounds wonderful," Krisztina said.

"It is. The land here is very rich—one can sometimes count perhaps fifty different shades of green in the grasses and trees."

Driving through the town of Barr, Krisztina was enchanted by the cobbled streets and multicolored, shuttered houses; in one street alone she saw red, pink, blue, ocher, beige, and cream-colored houses, most with window boxes. They reminded her, with a pang, of many small Hungarian towns.

"In summertime," Laurent said again, "those boxes would be overflowing with geraniums, and all the towns filled with flowers." He gestured toward a small, almost deserted square. "The old men would be playing *boule,* and the other townspeople would be sitting outside watching them and drinking beer."

"Not wine?"

"Yes, but beer too. Our beer is very delicious—in summer, you will see many fields of hops and barley."

In summer, Krisztina thought wistfully, shivering in spite of the car heater. *Everything good here seems to happen in summer. But will I survive until then?*

Her first glimpse of de Trouvère brought Krisztina closer to the brink of what might be called magic than any other experience of her life, with the exception of her afternoon of love with David.

They had approached the estate from the north side, and when Laurent stopped the car suddenly, without a word, looking at her oddly, Krisztina had gazed straight ahead at what seemed to be just another frosted pine forest.

"It's there." Laurent nudged her quietly.

Looking again, she saw that there was a parting in the center of the trees through which a long, meandering uphill path led out of the forest and past the now familiar *vignobles* to the small, cream-colored baroque château. It was perched on the summit of the hill, its whole right side bathed in the pale rose flush of the early sunset.

"O gyonyoru," she breathed in astonishment, and fell silent. Beside her, Laurent smiled, and did not trouble to ask her for translation, understanding only too well.

Still she stared, utterly absorbed. All her expectations, she now realized, had been either exaggerated or totally fallacious. Yes, it was certainly a most authentic château, and even from a distance of what she judged to be about three miles, it was clearly quite exquisite in both structure and setting. But what struck Krisztina so instantly and gratifyingly was that it was definitely, indisputably a *house;* not a Wagnerian fantasy, complete with pinnacles and turrets, nor a moldering, bleak nightmare, but a real, living, solid house, with foundations many generations old deeply entrenched in the earth on which it stood.

"Well?" Laurent's voice made her jump.

She tore her eyes away and looked at him. There was a curious glint in his golden eyes, a glimmer of tears, she saw with surprise. *Strange man,* she thought, *one part so tenacious and insensate that he can turn lives upside down for his own ends, and yet another part capable of such intense emotion about his home.*

"Tell me," he said, his voice husky.

She reached out, moved, and lay her hand on his. "It's very, very beautiful," she said softly. *"Gyonyoru,"* she added again, in Hungarian, and then, *"magnifique."*

He drew her hand up to his lips and kissed it tenderly. "Like you."

She waited a moment, not wishing to break the atmosphere, and then, very gently, she pulled her hand away.

"May we go closer, please?"

He put the car into gear and began the ascent. Just past the forest, the road split and then, rounding another bend, they approached a huge stone arch. Laurent drove beneath it and stopped the car again.

"Voilà," he said. "This is de Trouvère." He leaned back against the leather, and Mozes, instinctively aware of impending arrival, whined and stirred from his sleep.

"This is not the main entrance," Laurent explained. "The principal *allée* and front entrance are on the south side, and the bulk of the estate lies to east and west." He paused. "But this is one of my favorite aspects."

"I'm not surprised," she said warmly.

The château was now less than a mile away, standing in perfect symmetry beyond a sweeping expanse of garden, its landscaping and details shrouded by winter. In the middle lay a rectangular pool, its central fountain frozen into thousands of glittering icicles, the slender marble statue of a woman clasping bow and quiver, a hound at her heel, rising majestically from the heart of the spray.

"Poor Diana," Laurent chuckled. "She looks chilly today."

"How lovely she is," Krisztina admired.

Laurent raised an eyebrow. "Diana the Huntress? I thought you despised hunting."

"But she's also the goddess of domestic animals."

They fell silent, devouring the château with their eyes. It *was* a

feast, Krisztina decided—three creamy stories with a small pavilion on either side, linked to the main house by pretty galleries.

"It looks bigger from here," she said more tentatively, quite
nervous again now that they were almost at journey's end.

"Small enough to be manageable," Laurent replied easily.
"Châteaux come in many shapes and sizes. This might be called
'un p'tit château,' scarcely more than an overgrown villa. Actually, it was originally a seventeenth-century hunting lodge, completely rebuilt in the late eighteenth century by a follower of
Guêpière, who built several country palaces for the House of
Württemberg." He smiled at her expression. "I'll explain the full
history later, when you are rested, but make no mistake, *ma
chère*, in spite of its impressive pedigree, Château de Trouvère is
principally a home, not a monument."

"How could you have stayed away so long?" she asked in genuine puzzlement.

Laurent laughed, and turned the driving mirror so that it reflected her face. *"Regarde,"* he said. *"La cause."*

She flushed. "You were dancing and traveling long before we
met."

"True," he agreed, "though Alice Gébhard was from Colmar,
which is considerably more accessible than Budapest." He
paused. "I think, too, that knowing I would, in all probability,
spend the rest of my life at de Trouvère, it was necessary to make
use of my freedom while still young."

"Do you regard this as an end to your freedom, then?"

"In many ways, yes." He shrugged. "But it's no great hardship
to give up things you enjoy—*la danse*, for example—for something of far greater value. All this"—he indicated the estate with
a sweeping gesture—"was always the most important thing in my
life. Until I met you, my sweet Krisztina, it was the only truly
important thing."

"But how could I compete with this?" she asked with gentle
irony.

"Ah, but you did," he replied seriously. He reached out and
stroked her hair, still pinned in the chignon she had worn under
her hat for the wedding. "And now I am surely the most fortunate of men, for I possess you both."

There was a brief silence.

"Possess?" she echoed.

"You are my wife," he said simply.

"That does not mean I belong to you, Laurent."

"Nous sommes mariés." Still, his tone was easygoing. "We belong to each other."

She said nothing.

"Jusqu'au mort," he added. "Until death."

But not before God, she thought unexpectedly, *only before the deputy mayor.* A swift pang of guilt for the notion struck her, but she pushed it aside and was still grateful for the qualifying thought. *Possession,* she repeated in her mind. *My husband is a man of property.* Involuntarily, she shivered.

"Don't be afraid," Laurent said, misreading her reaction. "Death is a long, long way off." He leaned closer and kissed her cheek. "Today marks a new beginning, *chérie.* A new marriage for us both, a new home for you, and later tonight, a new year for the whole world."

Slowly, she nodded, pulling her fur coat more closely around her.

"Alors," he said, sitting straighter. "Shall we go home? Are you ready?"

No, she thought dully. *Not ready.* Not without David.

She twisted the new gold band on her hand. "Yes," she said softly.

Gently, but resolutely, she pushed David to the back of her mind, and looked straight ahead at the château.

Chapter 10

They sat, at five minutes before midnight, in what Laurent had described to Krisztina as the Salon Rouge, a warmly decorated, gently cluttered family drawing room; walls paneled in oak, windows hidden behind heavy red damask curtains, a richly woven late Gothic mille fleurs tapestry, the focal point of the room, hanging across one wall, two marble fireplaces and three well-trodden Persian rugs on the polished parquet floor.

The inhabitants of the room might well have been marble too, sculpted statues brought to life occasionally by hushed ripples of polite conversation. The three surviving members of the main core of *la grande famille de Trouvère*.

Geneviève de Trouvère, forty-four years old, sat still and erect in a large silk damask–covered fauteuil, her long-fingered, elegant hands unadorned but for her wedding ring and folded neatly in her lap. *How beautiful she is,* Krisztina thought, in spite of the severity of her black Balmain dress. Her remote, desolate expression was relieved only periodically by the fleeting deliverance of some sweet, private memory, when the clouds over her gray eyes would lift, a spark of past warmth kindling, and her right hand would rise absently to pat her thick, honey blond hair.

The newlyweds, too, sat in silence, oppressed by the gloomy atmosphere. In a corner of the room stood a Christmas tree, branches undecorated but for twenty or thirty small candles, all depressingly unlit. Laurent, dark-suited and smoking a cigarette, leaned casually at one end of a *dormeuse* couch, while his uncomfortable bride, clad in the only uncreased and fittingly somber dress she had been able to find, fairly bristled with strain as she perched on a rococo chair facing her mother-in-law. Her only distraction was the four dogs sharing the salon; the Irish wolfhounds, two brindle and one pure white, lolling in noble formation around the flickering central fireplace, while poor displaced Mozes lay, alert and tense, by his mistress's feet, one muscular shoulder pressed hard against her left leg.

From behind the drapes came a sudden whistling of wind, followed instantly by a creaking of branches and rattling of windowpanes. Krisztina imagined the snow already on the ground swirling icily through the air, and shivered.

Laurent glanced up at the handsome bracket clock over the mantel. "Almost time," he said, his voice reverberating in the room.

His mother stirred, and her gaze swiveled to focus on the bottle of Krug champagne that stood in a silver ice bucket on a gilded table near the window, the only concession to the occasion.

"By all means," she assented, her voice low but compelling. "*Le champagne, s'il te plaît,* Laurent."

He finished his cigarette and stood up to attend to the bottle. Slowly, Geneviève rose, and Krisztina followed suit, watching as the older woman moved to the main fireplace to warm her hands.

One of the wolfhounds thumped his tail, and Geneviève stooped to pat him on the head before turning toward Mozes.

"*Pauvre petit,*" she crooned softly, and scratched his chest with firm, practiced fingers. Mozes, able to recognize a true canine connoisseur when he met one, folded back his ears and grunted in appreciation.

"*Il est beau,*" she said to Krisztina. "He will help you to adjust," she continued in German.

"He likes you, madame."

She smiled. "Most animals like me."

"*Maman.*" Laurent handed Geneviève a glass.

"*Merci,* Laurent."

He passed another to Krisztina, took the last for himself, and came to stand between them. *How small his mother is,* Krisztina noticed with surprise for the first time, and realized that it was the force of the Frenchwoman's personality that gave an illusion of stature.

The midnight chimes began, their tone silvery but proud, as if the ormolu clock were aware that they had put their trust in its delicate mechanism rather than in the more majestic English grandfather clock that could be heard booming in the Salle Anglaise farther down the hall.

As the twelfth chime died away, Geneviève raised her glass. *"Bonne année, mes enfants,"* she toasted, her voice as steady as her hand, her eyes bright. "May 1939 bring us peace within and without." She paused. "And may your marriage be as blessed as my own."

"Merci beaucoup, Maman." Laurent put his glass on the mantelpiece and turned to hug her warmly, while Krisztina, moved but feeling more than ever an interloper, knelt on the rug and rubbed her cheek against Mozes' silky coat, murmuring fondly in his ear.

Feeling a sudden touch on her shoulder, she glanced up. Geneviève looked down at her, her eyes sympathetic. *"Glückliches Neujahr,* Krisztina," she said in her perfect German, and Krisztina rose quickly, remembering gratefully that Laurent had said how much she detested the language.

"Merci, madame." She took the other woman's outstretched hand and felt its chill. *"Pour tout."*

"For what?" Geneviève said wryly. "A glass of champagne?"

"For welcoming me into your home at such a difficult time."

"Château de Trouvère is *your* home now, Krisztina. This is your wedding night and New Year's Eve. There should be rejoicing, music and dancing . . ."

"Perhaps there will be, in the future," Krisztina said softly, "but now is not the time."

Geneviève shook her head. "No."

"Why don't we sit down?" Laurent said.

"Perhaps," Krisztina suggested abruptly, "you and your mother would like some time alone together? I could go upstairs. I'm very tired, and I wouldn't mind at—"

"Absolument non," Geneviève stopped her firmly. "I would not hear of it." She checked the time. "In any case, in a few minutes we must all go to the servants' hall, where they are holding their own party. It is traditional," she explained, "for us to share a small celebration on this night and on Christmas Eve."

Laurent touched his mother's arm gently. "Are you sure that you want to go, Maman? I'm certain they would understand if—"

"Of course I shall go," she interrupted quite tartly. "They were most generous," she told Krisztina. "They offered to cancel their *Réveillon* parties out of respect for my husband, but I told them it would have been the very last thing Armand would have wished." She reached up to pat her son's cheek fondly. "You must not start treating me like fragile porcelain, *chéri,*" she rebuked him tenderly. "Life must continue, especially in a family such as ours where history and tradition are paramount."

"You're right, Maman, of course." Laurent looked contrite. "Forgive me?"

Geneviève smiled. "Always."

He glanced at Krisztina. "My mother has courage, *n'est-ce pas?*"

"Yes," she agreed readily, and was suddenly aware that those were the first words he had addressed to her since midnight.

"One cannot run away," Geneviève said, and shrugged eloquently. *"On peut se cacher pendant quelque temps*—one can hide for a while within oneself, but there is no escape from the truth." Her eyes grew suddenly bright with tears, but she brushed them away quickly and retrieved her champagne glass from a small ornate table. "I said earlier, Krisztina," she went on in German, "that Château de Trouvère is now your home."

"Yes," Krisztina said softly.

"I realize, however, that it takes time to grow accustomed to new surroundings, however lovely, not to mention different customs and, of course, people. But I hope that the love you feel for your husband will fill the difficult early days with enough joy to make them worthwhile."

There was a brief silence.

"I hope so too," Krisztina said steadily.

"It's getting late, Maman," Laurent reminded them. "We should be going down."

"Very well." Geneviève handed him her glass and straightened her dress with a brisk patting of her hands. "Laurent," she directed calmly, "stand between us, please. We shall present them with a picture of continuity." Unexpectedly, she twinkled at Krisztina. "One baroness on each arm should serve well, don't you agree, *ma chère?*"

*

Krisztina would never forget that first evening at de Trouvère, any more than she would forget the first morning that followed. Surprisingly, only the night itself, which she had dreaded above all else, passed unmemorably, lost in deep, refreshing, uninterrupted sleep. Her husband, observing that she was exhausted, had allowed her to prepare for bed in the dressing room, after which he had kissed her gently on the cheek and wished her good night.

She was woken by a young dark-haired maid carrying a silver breakfast tray.

"*Bonne année*, madame." The girl placed the tray on her lap, tidied the quilt, and drew the curtains.

"*A vous aussi*," Krisztina said, embarrassed. "*Et merci beaucoup.*"

There was a knock at the door, and she looked up to see Geneviève, dressed in a dark chocolate-brown wool suit.

"*Bonjour*, Krisztina." The maid gave a tiny curtsy and left.

Appalled at being discovered still in bed, Krisztina started to push away the tray.

"*Non, non*," Geneviève said hastily. "*Reste tranquille.*" She remained in the doorway. "I only came to remind you that today is a holiday, and so there is no need to hurry. Normally, we would have attended the service in Colmar this morning, but under the circumstances, Père Perigot came from Riquewihr to say mass in our chapel."

"Why didn't Laurent wake me?" Krisztina asked with regret. "I should so like to have been there."

"We both agreed that you must be tired from the strain of the journey followed by such a late night."

"Where is Laurent?" Krisztina asked.

"Riding," Geneviève replied. "He has always loved the estate in the mornings, and as you see, it is a particularly beautiful day. Perhaps we may take a stroll together a little later?"

"I'd love it, madame."

"Good," she said. She turned to go, then stopped. "May I ask you to do me one favor, my dear?"

"Of course."

"Please stop calling me madame. I would so much prefer it if you used my name, or, if you wish, Belle-mère."

Just over an hour later they stood halfway down the stone steps on the east side of the château, gazing at the sparkling panorama. Krisztina tried to imagine what lay beneath the mantle of snow. Normally, she guessed, gardens, vineyards, fields and orchards would be clearly definable, but now it was all one vast, majestic splendor, without boundaries.

"And most of it de Trouvère," Geneviève said softly, reading her thoughts. "This is one of the great vistas of the region."

Krisztina shook her head slowly. "It's glorious. I feel I could stand here forever."

"And catch pneumonia." Geneviève looked down toward Mozes and the three wolfhounds—Vénus, Orion, and Perseus—who were already romping in the snow. "Come, let's walk."

They moved away from the château over pristine white lawns toward what Geneviève explained, mostly in German, was one of the estate's two classic baroque gardens.

"At one time," she said, "the whole area surrounding the house was laid out in this style, divided into what are called *compartiments de broderie,* but Armand's mother disliked exaggerated formality. She was a nature lover, she believed that it was pointless to try to improve on God's chef d'oeuvre and that the right place for marble, gilt, and geometry was in architecture. So now, though you will still find some sculptures and decorative fountains in the grounds, I hope you will feel that they're there to enhance what belongs there by right, rather than being part of some design."

"Belle-mère," Krisztina said, and Geneviève smiled, "it's very generous of you to speak to me in German."

"I want to make you feel at home, Krisztina. I only wish I spoke Hungarian."

"Surely it's for me to improve my French."

"It's already quite good, *ma chère,*" Geneviève assured her, "but it will inevitably take time for you to grow easy with it."

They left the ornamental garden and continued on a broad path, the dogs overtaking them and flying ahead at a noiseless gallop.

"I suggest a compromise," Geneviève went on. "The best way to become fluent is to immerse yourself in French as much as possible, so in future let's speak nothing else, when practical, during the daytime. In the evenings, until you are quite comfortable, we shall all speak German."

Krisztina nodded. "That sounds more than fair."

"Today, however, is a holiday, and there is more than enough for you to absorb without struggling for words." She clapped her gloved hands suddenly together. "We must move a little more briskly. I can do little more this morning than show you the parts of de Trouvère that are in walking distance. For a true idea of the beauty and character of the place, you must wait until spring."

Krisztina sighed appreciatively. "It looks wonderful even now."

"*Oui,*" Geneviève agreed, "*c'est un beau camouflage.* My husband always loved the snow, because when the light was as it is today, it was the only time he could easily survey all his lands from the house."

For an hour and a half they walked companionably side by side, and just as Laurent had described the countryside in summer, so Geneviève attempted to give Krisztina some notion of what each successive garden would look like in the coming months.

"To our left," she said in one tranquil, icy spot, "in the shadow of that old oak, will be a border filled with lilies, and to the right, in springtime, you will find narcissi, hyacinths, and primroses." They went on a little way, and near a pretty pond, she closed her eyes and brought forth a fragrant picture of irises, forget-me-nots, lilies of the valley, meadow rue, and bleeding hearts while her daughter-in-law listened spellbound.

Their boots making soft, scrunching sounds, they passed from the *jardins anglais* to the *japonais,* from the tangled, twisted splendor of the great wild garden that had been the favorite of Laurent's grandmother, to the tightly regimented vegetable plots and then into open parkland and a breathtaking arboretum of rare trees.

"The park, of course," Geneviève said, "is a mass of color when the azaleas and rhododendrons are in full bloom, and over there," she pointed, "is a Judas tree, whose flowers appear before the leaves."

On and on they went, through winter-barren pergolas and beneath wooden arbors of delicate latticework, along an avenue of noble Spanish chestnut trees and an alley of copper beeches. From a vantage point in the park, Geneviève showed Krisztina the distant fruit orchards that had been an autumnal magnet for Laurent as a boy. She pointed out the numerous bridle paths, bordered by flowering bushes, that led into the forest and out into the open, uncultivated fields where horses could gallop freely. They walked along the meandering, ice-covered little river, crossed at two points by charming arched wooden bridges. And finally, they came to a halt near a frozen lake, on the far shore of which stood an enchanting *temple d'amour,* lonely and isolated against a backdrop of snowcapped fir trees.

"Does anyone ever skate on the lake?" asked Krisztina. Mozes, having sniffed at the ice, trotted to her side and pushed her right hand with his nose.

"On the north side it's sometimes thick enough," Geneviève replied. "Do you skate?"

"Not since I was a small child." She paused wistfully. "When I became a dancer, my legs were too important for me to risk injury."

A silence grew between them, punctuated only by occasional bird calls and the regular panting of the dogs.

Geneviève spoke first. "Shall you miss it very much?" she asked gently.

Krisztina looked at her frankly. "I cannot imagine my life without dance." She waited a beat. "I can't believe that it's over." She laughed a little harshly. "But then, I haven't quite absorbed the fact that many other things are at an end for me too." Sudden tears had sprung into her eyes, but she controlled herself tightly.

"You are very talented," Geneviève said quietly. "A rare dancer."

"Better than average." Her voice was husky. "And fortunate with my partners."

"More than that."

"Of course," Krisztina said, misunderstanding. "Without Laurent, I would never have been a champion."

"I meant you. *Your* talent. You are the best I have ever seen."

Krisztina raised her eyes, bewildered. "You've never seen me dance."

"Not true," Geneviève corrected. "I saw you once in Baden-Baden, and again in Paris at the *Championnat du Monde.*"

A stray white cloud, puffing lazily across the blue sky, shadowed the sun briefly. Orion, the white wolfhound, thumped his tail impatiently, and Mozes whined.

"But we never met," Krisztina said, confused. "Laurent said nothing."

"We asked him not to."

"Why?"

"Because my husband wished to understand the object of his son's passion." Geneviève shrugged her shoulders lightly. "I should have liked to have met you, but Armand preferred to remain anonymous."

"And did he understand?"

"Of course." Geneviève smiled. "How could he fail to?"

"But he did not approve," Krisztina said thoughtfully, half to herself, as suddenly a whole new aspect of Laurent's courtship manifested itself in her mind. It had never occurred to her, though realistically it should have done, that he had even more to overcome than her own reluctance.

"I'm afraid not," Geneviève concurred. "At least, not wholeheartedly. Armand was no rigid martinet—he could be strict, even severe at times, but he would never, in the last resort, have forbidden Laurent to marry the girl he loved."

Krisztina fell silent for a moment. Then she looked directly at Geneviève. "And you? Were you against our marriage?"

"At first, I confess that I agreed with Armand. We felt that Laurent was merely infatuated with you."

"You said 'at first.' "

"That's right. The longer the partnership continued, the more persistent the wooing, the more intrigued I became by the mysterious young *Hongroise.*" She smiled wryly. "You must consider, too, Krisztina, the significance of snobbery to the aristocracy."

"Your husband wanted Laurent to marry someone with a better pedigree," Krisztina said, without rancor.

"As I did," Geneviève agreed. "There are great responsibilities attached to the perpetuation of a noble line, *ma chère,* which are generally easier for someone of similar upbringing to cope with." She shrugged again, elegantly. "We live, regrettably, in an imperfect world." She waited a moment, then continued. "So, as I was saying, I persuaded Armand that we should learn more about you before voicing our disapproval, and that is when he decided we should see for ourselves without committing to a formal introduction."

A pair of magpies, flying overhead, screeched, and Vénus and Perseus barked loudly.

"And was that when you changed your mind?"

"That was when I understood the importance of perfect partnership, and how such a blessed union—what seemed to amount

to a virtual fusion, on the dance floor, of two minds and bodies—
might easily grow to equate with love." She paused. "At least in
the heart of one of the partners."

Krisztina said nothing.

"That was when I understood my son." Again Geneviève
paused. "I admit, Krisztina, I have yet to understand you."

They had grown chilly, standing motionless by the frozen lake,
and they returned to the château by a more direct route, ending
their walk in the small private chapel, which was sequestered,
together with the family graveyard, in a silent walled garden.

It was cold inside, with lively little drafts that rose from the
stone floor and lapped about the hems of their coats. The light
was quite dim in spite of the sunbeams that penetrated the seven
stained-glass windows, so that the steaming of their breath
seemed to waft wraithlike in the air; yet as soon as the heavy oak
door closed behind them, Krisztina felt a marvelous, almost prim-
itive peace wash over her like a warming wave.

She watched as the Frenchwoman dipped her fingertips in the
stoup of holy water, made the sign of the cross, and knelt, and she
intended to follow suit, but found herself instead standing openmouthed, like an awed schoolgirl.

So this was what wealth and position could provide—a private
place to commune with God. She had always felt that she could
pray anywhere; she did not, like her mother, need plaster saints
or rosary or altar. She had never even felt the need, particularly,
to kneel. She had learned Catholicism at her mother's knee, and
she respected her religion, but if asked what she believed in, she
would have to reply that she simply had faith in the existence of
God, and that for her the solemn rituals, though of undeniable
comfort to millions, were little more than symbolic.

She gazed around, drinking in the remarkable serenity of the
place, admiring the snowy Ionic pillars and pure, arched roof,
and the delicately carved altarpiece depicting the Crucifixion,
topped with a small painted and gilded statue of the Blessed
Virgin. The symbols were present here, too, of course, but the
modest dignity of this chapel was both soothing and inspiring.

Geneviève crossed herself again, rose, and smiled at Krisztina's
rapt expression.

"The only example of the *néoclassique* at de Trouvère," she
explained. "It was a period of reaction, they say, against baroque

and the fussiness of rococo. Simple but effective, don't you think?"

"It's—" Krisztina sought the right word. "It's sublime. My mother would love it dearly."

"I hope she will be able to come here one day and see it."

A sudden, terrible pang of homesickness struck Krisztina with such force that she almost cried out. Sensing her distress, Geneviève reached out and touched her sleeve.

"I, too, have been in shock, I think, since Armand died," she said acutely. "Our losses are, of course, of a different nature, yet I cannot help feeling that yours are somehow greater than one might expect."

The tears that lately seemed an ever-present threat, swam again in Krisztina's eyes, provoked this time by the sensitivity of the older woman.

"True friendships," Geneviève went on, "are not created overnight, Krisztina. Like most growing things, they take time to root and become strong, but sometimes, like the Judas tree, they bloom with surprising speed." She paused. "I cannot replace your mother—I would not presume to try—but I hope that before too long you will feel you have a friend here."

Krisztina bit her lip, wanting to respond, to find appropriate words of gratitude, but knowing that if she spoke, she would weep.

"Perhaps," Geneviève went on, "you might like to spend a few minutes alone here. I have always found this a most comforting place."

Krisztina swallowed and nodded. "Thank you. I think I would like that."

"Shall you find your own way back?"

"We're so close now, I have my bearings. In any case"—she mustered a smile—"Mozes will show me."

Alone, Krisztina walked down the aisle to the front pews, the soft skin soles of her boots soundless on the stones, and sat down.

If only I could pray. She had found it impossible to do so since that hideous night at home with her father. Now she closed her eyes and tried valiantly to stem the tide of mutiny that seemed suddenly perilously close to bursting through the barrier of resignation that had held it in check since she had agreed to the marriage.

"Hail Mary, full of grace," she heard her voice whisper, a harshness in the hollow silence. Her eyes burned behind their lids.

No good, her heart rebelled. *I have betrayed David and Mama and myself. If the vows I took yesterday were a mockery, then so must my prayers be today.*

She opened her eyes, and the suffering faces of Christ and the two crucified thieves stared back at her from the altarpiece.

Where David is now, there will be no synagogue, she thought wretchedly.

Abruptly, her nerves too exposed by the tranquillity of the chapel, she stood, and hurried to the door.

Chapter 11

Laurent returned from his ride, his face flushed and his eyes sparkling. They ate lunch with Geneviève in a pleasant room on the first floor that overlooked the rose garden and was decorated in pale apple green, an eternal spring touched by autumn through the golden tints of the walnut furniture.

Shall we eat lunch up here every day? Krisztina wondered, watching the heavy silver trays being carried in and out and thinking of the kitchens in the basement. *Or is it just because today is a holiday?*

"The finest foie gras in the land," Laurent enthused, wiping his mouth with a napkin. "You're not eating, *chérie?*"

"Do you keep geese at de Trouvère?"

"Since the turn of the century. Do you know it was a *pâtissier* here in Alsace, a man named Jean-Joseph Clause, who perfected the pâté? A genius."

"I doubt if the geese would agree with you."

He cocked a surprised eyebrow. "Don't you like it?"

"It repels me. It's so cruel."

He shrugged. "This is farmland, Krisztina. Farmers cannot afford sentimentality, can they, Maman?"

Geneviève made no comment.

I have married a farmer, Krisztina thought abstractedly. *Not a dancer, but a farmer.*

Luncheon over, she found herself again alone while Laurent and his mother excused themselves to discuss matters arising from Baron Armand's estate.

And now what is expected of me? she wondered, kicking her heels in one of the empty corridors on the ground floor. *Nothing, I suppose, since it's a holiday. I could fetch Mozes and take another walk, or I could write to Mama, or I could explore the house . . .*

She set off, armed only with a jumbled mental list of the names of different rooms that Laurent had recounted to her just after their arrival the previous day. One by one, her heels clicking on parquet and stone and sinking soundlessly into the depths of Savonnerie and Aubusson carpets, she embarked on a private voyage of discovery, trying to link each name with what she found behind each imposing oak door.

Some were obviously identifiable—the Salon Chinois, full of exquisitely carved, lacquered furniture and jade; the Hunting Room, every art-filled cabinet, every wall, and even the ceiling dedicated to the chase; the charming Salon Bleu and the masculine Smoking Room, in which the air, despite two open windows offset by a generous blaze in the hearth, hung heavy with years of tobacco, wood smoke, and a definite hint of cognac.

She found two formal dining rooms, one immense, one more intimate, and adjoining the Salon Rouge she discovered what she presumed must be the room in which the family generally dined, no less handsome but obviously well used.

Dreamily, she climbed the fantastic baroque staircase, her hand stroking the cool surface of the ornate marble balustrade, pausing halfway up to decide whether to continue to left or right as the staircase split magnificently into two white wings to reach the slightly dizzying gallery on the first floor.

"It's almost exactly a miniature version of Rastrelli's great staircase, the Jourdain, in the Winter Palace at St. Petersburg," she remembered Laurent telling her the night before. "I like to think of it," he had added, "as the true core of the château."

On the first floor she came across the Music Room, silent as the grave but immaculately polished, with a Bechstein grand piano and a huge covered harp the only two permanent fixtures. Through a second door, in a large closet room, Krisztina found a veritable orchestra's worth of stringed and brass instruments.

Leaving the Music Room and closing the door gently behind

her, she almost collided with Sutterlin, the butler, a balding, distinguished, rather remote Alsatian who had been at the head of a receiving line when she and Laurent had arrived.

"*Bonne année,* Monsieur Sutterlin." She was conscious that both Laurent and his mother addressed him by surname only, but awkward with what seemed to her almost discourteous.

"*Bonne année,* madame."

"I've been enjoying a little exploration," she explained, with a newcomer's need to account for trespass into closed rooms.

"May I be of assistance, madame?"

She shook her head. "Unless you can tell me what I may have missed." She counted off the rooms she had already visited.

Sutterlin thought for an instant. "I think, madame, you might enjoy the Salle Fleurie and the Summer Room." He paused. "And the Mirror Hall."

"Thank you," Krisztina said quickly, and smiled. "Are they on this floor?"

Duly directed to the west side by Sutterlin, she found that the Salle Fleurie and Summer Room were a connecting suite. The former was a room created by some wildly feminine spirit, a dream of floral fabrics that Krisztina found quite overpowering. The latter was a delectable splash of contrast against the wintry landscape outside, an airy, terraced salon with trompe l'oeil walls depicting what she guessed was de Trouvère's lake in summer, a riot of blossom and smooth blue water, complete with swans and cygnets, the *temple d'amour* on the far side inhabited by a pair of unidentifiable lovers.

But it was the Mirror Hall that, unexpectedly, gave her real cause for celebration. In the eyes of most this was undoubtedly a remarkable example of rococo art. But in Krisztina's eyes the lavish silver stucco and carved wood that framed the enormous mirrors off which the early sunset bounced fire back and forth represented only one thing—the perfect, if somewhat extravagant, dance studio.

Quickly, she closed the door, found the light switches and was dazzled by the chandeliers. Even the door, its handle silver, was mirrored on the inside, making it difficult to recognize and giving the room an almost cloistered atmosphere.

Falling to her knees, Krisztina scrabbled and tugged at the edge of the carpet until it lifted up in her hands. To her delight, the floor beneath was parquet.

My first act as Baronne, she decided suddenly. *I shall ask them to take up this carpet and bring in a gramophone. If Laurent won't dance, I'll dance alone.* Her confidence wavered. *Unless Geneviève objects. This is still her house.* A gentle, warming conviction brought a smile to her lips. *She will not.*

At ten o'clock, Laurent suggested an early night since they were all tired. The glow of his narrow golden eyes as he looked at Krisztina sent a quiver of nervousness to the pit of her stomach.

They climbed the great staircase side by side but not touching, until they reached the halfway point, where Laurent took her arm and guided her to the left, which would bring them a few paces nearer to the private, more commonplace staircase to the second floor.

Even through her closed dressing room door and from a distance of two stories she could hear the faint booming of the grandfather clock as it struck eleven. She could delay no longer. She studied her pale face once more in the mirror, saw how her hair gleamed from her protracted, agitated brushing, raised her chin, rose, and walked into the bedroom.

All the lights were out, with the exception of her bedside lamp.

In the dark, she thought absently as she slipped off her white satin negligee and draped it over the back of a chair, *I can imagine that I am with David.*

Laurent half lay, half sat in bed, propped up by two large square pillows. He wore black silk pajamas with narrow scarlet edging and a tiny red family crest on the breast pocket. He seemed composed, his eyes open and watching her every move. Only the faint tremor of the scar tissue on his cheek betrayed his tension as she joined him under the duvet.

Krisztina turned her face toward him and managed a nervous, watery smile. He responded by taking her hand, stroking the wedding band on her finger for a moment and then raising the hand to his lips. His skin was warm and dry, his touch curiously comforting.

Thank God, in spite of everything, she thought, *we are at least friends.* This marriage might be strange, and it might be wrong, but it was a bargain, reached by her through despair and out of thwarted love. It was a bargain she intended to honor.

Looking into his face, she saw for the hundredth time how handsome Laurent was, and she realized, with a flash of relief tinged with guilt, that it would be no grievous hardship to lie beside that lean, well-muscled body at night. It was a body that, in a sense, she knew intimately, to which she had virtually made love under public scrutiny in ballrooms all across Europe. And his hands, which had held and guided her with such confidence and sensitivity, would in all probability be sensual, clever hands when it came to actual lovemaking. This might not, after all, be a hideous nightmare, for blended together with a host of conflicting motivations and emotions in Laurent de Trouvère was an oddly vulnerable streak that she could not help but sympathize with.

"Krisztina, *ma belle*," he said suddenly, his voice startling her from her thoughts, "do you know how long I have waited for this moment?"

She hesitated, and then replied, "No."

His gaze was steady. "For more than five years I dreamed of you almost every time I slept, but in those dreams you were made of marble, like a statue."

Krisztina said nothing. If that was true, it alarmed her, for once the magic of unattainability was lost, there would be little left of this marriage that would stand up to life's daily blows. And the marriage had to work! It was crucial to their bargain, for if it failed, who would there be to continue the fight for David's release?

Taking her silence for modesty, Laurent put his hands tentatively, almost reverently, on her arms and drew her close to kiss her. Krisztina shut her eyes for the duration of the kiss, sitting erect and passive, and when he released her, she reached back to turn out the lamp.

"Non, chérie, s'il te plaît."

She stopped and looked back inquiringly.

His eyes were intense and appealing. "It would give me particular joy," he said, almost humbly, "if you would leave the light on."

Her hand fell away from the switch. "All right," she said softly.

He smiled. "I want very much to see you."

"Yes." She nodded. "I know."

Slowly, his arms slid around her, and again she closed her eyes, this time thinking how different his scent was from David's, a spicier cologne, perhaps, and—smoke from the log fire, that was it, of course, lingering faintly in his hair.

Laurent's hands, strong but gentle, began to stroke her shoulders and arms, and it was not the same as with David, when her flesh had seemed to burn with desire, but it was far from unpleasant. And though at first when he caressed her breasts through the satin of her nightgown, she wanted to wrench away, she remembered her vows and commanded herself to relax. And when she opened her eyes and saw his face, rapt with wonder and delight as his fingers brought her nipples, under white satin, to hardness, she thought his lovemaking seemed almost like worship. The notion weakened her and made her tremble, in spite of herself, so that when he slipped the narrow straps from her shoulders, she had no real urge to resist, and the guilt she was trying so hard to suppress, magnified and threatened to suffocate her.

"Mon amour," he murmured, and buried his face between her breasts, and as his old recurring dream came true, as the marble of his lonely, frustrated nights turned into warm flesh and fragrance, he cried out briefly, and Krisztina thought she felt his tears on her skin.

"Naked," he muttered unexpectedly, and pulled away from her. Suddenly his silk pajamas felt unbearable, restricting and claustrophobic—savagely he tore off the jacket, sending a tiny scarlet button soaring through the air, kicked away the trousers, heaved off the duvet that had covered them both, and tugged the white nightgown from Krisztina—and then, for several long moments, he paused, motionless, on his knees, and stared at the staggering and utterly exposed loveliness of his bride.

Furiously he tried to unravel the sudden new imbroglio that raged between his heart and his senses. Part of him wanted to make slow, gentle, persistent love to her, to take her tenderly, to treasure every inch of her as befitted the earthbound goddess his interminable pursuit had created in his mind. But at the same time, his eyes roved over the enchanting breasts, the luscious curving hips, and the tantalizing golden pubic hair, and wholly carnal, unspiritual messages ripped through him, telling him that what he *really* wanted was to possess her, to violate that sweetness, to grapple and to rut, to plunge into her, and as his thoughts flayed him, his eyes darkened, his penis grew immense, and his heart pounded like galloping hooves. . . .

Krisztina watched him, and her body, too, seemed to part company from her consciousness. Her skin, from her cheeks down past her breasts all the way to her toes, began to flush rosy with anticipation, her breathing became shallower and more rapid, and she became aware of a wetness between her thighs that both surprised and embarrassed her. It was as if only her psyche remained aloof, remembered the agony of her betrayal of David, and counted the cost of her vows, while her flesh continued on its wanton, spontaneous way, preparing her for her husband with a soft, welcoming moisture . . .

Abruptly, with a groan, he was beside her on the sheet, and his arms were tight about her. What had for a few minutes seemed to her more like the contemplation of a work of art, became all at once tangible and frighteningly real, for this, on Krisztina's part, was sexuality without love. It was mating, coupling, animalistic and lusty and exciting and dreadful. And as Laurent's hands, fierce and acquisitive, parted her thighs, and she felt him beginning to enter her, she squeezed her eyes as tightly shut as she could, and tried to summon up her love in a dark, desperate fantasy.

And then suddenly, it struck her that this was perhaps the greatest betrayal of all, that all she would gain from such hypocrisy would be grief and shame. So she wrenched her eyes open and looked unblinkingly into her husband's eyes, dark golden slits that seemed half drowned in passion and desire. And as he ravened and thirsted for her, arms embracing, hands caressing, clutching, all sensation in Krisztina subsided and died, and a voice in her brain said over and over again: *Not David, never again David, but* for *David.* And as Laurent thrust into her, hips lunging eagerly, desperately, the sound of their skin meeting, smacking gently, began to beat a rhythm in her ears. It grew faster, rising relentlessly to the toneless crescendo of climax, and the incoherent, groaning rallentando that followed, and all through it another thought rode uppermost in her head, relaxing her, curiously comforting and absolving:

A bargain is a bargain.

It was minutes later that Laurent finally rolled over and sat up, sweat glistening on his chest.

"I caused you no pain," he said flatly.

She smiled a little, misunderstanding. "No."

"A virgin feels pain."

Her breath caught in her throat. "Often, yes," she managed steadily.

Seconds passed.

"I should like to hit you," Laurent said at last, his voice still empty.

She was silent.

"But I cannot beat my wife for my own folly." He smiled bitterly, wanly. "And because I love her," he added.

Slowly, wishing she could cover her nakedness, Krisztina sat up.

"You lost your virginity in Berlin," Laurent said.

Her cheeks grew hot. "You knew that," she replied, trying not to sound defensive, but failing.

"Tu as raison. You're right, of course." He laughed shortly, harshly. "But until tonight, it wasn't real."

Tentatively, sensing that he needed comfort, she put out her hand and touched his right arm, but he flinched and drew away as if she held a burning cigarette.

"And it is worse," he went on, "far worse, knowing that it was my fault."

She hesitated. "Because it happened—in your room?"

He nodded, his jaw clenched with pain.

"But you couldn't have known what would happen," she said quietly.

He looked away, as if her scrutiny was too much to bear. "No," he said tightly.

"You acted out of friendship, Laurent."

He shook his head, still unable to meet her eyes. "No," he said again. "Out of love."

A new kind of guilt began to surface in Krisztina as she became aware, perhaps for the first time, of how selfish her feelings were, as though she were the only person who *felt.* Maybe, she fumbled in confusion, if she began to try to separate emotions, to see them from Laurent's viewpoint as well as her own, it might help her to survive within this marriage. *No,* she corrected quickly, *help us* both *to survive.*

Still feeling uncomfortably exposed, she slid off the bed, found her nightdress on the floor and slipped it over her head.

"Krisztina!"

The sharp anxiety in his voice startled her. "What?"

Laurent's expression had changed again, was suddenly supplicating. "Don't leave me."

She smiled. "I'm only—"

"No! I don't mean . . ." He was like a boy in a nightmare. "Don't leave de Trouvère!"

Mystified, she came quickly around to his side of the bed and sat down on the edge. "Laurent, I'm not going to leave you or de Trouvère. We've only just—"

He grasped her hand. "I swear to you I will keep my word!"

"What?"

"I *will* try to find David, to have him released!" He was near hysteria, his grip almost violent.

"Laurent, my dear," she said gently, hiding her alarm. "I believe you. After all, that was the promise you—"

"And I shall keep it!" He released her hand abruptly, jumped from the bed and opened the drawer of his bedside table. "Shall I prove it to you? Do you want me to write it in blood?" He rummaged wildly in the drawer. "Let me find something to cut myself with, and—"

"Laurent, stop!" Wide-eyed, Krisztina pulled him away from the drawer and slammed it shut. "It's not necessary to prove anything to me. I told you I believe you. Please calm yourself."

"And what if I can't find him?" His face was chalky white and there were tears in his eyes. "What if they won't release him? Then you will leave me, won't you!"

Very gently, confused by his agitation, she put her arms about him and held him. For a few minutes he trembled violently, until gradually he quietened and at last they sat down together on the side of the bed, the husband cradled against the wife's breast, and Krisztina thought about the way his maturity had diminished. Until now, the difference in their ages had seemed so great, his experience so much vaster than hers. Now suddenly she felt that *he* was by far the younger, in need of protection from what she realized was his own instability.

There was no escaping the truth, she reflected. Theirs was a monstrous basis for a marriage. David might be a thousand miles away in a concentration camp, but he was still with her, here at de Trouvère, in a château upon which he had never set eyes—in her heart and in Laurent's bitter soul.

Slowly, patiently, one arm growing numb with Laurent's weight, Krisztina began to ease herself out of the weary embrace.

"Tu vas?" he murmured.

"Just to the bathroom," she reassured.

He took her hand again, calm now, and raising it to his lips he kissed it and let it go again. "So much emotion," he said quietly.

"Yes."

"Stored up for too long."

She kissed his cheek.

In the bathroom, she splashed her face with tepid water, patted it dry, and then sat heavily down on the towel-covered changing stool. Her legs were shaking. She felt as if she had locked horns with a cyclone, uprooted, twisted feelings whipping around her head. She could hardly recall ever being so exhausted. And *cold.* She hugged herself to find a little warmth, huddling in the marble splendor and trying to regain her equilibrium.

"Krisztina?"

She heard his voice through the door.

"Coming," she called.

A fresh and fearful thought struck her. What if she became pregnant? Laurent had already said that he wanted children, but at this stage it would certainly be a terrible mistake. If she was to create any kind of stability, that had to be achieved before an innocent child was brought into the world.

Please God, don't let me be pregnant. She took a deep breath. She must find a doctor, someone discreet and kind, to help her.

An image of her mother kneeling in church flashed through her mind, and she thought with sorrow how deeply grieved Ilona would be at the idea of birth control. She realized, too, that it was vital it should remain her absolute secret, for she had married into an old and stoutly Catholic family.

Contraception is sinful, they would condemn, and call for Père Perigot.

A baby born into unhappiness is a greater sin, she thought defiantly, and looking into the mirror that covered one whole wall of the bathroom, she saw that her eyes were clear with resolve.

No babies. Not yet.

The bargain was sealed.

Chapter 12

The situation in Alsace grew more perilous, and Krisztina, watching as winter melted into an enchanted spring and early summer, and settling gradually into her new role, became aware that they were being sucked, steadily and inexorably, into war.

Army reinforcements poured in, reservists were called up, money was withdrawn from Strasbourg's banks. In late August, the population were invited to leave "while they still could," but Geneviève was scornful.

"Lâches!" she dismissed. "Cowards! Our family have lived here since 1817, through peace, war, and invasion, and it will take more than a gang of Germans to move us!"

International telephone lines were cut, and Krisztina lost the weekly luxury of speaking to her mother; a blackout was requested, gas masks and evacuation cards were distributed, and a trickle of alarm developed into a stream.

On September 1, Germany attacked Poland, and the following day the army in Alsace was mobilized and a general evacuation ordered. More than three quarters of the work force left de Trouvère, but the family, as well as the loyal older generation of their employees, remained, with Laurent at the helm, exempt from call-up because their farm produce had been certified as an essential contribution to the war effort.

The military were everywhere, but it was not until May 1940 that the war began in earnest. Even in the heart of the Haut-Rhin distant bombing was heard; but the Maginot Line held until mid-June, when the French army began to retreat, to the dismay of the Alsacien stoics.

"Traîtres!" Geneviève railed in outrage. "They are abandoning us without a fight! For the very first time, I am glad that Armand is not here to witness such an abomination."

By dawn on June 18, Strasbourg was virtually a ghost town, open and defenseless to the enemy. The next night, the Germans crossed the Rhine and advanced to Benfeld, only about thirty kilometers from de Trouvère. By the time the armistice had been signed, ending the battle completely, the view from the top of the château was of long streams of French prisoners filing along the roads. It was abundantly, painfully clear that, while for most of Europe the war had barely begun, for France, and for Alsace, it was already lost.

On June 28, Adolf Hitler came to admire his new conquest; the Wehrmacht was promptly installed, German time was introduced and a curfew ordered. In just a matter of months, most of those evacuated to the southwest had come back, and the Germans set about trying to convince the inhabitants of the region that life under the Reich could and would be better than it had been under French rule.

The newly appointed head of the *administration civile* in Alsace, Gauleiter Robert Wagner, made it clear that they intended to align the province with the Reich in every imaginable way. Civil servants were to be immediately reeducated, German race laws were to be introduced and all "undesirables" and "politically unreliable" elements deported. They were the masters now, the new overlords, and if their early commands were couched in persuasive, almost benevolent tones, their voices quickly became strident and ruthless.

In July, *Hochdeutsch* became the only officially allowed language, and French was banned. Free German lessons were offered, but when the people declined to learn, the clampdown became tougher, extending to punishment by imprisonment. In August, the Alsatians were "asked" to change their French-sounding names. In December, a request was made to hand over all French books to assist the "purification" of all public and private libraries; members of the Hitler Youth marched from house to house in Strasbourg to receive the books, which were subsequently burned in the Orangerie before three thousand people.

"It's scandalous!" Geneviève reported to Laurent and Krisztina after a visit to the capital the following spring. "They have eradicated almost every vestige of French. The word *lettres* has been removed from the letter boxes. In the café where I ate my pitiful sandwich, I found that the bathroom taps had been painted over because they said *chaud* and *froid!*"

"How absurd," Krisztina laughed.

Geneviève nodded vigorously, her cheeks pink with anger. "I believe they are mad as well as evil! Madame Piquart, who owns a *papeterie* in the Place Broglie, told me they destroyed every photograph she had of our men in French uniforms—even the captions on her postcards had to be overprinted in German!"

They were sitting in the Salon Rouge after dinner, the wolf-hounds around the empty grate and Mozes, as always, at Krisztina's feet. Her husband, tired from the day's work, sat beside her on the couch, smoking.

"Shall I turn on the wireless?" Krisztina asked.

"For what?" Geneviève said drily. "To hear Nazi propaganda?" She looked coldly at her son.

"Maman," Laurent sighed, "wasn't it foolish enough to tear up the *étiquette?* Do you now want to break the law too?"

"Yes," she replied, her gray eyes quite steely. "As a matter of fact, it would give me considerable satisfaction."

Some months before, every household had been issued a label printed with a grim reminder that listening to foreign transmissions was now a crime punishable by forced labor. Laurent, upon receiving the label, had promptly fixed it to the wireless; his mother, incensed, had ripped it off.

It had by no means been the only heated dispute between them since the German invasion. The very day that the ban on French had been announced, Geneviève and Krisztina had by mutual consent finally ended their habit of chatting in German in the evenings. Laurent, on the other hand, began to allow German phrases to creep into his own conversation and to issue orders to the staff in either the regional patois many of them spoke or even in *Hochdeutsch* itself. Those employees who still remained found themselves in the middle of a bitter family disagreement, with Madame la Baronne and *la jeune Baronne* (as they privately referred to Krisztina) on one side, and the head of the estate "on the fence" but apparently teetering toward the other side.

Sutterlin was the only one bold enough to show open dissent.

"Sutterlin, please have Seigneur saddled," Laurent had requested one morning in German.

"*Immédiatement,* Monsieur le Baron."

Laurent had raised an eyebrow. "Are you not aware, Sutterlin, that it is now forbidden to speak French in Alsace?"

"*Mais oui,* Monsieur le Baron," came the steady, respectful answer.

Geneviève, just passing in the main hall, gave a small laugh. "I can't think why you don't change the names of the horses, Laurent. Though personally, I would find *Herr* an unattractive name for a handsome stallion."

Laurent flushed. "That will be all, Sutterlin." He waited until the butler had left, and turned angrily on his mother. "Is it necessary to try to make a fool of me in front of the servants, Maman?"

She stared at him coldly. "No more than for you to behave like a fool."

"I don't regard it as folly to obey the law."

"What law?" Geneviève retorted. "There was no mention of Alsace in the armistice agreement."

"Nevertheless they are here, aren't they, and in command." Aware that they might be overheard, he spoke more softly. "And I must tell you, Maman, that I find them just as civilized as I have always done."

"If you find thieves civilized."

"But in their eyes, it was the French who stole this territory from *them.* You forget that this was part of the German Empire for nearly fifty years."

"What is fifty years in history?" Her eyes flashed. "If your father could hear you now, he would despair!"

"He would consider the future of de Trouvère, Maman, just as I do," Laurent retaliated. "He was an intelligent man."

"He was a *patriot.*"

The situation between them had grown steadily worse, and now, as Geneviève continued to describe what she had found in Strasbourg, Krisztina found it disturbing to see that, though love undoubtedly remained, there was less and less affection and, worse still, less trust.

"There is almost nothing worth buying in the shops," Geneviève told Krisztina. "And if one did not know the city well, one would be constantly lost because of those ridiculous new street names. Place Broglie is now actually Adolf Hitler Platz—Madame Piquart and I spat on the sign."

"How dignified," Laurent said quietly, "and clever, too, if you want to be arrested."

His mother ignored him. "Avenue Jean-Jaures is Horst Wessel Allee, rue des Juifs is Mauerzunftgasse. My hairdresser is now a *Friseur* and the Banque de France is the Reichsbank." She paused for breath. "And when you have children, *mes enfants*, they will have to attend *Oberschulen* instead of lycées, and join the *Hitlerjugend!*"

Her voice, uncharacteristically passionate and loud, echoed in the silence that fell on the Salon Rouge. The merest mention of children was often enough to plunge Laurent into gloom, since not a month passed without his eager optimism being dashed, at which time Krisztina, guilty for her deception but more determined than ever that this was not the moment to usher new life into the world, would feign shared regret and pray for the mood to pass.

It was three days later that Geneviève, by pure accident, happened on Krisztina's secret.

The two women had been preparing to go for a ride when Krisztina found that she had forgotten her gloves. Since she was already in the saddle and since Geneviève wished to have a quick word about lunch with Marthe Schneegans, their cook, Geneviève offered to fetch them for her.

"Where are they, *chérie?*"

"In the top drawer of the chest closest to the dressing table, I think," Krisztina said. "Let me go, Belle-mère." She began to dismount.

"No, stay there, *chérie,*" Geneviève stopped her. "The horses will get restless—I shan't be more than a few minutes."

Having spoken to Marthe, Geneviève went to Krisztina's dressing room, but found only black suede and white cotton gloves in the top drawer. She tried the second, also without success, so hastily pulled out the bottom drawer and rummaged through a mixture of scarves, lingerie, and letters, smiling at the disorder. Krisztina always appeared so neat, so soignée—it amused Geneviève to discover that a chaotic condition within their wardrobes was yet another thing they had in common.

It was the photograph she found first, her eyes flicking over it with mild interest, thinking at first glimpse that it was just another of the scores of competition pictures taken of Krisztina and Laurent, since her daughter-in-law was wearing a frothy dance dress. But then she saw that her partner, his arm about her waist, was not Laurent but another man—dark-haired and merry-eyed —and on looking again at Krisztina's face, she saw an expression of pure joy that she had never seen before.

Ah, she thought, with a pang of realization. *The loss. The* true *loss.*

Slipping the photograph swiftly back beneath the pile of silk stockings, her fingers closed on a little box, and without really intending to, for she was not by nature an inquisitive woman, she glanced down at it and saw from the label what it contained.

Her eyes widened, and she sucked in her breath sharply. So the reason for Krisztina's failure to conceive was not God's will, as she had philosophically presumed until now.

A succession of emotions coursed through her. Shock first, and surprise at Krisztina's deception; then anger, clear and acute, in instinctive defense of her son; and finally, disappointment.

Tugging off her right glove, she opened the box and stared distastefully at the little diaphragm sitting snugly inside, then snapped it shut again and pushed it back to the bottom of the drawer, closing it with a bang.

"I couldn't find your gloves," she explained shortly, mounting her horse, "so I brought you a spare pair of my own."

It was not until they were back in the château two hours later that Krisztina had an opportunity to question her mother-in-law about her seemingly inexplicable change of mood.

"Is something wrong, Belle-mère?"

"What should be wrong?"

"You seem—distracted somehow—angry even."

Geneviève regarded her for a moment, and made a decision. "Let's go into the library. I think I should talk to you."

Inside the mellow, book-scented room, Krisztina looked at Geneviève with troubled eyes.

"What is it, Belle-mère?"

"Sit down, Krisztina, please."

They both sat in comfortable leather armchairs.

"First," Geneviève began, "I owe you an apology."

"Whatever for?"

"I have done something unpardonable. I have meddled in your privacy." She paused, then went on candidly. "I was looking, as you know, for your gloves. When I couldn't find them in the top drawer, as you had suggested, I opened the next, and so on."

Krisztina's face grew suddenly pale.

"I should, of course, have exercised proper self-control and looked away," the older woman said calmly, "but human frailties being such as they are, having seen the box, it was impossible to pretend even to myself that I had *not* seen it."

Krisztina remained silent, her hands folded tightly in her lap, the cravat about her neck suddenly constricting.

"It is not, I know, really my affair, *ma chère,*" Geneviève continued, more gently, "yet it does affect me deeply. I am sure that you have your reasons for deceiving my son—"

"To spare him the pain of the truth!" Krisztina broke in heatedly.

Geneviève maintained her composure. "Personally, I have always preferred honesty, even when it is painful."

"So have I," came the quiet reply.

Her mother-in-law reached out and patted her hand. "I believe you." She hesitated. "I often feel you are still lonely here, Krisztina, and I realize how much you miss your mother. I had thought we were becoming close, that you considered me your friend— but if you feel you cannot trust me—"

"I do trust you!"

"Then talk to me, *chérie.* I would like to try to understand your motives."

"Motives." Krisztina couldn't suppress the bitterness in her voice. "You make it sound like a criminal act."

"To many Catholics, that is what birth control represents. A crime against natural law. You know that, Krisztina."

"Of course I know. 'Procreation is the primary purpose of marriage'," she quoted harshly.

"That's right."

"But even the late pope understood that times were changing—"

"He approved *natural* means," Geneviève corrected. She

shook her head. "In any event, that is for you and your conscience, not for your mother-in-law. But it has everything to do with Laurent. If you've chosen not to have his children, surely he has the right to know why?"

"If he thought about it, he would know why."

"But he does not know you're using a diaphragm?"

"No."

Geneviève rose for a moment to remove her riding jacket, then sat down again, her expression intent.

"Is Laurent a bad husband, Krisztina?"

"Not at all."

"He loves you, doesn't he?"

"Very much."

Geneviève frowned. "Then is it because of his attitude toward Annexation?"

Krisztina met her gaze. "In part, yes, it is."

Her mother-in-law's eyes were sad. "With that I can sympathize, *chérie*. It has been quite a blow to me, as you know."

"He thinks he is protecting de Trouvère for the future."

Geneviève thought for a moment. "Armand would not have understood," she said softly. "He would have rebelled against the Nazis at every opportunity."

"I doubt if Laurent would have reacted this way if your husband were still here."

Geneviève smiled wanly. "You're probably right. My son is perhaps not suited to the kind of responsibility that has been thrust on him."

"He loves de Trouvère more than anything, Belle-mère."

"Yet he stayed away for months at a time."

"For the dancing."

Geneviève smiled. "And for you."

"Yes."

"Dance was, I think," Geneviève said slowly, "one symptom of his many confusions."

"I never used to think there were any confusions in Laurent," Krisztina said. "He knew exactly what he wanted."

Geneviève nodded. "To the point of obsession." She paused. "His dancing, for example. Laurent was—is—very talented, but to most men in his position, dance would have been a pastime, not the raison d'être that it became."

"And now he won't dance at all."

"Which must be very unhappy for you." Geneviève's eyes warmed a little. "Though at least you persist in your 'studio.'" She stressed the last word with amusement. The Mirror Hall that Krisztina had discovered on her first day in the château had become, in many ways, her salvation. Hardly a day passed when she didn't spend an hour or two bending and stretching in front of the steamy mirrors, jettisoning any stress and negative emotions in a sweep of pure physical effort.

"Laurent doesn't even want to talk about dancing, not even as a memory."

"It's one of his confusions," Geneviève said. "He misses it, but he feels guilty about it. He thinks he should have been here to help his father—and yet he wishes that he could have stayed away forever, a free spirit." She paused. "He always thought he had accepted the fact that de Trouvère would be his burden as well as his joy. From early childhood, he played at being baron, often put on airs and graces that we had to curb. He loved de Trouvère, as you say, because he felt it was *his,* his possession. Yet he still ran away from it. He is confused," she said again, and gave a small grimace. "In short, he is an unhappy man."

"And now I'm adding to his unhappiness because I don't want to draw another life into such—instability."

"Put that way," Geneviève said candidly, "I find it hard—as a woman, not a Catholic—to blame you."

Krisztina said nothing.

"But I cannot help feeling, *chérie,* that, putting Laurent aside, perhaps the young man in your photograph—" She stopped, seeing Krisztina's startled expression. "It was in the same drawer —I'm sorry." She went on. "I feel he may have something to do with your feelings." She paused. "Am I right?"

A deep, slow flush rose from Krisztina's neck into her cheeks. "Yes." Her voice was little more than a whisper.

"Your former partner?"

Krisztina nodded.

"But far more than just a partner."

Another faint "Yes."

"You said that you trust me, *chérie.* Won't you share this with me?"

Geneviève's tone was so infinitely gentle now, so filled with her wish to understand, that long-suppressed tears pricked Krisztina's eyes, and she knew that the moment for unburdening had come.

"So my son is little better than a blackmailer." Geneviève's face had grown pinched and pale, her voice dull.

"He acted out of love, Belle-mère."

"You defend him?"

"I think," Krisztina said softly, "that I have grown to understand him."

The Frenchwoman shook her head, still deeply shaken. "No wonder you don't want his children."

"Not now, at least."

They both fell silent for a while.

"You must realize, by now," Geneviève said at last, "that Laurent cannot help David anymore. Even if he could have achieved something before the war, it's too late now."

"Yes." Krisztina's lips grew numb as she tried to frame the question that had preyed on her mind for years. "Could—" She swallowed and tried again. "Could he have helped before?"

Geneviève looked grim. "You're asking me if he lied to you?" She gave a little shrug. "I hope not, with all my heart. It's true that Armand did have connections with the embassy in Berlin and they might have assisted him." There was real sorrow in her eyes. "But now it's all too late."

"I know."

"And still you're willing to stay with him?"

"I can't blame Laurent for the war."

"I doubt if I could be as generous, *ma petite*."

Krisztina stood up, her knees shaky from emotion and strain. "I took vows when I married Laurent," she said, "and I do, in spite of everything, care for him—though perhaps more as a friend than as a wife." She took a deep breath. "And then there's de Trouvère. I think it would be impossible for anyone not to fall in love with de Trouvère." She paused again. "And there's you."

Geneviève rose, and the two women embraced, fresh tears on both their faces.

"There's something I would like to show you," Krisztina said after a few moments. "A letter." She looked into Geneviève's eyes, and knew that she could trust her. "From David."

Geneviève looked startled. "But when? Oh, you mean an old one."

"Not so old. It arrived here just four months ago, but it was written more than a year before." She took Geneviève's hand. "Come. It's in my room."

In her sitting room, Krisztina handed her a small, rectangular envelope, shabby and slightly torn at the edges.

Geneviève stared at it. "Are you sure you want me to read it?"

"Quite sure." Krisztina's mouth quivered, and she caught at her lower lip with her teeth. "It looks so fragile, doesn't it, and yet it traveled from Germany all the way to Palestine, then to Hungary, and at last, thanks to my mother, to me." She paused. "Sit down, Belle-mère." Geneviève sat, and Krisztina pulled forward the footstool for herself. "Laurent was wrong about his being in Dachau or Buchenwald. He was in a camp at Sachsenhausen, just north of Berlin." She closed her eyes, and tears trickled from beneath her lashes. "Quite close really, and I never knew."

Geneviève looked down at the envelope. It was clearly old, reused, for an unfamiliar name and address had been carefully scratched out, before *Florian Krisztina kisasszonyt* and the Kalvaria Street address had been written in, in painstaking, spidery writing.

"It is his hand," Krisztina explained with pride, "though on all the other letters, the old letters I could show you, it was upright and strong." Seconds passed. She reached out and covered Geneviève's hand with her own. "Please read it."

With tender care, the older woman opened the envelope and removed a single flimsy sheet of paper, colored pale blue with a grease stain in the top right-hand corner. It was faintly crumpled, and Geneviève had the notion that a hand had smoothed it patiently, lovingly, perhaps for hours. The same, delicate writing covered one side only.

So short, she thought, her senses shocked by the meagerness of what must, to its recipient, have represented little less than a miracle. *So—pathetic.*

She read, in German.

Beloved.

Too little time, too little space, too little strength, but it must be enough for eternity.

Many have died here, are dying now, but I have gone on living—I am still your David. One hears rumors, some of us will be deported soon. To Riga, the whisperers say.

Riga is very far. Too far. I think I will not survive. But do not
cry, my beloved, my pure delight.

I wept when I found this paper, for it seemed so beautiful.
And then I remembered your eyes. My Kriszti. All grace and
softness and fragrance and love.

If you find my parents, share this with them. There was only
one piece.

My body is crumbling, my hair is white, but my heart and
soul are filled with you.

David

Geneviève put out her hand, blindly, to catch the tears, afraid
they might soil the paper. There were ghosts in the air—she felt
them stroking her cheeks, wrenching her stomach, prickling her
scalp, tearing her heart.

She looked up and saw that Krisztina, too, felt them, but was
unafraid.

"What you feel is evil, Belle-mère," her daughter-in-law said
calmly. "David wanted to spare me, but it comes from the page
into the atmosphere."

Geneviève could not speak.

"But the love is stronger," Krisztina added simply.

Geneviève nodded and, very gently, put the letter and envelope back into Krisztina's hands. They felt cold, and her own, she
noticed, were trembling.

"He thought that I was in Budapest, waiting for him."

"And that his parents were free." Geneviève's voice, un-
leashed from her constricted throat, was hoarse.

"No." Krisztina shook her head. "He knew too much to think
that. He may have hoped." The tears came back to her eyes but
did not fall. "But he was alone."

Neither spoke for a while.

"Do you think," Geneviève asked, carefully, slowly, "that he is
in Riga?"

"I don't know."

Geneviève forced herself on. "Do you think that he is dead?"

Krisztina gave a small, soft sigh. "I imagined that I would feel it
if he were."

"But you don't."

"No." Now the tears began to fall. "And I know now that I
never shall. He is too much alive inside me for that." She paused,

and looked into Geneviève's face. "But I feel, may God forgive me, that he is lost to me."

"Perhaps—" Geneviève swallowed hard. "When the war is over?"

"I don't believe that, Belle-mère." She held the letter to her breast. "I don't think that I will ever see him again."

Chapter 13

Sometimes the staff at de Trouvère believed there were two wars —one that spread destructive, fiery tentacles across the world, and another that raged more privately, but not much less passionately, inside the château.

Under German occupation, de Trouvère had become a hub of activity. Alsace had been cut off from the rest of France; all imports had practically ceased and the region was living on its own supplies, which had rapidly dwindled. Partly thanks to Krisztina's love of animals, however, the family's situation was remarkably healthy. During the evacuation prior to Annexation, livestock had been abandoned to run wild, usually starving and sometimes even used as target practice by soldiers. Upon learning of their plight, Krisztina had swept into action, organizing what was left of de Trouvère's work force to round up as many creatures as possible. Consequently they now had what amounted to a small dairy herd.

Laurent had been quick to capitalize on his wife's compassion. As soon as rationing was announced, he made contact with Gauleiter Wagner's office in Strasbourg, offering produce to the Nazis. With the evacuees' return and the appalling economic situation, unemployment was rife, but at de Trouvère new jobs were created as the grain crop was trebled, additional vegetable gardens were created, the dairy cattle were nurtured and the Riesling vines well tended, all with the blessing of the Germans.

The Nazis had believed that the war would end quickly, and any suggestion that Alsatians should be incorporated into the Wehrmacht was scorned. In any event, the defeat in the Battle of Britain and the earlier-than-planned aggression against Russia forced the Gauleiter to begin a huge recruitment campaign. Tempting promises were made, and the propaganda machine went into overdrive, but hardly any Alsatians volunteered. In August 1942, conscription came into effect. The same factors that had protected Laurent from call-up into the French army now saved him from the Wehrmacht, for de Trouvère produce was vital to the Germans' war effort.

When Laurent informed Krisztina and Geneviève that he had invited Hermann Bickler, the Kreisleiter of Strasbourg, to dine at de Trouvère, Krisztina was the first to express outrage. "You surely don't expect me to play hostess to that man, Laurent!"

"I do."

"It's out of the question!" Geneviève was livid.

"Please don't try to interfere in this, Maman. Bickler expressed a desire to visit de Trouvère, and to refuse him would be folly of the worst kind."

They were in the family *salle à manger* just after Sunday lunch, and Geneviève thumped the table with her fist, making the porcelain and crystal shiver. "They're murderers, for the love of God!"

"They care for Alsace, Maman, and they are patronizing de Trouvère, when they might easily have let it fall to ruin."

"You're an even greater fool than I thought." Geneviève's eyes flashed icily. "When it suits them, they will rape our land and leave us with nothing."

"That's nonsense," Laurent dismissed impatiently. "And when the Kreisleiter does come to dinner, you and Krisztina will please make the effort to speak German."

"My son the Nazi!" Geneviève spat.

"Belle-mère, don't," Krisztina said quietly. "There's nothing to be gained by our abusing one another." She was pale with strain. "Laurent believes he is protecting us. He is afraid to act otherwise."

Now Laurent banged the table in fury. "It's bad enough for my mother to insult me, but I will not stand being called a coward by my wife!"

Krisztina smiled thinly. "I'm not calling you a coward, only saying that you have fear. There is a difference."

"Cancel the arrangements, Laurent, please." Geneviève spoke more gently.

"Impossible."

"Nothing is impossible, if you have courage."

"I don't lack courage, Maman, I simply have foresight." His anger receding, he, too, spoke more softly. "You are living in the past, Maman."

Geneviève rose, and looked him in the eye.

"No, Laurent. I am living for the future."

"This man Bickler must think well of you," Krisztina said later that night as they lay in bed reading, "if he wants to come here for dinner."

Laurent laid down his book. "He is interested in the château and its history."

She smiled. "Don't be so modest, Laurent. He must be interested in you too."

Laurent shrugged. "He knows, perhaps, that my vision is less blinkered than that of some Alsatians—that although I disapprove of much the Germans stand for, I understand and appreciate their professionalism, just as he appreciates my efficiency." His eyes hardened. "He knows, too, unlike my own family, that I am proud to be a Frenchman, and I believe he respects that."

Krisztina closed her book. "Well then," she said amiably, "since you seem destined to become great friends, and since you may even, in time, find yourself in the good graces of the Gauleiter, you may be in a unique position to remember an old promise."

"Promise?"

"To your wife."

Laurent's face was blank.

"I seem to remember you even wanted to write it in blood."

He turned toward her, his brow furrowed. "You mean David?"

"Of course." She was perfectly calm.

Still he looked puzzled. "But surely, Krisztina, you must have realized once hostilities began that there was no more I could do for him?"

"I did." She paused. "Until now."

"What do you mean?"

"Until I learned with what goodwill you are regarded by the Kreisleiter and his colleagues."

"The Kreisleiter is responsible for political, cultural and economic activities in this region, *ma chère,*" he said. "He knows nothing about camps." He gave a small, defensive laugh. "What would you have me do? Ask Hermann Bickler about a single Jew who may or may not be in one of their concentration camps?"

"Exactly."

"But it's impossible! Even if he wanted to help, it would be like looking for a needle in a giant haystack."

"And if one knew which camp he was in?"

"But we don't," he said in frustration.

Krisztina stared at a speck on the wall straight ahead. "I think he is in Riga."

"Why do you say that?"

She said nothing.

"Krisztina?" His voice was sharp.

"I received a letter."

"From David?" He sounded incredulous. She nodded, still not looking at him. "When?"

"A long time ago."

"And you said nothing to me?"

She shook her head.

His voice became brittle. "He said he was in Riga?"

"He was in Sachsenhausen, but there were rumors that they were to be deported to Riga."

Laurent was silent for a moment. "How many more letters has your lover sent you?" he asked harshly. "Do you have a secret cache?"

She looked at him at last, her expression contemptuous. "Do you think they have a regular postal service in and out of Riga?" She paused. "It was the only one."

"And how did he manage that?"

"It must have been smuggled out of Sachsenhausen. It came to me via Palestine and Hungary."

"How touching."

"Don't make me hate you, Laurent."

"Don't you hate me already?"

"No." Her tone was gentler. "But to let your jealousy drag you down is unworthy."

"Don't you think I have a right to be jealous?"

"I'm your wife, Laurent," she said simply. "I'm here with you, while David is thousands of miles away, rotting in a camp, if he is alive at all. You have no reason to be jealous of him."

"Haven't I?" His eyes were dismal. "I still live with his shadow every day. It's still as it was when we were partners—even when we danced in each other's arms, I knew that Kaufmann was squeezed tightly between us, that you were still remembering how it was with him."

"That wasn't true, you know."

"Of course it was! And it's been the same ever since we married. We make love, and you're thinking of him." He laughed bitterly. "They say that ghosts haunt the places in which they lived. David Kaufmann never set foot in de Trouvère, but he inhabits you."

"It isn't true. Of course I think about him—how can I *not* think about a man I loved, who has been made to suffer God knows what torments, who may or may not be dead?" She laid a hand on his arm. "But I don't spend my time dreaming of the past—there's no point in that, it's a waste of life."

Laurent shook her hand away.

"I live my life, Laurent, as well as I can. You are my husband, for better or worse."

"And we made a bargain." His voice was like steel.

"Yes," she answered steadily. "That's how this conversation began."

"You want me to talk to Bickler."

"But you won't, will you."

"No." His intractability wavered. "It's impossible, Krisztina. He couldn't help even if he wanted to, and he will *not* want to."

"And you're afraid to ask."

"It would be pointless," he protested. "Like taking a hammer and smashing every advantage I've built up." He was almost pleading now. "Bickler is not my friend, *chérie,* you must believe that. But he is as important an ally as he would be an enemy."

Krisztina put her book on the bedside table. "I was wrong at dinner when I said you were not a coward," she said. "You are."

His face darkened again.

"And you are a liar too."

"I'm not breaking my word," he said stiffly. "It's just not possible for me to keep it."

She turned out her lamp and closed her eyes.

Laurent lay very still. There was a long pause.

"Do you love me at all?" he asked at last, and the fear was there again.

Krisztina opened her eyes and studied his arrogant, handsome, confused face.

"Less and less," she replied.

Kreisleiter Bickler came to dinner, bringing a colleague, René Schlegel, head of propaganda in Strasbourg's recently set up municipal commission, and good wishes from the Gauleiter. Geneviève, abiding by her principles, refused absolutely to attend, her absence explained by Laurent as due to a migraine. Krisztina, however, driven by a curious sense of destiny, wore becoming black velvet and sat opposite her husband, responding as cordially as she could.

The most repellent moment of the evening came when Laurent emerged from the Smoking Room, to which the men had retired after dinner, to ask Krisztina to fetch his camera from his dressing room.

"Komm herein!" he called jovially when she returned with his Leica. "Our friends have done me the honor of suggesting that we have our photograph taken together. Perhaps you will be kind enough, *Liebling?"*

"Better set it for her first," Bickler said patronizingly.

A few days later, Laurent had the best print copied, sent two—framed and signed *In recollection of a splendid evening*—to the Kreisleiter and to Schlegel, and hung the third opposite the tapestry in the Salon Rouge.

Within an hour, Geneviève had torn it down and smashed the glass. Laurent, determined to rehang it in the same place, had the frame repaired, but at the eleventh hour the courage necessary to confront his mother deserted him, and it was relegated to his private study.

Three months after the dinner, while the photograph of Laurent and his Nazi friends still hung above his desk, Krisztina thought that she began to understand the strange, fatalistic attitude that had swept over her on the night of Bickler's visit.

It was a cold, bleak December afternoon, and Krisztina was experiencing a rare and enjoyable few hours at her own stove while Marthe Schneegans took the day off.

She was making a favorite Hungarian dish, tossing paprika, peppercorns, and tiny whole onions into a huge, simmering pot of chicken broth, when she heard the knock at the scullery door. Mozes, his gleaming black coat lately grown a little duller and streaked with white, sat up from his patient, mouth-watering vigil, ears cocked.

The knock came again. Krisztina wiped her hands on her apron and went to the door.

A girl stood outside, aged about fifteen or sixteen, dark-haired and slant-eyed. She wore a bright blue skirt and a black knitted *gilet* over a high-necked white blouse, with only a crocheted black shawl for warmth, but though her exhaled breath steamed in the chilly air, she did not look as if she felt cold.

"*Bonjour,* madame." Her greenish eyes scanned Krisztina sharply.

Two or three seconds passed. Mozes, by her side, did not growl. Krisztina had the sensation that she was being assessed, yet oddly, the scrutiny did not annoy her.

"How may I help you?"

The girl's right hand brushed the red cloth that covered the wicker basket hooked over her left elbow. For another instant, she seemed to debate, and then abruptly she reached a decision.

"You are la Baronne de Trouvère?"

"I am."

The girl took her hand away from the basket.

"Were you perhaps hoping to find Marthe?"

"No," the girl answered. "I was looking for you, madame."

Krisztina's surprise lasted only for a moment. It was known that despite the stringent efforts of the Nazis to eradicate the *Résistance* in Alsace, active pockets still held out, fighting German propaganda, ferreting out information, and helping escaped prisoners of war. Spring of 1941 had seen an abortive attempt on Gauleiter Wagner's life, when grenades had been thrown at his car in Strasbourg. Since then the Gestapo had taken harsh measures, crushing many of the organizations, arresting dozens and condemning many to death, but still new networks were being set up all the time.

"Would you like to come in?"

The girl shook her head. "It's better I stay outside." She gestured to the basket. "If someone comes, I have preserves to sell."

"What do you want?"

"Your help." The slanted eyes looked coolly into Krisztina's.

A pulse throbbed in Krisztina's temple. "What kind of help?"
The girl glanced past her, trying to see into the scullery and
beyond.

"There's no one else down here," Krisztina said gently.

Again the green eyes fixed on hers. "You know there has been
some bombing?"

Krisztina nodded, hardly able to speak. A feeling of intense
excitement, tinged with fear, was beginning to flow through her.

The girl's voice was low. "Last night, a plane crash-landed near
Thannenkirch. British. Two men were killed, three survived."

"You picked them up?"

"They were found."

"Were they injured?"

"One has a broken arm, the other two cuts and bruises, nothing
serious."

Krisztina waited.

"We need a safe place," the girl said.

Krisztina looked at her blankly.

"Will you give them shelter, Madame?"

"That's impossible." Real regret pierced Krisztina. She wanted
nothing more than to help: in those few minutes, she had realized
that this was what she had been unconsciously waiting for—a
reason, a motive, for her purposeless existence.

"Why impossible?" The girl's voice had grown almost imper-
ceptibly harder.

"Because . . ." Krisztina wavered, hating to share private
fears with a stranger. She took a breath. "Because de Trouvère is
not safe."

"You have cellars."

"Yes, but they are used. For wine."

"They run under the whole château," the girl said. "There is a
whole section on the west side, near the furnace, too warm for
the wine." She paused. "They are safe."

"The furnace is fed several times a day."

"By Jacques Schneegans," the girl said, still with that remarkable certainty.

Krisztina was startled. "How do you know that?"

"It is our business to know." The girl waited an instant. "So may
they come? Just for a few days, until their escape can be arranged?"

The fear had lodged in Krisztina's chest, a hard ball of tension, but still that prickle of excitement, almost of exhilaration, danced in her blood.

"Madame?"

She stared at the girl. She knew so much—what did she know about Laurent? Disloyal or not, it was madness to pretend that he would want to protect three British airmen at de Trouvère.

"My husband—" she began.

"Monsieur le Baron has friends in high places," the girl replied promptly. "The Gestapo are not likely to consider a search."

Krisztina swallowed. "If he discovers them . . ." She licked her lips. "I cannot answer for his reaction. I don't believe he would report them, but—"

"There are always dangers, Madame. But Monsieur le Baron never visits the cellars on the west side, and it will only be for a very few days."

Krisztina's heart began to thump rapidly. Mozes, sensing her agitation, whined and pushed his body against her thigh.

"Well, Madame?"

"I must consult with my mother-in-law. I cannot make such a crucial decision without her consent."

"There is no time."

"Then I must refuse."

"You are the Baronne now, madame," the girl said evenly. "And besides, you know that she would certainly agree."

Yes, she would. Krisztina closed her eyes for a moment. *Geneviève would die rather than turn them away.*

She opened her eyes again and looked into that calm, seemingly invincible face.

"Bring them."

They were not as she had expected, but then she was not sure exactly what she *had* expected. Heroes? What did heroes look like? Much like everyone else, she realized, after her encounter with that nameless young heroine of three days before. She knew that these men flew unprotected through the night sky, ready to do battle with an unseen enemy, prepared to drop their deadly bombs, to destroy, to maim, to kill. Heroes. She supposed, if she had imagined them at all, that she had envisaged hussars, brightly colored, braided and flamboyant.

They were, as it turned out, pale and quiet, like vulnerable schoolboys drooping with exhaustion, fear, and misgivings. The one with the broken arm, his leather flying jacket draped over his shoulders, was the whitest-skinned of all, almost luminous, but Krisztina put that down in part to his reddish-gold hair, and in part to the pain of his fracture.

The girl had brought them, at a time when Laurent was safely engaged away from the house, to a disused cellar entrance she had previously spotted while reconnoitering the château, a half-overgrown hatchway, sealed ineffectively by nothing more than a few damp, rotting boards.

As noiselessly as possible, she eased the boards away, nudged the men to climb through, the injured one helped by the other two, and shook Krisztina firmly by the hand.

"Any trouble, tell Schneegans."

Krisztina's eyes widened. "He knows?"

"No. There's less danger for him that way, but if you have problems, he can be trusted to contact us."

It occurred to Krisztina to wonder, rather ironically, why her own safety should be of apparently less consequence than Jacques Schneegans', but she restrained herself from saying as much.

"You could claim ignorance," the girl explained, reading her thoughts, "and you might even be believed. Schneegans would be shot."

A shiver ran down Krisztina's spine.

"It should take only a few days," the girl said.

"I hope so," Krisztina replied fervently. "How will we know when you're ready?"

"You won't, if all goes well. You will not be asked to help in their escape. They will simply be gone."

Krisztina stared at her. "You're very brave."

The girl shrugged. "Not really." The green eyes were more enigmatic than ever. "It would be a humiliation to be otherwise." She paused, and gave a quick glance around. "*Allez,*" she said, and pushed Krisztina gently toward the hatchway. "I will replace the boards."

Obediently, Krisztina peered through the crumbling entrance, saw the faces of the airmen looking up at her from several feet below, and was briefly grateful that she had thought to wear her riding breeches.

"*Venez,* madame," the injured one encouraged.

She sat on the edge, put both hands firmly on the splintering frame, and propelled herself down. Strong arms circled her waist, and she came to rest gently on the stone floor.

"*Merci,*" she said, but no one responded.

In silence, she led them through the half dark, glad that she had investigated with the aid of a torch the night before, with Geneviève standing watch. It would be easy to become disorientated in this underground maze, which was divided into large, open areas and rooms of varying sizes, some stacked high with logs and furnace equipment.

The farther they got from the hatchway, the darker it became, and for a few moments their only source of light was the dull flickering from the furnace itself, about forty feet away.

Still hushed, they came even closer, and the atmosphere grew more strained as the captive flames roared like a caged monster and the air became almost unbearably hot. Glancing back, Krisztina caught sight of the face of the youngest man, and saw he was very afraid.

"Don't worry," she said in a low but clear voice. "It will be better where we are going." She was sure he didn't understand her, but the positive note in her voice seemed to comfort him a little. She led them around two more corners and into a room that had, she guessed, once been a kind of office, for it had a door, an old oak desk, and, greatest of all blessings, a tiny window high on the outer wall.

"It's a little cooler here," she said, and the men began to speak to one another in low, rapid English, of which she understood nothing at all. She thought at first that the injured man's name was Skipper, for that was what the other two called him, but then he turned to her and explained in French that his real name was William Hunter and that his comrades, who spoke no French other than *Bonjour* and *Merci, madame,* were called Jim Miller and Eddie Cox.

She smiled at the youngest, whose eyelashes were like a child's, thick and white-blond to match his hair. "Eddie? From Edouard?"

He said something to Hunter, and for the first time they all grinned.

"What did he say?" she asked.

"He likes your accent," he replied, but she was certain that Eddie had not put it quite like that.

"I thought your name was Skipper," she told Hunter.

He smiled again. "That's just English slang for captain."

"You are their leader?"

He raised his eyebrows self-deprecatingly. "Eddie and Miller are flight sergeants—I'm a flight lieutenant."

Krisztina thought how good-looking he was, and how utterly different to Hungarian or French men; very tall and slim, with a long, lean face that reminded her a little of a greyhound's but was saved from fragility by an oddly arresting broken nose. *A graceful man,* she thought, *yet not like a dancer, more rugged, more solid.*

"I was flying the Wellington when she came down," he said, "so I suppose that makes me their leader."

She sensed that he felt very bad about the crash landing, as if it was wholly his responsibility, not Hitler's. And then she remembered that two men had died, and that if he was the pilot, then it *was* his responsibility, and she felt a great compassion for him.

"Is the plane lost?"

"As good as."

She paused. "There are blankets under the desk," she said, changing the subject. "And some candles and matches." She glanced up at the window. It was almost four in the afternoon, and whatever light could filter through the grime was already starting to fade.

She looked at the dark-haired sergeant, Miller. They were all dirty, but he seemed the muddiest of the three, muddy and bloody.

"I wish I could invite you all upstairs for a hot bath and a good sleep," she said, aware that only Hunter would understand, but not wishing to seem to ignore the others.

"You've done enough already, madame," the lieutenant said. "We're very grateful."

"I'll try to bring you some hot water and towels later on, and I guarantee some kind of supper."

They heard a sudden rustling, and all three men froze.

"It's just the Baronne," Krisztina reassured them, seeing Geneviève materialize, like an elegant wraith, from beyond the furnace.

"I thought you were the Baronne," said Hunter.

"So I am, but this is my mother-in-law." She introduced them one by one, and Geneviève greeted them warmly and calmly, as if the hiding of RAF officers in her cellars was a perfectly commonplace event.

"I am afraid that you will not be as comfortable as I should like," she said in clear, fluent English, surprising everyone, particularly Krisztina, who understood not a word.

Hunter stared down at Geneviève, looking rather like a man regarding a mirage, and Krisztina thought she understood why. Dressed in a tweed skirt with Chanel blouse, cardigan, and pearls, her belle-mère had brought such style with her that the atmosphere of fear and uncertainty seemed, for a few moments at least, to have wafted away.

"It's far more than we could have hoped for, madame," the lieutenant said slowly.

"I didn't know that you spoke English," Krisztina said to Geneviève.

"Why should you?" She smiled. "I speak several languages that I have little opportunity to use." She looked at the men. "I admire the British very much, messieurs. Herr Hitler will never overcome the stoicism of the English, and if by some disaster he manages to cross La Manche, the Irish will confound the Nazis with charm, and the Scots and Welsh will slaughter them."

Hunter grinned broadly and translated for the other two, who eyed Geneviève with awe.

"Lieutenant Hunter speaks excellent French," she commented. "That may save them before the worst is over." She peered at her watch. "We must be upstairs before we are missed, Krisztina."

"I've told the men that we will bring them something to eat later."

Geneviève nodded. "But it will not be possible until everyone has gone to bed."

Krisztina spoke seriously to the lieutenant. "Please keep the door closed after we've gone. There is a *lavabo* just around the corner to your right, but wait until the man has come down to attend to the furnace." She looked apologetic. "The light from the candle cannot be seen from outside the door, but it might be wiser to blow it out whenever you hear footsteps."

"I think we'll sleep for a good few hours," Hunter replied. "At least in shifts. We're all pretty worn out."

Geneviève reached up and gently touched the sling in which his broken arm was resting. "You saw a doctor?"

He nodded. "Last night. He put the splints on—said that was all he could do."

"You should be in a hospital."

"That's what he said."

"Does it hurt very much?" Krisztina asked.

He smiled at her. "Not as much as it did."

It was after midnight when they returned to the cellar, carrying two steaming copper pots, one containing hot water for washing, the other filled with the remnants of Krisztina's Hungarian chicken soup.

"It's only us," Krisztina called softly as they approached the small, silent room. The door opened, and they heard the striking of a match as the hastily snuffed-out candle was relit.

The men were all awake and palpably tense, in particular young Eddie, whose pale eyes shone, scared and unblinking, in the candle's unearthly glow.

"All is well?" Geneviève whispered, uncertain whether voices might, in the night silence, somehow transmit through the labyrinth of heating pipes to the rest of the château.

"Perfectly, thank you." Hunter was on his feet again.

"Encore un instant." The two women vanished back into the dark, reappearing moments later with armfuls of supplies they had left at the top of the cellar steps.

"Towels and soap." Geneviève put them down on the desk.

"A razor." Krisztina added the small cutthroat that Laurent never used.

"And soup bowls." Geneviève sat down three delicate dishes decorated with tiny quails and sprigs of foliage.

Hunter's forehead creased into a frown as he looked down at them. "Good Lord," he said, and traced the overglazed color with a gentle finger. His eyes widened. "They're not copies!" he exclaimed in French. "Madame, these are very precious!"

Geneviève put a finger to her lips to hush him. "I know, Lieutenant."

"But they're genuine Kakiemon," he hissed with barely restrained excitement.

She regarded him curiously. "How does an RAF pilot come to know about Japanese porcelain?"

"My family are in the antiques business," he answered absently, and shook his head. "But they're not for *use*, madame, and they certainly shouldn't be touched by ham-fisted servicemen."

She smiled. "Three small items from a large collection are much less likely to be missed than pieces from our daily service."

"Spoons," Krisztina said a little impatiently. "The soup's getting cold, Belle-mère."

"D'accord." Geneviève handed her a gleaming ladle. While Krisztina served up the spicy liquid, thick with chicken pieces, potatoes, tomatoes, and onions, Geneviève plunged her hands into the large pockets of her fur coat. *"Et voilà."* With a triumphant flourish, she laid a small pile of books beside the white towels.

"Blimey!" Miller said, staring. "They're English! Agatha Christie!"

"A little escapism to refresh your spirit," she said.

"Look, Eddie," Miller said happily, *"The Murder of Roger Ackroyd*—that's a corker! That'll take your mind off your troubles."

Eddie managed only a weak smile, and Krisztina looked at him with concern.

"Sergeant Cox is a bit claustrophobic," Hunter explained. "He's not finding being cooped up in a small, dark place too easy on his nerves."

"Then how can he bear to be in an aeroplane?" she wondered. "Thousands of feet up in the sky?"

"He's a different man in the air—seems to belong there."

"Will he be all right? If this lasts a few days?"

"We'll look after him." He looked hungrily at the soup. "If you don't mind—?"

"Of course." She paused. "Oh, I nearly forgot." From her own pocket she pulled a corkscrew and glanced at Geneviève. "Belle-mère?"

"Bien sûr, chérie." Shining her torch in front of her, Geneviève disappeared for several minutes, returning with two dusty bottles.

"Château Pape-Clément," she announced, beaming.

No translation was necessary.

"Blimey!" Miller said again. "Red wine. Just what the doctor ordered."

Even Eddie, digging like a starving man into his chicken, cast an enthusiastic glance toward the bottles.

"I'm afraid I can't open them," Hunter said ruefully, touching his arm.

"You just sit there and eat, Lieutenant," Geneviève said. "We know how to use a corkscrew."

Hunter ate lustily for a few moments. "This is wonderful," he told Krisztina.

She smiled. "I'm glad." She looked with fleeting curiosity into his eyes. She had thought them a fairly nondescript hazel color at first, but now she saw that they were tawny.

"No glasses!" Geneviève exclaimed suddenly.

"That's all right," Hunter said easily. "We'll enjoy it just as much without."

"Pape-Clément has a charming history," Geneviève said.

"I know," Hunter nodded.

"You do?"

"Yes," he said, surprising them again. "The bishop of Bordeaux planted the first vineyards, and when he became pope, he so loved French wines that he transferred the papal offices to Avignon." He looked at the bottle in Geneviève's hand, and rose. "May I make a toast, madame?"

"Of course."

Hunter took the bottle and lifted it with his left hand. Miller and Eddie stopped eating and looked up.

"Tonight," Hunter began, somberly, "we might have been in prison camps." He spoke French, but the men seemed to understand. "We might even have been in our graves." He smiled. "Instead, I feel almost as if we have entered a kind of dream." He paused. "There's little time or room for grace and kindness in a Wellington bomber."

"There is courage," Geneviève reminded him quietly, "and purpose."

"There is also fear, and death." He smiled again, wryly. "There is war."

"There is war here too," Krisztina said.

"Not tonight." He looked at Miller and Eddie. "Tonight there is warmth and good food and fine wine and books to read by candlelight, and we can imagine an end to war."

"Not for long, alas," Geneviève said.

"Perhaps not, but I think it will linger long after tonight, a little solace for the colder, darker, hungrier nights to come." He fixed his attention suddenly on Krisztina. "Do you have children, madame?"

"No."

He smiled. "You should."

They stood in silence for several seconds, before he raised the bottle higher.

"To gallantry, to generosity, and to style." His eyes glowed. "To the Baronnes de Trouvère." He drank briefly but deeply from the bottle and passed it to Geneviève, who also drank and put it firmly in her daughter-in-law's hand.

Again, Krisztina felt the surging, piquant sense of new motivation that she had first experienced when the green-eyed girl had knocked on the scullery door.

She breathed in the stuffy cellar air and held the bottle before her like a trophy. She spoke in a soft voice, but her pulses were pounding.

"To your safe return home." She paused. "And to victory."

Chapter 14

Three days passed, days of unremitting tension, punctuated by moments of heart-stopping alarm for Krisztina and Geneviève. At breakfast on the first morning, Sutterlin complained that the heating system was playing up and that outside engineers must be called; by lunchtime, Schneegans reported that the problem had been nothing more than air bubbles. On the second morning, Laurent, reading the Nazi-controlled *Kolmarer Kurier,* observed that the missing British airmen had still not been found, and commented that only "abject fools" would risk martyrdom by sheltering them, since they were bound to be caught. And on the third day, at noon, Krisztina came close to fainting when a black Mercedes, sporting two swastikas, drew up at the front entrance to the château. As it transpired, it was only Bickler's secretary delivering an invitation from the Kreisleiter.

The men in the cellar grew paler and tenser, and when, on the fourth day, Laurent developed a bad cold and decided to stay indoors, it became harder than ever for Krisztina to visit them. At midday, after Laurent had taken to his bed, Geneviève told Krisztina that Eddie's claustrophobia was beginning to cause concern.
"He is begging the lieutenant to let him go for a walk."
"That's much too risky!"

"Of course, but he's becoming desperate. If they're not taken out soon, I'm afraid there may be serious trouble."

Just after four o'clock that afternoon, Laurent, growing increasingly tetchy and stifled lying in bed, decided that fresh air, provided he wore sufficient pullovers, would do him good.

Leaving by the east door, he spotted René the gardener, walking the wolfhounds.

"Give me Orion, René." His voice was husky from his sore throat.

"It's almost dark, monsieur."

"Give him to me." Laurent glowered impatiently, and seizing the dog's lead, he stamped away, kicking up little clouds of gravel on the path.

In the cellar, Eddie was on the brink.

"I'm telling you, skip," he gasped, beginning to hyperventilate, "if I don't get out of here right this minute, I'll do something terrible! I'll go off my head—I'll *bawl*—I'll—"

Hunter slapped him hard. Eddie gave one more shocked, heaving gasp, and then slumped. His whole body trembled and he was perspiring profusely.

"All right, Eddie," Hunter said quietly, "I'll tell you what I'm going to do. I'm going to let you go outside—"

"No, skipper!" Miller hissed, aghast.

"Don't panic, Jim," Hunter reassured him calmly. "There won't be any problems. It's dusk, nearly dark. The Baron's safely tucked up in bed and we've heard no one moving around out there since we arrived."

They both looked at Eddie, who was staring up at the tiny window, his eyes drawn like magnets to the scrap of sky above.

"He can't take much more, can he, skip?" Miller said in a low voice.

Hunter shook his head. "Afraid not."

"Think a few minutes outside'll do the trick?"

"Not for long, no. But it may get us through another night."

"Let's just hope it won't be much longer, eh, skip?"

Hunter glanced at his watch. "We should have plenty of time before they see to the furnace. Go and shift the boards on that entrance, Jim, and stick your head out for a second—make sure the coast's clear."

"Right, skipper."

Tramping disconsolately along the path that led to one of the baroque gardens, Laurent turned for a moment to survey the château, and a large patch of discolored stone caught his eye. He frowned and, pulling on Orion's lead, walked back toward the house to have a better look.

Peering through the fading light, he saw on closer inspection that the white wall was being infiltrated by a mossy growth of some kind, and that the area just below the windowsill seemed to be crumbling.

"Damned war," he muttered angrily, and sneezed loudly. "My house is falling apart." He bent and unclipped the dog's leash from his collar. *"Viens,* Orion. Let's check the rest of the building."

On the second floor, Krisztina tapped sharply on Geneviève's door and went straight in.

"Qu'est-ce qu'il y a?" Geneviève asked anxiously, seeing her expression.

"Laurent isn't in our room."

"He's probably downstairs reading."

"His boots are gone," Krisztina said tersely. "Belle-mère, I'm afraid."

Geneviève stood up. "Be calm, *chérie,"* she said. "If he's gone out, he'll almost certainly be in the gardens."

"At this time?" She ran a hand through her hair. "I just wish I knew where he was."

"Find him," Geneviève directed. "He can't be far. Say you're concerned about his cold, and get him back inside." She reached for her shawl. "I shall go to the cellar and make sure all is well."

"Are you frightened too, Belle-mère?"

"I just trust your instincts."

Hunter had gone out ahead of Eddie, with Miller staying behind to protect the rear. The two men stood on the hard turf and inhaled the evening air. It was wonderfully cold and clear after the mustiness of the cellar and the constant, oppressive warmth of the furnace, and for a moment they felt almost dizzy as they filled their lungs.

Eddie turned and threw the lieutenant a look of abject gratitude, and Hunter nodded. Silently, but for the soft brushing sound of the weeds against their trousers, they stretched their legs, walking in small circles and swinging their arms to get their circulation moving.

After three minutes, Hunter strolled back to the hatchway and peered down at Miller.

"Okay?" he whispered.

Miller's thumbs-up was just visible.

"Just one more minute." Hunter straightened up and looked at Eddie. The younger man was standing motionless again, his face tilted up toward the rising moon, his expression quite beatific.

Hunter smiled.

And then Eddie did the unthinkable.

His soul, almost unbearably uplifted by the pure joy of release, sent a subconscious, childish message to his lips. He pursed his mouth, closed his eyes, and, in a crystal-clear flute, whistled the three opening bars of "Wish Me Luck as You Wave Me Goodbye."

Hunter froze.

Eddie, realizing immediately what he had done, stopped in midnote, his eyes torn open wide in utter horror. A few feet below, Miller covered his face with his hands and Geneviève, just arriving at the top of the cellar steps, stopped dead in her tracks.

Outside, a little less than a hundred yards away, about to round the northwest corner of the house, Laurent stood still, the wolfhound pricked up his ears, and Krisztina, having spotted the white animal in the moonlight, clapped her hand over her heart.

A long moment of silence followed.

And then Orion, vigorously and persistently, began to bark.

"Are you *insane?*"

"I don't believe so."

"You must be! Or wicked, or perhaps just downright stupid!" Laurent shook his head in disgust. "But you're not stupid, are you, Krisztina? You simply hate me so intensely that you're prepared to endanger our whole existence—this château, the estate, our marriage—even my mother!"

"Your mother has a mind of her own."

"She's getting old, she's not responsible for her actions."

"She's forty-eight." Krisztina laughed scornfully. "And she has a better brain than any of us."

"She would never have dreamed of such a thing while my father was alive—his death has unhinged her."

"What rubbish!"

"Do you want to get her shot?"

"Of course not. Do *you*?"

"I haven't broken the law!"

"No, but your mother and I have, and I thank God for the opportunity."

He made as if to slap her, only just stopping himself.

"Well," she said through gritted teeth, "are you going to get your mother shot? If you report them, that's what will happen."

"No," he said.

Krisztina sagged with relief.

"But you will." His face was set.

Krisztina stared at him. "I'd sooner die."

"You will telephone Gestapo headquarters in Colmar and say that you have just discovered the missing RAF men in the disused part of our cellars, and that you have no idea how long they have been there."

"You're mad," she said flatly.

"If you don't, I will." He smiled harshly. "And since I can hardly report my own wife and mother, I shall have to say that one of the servants must be responsible."

"You wouldn't!"

He shrugged. "Certainly I would prefer not to, but—"

"Then for God's sake *don't*!" Krisztina seized his left hand, her voice imploring. "Laurent, please! Before it's too late, remember who you are, what your family stands for!"

"I have remembered. It's you who have chosen to forget."

"You've forgotten that you're a Frenchman. You think the Nazis are your friends, but they're your enemies and they will destroy you, just as they're destroying everything good!"

His mouth twitched cynically. "You think I'm good?"

"Fundamentally, yes!" Krisztina knew she was clutching at straws. "And I think you love your mother too much to betray her—"

"I have a right to live my life within the law!" he shouted suddenly, and began coughing, for the argument had hurt his raw throat. "I have a right to protect what I believe in!" The coughing became more violent. Krisztina began to move toward the decanter of water on the table, but stopped. If he wanted water, let him get it himself.

"I can't fight you anymore," she said bitterly. "You've chosen your course of action—you have free will—and if you don't see that those three men are not only human beings, but heroes who deserve our protection at any cost, I beg you at least to realize that if you do betray them, your mother and I will never, never forgive you."

Silence fell, thick with emotion. Laurent's face was flushed, his eyes red-rimmed, his breathing labored, and Krisztina hardly dared to move a muscle, aware that there was nothing else she could threaten him with.

The minutes ticked remorselessly by. Laurent seemed steeped in thought.

"Well?" she said at last, softly.

He blinked, as if he had forgotten her presence.

"What are you going to do, Laurent?"

He swallowed. "I shall wait until morning," he said hoarsely.

"And then?"

"I shall visit the cellars."

She waited.

"And if I find them, I shall telephone the Kreisleiter's office." He sat heavily on the edge of the bed.

"They can't leave in the middle of the night, Laurent. They won't have a chance."

"That, my dear wife," he said wearily, "is not my affair."

The dreadful quiet descended again. Krisztina's mind worked rapidly. She looked at the clock on the mantelpiece. Almost half past five. Slowly, she moved to her husband's side and laid a hand on his forehead. "You should go back to bed."

He nodded weakly.

"Would you like some hot tea?"

"Yes." He bent to remove his boots, then glanced back at her, his eyes narrow and bleary. "Till morning," he said again.

Krisztina felt very cold.

"I'll fetch your tea now," she said tonelessly.

Closing the bedroom door, she saw Geneviève coming up the staircase, and hurried to meet her. Gesturing her to be quiet, she drew her back down to the first floor.

"I only have a minute—he wants tea, and if I don't bring it quickly, I'm afraid he may call Bickler."

"He hasn't already?"

"He's waiting till morning." She saw the relief on Geneviève's face. "But I'll stay with him in case."

"What shall I do?"

"Find Jacques Schneegans and explain. Tell him they have to be out before dawn." Swiftly she kissed Geneviève on both cheeks. "Don't take any more risks, Belle-mère. Leave it to Jacques." She paused. "Tell them I'm sorry."

"Of course, *chérie.*"

"And wish them good luck."

They spent a fitful night, Laurent sleeping restlessly, Krisztina wide-awake and listening for any sound. At three in the morning, the already fresh wind whipped itself into a gale. At four, Laurent woke, his fever higher, and began to cough rackingly. At five, dosed by Krisztina, he lapsed back into an agitated, intermittent doze.

Just after six, Krisztina got out of bed cautiously, padded barefoot to the window, and saw, through a crack in the curtains, that it was snowing heavily. Her heart sank. It was already quite thick on the ground—had Schneegans got word through? Were the men still in the cellar, or were they out in the open somewhere, clear targets against the white landscape?

Laurent stirred, and she forced herself to return to bed. The worst thing she could do was to risk waking him just to satisfy her own curiosity, for if Laurent missed her, he might telephone Bickler on the spur of the moment.

At eight o'clock, he woke, sat up, and groaned. As if she, too, had been asleep, Krisztina stirred.

"What is it?"

"My head's splitting."

She sat up. "I'll fetch some tablets."

"I should get up."

"It's early yet." Her heart pounded as she went into the bathroom and brought out one of their last remaining aspirin bottles.

Laurent shook his head. "If I take those now, I'll go back to sleep."

"You're ill, Laurent. Sleep is what you need."

He shrugged. "You're right." He swallowed the tablets and got out of bed.

"Where are you going?" she asked, alarmed.

"Where do you think?" he said abruptly, and shut the bathroom door. A minute passed—she heard flushing, then running water, and the door opened again.

"How's your throat?"

"Sore. And my chest hurts."

"You should stay in bed."

He climbed back into bed and pulled up the duvet. "Wake me in an hour." He cast her a drowsy glance. "I have important things to do."

She said nothing.

At nine, no longer able to bear the tension, Krisztina got up, slipped silently into the dressing room, and pulled on trousers and a thick pullover.

In the hall on the first floor, she saw Sutterlin.

"Please don't disturb my husband," she said. "He's unwell and should rest as much as possible."

"*Bien sûr,* madame."

Geneviève was in the library, sitting in a straight-backed leather chair, a book open in her lap. She was staring into the flames that shot up the chimney.

Krisztina bent to kiss her. "*Bonjour,* Belle-mère."

"Laurent?" Geneviève asked tensely.

"Still sleeping."

Geneviève raised her eyebrows. "So late?"

"With a little help." Anxiously she regarded her mother-in-law. "Well?"

"Gone."

"When?"

Geneviève shook her head. "I went down just after midnight— I took hot *potage de légumes* and the remains of the pork, and I asked what they might need. Lieutenant Hunter was superb— very composed. He told me to go to bed, that we had done more than enough and that he felt that they would come through."

"How were the others?"

"Pale, but brave." She smiled. "That poor boy is horribly guilty, but I think he was relieved that the waiting was nearly over."

"And then?"

"When I returned at half past six, they were gone. Every trace of their presence was removed, with the exception of the Kakiemon bowls and the books, which were hidden in the desk drawer."

"And Schneegans?"

"I imagine he got word through." Geneviève hesitated. "But he has not yet come back."

"Are you sure?"

"I heard Sutterlin grumbling at Marthe that he had vanished from the face of the earth."

"Did Marthe know anything?"

"If she did, she gave no hint, but you know Marthe."

Krisztina walked over to the window. "This weather." She shivered. "It reminds me of my first winter here—it looked so bleak when the sun wasn't shining." She turned to Geneviève. "Do you think they'll be all right, Belle-mère?"

Geneviève raised her hands, and let them fall to her lap. "In the good Lord's hands."

When Laurent woke, Sutterlin brought a tray of tea and dry *biscottes* and, as he left the room, Krisztina drew open the curtains.

Laurent flinched at the brightness. "Snow?"

She nodded, and turned to look at him. "They've gone."

His shoulders stiffened. *"Vraiment?"*

"Oui."

"You swear it?"

"Check for yourself. Nothing remains." She paused. "No one need ever know."

He pushed away the tray and huddled back under the duvet. "Have the fire lit. I'm staying in bed today."

"Do you want a doctor?"

"I want the aspirin bottle, fresh water, and I want not to see you."

"That," she said calmly, "can be very easily arranged."

At one minute past five that afternoon, two Gestapo officers came to the front door, opened by Sutterlin.

"Frau Schneegans, *bitte.*"

"Tradesman's entrance," Sutterlin answered in curt French.

They glared at him, but he was implacable. "Go back two hundred yards and take the road to your left."

He closed the door smoothly, then, astonishingly, ran like a prize athlete for the kitchen.

"Where have they taken her?" Geneviève asked Sutterlin.

"They wouldn't say, but probably to Gestapo headquarters in Colmar."

"And they gave no reason?"

"None, madame."

She nodded absently. "Thank you, Sutterlin."

The butler began to turn away, then stopped. "Madame?"

"Yes, Sutterlin?"

His expression was as inscrutable as usual, but his voice was sympathetic. "There is nothing you can do, madame."

"Except wait."

"Yes, madame."

Marthe returned twenty-five hours after she had been taken away. She was alone.

Geneviève and Krisztina greeted her warmly in the kitchen, but received little response. She had always been a thin, angular woman, but now she looked, they later agreed in mutual horror, like an old chicken with its neck wrung—limp, cold, and dead.

"They have shot him," she said, her voice flat.

Krisztina stared at her stupidly. *Who?* her mind asked. Images of Hunter, Miller, and Eddie flashed through her brain.

"They have killed Jacques."

Disbelief, hatred, and guilt stalked the château. Everyone felt it, even the animals, who lay listlessly near the fireplaces, except for Mozes, who followed Krisztina like a shadow, and Vénus, the brindle bitch, who stayed close to Marthe whenever possible.

"She looks at me," Laurent complained to his wife about Marthe, four days later, "as if *I* had shot her husband." They were in the Salon Rouge after dinner.

"It's your imagination," Krisztina dismissed.

"Those sharp little eyes," he said, and shuddered, "the only living part of her miserable face—firing her loathing at me like tiny arrows."

She raised an eyebrow. "What do you expect her to do, kiss you? It's remarkable that she's working at all."

"I wouldn't be surprised if she were to poison me, old witch."

"Laurent, her husband has been *murdered.*"

"He wasn't murdered," Laurent said morosely. "He was punished for breaking the law."

Krisztina looked at him with fresh disgust. "Nothing changes you, does it?"

"It wasn't my fault Schneegans chose to help those men."

"Of course it was. But for you, he would never have been involved."

Laurent picked up a decanter of cognac and poured himself a double. "You blame me, my mother hardly speaks to me . . ." He gulped impatiently at the drink, and grimaced as it hit his throat.

She didn't answer.

"I didn't even *tell* Bickler!" he protested.

"We know that."

"Well then!"

She looked up at him. "There are times," she said quietly, "when threats are as dangerous as actions."

"I'm going to move my things out of our bedroom," Krisztina told Geneviève next morning at breakfast.

Geneviève lifted her cup of black coffee, her face calm. "Which would you prefer—the guest suite or the Chambre Rose? The clematis might be warming in this season, but the mattress is better in the suite."

"The suite is more practical." She looked at Geneviève. "Do you mind very much?"

"Of course—but if I were you I would do the same." She paused. "If I were you, I think I would leave him altogether."

"In different times, I probably would, Belle-mère," she said frankly. "And yet . . ." She hesitated. "At the same time I feel almost sorry for him." She fingered her butter knife. "He may never find the courage to admit it, but I'm sure he feels guilty."

They fell silent for a while, finishing their breakfast without appetite.

Krisztina spoke first. "Do you think they are alive?"

"Our British friends?" Geneviève nodded decisively. "Yes, I'm sure they are."

Krisztina sighed. "I wonder if life will ever be normal again."

Geneviève smiled. "And what is normal?"

"I don't really remember." She sat back in her chair, eyes hazy. "Perhaps life isn't meant to be normal, or at least not for long." She considered for a moment. "I suppose I meant to say that I wonder if this war will ever end."

"All wars end, *chérie*."

Chapter 15

What had begun as war, but transmuted into the bizarre "peace" of Annexation, turned another corner, drawing Alsace back into real, tangible war.

American bombs fell close to the capital on September 6, 1943, targeted on the railway between Strasbourg and Kehl but causing extensive damage on a broad scale, and killed over a thousand people. There were no more major attacks until the following spring, but then, on June 6, the Allied forces landed on the Normandy beaches. In Geneviève's private sitting room at Château de Trouvère, in the heart of the Haut-Rhin, she and Krisztina listened to illegal British and Swiss broadcasts and drank a toast to the beginning of what they hoped and prayed would be the final campaign against Hitler.

By August, hopes and fears were soaring and dipping in a dizzying spiral that would continue, at least for the Alsatians, for another seven months. Krisztina, additionally, was increasingly worried about her mother in an ever more confusing Hungary that had, since March, allowed the Nazis free rein and was now fumbling for peace with the USSR.

Closer at hand, the Germans, still reeling from the July plot to assassinate Hitler, had grown more savagely determined to hold on to Alsace. Strasbourg had been left in partial ruin after a massive bombing on August 11. Aggressively, they mobilized everyone still available to help with the emergency conditions, to fortify the now desperately struggling Wehrmacht. As shortages began to bite fiercely on all fronts, they seized produce and raw materials wherever they could.

At last, Laurent was aware that Geneviève's ominous predictions might, after all, be coming to pass. With growing concern, he observed the gradual diminution of his personal control of the estate, the systematic ransacking of the crops, the worsening condition of the surviving cattle, and, most worrying of all, the neglect of the Riesling vines, as de Trouvère's work force was once again decimated.

Under the circumstances, he found his mother's persistent optimism doubly infuriating.

"Not long now, Laurent," she said often.

"Until what?" he asked bitterly. "Our ruin?"

"Until our liberation."

"But don't you see what's happening here?"

"Of course I see," she said contemptuously. "I saw long, long ago, while your eyes were conveniently closed."

"For Christ's sake, Mother! Maybe if others had understood what the Germans wanted, we might be prosperous and peaceful today."

She laughed mockingly. "No, Laurent, they wanted to tyrannize, to enslave—to bludgeon." She went on with almost threatening softness, "And I warn you, my naive son, that a time is coming—and coming soon—when it may be too late for you to make the right choice."

"What would you have me choose, Mother?"

She looked at him with sorrow.

"I would have you choose sides."

Nothing Laurent did or said seemed to stem the flow of de Trouvère's lifeblood. Hermann Bickler had been succeeded at the end of 1942 by Paul Schall, and though dealings with the new Kreisleiter had been cordial, Schall had resisted all Laurent's attempts to draw him into a more personal relationship. Laurent was left feeling snubbed, depressed, and angrier than ever with his wife and mother.

For months after the incident with the RAF men, he had sat for hours at a time in his study, gazing up at the photograph of himself with the two Nazis and brooding over the fact that, though nothing had ever been said, Schneegans's guilt had almost definitely cast a shadow over de Trouvère itself.

On August 28, three days after Free French units had entered Paris, an SS colonel with a gleaming bald head, pale eyes and the name of Rahm, came to Château de Trouvère.

The purpose of his visit was simple. Former Kreisleiter Bickler —now a Standartenführer in the SS—had spoken in warm terms of Laurent's hospitality, and Colonel Rahm had hopes of prevailing on that same goodwill again.

They sat at the oak table in the Hunting Room, surrounded by assorted weaponry and gazed down upon by boars' heads and glassy-eyed roe deer.

"How can I help you?" Laurent asked, his stomach tense and his mind whirling. Paris was free, and the Allies, after landing in Provence, had formed a front from Switzerland right up to the North Sea and were pushing toward the Vosges and Alsace. In German terms, the "enemy" was knocking at the door; for Laurent, as Geneviève had predicted, the time had come to choose his own enemy.

"Three friends need shelter for one or two nights."

"Friends?"

Colonel Rahm nodded. "They are en route from Paris to the Fatherland, and have experienced a few delaying problems."

I'm sure they have, Laurent thought. It was rumored that a number of high-ranking Vichy officials had already moved eastward with the Germans ahead of the liberation, and were trying to establish a "government-in-exile" from the safe base of Sigmaringen Castle, about fifty miles south of Stuttgart.

"A passage has been arranged for them, and they will be here tomorrow afternoon," Rahm continued.

"I see," Laurent said noncommittally.

"Does it present a problem, Herr Baron?"

"Of course not," Laurent replied hastily. "Or rather, I hope not. I shall naturally have to consult with my wife."

"Isn't she here?" Rahm smiled. "Then you could *consult* with her right away." He stressed the word ironically.

"I'm afraid not. She has gone to Ribeauvillé with my mother."

Rahm stood. "Then perhaps if I telephone you this evening, you will have an answer for me."

Laurent, too, rose, glad of the reprieve, but abruptly the colonel sat down again.

"A small point, Herr Baron, that you might wish to take into consideration."

"Yes?" Laurent sat again, stiffly.

"You will be aware that the case of your employee, Schneegans, was never thoroughly investigated."

Laurent's spine prickled.

"Under most circumstances," Rahm went on, "a full inquiry would have taken place, and as Schneegans not only worked in but is believed to have given shelter to enemies of the Reich in your home—"

"Which I knew nothing about," Laurent interjected sharply.

"—you and your family," Rahm swept on, "would have been questioned. Former Kreisleiter Bickler, however, was consulted on the matter, and vouched for your integrity."

"I'm indebted to him," Laurent said, with a touch of asperity. "I am unclear, however, as to your reason for referring to a subject that was concluded twenty months ago."

"Nothing is concluded, Herr Baron, where doubts linger on."

"Doubts?"

Colonel Rahm smiled again, thinly. "You have proved yourself a good friend in the past, of that there is no question." He paused. "But nonetheless you were, I am led to believe, a loyal son to your father."

Laurent frowned. "Certainly."

"And the late baron was, I am also reliably informed, a patriotic Frenchman."

"Indeed he was."

"Your mother, too, is an intensely loyal *Französin* who has never bothered to hide the fact." Rahm's upper lip curled. "I can, of course, respect such a woman, my friend, but I cannot, in all conscience, trust her."

Since the start of the war, Laurent had seldom known real fear. So convinced had he been of German superiority, so adroitly had he steered his estate onto the course that would best serve their new masters, he simply had never considered that he was taking a risk.

"And then," Rahm pushed on, "there is your wife."

"My wife?"

"The beautiful, softhearted Hungarian—who once made an error of judgment that might, but for your intervention, have cost her dearly."

Laurent's mouth was very dry.

"But then again, but for you, Herr Baron, my colleagues in Berlin tell me that her 'error' might never have been discovered at all."

Laurent did not trust himself to speak.

Rahm's voice was smooth as silk. "But does *she* know that, I wonder?" He watched Laurent with mild, venomous amusement. "Well, Herr Baron? I asked you a question."

"She does not."

Rahm's tone grew harder. "Then I'm sure that she, and certain members of the *Résistance* with whom I believe she is acquainted, might find it a most enlightening piece of information." He stood again, and Laurent, numbed by shock, followed suit. "I shall telephone you later, Baron de Trouvère, when you have had an opportunity to consult with Madame."

He stepped two paces back and gave a smart salute. *"Heil Hitler!"*

A small spark of something vaguely related to free will, or perhaps even pride, held Laurent's right arm down by his side.

He raised his chin slightly.

"Au revoir," he said.

When Colonel Rahm telephoned at seven that evening, Laurent's fleeting bravado had long since evaporated.

"Your friends may come," he told the colonel.

"I'm glad to hear it."

Laurent replaced the receiver, and saw that his hand was trembling.

He had yet to tell Krisztina.

At twenty minutes past ten, he walked past the Mirror Hall, heard music filtering out from beneath the door, and knocked on the heavy oak. Getting no response, he braced himself and entered.

For a moment, he felt as if he had stepped from the bedrock of the corridor into the incorporeal world of one of his old fantasies.

The chandeliers were unlit, but a three-branched candelabrum at one end of the room spilled a phosphorescent glow through the dark, creating dreamy, dappled starlight in the mirrors and bathing the young woman who sat, center stage, on the floor. Eyes closed, Krisztina stretched her legs out before her, knees slightly bent and tiny specks of dust dancing around her silvery hair like a halo of microscopic fireflies.

"Begin the Beguine . . ." sang Bing Crosby from the gramophone in the far corner.

"Krisztina?"

She opened her eyes, startled. "Laurent!"

Trying to steady his heartbeat, he closed the door behind him. "I'm sorry to disturb you."

"That's all right," she said, not moving. "Join me." She indicated the floor beside her.

He took off his jacket, slowly sat down, and told her about Rahm and their visitors from Vichy.

She was appalled. "Did they order you, or ask you?"

"Ordered."

Her eyes narrowed. "I don't believe you. They asked you, didn't they? And you're still eager as a sycophantic child to please them."

"Not true," he said. "They gave me no choice. They made threats."

She looked away from him. "Then that's worse," she said flatly, "for it means you really are a coward."

The candlelight seemed suddenly hard, the music jarring.

"The threats were against you," he said quietly.

"Me?"

"And my mother."

She was startled. "How?"

"Schneegans."

"They know what we did?"

"Evidently."

"Why have they never said so before? Never arrested us or even questioned us?"

He waited a moment. "Because of me."

"I see." Her tone was cutting.

"Until today." He paused. "They want payment."

"Don't you think they've had enough? Our land is almost barren, our vineyards will take years to recover—" She stopped, her expression bitter.

"So you see," Laurent said, "why I had to agree?"

"No." She shook her head. "Not really."

"You want to be arrested?"

"They're as good as beaten, Laurent. They can't do anything to us now."

"They can still shoot you."

She glanced at him drily. "Would that really matter to you?"

It was his turn to be shocked. "Do you mean that?"

"I'm sorry," she said. "You might care, I suppose—at least about your mother."

He was intensely aware of the closeness of her body, of her fragrance. "You think I don't love you anymore?"

"I think you know nothing about love."

"I've always loved you, Krisztina—I've never stopped loving you!"

She stared at him, saw the misery, loneliness, and naked fear on his face, and suddenly something inside her softened.

"Tell them no," she said intensely. "If they have nowhere else to house them, they'll come anyway with guns at our heads."

He gazed down at the parquet floor. "They mentioned the *Résistance.*"

"What about them?"

He licked his lips nervously. "I think they might tell them that I betrayed Schneegans." He looked at her. "Don't you see? The *maquisards* are growing more powerful all the time."

"I have no doubt that they know exactly what you did and did not do about the airmen, Laurent," she said, calmly. "And we all know that, though you might have reported them later that morning, you did not." She paused. "This is your chance to exonerate yourself."

"How? By refusing?"

"No." Her eyes challenged him. "Let the Vichy men come—but get word through to the *Résistance.*"

"You want me to set a trap for them?"

"Exactly."

He looked aghast. "They'd be murdered in cold blood!"

She looked at him coldly. "It didn't seem to trouble you when Jacques Schneegans was shot, or when you've done business with men who've slaughtered multitudes."

"How do you know what troubles me?" he protested angrily. "Do you imagine that the last few years have been easy for me?"

"I think that you've always chosen the easiest route available," she said mildly.

"Was it easy when my mother turned against me? Is it easy, do you think, to hear the servants whisper about me? When Sutter-lin openly defies me?"

"All those things could have been avoided."

"*Everything* has preyed on my mind!" He got to his feet and began to pace back and forth, striding in unconscious rhythm to the music. "Ever since we came home to de Trouvère . . ." His face was contorted. "But nothing—*nothing* has been so bad as knowing I've lost you!"

She swallowed. "I'm still here, aren't I?"

"Not with me, no! Not by my side, not as my wife—not even in my bed!"

She watched him for a moment. "It might not be too late," she said quietly.

He stopped pacing. "If I believed that, I'd do anything."

She looked up at him. "Even betray the Vichy men?"

"Anything!" He flung himself suddenly down on his knees beside her. "Krisztina, if you only knew how empty my life has been without you—how desperately I've longed for you! I've driven myself nearly mad thinking that if only we'd had a child to bind us together, things might have been all right!"

"Children don't mend broken marriages," she said steadily, old guilt stabbing her.

"But they create love!" His eyes beseeched her. "Is there truly a chance, Krisztina? If I pass a message to the *maquisards*? Is there?"

Gently, she touched his hair, and a wave of pity and grief washed over her, the first trace of tenderness for the first time in months. "Perhaps," she said hesitantly.

With a small, hopeful cry, he seized both her hands and kissed them. "I swear to you," he whispered fervently, "I'll do it."

The candles flickered, wax melted and hissed and set in threads, and the crooning voice began to sing "In the Still of the Night", and an old, almost forgotten impulse crept over them both as they sat on the floor in the haunting light . . .

"Dance with me," Laurent breathed softly.

Krisztina sat very still.

"Please," he said, "just for a minute."

She looked into his face, and her legs yearned to move. "All right."

Slowly, carefully, he drew her to her feet, and his right hand slipped behind her back in the old, familiar steadying motion that was as instinctive and natural to them both as breathing.

It was years since they'd danced together, but the steps and fusion came as easily as a warm knife sliding through butter. Across the room they glided in a slow fox trot, their images floating from mirror to mirror—Laurent in white shirt sleeves, Krisztina in her summer dress so sheer that the curves of her body and thighs showed through against the light. And yet they danced in a way they had never danced before—not for judges or audience or the gregariousness of a social event, but for themselves, for their memories, for whatever pitiful shreds remained of their marriage—because they wanted to—and it was strangely tender and curious to them. . . .

The song ended, and they stopped dancing and stood perfectly still. Laurent's hand stayed at her back, and he looked down at her upturned, marvelously tranquil face, and he bent and kissed her.

"Laurent, no," Krisztina murmured against his mouth, but he could not stop and she could not tell if she wanted him to stop. She saw that his eyes were wet with tears, and myriad conflicts raked her like seductive demons with sharp fingernails. *Pull away,* they ordered her, *be alone again, like a stone, in your big cold bed.* And then, prodding her, urging her to stay and hold him, reminding her that she, too, had needs and desires . . . And she moaned with confusion, and her hands pushed feebly against his chest, but her lips parted and her tongue darted and tangled with his. Her breasts tingled and their nipples hardened, like small, astonished buds, rising at the touch of his left hand while his right, still at her back, slid down and caressed the curve of her buttocks, and she was conscious of his body growing, greedy and strong and acquisitive . . .

"*Mon amour,*" he whispered, and reaching behind her, he began to unfasten her dress.

"No, Laurent, not here—"

"Yes, here, now!" Quickly, he maneuvered her toward the door, and grasping the large silver key, turned it in the lock.

Her dress tumbled to the floor, and Laurent's hands and lips and tongue were everywhere. She sank down with him onto the cool, polished wood, and felt the shock of the parquet and the warmth of his skin, and she wound her arms and legs around him like tethering ropes.

"Merci, mon amour," he gasped as she opened herself to him, and there was such piercing love and gratitude in his voice that, with a feeling almost akin to happiness, Krisztina found that she was glad. . . .

Later, in their old bedroom, lying side by side in the lambent light of the candelabrum brought by Laurent from the Mirror Hall, he took her hand. The lines of his face were strong again, alive with the joy of having her there.

"I've been worse than a fool," he said huskily.

She returned the squeeze of his hand, and felt an urge to be kind—he was like a fish, trapped by his own naiveté and greed on a powerful hook.

His eyes were riveted on her. "You are all I need—I know that now."

She shook her head. "You need de Trouvère more than me."

"No!" he said vehemently. "I would give it up in an instant to have you back. I need *nothing* more than you!" A shadow flitted over his eyes. "Except your child—and in that, as in everything else, I've failed you."

She shut her eyes, unable to look at him.

He took her silence for sorrow. "Forgive me," he begged. "It's not too late. Perhaps now, if we continue to try—" He broke off, seeing the bleakness of her expression. "Krisztina, please, *chérie,* don't look that way."

She opened her eyes, but did not speak.

"Krisztina?"

She sat up suddenly and pushed back the covers.

"Where are you going?"

"To my suite." She got out of bed and put on her peignoir.

"No!" he cried, dismayed.

"I'm sorry, Laurent."

"For the love of God, Krisztina, don't leave me now!"

Krisztina went to the door, and did not turn back.

"I'm sorry," she said again.

In her dressing room, Mozes, grown ancient and snowy around the muzzle, thumped his tail in welcome.

Krisztina patted him absently on his old head and walked into the bedroom. For a few moments, she sat on the edge of the bed, her cheeks burning, her breathing unsteady. Then, slowly, like a sleepwalker, she rose again and went to the armoire. Opening one of the drawers, she took out the tiny box that contained her diaphragm.

So long unused. She thought about tonight. What an irony if . . .

She looked at it. For a moment, in his room, she had almost told him. She shook her head. *Madness,* she thought. Out of pity and guilt.

She had not heard the door, or his footsteps behind her.

"My God," he said quietly.

Krisztina spun around, shocked, and dropped the box.

Laurent picked it up.

She watched his jaw clench and his skin redden and his eyes harden, and all traces of vulnerability disappeared, and she was powerfully, acutely aware that if there had been a glimmer of hope for their future, she had, with this single, fatal blow, killed it.

"You bitch."

She said nothing.

He stared at the box. "And you accused *me* of betrayal." He tossed it onto the bed.

"Yes," she said, as steadily as she could. "I'm sorry."

He did not speak. She had the sensation that he no longer saw her.

Suddenly, he walked to the door, turned the key, took it from the lock, and pulled off his robe. He was naked.

"Laurent, what are you doing?"

She had never seen such absolute tautness in a body before. Every muscle was clenched—belly, buttocks, thighs, arms, neck . . .

"Laurent?"

Still he did not reply, and as he came toward her, backing her up against the wall, she saw that this discovery, this single deception of hers, had been too much. He did not see her—he seemed caught up in the creation of an image, a distorted vision, a *nightmare,* and Krisztina knew sudden, total, crystalline fear.

"Laurent?" Her voice was breathy with alarm. "Laurent!" she said more sharply.

As if in slow motion, his right arm swept up and around in an arc, and he hurled the key like a tiny, gilded cricket ball through the air. It struck the marble fireplace on the other side of the room and ricocheted away.

"Laurent!"

His arm kept moving, following through and swinging back—it stopped, hovered for a second, and then it came fast, very fast, like a streak of lightning, and his fist, like burning iron, struck her a mighty blow in her stomach.

"God in heaven!" she gasped, and slumped to the floor, fighting for breath, her stunned brain sending messages of agony and terror to all her nerve endings, telling her to prepare for more, to be beaten or kicked or even killed.

But the rage and anguish had left his hand, which burned from the contact with her soft flesh, and had traveled down, sucked like molten energy into his loins. He saw her, crumpled and sagging on the carpet, through a glowing filter, misty and distant.

Vaguely, he heard her speak his name, saw her put up her hands, shieldlike. But her chalky face and horrified eyes barely registered, took a paltry second place to the all-consuming need to pour every last ounce of his juices into the body that had deceived him, defended itself against him, and he stooped and took her by the arms, raised her up, and pinned her to the cold wall, wrenching away the belt of her robe.

Krisztina's head cleared. She stared into her husband's face and saw that his eyes were glazed and that his skin was scalding hot and that he was, at this moment, quite mad. For an instant she stood petrified and immobile, until she looked down and saw his huge erect penis. Then she began to struggle, but his right arm, flung horizontally across her breasts, was like a steel bond trapping her, and his other arm thrust behind her, the hand clamping over the base of her spine to drive her pelvis forward and up, while his right knee forced her thighs apart.

And then he plunged into her, and she screamed, piercingly. His penis was like a sword, impaling, bruising, and tearing at her flesh and her soul, until he was completely empty, and fell back, breath rasping, half dead with exertion and dementia. Krisztina hardly heard Mozes' barking outside the door. She felt an overwhelming dizziness and began to slide down the wall, robe rustling against paper, and she welcomed the dark, but there was a knocking that dragged her back, would not let her rest, became pounding, frantic and demanding, while the handle of the locked door jerked and rattled.

"Let me in!"

Geneviève's voice, afraid but authoritative, acted like a dash of ice water on Laurent's temporarily addled brain. With a kind of paralyzed fascination, Krisztina watched as he reacted to the dominant sound of his childhood.

Still naked, he walked slowly, mechanically, to the door and turned the handle, to no effect.

"Laurent?" Geneviève said tersely from outside. "Open the door."

"It's locked," he said hoarsely.

"Unlock it!"

He turned around and began to search for the key, apparently oblivious to Krisztina on the floor praying for him to find it quickly.

By the far window, he saw it, bent to pick it up and returned to the door, still moving with that strange, automatic quality, and opened it.

Geneviève swept in, dramatic in a royal-blue peignoir. Her eyes absorbed the scene, and alarm turned to horror.

"Nom de Dieu!" She rushed to Krisztina, took in her ashen face and shocked eyes, the disheveled robe and the blood traces on her thighs, and gasped again.

Swiftly, she tugged at the robe to cover the younger woman's nakedness and then, slipping one arm around her shoulders, she turned her face to her son.

"Dress yourself!"

It sounded like a whiplash, and he responded silently, staring at them both, seeming to see Krisztina for the first time, his expression inscrutable.

Geneviève spoke softly in Krisztina's ear. "Can you stand, *chérie?*"

"In a minute." Her voice was a faint whisper.

"Ça va," Geneviève soothed. "There's nothing more to fear."

Laurent, wearing his dressing gown, sat heavily on the edge of the bed and picked up the box from the duvet.

Geneviève's eyes narrowed as she recognized it. She looked at Krisztina. "He found it?"

Krisztina nodded dumbly.

"I see." The words were a sigh.

Laurent took the diaphragm out of the box, held it out before him like a tiny banner, took his gold cigarette lighter from his pocket and ignited it.

"Laurent, *arrête!*" Geneviève rapped sharply.

Ignoring her, he touched the flame to the base of the little cap, and immediately the smell of burning rubber wafted through the room. He dropped it to the carpet and stepped on it, shockingly, with his bare foot, grinding out the flame.

"Are you *mad*?" exclaimed his mother.

"At least now she cannot use it again," he said dully.

Krisztina gave a little whimper of pain and pressed a hand to her stomach. Geneviève frowned, parted the robe slightly, and peered with widening eyes at the already spreading bruise. Her anger intensifying, she glared at Laurent.

"If you even dream that she will ever need it again, then you are truly insane."

He stood up, the small pain of his burned foot beginning to refuel his strength. "You needn't worry, Mother," he said. "I shall never touch her again as long as I live." A flicker of anguish touched his eyes and he threw Krisztina a swift, bitter glance. "She was never really mine anyway."

"No one belongs to another person," Geneviève told him quietly.

"My wife does," he said. "She still belongs to her first love—to her beloved David. Do you know about David, Mother? I expect you do, since you have shared so much together."

"I know about him," she answered calmly.

"He's probably dead," Laurent went on, almost dreamily. "Gassed, like an animal."

Geneviève embraced Krisztina more tightly and stroked her hair.

"Such a waste," Laurent said.

"Yes."

"No, Mother, you don't understand my meaning."

"Laurent, for the love of God, stop this, *now*. Haven't you done enough harm?"

"It's a waste," he continued, still in the same vacant voice, "because she was supposed to forget him in time. I knew it would take time—I was so patient. Don't you think I was patient, Krisztina?"

She could not speak.

"But you never forgot, did you?" He shook his head, weary again. "A waste of all my efforts, all my strategy."

The two women listened, appalled.

"It was all part of my plan, you see?" His eyes were hazy. "Your father hoped that he might be arrested, just for being Jewish." He half smiled, ironically. "And of course he would have been, in time. But I didn't *have* the time—I'd waited so long already—so I made certain, the only way I could."

In Geneviève's arms, Krisztina felt her blood run cold.

"*You* reported us?"

He nodded.

"You arranged for him to come to me, and then you reported us?"

"Of course." He paused. "*Rassenschande.* The worst crime available."

It had become so hard to breathe, Krisztina thought she might die of the horror. "But you loved me!"

"More than anything."

She swallowed. "And you never tried to help him—never had any intention of helping him."

He smiled again, remotely. "I might have done, once you were mine." He thought for a moment. "But then the war came, and it was too late. And besides, you never *were* mine, were you?"

Geneviève stirred, as if emerging from a stupor. Gently but firmly, she drew Krisztina from the floor, holding her tightly in case she fell.

"*Viens, chérie.*" She kissed her tenderly on the cheek. "We'll go to my room—we'll stay together."

Slowly, they started to walk toward the door, leaving Laurent standing in the middle of the floor, staring into space. "Mozes," Krisztina murmured suddenly. "In the dressing room."

"*Bien sûr, ma petite,*" Geneviève comforted her. "Mozes must come too. We'll all be together, I promise you."

Leaving Krisztina in the doorway, propped up against the oak frame, she fetched Mozes, who came, quivering with distress, to his mistress's side.

"*Bien,*" Geneviève said softly. "Let's go."

She never looked back at her son.

The night passed.

In Geneviève's room, they lit a fire in the hearth, even though it was August, and Krisztina lay on the bed. Her mother-in-law sat beside her, holding her hand and smoothing her hair, talking when Krisztina felt like it, sitting silently when she slept in brief, fitful snatches, the old black dog stretched at the foot of the bed like a stoic, loving sentinel.

In his room, Laurent lit a cigarette and clutched a full bottle of cognac he had brought from the Smoking Room, and drank until it was empty. And by three in the morning, he was unconscious on the floor, and by four, he was up again and vomiting in the bathroom, and for the rest of the night, there was no sleep for him, and no peace.

He would never find peace again.

The three men from Paris arrived the following afternoon, two of them with their wives, plus five steel-framed portmanteaux and ten additional leather suitcases.

They stayed for forty hours.

For Laurent, the visit had the amorphous, menacing quality of a surrealist nightmare. Krisztina and Geneviève remained upstairs, descending only three times, for fresh air, and maintaining frigid silence when they encountered Laurent or the strangers. Sutterlin, René, and Marthe, despite Laurent's enraged threats, staged a mutiny.

At seven o'clock, Rahm telephoned.

"Your hospitality is appreciated, Herr Baron."

Laurent's voice was taut with strain. "You've placed me in a terrible position. My household staff are refusing to work."

"I could send you a BDM girl to help out." The pause was infinitesimal. "That would, of course, cost you your existing staff as a consequence."

The ghost of Jacques Schneegans danced, skeletal and bloody, before Laurent's eyes, and he shuddered.

"Thank you, but I'll manage."

"I will depend on it."

He became their servant as well as their host. He saw that they were comfortable, brought them champagne and even entered the kitchen—something he had seldom done since boyhood—to scavenge for cold meat and salad to add to the foie gras he had already found, which would, together with several chilled bottles of Riesling, stem their hunger.

Next morning, he found a young girl cleaning the scullery floor.

"Who are you?"

"*Je m'appelle Marie,* monsieur."

"How long have you worked here?"

"Six months, monsieur."

"Good. You can make breakfast."

"Monsieur?"

"*Oeufs au plat,* croissants, and coffee for six."

She looked blank.

"Go on!" he said impatiently.

"But Madame Schneegans said we must not work for the—"
She stopped, discomfited.

His remaining patience snapped. *"Merde!"* He towered over
her. "Make breakfast now, or I will send for the Gestapo and have
you shot!"

She cowered. *"Oui,* monsieur."

"Go on!"

By lunchtime, Marie, too, had vanished into thin air. Laurent,
in the depths of despair and fury, was forced back into servitude,
for it soon became clear that the Vichy men and women would
rather die of starvation than fend for themselves. He longed to
abandon them, or even turn them out, but the specter of SS
Colonel Rahm loomed threateningly, and so he swallowed his
humiliation and rage, and blundered on.

Rahm telephoned again at five.

"All well, Herr Baron?"

"As well as can be expected under difficult circumstances."

"Times are difficult."

"Yes, Colonel."

Laurent replaced the receiver, mopped his perspiring brow,
and glanced out of his study window to see André Sutterlin standing outside on the path, watching him.

A rat in a trap, Laurent thought, and his fear was like a cold
sickness in his belly. *With no way out, whichever way I turn.*

They left at nine o'clock the following morning, their luggage
loaded into a vast Mercedes by a driver in mufti.

Just before she climbed aboard, one of the wives, a tall, arrogant blonde, stepped up to Laurent to thank him for his hospitality.

"You'll never make a chef, Monsieur le Baron," she said in a
low, clear voice, "but if you ever find yourself near Sigmaringen,
I'm sure I would enjoy discovering your other talents." She kissed
him lingeringly on the cheek.

Laurent said nothing, for his eyes were focused on Sutterlin, who stood just twenty yards away, once again, undoubtedly, chillingly, staring at him.

A few hours later, he came across Krisztina in the main hall, and for the first time she acknowledged him with an icy nod.

"They have gone," he said.

"Yes."

"The *maquisards* didn't come."

"No."

"I thought you might inform them."

She stared at him evenly. "I would not publicly brand my husband a traitor."

He blinked. "Sutterlin will tell them, won't he?"

"Yes," she replied.

Next morning when he awoke, having drunk himself to sleep for the fourth night in succession, the first thing Laurent saw when he opened his eyes was the word *COLLABORATEUR!* painted on the wall opposite in large, blood-red letters.

He sat up in terror, the dregs of sleep scattered to the four winds, his heart pounding wildly.

Sutterlin, the thought came, clear and frosty and terrible. He shook his head, eyes fixed like magnets on the splattered wall. Surely not Sutterlin—not his style. But someone.

Someone, unknown, in his room.

He called Colonel Rahm from his study, the door locked, curtains drawn, afraid for a moment that they might not put him through.

"*Ja?*"

Relief steadied Laurent slightly. "I need your help, Colonel."

"In what way?"

He told him, briefly.

"What do you think I can do?"

"Give me protection. Send someone—two men—one, even, to guard the château."

Rahm sounded almost amused. "We have a country to defend, Herr Baron. Do you seriously think I can spare a single man at a time like this?"

"But I'm in danger!"

"Perhaps."

"For Christ's sake, I did as you asked, didn't I? I've given my cooperation since the beginning! Surely you can do something to help me now!" He was sweating profusely again.

"I can only advise you to stay at home, Herr Baron. There are many reports of summary executions, of both Vichy officials and their supporters, by *Résistance* bands."

"What use is staying at home when they've already got inside my house?" Laurent hissed in desperation.

Rahm paused a moment. "I could perhaps let you have a couple of *Hitlerjugend*—"

"How can *boys* protect me against the *maquis*?"

"Very likely they can't," Rahm answered calmly. "In any case, their presence is more likely to inflame your situation even further."

"And that's your final word?" Incredulity and violent hatred rose in Laurent's throat, choking him. "After all I've done for your people?"

Rahm's voice became impatient and hard. "All you ever did, my friend, was to line your own pockets and seek safe passage through the war."

"I fed your armies, for the love of God!"

"You merely gave, willingly, what we could almost as easily have taken for ourselves."

Laurent had been standing, rigid, over his desk. Now he sagged into his chair, knowing there was nothing more to be said.

"I wish you luck, Herr Baron," Rahm said.

The connection was cut. The line was dead.

He walked to the stables, saddled Seigneur, and took off into the forest.

He felt easier there, among the infinite browns and greens, protected by the ancient gnarled trees and thrusting, juicy saplings. Slowly, the horse moved, swaying gently, and Laurent inhaled the tangy mosses and listened to the steady sound of hooves plodding through Alsatian soil, and his senses were assuaged by the unfettered carpet of wild flowers, whose names he had never troubled to learn, even when his mother had taken him by the hand as a child and pointed to each one in turn.

If only he could stay here in this gentle light, he thought, nourished by nature, inanimate but surviving, season after season, year after year, removed from the château and from the beings who inhabited it. If he could remain here, safe and snug, like a mole, burrowing deeper and deeper into the earth, blind but certain, digging away until death . . .

But he stayed up in the saddle, his legs strong as iron around the flanks of the noble white creature who did not, could not, judge him. And he did not stay in the forest, but continued on the path toward the light and out into the open, where sunshine pricked his eyes and warmed his skin, and where the birds, released from the bondage of tangled branches, sang brightly. And slowly, instinctively, he rode on and on, until he reached the point, on the northern approach to Château de Trouvère, where he had first shown Krisztina his ancestral home.

Magnifique, he remembered she had said, very softly.

He looked again, and drank in the purity of the creamy baroque lines, and the splendor of the lands surrounding the house. And a sense of history and fate enveloped him, for it might have been any summer of any year, the overall picture untouched by war or Nazis or lusty young patriots who played with his terrors while they waited, in dark corners, to shoot him, or hang him, or chop off his head with an ax.

Seigneur quivered beneath him with sudden impatience, tossed his mane, and pawed at the ground with his hoof, and Laurent patted him.

"You don't want to wait any longer, *mon ami,* while I can do nothing else, for I don't know where or when or how it will happen."

Suddenly, recklessly, he began to laugh, violently, wildly, from his stomach, throwing back his head and opening his mouth wide, and he dug his heels smartly into the horse's flanks and flicked the reins, and together they galloped hard and fast up the road, back toward the home that was still his, and the people who shunned him, and to the end, which was assuredly, inevitably, close at hand.

He only stopped laughing after he dismounted, and was leading the horse back into the stable yard.

The words were clear, on the outside wall of Seigneur's stall, in yellow paint this time, and in a different hand.

MORT AUX COLLABORATEURS!

And the panic was with him again, searing and shameful and inescapable, and he turned, and flung his arms about the animal's great neck, and buried his face in the silken mane, and wept like a child.

There was nowhere for him to run, no place for him to hide. No one spoke to him. He had become untouchable as a leper.

He went to his mother's room and knocked at the door.

"*Qui est là?*"

"Laurent."

"Go away."

"Mother, help me, please."

"No, Laurent."

"*Maman!*"

"I cannot help you, Laurent."

He turned away.

Inside, Geneviève sat in a straight-backed chair. Her face was quite gray, and the tears ran down her cheeks, unchecked.

At the door of the blue guest suite, he stood silent and listened to the soft music from her wireless, and imagined Krisztina within, dancing alone, with no audience but her old black dog.

He knocked, and she came to the door and opened it.

"What do you want?"

"To be with you."

Her face was grave. "No, Laurent."

"Just for a while."

"It's finished, Laurent," she said.

"I know."

"Go away, please."

He thought her eyes the purest, sweetest blue he had ever seen.

"Help me," he whispered.

"I can't."

She closed the door.

He took the Mauser from the Hunting Room, and a bottle of precious malt whisky from the Smoking Room, and he went into his study, locked the door, and, again, drew the curtains.

From the bottom drawer of his desk, he took a large leather

album, opened it at the center pages, and stared down at his lost past.

Europa Meisterschaft, Berlin, 1937.

Gone.

He looked up at the wall, and saw three smiling faces. Bickler, Schlegel, and himself.

He reached up, unhooked it, and laid it down on the desk. His expression was ineffably sad.

The whisky was very fine.

My last taste, he thought.

He picked up the Mauser, and pressed the cold muzzle to his temple.

"Mea culpa," he said, looking down upon Krisztina's laughing, glowing face.

And pulled the trigger.

"He left no note."

"There was nothing more to say."

"I don't believe that."

"You must, *chérie.*"

"He tried to talk to us, Belle-mère."

"I know." Geneviève sighed. "We both know."

Both women, dressed in black, fell silent. On the table before them in Geneviève's sitting room was a silver tray with tea things, four thick albums, one bloodied, and the framed photograph of Laurent with the Nazis, the stains carefully wiped away.

"You should burn it," Geneviève said.

Krisztina shook her head. "He was proud of it. It made him happy, for a while."

Geneviève opened one of the albums, filled to bursting with pictures of Laurent's childhood and early youth.

"A record of a life."

Krisztina looked at another, and saw photographs of Laurent dancing with Alice Gébhard.

"He should have stayed with her."

"For your sake, perhaps. Not for his."

Krisztina touched the framed picture with her finger.

"The whole man," she said quietly.

Geneviève closed her eyes for a few seconds. "Was he whole?"

Neither spoke.

"I feel—" Krisztina broke off, her throat closing, tears threatening.

Geneviève nodded.

"I know."

PART THREE

Krisztina: Alsace, 1945–1958

Chapter 16

"Almost bankrupt."

"Practically no crops."

"More than eight months pregnant."

Geneviève smiled. "Alive."

Krisztina shifted uncomfortably in her chair. "What are we going to do, Belle-mère?"

"Do?"

"To survive."

"Call Sutterlin and Marthe and the others, and throw open the terrace doors in the Summer Room, and drink champagne, just as millions will be doing tonight all over Europe."

"I think they want to go to Riquewihr this evening."

"Do you want to go too, *chérie?*"

Krisztina shook her head.

"Then we'll drink champagne alone."

"And when the cellar's run dry, and the fields are still barren, and another hailstorm rips the vines apart, and the pickers won't come because we can't afford to pay them—what shall we do then?"

"Such dark thoughts," Geneviève said gently. "Don't you remember how long we prayed for victory?"

Krisztina's eyes were bleak. "Of course I do."

"Alors."

"But now that it's here, all I can think about is death and loss and failure."

"Laurent."

Krisztina nodded. "And Mama."

"It's hard, without news."

"I'm so afraid, with the Russians in Budapest—no post, no telephone." She reached down and absently fondled Perseus's ears; ever since Mozes had died three months before, the brindle wolfhound had taken his place by her side. "We must get them out, Belle-mère. Hungary is finished."

"A country with a strong heart is not so easily finished. You have the example all around you." She paused. "You're thinking of David, too, aren't you?"

Krisztina said nothing.

"Perhaps soon it may be possible to trace him."

"Perhaps."

Geneviève leaned closer. "But now, *ma petite*, you must consider the baby."

Krisztina laughed painfully. "I consider nothing else! I'm on the verge of bringing Laurent's heir into the world, and for all I know, there may soon not be a de Trouvère for him."

"Or her."

"It's a boy, I'm sure of it." She paused. "Poor baby."

"Why poor?"

"No father."

"But a wonderful mother."

Krisztina smiled. "And grandmother." She grew serious again. "But to be born into a life crumbling around him."

Geneviève shook her head decisively. "The crumbling is over, Krisztina—it ended with the war. Now the rebuilding starts."

"But how? You've said yourself that the *vignobles* may not recover sufficiently. Short of selling off land—"

"No one would buy now."

"So what can we do?"

"First, open a bottle of Krug." Geneviève stood up and gave Krisztina her hand.

"And then?" She struggled heavily out of the chair.

"Then we'll think."

"But of what, Belle-mère? We're two women on our own."

"You forget something, Krisztina."

"What?"

Geneviève's mouth was determined.

"We're *strong* women."

The child was born. A son, as Krisztina had predicted, and baptized in the chapel:

"Olivier Armand Laurent de Trouvère."

They brought him, blinking furious, dark eyes against bright sunlight, to his father's grave.

"Your papa," Krisztina told him softly, "who longed for you, and who would be infinitely proud of you."

The boy fought free of the de Trouvère baptismal shawl, tiny fists flailing in the mild spring air, and his red mouth puckered and stretched into a protesting wail.

"He cries so much," Krisztina said anxiously.

"It's healthy." Geneviève's eyes were hazy with memory. "Laurent was such a silent baby." She shrugged. "Perhaps it's better to let the emotions bubble and erupt."

"You think he's all right?" Krisztina rocked him gently.

"Tough as a little Trojan." Geneviève stroked the dark fuzz on his scalp. The wailing redoubled, accelerated to an angry scream. She smiled fondly.

"*Petit sauvage.*"

A letter came from Ilona at last, written in April and sent via the Soviet Embassy in Paris. It was only a few lines, with the stilted unnaturalness of censorship—all was well, Ilona tried to reassure her; Kaufmann's was no longer theirs, though Gabor was employed there, and their *lakas* (the modern luxury apartment Gabor had insisted they move to shortly after Krisztina's marriage), which had miraculously escaped bombing, had been requisitioned by the authorities to shelter other displaced families. *But we are glad to help*, she wrote, *and our room is quite adequate.*

Krisztina wept with relief and pity when she read the letter, grateful beyond words that her mother was safe, but knowing too how she had loved Kalvaria Street. She realized with an added pang of sympathy what misery it would be to live in one room with her father, to whom such a change of circumstances must have been an intense blow.

"If they can't leave, perhaps I can apply for a permit on their behalf," she said to Geneviève.

"You won't succeed, *chérie,*" Geneviève said gently. "You must be patient a while longer. Things will improve, settle down, and then maybe you'll be able to take Olivier on a visit."

Krisztina's eyes were desolate. "Maybe."

The scheme to save de Trouvère was born one month after Olivier.

It came naturally, like soft fruit, ripe and ready to be plucked at the right moment, and yet it came after endless hours of hopeless discussion during which the only logical means of escaping financial ruin still seemed to be to sell. But even if they were to find a buyer in such an appalling economic climate, both Geneviève and Krisztina felt they would sooner die than deprive the twenty-seventh baron of his rightful home.

Painstakingly, with help from Laurent's meticulous management books, they logged every acre, noted what had been earned when production was at full tilt, and compared the figures to what might reasonably be expected in the next year, allowing for the meagerness of the work force.

"I fear the land cannot help us this time," Geneviève pronounced wearily, laying down her pencil.

"Which leaves only the château."

"And our treasures."

"You wouldn't sell your collections, Belle-mère!"

"If it would save de Trouvère, yes, I would."

"But that would be like digging all the gold out of a vein just to preserve an empty mine. So much of the character of this place stems from the richness of the paintings and the sculptures, and the silver and the tapestries—"

"And the porcelain and gold and carvings and furniture," Geneviève finished for her. "I know, *chérie,* believe me, I know. In any case, it would not be enough in the long term."

They were in the library, sitting at the reading table, account books piled high and coffee, in fragile Dresden cups, gone cold. Krisztina stood up and walked over to the bookshelves, running her fingers over the leather bindings.

"I fell in love with de Trouvère the very first day," she said softly. "Do you remember, Belle-mère, you walked with me through the gardens and to the lake, and you showed me the chapel?"

"It was wonderful for me too. A chance to see it all through fresh eyes."

"It was all disguised by snow, yet you made me understand how it would be in spring and summer."

Geneviève smiled. "But the château itself—I wish you could have seen it in better times, happier times."

"Before the war?"

She nodded. "When Armand was still here, and still strong. Sometimes we gave house parties every weekend. Friends came from everywhere—from Paris and Lyon, and from Frankfurt and Zurich and even London. De Trouvère drew them like a magnet from all over Europe—sometimes they came en route to Baden-Baden, but mostly they came just for de Trouvère."

"It's a wonderful house."

Geneviève shook her head. "It was more than that. It had a kind of magic."

Krisztina sat down again. "So," she said resignedly, "that's our chief asset. A beautiful château with the ability to cast spells on people."

A silence fell.

"That's it."

Krisztina glanced at Geneviève. "That's what?"

"Our chief asset. Just as you said." Her cheeks had grown quite flushed.

"And?"

"A hotel," Geneviève said.

"I beg your pardon?"

"We can turn Château de Trouvère into a hotel."

Krisztina stared at her.

Geneviève smiled. "Not just an ordinary hotel, Krisztina. A splendid hotel. *Un grand hôtel de luxe.*"

Krisztina still stared. The room became so quiet, the atmosphere so intense and rarefied, that she could feel all her pulses keeping time, like silent metronomes.

"How?" Her voice was little more than a whisper.

"Work," Geneviève answered. "Imagination. Inspiration." She paused. "Struggle and toil." She beamed. *"Work."*

Krisztina swallowed. "And money?"

"The banks will recover."

"They'd never lend us enough to finance a project as huge as that, Belle-mère."

"I think they would. My husband had many friends in positions of power, not least the former manager of the Crédit Lyonnais in Strasbourg."

"This friend," Krisztina asked, "would help?"

Geneviève shrugged. "He has good reason to remember an outstanding debt to Armand. It's the place to begin anyway."

Krisztina sat back in her chair and briefly closed her eyes, quite dizzy with the whirlwind of ideas and visions rushing through her mind.

"Chérie?" Geneviève said, concerned. "Are you ill?"

Krisztina laughed. "Belle-mère, you've completely bowled me over, and you sit there as if you had just suggested a day trip to Paris!"

There was a knock at the door.

"Entrez," said Geneviève.

Jeanne, Olivier's nanny, looked apologetic.

"A problem, Jeanne?" asked Krisztina.

"Le p'tit is very fretful, madame. I've given him water and changed him, but he won't settle."

"He wants his *maman,"* Geneviève said.

Krisztina rose. "I'll come right away." She looked down at her mother-in-law. "We'll talk later?"

"Of course." Geneviève paused. "In principle, *chérie,* you approve?"

Krisztina bent to kiss her warmly on the cheek. "In principle, I think it's inspired, courageous, and just crazy enough to be the perfect solution." She straightened. "But one thing is certain."

"What's that?"

"It won't be easy."

Later, as Olivier slept snugly in his nursery, they walked every inch of the château, assessing it with fresh, critical eyes. They drank in its beauty, spotted its flaws, counted bedrooms, bathrooms, and storerooms and tracked the routing of water and heating pipes from the cellar up through the structure. From room to room they went, struggling to impose new identities on each one and meeting problems at every turn—the Salon Chinois, for example, would make a unique and exquisite bedroom, but lack of plumbing made an adjoining bathroom an impossibility, and in any case, it was important that the bedrooms be on the upper floors, for otherwise the guests would have no peace. And what a pity it was that the Summer Room and the Salle Fleurie were linked, for the former would make an excellent public room while the latter would quite easily transform into a romantic bedroom.

"It's a nightmare!" Geneviève despaired, her head spinning. *"Un grand hôtel de luxe* must be purpose-built, I see that now. It was a mad idea." She tapped her head energetically. "I am a *madwoman!"*

"Then perhaps I should be committed right away, for I think it could work."

"How? Without the west wing, there aren't enough bedrooms, and then where would we live?"

Krisztina waved the notes she had made as they had walked. "Discounting what would be our own rooms, there would be"— she referred to her figures— "three suites and three bedrooms, plus an extra bathroom, all on the second floor."

"Those bedrooms aren't large enough."

"And on the first floor," Krisztina continued, "there are another three bedrooms and two bathrooms, as well as three rooms that could definitely be turned into bedrooms."

"Which rooms?" Geneviève asked defensively.

"The green dining room, the Music Room and the Salle Fleurie, though that would exclude the Summer Room from daily use." She made a scribbled note. "That gives us twelve rooms."

"Surely not enough to make a profit."

"Perhaps not, but we shan't know that until we have a complete plan worked out." She swept on. "The ground floor has far too many small rooms, so some walls would have to be knocked down."

"Arrête!"

Krisztina stopped, startled.

"May I remind you that this is my home you're smashing to pieces," Geneviève said frostily.

"Our home, Belle-mère," Krisztina amended, still surprised.

"All the more reason not to get completely carried away." She softened a little. "The idea is to save the château, not to savage it."

Krisztina was stung. "That's exactly what I'm trying to do, surely?"

"Is it? Is that why you're already planning to wipe out the room where my husband used to play Chopin for me?"

A flush of shame colored Krisztina's cheeks. "I'm sorry, I didn't know."

Geneviève shrugged. "You couldn't, of course. But you talk of knocking down walls . . ."

A deep silence fell on them, both women wrapped in thought. From the depths of a venerable wall, a pipe groaned, and as if in reply, a floorboard creaked.

Krisztina glanced anxiously at Geneviève. "Would you like to forget the idea, Belle-mère?"

"I'm not sure yet."

"Why don't we sleep on it?" Krisztina suggested softly.

Geneviève nodded. "We need time to think," she said slowly. "About every aspect—what it would do to the château, to us, to Olivier, and to the others who rely on de Trouvère."

At dinner the next night, they hardly spoke. The soft scratching of silver on porcelain and the occasional creaking of their chairs lent an unusual quality of strain and formality to the atmosphere between them.

Sutterlin brought coffee to them in the Salon Rouge.

"Let's have some cognac too," Geneviève said, after he'd gone.

"Good idea."

They sat together on the *dormeuse*, a little space between them.

"For my part," Geneviève said, "I have decided."

Krisztina was silent.

"I am getting too old for new ideas," Geneviève went on.

"You're not at all old, Belle-mère."

"I am fifty-one," she said steadily. "And though I flatter myself I may have looked younger in the past, the last few years have taken their toll."

"Age is immaterial, Belle-mère," Krisztina insisted, a little exasperated. "And you're the most timeless woman I've ever met." She paused for a moment. "Fear," she said decisively. "That's the problem. Of change, whether it be to de Trouvère itself or your own way of life. Fear of betraying your husband's heritage. Of ravaging his ancestral home instead of strengthening it." She paused again, and repeated simply: "Fear."

Geneviève looked at her. "You're right. I am afraid."

"And that's natural." Krisztina stood up. "So am I—but that's not a good enough reason to reject the most brilliant, brave idea I've ever heard!"

"I agree."

"You do?"

"Please don't gape, *chérie.*" Geneviève smiled. "You've made it quite plain that you feel we should proceed. I am merely agreeing."

Krisztina sat down again. "But what about the changes? Some walls will have to be knocked down. Strangers will sit in our rooms and walk through our gardens. Won't you hate that?"

Geneviève thought for a moment. "Have you heard of Tagore?"

"The Indian poet?"

"He wrote very wisely about change. 'When old words die out on the tongue, new melodies break forth from the heart . . .'" She took Krisztina's hand and held it. "When the Music Room is transformed into a bedroom, I shall try to remember Tagore."

Krisztina felt choked. "The Music Room won't be touched, Belle-mère, you have my word."

"Don't make rash promises," Geneviève said with composure. "If it becomes necessary, so be it."

They sat in silence for a while longer, and Krisztina began to comprehend the enormity of the decision that had just been reached. She felt a great thrill—not the wild, galloping intoxication that had swept her yesterday, but a deep, intensely gripping exhilaration.

"Our *projet,*" Geneviève went on at last, "is exactly what we need. Before Armand's death, before the war, not a month went by when I did not go to Paris—I shopped, I visited friends, my coiffeur, even my dentist. I joined Armand for business meetings and traveled with him: I *lived.*"

"But de Trouvère always had the main place in your heart."

"Yes, of course, because above all it was home, a place to rest and be easy and to belong. The Nazis helped turn it into a kind of sanctuary—a safe, half-sane house in the midst of madness, but we have become a closed community in the process."

"And thanked God for it."

"Indeed," Geneviève agreed. "But it's another strong reason

for change." She smiled. "It's not so important for me, Krisztina, but it's time for you to learn to be fully alive again."

"You're right," Krisztina said quietly.

"And now"—Geneviève stirred—"we should drink a toast. But it must be in *vin rouge,* not cognac."

"Not champagne?"

"Champagne is for celebration, for festivity," Geneviève explained. "Matters of great significance require something more substantial, something to blend with the blood."

Krisztina smiled. "Let's go up to the nursery. I think Olivier should share this time with us."

"I agree," Geneviève said, standing up. "After all, it is his future that we're deciding."

Upstairs, Krisztina bent over the crib and regarded her son, his little face, so intense and mobile in waking hours, now serene and utterly seraphic, the almost black hair a striking silky halo against the white skin.

"Oh, Belle-mère, he smells better than anything in the world," Krisztina whispered, inhaling the unique aroma of baby and talcum, and a pang of ferocious tenderness clutched at her heart.

"Give him another hour," Geneviève murmured fondly, "and he'll have added a touch of piquancy."

Krisztina giggled.

Geneviève poured Château Margaux into two glasses on the changing table.

"And now," she said gravely, "let us drink our toast to the Grand Hôtel du Château de Trouvère."

Krisztina raised her glass. "May it provide security, shelter, and delight to the twenty-seventh baron." They drank deeply. "And to your bank manager," she added. "May his mind be broad, his heart generous—"

"And his pockets deep," Geneviève finished for her. They both laughed, and in the crib Olivier stirred, making small whimpering sounds. His mother turned him carefully onto his stomach, her hand gently rubbing his warm back until he was sound asleep again.

"Do you think you will persuade this banker, Belle-mère? It will be an enormous investment."

"I have not been a de Trouvère for nearly thirty years without learning something about determination."

Krisztina saw that Geneviève's eyes were keen and bright.

"Rest assured, *ma chère* Krisztina," the older woman went on resolutely, "by the time I have finished with Monsieur Jean-Joseph Dienheim, he will be a true believer."

Chapter 17

It took effort, charm, subtle threats, and time, but eventually, as Geneviève had predicted, Jean-Joseph Dienheim became a believer, and funds, subject to approval of all planning decisions, became available.

Their next task was to find the right architect to assess the château's potential and to recommend the necessary alterations. They rejected three men, none of whom seemed to understand their aims or share their sensitivities about the house—and then they found Alberto Giordano, who was, in fact, not an architect but an interior designer.

"But don't we *need* an architect?" Krisztina had asked him when he first came to call; it was he who approached them, a short, balding, attractive Italian with a sparkle in his dark eyes that spoke of a natural exuberance and a genuine enthusiasm that was most appealing to the two Baronnes.

"For advice on structural matters, surely," Giordano had answered, "and I would consult a team of experts at all times. But I think that your object is to utilize Château de Trouvère as she stands—to try to maintain her character, but to make it possible to share her beauty with the public."

Krisztina glanced at Geneviève.

"It's difficult for an architect to take on such work," he continued. "By definition, an architect is a designer of buildings, a creator. This house does not need creation, just imagination."

"Why are you in Alsace, signor?" Geneviève asked curiously.

He grinned. "I have gypsy blood, Baronessa. I have traveled through much of Europe, absorbing different cultures and working where and when the right situations have presented themselves."

Krisztina looked again at the portfolio he had brought with him, containing dozens of photographs, letters, and clippings related to his work; including the criticisms as well as the plaudits.

"You've achieved a great deal," she said, impressed.

"I am a happy man, signora." He smiled.

"Mightn't you have found greater fame and wealth if you had stayed in one place, one city?" asked Geneviève.

Giordano shrugged. "Probably, but I doubt if I would have the adaptability and vision that my travels have taught me."

"Do you have a home somewhere?" Krisztina probed.

"Not yet," he replied easily. "I am not ready. I live where I work—sometimes, if possible, I actually sleep there too. That way, I grow to understand the personality of the house, or the room, not just the structure and surfaces." He paused. "I have talked enough. I shall leave you now, Baronesse, and await your decision."

Geneviève and Krisztina eyed one another and nodded, their expressions satisfied.

"There is no need to wait," said Geneviève.

The Italian eyes grew even darker with anticipation.

Krisztina smiled. "We are in your hands, Signor Giordano."

It was time to share the news with the staff.

Sutterlin had already been consulted, partly because it was hopeless trying to keep anything important from him, and partly because they had a proposition to put to him.

He had known they were in financial straits, and was very relieved that they were not going to sell, but he was, at first, visibly shocked by the project, though prepared to give it consideration. It took him only twenty-four hours to decide that it was an idea he could live with.

André Sutterlin was the obvious choice for concierge, for no one else could possibly be as well equipped as he was to share his knowledge of de Trouvère and the surrounding area with hotel guests. When Geneviève and Krisztina offered him the post, he accepted with pleasure and dignity.

Over Marthe Schneegans, they worried themselves almost to distraction. Marthe had been with the household for as long as Geneviève could remember, but in spite of her thinness, she was as strong as a horse, and could certainly not be offered an early retirement.

"She'll want to cook," Krisztina said for the umpteenth time, "but it's out of the question."

"*Absolument,*" Geneviève agreed, twisting a strand of hair into a tight curl, releasing it, then twisting it again. "Marthe is a fine family cook, but she's no chef. Above all, the cuisine in our hotel must be beyond reproach."

"But what can we do?"

"We can't ask her to take orders from a stranger—she'd be outraged."

"And we can't send her away—de Trouvère is her whole life now that Jacques is gone."

"*Zut, zut, zut!*" exclaimed Geneviève, quite flushed with frustration and rare temper. "It's insoluble!"

"What does André say?"

"That we should speak to her, be honest with her."

"Perhaps he's right, Belle-mère."

It soon became clear that Marthe had known about their plans for some time, though no one, she hastened to reassure, had actually told her; she had merely paid attention to the unusual comings and goings in the house and had drawn her own conclusions. And since she had also foreseen the predicament her employers would find themselves in, she had taken it upon herself to devise her own future.

"I was afraid that you might ask me to remain as cook, but then, of course, I realized I am no chef de cuisine."

Geneviève and Krisztina were baffled.

"You don't want to stay on?"

"*Naturellement,* but not as cook. I am sick of cooking! I've done nothing else morning, noon, and night for more than twenty years, and I never wanted to be a cook in the first place. If I had a choice, I would be overjoyed beyond words if I never had to step inside another kitchen for the rest of my life!"

The two Baronnes were more confused than ever.

"So what is it you do want, Marthe?" Geneviève managed weakly. "I have the impression that you have worked it all out."

"I have, madame." With a resolute and symbolic flourish, Marthe removed her apron and laid it over the back of a kitchen chair. Her small, birdlike eyes were very sharp. "I have made inquiries, a little *recherche,* and I am aware that in every good hotel there must be a *gouvernante* to control the maids and the housekeeping in general." She paused. *"C'est moi."*

There was a moment's stunned silence.

"If you consider me unsuitable," she said rather stiffly, "I shall understand. But I believe I should make an adequate *gouvernante.*"

Geneviève and Krisztina shook themselves from their stupor.

"Of course you will, Marthe." Geneviève recovered first, and began to smile. "Forgive us if we're a little dazed. We were in despair—we made the mistake of seeing you only in the role you'd played for so long."

"It was unforgivably unimaginative of us," Krisztina said. "We knew it was impossible for you to cook for an entire hotel—"

"I daresay I could manage it if it was required," Marthe interjected smartly.

"Oh, I'm sure you could," Krisztina agreed hastily, "but you'll make a superb *gouvernante.* It's a wonderful idea."

If asked, Geneviève and Krisztina would have said that it was virtually impossible to imagine Marthe Schneegans glowing. In truth, she had rarely smiled, even in the happier days before Jacques was taken. Yet at that moment her whole personality seemed to alter. Her little eyes shone, her sallow cheeks flushed, she stood erect and she actually beamed. Marthe, the cook, had already disappeared; Madame Schneegans, *la gouvernante,* had taken her place.

Alberto Giordano became a fixture. It was hardly possible to turn a corner in the château without coming upon one of his huge pads of paper, covered with rough sketches and notes, or one of his "experts," or Giordano himself, either silent and absorbed, or aflame with new inspiration.

He was a gypsy. Almost every night for four months, he camped in the house, sleeping on a mattress on the floors of every room and hallway in turn. He worked like a dervish on one plan after another; he brought in architects, electricians, plumbers, builders, and decorators, chatting amiably with them, shouting at them, agreeing, disagreeing, praising them, throwing them out, and then usually cutting himself off to ponder and to draw.

He grew thinner, then rounder, then thinner again, the result of erratic bouts of eating and drinking. For days on end, he rejected every effort by Marthe (to whose hidden maternal instincts he appealed) to feed him, and let not a drop of alcohol pass his lips, and then, suddenly, as if acknowledging that a massive refueling was overdue, he would pound on the kitchen door and devour huge bowls of spaghetti, while draining sometimes two or even three bottles of *Chianti rosso*, which Krisztina ordered specially from Strasbourg.

There were countless problems, but Alberto was determined to solve them all. Nothing was outside his domain. "In our hotel," he vowed, "there will be endless supplies of hot water, and the wiring will be so sound that the entire hotel can be ablaze with light and no fuse will blow!" He improved, by two, Krisztina's early estimate of twelve guest bedrooms, finding a way to house the whole family in comfort and maintain rooms of importance, such as the Salon Rouge and the Music Room. He shared with both de Trouvère women their aversion to installing lifts in such a perfect baroque château, but recognizing their necessity, compromised by designing one passenger and one service lift, both wholly disguised by the original oak, meticulously sliced from the existing wall and replaced over the lift doors.

For every problem, he said, there was a solution. And where that was not readily available, there was his favorite word: *compromesso.* Compromise.

The planning stages completed, the operation moved into its next phase. Château de Trouvère lost every semblance of normality and became a hubbub of noise, grime, and chaos as the builders and their cohorts moved in and began, apparently, to tear at the beloved house like ruthless saboteurs.

"Calma, calma, miei amiche." Giordano tried to pacify the two distraught Baronnes. "All will be well, all will be returned to peace and beauty."

"But the walls! The oak! The marble!" moaned Geneviève. "You promised to keep them intact."

"And they shall be, *cara* signora, I give you my word."

"How can they ever look the same again?" Krisztina protested. "It's rubble! It's all destroyed!"

"*Ma no!* Each piece is removed *con tenerezza*. When the work is completed, there will be nothing to show that the walls were ever touched!" He lowered his voice. "These men are like surgeons, Baronesse. In order to enable the plumbers and *elettricisti* to do their work, they must first make incisions." He smiled. "A body under the knife must also look unpretty, but with a first-class surgeon, the scars disappear completely."

Geneviève stood very straight, a lethal gleam in her eyes. "Very well," she said, not unpleasantly. "We'll take you at your word." She waited a second. "But I warn you, Alberto Giordano, if you are wrong, I promise you will never have another peaceful night."

Giordano bowed from the waist. "Baronessa, I swear to you, there is not a grain of doubt in my mind that when our labors are ended, I shall sleep like an innocent *bambino.*"

On the twenty-eighth day of April, Krisztina was summoned by Sutterlin to the telephone in the study.

"Krisztina?"

It had been eight years, but there was not a grain of doubt. Her stomach clenched.

"Father?"

"*Igen.*"

"Where are you?"

"In Vienna."

"And Mama? Where's Mama?" Her legs trembled and her cheeks grew hot. "Father, tell me!"

"Your mother is here too."

"*Hala Istenek!*" she thanked God. "Let me speak to her, quickly!"

Gabor seemed hesitant. "She isn't actually with me this minute, Krisztina."

"Why not? Where is she? Why are you in Vienna? Is it a business trip? How did you get out? Where is Mama?" The questions tumbled out feverishly.

"*Lassan,* Kriszti—slowly! Give me a chance to answer."

"Is Mama all right?" she demanded.

"Yes. She's in hospital, but—"

"Why?" Fear wrenched her. "What's wrong with her?"

"She's had an operation, a hysterectomy, but she's—"

"Oh, my God!"

"Try to be calm, please, Kriszti, and let me tell you. Your mother had the operation three days ago—"

"Why didn't you tell me?"

"Because I wanted to wait for the doctors' verdict."

"And?"

"They're pleased, thank God. She was very sick at home, and it will take time for her to recover completely, but she will recover."

"But how did you get to Vienna? Why didn't Mama have the operation at home?"

The long-distance connection made Gabor sound tinny and harsh. "You haven't seen Budapest as it is now, Krisztina. The bombing destroyed so much—every bridge, our old house, nearly all the houses. And then the Russians—"

"Did they destroy the hospitals?"

"She was admitted to hospital in Pest, and her doctor, a good man, a fine young man, said if she didn't have top-class surgery, she would die. He said the place for her to be was here."

"So they let you go?"

"Not so easily, believe me. But he convinced the authorities that they would be killing an innocent woman, all for the price of an exit permit. He had influence."

"Thank God for him."

"Indeed." There was a pause. "We want to see you, Krisztina. Can you come?"

"Of course I'll come." She thought for a moment. "Did Mama receive any of my letters? Do you know about Olivier?"

"We do, Kriszti. Will you bring him?"

"It's a long journey, Father."

"It would mean so much to your mama."

She heard the humility in his voice, and the pleading.

"We'll leave tomorrow."

Ilona was thin and pale and weak, but when she saw her daughter, she cried out with joy. As they drew apart, having wept copiously in each other's arms, Krisztina saw that her brown eyes were as beautiful as she remembered, and a hint of color touched her cheeks.

"Hala Istenek, hala Istenek," Ilona cried over and over again,

staring into Krisztina's face as though she were trying to imprint a vision on her brain that could never be blotted out, whatever more came between them.

"You've changed, *dragam,*" Ilona said in wonder. "You're a woman, a golden beauty . . ." She smiled. "And a mother."

"And you, Mama, how are you feeling?" Krisztina asked anxiously.

"Me? I'm much better," she dismissed. "No need to fret over me, not now anyway."

Krisztina stroked her mother's cheek. "You'll get well and strong, Mama, and you'll come to de Trouvère and live with us."

Tears filled Ilona's eyes. "Did you bring Olivier? Gabor said you might."

"He's just outside, playing with a nurse. I wanted to be sure you felt strong enough."

"To meet my grandson?" Ilona laughed with an effort. "Could you doubt it?"

"And I wanted to have you to myself for a while," Krisztina added gently, squeezing her hand.

"God willing, we'll have all the time we need soon, *dragam.*"

Krisztina rose from the small, hard chair. "I'll fetch him."

When Ilona saw Olivier, she gasped with astonishment. "So dark! Like a little gypsy!"

Mindful of the intravenous drip in her mother's arm, Krisztina carefully deposited her son on the edge of the hospital bed, and waited for his protest. None came. Grandmother and child stared into each other's eyes with solemn fascination, Ilona mute with happiness, Olivier apparently too intrigued to scream.

Ilona stretched out her free arm. "Come, *baba,*" she beckoned softly.

Olivier turned his round, almost black eyes up to his mother, then gazed again at Ilona.

"Vas t'en, chéri," encouraged Krisztina.

Olivier chuckled. His chubby cheeks dimpled, his charming baby mouth stretched to display tiny white teeth, and he crawled close to Ilona and seized her arm.

"Dieu, Mama," Krisztina exclaimed. "He's happy to meet you."

Ilona looked surprised. "And why should he not be?"

"You don't know Olivier yet, Mama," she explained, amused.

"We love him dearly, but he's not easy to please, and I've never known him take to a stranger so quickly."

"Because you know, don't you, *baba*? You know I'm your grandmother, no stranger at all." Ilona examined him more closely, caressing the dark hair and tickling him under the chin, making him laugh. Her thoughts, though, were flying out of the Viennese hospital, back more than twenty-five years, remembering the exquisite infant, the child of her dreams that her cousin had entrusted to her love.

Kriszti blonde as flax, she thought, *and Laurent almost as fair* . . . She studied Olivier's eyes again, so dark they seemed almost jet. *A throwback?* she wondered, and thought for the thousandth time of the Star of David she had smuggled out of Hungary in her handbag, concealed from Gabor. . . .

"Mama?"

Ilona blinked.

"Are you feeling bad, Mama?" Quickly, Krisztina retrieved Olivier from the bed, where he was sucking on the corner of a sheet.

"I'm fine, Kriszti, don't worry. Just a little tired . . . so much excitement . . ."

"We'll let you get some rest." Krisztina stood up, and the boy began to squirm in her arms.

"You'll come back?" Ilona's face creased into lines that her daughter had never seen before the war.

"Persze," Krisztina soothed her. "Of course I'll be back tomorrow. We'll stay in Vienna as long as we need to." She stooped and kissed the top of her mother's head.

"Kriszti?"

"Igen, Mama?"

Ilona caught at her hand, and her grip was fierce.

"What is it, Mama?"

"We must never let anyone separate us again." Tears of intensity stood out in her eyes.

"Never, Mama."

Ilona gulped back a sob. "I couldn't bear to lose you again."

Krisztina shifted Olivier's weight, and gently stroked the thin, clenched fingers that held on as if she were a lifeline.

"Nor could I."

*

Krisztina and Gabor sat at a window table in a mediocre restaurant close to the Danube Canal. Half-eaten, overcooked schnitzels lay before them, half-finished glasses of too sour *Heuriger Wein* stood on the stained cloth. A candle, flickering wildly each time the restaurant door opened or closed, and clearly intended by the proprietor to inject romance into the drab postwar scene, only served to illuminate the strained faces of father and daughter as they watched each other closely for the first time in eight long years.

"Gone," Gabor said morosely. "All gone."

"What's gone?"

"Vienna, as it was. Finished. *Fertig.*"

"Did you expect it to be the same?"

"I don't know what I expected. Budapest looks so terrible, so completely destroyed. I remembered Vienna as it was." He shrugged. "Just idle hope."

"It's reasonable to hope, I suppose."

There was a short silence.

"You and I too," Gabor said quietly.

"What?"

"Finished."

She ignored the appeal in his eyes. "As we once were, yes."

He blinked hard, and cleared his throat, then continued with an attempt at jauntiness. "They tell me that your mother must have a good convalescence. They suggested Semmering, for the air. I thought we might rent an apartment for a while. It would be more relaxing than a hotel—a maid could see to the domestic affairs." He hesitated. "And it would be cheaper too."

"Will that be a problem? The cost?" Krisztina knew that the loss of Kaufmann's, their departure from Budapest, and her mother's medical bills must have drained whatever resources he still had after the war.

Gabor flushed. "Frankly, yes." The top of his balding head shone in the candlelight.

"Can I help?"

He averted his eyes. "Would you want to help me, Krisztina?"

No, she thought, *not you,* but refrained from saying so. Even now, after so many years, her feelings for Gabor were confused. He had played a major role in David's loss, but just as bad, he had destroyed so many precious memories, forever tainted by the shock and revulsion of a single night.

"Krisztina?"

And yet . . . She looked at him, and saw such weakness and defeat and guilt that in spite of herself, pity swept her.

"Of course I'll help, Father," she said calmly. "Though things have been far from easy at de Trouvère since the war."

Briefly, she told him of their struggles, outlining Geneviève's idea for the hotel.

"Is it really so very beautiful?" Gabor asked. "It seems to me you've grown fonder of your new home than you might have expected."

"That's true."

"Then perhaps . . ." He wavered, uncertain whether or not to continue. "Perhaps some good has come from your marriage after all."

"My marriage was wrong," she said implacably, "but it was my own sin, and I blame no one else for it." She paused. "And yes, much good has come out of it—my friendship with Laurent's mother, the château and estate, and most of all, Olivier."

"My grandson."

"Yes."

Gabor looked awkward again. "You know why your mother needed the operation?"

"Yes. I spoke to a doctor at the *Krankenhaus.*"

"She needs more rest. Semmering will be good for her."

"And then?" Krisztina looked at Gabor. "After Semmering?"

He could not meet her eyes. "Your mother, of course, longs to be near you and Olivier, but—" He broke off.

"But?"

"I know you don't want me, Krisztina, and I can't blame you." Again there was humility in his voice.

"Mama will need you," she replied evenly.

"I think so."

She paused. "And you're still my father."

At last he met her gaze. "When the hotel opens, I could work, be useful." He looked hopeful.

"Perhaps."

His face fell again. "They took the store away from me, you know."

"I know, Mama wrote me."

"And they gave me a job." He laughed bitterly. "Sweeping up, scrubbing the counters, washing the windows. In my own store."

He gulped, close to tears. "When I cleaned the chandeliers, I had to stand on top of a high ladder, and I was so dizzy—you remember I always hated heights—but they said either I did all the work or none at all."

She remembered him before the war, remembered the ambition and greed that had burned in him, and she saw his hopelessness and misery now. And though she recognized the justice of his downfall, she was surprised to find she had no appetite for revenge.

Gabor steadied himself with a drink of the sour wine. "So you see, Kriszti," he said, "I'm willing to work, to pay for our keep."

"That won't be necessary, Father," she stopped him, hating his self-abasement. "My home is yours; that's normal and right."

"What about Laurent's mother? How will she feel?"

"Belle-mère feels as I do." She frowned. "But I'm afraid you won't be able to come to the château for a good while yet."

"Why not?"

She smiled. "If you could see it, you'd understand. There's hardly a centimeter untouched by the builders. There's dirt and dust everywhere—it would be very unhealthy for Mama."

Gabor looked anxious.

"Don't fret about money, Father, not now," she said gently. "Let Mama get well at Semmering, and then perhaps, if the château is still not ready, you'll stay for a time in Ribeauvillé, which is not far."

Another flush darkened his cheeks. "It's hard, you know, Krisztina, to take charity from one's child."

"This isn't charity."

"Not for your mother, no, but surely when it's for a man you hate. . . ."

"I don't hate you, Father."

He looked up suddenly, and his spectacles glinted in the candle's flame. "Why not?" he asked, unbelieving.

Krisztina thought for a moment.

"I wish I knew."

Having seen Ilona well on the way to recovery, Krisztina returned with the baby to Alsace, and broke the news to Alberto that somehow, somewhere, another family suite was needed.

Giordano had proved as good as his word; the builders were indeed craftsmen, tender and loving with every task. But for

every blessing, it seemed, there was a setback to balance the book
of mixed fortunes. Foremost among them was money. Or, rather,
the lack of it.

It seemed almost vulgar to watch such wonder in the making
and to translate each ensuing achievement into francs, but the
overseeing and increasingly pessimistic presence of Monsieur
Jean-Joseph Dienheim and his delegates made more than a degree of frugality necessary.

For the first time, Alberto began to show signs of the tension
and irritability that were affecting everyone at de Trouvère.

"I cannot work like this! It is crippling us!"

It was Krisztina's turn to try to soothe. "We have no choice,
Alberto. The bank insists that the budget has been stretched far
enough. They have copies of your estimates, and—"

"Estimates!" yelled Giordano, further incensed. "This is not an
office block we are creating—this is a *vision!*"

Krisztina smiled sympathetically. "We know that, Alberto—
nobody better—but the harsh truth is that if Monsieur Dienheim
so decrees, our funds could be cut off like an amputated limb.
And if that does happen"—she shook her head morosely—"de
Trouvère will need more than one of your 'surgeons'—she'll need
an undertaker."

Giordano looked puzzled. *"Prego?"*

Krisztina sought a translation. *"Per la morte,"* she said.

"Ah, un becchino." His face cleared, then visibly darkened.
"Over my dead body!"

She didn't know whether to laugh or cry. "But Alberto," she
reasoned, "do you at least begin to understand? If we don't show
them that we can keep the costs down, there will be no hotel."

On the fourteenth day of August, Krisztina heard at last from
the International Committee of the Red Cross in Geneva. David
Kaufmann, they confirmed, had perished in transit from Sachsenhausen to Riga in January 1942, and both his parents had died
in Buchenwald.

A copy of a diary entry, passed to the ICRC by a survivor of
Salaspils labor camp near Riga, was enclosed for her attention.
Written with stark simplicity, it chronicled the horrors of a single
deportation of Jewish prisoners from Germany to Nazi-occupied
Latvia.

Naming numerous fellow travelers in his freight car, the diarist had recorded that, while stronger prisoners scraped icicles from the walls and windows and melted them for water, eleven men, women, and children, including David, already weak from typhus and malnutrition, had frozen to death.

For many, it might have been better to die on the train, the diary went on, *for we heard later that perhaps five hundred or more were taken to Rumbuli forest and shot.*

For four days, Krisztina spoke to no one and attended only abstractedly to Olivier, clutching the fourteen-month-old boy to her breast in a soundless, wild despair and releasing him only when he squirmed and yelled in protest. The news that *la jeune Baronne* had lost a loved one spread quickly through the château, and Alberto, out of respect, ordered his men to stop work. A hush filled the house.

"Wouldn't you like to go to Semmering to your mother?" Geneviève asked on the fifth morning. "Jeanne and I can easily manage Olivier."

At last, Krisztina spoke. "No, thank you, Belle-mère. It would only distress Mama to see me now." She shook her head slowly. "I feel so strange."

"How?"

"It's grief, I suppose." Her voice was dull. "But not the same grief one feels for someone who has shared one's everyday existence—no new void has been left in my life."

"I think it has, *chérie.*"

Krisztina was hardly listening. "You know, in spite of everything, even though I told you I believed he was dead, I never really stopped hoping that one day he might escape and come to find me. And now I know, really know, that he's gone forever, that he's never coming back." She swallowed hard. "But there's no body, no corpse for me to bury and weep over, just words on paper, and I think I still don't truly believe it."

"You must, *chérie.*"

"I know. I *know!*" Unshed tears glistened in her eyes. "But they said he was sick and weak," she said, her voice trembling. "That he froze!" She shuddered and clenched her fists. "I'll never allow myself to think of David that way, *never!* To me, he'll always be as he was—healthy, and handsome, and alive."

"That's as it should be," Geneviève said gently. "That's how I remember Armand."

Krisztina flushed. "And Laurent."

"Yes."

The pause was cumbersome, laden with memories and sorrow.

"But unless I acknowledge the truth, Belle-mère," Krisztina continued, knowing now that she needed to talk, trying desperately to maintain self-control. "Unless I stop dreaming that David may, by some impossible miracle, walk into Château de Trouvère someday, how will I ever forget him?"

"You don't want to forget him, *chérie*."

"Yes, I do!" Her face twisted with anguish. "I want to forget those sweet memories! I want to forget what I did to him!"

"But what did you do that was so terrible?"

"I betrayed him!" she cried.

"How?" Geneviève asked sharply. "By marrying Laurent?"

"Of course."

"You did that for him, Krisztina."

"Not only."

"Perhaps not." It was hard for Geneviève to go on, to quell her own sense of disloyalty to her son, but she wanted desperately to console Krisztina. "But if David had been safe, you would have married him, not Laurent, wouldn't you?" She stroked Krisztina's hair. "You don't want to forget."

"I want to forget that he's dead," Krisztina whispered.

Geneviève sighed, aware that before comfort must come acceptance and grief. "Perhaps," she said thoughtfully, "if you were to do something for his memory."

"Light a candle, you mean?" Krisztina's voice was quite bitter.

"Certainly," Geneviève replied steadily. "But I meant something more than that."

"But what? I can hardly have a service for him."

"Why not?"

"A Catholic service for a Jew?"

"No, of course not."

"What then? Go to a synagogue?"

Geneviève shook her head. "I doubt if that would give you the comfort you need, *ma chère*. No, I have in mind something different." She pondered. "A memorial service, yes, and in our chapel."

"But David—"

"I'm sure that Père Perigot would not object to a rabbi being present."

Krisztina was startled. "But wouldn't *you* mind, Belle-mère? Having Jewish prayers said in your chapel?"

"It's our chapel now, Krisztina."

Krisztina fell silent, and Geneviève, studying her pale face, guessed easily the pattern of her thoughts.

"You're considering Laurent?"

Krisztina nodded.

"Wondering if this might be an affront to him—perhaps even to me?"

Krisztina didn't trust herself to speak.

Geneviève's eyes were full of pain, though her voice was calm. "I try, as much as is humanly possible, never to remind myself of what my son did to your David."

"And God knows I don't *want* to remind you, darling Belle-mère!" Krisztina burst out miserably.

"I know that. But there are truths that are unavoidable."

"You mustn't lay the blame for Nazi crimes on Laurent's shoulders," Krisztina argued in distress. "There are millions dead—we both know that if David hadn't been arrested that night, it would probably have happened later."

"Or he might have escaped."

Krisztina stared at her helplessly.

"And there will be no grave for you to visit."

Krisztina shook her head, wordless again.

"And his mother and father cannot mourn him."

The banked-up tears began to flow, painfully, trickling down her cheeks.

"The Blessed Virgin will not mind," Geneviève went on quietly, "and *le bon Dieu* cares for us all equally."

They fell into each other's arms, both women needing to share their sorrow and finding solace in closeness. And as Krisztina sobbed away years of suppressed yearning and loss, Geneviève gazed down the futile avenue of might-have-beens, and was more awed than ever by life's ironies; for if Laurent had been less flawed—if this cherished stranger, this David Kaufmann, had lived—she would never have known Krisztina, never have had this tender, courageous friend, this daughter.

"*Alors, chère fille,*" she said softly, still feeling the sobs that shook the slender frame, "will you let me do this small thing?"

With an effort, Krisztina raised her tear-drenched face. "How can I ever thank you, Belle-mère?"

Geneviève held her at arm's length, and her eyes were filled with love.

"There is nothing to thank me for."

Jean-Joseph Dienheim no longer believed.

Financial support withdrawn, Geneviève was compelled to telephone Alberto Giordano at the small *pension* in Ribeauvillé to which he had discreetly withdrawn to give Krisztina peace.

"It's all over," she told him with deep regret. "The bankers have terminated the project."

"Ma non e possibile!"

"Sadly, Alberto, it is. We have to pay off the men and finish immediately, or there will be penalties."

"We cannot finish!" he erupted. "We cannot stop until the hotel is ready! I *will* not stop! I tell you, Baronessa, if these bankers are such cowards, I shall work for nothing until we find others with *coraggio!*"

"My dear Alberto, that is out of the question. You will all be paid, for everything. But we cannot continue."

"There must be a way!"

"Not this time."

"At least allow me to think!"

"By all means," Geneviève said gently. "But we have to face the truth. There is no more money."

Père Perigot came from Riquewihr, a rabbi from Colmar, and Krisztina, Geneviève, and little Olivier, supported by Sutterlin, Marthe, and Jeanne, knelt as the priest intoned a requiem mass. They then stood with bowed heads as the rabbi sang two psalms of David and recited the traditional Mourner's Prayer, after explaining that it was customarily the closest male relatives of the deceased who led the Kaddish.

"Would it be improper if I said this prayer?" André Sutterlin had asked, grave-faced and dignified. "Though I am no relative, and was not acquainted with Monsieur Kaufmann."

"Under the circumstances, Monsieur," the rabbi had replied, "I should regard it as a considerable *mitzvah*—a good deed."

He handed Sutterlin a card, upon which the Hebrew words were written phonetically, and the Protestant butler blushed crimson as he read, hardly faltering, his voice following less than a half beat behind the rabbi's. And when they were finished, the stillness in the chapel was so remarkable that, for once, even Olivier seemed hypnotized. And after Père Perigot and the rabbi blessed the small, gold memorial plaque that had been fixed to the wall near the door, Marthe's eyes were pink, Jeanne was openly weeping, and Krisztina's heart blazed with gratitude and pride.

"*C'était beau, chérie, n'est-ce pas?*" Geneviève said, embracing her, and her eyes, too, were wet with tears.

"More beautiful than I could have dreamed," Krisztina murmured, still absorbed in the tranquillity generated by the short service.

"It's extraordinary," Geneviève continued, her voice full of wonder. "The war has changed so much, and it's brought great good as well as evil." She watched as the others left the chapel ahead of them, Jeanne leading Olivier by the hand. "This could never have happened before. These people were always loyal, trusted friends, never just servants—but now I feel we have become a family."

They hugged once more, and then, sensitive as always, Geneviève crossed herself again, turned, and followed the others, leaving Krisztina for a moment's solitude.

She stared at the plaque.

DAVID KAUFMANN
1918–1942

There was another word, in Hebrew, which the rabbi had helped her to choose. *Shalom.* Peace. She raised the fingers of her right hand to her lips, then touched them to the engraved name. The first words of the Kaddish flickered into her mind:

Yis'gadal v'yis'kadash sh'mai raboh . . .

They tasted strange on her tongue, and she wondered what they meant. Then a picture of her mother came to her, devout and veiled in church, and a small tremor of confusion touched her, and quickly she, too, genuflected, made the sign of the cross, and left the chapel.

The others had returned to the château, and the afternoon was vivid with late summer sunshine and flowers, and birds sang jubilant hosannas in the trees beyond the garden wall.

She went out through the gate, and was just passing the graveyard when she noticed a man standing with his back to her, looking down at Laurent's tombstone.

He wore a lightweight summer suit, a raincoat was slung over his left shoulder, and he was very tall and, somehow, oddly familiar.

That hair, she thought. Red-gold in the sunlight.

He must have sensed her presence, for he turned to face her, and smiled.

"Hello," he said.

Chapter 18

Lieutenant Hunter and the two Baronnes talked all through the evening, through feathery vols-au-vent, grilled trout and *tarte aux cerises,* a feast put rapidly and enthusiastically together by Marthe—through two bottles of de Trouvère Riesling and a *vieille réserve* cognac, and on, late into the dark, warm September night.

He told them, in the excellent French they both remembered, of the shock of arrest following the three flyers' premature departure from their cellar refuge, and of the way their RAF uniforms had saved them from being shot as spies. He described their brief, unpleasant incarceration in a Gestapo prison, their transfer to two separate, adequately run prisoner-of-war camps near Augsburg in the south of Germany and, finally, the morning when he woke to find his own camp abandoned, the captors gone.

"The gates were wide open. We could have walked straight out."

"But you didn't?" Krisztina was still as rapt as she had been hours earlier.

"No. It was safer to stay put until the situation crystallized." He shrugged. "We organized ourselves, got wireless contacts set up, did what we could with what supplies were left, and waited." He smiled. "The American Seventh Army reached us first, on March twenty-seventh, and we were back in England two weeks later."

"So you were home for VE-day," said Geneviève.

"We certainly were."

"How's your arm?" asked Krisztina.

"Good as new." He flexed it. "It was a bit stiff for quite a while —the camp doctor wasn't what you'd call a specialist—but a physio back in London put it right."

"And the others? Eddie and Miller?"

A shadow crossed Hunter's face. "Miller's in good shape. He got married straight after he was demobbed."

"And Eddie?" Even as Geneviève spoke his name, she knew.

Hunter paused. "Eddie didn't make it."

There was a hush.

"What happened?" Krisztina was pale.

"It seems he couldn't stand it. Being cooped up. And he felt guilty, blamed himself for our arrest." His expression was grim. "Eddie was the least suitable candidate for escape. There were men in most of the camps who tried it," he explained. "Became almost professional escapologists. But with Eddie, it was too much like hysteria."

"He was caught?"

Hunter nodded.

"Shot?" whispered Krisztina.

"No. He saved them the bother. They put him in solitary, and he hanged himself with his belt."

The silence was horrified.

"If he hadn't been the one to whistle, I think he might have been okay." His eyes were remote and sad. "We were all warned, you see, about the good old tunes."

Krisztina closed her eyes. Geneviève stared into the empty fireplace.

Hunter drank some more cognac. "I get the chills whenever I hear that damned song. "Wish Me Luck as You Wave Me Goodbye." It's so bloody cheerful."

He had come to Alsace out of gratitude and because he wanted, intensely, to see them again under conditions of peace. He told them, too, that he had recommended them both for the King's Medal for Bravery. He hadn't known about Jacques Schneegans, and he resolved to see that Marthe might receive a posthumous award on her husband's behalf. They would all probably be asked to go to the British embassy in Paris for the presentation.

"But it's absurd," Geneviève protested in embarrassment. "Not for Jacques, of course, but we did nothing out of the ordinary."

Hunter smiled. "We all know exactly what you did, madame, and at what cost."

He stayed at de Trouvère as their guest for three weeks, growing more familiar with Geneviève and Krisztina, and taking an interest in Olivier, who was now increasingly active and as tempestuous a toddler as he had been an infant.

It was, of course, impossible to overlook the bizarre condition of the château, left as it had been in distressing disarray, but at first, when they dismissed it as "unfinished building work," Hunter was too discreet to comment further. But at last the moment came when they felt sufficiently at ease with him to disclose their problems.

He was appalled by their financial straits, fascinated by their solution, and disgusted with the bank's shortsighted attitude.

"Disgusted, but not surprised," he added. "Banks are notoriously fainthearted when it comes to medium-scale financing."

"They seem to regard this as rather large scale," Krisztina commented drily.

He laughed. "Don't believe a word of it. If you were multimillionaires, planning to build a hotel five times the size of de Trouvère starting from the foundations up, they would beg to lend you their money."

Geneviève's eyes narrowed. "Is it because we're women, William?"

He shrugged. "I'd like to deny it, but I have to admit it may be a factor—but it will only be part of their reason for backing out." He paused. "They'd be back with the right encouragement."

"Such as what?" Geneviève demanded. "We forget the fireplaces in every bathroom? Do without lifts? Paint the bedroom walls because the papers we've chosen are too dear?"

"Of course not," Hunter dismissed. "You both know as well as I that such retrenchment would only discourage them further."

"So what is this encouragement? This incentive to throw good money after bad?" Krisztina asked.

He waited an instant. "A backer. A backer is what you need."

"A backer?" Krisztina echoed.

"Yes. A patron. A guarantor."

Geneviève gave a snort of laughter. "Why not a saint? Or a guardian angel? Why stop there?"

"Because I can't sprout wings or a halo," he answered in amusement. "But I can back you."

They stared at him.

"Have I grown wings?"

Krisztina found her voice first. "You said you could back us."

"That's right."

"By which you meant what, exactly?"

He smiled. "I can't tell you exactly, not at this moment—that would require the presence of lawyers and accountants. But what I can say is that from all I've seen and heard, from the evidence of my eyes and from my own instinct, there is a distinct possibility that I—or rather, my family firm—might be able to supply the confidence your bankers lack."

"*Dieu,*" Geneviève said flatly. "I'm more confused than ever."

Hunter laughed. "Let me explain. This château is full—absolutely laden—with treasures. Gold, silver, porcelain, antiques that would make our auctioneers' eyes water, tapestries and works of art that some of the world's great museums would kill for."

"You think we can sell them?" Krisztina smiled wryly. "We've thought of it, believe me, but we'd never get anything close to what they're worth. And in any case, the hotel would need them in place, where they belong."

"Precisely," he said.

Geneviève frowned. "You mentioned *your* auctioneers."

"Yes."

"Your family firm—it's what, exactly?"

"An auction house, based in London, with branches in Paris and New York."

Her eyes widened. "Hunter's." She challenged him. *"Hunter's?"*

"That's right."

"But you said . . ." Her forehead creased with remembering. "When you were in the cellar, I asked how you knew so much about Kakiemon porcelain, and you said your family was in the antiques business."

"I did."

"But Hunter's is one of the great auction houses!"

"We're no Sotheby's or Christie's," he said modestly.

"And Olivier's great-great-grandmother was not Marie Antoinette," Geneviève retorted amiably, "but the de Trouvère family is still one of the most distinguished in Alsace." She grinned ironically. "Not that one would think it right now."

"I'm still finding this hard to follow," Krisztina interrupted them.

"I believe Lieutenant Hunter may be offering to sell some of our collections at auction," Geneviève ventured. "Though, even if such sales were to bring true value, we would still have stripped the château of its character."

"You're both under a misapprehension," Hunter said. "It's true that Hunter's is a firm of auctioneers." He paused. "But our buildings in London and New York also house two quite small but increasingly respected museums."

The Baronnes listened with new interest.

"I have an idea," he continued, "which, if it can be worked out both to my father's satisfaction and, of course, to your own, might resolve your cash crisis *and* restore the faith of your bankers."

The two women sat straighter, their mental antennae almost visibly sharpening.

Geneviève spoke first. "Dare we ask what your idea is, William?"

He shook his head. "I shouldn't like to suggest a commitment I may not be able to keep." He deliberated. "All I can say is that I see a situation where Hunter's might be able to assist you, without doing anything to detract from de Trouvère's beauty." He gave them a moment. "Will you trust me?"

They looked at his lean, intelligent face. There was something special about him, something fundamentally true.

"When will you leave?" Geneviève asked.

He laughed. "Not just yet. I need to do a little more groundwork before I go back to London with a solid proposal for our board. And I shall need your cooperation."

"Anything," Geneviève assured.

"Good. In that case, I shall ask certain colleagues of mine from our Paris office to join us here without delay." He hesitated. "They will need your permission to roam the château freely, perhaps for a week or even more."

Krisztina smiled. "There have been so many people in this house for so long now, it's been unnaturally quiet since Alberto took his men out."

"Has he left Alsace?" William asked quickly.

"Alberto?" Krisztina queried. "I don't think so."

"Then I think you should contact him without delay, and ask him to hold on." He rose. "And now, I need a telephone."

No less than eleven of Hunter's 'colleagues' came to call, sweeping down the south *allée* in a motley procession of automobiles, ranging from a magnificent 1939 Bentley Mark V ("They only built about twenty, you know," William told them), which bore Hunter's resident expert on imperial Chinese art, to a battered, pre-Depression Citroën, which carried the similarly battered-looking connoisseur of European porcelain. They arrived with small overnight bags, bland and expressionless, but more than a week later they were still ensconced in sundry unfinished bedrooms, increasingly prey to fits of jubilation, their often bespectacled eyes widening and glittering as de Trouvère's treasures unfolded before them.

If Krisztina and Geneviève had realized the splendor of their home, they had regarded it as an integral beauty. Now, for the first time, they had the opportunity to observe the many, varied components that made up the whole.

Almost every room yielded up glories, many far more valuable than they had ever paused to consider. In the Hunting Room alone, the experts had unearthed and certified ten Etruscan bronze and terra-cotta sculptures; two sixteenth-century Persian hunting carpets; a Cretan sword and two bronze daggers with handles inlaid with gold, silver, and niello; an exquisite nineteenth-century marquetry table and a pair of ferocious animal paintings by Antoine Barye; not to mention a remarkable English Coalbrookdale table supported by four Irish wolfhounds at each corner, a great favorite of the late Baron Armand.

William left de Trouvère at the end of the third week, one day after the specialists had packed up and departed for Paris. It was another three weeks before he telephoned.

"Well?" Krisztina demanded, after only the hastiest courtesies.

"The board gave their decision half an hour ago."

"Yes?"

"Is Geneviève with you?"

"Yes, she is."

"Good. Please give her my best wishes."

"William, please! What did the board say?"

The line crackled.

"William!"

The static vanished, and his voice, strong and distinct and so ineffably British in spite of his excellent French, breached the four hundred miles between them.

"Call Giordano. Tell him to collect his men, and to stand by."

Krisztina clutched at Geneviève with her free hand. "You mean it's all right?"

"There's a load of paperwork to be done, and we still need the bank's cooperation, but . . ."

"What if they won't?" Fresh panic rose.

Hunter's words rang with confidence.

"Believe me, Krisztina. They will."

He returned to de Trouvère, having spent three days with Dienheim at the bank, and over a resplendent dinner prepared by Marthe and Krisztina together, he explained the extraordinary bargain that Hunter's were ready to strike, should the two Baronnes agree.

The simplicity of his scheme was stunning. Hunter's would lease a great quantity of works of art, antique porcelain, silver and gold, furniture, and certain items of family jewellery, but everything would remain *in situ* at the château, on the written understanding that any piece, or group, could be withdrawn at any time, with reasonable notice, for exhibition purposes and also, in the last resort, for sale by Hunter's, though Geneviève and Krisztina would have first option to buy any item before it was offered to another party.

"And instead of paying you in cash," William finished, "we shall guarantee your bank loan. And if the building and initial running costs of the hotel exceed the bank's available resources, then we shall either back you ourselves, or arrange another loan."

"So all our problems are solved with a few strokes of the pen," Geneviève said slowly, hardly able to believe it.

"But why?" Krisztina asked, speaking for both of them. "What do Hunter's hope to achieve from this arrangement?" She shook her head. "After all, you could simply insist on buying some works for exhibition and auctioning the remainder—we're not in any real position to keep them here, no matter how painful their loss would be."

"Firstly," William answered, "we shall effectively own the pieces until such a time as the hotel is running at a healthy profit."

"Which might not be for years, if ever," Krisztina pointed out.

"Possibly," he agreed, and continued. "Which brings me to my second point. Hunter's has decided that de Trouvère is a worthwhile investment to add to our portfolio. It will, as you might expect, be necessary for our respective accountants and lawyers to set up an agreeable working company in which we shall be partners—but I can promise you both that, within reason, we shall be conscientiously silent partners."

"Surely your board will demand reassurances that we're running the hotel efficiently?" Geneviève asked.

"They've already had and, I'm sure, will continue to have such reassurances from me." He smiled. "Unless glaringly obvious mistakes come to our attention, we'll leave it to you. We are auctioneers, not hoteliers."

Geneviève pulled a wry face. "We can hardly claim to be experts ourselves, William."

"Perhaps not, but you've already demonstrated that you'll seek specialist help where and when you need it. And I'm also certain, Geneviève, that you've stayed in more *grand luxe* establishments than most people I know."

"If that were a qualification," she scoffed, "tens of thousands would open hotels."

"But how many have the desire or ability, let alone the raw material that you're blessed with?" He paused. "There's a third factor, though it's one that neither my father nor I put before our board."

"What's that?" Krisztina asked.

His face was somber. "I remember—indeed, I shall never forget—in the cellar that remarkable first night, I drank a toast in Château Pape-Clément, to gallantry, generosity, and style. To that, I should now add gratitude."

"For what?" Geneviève said ironically. "For more than two years in a prison camp?"

"You know very well for what," he said steadfastly, refusing to be put off. "The King's Medal for Bravery is fine, and a salute to your courage, but it won't open the doors to your hotel, nor will it save de Trouvère for Olivier."

Krisztina looked at Geneviève. "He's right," she said softly.
Geneviève nodded. "I know, *chérie.*"

Work began again, and the château was filled with vitality, the
air thick with grime and the smell of paint. The sound of ham-
mering and sawing and drilling and the amiable shouted abuse
hurled between men from Marseilles and Milan, and Lyon and
Naples—men who had come to de Trouvère as strangers, but
who now seemed as much a part of the house as Alberto Giordano himself.

Ilona, granted permission by her physicians to leave Semmering, came to de Trouvère with Gabor a few days before Christmas. Though it was understood that they would live in
Ribeauvillé until work was completed, Geneviève and Krisztina
both agreed that over the holidays they should all be together, *en
famille,* under one roof.

It was a golden time, a halcyon spell when it seemed possible to
believe that all trouble, all evil was behind them, and that only
peace and gladness lay ahead. Krisztina watched her father
quickly throw off the mantle of humility and despair with which
the Russians and his wife's illness had covered him, and she observed, with wry amusement, how his still-snobbish heart swelled
with pride at the sight of so much grandeur and beauty. This was
the genuine manifestation of the nobility to which he had always
aspired—daughter a baronne, grandson already a baron, his future home a château.

Yet it was Ilona, in her quiet, modest way, who seemed to slip
most easily into life at de Trouvère, who sat, with a natural grace
and refinement, beside Geneviève at their *Réveillon* dinner.
Ilona, thin, not yet strong and still mourning Hungary, became
effortlessly absorbed into the fabric of the de Trouvère family,
while her husband, yearning to belong, remained frustratingly
peripheral despite his own efforts and Geneviève's courtesy.

They attended midnight mass in Colmar and on Christmas
morning went to Père Perigot's service in Riquewihr. In the
early afternoon, having made certain that she was well wrapped
against the cold, Krisztina took her mother to see the chapel and
found her, for the first time, in awe.

It was as they were leaving that Ilona noticed David's memorial plaque on the wall. Swiftly, she turned to her daughter,
white-faced and shocked.

"You didn't tell me!"

"No, Mama."

"Why not?"

"I didn't want to distress you."

"You should have told me, Kriszti," Ilona said, without stricture. "When did you hear?"

Briefly, Krisztina explained, described the service they had arranged, and translated the Hebrew word on the plaque.

Ilona remained silent for several moments.

"Mama? What are you thinking?"

Ilona shook her head. "Many things." She smiled wistfully. "Geneviève is a remarkable person."

"I could not have survived the last eight years without her."

Her mother touched her cheek with one gloved hand. "I think you could, Krisztina, but I thank God for her all the same."

There was joy in the house of de Trouvère.

On New Year's Eve, William came from Paris to join them, and for the first time Sutterlin, Marthe, Jeanne, and the others came up from the basement to share the family celebration, to which Alberto, too, had been invited.

"It's extraordinary," William said, a half hour into 1947, as Krisztina strolled with him around the château, showing him the progress that had been achieved since his last visit.

"What is?"

"It's almost there. It's still, irrevocably, your home, and yet it is going to be the Grand Hôtel du Château de Trouvère that we've all dreamed about."

Emotion constricted her throat.

"How will we ever be able to thank you?" she asked, a sudden fresh burst of gratitude almost choking her.

William stared down at her, his expression cryptic.

"There is one thing that you can do for me, Krisztina," he said softly.

"Anything," she whispered fervently.

He smiled, and warmth lit up his face.

"Learn to speak English."

Chapter 19

"I never thought I would live to say this." Geneviève laughed as she passed Ilona another cup of coffee one Sunday morning in early March, "but yet again I thank the good Lord for the German language. Without it, we'd hardly be able to communicate."

"I wish my French were better," Ilona apologized.

"Why should your French be any better than my Hungarian? After all, I've lived with your daughter for years and still speak no more than ten words."

They were in the Summer Room, an oasis of calm in what still remained a sea of wood shavings, varnish, and general confusion. Krisztina smiled as she watched her father and Olivier playing on the rug with a spinning top the child never tired of. "At least my son will grow up mastering four languages—or five, if Alberto is with us much longer."

"Your English is vastly improved," Geneviève commented. "William was delighted on his last visit."

"He would be," Gabor said. "Romance is easier with a common language."

Krisztina's eyes widened. "Romance?"

"Any fool can see the man's in love with you."

"Of course he isn't," she denied hotly.

He shrugged. "If you say so. But you must have asked yourself why a stranger was so keen to do so much for you."

"I'm sure we've explained that more than once," Krisztina said peaceably. "We were able to help him during the war, and he's in an unusual position to repay us. It's just a simple business arrangement."

"Hardly simple." He spun Olivier's top again, ruffling his hair. *"Kis cigany,"* he said fondly.

"What does that mean, Gabor?" asked Geneviève.

"Little gypsy."

Krisztina laughed. "That's what Mama called him the first time they met."

Geneviève chuckled. "I often think he looks like a little Spaniard, or perhaps a Jewish child."

"Don't talk damned nonsense!" Gabor snarled, startling them all.

"Gabor!" Ilona, clearly upset, turned to Geneviève. "Gabor didn't mean—"

"Don't make excuses for me!" he shouted. "If she's going to insult our grandson—"

"I assure you," Geneviève interjected calmly, "there was no insult, and please don't forget that Olivier is my grandson too."

Krisztina had grown white with anger. "You'll never change, will you, Father?"

"Ça va, chérie," Geneviève said easily. "Don't upset yourself. It was just a misunderstanding."

"No misunderstanding." Krisztina stood up and retrieved Olivier from the floor. "My father has always been an anti-Semite, Belle-mère. Nothing has altered."

"Nem, Kriszti!" Ilona protested in distress.

"I'm sorry, Mama, but you know as well as I do that it's the truth."

Gabor, still scarlet with anger and humiliation, spoke tightly. "I'm sure Geneviève can understand, Krisztina. After all, her own son shared my feelings on that particular subject."

"Gabor, please!" Ilona appealed.

Geneviève sat stock-still, only the pallor of her skin revealing her emotion. "We all make mistakes, Monsieur Florian," she said evenly. "Some worse than others." Her eyes were gray and chilly. "My son made his share, perhaps more, but he is not here to defend himself."

Shutting her eyes, Ilona crossed herself, and Olivier, in Krisztina's arms, began to wail loudly, his sturdy legs kicking furiously at his mother's midriff as she attempted to quiet him.

"It's no good," she said, "I'll have to take him upstairs." The boy's screaming reached full pitch. "Olivier, *chut!*" she rebuked fiercely.

"Ilona," Geneviève said gently, "why don't you go with them? You're often the only one who can calm him when he's like this."

"Yes, please, Mama, do come up."

Ilona cast a doubtful glance at her husband, who now glared balefully out at the terrace. "All right, Kriszti." Wearily, she got to her feet and they left the room, closing the door softly behind them.

The room was silent but for the ticking of the old Italian clock on the mantel. Geneviève studied Gabor indifferently, taking in the disgruntled hunch of his shoulders, the downward tilt of his mouth, and the scowling bespectacled eyes.

How disagreeable he is, she thought.

The clock struck five.

"So, Gabor," she said quite pleasantly, "how are we to resolve this?"

"What have we to resolve?" He did not look at her.

"This—conflict."

"Can't we agree to differ?"

"Certainly we can, but I should like to ensure that there will be no repetition. It's most upsetting to us all, particularly to your wife, who is still far from strong."

"I'll look after my wife, thank you."

"I hope so." She found herself more than ever surprised that such a charmless man could have ever won a woman of Ilona's caliber, let alone have fathered Krisztina. "But I must make one thing perfectly clear."

He threw her a look of intense dislike. "And what's that?"

"I know what your prejudices and ambition cost your daughter . . ."

"That's hardly your business."

"You are mistaken, Gabor Florian," she said witheringly. "It has become my business, and when you come to live in my house, I intend to protect Krisztina from any more hurt."

"I'm not sure I wish to live in your house, madame."

"We both know you have nowhere else to go, so please hear me out."

He said nothing.

"I think we can all get along quite civilly," she continued, "so long as you keep your bigoted and unacceptable opinions to yourself. Have I made myself clear?"

"Quite."

"Good." She smiled, and picked up the silver coffeepot from the tray on the table beside her. "Another cup?"

Upstairs, in Olivier's nursery, Ilona sank into an armchair. "I wish you and your father could try to understand each other, Kriszti," she said miserably.

Krisztina watched her son, who had fallen into a deep sleep. "Some things are impossible, Mama."

"I thought that, too, until you met with him in Vienna and arranged all this. Then I began to hope . . ." She shook her head.

Krisztina came to her and knelt on the carpet. "I'm sorry, Mama, but you mustn't ask too much of me."

"Can you live with him, do you think?"

Krisztina hesitated, then saw the fear on her mother's face. "I think so. I hope so." She paused. "He has to understand that I'm no longer a child, Mama, that I'm a grown woman with a life and child of my own." Her mouth tightened. "And that I find his ideas repugnant."

Ilona sighed. "If only I felt stronger, I could cope so much better, try to make him see—"

"He was always too dogmatic for that. It was never easy to criticize anything he said or did."

"But if I were more myself, I could at least try."

"You're still weak, Mama," Krisztina reassured her. "It's natural."

"But that's just it—I don't *feel* natural anymore!" Ilona's eyes were filled with panic. "I feel I've lost everything, yet I know I haven't, that I'm being appallingly ungrateful and that God should punish me. . . ."

"You've lost your home," Krisztina protested. "You've been forced to leave your country and you've been very ill. Of course you have a sense of loss."

"But I still have my husband, and I have a grandchild, and, most important, I have you again." Tears came suddenly, splashing unhindered down her cheeks. "That's why I beg you to try again with Gabor, *dragam*! Otherwise I'm afraid I may lose you a second time, and if that happened, I think I would die! I would *want* to die!"

"Mama, don't!" Krisztina was horrified by her eruption of unhappiness. "Of course you won't lose me. You never lost me, not even for an instant, all the years we were apart."

"But I don't want us to be parted ever again!"

"Nor do I, darling, and we shan't be, I swear it." Krisztina stroked her mother's hair, neatly pinned back from her distraught, crumpled face. "The hotel will soon be finished, and then we can all be together all the time."

Ilona found a handkerchief in her pocket and wiped her eyes, recovering her composure. "I'm sorry," she said. She stood up shakily and looked down at Olivier, so tranquil in slumber.

"Kriszti?" she said pensively.

"Yes, Mama?"

"Was Gabor right about Lieutenant Hunter?"

"About what?"

"You know quite well, *dragam*." Ilona's voice was calm again. "Is he in love with you?"

Krisztina did not look at her. "I'm not sure. He may be. He's never said a word."

"I doubt that he would, at this stage. He's too English."

Krisztina smiled. "He's the first Englishman I've known—apart from the two sergeants who were with him during the war."

"And you? Are you in love with him?"

Krisztina shook her head. "No." She hesitated. "That is, not in the sense that I was in love with David."

"Or your husband?"

"I was never in love with Laurent."

"No."

"William is a very special man, Mama. A rare person."

"And striking," Ilona added quietly.

Krisztina nodded. "That hair is extraordinary—such red-gold, yet not a freckle on his face."

"And his eyes."

"You've noticed them too." Krisztina chuckled.

Ilona looked at her. "I think you are falling in love with him, just a little."

Krisztina's eyes were candid. "I've honestly never thought about him in that way, Mama. So much has happened, our lives have been so busy, and I'm so deeply grateful to him for what he's made possible—I should hate to confuse gratitude with anything stronger."

"That would be wrong," Ilona agreed gently. "But don't forget, Kriszti, that a good marriage, a lasting marriage, is built from many more things than idyllic, passionate love."

"Marriage?" Krisztina laughed. "Whatever are you saying, Mama?" Olivier stirred, and she lowered her voice. "Whatever are we both saying? Neither of us has the remotest idea of how William feels about me—or even if he feels anything at all."

William was biding his time.

He felt—he certainly felt. There was not an ounce, not a milligram of doubt about the way he felt about Krisztina. He had fallen in love with her at first sight, when the little *Résistance* girl had brought him and his companions to the château.

He supposed, in a sense, that he had fallen in love with both of them, Krisztina *and* Geneviève; two courageous, remarkable women, prepared to risk their home, even their lives, for three total strangers. But while his profound gratitude for the elegant Geneviève would never fade, it was Krisztina's beauty that had bewitched him. It had haunted him through the nerve-wrenching nights in the cellar, and bolstered him through the endless months in the POW camp where he had first begun to fantasize about her, a mingling of memories and dreams that had sustained him in the cold light of more than seven hundred German dawns.

He'd visited de Trouvère often—as often as he could find time or excuses—and he'd learned much about her. He'd seen sadness in her lovely face, and regret, frustration, anger and vulnerability, strength and determination too. He had experienced real joy when the board of Hunter's had delivered their positive verdict on the hotel project, and acute, trembling delight the first time Krisztina had felt comfortable enough with him to plant a kiss on his cheek.

He'd met her parents, been charmed by her mother and disturbed by her father, and he'd learned about David Kaufmann and Laurent de Trouvère. And though the still-pristine headstone in the family graveyard occasionally reproached him, it was the little gold plaque nailed to the chapel wall that troubled him and continued to warn him off. He knew that though she was the late Baron's widow, Krisztina was still grieving for Kaufmann, and was not yet ready for another man to enter her life.

William did not know if she would ever be ready, and so he was biding his time.

It was on a hot August afternoon, just after William had arrived for a few days' stay at de Trouvère before driving south to join his parents at their holiday villa in Villefranche-sur-mer, that life changed dramatically for Krisztina.

She was lying on a large white turkish towel spread on the grass about twenty yards from the *temple d'amour* near the lake. The afternoon heat was sticky and oppressive, but Krisztina had discovered the comparative coolness of this tree-sheltered spot during their last heat wave.

She had removed her cotton robe, sunbathed for a time, and then slipped into the cool, clear water of the lake before returning to lie on the towel. After a while, she took a plump mirabelle plum from a *panier* into which she'd tossed one of Geneviève's favorite Agatha Christie novels—which she was finding a great boost to her English—another dry towel, and a bottle of tanning oil.

Glory be, she thought, *this is even better than Balaton.* She smiled and stretched, catlike. *Who'd have believed it possible? My very own private Balaton.*

"You look happy."

She sat up with a start, her heart pounding.

Gabor stood on the temple steps, looking down at her. He was dressed in the short-sleeved white shirt and well-cut lightweight trousers that Ilona had bought for him as a birthday gift in Strasbourg, and with the suntan he'd acquired since they'd moved into the château, he looked a little younger and more relaxed than he had for years.

"Father! You frightened me."

"I'm sorry."

"How long have you been there?"

"For about an hour."

"Why didn't you tell me?"

"I was sitting in the shade, reading. And you looked as if you wanted to be by yourself."

"I did."

"I'm sorry," he said again. "I'll go."

She felt ashamed. "No, don't, please. It was only that you startled me. I thought I was alone."

"I often come here," Gabor said.

"Do you?"

"It's a little like Balaton, isn't it?"

She smiled. "Yes, it is."

He came slowly down the steps. "It's hot today." He took a handkerchief from his pocket and mopped his brow. *"Quelle chaleur."* He grimaced.

"Your French is getting better, Father."

"Little by little."

Krisztina was suddenly aware that her bathing suit had become slightly transparent with wetness, but Gabor's eyes were focused on the creamy château on the hill in the distance.

"So when will it be?" he asked. "The opening."

"Christmas, hopefully."

A pure white butterfly landed on her foot, and neither of them moved until it had flown away.

"That's good luck," Gabor said softly. "I hope so, Kriszti."

She was surprised. There had been few kind or sincere words between them since that unpleasantness earlier in the year. "Thank you, Father."

He looked down at her. "You'll burn."

"No, I won't."

"You haven't oiled yourself."

"I have."

"Not your back. Your shoulders are quite dry."

"I couldn't reach." She regretted the words the instant they were spoken.

"Let me."

"They're fine, Father."

Hurt flickered over his face. "I know you won't ever call me Papa again, Krisztina—I know we can't forget the past. But will you never allow me to do anything for you, even the smallest thing?" He gave a little smile. "I always did that when you were a child."

A brief memory of hot summer Sundays in the little garden at Kalvaria Street pierced her with long-forgotten sweetness. *Dishes of her mother's homemade ice cream, Miksa lying lazily in the sunshine, her Papa, so kind and gentle, rubbing cream into her skin . . .*

"I'm not a child anymore."

She caught a glimpse of pain in his eyes just before he turned to walk away, the weary, aging slump back in his shoulders.

"You're right, Father," she said quickly, stopping him. "I am a

little sore." She reached for the bottle, and held it out to him.
"Here, but not too much or it'll stain my costume."

"Thank you, Kriszti."

She heard the gratitude in his voice, and was glad she had
relented. She remembered her Bible lessons: *And be ye kind one
to another, tenderhearted, forgiving one another,* and she realized guiltily that worse than being a poor Catholic, she was not
even a good Christian, for she knew she would never be able to
forgive him for the loss of David.

Gabor unscrewed the cap of the bottle and crouched behind
her on the grass. She heard the little gurgle of oil as he tipped it
onto his hand, and then his palm touched her back, between her
shoulder blades and, involuntarily, she shivered slightly.

The hand moved over her skin, lingering, rubbing, sliding, and
another memory returned to the forefront of Krisztina's mind,
the one she had almost allowed to be submerged in the greater
sins against her love.

"So smooth," Gabor said softly, and must have felt the goose-
flesh rising on her, but continued regardless.

"That's all right, Father," she said clearly. "Thank you."

"Just your shoulders, *dragam.*"

With the dry fingers of his left hand, he tugged at the strap of
her bathing suit, and Krisztina felt suddenly sick. She reached up
and snatched the strap from his hand. "Then hurry, please, or it'll
hardly be worthwhile—I have to get back to the house."

"You've only been here twenty minutes."

He was watching me all the time, she thought, with revulsion.
Spying on me, like a loathsome peeping Tom. She jerked forward,
away from him.

"Kriszti, what is it?"

She turned to face him, was conscious of his eyes, magnified by
his spectacles, riveted, in spite of himself, by her erect nipples,
still visible through the damp costume.

"I should have known better."

"What do you mean?"

"So innocent," she said with contempt. "Just sitting reading."

"That's right."

"The gentle father, wronged by his daughter—"

"I never said that, Kriszti."

"And don't call me Kriszti!" She was aware of a growing hysteria that she was unable to control, of old horrors returning from the past.

"That's easier said than done," Gabor said, the wounded expression back on his face. "I called you Kriszti all through your childhood, just as you called me your Papa."

"That was before you stole David's business like a common thief!" Each word was like a whiplash. "Before you forbade me to see the man I loved!" She stared into his face. "You even used Laurent for your own ends—"

"Laurent used me!" he protested.

"I have no doubt that he did, but you were my *father.* You should have wanted only to protect me and those I loved."

"I did, Kriszti! Just see what you have now!" He gestured wildly around them. "All this beauty! And you do love de Trouvère, don't you?"

"I may have learned to love it, yes, but you should have let me stay at home in Budapest and marry David."

"If you had married him, you'd probably be dead now too."

"Perhaps that was my right, Father."

"You see?" he tried to reason. "You still need my protection, even if you don't realize it. You're *irrational,* Krisztina. You have everything, yet you hanker after one miserable dead Jew."

The desire to spit in his face was so intense that she had to clench every muscle to stop herself.

"You do need me, you know, *dragam,*" he went on, pleadingly.

"For what? To creep into my bedroom here some night, the way you did at home?" Her flesh crawled with repugnance at the memory. "To put your arms around me like my Papa, when all the time you just wanted . . ." Her eyes were dry, yet suddenly there were painful, gut-wrenching sobs contorting her voice and her face.

"My God, Kriszti, no! Of course not!" He came toward her, arms outstretched, face beseeching. "You don't know what you're saying!"

"Do you think I've forgotten that night?" she sobbed, and it was as if all her hard-earned maturity had deserted her, as if she were a young girl again, vulnerable and scared. "It was the thing that finally pushed me into leaving, into marrying Laurent, didn't you realize that?"

"No!"

"Of course you knew, you must have known! I did it because I thought it might save David's life, but you were the last straw—I couldn't stay in the same house as you, because I couldn't look at Mama, and I knew I could never tell her!"

"Kriszti, oh, Kriszti." With a clumsy, lumbering movement he came at her, tried to embrace her, but with a cry of revulsion she pulled away.

"Don't *touch* me!"

He persisted, his arms strong, seeming to her like steel bonds. She struggled violently, freed her right hand and swung it up to try to slap him away.

"Kriszti, stop it!" He caught at her wrist. "I only want to—"

"Let me go!" With her other hand she clawed at his face and he gave a little cry of shock, but instead of stepping away from her he tried one more time to grab her.

"Let her go, you bastard!"

The voice, thundering from behind, startled them both. The fist, strongly clenched and white-knuckled, smashed into Gabor's face and sent him reeling, blood spurting from his nose.

"William!"

He stood at Krisztina's side, his crisp flannels giving him the appearance of a cricketer about to stroll onto a tranquil English pitch, but his face so tightly drawn with fury that he almost frightened her.

"Are you all right?" he asked, his eyes locked on Gabor.

"Yes," she whispered.

"You're mad!" Gabor whimpered, dabbing gingerly at his nose with his handkerchief and staring at the blood on it.

"That's right, look at it!" William rapped. "That's your blood, Florian. And there'll be more of it shed if you ever, ever go near Krisztina again!"

"But you don't understand! She went crazy! She thought—"

"I know what she thought, and I swear to you that if she weren't standing here right now, and if it weren't for her mother, I would kill you."

"You *are* mad!"

"There are words for men like you, Florian."

"What?" Gabor began to recover. "Who do you think you are, Hunter?"

"I know exactly who I am. More to the point, I know what you are."

"What am I?" Gabor demanded, his face almost apoplectic.

William advanced again, and Gabor stepped quickly back in fresh alarm. "You're an evil bastard, and if that weren't enough, you're a perverted son of a bitch!"

"Perverted, am I?"

"William, please!" Krisztina pleaded.

"She isn't even my daughter!"

The words hung in the air, reverberating. Everything seemed to stop, even the birdsong stilled for a few stunned moments.

"Well, she isn't!" Gabor blurted, stupefied with growing panic, the flaming color dying from his cheeks except for two bright red spots. "We adopted her when she was a baby. We never told her, but it's true, I swear it!"

Krisztina was staring at him, her eyes torn wide with horror.

"Don't look like that, Kriszti," Gabor implored her. "I didn't mean to tell you now, it's only that he *accused* me . . ." He groped for words. "It makes no difference. You *are* my daughter, our child, just as if you were our own flesh and blood!"

She could not speak.

"In God's name, Kriszti, please!"

William recovered first. Ignoring the trembling older man, he turned to Krisztina.

"Come on," he said softly. "Let's get you away from here."

She still stared at Gabor, transfixed.

"You've had a shock," William cajoled her, as kindly as if she were a child. "Let's go home."

"No." Her voice was hoarse. She turned frantic eyes on him. "Not the house, not yet!"

"All right," he soothed. "Somewhere else. Somewhere private where you can take your time, as much as you need." He picked up her robe and put it around her shoulders, feeling her cold, quivering skin through the thin cotton. "Come on."

"My things . . ."

"I'll come back for them later. I'm going to fetch you something dry to wear before you catch your death of cold."

"No!" she said again. "Don't leave me!"

"It's all right. We'll go to the chapel—there'll be no one there now—and I'll be back with some clothes before you know it."

She looked up at him. "How did you get here?" Her voice was dull. "We weren't expecting you till tomorrow."

"I got away sooner. I saw Geneviève at the house, and she told me you'd come out here to get some sun."

Krisztina looked back at Gabor, standing silent now, shame, anguish, and resentment all visible in his expression and posture.

"*Venez,*" William nudged quietly.

Numbly, she nodded.

More than an hour later, they still sat in the chapel, side by side on a front pew. Krisztina huddled in the frayed cashmere pullover William had quickly dragged from his suitcase in the château, an ancient but favorite sweater that he took on all his travels. He'd turned his back while Krisztina removed her damp bathing suit, and when he looked at her again, he had thought that, in spite of the misery of the moment, he had never in his entire life seen anything quite so sensual as this shivering, unhappy young woman, clad in nothing but an oversized, almost dress-length man's pullover.

"Nothing really happened, you know," she said.

"I know." He paused. "But something happened before in the past?"

She nodded, wordlessly.

"Shall you tell your mother?"

Krisztina looked up, aghast. "Of course not!"

"No, not about that. I meant to say, will you ask her?"

"About what he said?"

"Yes."

She stared at the altarpiece. "I don't know. Not yet."

"Do you have a choice?"

She shook her head in confusion. "It's strange," she said. "There are so many turning points in life when you think, this must be it, the end of my childhood, or youth, or immaturity. Now I'm an adult, now I know better, now there can't be so many shocks. But I'm a grown woman, William, a mother, and there are *still* more, always more." She shrugged helplessly, tears in her eyes. "Does it ever end?"

"I wish I knew."

"But this is the best yet, isn't it?" she said bitterly. "If he was speaking the truth, then I don't even know who I really am."

William hardly trusted himself to move. The scent of her, a mixture of sun oil and perfume and her own natural fragrance, was almost too much to bear. He longed, more than anything, to hold her tightly, to brush that soft curve where her neck ended and her perfect, straight shoulders began, to comfort her with kisses—but he couldn't even take her hand.

"You know exactly who you are," he said huskily. "You're the same person, the same woman you were two hours ago."

"Am I?" she asked wanly.

To hell with this, he thought, finding her sorrow unbearable. With a sudden determined movement, he reached out and seized her right hand. It was as if he had made a statement; it was no simple gesture of friendship, but a declaration of solidarity and something more besides—a challenge.

He waited.

Her face itself showed nothing, no surprise, no displeasure, nothing at all, but her eyes grew perceptibly darker.

Still he waited.

Her hand, long-fingered and slender, wriggled slightly, seemed to understand that it was not to be released, and gave up. Then, slowly, and just as purposefully as his, though with greater delicacy, her left hand rose from her lap where it had lain, and covered his.

She had accepted his challenge.

A sharp tweak of memory nudged him.

"I hate to move," he said, "but I've just remembered that I brought something for you." He took a small velvet box from his pocket and placed it on Krisztina's left knee. "Open it."

She lifted the lid. A pair of earclips sat on black velvet, two square-cut sapphires surrounded by tiny diamonds, set gracefully in white gold.

"But why?" she asked.

"Don't you like them?"

"Like them?" Her mouth was dry with astonishment. "They're exquisite! How could anyone fail to like them?"

"So don't just sit there. Put them on."

Quickly, she obeyed, hands trembling, and turned her face up to him. "How do they look?"

His eyes scanned her face, took in each tender earlobe, swept up to her smooth forehead, then down past her straight nose and mouth and chin, down her neck and on. . . .

"What are you doing?" she asked weakly.

"Enjoying the view."

"I asked you how they look."

"The earrings?"

"Yes, the earrings."

He smiled. "How do you think they look?"

They sat a while longer, but some of the strain had gone out of her. Though the bulk of her thoughts remained concentrated on the distressing mystery Gabor had flung at her, a portion of her mind realized that she had another enigma to unravel, one that she already knew would be far less dangerous and infinitely more delicious.

"Krisztina?"

"Yes?"

There was a tightness in his chest. "I'm in love with you."

The chapel was very quiet.

"Krisztina? Did you hear me?"

"I did."

"So what do you think?"

"I'm thinking."

"Shall I say it again?" he asked pleasantly.

"Yes, please."

"Je vous aime."

"Rather formal," she said softly.

The late afternoon sunbeams spread light in great streaks over the stone and wood, and over them.

"I'd like to go now," William said.

"Would you?" She sounded disappointed.

"Do you want to know why?"

"Please."

"Because I want to kiss you. And I feel inhibited in here." He paused. "Do you mind?"

"Not at all."

They kissed, just outside the chapel, as soon as the door was closed, a long, searching, satisfying kiss, neither tentative nor a wild collision, but a confident, tender union, laden with warmth and pleasure.

When they finally drew apart, William felt his pulses racing with relief and joy, and his eyes were as moist as Krisztina's.

Ilona blanched when Krisztina came to her.

"Mother of God, *why*? Why did he tell you?"

"We had . . . words." Krisztina had determined that her mother would never learn what had really happened between them.

"Jesszus-Maria!" Ilona burst out in despair. "To tell you that in a fit of temper!"

"Perhaps he was right." Krisztina was oddly calm.

"Right?" The echo was incredulous.

"Isn't it time I knew the truth, Mama?"

Ilona seemed to shrink before her steady gaze.

"Won't you tell me now?"

Ilona sagged.

"I will."

Krisztina felt like a lone passenger on a small boat caught in a tumultuous storm, being tossed about on great, wild waves. She heard her mother—or rather the woman she had believed all her life to be her mother—tell her about a young, nameless woman murdered, dragged from a Hungarian river . . . about Jozsef Szabo, a priest with dark, sad eyes Krisztina recalled only vaguely from her childhood . . . about a man and a woman, dissatisfied and incomplete, whose lives had been transformed by what they saw as a gift from God . . . about happiness and confusion and torment . . .

"Kriszti?"

She hardly saw Ilona. "Yes, Mama."

Ilona was fearful. "What are you thinking?"

"I don't know." Krisztina shook her head. "I'm numb."

"Aren't you angry?" All through the telling of her story, Ilona had fought against tears. Now they shone in her eyes, still unshed. "Bitter?"

"No."

"Don't you hate me?"

"For what? For loving me?"

"For keeping the truth from you." Ilona's mind reeled, her guilt terrible. Truth? She still had not told the truth, not the whole truth.

Krisztina was struggling for comprehension. "Why didn't you tell me?"

Ilona stared unhappily at her. "There never seemed any reason. The time never seemed right." She took a big, gulping breath. "You made us so happy. You were our child. We never considered that we might be depriving you of anything, of anyone."

"Of my mother." Krisztina's voice was hushed.

"She was gone."

"And my father?"

"You could never have traced him, Kriszti." The tears began to fall.

"Did you ever try?"

"Jozsef tried."

Krisztina's brow was creased in helpless confusion. "And you never learned anything about her? Was there *nothing*?"

The knowledge of the hidden Star of David burned like a monstrous scar into Ilona's mind, and with it the cruel irony of the memorial plaque to David Kaufmann. *It's her* right *to know,* she thought desperately, and for one wild moment she yearned, as she had so often before, to share the secret she had carried for twenty-eight years. But then she remembered, as she had always done, Gabor, and she thought of the name of de Trouvère, and of little Olivier, the twenty-seventh baron, and of all the anti-Semites there still were in the world. . . .

"Mama?" Krisztina's face was so pale, so questioning. "Was there nothing?"

"No," Ilona answered absolutely. "Nothing at all."

"So how *do* you feel?" William asked her later, in the Salon Rouge.

"I just wish they'd told me," Krisztina said passionately. "I think that's the only part of it that really troubles me."

"But you understand why they didn't, don't you?"

"Yes, of course, but that doesn't make it right."

"No." He studied her.

"What about my real mother and father? How will I ever know anything about them?"

"You won't," he said gently.

"No." She bit her lip. "She said that it was a wild, insane time in Hungary."

"Not just in Hungary, darling."

"She's right about that, I know. There would have been no record of one tiny human tragedy when millions had just died— were still dying."

William frowned. "That's all very rational, my love," he said gently, "but it's not going to help you, is it?"

"And what is going to help me?" she asked bitterly.

"Talk to Geneviève."

"Burden her with more of my problems?"

"She's your closest friend, isn't she?"

"Yes, but—"

"And a very wise woman." William paused. "And then I think you should let go." He reached out and touched her cheek with tender fingers and saw her mouth quiver. "Let out some of that grief you're feeling, shed some of those tears you're holding back."

Krisztina shook her head. "I've wept too much today already."

He moved closer to her on the *dormeuse*. "As someone once said, there's a time and place for just about everything. And it seems to me, Krisztina, my love, that this, as sure as May follows April, is the time, and this"—he drew her head gently down onto his shoulder—"is the place."

Chapter 20

"Sheets."

"Fifty double, one hundred single."

"Pillowcases."

"Two hundred monogrammed, two hundred plain."

"Couvertures?"

"Same as the sheets."

"Saucepans."

"Twelve, different sizes, half copper, half silver."

"Cocottes."

"Five."

"Iron pans."

"Seven."

"Sauté pans."

"Five. And five omelet pans."

"Marmites."

"Five. Oh, and Marthe says that a tinker comes twice a year to reline the copper pans."

"André, has the champagne arrived?"

"Oui, madame."

"The Pol Roger?"

"Yes."

"The Perrier-Jouet?"

"Yes."

"And the Cristal?"

"Not yet, madame."

"Merde!"

"I agree, madame, but I'm assured the delivery will be here in time for the opening."

"I should hope so! Though I suppose we must be grateful there's any champagne left in France. Do you know that more than six million bottles vanished before the war ended, André?"

"The *Boches* have much to answer for, madame."

"The Clicquot! Has that arrived?"

"Yesterday."

"Thank God."

And so it continued, a frantic, sometimes crazed stocktaking that would, when it was completed, cover every item of every section of the Grand Hôtel du Château de Trouvère. That included everything, right down to the last duster in Marthe's linen store and the steel *vide-pommes* in the immaculate new kitchen, which was soon to become the exclusive province of Monsieur Luc-Alain Carême, whose early-nineteenth-century namesake, Geneviève and Krisztina were optimistically aware, was arguably the greatest chef of all time.

The seemingly endless and manic organizational frenzy left everyone in the château suffering from varying degrees of exhaustion and stress at the close of each successive day. It was also one reason why William refused, point-blank, to consummate his love affair with Krisztina.

The second stage of their relationship had unfolded as tenderly and inevitably as it had begun, without artifice or game-playing or histrionics on either side. William might have nosedived into passion, rather as Laurent had done more than a dozen years earlier. Like the Frenchman, he might have dreamed of her for an unconscionable time before seizing his opportunity to declare himself, but there any similarity ended. William Hunter had no wish or need to possess Krisztina, but he had, for the first time in his life, an absolute longing to give himself completely to a woman, to share his existence, his very essence, with her.

For Krisztina it evolved differently, yet the outcome was the same. Her love for David would linger in her memory with untaintable, savage sweetness, but he was irretrievably lost. At last she could accept the fact, and envisage a future that she had lately come to feel would be made complete only by the presence of this steadfast but indefatigably romantic Englishman.

And he was romantic, enough to want everything about their love to be perfect, including sex. When the time came, he told Krisztina, he wanted her full attention, wanted her to focus on him, on them, not on the cutlery or the wine cellar or the linen stocks.

And so they waited, like two virgins, for their marriage, which was to take place on December 23, the day before the opening of the hotel.

If Krisztina had been asked to find just two words to describe her wedding to William, they would have had to be "serene" and "right."

This time, there were two ceremonies, first the *mariage civil* performed by the mayor of Colmar, followed by a small and intimate gathering of family and close friends in the chapel at de Trouvère, presided over by Père Perigot.

William's parents and two sisters, Leslie and Wendy, were present, all damp-eyed but dignified. Ilona was weeping, Geneviève absorbing every second with avid joy, Olivier trotting up and down the aisle, complaining vociferously as usual when Jeanne tried to thwart him. And no less than seven Irish wolfhounds (including four puppies born to Vénus in September) waited impatiently outside in the icy air, pawing at the door and whining.

There was only a brief moment of awkwardness, when Gabor took Krisztina's arm to lead her to the altar. Having an urge to flinch from him, she quickly averted her head and was confronted by David's memorial plaque and experienced a sudden tremor of nerves.

And then she shifted her gaze to William, who was waiting for her, erect and composed and, she thought at that very instant rather beautiful with the Christmas sunlight streaming down on him. And she saw flowers strewn everywhere, white lilies, clematis, and soft pink roses, spirited into winter by Geneviève from heaven only knew where. And she observed, through the mist of her veil, the faces of the assembled guests, expectant and admiring and, in every case, glad for them both. And she turned her back, finally, on the past, able even to tolerate Gabor's proximity

for those few remaining seconds, and, with one more swift, resolute pat to the Dior peach silk of her dress, she smiled, clear and
sure, and stepped forward to be married to William.

The château seemed a little uncanny that afternoon and evening. It was not quite yet a full-fledged hotel, nor any longer quite
home, but still, it was all part of the metamorphosis that Geneviève and Krisztina had deliberately wrought. And so when
Krisztina's gaze fell with fleeting regret on the pristine halls and
corridors, their familiar, well-worn shabbiness lost forever, she
remembered the wisdom of Tagore's words about new melodies
breaking forth, and the regret vanished, the future beckoned,
and she became light-headed with anticipation.

There could be no honeymoon, but Krisztina did not care. It
was enough that they would finally be together, truly together.
So she was baffled when, at the stroke of ten, Geneviève ushered
her from the celebration to the front door, where she saw a small
suitcase and her fur coat awaiting her.

"*Qu'est-ce que c'est?*" she asked in astonishment.

Geneviève just smiled.

"Belle-mère, what's going on?"

"Our honeymoon, that's what." William, wearing a camel hair
coat, was suddenly at her side.

"What are you talking about? I can't go anywhere! There isn't
time!"

"We know." He picked up her case. "Come on, André's outside
with the car."

"Go on, *dragam*." Ilona, with Olivier sleepy in her arms, appeared from nowhere.

"Mama! You too?"

Geneviève helped her on with her coat. "It's unlucky to spend
the first night of your marriage at home."

"I've never heard that before. You invented it, Belle-mère."

"Will you come?" William pressured her toward the door.

"No! Wait a minute!" She refused to budge. "I have to be up at
dawn, and I have to be here!"

"And so you will be, *dragam*," Ilona reassured her, kissing her
on the cheek. "It's all arranged."

"But where are we going?"

William bundled her out. "To the forest."

There was a tiny lodge in the heart of the pine forest, one of the many assorted lodges, pavilions, temples, and follies scattered all over the de Trouvère estate, which it had become virtually impossible and impractical to keep in good repair. It was to this particular lodge, surrounded by tall, dark trees and accessible only by an unmade road, that André Sutterlin drove William and Krisztina that night.

"I don't understand," Krisztina muttered in vain as Sutterlin went ahead with the cases and unlocked the door. "This place is a wreck."

"Yes, darling."

"Then why have you brought me here," she asked reasonably, "when we have a perfectly wonderful suite waiting for us at the château?"

"A good question."

Sutterlin emerged and came to open the car door, his breath steaming in the frosty air.

"And what's the answer?"

William smiled. "Romance."

"Shall you need me, monsieur?" Sutterlin asked.

"No, thank you, André. We'll be fine now."

"I shall return at eight in the morning."

"Six," Krisztina amended.

"Seven," William decreed.

Sutterlin got back into the driving seat. "*Bonne nuit,* monsieur."

"Good night, André, and thank you."

"*Bonne nuit,* madame."

The car vanished.

"What now?" Krisztina asked. "Spiders? Mice, perhaps? I dread to think."

"Now," William said, "I carry you over the threshold."

"I'm heavy."

"Rubbish." He picked her up. "Close your eyes."

"Why?"

"Are you going to argue with everything now that we're married?"

"Probably."

"*Close your eyes.*"

She obeyed, felt a rush of freezing air, then a swoop of warmth,

and as the door banged, two familiar, separate aromas pricked at
her nostrils.

"What can I smell?"

"You'll see."

"Don't put me down!"

"Why not?"

"Because my feet are killing me, and I haven't been so comfortable all day."

He set her down, ignoring her groan. "Keep your eyes shut."

She felt his hand take hers, drawing her forward a little way,
then to the left a few more paces, and she heard a roaring,
crackling sound. *That's one of the smells*, she thought. *At least
someone's swept the chimney.*

"Open them."

She did.

"Dieu!"

"Like it?"

She was dumbfounded.

The room they stood in seemed hewn out of golden pine,
polished to a lustrous glow, and enhanced by the light from the
flames that leapt in a great stone fireplace in the center of the
plain, whitewashed wall they faced. On the opposite wall hung a
wondrously rich tapestry, and the stone floor was entirely covered with a wine-colored carpet, so thickly tufted that Krisztina
longed to kick off her high-heeled peach silk shoes and sink her
bare toes in the pile.

"Krisztina?"

Her eyes were huge. "I don't know what to say."

"That it makes you happy, I hope." He paused. "It's my wedding gift."

Still dazed, she shook her head. "It feels so secure," she whispered.

"That's what I hoped for. It's our safe haven, for when things
get too hectic at the hotel, and we can't get properly away." He
grasped her hand again. "Take a look. First, the bookcase." He
indicated beautiful mahogany shelves behind glass, already
thoughtfully stacked with a selection of French, English, and
Hungarian reading. "It's Sheraton—a gift from Clemmie."

"Your mother knew about this?"

William grinned. "Just about everyone's known. We were sure
you'd find out, but you were too busy to suspect a thing. And

this," he said, stroking an inlaid satinwood table, "is Hepple-white, and it's from Dad."

"It's wonderful," she breathed, "but much too generous."

"The tapestry's a Burne-Jones, with love from Wendy and Les-lie. And if you'll just accompany me . . ." He tugged her from the room back down the little hall and into a neat, gleaming kitchen. "This is what you've been sniffing at since we came in."

With a cry of pleasure, Krisztina whipped off the lid from a large copper *marmite* simmering on a low light on the stove. "I don't believe it—*gulyas*! But how?"

"Your mama, of course."

"But when? She's been with me all day."

"Marthe brought it over earlier. It's for our midnight feast, and that's to go with it." He pointed to a silver tray on a pine table, set with china bowls, spoons, and crystal wineglasses.

"The Kakiemon!" she exulted, seeing the precious porcelain that had last been used on the night that William, Miller, and poor Eddie had first come to de Trouvère. "And Pape-Clément too! This must be Belle-mère's doing."

"Who else?"

Krisztina's eyes filled with grateful tears. "So much thought . . ."

"No more than you deserve," William said softly.

She reached up and took his face in both her hands. "*You* are more than I deserve."

He shut his eyes. "Christ," he said, and his voice shook.

"What is it?"

"You. Your hands."

"What's the matter with them?"

He smiled, eyes still closed. "Not a damn thing." He put his arms around her waist and drew her close to him. "But I think that was the touch that broke the camel's back."

"I beg your pardon?"

His eyes opened, burning brightly and intensely, searching her face. "My darling wife. I'm talking about *desire.*" His voice lingered huskily on the last word.

Krisztina felt a quivering sensation sliding down her back, and involuntarily she shivered.

"Does this place have a bedroom?"

"A charming bedroom."

"May I see it? Or do we have to wait until our first anniversary?"

"What about the *gulyas*?"

Tenderly, she kissed him just under his chin, precisely at the point where she knew he was especially sensitive. "*A fenebe gulyasal,*" she whispered wickedly.

"What on earth does that mean?" He ducked his head and nuzzled her ear.

"To hell with the *gulyas.*"

Krisztina had been with only two other men in her life—the first experience, pure, magical enchantment; the second, sexuality without mutual love and, at the last, an invasion, ugly and savage.

Tonight, as she came to William, she reflected while still capable of rational thought, before sheer physical longing overwhelmed her, on how bountiful the fates were being to her at last. For here, in this sublime four-poster bed, were a man and a woman irrefutably, undeniably in love, two equals, sheltered and strengthened by certainty and readiness and optimism.

They made love that night on three different levels: the first time, face-to-face, eyes open, slowly, deliberately, and with joy, their nerve ends tingling, tenderly seeking and discovering, giving and taking; the second time, they came together wildly, lustily, without inhibitions, their hearts pounding, mouths gasping, limbs twisting, fingers grasping, climaxing together and crying out their passion in the night silence; and the third time, they felt as if they comprehended the essence of marriage, for they made love with all the calmness and sweetness of two human beings who knew that there were no ghosts to haunt them, no shadows, and no need for urgency. For this, truly, was just the first night, and there would be many, endless nights to follow. . . .

At five in the morning, Krisztina woke to hear a strange scuffling sound, and silently, loath to wake her sleeping husband, she got out of bed and tiptoed, naked, to the window.

She pulled aside one of the curtains, and gave a startled gasp.

William stirred, reached out for her, and finding her gone, opened his eyes. "Kriszti?"

She looked through the dimness back toward the bed. "I didn't mean to wake you, *chéri.*"

"What's wrong?"

"Nothing. Come and look," she whispered.

"It's freezing. Come back to bed."

"No, really, come and see."

He pushed back the warm quilt, grumbling softly, and joined her at the window, pressing himself against her nude back.

"Look," she hissed. "*Réveillon.* Isn't it perfect?"

William stared out over her shoulder, and jumped slightly as two large pairs of limpid brown eyes gazed unblinkingly back through the glass.

"Deer," Krisztina said happily. "Aren't they beautiful! They must be surprised to find this place inhabited after so many years."

"When did it start snowing?" he asked, astonished.

The sky had been clear when they arrived, the moon almost full, but now at least an inch of fresh snow had silently tumbled down, turning the little clearing behind the lodge and the pine trees beyond into an Advent calendar scene, to which the inquisitive deer added even more charm.

"*C'est une idylle,*" Krisztina sighed. "How could you have been so clever as to find this place, darling William?"

"Skill," he said, with satisfaction.

She turned slowly around, and was aware of a sense of consummate pleasure at being confronted by his body less than a hair's breadth from her own. "Do you know," she murmured, "that you have a rare and glorious fragrance?"

"Do I?"

"Definitely." She rested both her hands, palms down, on his chest, and let them glide over the soft hairs and hard nipples, and on down past his navel, over his belly and farther still, until her fingers joined, gently clasping his erect penis.

He groaned. "Back to bed."

"This carpet's very soft . . ." She tugged at him.

"Bed's better," he mumbled, kissing her mouth, "and we're neither of us twenty anymore."

"*Te mindent el rontasz,*" she complained tenderly.

"What?"

"Spoilsport."

With a swift movement, he plucked her from the floor, held her tightly in his arms, and padded back to the four-poster. "You're very Hungarian this morning."

Krisztina snuggled against him, and licked his shoulder experimentally. "Perhaps that's because I'm very *me* this morning."

"That's fine," he said, laying her down on top of the quilt and kneeling over her. "We wasted your mama's *gulyas*," he whispered apologetically.

"She'll understand."

"Kippers for breakfast. Very Scottish. I'm cooking."

"You're not Scottish."

"But I love Arbroath Smokies. Leslie brought them over for me."

She felt his hands, greedy again, on her breasts. "How can you even *think* about food at a time like this?" she asked, wriggling.

He smiled. "To some men, my love, food is an aphrodisiac."

Krisztina parted her thighs, as open and moist an invitation as she could signal. "Do you need an aphrodisiac, William?"

His fingers traveled rapidly, vertically downward, and tangled in her warm, silky curls. "Perhaps not," he said huskily.

"Really?"

He closed his eyes and slid inside her with a long, lavish, rapturous sigh.

"Even better than kippers," he said.

Chapter 21

From Yves Perrault's column in *Nouvelles d'Alsace*, September 5, 1948:

Let us rejoice! Let the great *châteaux-hôtels* of the Loire, the grand hotels of Normandy and even the Côte d'Azur, look to their laurels, for today I can confirm that a new star, one that exploded in the *grand luxe* firmament just over eight months ago, has stabilized into, I hope, a permanent, and certainly glorious, fixture.

The Grand Hôtel du Château de Trouvère, upon which I tentatively reported after their Christmas premiere, has since cut its teeth, stretched its legs, and walked. With admirable deftness, competence, and conviction, it has settled into a kind of dynamic serenity that captivates the newcomer on arrival, and enfolds each guest to its civilized and luxurious bosom.

What exactly *is* a great hotel? A dream, a notion, a beacon of imagination and optimism fired by its creators and passed, like the Olympic torch, from runner to runner, finally transmitting its flame to its undisputed raisons d'être, its guests.

De Trouvère appears to have it all; a house of history, distinction, and beauty, transformed by its instigators, two *belles dames* of flawless taste, the Baronnes de Trouvère, with the help of a man whose talents must be lauded, Signor Alberto Giordano; an estate, including its own Riesling vineyards, of breathtaking loveliness; and total commitment from its whole work force. Without doubt, millions of francs have been lavished upon its beloved baroque edifice, yet one is not left with the uneasy sensation of having registered in a palace, but rather in a home from home (as one might fantasize home) in which one may truly relax or romp or pet the dog (any one of a charming, benevolent troop of home-grown Irish wolfhounds) or actually touch (with care) the profusion of art works and antiques that enrich every part of the château, without fear of reproach.

Last Christmas, I arrived in the middle of a snow-storm, to be welcomed by blazing log fires in my bedroom, sitting room, and unashamedly hedonistic bathroom. Last week, the blaze was created by the massed forces of Nature, her rampant loveliness subtly tamed for tranquil strolls and invigorating horseback rides. On both occasions, I was greeted by René, the venerable doorman who apparently doubles as *directeur des parcs,* imparting his thirty years of de Trouvère gardening wisdom and expertise to a team of younger *jardiniers.* In fact, most of the managerial positions at this hotel have been filled by loyal family retainers. Perhaps it is these men and women who are the lifeblood of the château, and who have conveyed their own love and fervor to the newcomers like Bertrand Leclerc, the distinguished maître d'hotel plucked from comparative obscurity by the owners, and the redoubtable chef-de-cuisine, Luc-Alain Carême (possibly a descendant of Marie-Antoine Carême, the colossus of *cuisine française*), whose own personal genius made me remember, with gratitude, the true meaning of the word "restaurant"—restorative!

I ask again, what is a great hotel? There is, of course, no simple answer. It is the house itself, those who nurture it, its surroundings, comfort, facilities, its foods and wines, its employees, and ultimately, the clients it attracts. Whatever it is, I also say again, let us rejoice, for Alsace has not lost a precious historical relic but has rather gained a new and precious friend, with the freshness of the future and the dignity of the past.

One dimension of a critic's duties may perhaps be to act as a guardian of excellence, rejecting sham and inferiority and welcoming that rarity, the chef d'oeuvre. I welcome it now. I welcome the Grand Hôtel du Château de Trouvère, and I offer two predictions: first, that before long the *Guide Michelin* will add a new three-star establishment to its elite few; and second, that the two Baronnes de Trouvère will not now be sitting idly, smugly permitting their dreamchild to meander on its successful way. I am certain they will be maintaining their meticulous and intelligent control of every aspect of the hotel, with the assistance of their invaluable staff and, of course, the encouragement and plaudits of their blissful, fortunate guests.

Chapter 22

Four months after Perrault's lyrical review, another notice, far briefer but perhaps even more triumphant, appeared concurrently in *Nouvelles d'Alsace, Le Figaro, The Times,* and the *Surrey Gazette:*

> To William and Krisztina Hunter
> a daughter
> ELLA CLEMENTINE ILONA
> born 10 January 1949
> Clinique Kléber, Strasbourg, France

She was, even the baby-sated maternity nurses agreed, a rarely observed miracle, a truly exquisite newborn child. She was tiny but thriving, she had fragile, creamy skin without a hint of the wrinkled blotchiness that marred the perfection of so many babies, her eyes were the identical violet-blue of her mother's and the whole masterpiece was topped by a startling head of hair.

"Les cheveux sont divines!" cooed Soeur Mathilde, a middle-aged woman not known for her passion. "Half mother's, half father's—*chouette!*"

"She will have freckles, *pauvre petite,*" Soeur Joanne predicted dourly, though with pity, since she had always felt her own sprinkled pigmentation to be a curse from an otherwise merciful God.

"You are ginger," Soeur Mathilde dismissed with disdain. "Ella is golden fire."

When Krisztina first observed her daughter's glorious hair, apprehension stirred in her lest it signaled temper—an attribute already more than adequately distributed in Olivier's genes. But it soon became evident that she had no cause for concern—Ella was as calm as her half brother was turbulent; not placid, and definitely not impassive, but somehow blessed with a marvelous tranquillity.

Within weeks, she had developed a smile that transcended cynical thoughts of wind, and that was capable of spreading warm pleasure over anybody who was fortunate enough to witness it. One might enter a room feeling depressed or irritated, but if Ella smiled, one felt better; when she laughed, a rich, bubbling chuckle, one laughed with her; when she wept, which she did remarkably seldom, one's heart contracted with pity or remorse.

"It's like having one of Luc-Alain's *sauces mousselines*," William declared after a session with his daughter. "Other chefs may make the same sauce, yet it is not the same. I daresay other babies smile, too, but with Ella it is utterly different."

Olivier provided the greatest surprise.

Everyone, Krisztina most nervously of all, had anticipated an abominable display of jealousy, but the three-year-old adored his baby sister from the first moment they were introduced, cuddling and cosseting her at every chance he was given.

Since their marriage, William had contrived to be transferred to Avenue George V in Paris, from where he now headed Hunter's French operation and planned their forthcoming Swiss auction house, to be sited in Zurich. Still, his work necessitated his being away from de Trouvère more than he or Krisztina liked.

His unavoidable, week-long absences from the hotel had other, more annoying, implications too. The board of Hunter's were more inclined to skepticism than their chairman, Robert Hunter, or his son. And, more frequently than William, Krisztina, or Geneviève cared for, they were troubled by board members' time-wasting questions, requests for the disclosure of accounts or booking figures, and criticisms.

On one occasion, a board member named Bradley, staying for a few days at de Trouvère, had come across Ilona weeping distractedly in the library, and, assuming her to be a hotel guest, had summoned André Sutterlin. Upon learning that she was one of the family, he had disapprovingly reported the incident to William. Fully aware that his mother-in-law was in a fragile state, William had assured Bradley that there was no cause for concern, but the man's lack of tact had rankled badly with Krisztina.

In truth, Ilona had never fully emotionally recovered from her surgery, and was still grieving for her homeland, upon which the Communists had strongly tightened their grip. Lately, she felt as if her own identity, her individuality, had been left in Budapest, that she existed only for Krisztina and her grandchildren, and that her marriage was now almost completely loveless.

"I'm troubled about your mama," Geneviève told Krisztina shortly after the incident in the library. "She seems to be cutting herself off from us, from reality." Her forehead was creased with concern. "I'm the first to understand the consolation of prayer, but she's in the chapel every day, sometimes for hours at a time."

"But it's the only thing that *does* console her lately, Belle-mère. I have the feeling she'd gladly give up every material comfort if she could keep the chapel."

"Lighting candles for the past is one thing, but she has to be able to see a future, *chérie*. André is quite worried about her, too, you know. He told me the other day that some of the guests had asked about the 'lady in the black veil'—they seemed disturbed by her obvious unhappiness."

"I hope he told them to mind their own business," Krisztina rapped sharply.

"I'm sure, and grateful, that he did not. This is a hotel now, Krisztina. We cannot afford to forget that, however tempting."

"It's also a home, and I shall always put the interests of my family first."

Geneviève spoke gently. "Where Hunter's are concerned, however, I think we might be wise to be tactful, no matter how we feel."

"What do they want of us?" Krisztina asked frustratedly. "The hotel is booked for months—Christmas and New Year's are already full. Bertrand reports that the locals have begun trying to bribe him for tables. . . ."

"I think they want a profit," Geneviève suggested mildly.

"That's going to take at least three years, and they're perfectly aware of the fact."

"They're also aware that we shall have to borrow more money rather than pay it back before they can even dream of a profit, but that won't stop them trying to help us achieve one in the shortest time possible."

Krisztina's eyes glittered with determination. "We'll give them a profit, Belle-mère, I guarantee it. But we'll do it our way, not theirs."

Space in the family quarters was already at a premium, but when Krisztina learned in December that she was expecting another child, it became apparent that somehow more rooms would have to be found.

Alberto arrived a month later.

The answer, he told them, lay in the two pavilions linked to the north side of the château by the airy, bright galleries. The pavilions had never served as anything more than attractive, balancing extensions of the main torso of the house, but Alberto decided that they were the ideal solution.

"They're much too small," Geneviève argued.

"Not much."

"Too small is too small."

"Not if they are enlarged."

"Enlarged?" Even Geneviève's equilibrium was shattered. "Alberto, I thought you understood that we would never meddle with de Trouvère's basic structure."

"Not even if it is an improvement?"

Krisztina's brow was furrowed. "But you've always told us how perfect everything is."

"Not quite everything, signora."

They were, as usual, in the Salon Rouge, drinking coffee and eating some of their *pâtissier*'s sublime *tartes aux fraises*. Now William rose from his armchair and fixed Giordano with a challenging stare.

"Since it seems you are nearly always right, perhaps you'd care to point out whatever faults the de Trouvère family have failed to notice for over a century?"

"With pleasure." Alberto pushed aside his untouched pastry. "The pavilions," he said again.

"What's wrong with them?"

"They are spindly, like the legs of an undernourished girl."

No one spoke.

"They should, however, be firm and ripe, like the legs of a great courtesan at rest."

Krisztina smiled. "I never thought of them that way."

"Also, the galleries—most charming, of course—but they turn the *padiglione* into separate units, as if they were detachable from the rest of the château. They should be indivisible." He paused. "And by making them larger, with the utmost care, I believe I can achieve the unity that is now lacking, and at the same time give you comfort, space, and privacy."

William glanced first at Geneviève, then at his wife. Finding assent on their faces, he turned back to the alert eyes of the designer.

"Well," he said, "if you put it that way, what can we say?"

"You can say yes, signor."

"Can it be finished by August?"

Giordano beamed in the direction of Krisztina's still flat stomach. *"Naturalmente."*

William, too, smiled. "Then, yes."

The great advantage of Alberto's plans was that they were always as sound in practice as in theory.

With a remarkable lack of disruption to the life of the hotel, the west pavilion became home for Geneviève, Ilona, and Gabor on the twenty-second day of July. The opposite side, though maintaining a perfectly trim exterior, expanded internally as if its walls were made from elastic, to provide the Hunters with everything they needed—even a small dance studio to replace Krisztina's beloved Mirror Hall, which was now, of course, a public room.

On August 23, Orion, the oldest of the wolfhounds, died in his sleep. The next afternoon, Giselle, one of the young bitches, always less placid than her brothers and sisters, took off at a mad gallop down the main driveway and was knocked down and killed by a black Mercedes.

"Something else is going to happen," Krisztina fretted miserably, distressed by the double loss.

"Of course it won't," William soothed her.

"They say disasters always come in threes," she insisted.

"You've never been superstitious, darling," William said. "In any case, Orion was a very old dog, and he died very peacefully. You can't call that a disaster."

"Perhaps not." She sighed, her eyes troubled. "Pregnancy must be making me foolish."

Two days later, a large antique mirror in the hall fell inexplicably from the wall, shattering into thousands of fragments.

"Well, at least that's your number three safely out of the way," William joked to Krisztina, who appeared just as he was sweeping up the mess.

"Dear Lord," she whispered.

He straightened up, seeing her ashen face. "What's wrong?"

"Seven years' bad fortune."

He smiled. "More superstitious rubbish, darling? I'm surprised at you."

"Are you?" She clutched her swollen belly with both hands and shut her eyes. *"Jesszus-Maria,"* she murmured, *"Istenem segits rajtam."*

"What does that mean?"

She opened her eyes, and he saw dark fear in them. "I'm praying for our baby."

William put his arms around her. "Our baby's fine, Kriszti."

"I'm not so sure."

"Because of a mirror? You're too wise for that, darling."

"I know," she said, and then shivered.

Seven years, she thought.

On August 30, at three o'clock in the afternoon, while Krisztina was standing in reception talking to Sutterlin, her water broke.

A strong and healthy eight-pound son was born just four hours later, complete with ten fingers and just as many toes.

"And in time for dinner," his father said with delight. "He'll probably be a gourmet."

Krisztina stared down at the bundle in her arms, taking in every detail incredulously. "So much hair," she crowed joyfully, "and pure, true red, redder even than you!"

"And fighting fit," William pointed out soberly, "thank God."

Tears of relief poured down Krisztina's cheeks. "I've been so terrified," she confessed.

"I know, darling, but that's all over now."

"He's so wrinkled," she breathed. "I always used to think that all new babies were the same, but mine have all been completely different."

William gently stroked the sleeping infant's diminutive fingers. "Are we still set on Michael?"

"I think so." She kissed the soft fiery hair. "Michael Armand Robert."

William smiled. "Dad will be thrilled."

A nurse bustled into the room. "We'll just let baby have a little rest now, shall we? And Maman needs to sleep too, *n'est-ce pas?*"

Reluctantly, Krisztina passed the dozing child into the other woman's secure plump arms.

"We're calling him Michael, Soeur Juli."

The nurse beamed. *"Un p'tit Anglais."*

"His brother and sister will want to visit as soon as possible," Krisztina added. "Not to mention his grandparents." Just as with Ella, it was a wholly accepted fact that Geneviève was as much the baby's *grand-maman* as Ilona or Clementine Hunter.

"In the morning," Soeur Juli decreed. "The first evening is just for Papa. The rest may join in tomorrow."

Before his first month of life was accomplished, the little boy had no fewer than four names. To his sister, he was Mischa, to Geneviève he was Michel, and to Ilona and Gabor he was Mihaly. Only to Krisztina and William was he known as Michael, or sometimes, to his father, as Mike.

Everyone adored him. Whereas Olivier had, from birth, been a creature of temperament, and Ella had been possessed of a quality of tranquillity, this child was, purely and simply, an innocent.

Everyone adored him.

Except Olivier. Whereas he had loved Ella from the moment she was born, Michael was different. He was a boy. An interloper. A threat. Olivier loathed him.

On Michael's first birthday, William tried to take a family photograph. "Kiss your little brother, Ollie," he called.

Olivier kept his arm around Ella.

"Come on, Ollie, I want you on Michael's other side."

The six-year-old remained stubbornly still, not giving in until William ordered him to move.

"Vas t'en, chéri," Krisztina prodded, "smile."

He gave a grudging grin.

"And kiss your brother, as Papa told you."

Cornered, Olivier bent down and pecked Michael's chubby cheek.

"That's better. Now put your arm around him." William focused the camera.

It was more than Olivier's piqued and childish flesh could bear. Slipping his left arm round the baby, he dug in his fingers and gave a swift but thorough pinch.

Michael began to cry, Krisztina scooped him up in her arms and the photo session was wrecked.

Olivier smiled.

"I thought Ella had changed him," Krisztina said later that evening when the children were all in bed. The hotel was running along smoothly and the Hunters and Florians were assembled for a nightcap in Geneviève's drawing room.

"He'll adjust." William poured cognac for everyone.

"But we had no trouble like this after she was born."

"He wasn't jealous of Ella," Geneviève said.

"Why should he be more jealous of Mihaly?" Ilona asked anxiously.

"Ella was no rival. She's a girl."

Krisztina shook her head. "That doesn't really make sense, Belle-mère. Olivier's already aware of his title, and he knows that Michael's a Hunter, not a de Trouvère."

"Exactement."

"What do you mean?"

"Olivier worships William, but William will never be his father."

"But William treats him exactly as his own son," Krisztina defended.

"I know he does, but our Olivier has a complicated mind." Geneviève smiled. "Not like Ella, who accepts life at face value, who trusts everyone. Olivier is proud of his name, yet he yearns to be a Hunter."

William nodded. "Not long ago, he asked me if he should call me Beau-père instead of Papa. I told him I *was* his papa, but I think he's still troubled about it."

"Families," Gabor grunted from the corner.

"What about them, Gabor?" William asked tersely.

"The larger they become, the more problems there are."

"So what should we do?" Krisztina asked, ignoring Gabor. "Treat Olivier specially in some way?"

"And encourage him to think he *is* different from the others?" William shook his head emphatically. "We'd end up with a spoiled, neurotic boy."

"Ignore it," Geneviève said.

"But if he's unhappy, surely one must do something to help?" Ilona looked more worried than ever.

Geneviève patted her hand warmly. "Olivier is greatly loved, and he knows it." She smiled again. "The youngest of three often has a trying time. They are inevitably babied for longer than other children because they are quite often the last, and resented for that reason."

Krisztina looked wistful. "Michael's only a year old, Belle-mère. We don't want him to grow too fast."

"He'll grow at the rate that suits him," William said. "Geneviève's absolutely right. We have to give them time, let Michael expand a bit, assert himself." He sat down, and relaxed. "I think we can trust them to have the sense to sort themselves out."

Chapter 23

They all grew.

Like marvellous weeds, Olivier, Ella, and Michael stretched and thrived. Their bones lengthened, their muscles strengthened. They quaffed new experiences like seasoned drunks, and absorbed everything around them like constantly mobile, natural sponges.

To the guests who slumbered in Château de Trouvère's suites, the family's private apartments set apart from the rest of the house, must have resembled a kind of fairyland, removed as they seemed to be from commonplace realities and worldly problems.

As with many living fables, it was half true, half false. Krisztina, for example, knew she was very happy, understood her great good fortune, but considered herself a hardworking mother with too little time by far to spend with her children or her husband. To the three youngsters, de Trouvère life was all they knew.

"Time for our walk, children."

Thus came the command that could be heard twice each day in the schoolroom in the west pavilion.

"But it's cold, Miss Herrick."

"Nonsense, Olivier. Go and fetch your coats, and you'll need boots and scarves."

"Mischa was sneezing," Ella volunteered.

"Michael always sneezes when the blackboard is cleaned. It's the chalk dust."

"Mais, Nannee . . ." This from the youngest, who actually enjoyed the walks but supported his older brother and sister in everything.

"Speak English, Michael, and all of you kindly do as you are told."

"Yes, Miss Herrick."

Since Michael's third birthday, the children's feet had been kept solidly on the ground (in an unflattering though sensible array of British shoes, sandals, and Wellington boots) by Annabel Herrick, an authentic English governess brought from her native Devon by William and Krisztina, who had decided that their children's primary education should take place in the home.

Annabel Herrick was thirty-nine, just five years older than Krisztina, with gently curling brown hair, a clear, unmade-up complexion, and a trim, narrow-waisted figure dressed invariably in Jaeger skirts and twinsets. Only too conscious that her latest charges could easily become unpleasantly spoiled (the young Baron was already a most willful boy), Miss Herrick had agreed to a policy with their parents that would ensure a healthy degree of discipline but still leave enough time and scope for relaxation, warmth and fun.

The official timetable of their lessons was pinned to the noticeboard on the schoolroom wall, but the children bemoaned the fact that they could predict almost every minute of every weekday.

Breakfast: Wholesome, to be eaten to the last morsel, followed by vile, pernicious cod-liver oil.

Lessons: Never to be interrupted, even by William's return from a trip, bearing gifts.

Walks: Twice each day—once only, Miss Herrick's special dispensation, in torrential rain.

Afternoon tea: Sometimes delicious, with English treats such as cucumber sandwiches or scones with strawberry jam; more often than not, bowls of milk with bread and butter.

Bedtime: Eight o'clock for Olivier, seven for Ella, and six-thirty for Michael.

Sundays were an improvement, except for the obligatory visit to church and the uncomfortable suits they were made to wear.

But it was Saturdays, glorious Saturdays, that were emblazoned on their mental calendars in great glowing letters. On that day they had only one lesson in the morning, ate what they liked (within reason) for lunch—picnicking if the weather was fine—ran free on a blissful, unfettered cross-country ramble with the dogs, and stayed up for dinner with the grown-ups.

If discipline was ever present, however, the three children frequently found ways and means of escaping its confines. On these forays into mischief, the ringleader was invariably the young Baron, with Ella his courageous disciple and little Michael their willing stooge and satellite.

Olivier had developed an appetite for practical jokes, and with an entire hotel and a small army of staff and guests as potential victims, he found ample scope for his energies.

The telephones on André Sutterlin's desk jangled at least once a week with news of the *enfants terribles'* latest villainy.

"Fir cones!"

"My husband has a weak heart, André. It was a dreadful shock for him."

"The cones were meant for scenting the fireplace, madame . . ."

"Then how in God's name did they come to be in our *beds*?"

"André, call Docteur Schaeffer!"

"For whom, Bertrand?"

"For everyone who ordered consommé!"

"Food poisoning?"

"Chef Carême is beside himself—he almost murdered the *entremetier*!"

"*Oh, mon Dieu!*"

"What, André?"

"Cod-liver oil again?"

"Could be."

"I'll call the doctor."

"Better hide the children. If Carême finds them, their bones will be in tomorrow's consommé!"

"André, come to the second floor, *vite!*"

"*Pourquoi*, Marthe?"

"I can hear screaming in one of the suites."

"Je viens tout de suite."

"No, wait, André—one second! Monsieur Sondheim is coming from his room."

"Marthe?"

No reply.

"Marthe?"

"André, where are those children?"

"Why?"

"Frogs! In the bathtub, in the bidet, jumping everywhere!"

"Merde!"

"Precisely, André. Now would you please get someone up here to help me catch them."

After every misdemeanor, Krisztina made sure that the culprits apologized humbly to their victims and accepted suitable penance. The children generally had a good instinct for choosing targets possessed of a sense of fun, but occasionally, usually when Olivier had failed to heed Ella's warnings, their jokes misfired badly. At those times the penalties were really designed to hurt—Saturday rambles were tabooed, they were sent early to bed on Saturday evenings, and after one truly catastrophic incident that resulted in a lost booking for the hotel, an entire week's holiday in Normandy was scrapped.

Anyone wishing to punish Ella, however, had only to separate her from the dogs. Soon after her birth, it became apparent that she had inherited her mother's rare affinity with animals. The wolfhounds stood vigil over her night and day as an infant, and permitted her almost anything as a toddler, unstintingly indulgent of her clutching fingers and pummeling feet, even vying with one another for the pleasure of having her ride on their backs. Now that she was older, Ella's favorite time of day was when René, still charged with the animals' welfare, allowed her to help with their feeding and grooming. Even a one-day ban on that precious hour was enough to bring contrition to her heart and tears to her eyes.

The children were, like all children, absolute individuals with separate personality traits, likes and dislikes, but knotted together by a series of emotional tethers. Ella worshiped her older brother, felt with sympathetic pain his complex mood swings, and unconsciously dedicated herself to his defense. Her feelings about Mischa were simpler. She loved him—*everyone* loved him

—so open displays of solidarity were unnecessary where he was concerned. And Michael, with his carrot head, expandable heart, and ready grin, stumbled after both Olivier and Ella with the blind faith of a puppy.

Olivier's attitude toward Michael was simple too. As irrevocably yoked as he was to Ella by adoration, he was also tethered to his charmingly vulnerable little half brother—by hatred.

Olivier took a tremendous perverse pleasure in their communal games. He was the twenty-seventh Baron and the oldest sibling, therefore he was, by right, the leader and instigator, and he used young Michael unkindly. Sometimes, when Ella was not looking their way, he even ill-treated him physically, so that at the end of a day, the little boy's tender white skin would be marked with extra little scratches and bruises not gained in the honest rough-and-tumble of normal, healthy children's play.

"You must be more careful, Michael," Annabel Herrick would say, after dabbing iodine on the injuries.

"Oui, Nannee."

"Why do you fall over so much more often than the others?"

Michael blushed. "Olivier calls me 'clumsy oaf.' "

"That's not very kind of him." She looked at his left knee. "But he does have a point—that's a very nasty bruise."

Her fingers were gentle as they touched the aching bone. Michael's lower lip quivered, but he said nothing.

The children's mischief, which might have been a detriment to the hotel, actually seemed to be creating an opposite effect. Château de Trouvère had begun to develop a unique reputation for warmth, charm, and a true family atmosphere. So many *grand luxe* establishments shunned small children and banned dogs; Geneviève's and Krisztina's policy was to welcome almost anyone, trusting to their guests' good taste and sense not to create any situation that might compromise the serenity of the house or damage the lovingly tended parks or gardens.

They were under no illusions—they were still novices in a highly competitive world—and each ensuing day was a time for learning. But like most eager students, they learned swiftly and thoroughly.

They learned, for example, that it was necessary to assess in advance the clients who would be filling the hotel in any one period. If more than two reservations including children had been made, then it was vital to make special arrangements to keep the youngsters happy. The key to successfully allowing children and animals in the same hotel as bankers, duchesses, film producers, diplomats, and fashion designers, was to cater to the whims and exuberances of each peer group and to keep them subtly separated.

For the energetic at de Trouvère, there were the stables, the walks, swimming in the lake in summer and skating in winter. By the spring of 1955, there were four tennis courts, and by the following winter a tobogganing hill had been specially created. There were other changes too: The pretty gazebo in the park was used for periodic readings from Hans Andersen or the Brothers Grimm; the *temple d'amour* near the lake, for occasional concerts or plays; and for children of an adventurous age, there was the slightly decaying belvedere whose potential as a "haunted house" Krisztina had spotted, transforming it into a kind of stationary ghost train, from which screams of delicious terror regularly wafted across the lawns.

Animals were predictably given a warm welcome. The smaller cats and dogs were permitted in the bedrooms, while the larger pets were housed in centrally heated kennels, to which their owners had access at any hour of day or night.

By such means, the Salle Anglais could remain a peaceful adult enclave; the Salon Bleu, now one of the hotel's two bars, was able to retain its air of lighthearted sophistication, and the decorum of the baroque gardens would not be polluted by the shrieks of children's games or the barking of uncontrolled dogs.

De Trouvère was a resounding success. As Perrault had predicted in his critique six years earlier, *les deux Baronnes* had not lapsed into complacency. They worked grindingly hard, made their staff feel that they shared a real vested interest in the future of the hotel, cared passionately for the comfort and pleasure of their guests. And, miracle of miracles, in spite of costly improvements and annual decorations, they were even showing a healthy profit!

One rainy Sunday afternoon in October 1955, while William was in Paris, Krisztina and Geneviève were in Strasbourg, Miss Herrick was ensuring that Michael took a nap, and Ilona was in the chapel, Gabor and Ella were in his room.

"*Je t'aime,* Grand-père," Ella said, hugging the grandfather who often seemed, to her tender heart, to be lonely and sad.

"And I love you, *kis szivem,*" Gabor responded, his arms folded around the little waist, so neatly trimmed by the broad blue satin ribbon tied in a big bow at the back.

"I wish it weren't raining, Grand-père. Miss Herrick doesn't let us go outside on Sundays in the rain."

"Why not, princess?"

"Because we have to keep our best clothes on."

Oh, that voice, Gabor thought. So sweet and clear, it tweaked at his heart to hear it.

"It's a foolish rule," he said. He kissed her hair, that untamable cloud of fire that brought the sun into the darkest room on the bleakest day.

Ella shifted on his knee. "Can we play a game, Grand-père?"

"What would you like to play?"

"I don't know."

"Sit on my lap a moment more, *kis szivem.* I so rarely get a chance to cuddle my little princess."

His aging memory bank gave a little spark of remembrance. *Kriszti was my princess* . . . Six years old. If he closed his eyes, he could still see Kriszti, pure spun gold instead of molten flame, but the same beautiful eyes, the same fragrant skin.

Ella put a soft hand up to his chin. "Like a baby hedgehog." Her cheeks dimpled. "Papa shaves his face every morning."

"So do I, little one, but it always grows again."

His right hand reached down and encircled one small ankle, just above the gleaming white sock. *Baby flesh* . . . *Nothing as pure and glorious as the skin of a girl-child* . . . He stroked her leg, and Ella smiled and rested her head against his shoulder.

"Nice, Grand-père," she murmured.

Gabor shut his eyes. Her scent was in his nostrils, flowery, milky, like nectar, irresistible as . . . *as Kriszti at six* . . . *and twelve* . . . *and twenty* . . . *and* . . . His hand continued its path, tracing a route along innocent, soft silk that sent tingling messages through his fingers and up through his arm toward his throbbing heart.

Reflexively, Ella's left hand darted down to push him away. "Tickles," she giggled softly.

He could not stop.

Beneath the pretty blue skirt his hot fingers wandered, under the creamy petticoat, like little creatures of instinct, stalking a prey that would only be found farther still, in the warmth, past the snug cotton panties and inside the hallowed, undefiled folds of little-girl flesh . . .

Ella wriggled. "No, Grand-père."

"It's all right, princess, don't move."

A frown puckered her forehead, but she stayed obediently still, not wanting to hurt Grand-père's feelings. He wasn't tickling anymore, he was tugging at her panties and his eyes were still tightly shut in a strange way, his mouth slightly open . . .

"Grand-père, I don't like that . . ."

She had to get down—she had a funny, unpleasant feeling, and suddenly her grandfather's particular smell, of cigars and something he put on his hair, a smell that had always been comforting and solid to her, made her feel sick, and she began to struggle out of his arms.

"No, *kis szivem.*"

She gave a little cry of terror and shock. His fingers had pulled her panties away and were pushing painfully, horribly, into her—

"*No,* Grand-père!"

He held her even tighter. Kriszti—his aching, desperate need for her, for her body, for her love, for her soul . . .

"*Let go of her!*"

Gabor jumped as if he'd been shot. His eyes tore open wide, his face was white with two great blotches of heat scorching his cheeks.

He stared at the small, dark-haired avenging figure standing in the doorway.

"Olivier!"

"Let her *go,* I said!"

"But I . . ." Gabor's hands flew guiltily from their target, and Ella scrambled down from his knee.

"Ollie, I didn't want—"

"Stay back, Ella!" Olivier commanded, with all the power his ten-year-old voice could muster. Then suddenly, with an almost mad howl of fury, he sprang at his grandfather, raining sharp blows wherever he could land them.

"Olivier, stop, please! What are you doing?"

The boy's contempt showed on his livid narrow face. "You're a horrible old man," he cried. "You were hurting her—I saw you!"

He pummeled Gabor wildly, still in a frenzy of rage, appalled by what he had seen, not quite sure what it meant, but instinctively aware that it was evil, and that it was directed against his own beloved Ella!

"Olivier, for God's sake!" Gabor panted, trying to catch the boy's flailing arms.

"Ollie, arrête-toi!" Ella pleaded, tears rolling down her cheeks, more terrified than ever by what was happening.

Abruptly, Olivier stepped back, and his hands fell to his sides, still clenched into fists, the fine veins in his temples standing out visibly.

"Don't be afraid, Ella," he said softly. "I'm here now. I'll protect you."

Gabor's face was even chalkier than before.

"Olivier," he said feebly. "You've misunderstood. I don't know what you thought, but you were wrong, terribly wrong."

Olivier's dark eyes narrowed with an astuteness far above his years. "If I'm wrong, Grandfather, then why are you frightened?" he challenged. "If I was wrong, then you'd be angry, wouldn't you?"

"I *am* angry, but I can understand how—"

"Be quiet!"

"How dare you speak to me like that!"

The boy's back was straight as an arrow. "Oh, I dare, Grandfather." His voice was loaded with menace. "And I promise you that if you ever, ever touch my sister again, I'll kill you."

"Olivier, I'm your grandfather," Gabor moaned incredulously.

"I wish you weren't."

"Ollie, please let's go." Venturing closer for the first time, Ella laid a hand on her brother's arm.

He ignored her. "And I think that Maman and Papa will feel the same way after I tell them what you did."

"You wouldn't!"

"Ollie, stop!" Ella clutched at him again and began to pull him away.

"And what will Grandmother think?" Olivier hurled in a final, breathless salvo of malice.

Gabor made a choking sound, and his eyes rolled. "You mustn't tell lies!" Gabor's mouth was contorted in a wide gash of panic. "It isn't true, Olivier!"

They'd thought he was white already, but now every last remaining drop of blood seemed to drain from his face.

Olivier took Ella's hand and tugged her toward the door, then turned back again.

"I'm warning you, don't you ever come anywhere near Ella again. Don't even *talk* to her!"

"Olivier!"

"And by this evening, no one will want to talk to *you!*"

They were in the playroom two hours later when they heard a commotion.

"Wait here," Olivier told Ella.

"Don't leave me!" Still close to tears, she had huddled beside her brother ever since they'd left the west pavilion.

"Something's going on, I want to know what."

When he returned minutes later, there was a strange expression on his face.

"Ollie, what is it?"

"Grandfather's ill."

"What?"

"They've just taken him away in an ambulance."

Ella gasped.

"He looked bad." Olivier sounded satisfied.

Ella's violet eyes were dark with anxiety. "Is he going to die, Ollie?"

"How should I know, Lalla?" At the time of her birth, Olivier had found 'Lalla' more satisfactory for his three-year-old tongue, and he still often used it.

"If he dies, we'll have killed him!" The words were a horrified hiss.

Olivier's face creased with scorn. "That old pig?"

"Ollie, don't!"

His eyes were hard. "This is probably God's way of punishing him."

"You always say you don't believe in God."

He shrugged. "I don't, usually."

Gabor had suffered a stroke. He was conscious, but paralysed and unable to speak.

Late that night, Olivier crept into Ella's room. She was lying awake, her cheeks luminous in the moonlight that came through the crack in the curtains.

"Ollie, what's happened?" she asked, terror mounting anew as she saw him tiptoeing in. "Is he dead?"

He raised a finger to his lips to hush her. "No." He sat on the edge of her bed.

"Are you cold? Get in with me."

"No, Lalla, listen."

She sat up, her hair cascading over her shoulders.

"We mustn't tell anyone what happened today."

She frowned. "But you told Grand-père you were going to tell Maman and Papa."

"That was before he got sick. It's different now."

"Because you think they might blame us?"

"You never know with grown-ups."

"Isn't that dishonest?"

He looked cross. "Who matters to you more, that man or me?"

She wriggled out from under her quilt and sat beside him. "You, of course, Ollie."

He looked dubious. "Can I trust you, Ella?"

"You know you can."

He stood up abruptly. "Tomorrow morning, before lessons, meet me behind the stables."

"But I visit the dogs then."

"You'll have to give them a miss for once."

"But René will—"

"Meet me." It was a command.

"Yes, Ollie."

It was a crisp autumnal morning, chilly enough for their breath to form a visible mist in the clear air. The tangy smell of the stables, that wonderful blend of muck and hay and oats and the creatures themselves, wafted into their nostrils.

Ella and Olivier eyed each other nervously.

"Have you heard anything?" Ella asked.

He shook his head.

She waited another moment. "Why did you want us to meet?"

"To talk about things some more."

"Make sure I won't tell?"

He nodded.

"I won't. Not if you say I mustn't."

"It's for your sake, you know, Lalla. They might think it was all your fault."

"What happened to Grand-père?"

"No, what happened before."

She stared at him. "But I didn't do anything," she said. "I just sat on his knee for a cuddle. Like I do with Papa."

"It's not the same."

"Why not?"

"I don't know. It just isn't."

"Oh."

He glanced at her out of the corner of his eye. "So you won't tell them?"

Ella still looked troubled. "I don't think they would blame me, you know, Ollie. And Miss Herrick says it's always better to tell the truth."

"If you tell," Olivier said, changing tack, "I'm bound to get it. They always blame me for everything."

"I won't let them. I'll tell them the truth."

"They'll think you're protecting me." He looked into her eyes. "You know I saved you, don't you, Lalla?"

"Yes, Ollie."

"He was doing terrible things to you."

She blushed, hotly and unpleasantly.

"I rescued you."

She nodded dumbly.

"So will you do something for me?"

"Anything," she said eagerly.

"Make a pact with me."

"What's a pact?"

"It's where we take an oath—that's the same as making a promise, only you die if you don't keep it."

"I always keep my promises," Ella said stoutly.

"And it has to be sworn in blood."

The eagerness vanished. "How . . . how do we do that?"

"It's easy." He took her by the hand and pulled her away from the stables, into a clump of shrubs and bushes. "We both make little cuts in our thumbs."

Shocked, she tore her hand from his. *"Cuts?"*

"Just teeny scratches, really. Nothing to worry about—it won't hurt." He produced a small piece of glass from his trouser pocket.

"Ollie!" She stared at it in horror.

"Don't be a coward," he condemned. "I always thought you were brave, for a girl."

"I am, but—"

"Now's your chance to prove it." He played his trump card. "And to prove how much you love me."

She was beaten.

"Okay?"

She nodded again.

"Hold out your hand. Your left one."

Trembling a little, Ella obeyed.

Olivier brandished the sliver of glass. "I'll do it very quickly so it won't hurt."

Ella squeezed her eyes shut. She felt his tight grip on her wrist, then a hideous, sharp pain in her thumb, and involuntarily she jerked away, trying to stifle a cry.

"There," she heard him say, and opened her eyes.

"All right, Lalla?"

She swallowed the tears rising in her throat with a gulp. "All right," she whispered, transfixed by the vivid blood streaming from her wounded thumb.

"Now me." He paused. "Do you want to do it?"

"No!" She closed her eyes again, unable to watch. She heard the smallest intake of breath, then a tiny pause.

"It's done."

She looked. More blood. She felt nauseous.

"Now," Olivier said, "we have to mix our blood together."

"Why?"

"That makes us a brother and sister in blood."

"But you're already my brother."

"Only your half brother, Lalla. This will make us even more special than a real brother and sister."

"It will?"

"Of course. It's the pact. It means you swear to be completely loyal to me—above anyone else in the world."

"Even Maman?"

"And Papa."

"And Mischa?"

"Yes, Michael too," he said impatiently.

Ella winced at the throb in her thumb.

"Come on," Olivier said. "If we don't mix it now, it'll dry, and then we'll have to do it again."

Swiftly, she thrust out her hand again. Olivier stepped side-

ways so that they faced each other, and, raising his own right
hand solemnly, took her left thumb and rubbed it against his.

"It is done," he said gravely.

"The pact?" she breathed.

"Sealed in blood." His dark eyes scanned Ella's awed face.
"Loyal to each other, or we die."

Gabor did not die.

Paralysed down his right side from head to toe, he sat in his
wheelchair or propped up on pillows in bed, focusing one mobile,
resentful eye on those around him. He refused to cooperate with
doctors or nurses or any of the succession of physiotherapists who
tried to teach him to cope with his limitations or improve his
condition. At last, too frustrated to carry on, they abandoned him
to the one person prepared to put up with anything from him:
Ilona.

He grew obese and lost his remaining hair. Most who came into
contact with him felt uncomfortable with or afraid of the man
who had, even in health, been a depressing, contaminating influence, but who now put people in mind of a malevolent slug.

The two younger children, brought periodically to his room,
were petrified of him—Michael, because Gabor's appearance,
and the pitiful, unintelligible sounds that emerged sporadically
from his distorted mouth, gave him shrieking nightmares, and
Ella because each time she looked at him, she imagined she saw
hatred in that grotesque, swiveling eye—hatred, despair, and
vengeance. And though Olivier had said that God had punished
Grand-père for what he had done to her, in truth, she believed
that He was punishing *her*.

Krisztina, mercifully occupied by the hotel, felt a greater compassion for Gabor than she would have thought possible. From
time to time she came to sit with him, to read to him from his
favorite Hungarian books, or to try to communicate with him.
But the barrier between them—his animosity and the awful,
irrational guilt that his helplessness induced in her—was absolute
and unyielding.

Ilona, alone, tended him without complaint and even, sometimes, with something akin to joy. Others might experience fear
in his presence, but for her, Gabor's apoplexy had brought an end
to fear. It had also brought an end to her own futility; at last the
good Lord had seen fit to bring her from her knees and had

granted her new purpose. Ilona had motivation once more—her husband needed her again, she had a new child to tend, to feed and bathe and dress and comfort. Even if she saw that he despised her more than ever, this, at least, was a contempt she could comprehend and tolerate without anguish.

Chapter 24

Krisztina knew that being Olivier de Trouvère, aged twelve, was not an easy matter. After much heart-searching, they had decided to send him to the lycée in Colmar in preference to a more exclusive private school, hoping that a "normal" education in the company of less privileged children might be character-building —might scrape away some of the rarefied snobbery that lay upon him like a veneer.

Olivier, however, had regarded the choice of the lycée as a direct insult to his heritage, for which he blamed William more than Krisztina. Every morning, as Ella and Michael waved *au revoir* from the playroom window, Olivier stared up with distaste at the eagerly smiling, freckled face topped by that *common* red hair, and was assailed by uncontrollable envy that Michael was staying in the bosom of the family, in the château that was *his* by right, while he was packed out of the way.

Arrangements for the family's annual summer holiday at their villa in Cabourg were always a headache, since it was unthinkable for them all to leave the hotel at any one time, and the month of August, when Olivier had his school vacation, was the time when Krisztina had to be at de Trouvère.

They had decided this year that William and Krisztina would spend July at the villa with Gabor and Ilona, and that Geneviève would take the children for three weeks in August. In late June, however, Michael suffered a bad bout of influenza, and the doctor suggested that he should go to the sea right away. It seemed only sensible for Ella to come along for company, while Geneviève waited for Olivier's vacation to begin.

July on the Côte Fleurie was bliss. The villa, given over several years earlier to William and his sisters by Robert and Clementine Hunter, and lyrically named "L'Idylle," stood a mere few hundred meters from the flat, broad Normandy beach. It was a large but cozy rose-colored house, half-timbered and topped with thatch, backing onto four charmingly unruly acres of garden, with its own apple and pear orchard and threaded by a tiny stream.

In the evenings, when Ella and Michael were sound asleep in bed, and Gabor and Ilona had retired for the night, William and Krisztina headed for dinner and an hour or two at the casino in Deauville. They usually ended their evening with a hand-in-hand stroll along Les Planches before returning to Cabourg. During the day they either remained ensconced at "L'Idylle," reveling on the beach, picnicking on the sand or in their own garden, or drove to Honfleur or Pont-l'Evêque, where the children gorged themselves on local specialties. With Annabel Herrick safely liberated on her own holiday in England, William and Krisztina allowed Ella and Michael almost all the shellfish, creams, and cheeses they could eat, even permitting Ella (for once the "oldest") an occasional sip of Calvados.

"Eh bien, mes enfants," William said the day before Geneviève and Olivier were due to arrive, as they sat at the rough pine table in the garden eating lunch, "are you happy?"

"Yes, thank you, Papa," answered Ella, her eyes even more vivid than usual against her golden tanned skin. "Very happy."

Ilona and Gabor were sitting inside, because the midday sun was too hot for Gabor, and William and Krisztina had observed that the children were always more at ease when their grandparents were not present.

"And you, Mike?" William asked.

Michael was a glowing mass of freckles, restored to obvious health. "Super duper!" He beamed ravishingly at them all, and knocked over the salt.

Krisztina brushed most of it away with a napkin, then threw three tiny pinches over her shoulder.

"What are you doing, Maman?" Ella asked.

Krisztina smiled. "It's a superstition, *chérie.*"

"What's that?" queried Michael.

"It's like believing in good luck or bad luck," his sister explained.

"It's really a lot of nonsense," Krisztina said.

"Then why do you do it?"

"Because she's silly," Michael said.

"Don't be cheeky," William rebuked. "And don't call your mother 'she.'"

"Sorry, Maman."

"That's all right, *chéri.*" Krisztina looked back at Ella. "Superstitions are quite good fun if you don't take them too seriously. I remember breaking a mirror years ago." Krisztina glanced at William. "And I got myself in a dreadful state about it."

"Why?" Michael gulped Evian noisily.

"Drink quietly," William said.

"Because one superstition says that if you break a mirror, you can have seven years of bad luck." She laughed. "That taught me a lesson though."

"Why, Maman?" Ella dipped a hard-boiled egg into the salt on her plate.

"Because I can't imagine anyone alive having seven happier, luckier years than we've had."

"So the moral is," William said, "breaking mirrors, spilling salt, or walking under ladders can do you no harm."

"Touch wood," added Krisztina.

"Love is strong as death; jealousy is cruel as the grave."

Olivier had paid unusual attention to those words of the Song of Solomon during one of his terminally dull Bible lessons, not because he really understood them, but because they struck a chord in him.

As July passed, his mind riveted itself on Michael, the ginger-haired runt of the litter, who had Ella and William all to himself while *he* slaved away at school. Somehow Olivier's first three weeks of August without his parents had not made up for it.

His jealousy of Michael had begun as a small, hard seed, rooted in his gut at the time of his half brother's birth, but it had grown over the years into an amorphous, oozing creature with a vast, repellent appetite, munching on what peace of mind he might once have had, gulping it down, absorbing it into itself and then spewing fresh malignance into his system.

One week of summer freedom remained before he was due to return to the lycée—one week to punish Michael for the expression of radiant joy on his simple, puerile face.

Olivier had for years been a deviser of games, most of them founded in fantasy, and his newest creation was named "Chevaliers et Dames," during the course of which the Knight was called upon to rescue his Lady from the clutches of the Enemy. The game was tailor-made for Olivier's purpose, and every afternoon that week they played it in the gardens, behind the stables, in the forest, and sometimes in the "haunted" belvedere. And each time, as Olivier flung himself wholeheartedly into his pursuit of the small, freckled, and unlikely Enemy, his persecution became more frenziedly true-to-life.

"You mustn't be so rough, Ollie," Ella chided him after their fourth game. "You really frightened Mischa before."

"He's such a baby—I didn't hurt him."

"You made him cry."

"He should realize it's only a game," Olivier argued defensively.

"We know that, Ollie," Ella said, "but he's only six."

"He'll be seven on Friday."

Ella hesitated. "Perhaps you could let him be the Knight one day, and you could be the Enemy."

"Me?"

"Why not?"

"He wouldn't know how to rescue you. He'd mess the game up."

"That wouldn't matter just once, surely?"

Olivier's eyes narrowed and grew quite black. "Have you forgotten who saved you from the old man?" he hissed.

"Ollie, this is only a game—you said so."

"I won't be the Enemy! This is *my* game. I invented it!"

Ella looked surprised. "All right, please don't get so upset."

"You like the game, don't you? I only thought it up because I thought you'd enjoy it."

"I love it," she reassured.

"So we leave it as it is?"

Ella sighed. "Yes, of course."

He saved the best for last.

Friday, Michael's birthday, would also have to be the final "Knights and Ladies" game of the holiday, since they were picnicking on Saturday and would not be allowed to play on Sunday. They all gave Michael his presents in the morning and then had lunch in the hotel restaurant as a special treat, all of them even being allowed (since Miss Herrick was not returning until Sunday evening) sips of wine with their food.

Olivier drank his own glass, then most of Michael's, which had been watered down, and was about to take Ella's when William spotted what he was up to and firmly put paid to it.

By the time they went out to play, Olivier was more than a little drunk.

"We're going to the riverbank," he told the other two, while three of the younger dogs, Apollo, Ceres, and Juno, danced about their heels. "I set it all up this morning, while you were still asleep." He grinned, flushed with excitement and wine. "It's going to be the best yet."

They arrived at the narrow river, near the point where one of the little flower-twined bridges crossed the river. There was a tree house up in the branches of an old oak, with a rope ladder leading up to it.

"Look!" cried Michael. "Swords!"

Olivier had left a small pile of props for them, including two plastic swords, two shields, a toy dagger and two gaudily painted cardboard crowns. He passed one crown to Ella and placed the other on his own head.

"Can't I have one?" Michael bounced up and down, making the dogs bark.

"You're the Enemy, and he's a commoner. But you can have a sword and a shield."

"And a dagger?"

"No, there's only one, and that's for me."

Michael beamed, docile as usual.

"Right," Olivier announced, "you climb up to the tree house, Ella. The Enemy's locked you into his prison and if I don't rescue you in time, he's going to kill you."

"Will you hold the ladder still, Ollie?" Ella was nervous of heights, but didn't want to admit to it.

"Of course, Lalla."

Gingerly, she clambered up and knelt on the wooden floor of the "prison."

"Now undo the ladder and throw it down!" Olivier shouted.

"But then I'll be stuck."

"That's the idea, stupid. If you could get down, why would I need to save you?"

"Oh, all right." She unhooked the end of the rope ladder and let it fall to the ground. Ceres and Juno skittered out of the way, while Apollo leapt into the water for a swim.

"Now you, Michael," Olivier ordered, "are the miserable pretender to my throne. You've captured Princess Ella and you're holding her for ransom."

"What's that?"

"It means if I don't pay you one thousand francs, you'll kill her."

"Yes, I will, I will!" Michael cried, entering into the spirit, knowing that Olivier got annoyed if he did not.

"I'll count to one hundred while you hide, and then I'll be coming after you."

Michael looked anxious.

"I'll count for you, Mischa!" Ella called from the top of the oak.

Olivier checked his watch. "The time starts *now!*"

"One, two, three, four, five—" Ella counted in her clear, high voice, looking down with a smile as Olivier disappeared and her little brother began scurrying around for a suitable hiding place.

"Mischa," she hissed loudly, "he'll find you wherever you choose, so why don't you surprise him?"

"How?" He looked up at her.

"Ssh! He'll hear." She paused. "Why don't you ambush him?"

"What's that?"

"It means you just hide in one of those bushes, and when he comes back looking for you, you jump out and wave your sword and fight him."

"But he'll win."

"But you'll have beaten him by surprising him."

"Ollie always wins," Michael said a little wistfully. His eyes grew round. "You've stopped counting!"

"Hide quickly—time's almost up."

With a flash of inspiration, Michael looked up again. "Lalla!"

"Yes?"

"Tell the dogs to stay, or they'll give me away."
"Good idea, but *hurry!*"

Michael crouched low behind a great glowing clump of roses
and hibiscus, his own brilliantly colored hair just another patch of
radiance camouflaged in the general blaze of reds and pinks and
mauves.

He couldn't tell exactly why, but he was afraid. Decidedly
afraid. His chest was tight, his breathing shallow and rapid, his
mouth dry.

Only a game, he told himself. *Like always.*

But Ollie always caught him in the end, and he always hurt him
in some small way that was definitely real, like a pinch or a kick
or, once, an honest-to-goodness punch.

I'm seven now, he remembered with a flash of pride. *I'm older
than I was yesterday, so maybe Ollie will respect me.* He remembered once, after Olivier had been mean to him, he'd asked him
why, and Ollie had said that he was just a baby, and he couldn't
respect a baby. *Seven isn't a baby.*

He heard a sound, like feet kicking leaves and coming closer.
He knew it was Olivier, and that any second now he would have
to leap out at him as Lalla had said, and he wasn't at all sure that it
was such a good idea.

And then Olivier passed very close to the bushes, and Michael
caught a glimpse of his face, and he saw his eyes, and there was a
look in them that curdled his blood and sent great warning signals to all his nerve ends. And in that last split-instant before he
jumped out from the bushes, Michael realized what the look said.

I'm not your brother. I'm the Knight.
And you're my Enemy.

Ella knelt on the planked floor of the tree house, pins and
needles cramping her legs. But she didn't want to move, feeling
more secure staying absolutely still.

A breeze ruffled the branches and her perch creaked. She
froze, and a small attack of panic rose inside her.

She peered over the edge, her fingers grasping tightly to the
frame as Olivier approached. Looking at the bushes, she tried to
pinpoint Mischa's carrot head. *There? No, there!*

Olivier's sword and dagger were both sheathed in his belt. Ella
smiled. If Mischa took her advice, for once he'd have an edge on

Ollie—and wouldn't it be nice if Ollie let him win because it was his birthday.

But he won't.

Olivier's head moved from side to side, his eyes scanning every nook, cranny, and shadow, like a seasoned hunter stalking his prey.

I'll find him.

I'll teach him.

He saw the dogs, three in a row, sitting like obedient children, tails wagging. Out of the corner of his right eye, he saw two ducks waddling down to the water's edge and setting sail downstream toward the little footbridge.

Where is he?

I'll thrash him.

There was a rush of leaves and twigs and air, and a loud whooping noise, and a cloud of insects rose out of the bushes just as the boy, small and quivering and resolute, launched himself into the air with a flourish of a plastic shield.

Ella looked down.

"I've won! I've won!" Michael shrilled with pure joy and the outstretched arms of a victor.

She saw Olivier stumble and his crown fall from his head, watched Michael crash against him, yelling and brandishing his sword. She saw Olivier recover his balance, draw his own weapons, and push the younger boy away from him with a sound that was half shout, half roar.

"I *ambushed* you!" Michael's triumphant voice soared. "It was Lalla's idea!"

Olivier glanced fleetingly up at the tree house, and Ella saw something in his face that scared her, absolutely, utterly terrified her.

Olivier raised his sword high in the air—a salute by the Knight to his Lady, especially for her.

"I'll save you!" he bellowed.

Suddenly, his moment of delirious pleasure over, Michael realized that the game was not at an end, and worse, far worse, that his seconds of terror in the bushes had not been foolish—they had been sound as the ground beneath him.

The chase began.

Into the bushes and out again, around the oaks, over hedges, along the path and off into the rough turf, while the wolfhounds barked madly and Ella shrieked for help piercingly—not for herself as the rules of the game decreed, but for her baby brother.

It is *a game,* she tried to tell herself. *It* is!

And then Olivier began to laugh, and the sound was as great a relief to her jagged fear as cool water might be to scalded skin, and then she heard Mischa, too, as far as his breathlessness would allow, yell with laughter as he evaded his brother yet again, and dashed past him onto the arched bridge.

"Right, you fiend!" Olivier yelled, leaping onto the planking, sword swishing. "Let's fight for her! Let's fight for Princess Ella!"

Ella got closer to the edge, craned her neck to see them, and her cardboard crown fluttered to earth.

"Yes, help me!" she cried loudly, actually having fun for the first time, and wondering just why she had gotten so upset about nothing at all.

"I'll save you!" Olivier shouted again, and gave a whack at Michael's shield, which fell with a clatter against the side of the bridge. He thrust again, and Michael's sword, too, tumbled out of his hands.

"I've got you now! Do you surrender?"

Michael tried to pass him, failed, and made a frantic scramble up the parapet on his right.

"No, Mischa, *don't!*" Ella screamed.

It seemed to happen in slow motion.

Ella saw Olivier's arms stretch out toward Michael, watched as the sword and dagger flew from his fingers, saw the expression on Mischa's rosy face change yet again from excitement to fright.

And then he fell. . . .

Down, down, twisting like a diver, tumbling, spiraling headfirst toward the dark water below. And as Ella began to scream again, he disappeared from her field of vision. She could only see Olivier standing openmouthed on the bridge, staring down as a great echoing splash reverberated in the air about them.

"Ollie!" she heard her own sobbing shrillness. "Save him! For God's sake, save him!"

Olivier looked up briefly, then suddenly, with an almost theatrical boldness, as if he were still quite immersed in his role of *chevalier,* he planted his hands firmly on the parapet, wrist-deep in thorns and petals, and launched himself into space.

Now they were both out of sight, and Ella saw Apollo hurtling toward the bank and into the water, with Juno and Ceres barking wildly. Frantically she cast around for a means to get down to the ground, but the rope ladder was still heaped uselessly at the foot of the tree.

For just a single, fleeting second, she hesitated, shrank from the terrifying sheer descent. But then she thought of Mischa and Ollie both in the water, and with tears of panic pouring down her cheeks, she forced herself out of the tree house. Somehow, half sliding, half clinging, she clambered down the trunk, fingernails gouging into the bark, hands and feet grappling with branches, hardly aware of the burning scrapes on her arms and legs and face, until she hit the ground, rolling over, the breath knocked out of her.

"Ollie! Mischa!"

Olivier had not intended for it to happen.

He had jumped into the water to save his brother, not especially for his sake, but for Lalla, whose white, horrified face had stared down at him from her treetop prison.

It was when he was *in* the river, chest-deep in the murky, rushing cold, with the small carrot-topped boy beneath him, eyes torn wide with fright, mouth open and gasping for air like a hooked fish, that it had come over him like a powerful wave, an almighty torrent smashing into him, taking him over.

"Ollie, save me!"

Those eyes, hazel and trusting and helpless.

"Ollie, help me!"

And then the dog was beside them, great, gray, muscular beast, its big mouth snarling, the large, sharp teeth trying to grab hold of Michael's shirt collar. Olivier put out his hands and shoved the dog away, and Apollo growled from deep in his throat, but Olivier pushed harder.

And as the struggle continued, he was no longer aware of Michael's stark, petrified face, or his eyes, no longer trusting, merely disbelieving, not condemning even now, even as his brother's strong arms held him under the water and the last bubbles of air squeezed from his bursting lungs past his aching throat and out through his nose and mouth.

Nor was Olivier conscious of the pain in his hands where Apollo's teeth had seized his flesh, nor of his own blood swirling in the water around them, nor of Ella, who stood on the riverbank, no longer able to scream, her face a ghastly mask of dread and agony.

He only knew that at last the thrashing had stopped, and with it the bubbling.

He only knew that the Enemy was gone.

"It was Apollo," he told her, in a dull, flat voice. "He wouldn't let me pull him out."

He laid Michael gently down on the grass.

"Look," he said. "My hands."

Ella stared at them, saw the deep wounds and the blood, and her knees buckled and she felt sick.

"Apollo?" she whispered.

"Yes."

She sank to her knees, put out a hand and touched Michael's cold, clammy skin.

"Mischa?"

"It's too late, Lalla," Olivier said, and began to cry. "He's dead."

"Dead?"

She began to tremble, so uncontrollably and violently that Olivier squatted down beside her and put his arms around her, but she wrenched away from him and he saw his blood staining her muddy, torn dress.

"*Mischa!*" she cried piteously, and flung herself at him, folding him into her arms and cradling him to her breast.

"I tried so hard to save him," Olivier sobbed, "but Apollo wouldn't let me. He went crazy all of a sudden! Maybe it was the water, I don't know . . ."

Ella glanced up and saw the dog, twenty yards away, standing head down, quivering and dripping, a strange, continuous low growling rumbling in his chest.

And then she looked down again.

And the screaming began again, and didn't stop, *couldn't* stop, until strong adult hands reached down and tugged her gently, but firmly, away.

Chapter 25

Michael Armand Robert Hunter
30.8.50 – 30.8.57

Seven years.

Krisztina, standing very erect, felt William's hand gripping her elbow and heard her mother's quiet weeping, and remembered her own words, tossed so lightly into the fragrant Normandy air just a few weeks before:

Seven years of bad luck.

She shut her eyes. They had had seven years with Michael, years of joy and beauty and love. An end to superstition.

She opened her eyes and looked at William, saw the gray bleakness of her own face mirrored in his, then turned to see little Ella, ashen and grieving, with Olivier's protective arm around her and Geneviève standing behind them.

Krisztina looked back down at the ground, at the coffin, so small, so alone. It was early September and still warm, but she felt icy cold, had never felt so cold in her life.

Michael was down there in that cold earth, and a whole part of her lay with him.

Some things are unbearable, she thought.

Unbearable.

For Ella, as for the others, life went on.

She had lessons with Miss Herrick, and she tried to forget,

though she never quite could, the two graves—the one with Mischa's name on it, and the other with poor, mad Apollo's, in the animals' graveyard not far away.

Papa sat alone a great deal, drinking whisky and crying, which Ella had never seen him do before. Maman was kind to her and to Ollie, and brave, but though they never saw her weeping, her beautiful eyes were always red and sore, with dark circles under them.

Ella had nightmares all the time, and woke up screaming, and then Ollie would come and sit on the edge of her bed, and she would sob in his arms until she could sleep again.

Life went on.

Maman began working all the time, every day, even harder than she had before, often not stopping for lunch or dinner. Papa seemed a little better, and started going away again on business, and when he came home on Friday evenings, he didn't drink whisky or cry anymore. And after a few weeks, he talked Maman into going with them all down to the villa in Villefranche-sur-mer, where they stayed for two weeks, and Ella thought it was very nice, but not the same as it would have been with Mischa.

One afternoon in December, Olivier found a tiny mongrel puppy sheltering from the rain in the *temple d'amour*, and brought it to Ella, hoping to cheer her. The pup was coal black, with little streaks of beige on its paws and on the tip of its tail. In spite of its lilliputian size, it displayed great confidence and audacity with the wolfhounds, and so Ella named him Titus.

She lavished love on him, and even Miss Herrick was so taken with the creature that she occasionally permitted it in the schoolroom, aware that Ella found lessons intolerably lonely without her brother. But nothing really helped for long, for Ella was tormented by pain and guilt and confusion.

She had accepted Olivier's account of what had happened that day, for she had no reason to doubt him, but she was still haunted by memories. Of the game, of the chase, of her own inexplicable terrors—worst of all, of Mischa's face as he plunged from the parapet. But even more than that, more than anything, no matter how normality seemed to return to their lives at de Trouvère, her own sense of guilt hounded her mercilessly, for Ella felt, truly believed that, in many ways, she was to blame. For she had known that she was frequently far more responsible than Olivier, yet she had always let him have his way, had participated willingly in his games, too often at Mischa's expense.

And now Mischa was gone.

In a few weeks time, Ella would be nine years old, in the very heart of childhood. But though she had come to understand that, in spite of everything, life did continue, and that she might even be happy again someday, a segment of her mind recognized that the joyous, unfettered summers and the sublime, ineffably snug winters that had embraced her in their sweet, tender blanket of protection, were also gone.

And they would not return.

PART FOUR

ELLA: Alsace and New York
1968–1974

Chapter 26

Ella could hardly believe her eyes.

KINGS ROAD, CHELSEA.

The sign said it all, and she supposed that many of the tourists thronging the famous London street were not particularly surprised. To a nineteen-year-old girl, however, who had done almost all her growing within the confines of the same few hundred acres of French countryside, the sights and sounds of this wild, extraordinary, milling peacock society were almost too much to absorb.

It was fresh, it was new, it was unceasingly mobile, it was brash and it was loud—it was another world.

They had come, *en famille*, to England for Robert Hunter's funeral ten days before, and had stood in a pleasant rural churchyard, gray November skies pressing down over the steeple, threatening rain, paying their respects in an atmosphere of controlled grief and composure to a man some of them had hardly known.

Robert and Clementine Hunter had moved to New York three years earlier, because it had no longer been possible to ignore the fact that the Manhattan branch of Hunter's was now their flagship branch. When Robert had died suddenly of a heart attack while chairing a meeting, however, there had been no doubts that he must be buried in his native land.

William and Krisztina stayed with Clementine at her London flat for a few days after the funeral, while Geneviève, Olivier, and Ella stayed at the Connaught Hotel. On the sixth day, however, William knew that it was vital he appear at the New York office. Krisztina and Geneviève returned to de Trouvère and Ella and Olivier decided to remain in London for a short holiday.

Olivier enjoyed squiring his sister around the great city, observing with pride the admiring glances thrown her way wherever they went, for he recognized as well as anyone that Ella had indeed become a rare beauty.

They went everywhere—to Hampstead, Kensington, Chelsea, Knightsbridge, Bond Street, Carnaby Street.

"But Ollie, I want to do more than shop and eat!"

"All girls love to shop."

"I want to go to the theater."

"All right," he said easily.

"And the cinema."

"We have cinemas in France, Lalla."

"But we never go. And museums—I want to see the V and A and the British Museum and—"

Olivier put his foot down. "If you want museums, *ma chère,* you'll have to find someone else to take you."

Ella went to the museums on her own. With her brother, she did all the things they normally had no opportunity to do, eating at in-places such as The Spot and 235 Kings Road, tossing back Pino Frios and spare ribs at Trader Vic's, carving up great rare slabs of beef in the Rib Room at the Carlton Tower Hotel, dancing at the Ad Lib and the Revolution, and watching *If, Barefoot in the Park* and *2001: A Space Odyssey.*

"They say," Olivier told her knowingly afterward, "that the last part was Kubrick's impression of an LSD trip."

Ella shook her head. "It was beautiful, not ugly and frightening like that stuff."

"How would you know, Lalla?"

"I wouldn't really, thank God, but I know it's dangerous and crazy and I want nothing to do with it."

Ever since Olivier had returned from his compulsory military duty with a cache of cannabis, Ella had been uneasy about drugs. She had found him one afternoon shortly after her seventeenth birthday, staggering like a blind man around their old "haunted" belvedere, and had pleaded with him never to touch the stuff again.

But the too common use of drugs was not all that had begun to trouble her about the London scene. The incessant noise and traffic gave her headaches; the palpable tension in the air discomfited her; and the sudden exposure, through Olivier and some of the friends he had swiftly made, to men, both excited her and sent warning prickles down her spine.

Olivier and Ella were indisputably two of the most eligible young people in the Haut-Rhin. Olivier, physically striking, with dark good looks and a muscular body kept trim with exercise and weight-training, had his pick of local girls, and it had lately become a ploy of his to make advances to hotel guests, advances that were often welcomed by their recipients, though, of course, strongly deplored by Krisztina and William.

Ella, on the other hand, was reticent with the opposite sex, even shy. Undeniably, her looks had already sent dozens of young and older men reeling, but the fact was that Ella, with her fiery mane of hair, her intense eyes, ripe, soft mouth, and lithe, high-breasted body, was simply not ready.

Her ambivalent attitude to boys had already caused her one moment of unpleasantness in London. Ella loved to dance, adored the thumping beat of the discotheques, found it easy to let herself go on the open dance floor, to allow the music to take her over and to shake her body without a hint of her natural restraint. One young man she'd danced with at the Revolution, a dark-eyed economics student called Tim, with a fine sense of rhythm but no experience of a girl like Ella, took her for what he said would be a "breath of air," and promptly pushed her up against a wall outside in Bruton Place.

Ella froze. "No, thank you," she said as pleasantly as she could.

Tim bent his head and kissed her moistly, his tongue trying to part her tightly clenched lips. Ella tried to extricate herself, but he held on to her firmly, one hand against her shoulder, the other groping at her left breast.

"No," Ella said, more sharply.

His face loomed close for another kiss, his eyes closed, and the roving hand left her breast, snaked down to the hem of her white Courrèges mini dress and up between her legs—

"*No!*" Ella shoved him away, feeling sick and angry.

Tim looked startled. "What's wrong?"

"I don't want to," she said tautly.

"You don't?"

"No."

"Well, you sure give out mixed signals."

"I don't." Ella was indignant.

"Dancing the way you do?" Tim raised an eyebrow and turned away in mild disgust, just as Olivier emerged from the nightclub looking for her.

"Lalla?"

Ella still stood by the wall, flushed and upset.

"Qu'est-ce que tu as?"

"Rien."

He came closer and tilted her chin. "What happened?"

She shook her head. "It was nothing."

"That boy—what did he do?"

Ella saw the anger sparking in his eyes, and forced herself to smile. "Nothing, Ollie, honestly. I just have a slight headache, and I want to stay out here a moment."

"I'll stay with you."

"No, you go back inside. I'll be there soon."

She waited until he had disappeared before she put her hands to her face, wanting, unreasonably, to cry.

Ridiculous.

She was nineteen years old, and she knew she was pretty. She knew from other girls her age that this was to be expected and that she was supposed to feel gratified. Not nauseated.

It had only been when he'd put his hands there, tried to probe between her thighs. No one else had done that—boys had kissed her, and sometimes she'd even enjoyed it—but no one had done *that.*

Except Grand-père.

She took her hands from her face and the lamplight shone on them, and Ella looked at the tiny scar on her left thumb, so small that no one else would even know it was there. Only Ella knew, and Olivier.

The past, she thought, was always with her. It never really went away.

London was teaching Ella something important about herself. Perhaps, she reflected, it was having a real taste of freedom for the first time, or rather of the outside world, since the only other time she had spent away from de Trouvère had been during her one year of business studies at the *polytechnique* in Paris.

Maybe it was liberty, she mused, that showed you what it really was you wanted to do, where you wanted to be, where you belonged. And she belonged, she now knew, at de Trouvère. Not only was it the only home she had ever known, but Ella was suddenly more intensely conscious than ever that the château itself truly returned the love and care lavished on it. De Trouvère actually nurtured them, granted her family immense security and comfort, and gave their guests pleasure and respite from their daily lives.

She was ready to go home.

The night before Ella and Olivier returned, they were sitting in the lounge at the Connaught having a drink, when Olivier confided in her his suspicion that William and Krisztina might be forced to move to New York.

"That's impossible!"

He shrugged. "It's Hunter's premier house—the head office. With Robert gone, they'll be wanting reassurance."

"What sort of reassurance?" Ella had grown pale.

"That life will go on," Olivier said simply.

"They would never expect Maman and Papa to live there. Their home is de Trouvère."

"Things change, *chérie.*"

"I don't like change."

Olivier squeezed her hand. "I know."

William spent two weeks in Manhattan, returned to Alsace for four days, collected Krisztina, and flew back again for another week, leaving Geneviève, Olivier, and Ella in charge of the hotel.

"Something's definitely going on," Olivier said late one evening as they sat in the office, checking purchase ledgers.

"What do you mean?" Ella asked.

"This New York business." He paused. "Big changes."

"Don't," she said quickly, and stopped punching figures into her adding machine.

"We have to be realistic, Ella. If they're going to move over there, it'll have to happen soon."

Ella threw down her pen and it rolled off the desk onto the floor. "Ollie, you're really serious about this, aren't you?"

"Sure I am."

"But you sound so matter-of-fact about it."

He shrugged. "I've done some thinking, and I've decided, quite frankly, it would be fabulous."

"Ollie!"

"It's just what we need, Lalla."

"To lose Maman and Papa?" she said incredulously.

"You've heard of abdication, surely?"

"Ollie, we're not royalty."

"Comes to the same thing though, doesn't it? So long as our parents are in control, we'll never be much more than bookkeepers, no better than the hired help."

"Speak for yourself!" Ella was indignant. "I've done almost every job there is in this hotel . . ."

"But to what end?"

"To learn, obviously."

"For what?"

"For the time when we have to run the business."

"And when will that be? When we're both silver-haired?"

"When the time is right."

Olivier shook his head. "The time is perfect now. Hunter's is basically still a family concern, and with the old man gone, Papa has to take over."

"That doesn't mean he has to live in New York."

"Of course it does. Don't be naive, Ella."

"If it's naive to be sorry that our grandfather's died, or to want my parents living in the same country as me, then that suits me just fine!"

"He wasn't *my* grandfather."

"Oh, Ollie, for heaven's sake!"

Olivier was unmoved. "You have to realize this is our chance, *chérie*."

Ella stared at him. "You can be so hard sometimes. It really troubles me."

Olivier tossed his hair, grown fashionably long. "There are moments to be soft, Lalla. This is not one of them."

"I don't understand why you're suddenly unhappy with the way things are. You have all the privileges that de Trouvère gives you, with very little responsibility."

"Does that rule out all ambition?"

"Of course not, and I have ambitions too. But I'm in no hurry—

I love my life the way it is, and I pray that you're wrong about New York. Apart from anything else, this hotel is Maman's world —she'd be lost without it."

"She'd get over it."

Ella flinched at his callousness. "Maybe," she said, her voice steady, "but I still pray that you're mistaken."

Olivier leaned over and kissed her cheek. "Pray all you like, *petite soeur,* but you'll see that I'm not."

He was right.

Less than a week later, the ax fell.

"We have to go, darling," Krisztina told her for the umpteenth time.

"I can't believe it."

"We have no choice."

"I still don't understand why Papa can't just go there more often," Ella tried again, though she knew perfectly well that he could not.

"For exactly the same reasons that his father had to leave England." Krisztina was pale and tired, for once feeling every one of her forty-nine years. "Ella, my love, I'd hoped for more objectivity from you."

"You want me to be objective about the loss of my parents?"

"You're not losing us, *chérie,* you know that."

Ella sighed. "Yes, of course I do." With a great effort, she brought her turbulent feelings under control. "All right, I give in."

"This isn't meant to be a battle," Krisztina said, distressed. "This is a decision for the whole family to be involved in."

"No, it isn't."

"Yes, it *is.*"

"This family is not a corporation, Maman. We can't have a nice civilized meeting and lay out our strategy and vote on it." Ella's eyes were intense. "We're human beings, with sensitivities and emotions and needs." She shrugged. "Maybe I'm supposed to be very adult and wave you off with a cheery *au revoir,* but I still want my mother and father in place."

"It is all wrong, isn't it?" Krisztina agreed. "It's the sons and daughters who are meant to leave home, not the parents."

"But this isn't just a home you're leaving," Ella persisted. "It isn't even just your business either—it's your creation, your masterpiece."

"Which I can, thank God, pass on to you."

"And Ollie."

"Of course. It was your brother for whom the hotel was first thought of."

"I know."

"So this is perhaps, after all, the right way for it to happen. Better than waiting for me to retire, or even die, by which time you and Olivier could be bored and embittered, or perhaps thousands of miles away involved in something else." Krisztina frowned. "That aspect does worry me as much as anything else."

"Which aspect?"

"The fact that William and I are effectively tethering you both to de Trouvère when you might in the natural course of events have wanted to leave."

"I can't imagine ever wanting to leave," Ella said truthfully. "But then again, I couldn't have conceived of your wanting to either."

"I don't."

"But you want to be with Papa."

Krisztina smiled. "Of course." She paused. "And you have to realize that he is appalled at the notion that he's stealing me away from you and de Trouvère. He would never consider such a move it it weren't one hundred percent necessary."

Ella chewed her lip. "I suppose Hunter's is important. More important than the hotel."

"Not more important—much larger, of course, with many more people dependent upon it—but your father would not, for an instant, minimize the value of Château de Trouvère, in both its financial and more abstract roles."

"But if Papa doesn't go to New York, he may lose control of Hunter's, whereas if you do go, de Trouvère stays with us."

"Precisely." Krisztina spoke the word with no hint of satisfaction, only deep wistfulness.

Ella was silent for a few moments, then she raised her head. "Do you think this is permanent, Maman? Do you think you might come back?"

"Nothing is forever, *dragam.*"

"Do you like New York?" Ella asked curiously.

Krisztina laughed. "In many ways, yes, I do. It horrifies me sometimes, but that's because I've spent thirty years in the countryside. But any city that can hypnotize its inhabitants into believing that it's the center of the universe must have remarkable powers."

"London made me feel like that."

"But London's utterly different—like Paris, or even Budapest, it has so much dignity, venerability. Manhattan is *now*."

Ella chuckled. "London seemed pretty 'now' to me when I was there."

They fell silent for a few moments.

"When will you go?" Ella asked.

Krisztina shook her head. "Papa will have to go fairly soon, but I shan't be able to leave de Trouvère for quite a long time." She paused. "Do you feel any better, Ella? Any more understanding?"

Ella made a wry face. "How does 'resigned' sound to you?"

"Better than we deserve."

"That's not true," Ella said quietly. "You deserve support and reassurance." She took a breath. "And you're going to get it."

"Do you think you'll be able to cope, *chérie*?"

Ella smiled. "I know I will."

Late that night, after Ella had gone to bed and before Olivier had come home, William and Krisztina sat with Geneviève in her drawing room, sipping cognac before a roaring fire.

"Do you think they're really ready?" William asked them both. "Ella's only nineteen."

Geneviève smiled. "But what a nineteen."

"She's more mature than Olivier," Krisztina pointed out.

"And *she* thinks she's ready," added Geneviève.

"So does Ollie," said William. "I suppose this might be the making of him. A chance to utilize his assets in a practical way for a change."

"He'll have to stop trying to seduce every attractive woman in the hotel."

"I'm sure he will, Belle-mère," Krisztina smiled.

"Are you? I'm not."

"They just may make one hell of a team." William stroked the small beard he'd recently grown. "Olivier has natural dynamism, ambition, and great charm when he wants to be charming, and we all know that Ella's given herself a finer all-round training course than any hotel school could offer."

Geneviève, still as superbly elegant as ever, in perenially chic Chanel skirt and blouse, beamed as she thought of her glorious granddaughter who was not, of course, any part of her flesh and blood, but who was equally as precious to her as Olivier.

"Ella is extraordinary," she said. "Efficient, talented, strong, and calm enough to smooth down her brother's brusquer edges." She paused for a moment. "What about Ilona and Gabor? How will your mama cope without you?" In recent years, Ilona had become increasingly confused, and a full-time nurse had been engaged to look after Gabor.

Krisztina looked unhappier than ever. "It's so hard to know what she wants, Belle-mère. You know how it is—sometimes she's quite lucid, other times she seems to believe that she's in Budapest. I think it would be almost impossible to drag them to another continent. They need stability, normality, their home."

"And Ilona needs her daughter too." William winced. "I feel such a complete swine, you know. So much disruption, so much pain."

Krisztina got up from her armchair and sat down very close to him on the sofa. "It isn't your fault, William. No one blames you."

"That doesn't alter the fact that I'm tearing you from thirty-year-old roots."

Geneviève put down her glass. "Your wife, mon cher, is a survivor. She was torn from other roots far more violently once before in her life."

"It wasn't so hard, Belle-mère," Krisztina said, "not once I'd met you and fallen in love with de Trouvère."

"Our home is very special, yes, but I think you have the ability to seek out beauty wherever you are."

"I must admit," Krisztina said slowly, "that I never for an instant imagined that anything or anyone would persuade me to leave de Trouvère." She took her husband's hand. "But I don't feel that I'm abandoning the château—not with you and the children, not to mention André and Marthe and the others. It isn't as if we're still building it up. Our hotel exists."

"And what about them?" William asked, gesturing toward the two dogs that lay at her feet; Janus, a magnificent descendant of Perseus, one of the first wolfhounds Krisztina had met when she came to de Trouvère, and Titus II, the oldest son of the little black mongrel Olivier had found for Ella years before.

Krisztina reached down and tickled Janus behind his ears. "These two will have to come—there's no possible way I could leave them behind. And young Vénus will make a splendid *maman,* if Belle-mère and Ella will give her up."

Geneviève smiled. "You're going to breed?"

"Did you think I was going to do nothing? After the life I'm used to?" Krisztina grimaced. "I'd go insane within a month."

"That means we'll need space, which means that I'll have to commute," William sighed.

"Since you've been doing that for the past twenty years, I can't see that should matter too much."

Geneviève stifled a yawn and glanced at her watch. "It's after two, *mes enfants.* I'm an old woman and I need my bed."

Krisztina raised an eyebrow. "You have more energy than any of us."

"Not anymore." Her face grew serious again. "That's why I'm glad we have the young ones to take over. It would be too much for me alone."

"They certainly won't be able to manage without you," Krisztina pointed out. "Ella may have taught herself brilliantly, but they lack expertise."

"Did we have experience when we began?"

"No," Krisztina replied, "but things were different in those days. There's more competition now, more to gain, more to lose."

"Don't worry, *chérie,*" Geneviève reassured, "I shall be the stabilizing influence they need. But I shan't interfere with everyday decisions. If I do that, they'll never have a chance, and the spirit of the place will suffer."

There was another silence.

"So it's all decided?" William said at last.

"It seems so," Geneviève replied.

"Kriszti?"

Her eyes were suddenly damp, but she swallowed down the tears that threatened.

" 'New melodies,' " she said softly.

"What, darling?" William looked blank.

She squeezed his hand. "One of Belle-mère's wisdoms. About change."

"Oh." William nodded. "One of those."

Geneviève smiled and waved a hand. "Not my words."

"But so very apt when we were wavering over whether to turn the château into a hotel," Krisztina said. "And just as fitting now."

William found them a home, a handsome, six-bedroom stone house near Rhinebeck in Dutchess County in the heart of the Hudson River Valley. Though no match for Alsace or California, it was wine-growing country, so Krisztina could relate to the land, and they had a charming landscaped garden that backed onto five untamed acres that had come with the house.

"Isn't it a little too far from the city?" asked Ella anxiously when Krisztina told her about it.

"Haven't we always been?"

"But this is home."

Krisztina hugged her. "Not when I first came."

On the morning that they left, shortly after seven o'clock, Krisztina went alone to the chapel and graveyard.

She stood on the stone floor, with the early May sunlight breaking through the stained-glass windows. She remembered the first time she had stood there—and all the others too—and her thoughts drifted back to David and Laurent, and to her father and her mother, to the days when Ilona Florian had been calm and strong, not the often bewildered old lady who had sat just now, beside her paralyzed husband, not quite realizing that the kiss her daughter had given her might be the last. . . . And to her wedding, and to the baptisms and the funerals and to Michael . . .

She walked out, past David's gleaming golden plaque, into the churchyard, where the graves confronted her, strewn as always with fresh flowers, the headstones well tended and somber. And as she knelt at the smallest, Krisztina was overcome by a strange feeling of unreality, as if none of this were happening, almost as if none of her memories had ever been real, as if she were still a child in Hungary, dancing before the long mirror in her parents' bedroom, with Miksa and then Mozes lying patiently, watching her. . . .

"Maman?"

She turned her head slowly, and saw Ella standing on the gravel path.

"Yes, *dragam*?"

"I'm sorry, Maman," Ella said softly, "but Papa and Ollie are waiting. It's time."

Krisztina nodded. "Yes."

She looked down again at Michael's grave, and the old, intolerable yearning to hold him in her arms was as strong and undeniable as it had been more than ten years before.

"He'll never be more than seven," she whispered.

"No." Ella came and stood close to her.

And David will never grow older than twenty-four, nor Laurent more than thirty.

"I'll see that they're looked after," Ella said tenderly.

"I know you will."

Her vision blurred, and Krisztina closed her eyes tightly, as if the fleeting blackness might blot out the awful, dull pain of the moment.

"Maman, you have to drive to Paris."

Krisztina opened her eyes, and all the loveliness and softness and fragrance that was de Trouvère brushed her cheeks and her bare forearms, and filtered, like gentle breath, into her lungs and into her brain, for posterity.

She rose from her knees, and took Ella's hand.

"I'm coming," she said.

A half hour later, their car purred along the main *allée*, away from the house, toward Paris, and America.

Ella went numbly to her office, sat down at her desk, and turned over the page in her diary.

26 May, 1969.

The second generation of the Grand Hôtel du Château de Trouvère had begun.

Chapter 27

It should have been easy.

With so much prevailing bonhomie and such a fine, twenty-year-old reputation, it should have been fairly simple, with dedication, hard work, and common sense, to maintain the smooth running of the hotel.

Though Ella was aware of Olivier's faults, she never for a minute considered him a bad man. Apart from the fact that she loved him, she believed that he had many good qualities—he was fond of his mother and looked up to William; he was proud, beyond most people's imagination, of his heritage; he adored his sister and loved de Trouvère desperately.

He could also be ruthless, she reluctantly conceded, even merciless; increasingly, he liked to gamble for high stakes and hugely enjoyed the seduction and subsequent discarding of women; he often drank heavily; he despised anyone and everything old, with the exceptions of antiques, the château, liquor, and his own ancestry; and he was a hopeless spendthrift.

Olivier, too, recognized and accepted these aspects of his own character with equanimity, for he was wholly and genuinely amoral, and if he did ever experience any feelings of guilt, they were buried deep in his subconscious. The more he had learned about his late father, the more his inheritance compelled him and the more confident he became. Even if others sometimes found his conduct or attitudes reprehensible, it hardly mattered, for they were of little consequence. He knew that he was different from them—he was an aristocrat, and that both explained, and excused, *anything*.

His time was coming—his and Ella's, for she, at least, could be depended upon to respect her older brother's domination—but it had not yet arrived, for his grandmother still held the whip hand. He felt that they formed a triangle—he and Lalla at either end of a solid, youthful base, looking to the future, with Geneviève sitting, like an elegant impediment, on the apex. And though she pretended not to interfere with the hotel's daily running, her presence was a constant threat to him, because he knew that she, more than anyone, saw through him.

It's enough, he often thought when infuriated. *I'm not a child anymore. I'm twenty-five years old—a man! A baron!*

He had, for the most part, disliked childhood, because children had too little control over the factors governing their lives, and it had been a relief when boyhood had officially ended and he had been called up into the *militaire*. Though, that, too, had been a struggle, for in place of grandparents, parents, and teachers, there had been others in command, men who dared to scream and shout at him, to punish and humiliate.

But now the military was behind him, and a brand-new liberty beckoned, a sense of freedom he had never known, represented by a time when he could truly claim his rightful inheritance, determine his own future.

"She's seventy-six, for Christ's sake," he snapped at Ella one day in the autumn of 1970. "Why doesn't she just retire?"

"Because she isn't old," Ella answered.

"Jesus, Lalla! Of course she is!"

"Don't swear at me, Ollie." She paused. "And you're quite wrong—Grand-maman is still the least old person I know, and I, for one, would be lost without her."

"You wouldn't. Neither of us would. We'd have a chance to forge ahead instead of stagnating."

Ella stared at him in confusion. "How can you associate de Trouvère with stagnation? It's a vibrant, living, breathing thing."

"Populated and run by old people with old ideas."

"Ollie," she said more gently, "I don't understand how you,

who are almost fixated by traditions, can have such absurd thoughts."

"Don't call me absurd!"

"It isn't you, it's your ideas! We're listed in the *Michelin* as *grand luxe et tradition.* You sound as if you'd like us to sling out our rococo chairs and bring in tubular steel!"

"Now *you're* being absurd, Ella. I'm talking about people. Fine, I'll admit Geneviève's in good shape, but how long can that last while she has to share the west wing with a cripple and a mad-woman?"

"Grand-mère isn't mad!" Ella was outraged. "She's a little se-nile, poor darling."

"They should both be put away, if they haven't the good grace to die."

"Olivier!" She stared at him in horror. "You don't really mean that."

He saw the intensity of her expression and gentled his attack, never keen to antagonize her. *"Ça va, Lalla, ne te fâches pas,"* he said more softly. "You're right, of course I didn't mean that."

"Then why say it?"

"Because it's one way of getting you to see that because we all live 'over the shop,' our home life is reflected in the hotel itself. Look at old Sutterlin, for example. He's an ancient monument— he should be cast in stone, but he's still our head porter. It's ludicrous. The man's a menace."

"In the first place," Ella replied quietly, "he's semi-retired, as you very well know, though it's true he still works harder than he should—"

"Wouldn't it just be great for business if the concierge had a stroke from lifting too many door keys."

"And in the second place," she went on, trying to ignore his callousness, "he's a highly distinguished member of the Clefs d'Or."

"I don't care if he's their president, he's still well into his seven-ties."

"Well, Jean-Martin Lalouche isn't ready to manage without him yet. None of us are."

"There you go again! Why do you have so little confidence in yourself? In us?"

"I have every confidence in us," she said with dignity. "But I have great respect for experience, and I happen to believe there's no replacement for it. What would you do, Ollie? Fire everyone over the age of fifty?"

"Sounds sensible to me."

Her eyes narrowed. "What about all the extra work you'd have to do without them? How would you find the time to saunter back and forth to Baden-Baden to throw away all your cash on roulette and baccarat?"

"Would you have me molder in Alsace *all* the time, *petite soeur?*"

She shook her head. "Not molder, no. Just take real responsibility, instead of complaining all the time about those who do."

He frowned. "Sounds like you and my dear Grand-maman have been exchanging complaints about me."

"Don't be silly, Ollie, of course we haven't."

"Be careful, *chérie,*" he teased, chucking her under her chin, "or you'll be growing old before your time. You take life so seriously."

Ella ran her fingers through her hair, which she still kept thick and long. "I honestly don't understand you," she said. "One second you want to cast aside everyone that de Trouvère has depended on for years, and the next you want freedom and fun with none of the liabilities or obligations that an estate like this has to entail. You can't have it both ways, Ollie."

He shrugged. "I can try."

"You'll fail." She frowned. "Why don't you make use of this period? Get used to being the boss gradually—make the most of Grand-maman's support, and people like André, who don't need to be told what to do every five minutes."

"Because I've waited long enough. I've been Baron de Trouvère since I was born, yet for almost twenty-three years my lands and this château have been controlled by Hunters."

"Grand-maman isn't a Hunter, and Maman is still often thought of as La Baronne. You're oversensitive, Ollie—there's no foundation for it."

"My father is the foundation for it, Ella," he said harshly. "The last baron. He died at thirty, driven to his grave by hypocrites."

"He was an unhappy man in terrible times," Ella said, aware of how troubled he had been ever since learning of his father's suicide.

Olivier had begun asking searching questions at an early age, confused by his family's paradoxical approach to Laurent; he had always been encouraged to visit the well-tended grave on anniversaries, and to honor the man he'd never known; yet there was so little physical evidence of him—just a single silver-framed photograph in his grandmother's bedroom and one other in the Salon Rouge, tucked away among the litter of family memorabilia. His parents' gold, silver, and porcelain trophies were shut away in glass cabinets in a seldom-used room, and when his father's name was spoken, Olivier observed that his mother and Geneviève's faces and voices were shaded with a regret that seemed deeper-etched than a normal grief for a premature loss.

So he had persisted with his questions, and in his midteens, Geneviève and Krisztina had agreed that truth, softened with love and tact, was best. Their honesty, however, had led to more and more rooting around in a past they believed would have been better forgotten. Yet the more Olivier discovered about Laurent's instability and his associations with the Nazis, the more the boy, and later the man, became fascinated by his father.

For several days after his return from military service, Olivier had locked himself away in his bedroom, refusing to allow even Ella to enter. When finally he had summoned her, she found what appeared, to her uneasy eye, to be a kind of shrine to the late Baron. One corner of the room was filled with leather albums of newspaper cuttings, newly framed photographs, a number of dance trophies, and, chillingly, the snapshot of him with the two Nazis, Bickler and Schlegel, all crowned with a specially made bronze replica of the de Trouvère family crest.

"*C'est beau, n'est-ce pas?*" he had said, smiling at her astonished face.

"*Oui . . . très beau.*"

"You don't seem very sure."

"I'm . . ." She hesitated. "It's a surprise."

"He was my father, Lalla," Olivier said softly, "as William is your Papa. Aren't I entitled to have pride in his memory?"

"Of course you are, Ollie." She looked at him. "As long as it makes you happy."

Absently, he ran his fingers over the leather cover of an album.

"It does," he said.

The "shrine" was still there, together with the thrusting appetite for self-determination and dominion, and a constantly gnawing resentment of anyone who stood in his way.

"I suppose Grand-maman still reports every misdemeanor to New York," he said ironically to his sister.

"I don't think she ever has."

"She certainly told them about Brigitte. I had a stern, very British letter from William, pointing out my duties as a gentleman, even where chambermaids are concerned."

Ella frowned. "Why don't you ever call him Papa anymore?"

"Because he isn't."

She shook her head. "I expect Grand-maman thought you'd pay more attention to Papa about Brigitte than to either of us. And surely you think it's right that you look after her."

"Brigitte had already had two abortions before she came here, you know. She's no little innocent—she knew the ropes, and she has the mental and physical constitution of a cow. I provided her with the funds, she checked into the clinic, and *voilà,* now she's having a free convalescence in Cannes."

"I wonder if we'll see her again."

"Depends who she finds down there."

"If she does come back," Ella warned, "we'll have to keep her on. We can't deprive a girl of her job because of your philandering, Ollie."

"Why should we? She's a good worker."

"And you'll have to keep away."

"Do you think I'm a fool?"

"At times, yes."

"Never drink twice at the same well." Olivier grinned.

Ella shook her head again and looked at the clock on her desk. "Oh, go away, Ollie, and let me get on with some work. You're such a time waster."

"Bien." Olivier rose. "But I still don't like feeling that my slightest sin is conveyed to New York. Grand-maman has no right."

"Actually," Ella said, already bending over the papers on her blotter, "she has every right."

Olivier's face was grim. "Perhaps that's just the trouble."

In fact, Geneviève seldom reported her grandson's misdeeds either to Krisztina or to William. She had made up her mind that Olivier deserved a real chance to find his path, if he could, and stick to it. She had serious misgivings—it was impossible not to remember Laurent, who, by the time he had returned to de

Trouvère in 1938, had at least had his years of liberty, with ample scope for sowing his wild oats; yet Laurent had still suffered a desperate internal struggle, albeit magnified by war and annexation.

But this isn't Laurent, she reminded herself frequently. *This is another man, and it isn't fair to tar him with the same brush.* If they didn't give him some freedom of choice, it would be like condemning him, declaring him irredeemable.

In any case, she mused, lying sleepless in bed, listening to the dawn chorus, *with Ella at his side, and the hotel almost running itself, what real harm can he do?*

Alex Monselet, the chef-de-cuisine who had replaced Luc-Alain Carême seven years earlier, and who had taken the hotel's reputation to even dizzier heights, handed Ella his resignation on the last day of January 1971.

"I thought you were happy here," Ella said in dismay.

"I was." Monselet paused, weighing his words.

"Please, Alex, be honest with me."

The chef made a grimace. "It's your brother."

"The Baron?"

"Oui," Monselet said shortly. "He does not understand the basic rules of the kitchen, mademoiselle."

"Which rules?"

"Chiefly the paramount rule: My kitchen is exactly that, my kitchen, my domain."

Ella smiled gently. "Of course, Alex. We all know that. We respected it all the years that Chef Carême was with us, and we have continued to respect it with you."

"Not your brother."

Ella looked up at him. He was standing rigidly behind her desk. "Won't you please sit down, Alex. We can talk."

"There is nothing to talk about."

"But what has he done to offend you?"

Monselet laughed harshly. "What has he not done?"

"Dieu," Ella said in alarm.

"Eh bien, mademoiselle," he erupted suddenly, "I will tell you."

"Good."

"Your brother has not only taken to invading my kitchen on a daily basis, to check my work—to check my work!—to taste the soups of my *entremetier,* to criticize the buying methods of the *gardes-manger*! He has also attempted to brutalize my second *commis-pâtissière,* a most gifted girl from Toulouse."

Ella's eyes were enormous. "What exactly do you mean by brutalize, Alex?"

His clenched fists banged on the desk and he leaned over her. "I am a Frenchman, mademoiselle," he boomed. "I understand the delights of seduction as well as the next man—but not in my kitchen!"

"But what did he actually do?" She paused, and rapidly skimmed a mental register of those currently employed in the hectic kitchens. "To Marguerite?"

The chef's face purpled at the memory. "He tried to make love to her! In the *garde-manger,* while she was fetching flour and sugar, and then again at her table, while she was rolling out pastry, he made most unwelcome advances."

Ella stifled a grin at the image.

"You find it amusing, mademoiselle?"

She shook her head. "Not in the least," she said firmly. "And I assure you, Alex, I shall speak to my brother immediately."

"To what end?"

"To learn more about the matter."

"You don't believe me?"

"Yes, I do," she assured him. "But obviously I must find out what he has to say."

"You think he will offer an explanation? For attempted rape?"

"Aren't you exaggerating, Alex?"

Monselet's voice grew quieter. "You are right, Mademoiselle Hunter. There was no rape as such, and if we were discussing another man—someone more simply addicted to joie de vivre—it might be less distasteful." He took a breath. "But I am sorry to tell you that Monsieur le Baron is not an amusing young man—far from it."

Ella remained silent.

"He is, however, your brother, and he is, *en effet,* my employer, and therefore you will see that it is now impossible for me to remain at de Trouvère."

Ella swallowed. "I do see, Alex. And I'm extremely sorry." She stood up.

"I, too, am sorry."

She felt sick and angry. "We'll miss you." Any amusement that had briefly flickered inside her had vanished completely.

Monselet gave her his hand.

"You will always have problems, mademoiselle," he said frankly, "so long as he is allowed a free hand. He is not like you."

Honesty stopped her from denial, loyalty, from agreeing.

"I shall eat more often in the restaurant in the two weeks you remain, Alex," she said softly.

"Then I shall try to excel myself."

On March 5, one day after Krisztina had flown back to New York following a two-week visit, Olivier dictated letters of termination to André Sutterlin, Marthe Schneegans, and two other members of staff recently past their sixtieth birthdays.

"You can't do that!" Ella exploded in his office when she found out.

"I've already done it."

"Grand-maman and I will countermand you, Olivier."

He smiled. "Even if you do, they'll all leave—at least Marthe and André will after this. Their pride is wounded."

Ella stared at him. "Do you realize what damage you've done?"

"To our hotel, none at all."

She shook her head in frustration. "You're wrong, so very wrong." She sat down in the leather chair opposite him, her face pale.

Olivier stood up. "Sutterlin and Schneegans were not always as loyal as you seem to believe, Ella."

"Of course they were."

"Not to my father." His face was stiff. "Not at the end. In any case, there's no longer room at de Trouvère for deadwood."

"André and Marthe aren't deadwood," Ella argued. "Their bones may be less strong than they were, but they're both still vital and capable, and they are loyal, whatever you may think." She glowered at him. "And I assure you that when Grand-maman gets back from Strasbourg, we are going to tell them that a mistake has been made."

Olivier smiled again. "By all means. So long as you don't expect me to retract."

"I certainly do, and so will Grand-maman."

"Then you'll both have a long wait."

There was a pause.

"If they were to leave," Ella said slowly, "have you their replacements in mind?"

"We don't need a replacement for Sutterlin, do we. Jean-Martin is ready to take over. And as for Schneegans, I have a young woman for you to interview as soon as you like."

"I don't like."

"Suit yourself. I'll have her contract drawn up without you."

"You will not!"

Olivier sat down again and played with a gold pen. "Don't you want to know who she is?"

"Probably one of your girlfriends."

"Actually she isn't, though I'll admit she's pretty enough. But in this instance, *petite soeur*, I was drawn to her other qualifications."

"Where has she worked? Probably some ultramodern chain," Ella challenged, angrier than ever. She drew breath. "And don't call me *petite soeur*, Olivier—I'm your business partner."

"Her name is Paula Müller, and she's from Graz."

"And where has she worked?"

"She's only had two senior jobs. She spent nearly four years at the Kempinski in Berlin."

Ella said nothing.

"And then she worked for three at Brenner's."

"Baden-Baden?"

Olivier smiled. "I've actually impressed you. Yes, Brenner's Park."

"Why did she leave?"

"To nurse her father back home in Graz."

"You've confirmed that with Brenner's?"

Olivier leaned back in his chair. "What exactly do you take me for, *chérie*?"

Ella waited a moment. "I'm not sure."

"A swine?"

She met his gaze. "In this case, a swine and a fool."

The telephone on his desk rang. He picked it up, spoke for a moment, then replaced the receiver. His face was inscrutable. "Grand-maman seems to have returned from the city. She wants to see us both."

"Has she spoken to Marthe or André?"

"Presumably."

Ella looked at him. "You know you've gone too far this time, Olivier. I won't support you. I can't. Grand-maman will insist on reinstating them all, not just André and Marthe."

"Ah well," he said, "it won't make a jot of difference. As I've said, I won't retract, and anyway, neither Sutterlin nor Schnee-gans will feel that they can stay."

"Don't," Ella said abruptly, standing up.

"Don't what?"

"Don't make me hate you, Olivier."

He looked up at her obliquely. "Strange—I thought I never paid much attention to Miss Herrick, yet I suddenly remember a line from her precious Browning." He stood up too. " 'When I love most, Love is disguised in hate . . .' " He looked directly into her eyes. "Appropriate, don't you think, Lalla?"

"Maybe it is. But don't think that it makes it any easier."

The afternoon that André and Marthe left the hotel, both Geneviève and Ella wept openly as they embraced.

"You *will* visit, won't you," Ella urged for at least the tenth time. Marthe would be remaining close at hand, in a house bought for her by Geneviève in Saint-Hippolyte, but André was going to his sister's home in Grenoble.

"I'll come when I can," he reassured her, and turned to Gene-viève. "And if ever you need me, madame, you have only to lift the telephone."

"Oh, André, we'll never stop needing you."

Sutterlin looked back through the doors toward the front desk, and saw Jean-Martin Lalouche in full swing, eyes intent upon the guest to whom he was giving directions for the Route du Vin, while at the same time accepting airmail letters and room keys.

"Jean-Martin is now a member of the Clefs d'Or. He is more than ready to be left in control."

"But you're so much a part of de Trouvère," Ella said. "Just as you are, darling Marthe." She squeezed the older woman's thin arm affectionately.

Marthe made a face. "I wish I could be sure that Fräulein Müller is the right *gouvernante*."

Sutterlin snorted rudely. "You're just prejudiced, Marthe. The girl seems most efficient to me."

Marthe gave him a tart look and turned back to Ella and Gene-viève. "You know what I shall miss the most?"

"What?" Ella asked.

"Chef Gérard's cooking."

"Really?" Geneviève was surprised. "He's wonderful, we all know, but you've never cared that much for haute cuisine, have you?"

Marthe gave a watery grin. "But the chefs have kept me out of the kitchen for more than two decades. Now I shall be forced to cook for myself again."

"You were a superb cook, Marthe," Sutterlin said. "I have never come across a better *Schifela* than yours in all Alsace."

Now it was Marthe who looked astonished. "You remember that? After all these years?"

"André remembers everything." Geneviève's eyes were wet with tears. "And so do I."

In his bedroom in the east wing, Olivier poured another glass of champagne for the curly-haired blonde beside him on top of the duvet.

"It's only four in the afternoon," she murmured. "I have work to do."

"*Chut*, Paula," he hushed her. "There are other things beside work."

"Some boss," she chuckled, admiring his narrow frame, still quite well muscled in spite of too much alcohol. "But I doubt if your sister or grandmother would agree with you."

"Oh, they would, believe me. They're both big on sentiment."

"And what, may I ask, has sentiment to do with this?" She licked at her champagne and then began to flick her tongue over his chest.

"Not a thing," Olivier said, and lying lazily back, solemnly regarded his penis as it grew rock-hard and rose, tumescent and huge.

"It's curious," Paula whispered breathlessly, beginning to straddle him, "but you never gave me any hint at my interview that you wanted me." She closed her eyes and smiled as Olivier's hands reached up to grasp her breasts. "You were strictly business."

"That's me—always business."

Paula giggled throatily. "This too?"

"Sure." Her breasts felt marvelous in his hands. "What is the paramount role of the *gouvernante*?"

She raised her hips and then, with tantalizing slowness, started to lower herself onto him. "To see to the complete comfort of each guest," she replied demurely.

"This, *Liebchen*," Olivier explained, giving both erect nipples a simultaneous, savage tweak, "is simply basic training."

"Any awards for initiative?"

"Quite likely."

"Then keep your eyes open, Monsieur le Baron." She arched her body, rounding her back and tightening her stomach, so that his view of his own genitals was unimpaired. With a sudden, violent, surging motion, she thrust herself down on him, like a Japanese woman committing ritual *seppuku* on a sword.

Less than five minutes later, the telephone on Olivier's bedside table rang.

"*Oui?*"

"Olivier, have you seen Paula Müller?"

"A little while ago, yes."

"Do you know where she went?" Ella sounded irritated.

"Am I our *gouvernante's* keeper?"

"Probably, yes."

Olivier glanced at Paula, prone at his side, and gave her a sharp dig in the ribs, quickly hushing her as she opened her eyes and groaned.

"Well, you'd better look for her somewhere else," he said into the telephone.

"This is one of the busiest times of day for her. You can tell your protégée that if she's going to perform vanishing acts on her first solo evening, she won't be here long."

Olivier put down the receiver.

"Get up," he said roughly.

"I'm too comfortable, *Schatzi*."

He sat up and slapped her buttocks once, hard. "I said get up, Fräulein Müller. It's time for work."

She rolled over, her eyes enquiring. "What happened to *Liebchen*?"

"*Liebchen* has to get dressed."

"What happened to basic training?"

"*Terminé*." He pushed her. "You're on the job now, Paula, and you'd better be terrific."

"Don't you think I was terrific, *Schatzi*?"

"Not bad. Not bad at all." He grinned. "You've convinced me you know how to lie on a bed. The question is, can you still make one?"

Chapter 28

There are some things in life one chooses not to believe, even if one knows that they are true.

In Ella's case, it was the ever-increasing knowledge that Olivier's true soul was sealed to her.

That his dark side was darker than she'd realized.

Perhaps she had always known.

But she loved him anyway.

In September of that same year, 1971, Ella came upon Olivier standing in front of the cheval glass in his bedroom, inspecting what appeared to be a new jacket of burgundy velvet.

"Very dashing," she said, smiling. "What's it for?"

"Why should it be for anything?"

"Well, it's hardly your usual style, is it?" she commented, eyeing the heavy gold braiding on the lapels and shoulders. "It looks like a uniform."

"It is."

"So why are you wearing it?"

"Because I'm entitled to."

Ella shrugged. "If you're going to be mysterious, I really don't have time."

Olivier turned away from the mirror. "I've joined a fraternity in Paris."

"Really? Which one?"

He began unfastening the gilt buttons. "It's called Confrères de La Fontaine; though that's simply because we meet in an apartment on the rue La Fontaine."

"What kind of fraternity is it? Who are your fellow members?"

Carefully, he slipped off the jacket. "Young men proud of their country and their birthright."

"Birthright? Are they all aristocrats?"

"Not all."

Ella smiled. "You *are* being mysterious, Ollie."

"Not really. It's just private, that's all."

She raised an eyebrow. "A secret organization?"

He shook his head. "Just private."

The next time she saw the jacket, it was partly concealed under a Burberry trench coat, just as Olivier was leaving the east wing one afternoon in November. He was carrying a long, thin leather case.

"What's that?" Ella asked.

"A rapier."

Her eyes widened. "For what?"

Olivier didn't answer, and her voice sharpened. "Ollie, what's it for?"

He smiled. "It's purely ceremonial, Lalla, don't worry."

"Your fraternity?"

"A special gathering." He paused. "The rapier's part of the uniform."

"That's all?" She relaxed and kissed his cheek. "Have fun."

"I will."

Three weeks later, after a weekend excursion to Baden-Baden that turned into a six-day stay, Olivier returned to de Trouvère with a large sticking plaster on his left cheek.

"What happened, *chéri?*" Geneviève asked the next morning as they passed in the hotel reception.

"Rien."

"It doesn't look like nothing."

"Un petit accident," Olivier said casually. "I tripped in the bathroom and cut myself."

"Too much to drink, I suppose," Geneviève said drily.

"If you like."

When the plaster was removed a week later, and Ella saw the

scar, long and fine, like a wound left by a razor's edge, she went silently to the library and took down a book.

An hour later, locating him in the Salon Bleu bar, she asked Olivier to come to her office.

"Well, *petite soeur*," he said lazily when he arrived, a bottle of old malt in his right hand, "why have I been summoned? Have I misbehaved again?"

"I don't know. Have you?"

He grinned. "Probably." He poured whisky into the glass in his left hand. "On second thoughts, definitely."

"The casino?"

He grimaced. "God, yes."

"You lost a lot."

He shrugged. "No more than I can afford."

Ella sat beside him on the couch. "Drinking too?"

"Sure." He put the bottle down on the carpet. "And sex. You forgot sex."

Ella looked at him. "What about dueling?"

Olivier blinked. "What?"

"Have you been dueling?"

"What a question! Of course not."

She continued to watch him.

"Oh, you mean this." He fingered the scar. "Dueling is illegal, Ella."

"Not student dueling, not in Germany—what they call *Mensur*."

"I'm not a student."

"Ollie, you lied to me about the rapier's being ceremonial, didn't you?"

"It is."

"Oh, tell me the truth for once in your life, Olivier! Does your little fraternity practice *Mensur*?"

"No."

"Oh?" It was clear she didn't believe him.

He sighed. "The members of Fontaine have never dueled, or even practiced *Mensur*. We do, however, fence, with full protection and face masks."

"So how did you get that?"

"We met with an associate brotherhood over the border."

"Students?"

He shook his head. "They've just adopted some aspects of student fraternity life."

"Like *Mensur*?"

"Yes."

Ella stared at the scar and shuddered. "How horrid."

"Not at all. It isn't like dueling, Lalla—there's no enmity involved, far from it."

"Olivier, many people associate fraternities like yours with neo-Nazism."

"Which is outrageous."

"Is it?" she asked quietly.

"Absolutely. Would you ally me with thugs and lefties?"

"I'm talking about the extreme right, not left."

Olivier drained his glass. "The so-called neo-Nazis have far more in common with the Commies than with the real Nazis, Ella. They're opposed to capitalism, to most things that I believe in."

"You seem to know a lot about them."

"Fontaine is aware of the criticisms leveled against us. We need to be able to defend ourselves." He poured himself a double shot of malt. "Most neo-Nazis are *old* Nazis, the aging party faithful cluttering their homes with Third Reich memorabilia, waiting for a second coming of their Führer. The young ones are sucked up out of the football crowds and from street gangs." He made a disdainful face. "Hardly our sort."

Ella was unimpressed. "So what does Fontaine stand for?"

Olivier looked irritated. "I told you when you first asked me. Don't turn something honorable and pure into something sinister and wrong."

She remembered his words. "Just a group of young men proud of their birthright."

"Exactly."

One of the telephones on Ella's desk rang, and she stood up to answer it. "*Oui*, Paula." She listened for a moment, answered briefly, and put down the receiver. "A problem in our linen store. I have to go."

"What do you think of our *gouvernante* now, Ella?"

"Effective and efficient." She paused. "More so now that you've stopped inviting her to your rooms."

Olivier shrugged. "I thought it was better for business."

"I'm glad to hear it."

"Perhaps I'm not such a lost cause after all," he said lightly.

"I've never thought that you were." She walked to the door, and looked back down at him. "That doesn't mean I must agree with many of the things you do."

"Fontaine, for example."

"Quite."

He smiled up at her, his dark eyes damp and blurred with drink and brotherly love. "There's nothing for you to worry about, Lalla."

"Good." She opened the door, glanced back once more, and added softly: "Be careful, Ollie, please."

Olivier raised his glass in a salute.

"I will."

On the eleventh day of 1972, while William and Krisztina were still in Alsace following the celebration of their wedding anniversary and Ella's twenty-third birthday, a bad cold from which Ilona had been suffering developed into pneumonia.

"I'll have to stay," Krisztina told William after an unhappy night at her mother's bedside. They had planned to return to New York the next day.

"Of course." His own face was creased with concern. "It's damnable enough that I have to go."

"Well, you do," Krisztina said firmly, aware of the pressures that always built up on him when he was away from Hunter's. "Docteur Freitag says that the antibiotics should have an effect quite soon, and then I'll be on the earliest possible plane."

William noticed that she was shivering slightly. He went over to the fireplace to throw fresh logs onto the dying flames, before returning to her side on the sofa. "She's eighty-two, Kriszti, darling," he said gently, putting his arm round her. "Do you think she'll beat this?"

"I don't know." Krisztina looked helplessly into his eyes. "Look at Gabor—all those years in a wheelchair, so many years unable to talk or do hardly anything for himself, and still alive." She sighed. "It's strange. Here I am, the mother of grown-up children, and I know I should be able to cope with this easily, to say that Mama's a good age, that she's been unhappy for years . . ."

"I don't think she's been so unhappy," William disagreed softly. "She just stopped being able to communicate her feelings as she used to, and with Gabor as he is, maybe a part of her mind chose to dwell in the past."

"I feel so guilty for leaving her alone." Tears began to rise in Krisztina's throat. "When they got out of Hungary after the war, I promised Mama that we'd never be separated again."

"That's my fault," William said, "not yours."

She shook her head, her usually immaculate and still golden hair in disarray after the night's vigil. "No, it isn't. Don't start blaming yourself, William. It was my own decision." She shrugged, hopelessly. "Maybe we should have asked them to come with us. Maybe it was wrong to leave them behind."

"This had become their home by then, Kriszti," William insisted steadfastly. "They had familiar surroundings, comfort, doctors who knew their histories, their grandchildren . . ."

"I don't think Olivier's been much use."

"Ollie's a selfish young man," William said drily. "But Ella more than makes up for him."

Krisztina smiled wistfully. "Our daughter." Her voice was soft. "She's rather spectacular, isn't she?"

"Like you, thank God—spunky, strong, yet tender as marshmallow."

"You might just as well be describing yourself, you know."

"Me? Really?" He stroked her cheek.

"Really."

Krisztina was sitting in her mother's bedroom at eight o'clock in the evening three days later when Ilona, who had been sleeping fitfully for hours, awoke and sat up abruptly.

"Mama?" Krisztina leaned forward.

"Kriszti." Ilona's voice was hoarse, and there was a curiously intent expression on her face.

"Mama, what's wrong?"

Ilona's cheeks were a ghostly translucent white, and her feverish eyes were fixed on her daughter's. "Tell you," she murmured.

"What?" Krisztina came to the bed and took her hand. "You're so hot, Mama. Shall I call Docteur Freitag?"

"No! No doctor. I have to tell you."

"Tell me what, darling?"

"The truth." Ilona began to cough, the awful, racking cough that had tortured her for days. Krisztina gave her some water to sip, and the coughing eased, though her breathing was still labored. "Truth," she said again.

"Shall I fetch Father?"

"No, Kriszti."

"He's just next door, Mama—"

"*Nem!* Not Gabor! He mustn't hear . . ." Ilona struggled for breath, then made a great effort to compose herself. "This is for you, *dragam,* only for you."

Krisztina stroked her mother's hair back from her forehead. "All right, Mama. I understand."

"Sit with me, Kriszti."

She sat on the edge of the bed.

"Closer."

Krisztina moved as near to Ilona as she could. "What is it? What do you want to tell me?"

"What I should have told you long, long ago." Ilona's voice was suddenly clearer and calmer than it had been for many months.

Krisztina waited.

"In the bottom drawer," Ilona said.

"What, Mama?"

Ilona gestured urgently at the bedside chest to her right. "In the bottom drawer, Kriszti, underneath everything. A pouch."

Krisztina opened the drawer and, after a moment, withdrew the small leather pouch. Bemused, she placed it into her mother's shaking hands.

Ilona's eyes filled with tears. "I have sinned."

Krisztina jolted with shock. "Do you want Père Beurmann, Mama?"

Ilona nodded weakly. "Soon."

Krisztina started to rise, but Ilona tugged at her arm. "Not yet," she protested. "This is for you, Krisztina. For no one else."

"All right, Mama, all right." She sat down again. Ilona began to struggle with the little drawstring at the neck of the pouch. "Shall I help you?"

Ilona shook her head and tipped the pouch upside down. Something golden spilled onto the white sheet. "Yours," she said, her voice strange again.

Krisztina looked down.

"Take it, Kriszti."

"What is it, Mama?" Krisztina picked up the fine chain and

looked at the six-pointed star. Her forehead puckered. "I don't understand."

The tears in Ilona's eyes began to stream down her wrinkled face, tears of long-pent-up remorse and fear and secrecy. "Yours," she said again, chokingly. "From birth."

Krisztina stared, too confused to speak.

"It was on you when Jozsef found you," Ilona sobbed, and the sobbing made her cough again, and gasp. Krisztina dropped the star and gave her more water and waited, ashen-faced, until the spasm had subsided.

"All right?"

Ilona nodded weakly, and forced herself to speak again. "You know what it is, Krisztina? You understand what it means?"

Krisztina picked up the star again, held the cool gold in her palm, and her heart began to pound, her breathing to quicken. She touched the points with her fingers, felt their sharpness, and suddenly an extraordinary mixture of awe and comprehension and wonder swept over her, for in that instant, holding that fragile link to the past, to *her* past, so many things became clear.

"Father didn't know?" She, too, was trembling. "Doesn't know?"

Ilona shook her head. "I was afraid for you." Her mouth quivered.

Krisztina nodded. Easy to understand—oh, how easy—after the years that they'd all lived through. Her mind twisted and turned. "You've kept this hidden all these years?"

The tears were still rolling down Ilona's cheeks. "It was my great secret, my great sin . . ."

Krisztina shook her head. "Not a sin, Mama." Her own eyes were wet.

"Yes, it was. I knew it, and Jozsef knew it, but what else could I do?" It was a wail, a plea for understanding.

"You could have told me later, when I was grown." The words slipped out quickly, thoughtlessly. Krisztina wanted desperately to comfort her mother, but it was impossible not to say what was in her mind. God alone knew how much torment that kind of silence had cost her mother over the last fifty years. She shook her head, trying to clear it. "You could have told me after I found out I was adopted."

"I wanted to, dear Jesus, how I longed to tell you! But I was still afraid. Your new life, your son, the twenty-seventh Baron—how could I have told you without changing everything?"

Krisztina still gazed at the star, and now her mind was traveling back through the years, and a voice was jangling in her head, repeating over and over again: *David.*

Ilona, watching her, knew. "You're thinking about David."

Krisztina's heart contracted painfully. "If I'd known—" She stopped.

"What would you have done?" Ilona's voice grew a little stronger. "Declared yourself Jewish? Would you have condemned yourself to death?"

Krisztina looked honestly into her mother's face. "I might." She paused. "That might have been my right."

"You think I don't know that?" Ilona sagged back against her pillows, weakness overwhelming her again.

"Mama?" Krisztina said, alarmed.

"Oh, Kriszti . . ." She reached for her hand and clung to it. "Can you ever forgive me?"

Hot tears cascaded down Krisztina's cheeks, scalding her skin, tasting salty, tumbling onto their entwined fingers. "There's nothing to forgive, Mama."

"Lies. Terrible, wicked lies."

Krisztina shook her head. "For love."

"My greatest sin." Ilona's mouth worked wearily, her whole being drained by guilt and irony. "Père Beurmann waits to grant me absolution, while my daughter, my own child, learns that she is a Jewess." She grasped at Krisztina's hands even more piteously. "How can you forgive me?"

"I can, Mama, of course I can."

Ilona pressed Krisztina's fingers to her cheek. *"Koszonom, koszonom . . ."*

"Why do you thank me, Mama?" The tears were blinding now. "It's I who should thank you."

Ilona managed to smile. *"Koszonom, Kriszti,"* she whispered again.

"For what? For loving you? It's impossible not to love you, Mama."

"For coming to me from nowhere," Ilona breathed. "For being my daughter, my child."

"You're my mother," Krisztina said quietly, simply. "You always were. You always will be. Whether I am a Catholic or a Jew makes no difference to that."

The sound came from behind, startling them both.

It was a grotesque, rattling sound, scarcely human, a rasping struggle for breath.

Ilona's eyes opened wide with shock.

Krisztina turned around.

Gabor sat in his electric wheelchair, in the doorway. With his good hand, he grasped at the air as if he were clutching for something, for someone. His spectacles hung askew from one ear, and his left eye—his one good eye—stared at Krisztina with incredulity and absolute, all-consuming horror.

"So now you know." Ilona's voice was shockingly loud in the evening peace.

Still the eye stared.

"So now you know, at last, my great sin, Gabor Florian." Ilona sat forward, using the last vestiges of her strength. "And you know your own."

"Mama, don't," Krisztina said, starting toward her father.

Ilona could not stop. "Now you know, Gabor Florian, that your daughter—the daughter you professed to love, and betrayed in more ways than you even knew—is Jewish."

Gabor had not spoken a word in more than sixteen years.

Now he struggled, and his eye bulged, and saliva trickled down his chin, and his chest heaved.

And he managed one word.

"Kriszti."

And then he died.

Père Beurmann came to hear Ilona's confession and to give her the last rites, and then to pray over Gabor's shriveled body. And Docteur Freitag and Krisztina and Geneviève sat with Ilona as she sank into her final sleep, until at last she, too, died at four o'clock that same morning.

"I don't know if she meant me to tell the rest of the family," Krisztina said pensively to William three nights after the bizarre double funeral, as they lay wide awake in their bed in the east pavilion.

William reflected for a moment. "I expect she felt that you'd make the right decision when you were ready."

"But what do you think?"

"It's not my secret, darling."

"But I don't want it to be a secret!" Krisztina twisted her body so that she faced him. "It isn't a thing I could possibly be ashamed of."

"So tell them."

"Just like that?"

"Why not?"

"I don't know, I guess I think it might come as a shock to a solidly Catholic family."

"It didn't shock you, did it, Kriszti? Not in that sense."

"No, it didn't."

"So why should it bother your children? I'm sure it won't worry Geneviève."

Krisztina smiled. "You're probably right." She deliberated. "Although even Belle-mère . . ." She hesitated. "Her faith is very important to her."

"You said it never troubled her that you weren't as staunch a Catholic as she was. And think about what she did for David."

She shook her head. "You are right, of course. It won't make an iota of difference to her, except that it may help explain a few things about me."

"As it has for you." William drew her closer.

She paused. "You can't really understand why Mama didn't tell me before, can you?"

"No, I can't. But you can, and that's all that counts."

"Yes, I can," she said fervently. "I've had an anti-Semitic father and husband, and I've only lived through one war. Mama had seen it all before. She knew I'd found happiness and security, and she simply couldn't bear to endanger it."

"And now you're left wondering the same thing—should you risk a little disruption to our well-ordered lives, or should you take that Star of David and hide it in a drawer for another fifty years?"

Krisztina sighed. "Yes."

"Except that by hiding it, you're perpetuating every monstrous thing that Adolf Hitler and all the anti-Semites before him stood for."

She was taken aback. "Am I?"

"Think about it, my darling—it's absurd, it's ludicrous! For God's sake, think about the State of Israel. Think about all that those people have been through in just the last ten years. And to what end? To have a woman of your high intelligence and moral values feel ashamed of being Jewish?"

"But I'm not ashamed, William."

"No, of course you're not. I think you're actually rather proud of it, aren't you?" He went on. "It isn't as if you were making drastic decisions, as if you were wondering whether to convert to the faith. It's merely a matter of identity."

She was silent.

"Look, my love." He reached past her and took the faded leather pouch from her bedside table. "This is what you are— what your mother by blood, and probably your father, were. Truth, Krisztina. Simple, honest truth."

For one more moment, Krisztina said nothing, then suddenly she scrambled out of bed and reached for her peignoir.

"Where are you going?"

"To call a family meeting."

"Now?"

She tied the silk belt in a strong, decisive bow. "I can hardly believe I've been so idiotic!"

William sat up. "Kriszti, it's two o'clock."

She stared at him. "Oh."

"I think morning will be soon enough, don't you?"

She got slowly back into bed. "Can I have the star, please?"

They turned out their lamps, and lay in each other's arms. For a little while longer Krisztina fought sleep, welcoming the new peace that was gradually invading her, until finally she slept, the little scrap of gold clasped in her hand.

She told them.

As predicted, Geneviève took the news with her accustomed equanimity, while Ella, over a generation removed from the climate that had made clandestinity of this kind necessary, was fascinated but fundamentally undisturbed.

Olivier was aghast.

"I don't believe it," he said flatly.

"It's the truth, chéri." Krisztina spoke gently.

"On whose word?"

"On the word of a priest. My mother's cousin."

"It really is amazing," Ella said. "Thank God she was able to tell you at last." She smiled. "I've always loved the story of the dog—it's all like some fantastic fable."

"No doubt that's what this is," Olivier dismissed acidly. "Myth, pure and simple. Let's face it, Grandmère hadn't made much sense for years."

"I assure you she made perfect sense when she told me."

His eyes were black. "I refuse to believe it."

"And this?" William picked up the Magen David from the marble coffee table in Geneviève's salon. "Was this a figment of your grandmother's imagination too?"

"She wasn't my grandmother," Olivier said harshly.

"Answer the question, Olivier. What about this?" William held up the star.

"She could have found that."

"Don't be childish."

Olivier ignored William and directed his angry stare at Krisztina. "You, a Jewess?" He shook his head vehemently. "Impossible."

"Why?" She smiled. "Because of my hair? My eyes? Mama's cousin told her that my real mother was blond too."

"Is there something wrong with being Jewish, Ollie?" William asked quietly.

"Don't ask ridiculous questions," Olivier snapped.

"I'd say that it's a highly pertinent question."

Again, Olivier ignored his stepfather. He felt sickened, repelled, and, more than anything, betrayed.

He gave a bitter laugh.

"What's so amusing?" Geneviève asked.

"That all these years, all my life, my father—my true father—has been the family scapegoat, the sinner."

"That's not so, *chéri*." Krisztina was pale.

"Of course it is!" His lip curled. "And you—especially you—were so generous in your forgiveness, when all the time, there's no question that he was above you in every way."

"Olivier!" Ella was appalled.

"It's different for you, Lalla—you're my sister, and you know I love you, but you've never borne the de Trouvère name, so it can't matter to you that they're trying to tarnish it."

Ella's eyes were full of pain and bewilderment. "I don't even begin to understand what you're talking about, Olivier."

"I think, Ella, my love, that what he's talking about is racial superiority." William's expression was grim.

Silence fell in the room.

"He isn't, Papa," Ella whispered. "That isn't what you mean, is it, Ollie?"

Olivier rose from his chair and faced them all, his eyes filled with antagonism. "Your father's right, Lalla, though perhaps a trifle melodramatic. I do care about the purity of our line—the de Trouvère line." His mouth was tightly compressed. "And until our mother married my father, we *were* pure, pure and undefiled."

Geneviève was on her feet, the sound of her slap resounding through the shocked room before anyone else could move.

Olivier stared at her, then gave an ironical little bow from the waist. *"Merci,* Grand-maman." The scar on his left cheek glowered angrily.

Geneviève's hands were trembling, but her chin was high as she looked with dismay into her only grandson's face. "Sometimes, Olivier," she said, "I think that you would have made a first-rate Nazi."

Ella sat rooted by horror to her armchair, her gaze fixed on the scar that Olivier had explained to the others as an accident, her mind shooting like a reluctant arrow to the gold-braided uniform that she knew still hung in his wardrobe.

"Ella? *Chérie?"* William looked drawn and anxious. "Are you all right?"

Ella nodded, unable to speak, all the time trying to push unwelcome thoughts from her brain, pushing them, willing them to be gone. *There are things in life it is better not to think about.*

Krisztina sat very still, her own eyes wet with unshed tears.

"How can she be all right, William?" Her voice was faint. "How can any of us be?"

Chapter 29

Olivier wanted revenge.

More than ever before, he wanted control over the estate, and now he was determined, hell-bent on having it.

William and Krisztina were back in the United States—mercifully, for every time he looked at his mother, he was reminded of the truth about her and the monstrous fact that there was a part of himself, one half of his blood, that he despised. But at de Trouvère, there was still the same damnable triangle, still dominated by his wretched, imperious grandmother.

On the second weekend of April, the combined membership of Olivier's fraternity, Fontaine, and their associates from Germany, assembled at the hotel for a "seminar." Olivier had preempted Ella's disapproval of such a plan by arranging for each member to make his own reservation, so that by the time she learned of their arrival, it was too late to alter anything.

It was well after midnight on the Friday night when, working on overdue correspondence in her office, Ella was summoned by a red-cheeked night porter, Louis Dettlingen.

"Whatever's the matter, Louis?" she asked as she hurried after him.

He muttered something.

"I beg your pardon?"

The young man ground to an abrupt halt and swung around to face her. *"C'est une orgie,* mademoiselle!" His expression was an agony of embarrassment.

"What?"

"Une orgie," he repeated.

"Where?"

He shrugged in desperation. "Everywhere!"

For Ella, the next two hours were ones of revulsion and blazing anger.

The night porter was right—the dinner laid on for the two brotherhoods in the Summer Room and Salle Fleurie had rapidly turned into a wild drinking spree, spreading itself over much of the château, soon becoming a full-blown bacchanal.

"Where did those women come from?" Ella demanded to know, after finding two seminaked couples on the Persian rug in the Salon Rouge.

"They weren't here when I went off duty," defended Jean-Martin, summoned from his room.

Ella turned to the junior man. "Louis?"

"They arrived during the evening," he said, flustered. "Monsieur le Baron said they were invited."

"Poules!" Jean-Martin spat disgustedly.

"What could I do?" pleaded Louis, wringing his hands. "How could I know?"

"It is your job to know," Jean-Martin castigated him.

"All right," Ella broke in. "Let's just concentrate on clearing up this mess. Louis, are any of the other guests still up?"

"Malheureusement, the Livornes were in the library trying to read. They came to reception to complain about the noise."

Ella made a swift mental check of the register, thankfully aware that Olivier's group had virtually taken over the whole hotel. "What about Maître Galle?"

"He went to a function in Colmar this evening. He isn't back yet."

Ella ran tense fingers through her hair. "Then let's get to work right away."

"Shall I wake Madame la Baronne?" asked Louis.

"Whatever for?"

"Madame told me always to inform her in the event of a crisis."

"You will certainly *not* wake her," Ella retorted crisply.

Jean-Martin looked more displeased with the night porter than ever. "Shape up, man, for God's sake."

"*Oui,* Monsieur Lalouche."

Ella had never seen or even imagined anything like the scenes that awaited her. This was single-minded debauchery, decadence on a grand scale, and she was ill-equipped to handle it.

But handle it she did, with the assistance of her two porters. Together they dragged eight dripping, half-clothed fraternity members from the chilly waters of the pool, put a stop to a nude wrestling match in progress at the summit of the great baroque staircase, locked away every visible bottle of liquor, swept up broken glass, cleaned up vomit, and physically put nine men to bed, having first sent seven disgruntled prostitutes back to Colmar in gratis taxis.

"Why can't we wake Fräulein Müller?" Louis asked reasonably enough as he scrubbed away at yet another odious section of carpet in the bar. "I'm sure she would make a better job of this than I can."

"I'm sure she would," Ella agreed gently, "but the fewer people who learn about this debacle, the better, don't you think?" She got down on her knees and helped him for a moment, then wrinkled her nose. "This one needs professional treatment, I'm afraid."

"*Merde!*"

They glanced up as Jean-Martin swept into the bar.

"What now?" Ella asked.

"Did you look in the Hunting Room, mademoiselle?"

"Not yet."

"Then do not, I beg of you." He dragged Louis to his feet. "*Venez, vite,*" he commanded.

Ella got up. "I'm coming too."

"No, mademoiselle, please! There are things that a lady should not see, even in this enlightened age."

Ella looked him in the eye. "This is my family's hotel, Jean-Martin, and it is my responsibility. There is nothing that goes on in this house that I should not know about."

"Forgive me for disagreeing with you, but there are exceptions to every rule."

"Oh, for heaven's sake," she exclaimed, irritated, "we're wasting time. Are you two going to accompany me, or shall I go alone?"

"*Nom de Dieu,*" Louis murmured as he opened the door.

The Hunting Room was in total disarray, furniture turned over, two showcases smashed, an appalling smell filling the air—but what transfixed Ella and, for just a few moments, both Louis and Jean-Martin, was the sight of two young men, wearing only their torn white shirts, lying motionless, their limbs entwined with the limp, apparently lifeless legs of Artemis, a five-year-old Irish wolfhound.

Ella's head spun.

I must not faint, she forced herself to think. *I* shall *not faint.*

In the other corner of the room, a third man, half slumped against the trompe l'oeil wall, urinated into an Etruscan terracotta vase.

Blood roared in Ella's ears.

"That is *enough!*"

The sound of her voice, clear and sharp as a stiletto, momentarily stunned the man, who dropped the vase onto the parquet floor, where it shattered into hundreds of fragments.

Ella kept her eyes deliberately away from the sight of the dog, unaware that her own nails were gouging at the flesh of her palms. "Louis, please escort that person to his room and lock him in."

"*Oui,* mademoiselle."

There was a tone in the night porter's voice that she had not heard before. She glanced at him. "Can you cope?"

"Assuredly, mademoiselle."

Swiftly, he marched over to the offender and took his arm. The man wrenched free.

"Take your hands off me!"

"Don't be more of an idiot than you already are," snapped Louis. He attempted to take hold of him again, but the broader, taller man lunged at him and struck him hard in the chest.

There was a brief, gaping silence while Louis appeared to draw breath. Then, quite unexpectedly, he inclined his head toward Ella.

"*Excusez-moi,* mademoiselle," he said pleasantly, and then, spinning agilely on his heel, he swung his right arm, fist clenched, and connected expertly with the other man's chin, catching him easily as he sank to the floor.

"Merde!" Jean-Martin said again.

"I'm sorry," Louis said, red-faced. "Shall I remove him now, mademoiselle?"

"Please do." Ella watched, in continuing surprise, the slight porter toss the unconscious man over his shoulder as if he were no heavier than a large bag of potatoes. "And Louis."

"Yes, mademoiselle?"

"That was superb."

His blush deepened. "Thank you, mademoiselle. I'll return in a moment."

Ella steeled herself to look down at the other two slumbering men, sprawled beside her beautiful Artemis.

Jean-Martin knelt down, rolled one of them away, and laid a gentle hand on the dog's side. "She's alive." He frowned. "I think she's been drugged."

Ella began to burn with uncontrollable fury.

Jean-Martin stared at the men. "They're okay, too, I think. Out of their skulls with drink and—" He stopped abruptly.

Ella shut her eyes.

"Mademoiselle?"

She opened them again. "I'm all right."

"Shall I telephone the police, or do you wish this to be forgotten?" The head porter was poker-faced.

She didn't answer.

"Perhaps," he volunteered, "you would prefer to wait until later before deciding?"

With his left foot, he prodded the second man, who shifted in his sleep and revealed a ruby-colored wound in his right thigh.

"Artemis must have bitten him."

Ella swallowed, nauseated. "Get rid of them, Jean-Martin," she begged him suddenly, through clenched teeth. "For God's sake, get rid of them!" She sank onto the floor and touched the animal's shaggy fur, her eyes filling with tears, which she blinked furiously away. "I'd better call the vet."

"I'll do it, mademoiselle, as soon as I've locked these two monsters away." He paused. "Can I shut them in the cellar? That will give them something to think about when they wake."

"An excellent suggestion," Ella agreed, "but we can't afford to take the risk."

"They wouldn't dare make a complaint."

She shrugged wryly. "Just the same, we're obliged to put them to bed, *and* to call Docteur Freitag to check them over and deal with that bite."

"Won't he make an official report?"

Ella shook her head. "Not unless there's anything seriously wrong, which I doubt."

Louis returned, pushing a baggage trolley.

"What's that for?" Jean-Martin inquired.

"I thought it would be good enough transport for them, Monsieur Lalouche."

Ella nodded. "Excellent."

"How is Artemis, mademoiselle?"

She felt steady breathing under her hand. "She seems to be asleep, thank God. Jean-Martin thinks she was drugged."

Louis looked horrified. "With what?"

"God alone knows." Her face was grimmer than ever. "But I'm going to find out."

Forty-five minutes later the hotel had been, superficially at least, returned to a reasonable semblance of normality. At ten minutes before three o'clock, when Maître Galle, a distinguished Parisian lawyer, strolled contentedly through the front door, Louis was back at his post in a clean uniform, offering the guest the key to his suite with a smile.

"Quiet evening, Louis?"

"As the grave, Maître."

"Good night, Louis."

The night porter bowed. "Sleep well."

In her office, Ella, hands cupped around the glass of cognac that Lalouche had poured for her, looked at him. "Have you seen my brother, Jean-Martin?"

The head porter's face was impassive. "No, mademoiselle."

She paused. "Is the doctor still here?"

"He'll call down before he's ready to leave." He stared down at Artemis, whom they had laid on a blanket on the floor. "And the vet is on his way."

"Good."

"Try not to dwell on it, mademoiselle," he said gently. "You must put it out of your mind as quickly as you can."

The image of the Hunting Room, now firmly sealed to the public, flashed into her mind. She blinked it away.

"Would you like to go to bed, mademoiselle? I could wait for the vet."

She smiled at him. "No, thank you, Jean-Martin. I'd prefer to wait myself."

He nodded. "Then I shall see if Docteur Freitag needs any assistance."

"And after that, get some rest. Tomorrow will be a tough day."

After the vet had come, and Ella was satisfied that Artemis was in no danger and had suffered no injury, she went into the hushed reception hall to see Louis Dettlingen.

"I want to make absolutely certain that there are no more uninvited females in the house, Louis."

"There are none, mademoiselle," he answered emphatically.

"How can you be sure?"

"Because I counted them when"—he looked acutely embarrassed again "—when they arrived."

She nodded. "Good."

There was an awkward pause.

"Mademoiselle?"

"Yes, Louis?"

"I very much regret what has happened tonight."

"We all do," Ella said wearily.

"And I must ask you to accept my resignation." He stared unhappily at the floor.

"Why?" she asked, astonished.

"Because it was my fault."

"Of course it wasn't."

"Not all of it, no, but the"—he stumbled over the word "—the prostitutes. Monsieur Lalouche was quite correct—I should have known better."

Ella smiled. "It was a new experience for you, Louis. Everyone makes mistakes, you know that."

"But at what a cost!" He shook his head in an agony of misery. "No, Mademoiselle Hunter, I was to blame, and I must leave."

"Oh, nonsense, Louis," Ella said briskly. "Don't be so dramatic. You've been a tower of strength for the last few hours, and if you did make an error earlier this evening, you'll certainly never fall into the same trap again, will you?"

"Never!"

"That's settled, then."

"Is it?"

"Totally." She regarded him. "I suspect that you'll make an excellent head porter one day, if not here, certainly somewhere else."

"I don't wish to work anywhere else."

Ella smiled. "Then you'll have to be extremely patient, for Monsieur Lalouche is still a young man."

"I am happy to serve him, mademoiselle," Louis assured her fervently.

"Then we're delighted to keep you. Just one question, Louis," she said as an afterthought.

"Mademoiselle?"

"Where did you learn to box?"

He grinned. "At school."

"I imagine you were rather good at it."

"The uppercut was always my best punch," he confided, now beaming broadly.

"I'll remember that."

After patrolling every floor of the hotel, Ella went to the east wing in search of Olivier. He was not in his room. She thought for a moment, then walked back into the main house, took the lift down to the basement, and marched directly to Paula Müller's room.

She rapped sharply on the door. There was a deathly silence, followed by scuffling and voices.

"Fräulein Müller, please open the door."

It opened a crack. The *gouvernante* stared out at her, hair tousled, mascara smudged, a satin robe drawn around her.

"What is it?"

"Is my brother here?"

"No, of course not."

"I don't believe you," Ella said loudly.

She heard Olivier inside the room. "It's okay, Paula."

Paula shrugged and opened the door wider. Ella saw her brother sitting on the bed, his uniform jacket over his shoulders, pulling on his trousers.

"What do you want, Lalla?" His voice was slurred.

"To speak to you," Ella said calmly.

"In the middle of the night?"

"Yes."

Paula Müller's face had grown pink. "I expect I'll be made to suffer for this," she said angrily.

"Whatever can you mean, Paula?"

"You won't be giving me notice?"

Ella smiled. "You're far too valuable to us right now for us to let you go."

The Austrian girl looked confused.

Ella glanced at her watch. "Better get a little sleep—though maybe it's not worth it, since you have to be up in a half hour."

"I don't have to be up till seven today."

Ella smiled again. "Correction. You'll be on duty at five sharp. Monsieur Lalouche will give you instructions first thing."

"Since when does he tell me what to do?"

"Since today." Ella paused. "I think you'll find rather a lot of extra cleaning in the bedrooms this morning—some of the guests seem to have had more to drink than they could handle."

Olivier came to the door. "What's so important that it can't wait?" he demanded, though Ella sensed a degree of apprehension behind the bravado.

"I want to take you on a little tour, Olivier."

"What?"

"You heard me." She drew him out of the room by his hand. "Good morning, Fräulein." She closed the door.

"Ella, for Christ's sake what is this? How dare you interfere with my private life this way?"

Ella's eyes were unaccustomedly hard. "I dare, Olivier," she said quietly. "Right this minute, I dare a great deal."

Half an hour later, back in her office, she faced him.

"Well, do you like it?"

"What?"

"Your friends' work."

He said nothing.

"Do you?"

He flushed. "Of course not. It's disgusting."

"Confrères de La Fontaine." She waited a beat. "Aristocrats?"

Again he was silent.

"I have a better word for them," she said. "It's German, but it applies to them all. *Untermenschen.* Subhumans."

Olivier's chin went up. "Don't go too far, Ella. You're insulting my friends."

"So you still call them your friends, do you? Men who vomit and defecate in public rooms—"

"They got drunk, that's all."

"Men who scrawl obscenities on hotel walls—on your walls, Olivier, on de Trouvère walls."

"They didn't know what they were doing."

"I'm sure they didn't." Tightly controlled rage swept her on. "I'm sure they didn't know that the women you invited into *our* hotel were whores!"

Olivier was white-faced. "Stop being such a prude, Ella!"

"*A prude?*" Ella jumped up from her chair, fury pumping more and more adrenaline through her system. "Your so-called friends smashed priceless antiques, destroyed valuable carpets, behaved like wild beasts and terrorized decent people!"

He dragged himself up from the sofa, his fear suddenly more evident. "Ella, please . . ."

Her voice grew icy cold. "They dragged a beautiful, innocent creature into their fun—poisoned her in order to commit God alone knows what loathsome assault on her—"

"That wasn't my fault! I'd never have allowed it!"

"Well, thank the Lord for small mercies!"

"Then why accuse me?"

"Because it was you, Olivier, twenty-seventh Baron de Trouvère, who invited those vandals, those sodomites, into our hotel!" She sagged, suddenly exhausted, back into her chair. "And now it's you who are going to get rid of them."

"I will, of course."

"This morning."

"But they just arrived! I can't just—"

"Olivier, they're lucky they're not in prison tonight. Don't push their luck."

"Okay, okay." He raised his hands defensively. "I'll get them out first thing."

"And the damage?"

"What about it?"

"Do you expect the hotel to subsidize wanton vandalism?"

"I'll pay for it."

"Why?" she demanded.

He looked confused. "Because it's down to me. You said as much."

"Did *you* smash sculptures and vases?"

"No, but—"

"Did *you* throw up all over our sixteenth-century silk hunting carpet?"

"For God's sake, of course I didn't!"

"I thought not," she said quietly. "I thought that perhaps some vestige of your upbringing must have lingered."

"Lalla, I said I'll pay. Why not leave it there?"

"Because you're too embarrassed to demand payment from the men who are responsible?"

"No!" he shouted hotly.

Ella studied him. "You are at least going to resign, aren't you?"

"Resign?"

"From Fontaine."

He hesitated. "I don't know."

"Maybe you admire the way they behave?" she asked with heavy irony.

He flushed darkly. "Not tonight, of course not."

"But that's exceptional, is it?"

"Yes."

"Generally," she went on, "they act like the well-bred, civilized aristocrats they are."

"That's right."

"Except for the occasional duel."

He fell silent.

"One of the men we found in the Hunting Room—one of the swine who poisoned Artemis—had a scar just like yours, Olivier. A *Schmiss*, it's called, isn't it."

Olivier was like a fish silently wriggling on a hook.

Ella had sudden tears in her eyes. "Friends to be proud of, Ollie."

He stared at her. "I expect my dear grandmother will hear about it." A note of defiance crept back into his voice.

"I expect she will."

"You'll tell her, then?"

Ella smiled sadly. "Do you imagine she'll need telling? There's damage to every public room, there's an appalling stench in the Salon Rouge and in the main bar, and the hotel will be virtually empty by midday." She paused. "There's only one reason I haven't called the police, you know."

"Bad press."

"No, Ollie." Her tone was gentler. "De Trouvère is strong

enough to survive a small scandal, though it's hardly the kind of publicity I'd seek."

"What, then?" He sounded resentful.

"You," she answered simply. "Olivier, Baron de Trouvère. Your precious name."

There was another silence.

"*Shall* you leave the fraternity?"

An expression of desolation entered his eyes, but he did not reply.

"You won't, will you?" She paused. "Why not? Are you afraid of angering them? Why?"

He reddened.

Ella regarded him thoughtfully, realization dawning on her. "Has it something to do with the fact that you're half Jewish?"

Olivier's chin jerked up and his eyes flashed. "Don't you dare say that!"

"Why not? It's a fact. Which you don't want them to find out because you're scared you would lose their esteem." She shook her head sadly. "As if their esteem mattered."

He stared sullenly at the carpet.

Ella realized that she was trembling with exhaustion. "I'm going to get some sleep." She rose, unsteadily, and regarded him. "Get them out, Olivier. I don't care how you do it, just get them *out.*"

Geneviève, Olivier thought, was like an imperious magistrate, administering clemency tempered with righteous outrage.

"Nothing like this has ever happened before in this family."

"Not even with my father, the black sheep?" he queried arrogantly.

"Your father lived in troubled times, Olivier, but he had a dignity, and a desire to protect his family's honor, which seems to be astonishingly absent in you."

He glared at her, livid that at the age of almost twenty-seven years he should still have to stand meekly before his grandmother, accepting reproofs like a boy.

"Any employee who brought such disgrace to the hotel would have been instantly dismissed and probably prosecuted."

"A pity for you that I'm your only grandson," he said sardonically.

"Sad, but true."

"Look, Grand-maman, I've accepted responsibility for the whole rotten mess," Olivier said with a first touch of humility. "I've said that I'll pay for the damage, though I realize certain things can't be replaced. And I've given you my assurance that it will never happen again. Can't we leave it at that?"

"Certainly we can," Geneviève said crisply. "With one stipulation."

"I might have known."

Her eyes were narrow. "Sit down, Olivier." They were in her private office. She indicated a straight-backed chair, and he sat. "A few simple facts." She folded her hands in her lap.

"By all means."

"Firstly, the ownership of this hotel has for nearly six years been split equally between your mother, myself, and you."

Olivier nodded.

"Secondly, my will."

The room was quite silent.

"Upon my death," Geneviève continued, "my shares will pass in equal halves to you and Ella, as I imagine you have presumed."

"I take nothing for granted, Grand-maman."

Geneviève slightly lifted an eyebrow. "At such a time, your mother and your half sister's combined holdings will match yours. Whether or not it is fair to Ella that she should own just one-third of the value of your own stock is extremely debatable, but since it was my decision to create a trust for you on your third birthday, it is not for me to argue the point, however much I may regret it."

Olivier was impassive. "You decided that I would be a responsible adult on my twenty-first birthday." He smiled wryly. "Yet here I am, still subject to your authority more than five years later."

"Don't exaggerate, Olivier. You know quite well that you would not accept any authority if your mother and I did not still hold controlling interest in the hotel."

"Until your death."

"Yes."

"And you are reminding me that wills, unlike trusts, can be altered."

Geneviève's gray eyes were grave, and she leaned slightly forward, one hand moving up to finger her pearl necklace. "It is a point you would be wise to remember, *mon cher.*"

Olivier's chin jutted up. "Don't *you* feel it would be wise to make a change now, Grand-maman?" He looked at her directly. "After what has happened?"

"No."

"Why not?"

"Because you are still my grandson," she replied composedly. "Because I sense, despite your arrogance, that you know you have been a fool." She smiled. "And because I am still, remarkably, *une optimiste*—I hope that you can learn."

"Learn?"

"If nothing else, Olivier, priorities."

Olivier did not need either a business mind or anything more than the most elemental arithmetical skill to conclude that he was at risk. If he did nothing more to incur the wrath of his grandmother or his mother, and if Maman lived to a reasonable age, it would take at least another two decades till he could achieve control of de Trouvère.

Geneviève might have decided to let her will stand for the time being, but Olivier guessed that it must distress her to know that after her death, every policy decision might turn into a battle, with Krisztina and Ella forced to group together against him. And what if he did, as he more than probably would, sin again?

Every day, Olivier found himself watching his grandmother, now an indomitable, remarkably youthful seventy-eight years old, for signs of frailty, either mental or physical, but he detected nothing graver than an occasional slowing of a step that had always been brisker than most, and the need for an early night every now and again.

How long could she go on?

Women of that type live to be a hundred, he answered himself despondently.

If only she were not quite so vigorous.

If only she would go to bed one night, do the decent thing, and simply *die.*

If only . . .

It was her annual checkup that made up his mind.

She had returned from Strasbourg, as elegant as ever, but with a gleam of pleasure in her eyes that had been absent for some time.

At dinner that evening, which he and Ella shared with her at their table in the restaurant, Olivier had commented on her special gaiety.

"I am in a fine mood," she admitted.

"Any special reason?"

Geneviève sipped a little red wine. "Only that I had been a little concerned about seeing Philippe Freitag today."

"Why, Grand-maman?" Ella asked anxiously.

"I was waiting for the results of some tests."

"I thought this was just your regular check," Olivier said quickly.

"That was what I wished you to think."

"And?"

Geneviève cut into her châteaubriand.

"And?" Ella echoed Olivier.

Their grandmother smiled. "And I'm fine."

"Truly?"

Geneviève reached over and patted Ella's hand. *"Oui, chérie."*

"What was it?" Olivier asked.

Geneviève shrugged. "Just a symptom that worried me a little."

"What kind of symptom?"

"Nothing that need concern you, Olivier."

"Clearly it concerned you."

"It was *my* symptom," she replied gently, "and now that I know it was nothing of the slightest consequence, it no longer concerns me either."

"So you're in good health?"

Again, Geneviève smiled. "Thank the good Lord, I am apparently in extraordinarily fine health."

Ella leaned over and kissed her cheek. "What lovely news to end a perfect summer's day."

Olivier raised his glass. "Isn't it," he said.

The strain of being the ideal grandson—or, at least, the reformed grandson, since Geneviève would have been the last person to find a wholly changed character credible—had begun to tell on him. With Ella, too, he had lately made a real attempt at keeping the peace—not going to Fontaine meetings, making the kind of conservative decisions he knew she would approve of, being as tolerant of employees and associates as he could bear to be. But now it had become abundantly clear to him that this situation might last for an appalling number of years. Their grandmother had the type of constitution that really might endure to something like a century. Even if she only survived to ninety, he'd have to put up with another twelve years of having to pussyfoot around her like some feebleminded boot-licker!

Twelve years!

Intolerable.

The opportunity came in September.

By that time, Olivier had toyed with every conceivable plan, but all the most feasible methods had been checked off his mental list.

Slow poisoning? Geneviève was far too observant and intelligent for that.

A fall? She had never been, nor was she now, a clumsy woman. In any case, one could never be sure that a fall would be fatal.

Suicide? A laughable idea, for even at her lowest ebb, after losing Armand and Laurent and Michael, Geneviève had considered life sacred, and there was no reason on earth for her to wish to terminate her own now.

He didn't really want to do it, that was the truth of the matter. He had no desire to hurt her, no urge to kill her. He just wanted her—needed her to be gone.

If only she would die—simply die—he would recite blessings over her grave and almost mean them.

But she wouldn't.

"I'm going to Paris next Thursday," she announced at their Friday morning meeting in her office.

"For what?" Olivier inquired politely.

"For fun."

Ella smiled. "More shopping?"

"Of course."

"Will you be taking the helicopter?" Olivier asked.

"Definitely."

"Do you want me to call Paul Moritz for you?" Ella volunteered.

Geneviève shook her head. "It's already arranged, thank you,

chérie. He'll come here the evening before, as usual, for dinner."
She rubbed her hands together gleefully. "I can hardly wait."

"You really love that awful machine, don't you, Grand-
maman?" Ella marveled.

"It's an adventure, *ma petite,*" Geneviève replied. "You know
how I still adore adventures, even if I am an old woman."

"I don't think you'll ever be old," Olivier said, so sincerely that
his grandmother smiled at him warmly.

"Thank you, Olivier. I believe that was a compliment?"

He nodded. "Absolutely."

It would be a relatively simple matter, he decided, to doctor
the pilot's food. The only two problems were selecting the right
drug, and acquiring it.

The ideal drug had to fulfill three requirements.

It had to have little or no taste.

Its effect had to be delayed.

The symptoms it caused had to be disabling.

Having driven to the main library at Mulhouse where he was
unlikely to be recognized, Olivier spent three hours poring over
medical textbooks and a massive pharmacopoeia, his mind beginning to spin with fatigue and confusion. He wrote note after note,
scratching each one out and starting again—until suddenly he
stopped.

An image had flashed across his brain.

Words on paper.

Olivier shook his head. He'd read for too long, was getting
overtired.

But the image persisted, and he closed his eyes, forcing himself
to concentrate. A memory was returning . . . something he'd
read, at another time, another place . . .

Olivier opened his eyes and thumped the desk in sudden triumph. The words he remembered were fiction, from one of his
grandmother's innumerable crime novels that they'd all read at
some time or other. There was a drug—no, a poison—and it had
no taste and no odor, and, in the book of which he was thinking, it
had been easily available as a commonly used rat poison.

Thallium.

Alert again with excitement, Olivier found the reference he
needed. Acute thallium poisoning, he read, caused severe ab-

dominal pain with vomiting and diarrhea—and in very serious cases, tremors, delirium, convulsions, and paralysis.

Olivier read on feverishly, skimming the minute details now that he had what he wanted. Symptoms occurred within twelve to twenty-four hours after a single toxic dose. *Oh God, oh Christ, what if the timing was off?*

But it wouldn't be. He'd make sure. He'd test it and adjust the dose, and it would work. It was his destiny to *make* it work, just as he'd been meant to remember thallium in the first place.

He closed the pharmacopoeia and thought again about the symptoms: tremors, pain, convulsions.

More than enough to incapacitate Paul Moritz.

It was remarkable, he reflected, how swiftly and easily he found the dusty old container, in the first of three gardeners' outhouses at de Trouvère. The next step, the test, went equally well, as he knew it would.

He cooked a little fish in his own small kitchen, added a dose of the rat poison, and took it in a covered plastic bowl to the stables, where he knew several hungry cats resided.

"Viens, mon p'tit," he encouraged a lean ginger cat, who came eagerly, rubbing its head against his ankle and sniffing at the bowl.

He removed the lid and set it down. *"Alors, mange."*

He buried the cat just after sunset.

All he really had to do in order to poison the pilot's food was to transport himself back to childhood and remember again the tricks he had so excelled at. If he'd managed in those early days to add cod-liver oil to consommé without discovery, he could surely, now that he was allowed into the kitchens, manage to ascertain which dishes were for Moritz alone. He did not, after all, want to cause his grandmother unnecessary pain.

It went perfectly.

From the instant Olivier woke on Wednesday morning, early enough to see the sun rising over his vineyards on the horizon, he had known with absolute, calm certainty that all would go well.

That calm, that sense of infallibility, enabled him to influence Moritz and Geneviève's arrival in the restaurant that evening at the time he had calculated—using the stable cat's relative body weight as his guide—would be most suitable for Moritz to take the poison in his main course. It was the same calm that helped him to create just enough of a diversion at the *entremetier*'s table for the *saucier* to leave the pot of morel sauce ordered by the pilot long enough for Olivier to slip in the thallium—just *after* Chef Gérard had sampled the sauce and had declared it excellent. And it was exactly the same cool nerve that allowed Olivier to remain in the kitchen after the waiter had carried away the finished dishes, and to observe every trace of evidence being washed away by the *plongeurs*.

Outside, after a late breakfast, on the broad expanse of clear lawn where landing markings were regularly repainted on the grass, Paul Moritz—looking, Olivier thought, paler than he had the previous evening—loaded Geneviève's luggage and took his seat at the controls while she and Olivier stood waiting for Ella to appear to say *au revoir*.

"She must have been held up," Olivier said after a few minutes, anxious for them to be on their way. "You'll have to go." He cast another glance at the pilot's face, then scanned the sky. "It's getting pretty gloomy—you don't want to fly in bad weather if you can help it."

Geneviève patted his arm. "It's good of you to be concerned for my safety, Olivier."

"I'm sure you'll be safe enough, Grand-maman, but I don't like to think of you flying in a storm. These machines aren't as comfortable as jets, are they?"

"I'm sure you're right. Anyway, thank you, *chéri*."

Olivier bent and kissed her on the cheek. "How many grandmothers do I have?"

Her eyes twinkled. "One too many, I suspect you've sometimes thought."

"Why? Because you've disagreed with things I've done? I thrive on our clashes, Grand-maman."

It was a cool morning, but Geneviève felt a warm flush of pleasure course through her. "I'd better get aboard," she said. "When you see Ella, give her a kiss from me and tell her I'll telephone later."

He helped her to her seat, saw that her belt was securely buckled, and gave her one more farewell kiss. "Bon voyage." He turned to face the pilot. "Take care of her."

Moritz nodded. "My favorite passenger."

Back on the ground, standing well away from the helicopter, his hair blowing wildly in the backwash of the powerful rotor blades, Olivier saw Ella running toward him, Artemis, as usual, loping easily beside her.

"Damn, I missed her!" She was panting, waving furiously as the machine lifted off into the air. "Was she all right?"

"Why shouldn't she be?"

Ella's cheeks were pink. "I don't know. I always worry when she rides in one of these things."

Olivier slipped an arm about her shoulders. "She asked me to give you a kiss. She said she'll call from Paris."

"Good." She frowned. "It's windy."

"Don't worry, Lalla. A chopper's tougher than it looks, and Moritz is a good pilot."

It was a curious sensation. A feeling that his brain had been sliced into two separate segments—one able to assess with icy, trancelike composure just when the pilot might experience the first surge of discomfort, when he might realize the danger, when the symptoms might overwhelm him—and the other, the smaller, less potent segment, tinged with a faint, curious sorrow and a sense of true, unmistakable grief.

Ella found him in the Salon Bleu just over three hours later. Her face was pale, her eyes wide and anxious. "Ollie, they haven't arrived."

"Who?"

"Grand-maman and Paul. They haven't checked in at the Ritz."

"Maybe they've gone somewhere else first," he said easily.

"With her luggage? Ollie, she always checks in and has a rest before anything else."

"Have you called the airfield to see if they landed?"

Ella bit her lip. "I thought you might."

Olivier stood up. "Right away."

It was air traffic control at Nancy who had heard the Mayday, and who had watched as the helicopter vanished from their radar.

"It seems there's been a storm over that way, so they haven't been able to start a search yet," Olivier reported tensely.

"But it's dark now," Ella said tearfully. "It'll be cold—they *have* to find them!"

He took her in his arms. "Lalla, we have to be brave and patient. They think they may have come down somewhere in the Forêt de Haye west of Nancy. There's no point searching before daybreak—they'd simply never spot them."

"With special lights?" Ella clung to his lapels, her face urgent. "Surely it's worth trying! Ollie, you have to make them try, please!"

"That's why I'm leaving for Nancy now. The roads won't be bad at this hour. I should make good time, and perhaps I'll be able to persuade them to make a start."

"I'm coming with you."

"No, Lalla."

"I am!"

"There's no point, *chérie*—"

"There's every point! I want to find Grand-maman!"

"The authorities won't let you go into the forest. *I* can insist. I've had army training so I shan't get in the way." He held her at arm's length. "Anyway, what about de Trouvère?"

"To hell with de Trouvère!"

Olivier gave her a tender shake. "You don't mean that, and Grand-maman would be furious if she heard you say it." He paused. "She'd much rather you stayed here, Lalla, and I swear to you I'll make sure you're informed every step of the way."

The day had begun with that astonishing clarity of purpose, that amazing calm, and so it went on. If Olivier had needed any proof that he was merely nudging destiny forward, that it was right for him to seize his own fate with both hands and run with it, then the chain of events that had first started with his remembering that novel—it had been an Agatha Christie, he'd realized later—the chain that seemed to go unerringly on and on, provided all the proof, all the conviction he required.

Ella had stayed at de Trouvère, ashen-faced but clinging to hope. Olivier drove on dark, wet roads toward Nancy, his E-type Jaguar devouring the miles while his mind, still stingingly keen, sorted through the risks that lay ahead.

The thallium might not have affected Moritz, or it might have worked at the wrong time. But it had worked, he reasoned, or there would have been no Mayday call.

The helicopter might have landed safely, or if it had crashed, they might have survived.

Olivier's hands tightened on the steering wheel, his face composed while his brain worked.

Even if they are dead, if there's been no explosion, a post-mortem will find the cause of his collapse. Thallium causes loss of hair. They'll know . . .

Olivier began to perspire as the lights of Nancy came closer. He signaled to the right, and the car roared off the *autoroute* onto the exit road.

If only I could find them first, get there before anyone else. That way, I could make quite sure. That way, I'd be safe. . . .

Fate stayed with him all the way.

He left before first light with a group of four men, having split from the larger rescue team at the edge of the forest where it was believed the helicopter must have come down.

One hour into the search, the four agreed that efficiency would be best served if they, too, each took separate routes, since they were all equipped with flares and whistles.

Olivier could not tell if it was old army instincts or a presentiment or sheer dumb luck that told him to choose to move east.

He knew he was going to find them when the smell touched his nostrils.

Fuel.

He halted and closed his eyes.

Smoke.

He found them both within yards of each other, Moritz facedown in the mud, clothes badly torn, and Geneviève, still strapped to her seat, though the seat itself had been uprooted from the cabin and slammed against a tree, which bore a deep, gashing scar.

He knew, immediately, that they were dead.

For a few moments, Olivier stood stock-still, transfixed by the sight of his grandmother slumped over at the waist like a rag doll, her beige silk Paris hat clutched bizarrely in her still-clenched hands. His head began to spin, his legs trembled, and he thought he might have to vomit.

The helicopter's tail section was some distance away, hanging askew about twelve feet up, supported by strong branches. As his reeling senses steadied themselves, and the first real perception of the success of his strategy began to filter through to him, Olivier saw that although a great pool of what he guessed must be kerosene had spread over the ground around the crumpled body of the machine, and smoke was still issuing from the smashed controls, the night's heavy rainfall seemed so far to have prevented an explosion.

He looked back at Moritz.

Postmortem, he thought.

Not if there's a fire.

He paused to listen for the others, but there was no sound other than the soft pattering of raindrops from branches.

He's close enough to the helicopter to burn with it.

His breathing suddenly shallow and rapid, his pulses drumming, Olivier fished in the pockets of his jacket and found a small box of de Trouvère matches.

How long will it take? he wondered. *Christ, how long do I have?*

And the answer came back, calm and sure.

Long enough, if you do it now.

Moving silently, quickly, he went over to the wreckage, seeking the source of the fuel leak. He found it easily. Quite probably it would catch soon anyway, since the controls were still smoldering, sparking every now and again.

It may explode. You'll have to get away as soon as you've dropped the match.

Still thinking with the same resolute composure, he checked back over the area, making sure he'd left no footprints. If he was going to claim he'd only found them after the fire had started, there must be no evidence that he'd been there earlier.

The sound came so softly that at first he did not register it as a voice at all.

"Olivier."

It was hardly a voice, not even as loud as a whisper, but it was enough to freeze the blood in his veins.

"Olivier."

He turned his head slowly, his eyes wide with horror.

She was not dead.

Not dead.

He stared at her. Geneviève was still slumped over, not moving at all.

He'd imagined it.

And then suddenly, quietly, the hat slipped out of her fingers and slid down to the ground.

Olivier gasped.

Her right hand was moving, the fingers straightening out, trying to stretch.

Oh Jesus and Mary, he prayed suddenly, though he never prayed. *Oh God, oh Lord, help me!*

He found the strength and courage to go to her then, to kneel at the side of her twisted, bent-over body, to crane his head, while his heart pounded deafeningly, and to look into her face.

There was dust on her right cheek, and a little blood and spattered mud on her left, but her makeup was as fine as it had been when he'd waved her good-bye, and her honey-blonde hair, tinted until the last, was almost immaculate.

A surge of admiration filled him for an instant. Dear God, this woman was *truly* indomitable.

And then her eyes opened.

He jerked back as if struck, terrified.

"Olivier . . ."

He swallowed. His throat felt parched.

The hand stretched again, as though trying to reach for something.

"Olivier . . ."

He licked his lips. "Grand-maman?"

With an immense effort, Geneviève managed to move her head a little way so that she was looking at him, and he realized that she saw the matches in his left hand, and that her gray eyes were still as all-seeing as they had ever been.

His whole arm quivering, he reached out and touched her cheek. It was icy cold, the skin of a dead person, and he knew then that Geneviève, Baronne de Trouvère, was, after all, going to die.

He stroked her cheek, and said again, in a soft, tender voice: "Grand-maman."

She gave one of her small, wry smiles, and for just a moment her voice was stronger, carrying high and clear to his ears.

"One too many," she said.

And she died.

Olivier stood up.

He remembered their conversation before they'd taken off from de Trouvère.

One too many, I suspect you've sometimes thought.

So she knew. He didn't know how, but there was not a doubt in his mind that she knew.

There was a shoe lying under a tree a few feet away, and he went and picked it up. It sat snug in the palm of his hand, small and elegant, beige and white soft calf with an unblemished heel, and as he slipped it back onto Geneviève's stockinged right foot, Olivier was oblivious to the tears that ran down his cheeks.

"*Au revoir,* Grand-maman." His voice was gentle.

He straightened again, and walked past Paul Moritz to the place where the kerosene ran down over crumpled steel to the ground.

And he struck two matches, smelled the sulfur, and dropped them.

Chapter 30

There had been many funerals at de Trouvère since Krisztina had first come to Alsace, too many, and each had, in its own way, been an occasion for grief, sometimes stark and unbearable, sometimes softened by small splashes of relieving remembrance to make it less intolerable.

The memorial service for Geneviève de Trouvère was like no other had been, for it represented not just the passing of a magnificent woman loved by many, but the passing of an era that would never return.

They had come from far and wide to pay their final respects: Clementine Hunter and her daughters from London; Alberto Giordano from Rome; Marthe Schneegans, of course, from Saint-Hippolyte, André Sutterlin from Grenoble and Chef Carême from Geneva. A host of friends stood silently outside the over-crowded chapel in the early October rain while Père Beurmann said mass, and William, Krisztina, Olivier, and Ella spoke of Geneviève and read and sang specially chosen psalms and hymns and poetry.

Krisztina and Ella were both equally bereft, for the ageless Baronne had been far more than Belle-mère and Grand-maman to them—she had been their wisest counselor, their most loyal partner, their best friend. Geneviève, they silently, bitterly protested, should have died peacefully in her bed at de Trouvère, surrounded by loved ones—not tumbling violently from the sky to a cruel and lonely end in an accident that had been analyzed, after the investigations, as "probable pilot error."

Ella, more than she had ever done, felt frighteningly alone in the world, felt more keenly than before her isolation from her parents, was more aware than previously of the problems created by her tempestuous, complicated brother, and knew that her greatest anchor at Château de Trouvère had gone forever.

For a time after the crash, Olivier flourished.

It was as if a tightly coiled spring within him had relaxed, as if he were finally reaching toward his true potential.

His new happiness affected everything about him; he stood taller, his already striking good looks began almost to border on beauty, he moved with a less-pent-up grace, his dark eyes and hair gleamed, and most of all, his approach to those around him grew gentler the more buoyantly optimistic he became.

He observed it in himself every day, took pleasure in the image that his mirror threw back at him, and was determined to go out of his way to be worthy of his hard-won good fortune. With Ella, particularly, he was pleasant and soft and kind, aware of how badly the loss of Geneviève had wounded her. He could afford to be more generous now, he reasoned, for at last he had what he had wanted for so long.

It lasted just over four months.

Then, abruptly, the spring grew taut again, the glimmer of warmth and peace dimmed, and as the aura of confidence dispersed, so did his newfound composure.

The reason was simple.

He had begun having nightmares.

Every night, lying in bed in the west wing, which he and Ella had agreed should now be his, Olivier was haunted in sleep by bad dreams, by horrific, grisly images of Geneviève and Paul Moritz being consumed alive by flames, their eyes accusing, their charred fingers pointing at him. He would wake, drenched in sweat, gasping for breath, terrified to go back to sleep in case they returned.

Every night, every single night, they came to him. His grandmother and the pilot, suffering agonies, denouncing him.

And another figure too.

A small boy with bright red hair.

Guilt was a new experience for Olivier, and as with most emotions he experienced, his guilt was outsized, acute, ever present, and wholly damning.

Permanently exhausted and drained, unable to confide in anyone, even Ella, he slipped back into old habits. He made poor decisions, grew discourteous and disconsolate, snarled when anyone tried his patience, and hired and fired as the mood took him. He began driving over the frontier to gamble in Baden-Baden whenever possible, even held private poker parties at de Trouvère, much to Ella's chagrin. He took out the Fontaine uniform that he'd hung away after Geneviève's death and joined forces again with the *Bruderschaft* whenever he entered Germany.

Life grew increasingly difficult for Ella.

The only way she could keep the hotel on an even footing was to go against her brother, and to drag her mother from William's side, an unhappy predicament for them all and a damaging situation for the hotel itself.

"I don't understand him anymore," Ella appealed to Krisztina in October 1973, a year after Geneviève's memorial service, following yet another emergency board meeting. "If I didn't know better, I'd think he was trying to destroy de Trouvère, yet we both know it's the most important thing in his life."

Krisztina sighed, still weary from jet lag and from hours of wrangling with her son. "He's his own worst enemy, Ella, *chérie.* He's been that way since he was a tiny boy, and I fear he'll never change."

"But he did seem different for a while after the accident. He was grieved, but it was obvious that he knew his time had come."

"His time?"

Ella nodded. "He'd felt for years that Grand-maman was here to keep an eye on him."

Krisztina smiled ruefully. "In a way, she was."

"Ollie often felt slighted by that, resentful of anyone who questioned his actions."

"Nothing much has changed, then," Krisztina said, thinking of their angry meeting. "He misses her, though."

"Has he said so?"

"He doesn't need to." Krisztina was pensive. "You're closer to him than anyone else, Ella, but your name isn't de Trouvère. He's the only one left now, and I think that sometimes frightens him, makes him lonely."

Ella sagged back in her armchair. "We seem to have spent more years than I can remember finding excuses for Olivier's behavior, Maman. Sometimes even I get tired of it."

Krisztina regarded her. "Perhaps you need a holiday."

Ella laughed. "Maybe I do, but I can't take one."

"Why not?"

"Because I can't leave de Trouvère, obviously."

"Of course you can."

"In Ollie's hands?"

"And mine."

Ella looked astonished. "Yours?"

"No need to look so baffled. I did more or less run this hotel for more years than I care to remember."

"Yes, of course you did, Maman, but you don't live here anymore."

Krisztina smiled. "That doesn't mean I can't stay for a while, does it?"

"But what would Papa say? He hates it when you go away."

Krisztina mused for a second. "How about a direct swap? He can have you in place of me. He won't mind that at all."

Ella's eyes lit up. "New York?"

"Well, it's about time, I'd say. We've been living there for four years, you've never found time for a visit, and with some enormous Hunter sales coming up in Manhattan, your father won't get over here for months."

"I'd have loved you to have shown me the city," Ella said wistfully.

"We can share it next time, *cherie.*"

Ella paused.

"What are you thinking?" Krisztina asked.

"That Ollie won't like it."

Krisztina grinned. "Having his mother back to bully him?"

"You're not a bully. You don't even know how to bully."

"Wanna bet?" Krisztina's accent was pure New York.

Ella grimaced comically. "I wish you luck."

"So you'll go?"

"If Papa agrees."

"He'll agree."

*

The afternoon she arrived, sweeping over the 59th Street Bridge into Manhattan in the back of the most remarkable vehicle she'd ever sat in, Ella was at a loss to know where to look first —at the interior of the "stretch" limousine her father had sent to Kennedy Airport for her, or at the glories of the city unfolding on her left.

Ella had been born into luxury, but this car made her chuckle with sheer, undiluted pleasure. She kicked off her shoes and buried her toes in the amazingly lush white rug, rested back against the soft white leather seat, and gazed at the walnut bar, stocked with Krug champagne, fresh-squeezed orange juice, tiny bottles of Evian water, and two small silver bowls of caviar on ice.

"It was absolutely outrageous," she told William after hurling herself joyously at him in Hunter's main lobby on Madison Avenue.

"Didn't you like it?"

"I loved it!" She smothered him with kisses while he tried to steer her toward the private elevators at the rear of the marbled hall. "But the TV! Who on earth would want to watch television on their first car ride in America?"

"I wanted to impress you."

"You succeeded."

They got into the elevator and the doors shut silently as William touched the top button.

" 'P'?" she read.

"Penthouse."

"Forty-eighth floor?" Her eyes widened and her stomach lurched.

"That's pretty low for Manhattan."

The doors opened. "Don't people get vertigo here, Papa?"

"Not if they want to be New Yorkers."

It took a week for her to make up her mind. To be exact, it took seven days, two and a half hours, but at that very instant, as the great bells of St. Patrick's Cathedral chimed half past five on that early November Wednesday, Ella, marching down Fifth Avenue with the masses, stopped walking and stood stock-still.

Suddenly she could see through the blur of people and traffic, through the facade of steel and glass and concrete. Suddenly her ears penetrated the cacophony of horns and the indistinguishable fuzz of voices, and she fancied abruptly that she had pierced the flinty outer layer of the city and found flesh and blood.

"Well? What happened?" asked William later in his office.

Ella looked puzzled.

"I mean, when you found Manhattan. Was it a *coup de foudre*? Did you fall in love?"

"With the city?" She considered for a moment. "Well, I felt, for a little while at least, that I could belong to it, even survive in it."

"That doesn't surprise me."

"Doesn't it? It amazed me. Manhattan seems such a jungle, so fearsome, that I was astonished to find that it has a heart, a kind of quietness at its core. It's just that you have to work hard to find it, and I suspect that even then you don't find it that often."

"You have to have strength to live here," William said. "And you have that strength, Ella."

"I think perhaps I do."

"But de Trouvère still tugs at you."

"Of course."

He looked at her. "That doesn't sound quite as absolute as it has in the past."

Ella shrugged. "I'm a little tired, Papa."

"That's why you're on vacation."

She sighed. "I think it'll take more than a week or two away to cure what ails me, Papa."

"Ollie?"

There were sudden furious tears in her eyes. "I love him, Papa, just as much as I've ever done—nothing on earth could ever change that. But I love de Trouvère, too, and I know he does— more than anything else in life. Yet he's dragging her down and I can't find a way to stop him."

"Maybe he's unstoppable," William said quietly.

"Give up, you mean?" She shook her head. "Never."

"Never's a long time, Ella." He paused. "You know what I think? It's time we went home."

She was startled. "But I've only just come."

"I'm not talking about Alsace. I'm talking about our home— your mother's and mine. You're tired, and Manhattan's no place to rest. Come up to Rhinebeck, sweetheart."

"I was planning at least another week in the city."

"You can come back—it's no distance, yet it's another world

entirely." He smiled. "We can take a boat up the Hudson, we don't have to drive."

"It's November."

"So we won't sunbathe. You've brought sweaters, haven't you? A country girl like you knows how to pack, surely."

"Of course. And boots, *and* walking shoes."

"Good. You won't need any city clothes, so we'll keep your suite at the St. Regis and you can just bring a bag."

She laughed. "That's taking the natural look a bit far, thank you —I'll need a case *and* a bag."

William surveyed her warmly. "Bring a trailer if you like—just come."

"Can you really spare the time, Papa?"

"No, but I'm going to. I'll settle you in, then drive back down."

"You'll leave me alone?" She looked dubious.

"You won't be alone. Alice will be there to cook for you and take care of the dogs."

Ella brightened. "I'd almost forgotten about the dogs—I can't wait to see them."

"You'll love it." He looked positive. "You can do exactly as you please for a change, rest up for a while, and then decide if you still want more of this crazy place."

The house, a mile outside Rhinebeck, was, in Ella's own breathless words, "delicious." It had begun life as a small Dutch farmhouse in the middle of the seventeenth century, and many of its original features remained, including the gables, the two-foot-thick walls, delft tiles in the kitchen, and the front pathway made of crushed oyster shells. At least four bouts of modernization, however, had insured convenience and comfort while maintaining charm and history.

Alice, the Hunters' housekeeper and kennel maid combined, had fires lit in every hearth, a pot roast in the oven, the aroma of fresh baking in the air, and Krisztina's two most beloved creatures at her side.

"Janus!" Ella fought to withstand the wolfhound's rapturous greeting so that she could pay attention to the little black dog yelping with joy behind her. "And Titus too! I've missed you both so much!"

Alice, a tall, handsome woman in her mid-forties, smiled at

them all. "Your mother told me that these two, more than any luxury, would make you feel at home."

"She was right." Ella beamed. "And those smells are wonderful."

"I thought you'd both be hungry as pups after your boat ride. I wasn't sure if you'd want me to set the dining room table, Mr. Hunter—"

"We'll eat in the kitchen, Alice. Okay by you, sweetheart?"

"Fine." Ella sank happily into one of the wicker chairs by the fireplace, the informality of the household washing over her like soothing balm.

William looked at her. "I said you'd like it, didn't I?"

Titus sprang neatly up onto her lap, while Janus rested his noble, shaggy head on her knee and gazed into her eyes. Alice busied herself at the stove, humming while she worked, and her father, glancing over some mail, tucked one envelope into his jacket pocket before tossing three others onto the fire.

"Junk mail," he explained. "There's no escaping it wherever you are, even in paradise."

"Is that where we are, then?" Ella asked, amused.

William lit a cigarette. "I think it might almost qualify, if the whole family could be here at any one time."

"That's what comes of having more than one paradise, I'm afraid, Papa."

"I hardly think that life at de Trouvère has been all that Elysian lately, has it?"

"That doesn't stop me loving it," Ella answered softly.

William stooped and stroked her hair. "I know."

After William had left for the city, Ella rested for four days, retiring at ten and rising at seven. Each morning, she spent an hour with Alice and the puppies in the large, purpose-built kennel area near the garden—Janus and Titus seemed resigned to sharing their humans with the unruly bunch born six weeks before to Vénus. After breakfast, Ella would collapse into one of the big, soft armchairs in the sitting room, where she alternately read, listened to Vivaldi and Mozart, and dozed until lunchtime.

"Hungry?" Alice asked each day at noon.

"Not really," Ella said on the fifth day.

"I'm not surprised. You're an active woman—your metabolism doesn't know what's hit it."

"Too much rest, do you think?"

Alice shrugged. "You'll know when you've had enough, honey."

"How?"

"When you start to sit up and take notice."

"Of what?"

"Of Dutchess County, for a start. If your folks were here, they'd have you seeing all there is to see."

"I suppose you're right," Ella said guiltily.

"Now don't start being ashamed of feeling tired," Alice hastened. "We all need to stoke the furnace from time to time." She placed a bowl on the table.

"What's that?"

"Clam chowder."

"More stoking?"

"You'll need something if you're going to make that start. The car, by the way, is right outside with a tankful of gas."

Ella smiled. "Where do I go first?"

"Ryn Beck."

"I beg your pardon?"

"I think that's what the Dutch called Rhinebeck, though it might have been the German settlers who named it after their own river—I've never been much for history."

"Were you born here?"

Alice shook her head. "No, I came up from Washington, D.C., for some skiing about twenty years back, went to Hunter and to Bobcat, liked what I found, and stayed." Alice paused. "Eat your soup while it's hot."

Ella took a spoonful and found it thick and delicious. "So you think I should start with Rhinebeck."

Alice nodded. "It's just a village really, but worth seeing. Go take a look at the Delameter House even if you don't bother with anything else—it's a genuine gingerbread house."

"Then what?" Ella dipped a large chunk of home-baked bread in the chowder. "I'm too impatient to spend long on one place, and I detest guided tours."

"Take a drive. I'll give you a good map so you won't get too lost, and even if you do go astray, just ask—you'll find the folk round here are pretty friendly. It's lovely, rolling country, though of course November's not the best month to see it."

"I gather there's quite a lot of wine."

The American woman smiled. "No match for France, obviously, but enough to make it quite a magnet for the wealthy. There's a whole bunch of great houses and mansions if you're interested, but somehow, with Château de Trouvère for a home, I doubt you will be."

"You've never seen it, have you?"

"Only in photographs, but Mrs. Hunter's described just about every nook and cranny."

"Do you think she still misses it?" asked Ella.

"God, yes. She was tickled pink about spending some time there now."

"Yet she seems to love it here."

"She does." Alice smiled again. "It's possible to love more than one place, you know, Ella."

"Is it?"

Alice nodded sagely. "Oh, yes."

Ella drove all that afternoon, lost her way three times, but somehow found her way back to the house with enough confidence remaining to climb back into the car early next morning. This time she brought Janus and a picnic hamper for company.

She drove north, zigzagging back and forth across the Hudson, staying mostly in the valley with occasional forays up into the low mountains of Ulster County. By the side of a vivid turquoise lake called, enchantingly, Minnewaska, she munched on Alice's fried chicken legs and watched Janus frisk like a pup, while she spread the map out on the grass and grew entranced by the magical quality of the names—Shawangunk, Phoenicia, Stone Ridge, and Esopus . . .

And then she began to drive again, forgetting the restrictions of the map, willingly losing herself in the countryside. She came upon a massive Victorian hotel, the Mohonk Mountain House, sprawled next to a lovely lake above the Hudson, and then she traveled farther north, bypassing Kingston and driving around the Ashokan Reservoir to Woodstock. A little later, she left Ulster for Greene County, and stopped for coffee at a roadside diner, chatting with a dark-eyed waitress who gave Janus a turkey sandwich with gravy and told Ella that she was not too far from one of the greatest views of all creation.

"Catskill Mountain House," she said, and there was reverence in her voice as she poured Ella a third cup of coffee and patted the dog's head. "It was *the* greatest mountain resort until the early forties."

"What's it used for now?"

"It isn't there anymore. They burned it down in sixty-three."

"So why go there now?"

"The site's still the most beautiful place on earth, that's why." She polished the steel coffeepot with her cloth, and there was a dreamy glint in her eyes.

"Even in November?"

The waitress shrugged. "May not be the best time, but when God decides to build glory, I guess he does it for all seasons. You go see it, miss."

The drive itself was worth the extra time, since part of the route took her through Catskill Park, with forests, rushing streams, dramatic precipices, and gorgeous waterfalls, though the terrain became gentler as she drove through Haines Falls and took a right turn up to North Lake, where she found she had to park the car and walk the rest of the way.

"Bon Dieu," she whispered when she arrived.

Beside her, Janus sat motionless, his dark eyes also calmly surveying the scene at their feet.

For a time, Ella just stared, trying to take in the entire majesty of the sweeping panorama, soaking up every particle of what she saw, attempting to turn vision into a total, consummate experience.

Finally, she blinked and stirred.

The map.

She knelt on the ground beside Janus and tried to get her bearings, using a map she'd picked up from the library down in Haines Falls.

They were on South Mountain, at a place called Pine Orchard. There was no mistaking the Hudson, of course—there it flowed, far, far below, through the valley, a luscious bright blue in the crisp November sunlight. Looking straight ahead, Ella saw the Berkshire Hills, the Green Mountains, and Albany and Bear Mountain State Park, and tried to imagine where New York ended and where Connecticut and Massachusetts and Vermont all began. Everything except the mountains themselves was miniaturized—specks that were houses, flecks of woodland, dots that were small lakes, some sparkling, some lazing in deep, dappled shadows—and yet the entire effect was enormous, inspiring, and somehow intensely moving.

No wonder her mother had been able to settle here. If one had to move away from a beloved, secure place, then one was certainly fortunate to find new territory worth belonging to.

The waitress had been right, more than right. This was surely glory.

Ella looked at the small guide she'd received with the map, wondering about the hotel that had stood on such a unique spot.

There was a photograph. An example of the Greek Revival style so popular throughout Europe and America in the first half of the nineteenth century, fronted by thirteen Corinthian pillars, with three hundred rooms. And what guests! Ella's envious *hotelière's* eyes scanned the list of names—Alexander Graham Bell, Jenny Lind, Henry James, Mark Twain, Oscar Wilde, Ulysses S. Grant—in God's name, who hadn't stayed there?

"The first great mountain resort in North America," the book told her. "A symbol of the wealth of the country. . . . One of the most romantic places on earth."

Yet they'd declared it a dangerous structure and burned it to ashes one January dawn in the early 1960s, after it had been empty for almost two decades.

Ella thought of de Trouvère, and shivered.

Janus whined.

"Okay, boy, we're going."

For the first time, she noticed two other visitors not far away. She'd been too immersed to see them.

She smiled.

Magic in the air, she thought.

"Well, it certainly was famous," Alice confirmed later that evening after dinner.

"Sounds as if it was almost a national monument."

"I think it was, in its heyday. Everyone who was anyone stayed up there at Pine Orchard. Must have been some place."

"It was gone before you came up here, wasn't it?"

"Oh, quite a while before, but in any case, there wasn't much left worth seeing. It was rotten, but people still kept going to see it, so they pulled it down."

"But they didn't pull it down, they set fire to it."

Alice smiled gently. "That really bugs you, doesn't it?"

"Yes, it does."

"I guess you can relate to it better than most folk, what with having your own hotel."

"I suppose I can." Ella frowned. "I keep thinking about the man who built it—what was his name? Erastus Beach." She shook her head. "I suppose he was dead and gone before they burned it."

Alice put down the knitting she'd been toying with and looked at her. "Do you think of de Trouvère as a hotel or a house?"

"Both," Ella said quickly, then considered. "Perhaps more as a hotel—it was that way when I was born." She paused. "I think it's different for my brother. He cares more about the château itself than the hotel—one's just a business, while the de Trouvère es tate is part of him." She smiled. "Or maybe it's the other way around—he is part of the estate."

"I gather you two don't see eye to eye about the running of the hotel," Alice said carefully.

A momentary surprise registered in Ella. Evidently Alice was far more than a housekeeper or even a manager: a trusted confidante of both her parents.

"Do you think it's a problem you're going to be able to resolve?" Alice asked.

"I used to think so," Ella answered slowly.

"But it hasn't worked out." It was a statement, not a question.

"No."

"What are you going to do?" Alice took up her knitting again, and the quiet clack of the big needles made a comforting sound in the room.

Ella rested her head wearily back against a quilted cushion. "I don't know."

She woke next morning with an urgent desire to see her father, sufficiently revived to withstand another buffeting by the city.

She stopped for nothing on the way, simply drove south, thirsty and impatient for the warmth that enfolded her whenever she was anywhere near William. The weather had changed; suddenly it was true November, murky and dismal, with heavy gray clouds overhead spitting down a constant, irritating drizzle that kept the windshield wipers languidly busy all the way from Poughkeepsie to Yonkers.

In spite of the dank weather, the first sighting of Manhattan

from this new angle of approach stirred Ella to totally unexpected heights of excitement. The Empire State Building, which
had disappointed her when she'd viewed it from the street below, looked utterly remarkable from the highway, looming
through the mist, summoning home its natives and beckoning its
newcomers. It created a tightness in Ella's throat she had only
previously experienced whenever she caught the first glimpse of
Château de Trouvère through the trees on the road from
Ribeauvillé.

"What's wrong?" William asked when she arrived in his office.
"Nothing."
"What are you doing here?"
"I missed you," she said simply.
A beam wreathed his face. "Good."
"Lunch, Papa?"
The smile vanished. "I can't, darling—too much on. Two im-
portant sales later today and tomorrow morning."
"What are they?"
"Rugs and carpets this evening—Impressionist and modern
paintings tomorrow. Why don't you come?"
"Carpets," Ella mused, thinking of the lovely rugs at de Trou-
vère that had suffered badly at the hands of Olivier's acquain-
tances. "I might even take a serious look."
"Do you have something in mind?"
"I'll know it if I see it."
"Then you'd better take a look if you're going to consider
bidding. Your rivals have had a head start." He stood up. "I'll find
an expert to take you down."
She kissed his cheek. "What time tonight?"
"Seven forty-five or eight. Be up here at seven, and we'll have
some champagne."

The colors were sumptuous, some wonderfully faded, others
astounding in their brilliance. The carpets were well-displayed
slices of history dating from the fifteenth to the nineteenth centuries, coming from Persia, Egypt, China, Turkey, India, France,
and Spain. The wealth of designs and styles was both inspirational
and confusing, but Ella had targeted her choice within twenty
minutes—a lovely, small seventeenth-century Turkish silk rug of

Persian design, with ethereal clouds and songbirds flying over a background of pale rose, emerald green, and indigo.

"That's it," Ella told her expert, a bespectacled, dark-suited young man.

"It is a gorgeous rug, Miss Hunter—the green, especially, is very rare."

"Do you think I stand a chance?"

He smiled. "It's an auction. Everyone stands a chance."

"Not unless I get into the bidding in the first place," she said worriedly. "The auctioneer only takes bids from two people at a time, doesn't he?"

"That's right."

"It's all so complicated. Commissioned bids, secret reserves . . . I need someone to bid for me."

"That could be arranged, Miss Hunter, though I doubt you'd have as much fun."

From William's office window, Ella watched the patrons arriving, some emerging from chauffeur-driven limousines, some clambering out of yellow cabs, and others hurrying along the pavement under big black umbrellas.

"Shouldn't I be downstairs finding a seat?" she asked her father anxiously. "It's important to be in the auctioneer's eyeline, isn't it?"

"A good auctioneer will see you even if you're right at the back, but I've reserved your seat, so you've nothing to worry about." He glanced at the catalogue in her hand. "Which is your lot?"

"Lot twelve." Ella smiled. "Perhaps nobody else will want it."

"You won't know that even if it happens," William said. "David van Street, the auctioneer, won't let you know, just as he'll seldom let it be known if an item isn't sold at all. Many of the bids at an auction are fictitious, as are the names of the buyers."

"Why make it so difficult?"

"It isn't really difficult, darling, not from your point of view. All you need to do is to know what you want and how much you're prepared to pay for it." He looked at his watch. "Time to go."

Ella put down her champagne glass and scanned her reflection in the long mirror on the wall. She'd had no real idea what to wear for an evening like this, and had finally settled for simple black satin pants and jacket with a white blouse, a big bow tied at the neck.

William scrutinized her. "You're gorgeous," he said with total sincerity, and then, as an afterthought, he leaned back, plucked a deep red rose from a vase on his coffee table, and secured it in her buttonhole. "Now go and buy your carpet."

The sale began so subtly that Ella hardly realized they'd started at all until David van Street banged his gavel and announced that the first lot had been sold to someone with a name she couldn't understand.

Maybe it was a fake sale, she thought, and settled back in her chair to absorb the atmosphere, fascinated by the faces around her—poker-faced clerks, agitated-looking rivals, and numerous men and women who were so relaxed that Ella thought they must be there simply to observe.

The next four lots were hammered down rapidly, and Ella's fingers gripped her catalogue tightly as bidding commenced for a lovely little silver-and-gold brocaded rug from Persia, unsigned but rare. Now she forced herself to concentrate on the different methods people employed to make their bids—some by nodding, one man by tapping his cheek with a gold pen, several by discreetly raising their hands, and one woman who shrugged her shoulders.

The gavel struck the rostrum, and Ella gave a small start, aware that she'd lost track of the bids and that the item had been sold. The next lot was put up, and she turned her attention to the auctioneer, trying to master the way the prices rose by increments, rising more dramatically the more valuable the lot on sale.

The next three carpets were swiftly dispatched, and Ella grew hot with excitement. A girl at the end of the second row dabbed at her nose with a white lace handkerchief—was she bidding or did she have a cold? She sneezed abruptly, and Ella grinned.

Lot 11 was under the hammer, a handsome wool Caucasian dragon carpet, and was soon sold, after a brief skirmish, to a rather handsome young man with a golden moustache sitting three places away from Ella in the front row.

"Lot twelve."

The skin at the back of Ella's neck prickled.

Two of the porters standing behind David van Street presented the tenderly colored Turkish rug, and she felt her heart begin to pound.

"Nine thousand dollars I'm bid."

Who? Ella blinked and her hand began to rise.

"Nine thousand five hundred."

She dropped her hand, dismayed. She'd as good as lost it already if there were two bidders in the race before her.

No, no, keep calm and wait. There'll be another chance.

The bidding rose swiftly to thirteen thousand dollars, and then suddenly there was a pause—no longer than two seconds, but palpable.

"Thirteen thousand dollars," repeated van Street.

Ella's hand shot up, like a child's in school.

"Thirteen thousand five hundred—thank you, madam."

Her cheeks flushed, her eyes sparkled—she was in it at last!

"Fourteen thousand."

Up went her hand. "Fourteen thousand five hundred."

Her eyes darted around. Who was her rival?

Another of those gaping pauses. That meant the other bidder had given up, didn't it? *She'd won!*

"Fifteen thousand. Thank you, sir."

Damn him! Ella's hand, with a will of its own, flew back up.

"Fifteen thousand five hundred." Brief pause. "Sixteen thousand."

Who was it now?

"Sixteen thousand five hundred. Seventeen thousand."

Out of the corner of her eye, Ella saw the man with the moustache lowering his right hand to his knee.

But that's greed! He just bought the dragon carpet.

Furiously she waved her hand.

"Seventeen thousand five hundred."

Go on, you swine, I dare you!

Silence reigned.

"Seventeen thousand five hundred dollars, I'm bid."

Ella held her breath.

David van Street's eyes scanned the room, searching for the tiniest movement.

"Seventeen thousand five hundred dollars."

For pity's sake, shut up!

The auctioneer's attention swiveled back to her and her alone.

"All done," he said.

The gavel banged.

They met outside in the lobby.

Her rival was very tall, over six feet. His hair cut neatly short, gleamed, his blue eyes twinkled and his mouth, beneath the moustache, smiled down at her.

"Congratulations."

Ella flushed. "Thank you."

"You did well."

She wondered if he was patronizing her, then decided he was not. "Thank you," she said again.

"How far would you have gone?" he asked.

"I don't know."

"But you had a cutoff figure, didn't you?"

Ella grinned. "I'd passed that before you came into it." Victory made her generous. "I'm sorry you lost. Did you want it very much?"

"I didn't want it at all."

"I beg your pardon?"

"I didn't want the rug. It's very pretty, but I have what I came for."

"But you bid seventeen thousand dollars!"

"True."

"Why?"

"Because I wanted to meet you."

She was speechless.

He smiled again. "It's true."

Ella stared at him. "I don't believe you."

"If I hadn't entered the bidding, you'd have got the rug for fourteen and a half thousand, but you'd never have noticed me."

For the second time, she found she could not speak.

"Are you angry with me?" he asked.

"Do you mean to tell me that you forced me to spend three thousand dollars just so that I'd notice you?" Ella demanded.

"That sums it up."

"Then yes, I am angry with you."

"Don't be."

"You must be crazy."

He shook his head. "Not at all. You know, I could easily say that I desperately wanted the rug, but saw how much you liked it and gave it away. That way you'd think me a fine gentleman, wouldn't you?"

"Possibly."

"But isn't honesty a greater attribute?"

"Not always."

The crowd around them was beginning to break up, and Ella, gathering up her dignity, prepared to leave.

"You're not going, are you?" he asked.

"I am."

"Haven't you forgotten something?"

"I don't think so."

"Your rug."

Her voice was acid. "I wasn't thinking of carrying it home."

"Where is home?"

"None of your business."

"Quite right."

Ella tucked her purse and the catalogue under her left arm. "Good night."

He stood between her and the doorway. "Will you have dinner with me?"

Her eyes widened. "Of course not."

"Why not?"

"Because I don't like you."

His eyes twinkled. "Because I wanted to meet you so badly, I was willing to risk seventeen thousand dollars?"

"You knew you weren't risking a penny," she retorted.

"You might have withdrawn."

"You knew I wouldn't."

He bent his head in feigned humility. "Please have dinner with me."

"No," she said firmly.

He looked up. "Aside from the fact that you don't like me, why won't you?"

Ella searched for a reason. "Because I hate moustaches."

He looked surprised. "Really?"

"Really."

William appeared at her side. "There you are—I've been looking for you."

"*Bonsoir,* Papa." She kissed his cheek.

"I gather you were successful." He looked at her rival. "Hello, Harry." They shook hands.

"A good night, William."

"Excellent. And for you?"

"Mixed."

"C'est la guerre," William said lightly. "I see you've already met my daughter."

Ella was staring at them both.

"I'm afraid she doesn't like me very much."

"Why? What have you done?"

"I've been a cad."

"Oh? That's not like you, Harry."

Ella began to feel annoyed. "Would you two mind not discussing me as if I weren't here?"

William smiled. "I'm sorry, darling. What's this man done to annoy you?"

"I think you'd better introduce us," suggested Harry.

William slipped an arm round Ella's shoulders. "This is Ella, my daughter. Ella, this is Harry Bogarde, a friend."

"Of yours?"

"That's right."

Bogarde grimaced. "Ella says that she doesn't want to have dinner with me."

"I thought we could all dine together," William said.

"You did?" Ella grew more irritated. It wasn't like her father to treat her in a cavalier manner.

"If you don't mind, that is."

"I don't see that I have much choice."

"I thought you might be tired, so I made a reservation at the St. Regis. Okay with you, Harry?"

"Wonderful."

"Do I have to make arrangements now for my rug?" Ella asked.

William shook his head. "They know you." He smiled at them both. "Shall we go?"

"I'm afraid I need a half hour," Bogarde said.

"Why's that?"

"I have some unexpected business to attend to."

"Anything I can help with?"

Bogarde chuckled. "I'm afraid not. You two go ahead, and I'll meet you at the hotel."

William and Ella were sipping champagne in the King Cole Room when Bogarde arrived at their table.

"I need some of that."

Ella gazed up at him in shock. "Your—" She blinked. "Your moustache—"

"Has gone." He sat down.

"But why?"

He shrugged. "You said you hate moustaches."

William laughed. "Did you?"

"Yes, but I never meant . . ."

Bogarde leaned toward her gravely. "Having you dislike me was as much as I could handle. Fixing that's going to take longer, but the moustache I could get rid of right away." He rubbed the skin over his upper lip. "I must admit I'd rather have done it less hastily, but anything for a beautiful woman."

Ella blushed.

"I didn't know you hated moustaches," William said curiously. "Why do you?"

"They hide things," she replied awkwardly.

"What kind of things?" Bogarde asked.

"Mean lips. Things like that."

"I don't have mean lips, do I?"

She grew even pinker, casting a swift, unwilling glance at his mouth. It was, in fact, not at all mean—it was a well-made, rather sensual mouth, now that she saw it clearly.

"Do I?" he repeated.

"No."

"Thank the Lord, that's one problem solved." Bogarde picked up his glass and drank a little champagne. "Now, the rest." He considered for a moment. "Ella, I'll bet you take your father's word as gospel on most subjects."

"I suppose so."

Bogarde looked at William. "Would you say that I'm a likable man?"

William grinned. "Fairly."

"Trustworthy?"

"That I can vouch for."

"Am I married?"

"Not to my knowledge."

"Sober?"

"In public at least."

"Would you let your daughter date me?"

"If she wanted to."

Bogarde turned back to Ella and saw, to his great relief, that she was laughing.

"Do you think you could stop hating me?"

"I didn't say I hated you, just that I didn't like you."

"Will you have dinner with me?"

"I'm about to, aren't I?"

Again, he raised his glass. "To our first date. Even if it is with a goddamned chaperone."

In the hotel lobby, after William had gone back to his apartment at the Hunter's building, Bogarde and Ella stood by the elevators.

"About the auction," he said quietly, and Ella noticed again the warm, pure American lilt to his voice. "If I hadn't known who you were, I'd never have played that game. I knew that—" He stopped, suddenly surprisingly awkward.

"That I could afford it?" Ella supplied.

He nodded. "I don't want you to go to sleep tonight thinking that I'm a complete cad."

"Cad." Ella smiled. "What a nice, old-fashioned word that is."

"Very English," he agreed. "Like bounder, or rotter. I can't think of a French equivalent."

"I don't think we have one. *Goujat* is a little harsh."

"I'm glad you think so."

"Do you speak French?" she asked with interest.

"We're quite well educated this side of the ocean, you know." He studied her for a moment. "So what *will* you be thinking? When you go to sleep tonight."

Ella pushed the call button, the elevator doors opened, and she stepped inside. "About my lovely silk rug, of course."

Upstairs in her suite, Ella leaned against the wall and shut her eyes. A picture of Harry Bogarde danced before her, tall, clever, and merry-eyed. She opened them again and saw herself in the mirror.

"Dieu," she said softly.

When she'd looked at her reflection earlier that evening in her father's office, she'd seen a pretty, chic, excited young girl.

Now, staring back with a startled expression, was a slender, glowing, unquestionably beautiful young woman.

Ella smiled.

"*Enfin,*" she said.

It was nearly two o'clock in New York, but a civilized morning hour in France. Ella picked up the telephone by her bed and placed a call, person-to-person.

"Maman?"

Krisztina's voice, slightly delayed by echo, sounded anxious. "Ella? Is something wrong?"

"Of course not. Can't I call you without having a problem?"

"It's late there."

"Not for New York."

Krisztina audibly relaxed. "How was the auction?"

"How did you know I was going?"

"Your father told me."

"How are things with you?" Ella asked.

"Fine."

"I mean the hotel."

"I know what you mean. The hotel, the château, the guests, the staff, even your brother—all fine."

"Ollie too?"

"On his best behavior, though I'm sure he can't wait to be rid of me."

Some of the tension that had steadily slipped from Ella since her departure from de Trouvère, crept back. "It's a strain, isn't it, Maman?"

"A little," Krisztina admitted, then brightened her voice again. "But you're not to think about it while you're having a holiday." She paused. "So how was the auction?"

"Thrilling."

"Did you get your rug?"

"Is there anything you don't know?"

"I'm sorry. Blame Papa. Tell me, *chérie.*"

"Yes, I got it." Ella hesitated. "But that wasn't what made it thrilling."

"No?"

Ella's eyes narrowed with sudden suspicion. "Maman, did you know who Papa and I were going to have dinner with?"

"You mean Harry Bogarde? I knew you *might* be having dinner with him." She paused. "Did you?"

"We did."

"And?"

"Maman, was this a setup? Was Papa matchmaking?" She was incredulous.

Krisztina laughed. "Of course not! But we did both think that you and Harry might get on."

"Well, we didn't. I loathed him."

"I don't believe you."

Ella grinned. "You're right." Exhilaration began to bubble up inside her. "Maman, tell me about him. Who is he? What is he? What's he like?"

"His name is Harry—not short for Harold or Henry, just plain Harry. He's what used to be called a property magnate, but his companies seem to be capable of running themselves, because unlike most businessmen, Harry seldom talks about business. What he really does on an everyday basis is, he collects."

"Collects what?" Ella asked, fascinated.

"Beautiful, precious things. Antiques, art, houses, small galleries. Anything that interests or excites him."

Ella fell silent.

"So?" Krisztina probed.

"So what?"

"Has he asked you to go out with him?"

"No."

"Do you think he will?"

"I don't know."

"Did he seem interested?" Krisztina asked patiently.

"I think so." Ella giggled. "He shaved off his moustache for me."

"What did you say?" her mother asked. "The line's crackling, I don't think I heard what you said."

"You heard."

"Why did he shave off his moustache, Ella?"

"Because I said I hated it."

"You did? That's not like you."

"No."

"And he shaved it off, just like that."

"In between the auction and dinner."

"Ella."

"Yes, Maman?"

"He's interested."

Ella was just dozing off when the telephone's ring startled her. Quickly, she snatched up the receiver. *"Oui?"*

"Stop dreaming of Persia and start thinking about me."

A large smile transformed her face. "Who is this?"

"And stop horsing around. How many lovesick swains call you at three o'clock in the morning?"

"Too many to count."

"Shit."

"Swains don't swear, Harry."

"The hell they don't."

"Harry Bogarde, what do you want at three in the morning?"

"To know if you'll have breakfast with me."

"Breakfast?" she said, horrified.

"Don't they have breakfast meetings in France?"

"France is a civilized country."

"I'm talking about nine o'clock, not six."

"Make it ten and I'll consider it."

"Let's say ten-fifteen, and I'll even shave again."

"Where? Here?"

"The Plaza—it's more romantic. We can stroll into the Edwardian Room arm-in-arm, and I can fantasize we spent the night together."

"Harry!"

"Can't a guy dream?"

Chapter 31

They breakfasted on bacon and eggs, muffins, and coffee. Afterward, they adjourned to Central Park where they walked for two hours, visiting the zoo, kicking up sodden leaves and talking, talking, talking, and then sauntered lazily into the bar of the Sherry-Netherland, where Bogarde was greeted with gusto.

"Bloody Mary?" he suggested to Ella.

"I can't drink before lunch."

"Not even champagne?"

"I've never tried."

"That can be arranged. Virgin Mary?" He paused. "That's the same, without the vodka."

"I know what it is," she said. "I do run a hotel."

"It's hard to believe. With that face and that hair"—he stared at her for a long moment, as if bemused—"you look like a cross between angel and devil. What you don't look like is a businesswoman."

"I'm not."

"If you run the Grand Hôtel du Château de Trouvère, one of the great hotels of France, that sure as hell makes you a businesswoman."

Ella shook her head. "It makes me a hotelier."

"Is that different?"

"Very much so."

"I'd like to see you in action."

Ella felt a happy glow. "Perhaps you will."

They had lunch at "21," tea back at the Plaza in the Palm Court and then, after a two-hour respite during which she visited William and bought black silk stockings and a lipstick at Bonwit Teller, Ella shampooed her hair and changed into a fluffy crimson dress that clashed effectively with her shining, madly electric, flaming hair.

Makeup completed, Chamade perfume dabbed in all the right places, she studied herself in one of the full-length mirrors in her bedroom.

"Merde!"

Bogarde had said she had a touch of devil in her, and suddenly Ella realized that, whether subconsciously or not, she had dressed for the part. The cashmere and angora mixture clung seductively to her small, round breasts, the new vivid lipstick made her mouth seem fuller and quite blatantly sensual, and her blue-violet eyes positively crackled with anticipation.

Dear Lord, I look like a trollop! He'll think I'm out to seduce him.

Panicking, she grabbed a tissue and wiped away the lipstick, but somehow her naked mouth seemed only to heighten rather than diminish her new abandoned image.

Be honest, Ella Hunter, a voice in her head said scornfully, *you've never looked better and you love it.*

The telephone rang.

"Are you ready?"

"No!" Her voice was a frantic squeak.

"Shall I come up?"

"No!"

"Okay." He paused. "Will you be minutes or hours? Shall I wait in the bar or come back tomorrow?"

She took a deep breath. "It's all right, I *am* ready. I'll be right down."

There was a smile in his voice. "I can hardly wait."

He was standing a few feet away when the elevator doors opened and she stepped out.

He stared at her. "Good Christ." The words were soft, hardly more than an exhalation.

"Hello." She felt appallingly shy, yet at the same time outrageously pleased at the effect she was obviously having.

Bogarde stirred himself and took her hand firmly in his. "I'm horribly torn," he said.

"Why?"

"Because we've been invited to a party, and now I can't decide whether I want to show you off or keep you all to myself."

"What kind of a party?"

"On a score of one to ten, I'd guess it'll be at least a nine."

Ella's eyes sparkled. She'd never felt so much like going to a party in her life.

"Would you rather just have dinner?" she managed to ask politely.

He drew her hand up to his lips and kissed it. "I'd rather make you happy."

Ella had never felt such an atmosphere.

They were in a duplex apartment at the Dakota on Central Park West, and it seemed to her that they'd had to pass through as many security checks as for a high-risk flight to the Middle East, though when they finally made it through the front door, she began to understand why.

It was a palace of luxury, wealth, and art—not in the same way that Château de Trouvère was, of course—but every single wall of every room on both floors had been painted by one of the great names of modern art. Pushing her way through the mass of guests, Ella gave little whoops of delight as she pounced on plaster, wood, and glass anointed by Chagall, Picasso, Dalí, and Warhol, as well as two collages by Robert Rauschenberg and a Calder mobile.

"What if there was a fire?" Ella exclaimed, her eyes huge. "Or a flood? What if they ever pull down the building?"

"Do you worry about the Louvre or the Metropolitan? And what about de Trouvère? I gather it's fairly crammed with objets d'art. Do you have nightmares about those?"

"All the time," she said fervently.

"Poor baby," he sympathized, and kissed her very gently on the lips.

An hour or so later, when Ella had grown more accustomed to brushing shoulders with men and women who bore uncannily close resemblances to Beatty, Hoffman, Dunaway, and Bacall, they sat on huge fur-covered beanbags with scarlet plastic bibs around their necks, munching blissfully on broiled lobster claws.

"This is heaven!" Ella sighed. "I've never, ever been to a party where it was okay to get so mucky."

"You look like a little kid." Bogarde grinned. "With butter running down your chin."

"Pass a hot towel, please," she said, then tossed it aside. "Better yet, pass me another claw—no sense getting cleaned up till I'm full." Her eyes rounded again. "Harry, is that really who I think it is?"

Bogarde looked up. "Sure is." He was amused. "I never would have thought you were so starstruck. Do you get this excited when famous people check in at de Trouvère?"

"Of course." She shrugged. "But I'd die before I let anyone know about it." She licked her fingers. "Now pass me a hot towel."

The thump of disco music from the next floor got their feet tapping.

"Do you dance?" Ella asked Bogarde.

"Why? Think I'm too old?"

"I don't know how old you are."

"Thirty-five."

"Do older men like dancing?"

The music accelerated from a healthy sixties' beat to fifties' rock 'n' roll, with Ella—as usual when given an opportunity to dance—wild and insatiable. When Presley gave suddenly way to Charles Aznavour, Bogarde, totally out of breath, drew her close with a long sigh of relief.

"Heaven be praised, I thought they'd kill me." He drew her into his arms and they held each other closely, swaying gently, letting the lush strings and uniquely French voice overwhelm them both with nostalgia.

And then abruptly it was over, and the music thrust them mercilessly into the seventies, and suddenly Ella and Harry stood motionless, just inches apart, scarcely knowing where they were and both longing, above all, to be elsewhere.

"Come on," Bogarde said abruptly, seizing her hand.

"Where?"

"Out of this."

Outside, on the sidewalk, he looked down at her, his eyes

veiled by the dark. "If it were summer, I'd drive you to the beach, and if it were winter, I'd whisk you up to a log cabin in the mountains, but it's November, and all I can offer you is an apartment with a log fire and one of the greatest city views in the world."

"It sounds perfect."

"Thank Christ." Briefly, Bogarde shut his eyes. "Now I *know* I'm the luckiest son of a bitch in America."

It was only at that instant, observing the undisguised joy in his expression, that Ella understood what she'd just assented to.

For several seconds, as Bogarde sprinted away to flag down a cab, alarm churned in her stomach, and she considered making her excuses or just fleeing. But then, as he returned to her side, his hand at her back, steering her into the battered cab, the fear all but disappeared, and only her desire to be with Harry remained—that, and an entirely brand-new trembling in her knees.

It was a glorious view, and as Ella stood out on the wide terrace, hands grasping the chilly rail, staring at the millions of shimmering lights and waiting for the champagne Harry had gone to open, she found herself thinking about that other view she'd seen just two days before, up in the Catskill Mountains.

"Penny for them."

Bogarde appeared holding two steaming pottery mugs.

"Doesn't look like champagne to me."

He handed her one. "Cocoa."

"Cocoa?"

"What every sensible man and woman drink at this hour."

"It is?"

"Don't look so suspicious. I make outstanding cocoa—I had an English nanny, you know."

"So did I. Miss Herrick's cocoa was ghastly."

"Probably didn't have my magic ingredient."

Ella sniffed, then tasted tentatively. "Cognac?"

"Napoléon. And actually, it's Suchard chocolate, but I feel more virtuous calling it cocoa."

"Cheat."

He watched the wind ruffling her hair. "Come inside. I've lit the fire."

He shut the French doors and set down his mug on a marble coffee table. "Now we could roast chestnuts."

"Or marshmallows."

"Drink your chocolate."

"I don't feel like it."

He paused. "What do you feel like doing?"

Ella blushed hotly, and silently cursed herself.

"Viens," said Harry, and took her hand.

"Where to now?"

He guided her out into the square hall and along a corridor into another room. It took Ella a few seconds to absorb the fact that this was his bedroom, for the bed itself, king-size and covered with a pale gray satin spread, was set into an alcove at the far end.

"How about a cognac?" He drew her to a large soft-cushioned sofa opposite another fireplace, already lit.

"Without chocolate?"

"Definitely." He opened a beautiful enameled cabinet and took out a bottle of Delamain. "The cocoa was just to make you smile."

Ella sat on the sofa. "You do make me smile."

"That's nice." He poured into two crystal snifters. "How else do I affect you?"

With most men, Ella knew she would have felt embarrassed by the question, acutely uncomfortable at being in their bedroom, but everything with Harry seemed to be natural—his question, too, seemed to have sprung from genuine curiosity, a need to know how she felt about him.

She took one of the glasses from him and cupped it firmly in both hands. "I'm not sure exactly how you affect me, Harry," she began, with a new and pleasantly relaxing feeling of candor. "I just know that I've spent more time with you in the last twenty-four hours than I've ever spent with any man, and that it's after midnight and I still don't want it to be over."

"It doesn't have to be over," he said, and sat down beside her.

For a few moments they watched the flames and sipped their cognac, and gradually Ella became aware of a new tension creeping into Bogarde and lapping over into herself.

"Put that down," he said suddenly, softly.

Startled, she set the glass on the floor at her feet and looked at him expectantly.

"Ella, you confuse me."

"Do I? Why?"

"Because I look at you, and I see one of the loveliest young women I've ever laid eyes on, and believe me, I've seen a few." His eyes were burning blue, devouring her face. "I see a startling, almost feline quality. I see unbelieveable bone structure, incredible, almost translucent skin, and a body, alive and warm and quite unbearably sensuous, that makes me long to touch it . . ."

He paused, his mouth taut, and Ella closed her eyes for a moment, abruptly weak with the astounding, quivering sensations that the strange new harshness of his voice was setting up in her.

"But at the same time," he went on, "I see such a purity in you, such a trusting innocence, that suddenly all that honest-to-goodness lust I felt at the party and out in the street and in the back of the cab, seems not quite right—if you know what I mean."

"No," Ella said, softly but clearly. "I don't know."

"That's because you can't see yourself."

"I see you, Harry."

He said nothing.

The trembling was still coursing through her, giving her an odd emotional strength, acting on her like rare, intoxicating wine. "I see a beautiful, tall, strong man," she said, "with straw-colored hair and electric blue eyes with wonderful crinkling lines around them, but who would probably be just as beautiful if he were ugly because of his personality and his perfectly disgusting charm . . ."

Bogarde was staring at her, dumbfounded.

Ella took a deep breath. "I'm also seeing a man who's had a sudden attack of funk because he's brought home the daughter of a friend."

"William has nothing to do with it, believe me."

"Then it must be because I'm a virgin."

"You are?" he said, in awe.

"Yes, I am," she said hotly, a corner of her brain wondering where in heaven's name her inhibitions had vanished to. "But I'm a virgin because I've chosen to be, because I haven't, until now, met a man I wanted to make love to. So there's no need to make a great big deal about it!" She stopped suddenly, panting.

"Until now," Bogarde repeated.

"What?" Now, after all that, she was blushing again. All that bravado, and she wanted to sink into the ground, to disappear through the rug at their feet.

"You said you hadn't met a man you wanted to make love to until now," Bogarde persisted.

She swallowed. "No."

"But now you have?"

Ella nodded.

"Hallelujah," he said fervently, and drew her into his arms.

Their mouths met, lips grazing, closed at first, then opening, willingly, tongues darting, exploring. Ella felt a lovely fever spreading down past her neck, flooding every part of her right down to her toes.

Bogarde pulled away, gasping slightly, and stood up, taking her with him and leading her slowly, tenderly to the bed, where he pulled off the satin spread and let it fall to the floor.

"Ella?" he whispered.

She nodded wordlessly.

Turning her around, Harry unzipped her dress, felt the fluffy fabric, warm from her skin, and then her flesh, her straight shoulders, soft, smooth arms . . . and then his hands were on her body, stroking their way over her navel and down over her abdomen past her lacy apricot garter belt, toward tiny satin briefs . . .

Ella froze. For a moment, she was rocketed back in time, to a terrible childhood afternoon when so many nightmares had taken root.

Harry sensed her fear, felt the change in her, and stopped. "Ella?"

She couldn't speak.

"Ella, what's wrong?"

It was the concern in his face—the care in his lovely, warm eyes—that brought her back, that blotted out the past, wiped away the associations that curious, invading hands on her body had until tonight triggered. . . . This was different, at last. This was Harry Bogarde, and these were hands she *wanted* to touch her.

And she reached out to him and took his hands and drew his arms around her, welcoming him. He sighed with pleasure and relief, and his eager fingers unfastened her brassiere, and for just an instant, Ella stiffened again, before she moved closer, huddling against his chest like an animal seeking shelter and warmth.

"I want to see you," Bogarde whispered, and as she stepped tentatively back, he stared in wonder, for she was even more exquisite than he'd imagined. Her breasts were small, but full and perfect, breasts of poets and painters and sculptors, and Harry felt himself grow hard as iron, and he groaned with joy and anticipation. Unbuckling his belt, he took off his shirt and trousers, leaving only his underpants, so that they stood face-to-face, like a pair of virgins holding back before the final plunge into total nudity.

"Will you come to bed with me?" he asked, and his voice was a plea, shaken by desire.

"Yes, please," Ella whispered, her own eyes riveted by his leanness, his fineness, by the marvelous, elegant way he was put together, like an athlete, with no spare flesh anywhere.

He is beautiful, she thought as they lay down together on the big bed and Harry drew the snowy duvet lightly over them before reaching down to tug away her briefs and release his own nakedness. And she experienced a vast, rushing, soaring excitement, as if she were a young bird launching into the sky for the first time, and there were tears of happiness in her eyes.

"All right, Ella?"

She nodded mutely, and kissed his forehead. And then she couldn't stop kissing him, his cheeks and his straight nose and his eyelids and his tousled fair hair and lines that flared from his nostrils to the corners of his mouth . . .

And then Bogarde began to move, could restrain himself no longer, and he caressed Ella with every part of himself, with his fingers and palms and his mouth and even his feet, kissing and licking and tickling and stroking and probing. And it wasn't a case of awakening her body, for it was immediately, shockingly alive—for Ella's soul had yielded, all doubts banished, and she was conscious that it was all for him, that she wanted him to have it all, to know it all. . . .

His fingers were buried in her flaming pubic hair, and she was being driven wild with longing, her body beginning to shake with it. She was hardly aware that every time he brushed her clitoris she moaned for more, spread her thighs farther apart and opened herself to him, unable to tolerate the waiting any more.

"Wait," Harry said suddenly.

Ella opened her eyes and saw his face, saw the look of near pain, of blunted concentration, and felt him move away from her.

"No! Don't go," she begged, clutching at him, knowing that she was wholly, utterly ready for him, that it was vital that this moment not be lost.

"I have to use something," he muttered, and abruptly she realized what he was doing, and gratitude and relief swamped her.

He rolled back into her arms and kissed her mouth with tenderness as well as passion, moved and delighted by her eagerness. Then desire overtook them both again, and she was on her back beneath him and he was inside her, penetrating her, making her his, and Ella was conscious of pain, but it was nothing compared to the happiness she felt at being so completely close to him, moving with him, rocking to and fro until the pain receded and a million other sensations took over. She knew that she cried out his name, and that he was saying over and over again, in a desperate, wild voice, that he loved her and that he wanted her, forever and ever. . . .

They slept until dawn, curled together, and then they made love again, and afterward they dozed until breakfast, which Harry made himself and carried in on a tray, complete with the champagne he'd promised her the night before. They ate croissants and dunked them in Dom Pérignon, and got crumbs on the sheets and sent the tray crashing to the floor, and made love again, continuing off and on until noon, when Harry remembered an appointment and staggered wearily off to get dressed while Ella slept happily in his bed until four in the afternoon.

"You look tired," William said, when she stopped by to see him at six.

"Do I?"

He drummed his fingers on the blotter on his desk. "How's Harry?"

"Pretty good, I think."

"Like him a little better now, I gather?"

"A little." She paused. "You're busy tonight, aren't you, Papa?"

"Unfortunately, yes."

"I think I'll drive back up to the house."

He smiled. "Had enough of the city?"

"Not exactly. I just think it would be good for me."

"Does Harry know you're going?"

"Not yet."

"Are you going to tell him?"

"I'm not sure."

"I see."

"Do you, Papa?"

"I think so." He got up, came around the desk, and hugged her hard. "Drive safely."

"Don't worry about me."

William tilted her chin so that he could see into her eyes. "I'm not."

She got to the house at nine to find Alice at the front door with Titus, tail thrashing joyfully.

"No Janus?"

"He's visiting with Venus and the kids."

"Good for him."

"Hungry?"

"I could eat."

"Omelets okay?"

Ella kissed the tips of her fingers. *"Parfait."*

She sat up until midnight, refusing to admit to herself that she was waiting for the telephone to ring, then went listlessly to bed with a book.

The roar of the engine woke her first, then the brief flashing of headlights before they were turned off together with the motor.

Ella tumbled out of bed and gazed out of the window, peering into the darkness. The shadowy shape of a man was emerging from a long, low sports car, and the moonlight caught a glimmer of gold in his hair before he vanished under the porch and the doorbell began to ring.

Ella squeaked with joy, switched on the light, and searched frantically for her hairbrush while the dogs began to bark and Alice's bedroom door crashed open.

"It's all right, Alice!" Ella called, rushing out onto the landing in her pajamas.

"It's two in the morning!"

"It's for me. I'm sorry."

"Are you sure?"

"Perfectly."

The doorbell was still ringing as she scurried down the stairs. "Will you stop that! You'll wake the neighbors!"

Fingers trembling, she pulled back the bolts and flung open the door.

Harry stood on the mat, grim-faced. "There aren't any neighbors," he said flatly.

"You're disturbing the peace."

"Screw the peace."

"Why didn't you call first?"

"Why didn't *you*?"

"I didn't know where to find you," she said.

"Crap!"

"Well, I didn't," she insisted lamely.

"You could have left a note—hotelkeepers can write, can't they?"

"In four languages." Ella was shivering with cold. "Perhaps you should come in."

"If you're sure you don't mind."

"I wish you would."

In the sitting room, he glared at her. "Why did you do this?"

"I'm not sure. I think I wanted to be enigmatic."

"Bull."

"I don't know why, Harry. Please don't be angry with me."

His eyes narrowed. "You wanted to test me out."

"Did I?"

"Wanted to check how much you meant to me."

"I just wanted to get out of the city."

"Did you or didn't you want me to follow you?"

Ella flushed. "I did."

"So now what?"

She tried to smile. "We go back to bed?"

"I didn't drive all the way up here to make love to you," he said tersely.

"Oh." Her disappointment was plain.

Harry sighed. "I guess this is what I get for deflowering a twenty-four-year-old, worldly-wise virgin. A scheming, shameless hussy."

"Is that what I am?" she asked, surprised.

"Apparently."

"Thank you."

"It wasn't intended as a compliment."

"Just the same, can we go to bed?" Ella asked pleasantly. "I'm sleepy, and I'm freezing to death down here."

"In your blue silk pajamas." He looked at her appraisingly.

"Do you like them?"

"Very chaste."

"They're supposed to be slinky." She saw him glance at his wristwatch. "You are staying, aren't you?" she asked anxiously.

"Maybe I have better things to do than hang around in the country."

"You told me you like the country."

Harry eyed her thoughtfully. "What I ought to do is put you over my knee and give you a good old-fashioned rural spanking."

"You dare!"

"Oh, I dare all right."

"I'll set the dogs on you."

"I'm scared to death." He looked at Titus, sprawled out on the hearth, black ears twitching, tail thumping amiably.

"There are six Irish wolfhounds out back."

"You told me—four pups and their gentle-giant parents."

"You wouldn't really spank me, would you?" Ella cajoled, moving closer to him.

"I might."

"I'd rather you did this instead." Gently but firmly, Ella reached for his hands, removed his car keys, and pressed his palms against her breasts.

Harry closed his eyes. "Shit," he groaned.

"You said I'm a hussy," she grinned, delighted at the effect she was having. "I'm just trying to live up to it."

"You've succeeded."

"Good," she purred. "Now come to bed."

Harry and Alice got on famously, and after breakfast, while Alice pulled together a picnic lunch for them, Harry and Ella took a stroll in the big back garden and went down to the kennels.

"So where are we going today?" Harry asked, fondling Venus's shaggy ears.

"I want to show you something special."

"What?"

"You'll see." Ella paused. "It's just something I'd like to share with you."

She'd known, somehow, when she'd left it four days earlier, that she would be drawn back again to Pine Orchard, for there was magnetism about the place.

"What *is* it?" she asked Bogarde as they stood, arms linked, gazing down from the site. "I've seen plenty of wonderful views before."

He shook his head. "Not many like this." His voice was soft. "This is special, you were right."

"But it's more than just spectacular." Ella tried to find the right words. "Do you know what a camera obscura is, Harry?"

"Latin for 'dark room'—and some kind of ancestor of photography."

"I saw one once, at the top of a hill. Somehow, the whole surrounding area was captured by this camera obscura and its image reflected on a kind of dish. It looked just like a great map, only the difference was that it was *alive*. If you looked closely, you could see tiny little people and cars and specks of animals going about their daily lives, quite oblivious that they were being watched. It was a curious sensation—*puissant*—powerful."

"And that's how you feel up here?"

"A little, yes."

"That's probably one reason why the Mountain House attracted all those wealthy, influential folk. They must have liked that feeling, too, made them feel at home."

"It makes me sad," Ella said.

"Why?"

"Because it's gone, without a trace."

The clouds that had been threatening since midmorning began to spit rain down on the mountain in big round drops.

"Come on," Harry said, "let's get back to the car."

"I wanted to see the Kaaterskill Falls. The waterfall's longer than Niagara, apparently."

"We'll get soaked."

"What are you, a man or a mouse?" Ella scorned.

"A New Yorker with a beautiful, dry Aston Martin just waiting to be sat in."

"I may never come here again, Harry. You go back to the car, and I'll see the falls alone."

Bogarde sighed heavily. "William tells me that Krisztina can be stubborn. It's easy to see you've inherited it."

They started along the road that led to the waterfall, and turned down a narrow track, where Ella stumbled slightly and fell against Bogarde.

"Kiss me," he said huskily.

For a long moment their lips met, while the raindrops grew even larger, splashing them, drenching their hair and turning the track to mud. When they drew apart for breath, Bogarde stared intently at Ella and kept a grip on her shoulders.

"Marry me," he said.

"*Quoi?*" She was startled.

"You heard."

"You want to marry me?"

"I do."

"But we've only just met," she breathed.

Harry checked his watch. "We met almost sixty-two hours ago." He looked at her. "Will you marry me, Ella?"

She couldn't tell if her eyes were wet with tears or with rain. She gazed up at him, her expression nakedly adoring. "I can't."

"Why not?" His eyes were more savagely blue than before. "You can't stand there looking at me like that and—"

"Like what?"

"Like you're . . . as if you love me. . . ."

"I do."

"Well then?" He was very tense. "Don't you want to marry me?"

"Yes. Oh, God, yes!"

"Then why can't you?"

"Because I live in France."

"Is that all?"

"It's quite crucial, isn't it?" Ella asked.

"Of course not!" He laughed, relieved. "You can move. People do, you know."

"Not me."

"Why not you?"

"Because I belong there."

"Your mother moved."

"True."

"Well then?" he said again.

"Don't be angry with me, Harry," she pleaded.

"I'm not angry, I just don't understand."

Ella reached up and stroked his face. "You're an American, *n'est-ce pas?*"

"So?"

"Would you come and live in Alsace?"

"I might."

She shook her head, her saturated hair clinging to her face. "No, you wouldn't."

"I have homes all over. Why not one more?"

"Where are these homes?"

"Long Island, Manhattan, Chicago, and San Francisco."

"All in America."

He changed his tack. "From what you told me in the park the other day, things aren't exactly joyful in the land of de Trouvère."

"No, they're not," she agreed quietly.

"So I'm offering you an alternative."

"What if I don't want an alternative?"

"Perhaps you do, and you just don't know it yet."

"Don't presume to know everything about me, Harry," Ella said tightly.

He let her go and ran a frustrated hand through his wet hair. "I just don't understand."

"How can you?" She was gentler again.

"What does that mean?"

"Unless you visit de Trouvère, how can you begin to understand anything about me?"

"Don't dismiss the last three days, Ella."

"How could I? They were the most wonderful days I've ever spent in my whole life."

"Then don't say no."

"Harry, I—"

"Say you'll think about it."

She was silent.

"Please!" His voice was desperate, his eyes beseeching. "I'm thirty-five, Ella, and I've never before found any woman who I wanted to marry." He paused. "Just tell me you'll give it some thought."

Ella shook her head helplessly. "I don't see how I'll be able to help thinking about it."

"Thank God for that, anyway."

*

A week later Ella flew home feeling bereft and utterly wretched.

At de Trouvère, Krisztina greeted her in the reception hall. "Let me look at you."

"Hello, Maman."

"Your eyes are pink and your mascara's smudged, but still you look wonderful."

"So do you." It was true—her mother looked sparkling and beautiful in a gray Balmain suit. "You've been shopping."

"Just two days in Paris. You wouldn't have expected me to be this close and not have some fun."

"I should think not."

"Come on, *chérie,* let's go and sit down." She linked arms with Ella. "First you can tell me all about your papa, and then you can explain why falling in love with Harry Bogarde has made you cry all the way across the Atlantic Ocean."

Later, Krisztina stroked Ella's hand. "Do you think he'll come?"

"Yes." She paused. "I hope so."

"Perhaps you should have accepted him. He's a good man."

"I know, Maman. But how could I? I don't want to give up de Trouvère."

"Maybe you should."

Ella paused. "Where is Ollie?"

"Out somewhere, I don't know. I think he made a decision when I arrived that there was only room for one of us at a time."

"So he hasn't been working?"

"Not much."

Ella slumped back in her chair. "Maman, what am I going to do?"

"About your brother or about de Trouvère or about Harry?"

"All three."

"Take the last first, *chérie.* Tell me one thing—would you rather you'd never met him?"

"No!"

Krisztina smiled. "Even though making a decision one way or the other is going to tear you into pieces, whichever way you choose?"

Ella was quiet for a moment before answering. "Meeting Harry has been the most splendid experience of my life."

"Then don't let him go, *dragam*. Don't throw such feelings away." Krisztina's eyes were serious. "I had them once, and I had no choice but to put them aside, and I married the wrong man."

"But then you found Papa."

"Not every woman gets to be that lucky, Ella."

"Do you think Harry's right for me, Maman?"

Krisztina laughed. "Don't lay that in my lap, *chérie*. Your father and I have known Harry Bogarde for a few years and we like him very much—because he's honorable, generous, kind, and likeable." She paused. "What you have to do is decide if Harry Bogarde is right for Ella Hunter."

"But even if he is, can I bear to give up this hotel, my home?"

"The trouble is, Ella," Krisztina said slowly, "that it isn't entirely your home."

Ella was surprised. "Because of Ollie, you mean?"

"Yes, because of Ollie. This whole estate bears the name of de Trouvère; his name, not yours."

"But we're brother and sister."

"He's your *half*-brother. It makes a difference—most notably that your name is Hunter." Krisztina spoke gently. "Olivier loves you more than anyone else on earth, Ella, I wouldn't dispute that for an instant, but he does not sufficiently respect you."

"I don't think that's true."

"He uses you, *chérie*. He manipulates you."

"I'm not so easily manipulated," Ella defended.

"Not by most people, but we all have our blind spots."

"He depends on me so much, Maman. You're not here, you don't see how lost he can be sometimes."

"I don't doubt that he relies on you, because he's not stupid. My son may be many things, foolish and arrogant and deeply unhappy, but stupidity is not one of his shortcomings."

"You make him sound so terrible."

"I'm his mother," Krisztina said sadly. "I don't say that he's a terrible man, Ella, but I see his faults more clearly than anyone." She took Ella's hand again. "There are too many differences between you and Olivier to count, my darling, but one is fundamental: You could leave de Trouvère and still be whole and happy—perhaps even happier than you've ever been. Olivier could not. He believes that he and the estate are one and the same, that the château and his lands are vital for his survival."

"But if I leave him—desert him—I'm afraid he'll destroy de Trouvère, and himself with it."

"Olivier had a self-destructive father, and the signs of that heritage are clearly there." Krisztina's face was pained. "It may take him a while, but if he is going to destroy himself, he'll do it with or without you." She paused. "Maybe it's kismet that's brought Harry into your life at this time."

"I don't want him as an escape hatch, Maman."

"No, of course not. That would be a disastrous basis for a marriage. But I think that's beside the point, because you've fallen in love with Harry, haven't you?"

"I think so."

"I know how you feel about this place, Ella, if anyone does," Krisztina went on. "You feel it has a life force of its own, that it's an extension of our family, that in leaving you might be betraying that family, not just Olivier."

Ella nodded. "Grand-maman, especially."

"You're wrong. Grand-maman and I felt the same way, and yet we knew when the time was right for me to leave."

"There are people who spend their whole lives in one place— generations of families living and dying in the same house," Ella argued. "Are you saying that isn't right?"

"I'd never presume to say such a thing. Laurent's destiny was bound up in de Trouvère and so is his son's. But mine wasn't, at least not irrevocably." Krisztina's eyes were penetrating. "Neither, I believe, is yours."

Chapter 32

In spite of their separation, Harry and Ella spoke every day and wrote long, lovesick letters or brief, romantic notes. She had managed to persuade him to wait until Christmas to fly over, since in the first place the week before New Year's was the crazy season for de Trouvère, and in the second place it gave her the time and space she knew she needed.

Ella did not notice that she'd missed her period until a fortnight before Christmas. They'd been so frantically busy, and the American trip had so disrupted her schedule, that she was never even suspicious until the nausea began.

Her initial reaction was terror.

Then confusion. How could it have happened when they'd used condoms? And then she remembered Rhinebeck—the first time that night, that one single time when they'd both forgotten, swept up in the heat of the moment. . . .

Next came wonder. Harry Bogarde's child in her body!

And excitement and renewed panic, and an intense, unbearable yearning to share her secret.

But with whom? Not Harry, who wouldn't be with her for another two weeks. Not her mother or father, who would do nothing but worry about her.

If only Geneviève were still alive. . . .

But there was only Ollie.

She wasn't sure why she told him, why she thought she could still trust him after so much bitterness—but he was still her brother, wasn't he, no matter what?

She knew that she'd made a mistake the second she'd finished speaking.

"I don't believe it," he said flatly.

"It's true."

"How many periods have you missed?"

"One. It's enough."

"What else?"

"Morning sickness. Ollie, I'm pregnant."

Olivier was silent for a long time. Then suddenly he looked up. "What are you going to do?"

"Do?"

"About getting rid of it."

"I have no intention of getting rid of it."

"You *want* it?" He looked incredulous.

"Certainly."

"You're crazy."

"No, I'm not."

His mouth twisted. "My sister the prude, my innocent little Lalla, knocked up like the commonest slut. It's almost funny."

Ella stared at him. "I wish I hadn't told you."

"You know you always tell me everything in the end. What about the father? Does he know?"

"Not yet."

"Ah, it's a Christmas gift for him—*un joli cadeau.* Will he marry you?"

"You know he wants to marry me."

"That was before you were pregnant."

Ella's eyes were bright. "I'll have this child whether we marry or not."

"That'll be good for business."

"Less harmful than many things you've done."

"Don't be superior with me, Ella, not now. You're no better than me, and now you've proved it." He leaned forward and patted her stomach. "And before long, everyone will know it."

She felt tears threatening. "I wish I hadn't told you," she said again. "I should have known better."

"If you're worried that I'll be indiscreet about it, don't be. I don't want to bring shame on our family."

"You *hypocrite*. After what you've done, right here at de Trouvère."

"This is my home."

"Mine too."

"Questionable."

"I beg your pardon?"

"This is not your father's house."

"For God's sake, Olivier!"

"At least our mother had the good taste to leave once she knew the truth."

"What truth?"

"About her parentage."

"And your own ancestry," she reminded him.

Olivier gazed at her in cold disgust. "You've grown pale, Lalla. Perhaps you should lie down. In your condition, you should take no risks."

Abruptly, he stalked from the room. Ella put a hand up to her cheek. It was wet with tears.

Late that night, when she was lying sleepless in bed, there was a knock at the door. "Yes?"

Olivier stood framed in light from the hall.

"Go away," she said.

"Lalla." He came in and closed the door.

"I don't want to speak to you."

"Please."

Ella switched on her bedside lamp and glanced at the clock. "It's nearly three, Olivier. What on earth do you want?"

"To be forgiven." He came closer, and she saw that his eyes were red.

"Leave me alone."

He sat on the edge of her bed and she could smell whisky on his breath. "Lalla, I'm sorry. I shouldn't have said what I did."

"How right you are."

"I didn't mean it. I was shocked."

"You meant every word."

"No! I love you, you know that."

"You have the strangest way of showing it."

"Don't be this way, Lalla, for God's sake." He tried to take her hand, but she wrenched it away. "I do love you. I *need* you, you know that. You're the only one that matters." He looked wild, desperate.

"You're drunk," she said in disgust. "Try telling me how much you care when you're sober."

"Lalla, please, please forgive me!" The words wrenched from him, almost in a sob.

"Get out of my room."

"Lalla—"

"Now!"

Harry arrived at lunchtime the day before Christmas Eve. He had three suitcases, two containing his personal effects, the third packed full of gifts.

"They're not all from me—two are from your parents and there's one from Alice."

"How nice of her." Ella peered into the case. "Harry, there are at least twenty packages in there!"

"And all for you."

"You're crazy."

"Just in love."

"I haven't had time to buy anything for you."

"That's okay, I've already got what I want." He drew her close, and for a long moment they held each other. "Christ, how I've missed you."

Ella had asked her parents if she might use their special place, the tiny lodge in the north forest which William had "given" his wife for a wedding present exactly twenty-six years before.

"I can't think of a nicer idea," her mother agreed, after a brief conversation with William. "I often think it's sad it's so seldom used."

"You're sure you don't mind, either of you?"

"We're both delighted."

Ella grinned. "I'll bet there aren't many parents who'd loan their daughter a love nest."

"But then there probably aren't many parents with such a daughter," Krisztina said warmly. "Give our love to Harry, and have fun."

"We will."

It was rarely used, though carefully maintained, but the air of romance that had greeted Krisztina for the first time so long ago was still vibrant in the air, as if it had been captured in the golden pine walls and held in trust for just such a time.

Ella and Harry spent two glorious hours in blessed privacy that afternoon, before she was forced to return to duty, promising that they would have dinner à deux at the Hepplewhite table, even if they had to wait until midnight to find the time.

When they finally fell asleep in the snug, fire-lit bedroom just after three in the morning, Ella had still not told Harry about the baby. She'd promised herself twenty-four hours, at least, to be sure things were still the same between them. Besides, *Réveillon* would be a properly auspicious occasion for such news. . . .

The telephone jangled her out of a happy dream, and she reached for the receiver swiftly, hoping not to disturb Harry.

"*Pardon*, mademoiselle."

"Louis? What's wrong?"

"A problem. A small fire—"

"Fire!"

"Don't distress yourself, it's already out."

"Where?"

"The kitchen—in the *vestiaire*. As I said, we put it out."

"Who's we?"

"Myself and Christine Vernier, one of the *femmes de chambre*. She smelled smoke even before the sprinkler had activated."

"I'll be right there."

"I was sure you would wish to check, mademoiselle, though there's little damage."

"You were right, Louis."

She put down the phone. Beside her, Harry stirred. "What happened?"

"Nothing much." Ella kissed his hair. "A little problem at the hotel. I'll have to go over."

"Did I hear the word 'fire'?"

"Only a tiny one, and it's out. Go back to sleep—I shan't be long."

"I'll come with you," he mumbled, only half awake.

"You won't. You're exhausted and I need you strong for Christmas."

Harry forced himself to sit up. "We're in the middle of a forest. You shouldn't drive by yourself."

Ella smiled. "This is Alsace, not Manhattan. I'll be fine! Now go back to sleep."

She'd been gone about ten minutes, and Harry was lying on his back, now maddeningly awake, when he heard a sound from the front door.

"Back already?" he called, pleased.

There was no reply.

"Ella?"

Something creaked, and then, very slowly, the door handle moved, gleaming in the firelight.

Harry froze.

"Ella? Is that you?"

The door opened slowly, eerily.

A man stood in the doorway, motionless.

Harry snapped on the light.

The man wore a uniform of burgundy velvet with gold braid and buttons and black immaculate trousers.

"Who the hell are you?" Bogarde's voice rapped through the silence.

That was when he saw the rapier.

"I didn't know who it was until he started raving about his sister," he told Ella between sips of cognac. "You told me he wouldn't be back till late tomorrow."

"That's what he told me," she said quietly.

"I thought for a moment I was dreaming. He looked so . . . so *absurd*—like someone from another age. I wanted to laugh, except I was too shit-scared. And then I saw the sword."

"Rapier."

"Ella, darling, it looked like a fucking sword to me, and since I didn't even have my pants on, let alone a gun, let's just say I felt the odds were against me."

She smiled in spite of herself.

"It wasn't funny."

"I know." She stood up and began to pace, trying to clear her head. "But you say he didn't attack you?"

"No, darling, I told you—he challenged me to a duel. A duel!"

"He must have been drunk."

"He was roaring drunk! But I've had too much to drink in my time, too, and I can't say I've ever climbed into fancy dress and staggered into a perfect stranger's bedroom to demand satisfaction!"

"I don't suppose you have."

Harry looked at her quizzically. "Is that normal behavior for Olivier, would you say?"

Ella shook her head. "Not even for Olivier." Her voice was suddenly very sad.

"Drunk or not," Harry went on, "I'm afraid he seemed totally unbalanced to me."

She said nothing.

"Come and sit down," he said gently.

She came and laid her head on his shoulder, longing to cry.

"How did he know you weren't here?" Harry asked.

Still Ella could not trust herself to speak.

Harry hesitated. "Might he have started that fire, as a diversion, do you think?" He paused. "You said it was small. Could it have been deliberately small?"

"Not if no one had found it," she whispered.

"You have sprinkler systems, don't you?"

"Yes, of course."

"So he'd know they would put it out."

"I suppose so."

Tenderly, he turned her face up to his. "Why didn't you tell me?"

"About what?"

"About the baby."

Ella stiffened. "You know? Olivier told you?"

"Why do you think he wanted a duel?" Harry asked wryly. "He was raving so wildly that it took a while before it sank in. I'd taken advantage of his sister, he said, and I'd pay for it." He shrugged. "I thought at first he just had a thing about your virginity, but then he accused me of abandoning you with a child."

"Oh, my God . . ."

"So why didn't you tell me?"

"I was waiting for tomorrow."

"Something to do with Christmas?"

"Partly. And partly because I wanted to be sure we were still okay."

"I see," he said.

"Do you?"

"I think so. You're not the kind of woman who'd want to marry for the wrong reasons."

"That's about it."

"Would it make any difference to know how I feel about the baby?"

"Of course."

"Look at me, Ella."

She faced him.

"I feel overcome," he said.

"Oh."

"With joy."

She smiled. "Oh."

"I find it hard to believe that there's even a chance that I might have everything I want, in one fell swoop." He stared at her. "Everything, by the way, being you and our child."

"Thank you," she said softly.

"What about you? How do you feel about being pregnant? About having a child so—abruptly?"

"Like you," she replied. "Overcome."

"And if you were to decide not to marry me, you'd still want to have the baby?"

"Definitely." Ella shook her head. "I could never have an abortion."

"Because you're Catholic?"

"No." She paused. "Anyway, I'm not really, as it turns out."

"Kriszti and William told me about her adoption."

"So how do you feel about marrying a Jewish girl?"

"It makes no difference to me." He thought for a moment. "Would you want to marry in a synagogue?"

Ella laughed. "I think that might be a little complicated, since my mother spent most of her life in the belief that she was Catholic."

"What about your chapel here? Would you like to be married there?"

"Harry, I haven't said that I want to be married at all!"

"I know. I'm sorry." He couldn't keep the grin off his face. "It's just that since you love me, and I love you, and we're going to have a baby that we both want—" He stopped, a little lamely.

Ella clambered to her feet, walked over to the fireplace, and stood for a while thinking.

"Oh, all right," she said at last.

"What do you mean?"

"Oh, all right, I'll marry you."

Harry sat back on the sofa, watching her. "Let no one ever accuse you of overromanticism, Ella Hunter."

She smiled and turned around. "Sorry."

"Come over here and do this properly, where I can see you. I want a little joyous weeping, or at least a kiss."

She came to him and fastened her arms around his waist. He kissed her for a long time, breaking off only for a second or two to say: " 'Ella Bogarde.' It has a nice ring." He hesitated. "Or do you want to keep your own name?"

Ella smiled. "Wouldn't you mind?"

"Not enough to divorce you."

"It so happens, I like 'Ella Bogarde' too."

Harry went back to kissing her, then stopped again. "We've forgotten the hotel." He looked suddenly afraid.

"I haven't."

"And?"

"We'll work it out somehow," she said. "Suddenly it doesn't seem like a good enough reason to stop us being husband and wife."

All the next day he watched her, hard at work, in the setting she loved, wholly embroiled in every heartbeat of the hotel. At lunchtime he sat alone at a table in the restaurant while Ella spoke to guests and staff, and when she returned for a while, he told her that she had never looked lovelier.

"Thank you." She smiled.

"Your work adds to your beauty, Ella. It rounds you, makes you complete."

A flicker of pain crossed her face, but she said nothing, just sat down and ate her cheese and drank a little wine.

"I'm going to the lodge after lunch, to do some thinking," Harry said.

"About what?"

"An idea. No sign of Olivier today?" Harry asked as they stood to leave the restaurant.

"He's probably nursing a hangover."

"Leaving you with the Christmas rush."

"It's not so bad," she said quickly. "The guests are mostly checked in and happy with their rooms."

"So you have nothing more complex than this evening's feast to mastermind," he said ironically.

"We have a wonderful chef."

"I know." He hugged her briefly, aware that she did not care for affectionate displays in the public areas. "If you want me, I'll be at the lodge."

"I want you all the time," Ella said ruefully, "but it's time I don't have."

The festivities went superbly well. Wearing a figure-hugging scarlet velvet gown, aware that she wouldn't be able to wear clothes like that for much longer, Ella managed to play her role and to enjoy herself with Harry, who seemed to take to the part of temporary adjutant with remarkable ease.

Olivier did not appear until just before midnight, when he came into the candlelit ballroom wearing a tuxedo and his most charming smile. He greeted Harry and Ella as if the previous night had never happened.

"Maybe he doesn't remember," Harry suggested in a low voice.

"He remembers." Ella was momentarily pale.

"Hey." He squeezed her hand. "Don't let him wreck your evening. You're the triumphant hostess at the greatest party I've ever been to."

She managed a smile. "It isn't a party, Harry."

"Not for you, no." He shook his head. "I don't know how you can control something as big as this. It must require immense stamina."

"It requires planning and the right staff," Ella explained. "It's a little like producing a fine play—you have to get the casting just right."

"And the set."

She nodded. "The set, in this case, is everything."

It was four o'clock before they were able to kick off their shoes and bury their feet in the soft carpet at the lodge.

"We need to talk," Harry said, "but I guess you're ready to collapse."

Ella shook her head. "Not quite. I've been waiting for hours to hear about your idea."

"It might be better to wait till you've slept."

"Unless I know what you're cooking up, I won't be able to sleep."

He made her drink a whole cup of coffee before he began. "In America," he said, "up on that mountain, you said that I'd never be able to understand you unless I came to de Trouvère."

"I remember."

"Well, I'm here, finally, and I've been watching you, and you were right. It would be wrong to take you away from the hotel. It's part of you; it doesn't just take your strength, it gives it back to you."

"But you wouldn't be happy living—"

"Wait until I've said my piece," he interrupted.

"All right."

He went on. "I don't want to live in Alsace, Ella, you were right about that too. It's a wonderful place, but as you so accurately pointed out, I'm very much an American."

"So what do we do?" she asked wearily.

"We take the hotel with us."

"What?"

"Leave de Trouvère with Olivier, for better or worse, and build a second hotel, identical in every way, if you like, though I think it has to be bigger—in New York."

Ella stared.

Harry grinned. "What do you think?"

She was too stunned to speak.

"I think it's the perfect solution," he said, "and what's more, I think it could work."

Ella put down her coffee cup, afraid of spilling it. "It's impossible." Her voice was hoarse. "Château de Trouvere is old. You can't replicate it, it would never be the same."

"With enough funds, you can have a damn good try."

"That's another reason—the biggest reason, I suppose. Money."

Harry smiled. "I'm rich, Ella. Filthy rich."

"No one's that rich," she retorted. "A project like that would cost millions."

"Probably around twenty million," he agreed easily.

"Well then."

"I told you, I'm rich—megarich."

"But you don't *do* anything!"

"Inherited wealth, my darling. Though it's not quite true that I don't do anything—I just don't talk about it much."

"Well, you should. A wife has to know how her husband makes his money. For all I know, you could be a criminal!"

"I'm not."

"I know."

"So?" Harry paused. "I can raise the money, Ella. We can locate the guy who turned the château into a hotel—what was his name?"

"Alberto Giordano." She shook her head. "That was thirty years ago!"

"He's alive. You told me he just sent you flowers."

"But he must be seventy!"

"That's no age if he has his health—anyway, at the very least he could supervise."

"Harry, wait, for pity's sake!"

"What for?"

"You're going too fast."

"I'm sorry, baby."

She shook her head again. "It's impossible."

"Nothing is impossible." He waited an instant. "You haven't asked me where I think the hotel should be."

Ella stared at him and, with a small, almost electric, shock, read his mind. "I think I can guess."

"It's the perfect spot."

Ella shut her eyes, and immediately the view that had so captivated her sprang back into her mind. For a few moments she let herself go, imagined Pine Orchard and the mountain in spring and summer and, better still, in autumn, when the colors must surely be glorious, tumbling away down into the valley.

She opened her eyes again. "It could never be another de Trouvère. Not without history, without family."

"Of course not," Harry said softly. "But you'd be giving birth to a *new* de Trouvère. Who knows, it might even be better."

Suddenly remembering, she laid a hand on her flat stomach. "I'm going to have a baby, Harry," she reminded him. "It's one thing running an existing hotel through a pregnancy; it's another matter entirely building one."

"I'd say it's ideal for you. Not the way it was for your mother, with workmen crashing all around her. You'll be able to tell people exactly what you want, then sit back and watch. Our child will be up on its feet by the time the doors open."

"Our child," Ella echoed, more than a little dazed. "A château in New York . . ."

"It's a lot to absorb, isn't it?" he agreed.

Reality stabbed at her again. "What about Olivier?"

"What about him?"

"He'd never let us duplicate de Trouvère."

"Depends on how it's presented to him. If he sees it as a path to greater autonomy, I doubt he'll put up too much of a fight."

"You realize that the bulk of my capital's tied up here, don't you, Harry?"

"I do."

"Doesn't that bother you?"

"Only from the point of view that with a man as unstable as your brother controlling it, this hotel's as good as lost." He reflected. "Would he buy you out?"

Ella shook her head. "I'm not prepared to offer him my shares. Even if I did consider getting out, I owe it to my mother and grandmother not to let go completely."

"Not yet, at least," he said quietly.

"No, not yet." She yawned. An immense weariness was at last stealing over her.

"You should be in bed." Harry reached for her hands to help her to her feet.

"In a minute." She rubbed her eyes, smearing mascara. "Do you realize how absurd, how insane, this is? We're sitting here in the middle of the night discussing the craziest idea I've ever heard—and I'm taking it seriously."

"Of course you are, Ella, my love, because when you stop to think about it, it isn't crazy at all, just imaginative."

Ella reached up and unpinned the chignon her hairdresser had constructed eleven hours earlier, and her hair cascaded down over her shoulders.

"God, that looks wonderful," Harry murmured.

She stood up. "I can't think any more tonight, I'm too tired."

She was just crawling under the duvet when Harry placed a small jeweler's box in her hand.

"What's that?"

"Something that can't wait."

She opened it with fumbling fingers, and gasped. It was a

diamond ring, the perfect central stone emerald-cut, set in platinum with delicate groups of baguettes.

Harry took it from her. "Let me put it on you." It fitted snugly.

"How did you manage that?" Ella asked.

"Kriszti lent me one of her rings—she said your hands are virtually identical."

"I love you," she said weakly.

"I know."

"It's just . . ." She lay back against the pillows. ". . . that I'm so . . . sleepy . . ." Her eyes closed.

Harry stared at her long and hard before he turned out the light.

"Merry Christmas," he whispered.

Harry left on the fifth day of 1974 to consult with lawyers, bankers, and local authorities about the possibility of building a new hotel, a French château, in the Catskill Mountains.

"I won't give it another second's thought unless all the answers are positive," Ella insisted before he left.

"They will be."

"I'm not so sure."

Harry looked at her searchingly. "You do want this to happen, don't you, sweetheart? I mean, you're certain now—no more doubts?"

"A zillion." She smiled. "But yes, I want it. Under the circumstances, I'd be an idiot not to."

Harry took her hands in his. "I'll make it happen, Ella."

She looked up at him. "I almost believe you."

It was a month before he returned.

"All set," he said casually in Ella's sitting room after they'd embraced. "It's done. We can build."

"I don't believe it!"

"Believe it."

Her eyes were bright with tears of wonder. "How?"

"I told you I'd make it happen." Harry paused. "Have you thought of a name?"

"Have you?"

"It's your hotel, Ella."

It came to her instantly. "Château Bogarde."

Harry smiled. "Château Bogarde . . ." He said it slowly, lazily, letting it roll off his tongue as if he were tasting wine.

"Like it?"

"Sure I like it, but it's your hotel, not mine."

"In case you've forgotten, it's going to be my name, too, pretty soon."

A large grin spread over his face. "When?"

"Soon as you like."

"Here?"

She loved the way they talked to each other, in a kind of verbal shorthand. There rarely seemed a need for long, drawn-out conversation because from the very beginning they'd both felt a deep, natural communication that went beyond words.

"If Maman and Papa can come."

"They're waiting for your call."

"Are they my parents or yours?" she demanded.

"Can't stop a man talking to his friends."

A shadow fell over Ella's face.

"What's the matter?"

"Ollie."

"Do I take it you haven't broached the subject with him yet?"

She shook her head. "It seemed pointless."

Harry frowned. "You shouldn't be frightened of your brother."

"I'm not frightened. I'm reluctant to cause someone I love pain."

"Pity the same can't be said of Monsieur le Baron."

Ella's voice developed a sharp edge. "Maybe you don't know me as well as you think, Harry—and you certainly don't know anything about Olivier's feelings for me."

"You're right," Harry said steadily. "And I don't want to make presumptions. I don't blame you for caring about your brother, Ella, darling." He sighed. "It's just that I don't want you suffering any more pain than you have to, and you'll have to forgive me for being more concerned about you than about Olivier."

Olivier took the news of her impending marriage quietly, if stonily. When Ella told him about the plans for the new hotel, he looked as if she'd kicked him in the groin.

"Over my dead body!"

"It took me by surprise, too, when Harry first came up with the idea. Until I saw the light."

"The man's a barbarian, polluting your mind!"

"Hardly," she said mildly.

"You would never buy reproduction furniture, would you?"

"You know I wouldn't."

"Yet you agree to build a reproduction château. It's obscene! I suppose you and your philistine hope to steal the odd antique sideboard or vase—or why stop there? Why not just rip out everything?"

"Nobody's going to take a single thing out of this hotel, Ollie. I'd never damage de Trouvère. I love it as much as you do."

"Is that why you want to leave?"

"I'm going to be married," she said simply, "to an American."

"So marry him," Olivier snarled bitterly. "Have his brat if you must and live miserably ever after—but I will not let you steal my family's property!"

"Stealing doesn't enter into it," she said coldly. "And perhaps if you were not so obsessed with what you call *your* family—since you conveniently forget that we share a mother—I wouldn't want to leave my home, wouldn't feel that it's the only sane, safe thing for me to do!"

"What do you mean by safe?" His eyes burned black in his narrow face.

"I can't cope with you anymore, Ollie," Ella said wearily. "With what you're doing to our hotel, to our lives."

"I love de Trouvère," he burst passionately, "and I love you, Lalla! Is that a crime?"

"Is that why you gamble? Why you drink? Is that why you make awful, destructive decisions about the hotel without ever consulting me or Maman?"

"No!"

"Why then? *Tell* me."

His face was contorted with anguish. "Because I'm so bloody unhappy."

"But why, Ollie? Why are you so unhappy?" She shook her head in bewilderment. "You have everything that's important to you—your title, your lands, good looks, money—and you still have people who love you in spite of everything."

His mouth twisted. "I'm not loved."

"You may not be lovable, but you know damned well you are loved."

"Then why are you going to leave me?"

Ella's shoulders sagged. "Maybe it's because I do love you that I have to leave. If I stayed, there's a terrible possibility that I might grow to despise you."

He stared at her. "Do you despise me?"

"No, Ollie. Not yet, thank God. You've disgusted me at times, made me ashamed for you—but you're still my brother. Nothing in the world can ever change that."

Suddenly he seized both her hands and gripped them tightly. "Don't go, Lalla! Please, for my sake, don't go!"

Her eyes burned, but she knew she would not shed a tear. "I will go, Ollie, for *my* sake."

He dropped her hands, and the stony resentment was back. "Go then. Marry your barbarian, bear his children, and try to reproduce de Trouvère." His eyes narrowed. "Just don't even think of using my name, or I'll drag you through every court in France and America."

"We're going to call it Château Bogarde," she told him quietly.

"How touching."

"Don't sneer."

He laughed harshly. "I'll sneer even more when your new creation and your marriage are both disasters, when you come crawling back on your knees."

Ella controlled her anger, aware that he was striking out in pain. "You have to try to see that we're building this hotel because I'm a hotelière—that's what I do, what I am."

"You're my baby sister." His voice cracked. "I thought I could depend on you."

"You can. Always. I wish you'd understand that."

"I only understand that you're going."

"I am."

"You'll fail," he said.

"You're wrong," Ella replied, and walked toward the door. "I'm going to succeed."

Ella and Harry were married two weeks later in judge's chambers in New York City. They had decided against the chapel because the contentment and peace she had hoped to experience were destroyed. In a way, Olivier had already wrought his revenge on Ella, for her joy in de Trouvère had gone.

She wore a short white Givenchy dress with a veil. William gave her away, and Krisztina wept with delight, and Harry's brother Saul, who had ridden for five days on his motorcycle from his beach house in Santa Monica, was best man, and he was the only member of the Bogarde family present, for both Harry's parents were long since dead.

Alice came down from Rhinebeck, Alberto Giordano from Rome, and Annabel Herrick, now white-haired, from Devon. While the judge was speaking, Ella glanced back at the little sea of faces and saw, in her mind's eye, those who were not there, and longed, as she always would, for Geneviève's wisdom and Mischa's bubbling laughter.

And then her vision cleared, and she saw what a fine and enviable representation there was of her past, and of her future. And she felt—or imagined that she felt—the stirring of her un-born child deep inside her, and she looked up at Harry, sober-faced and tall, and very handsome and dignified. And though she was grieved beyond words that Olivier had not come, a quiet, calm bliss stole over her, like a tender and protective embrace.

A small skeleton team assembled at Harry's Long Island house, a large mansion in Southampton, referred to euphemistically by the locals as a "cottage."

Krisztina, after dealing with both her own and William's mis-givings, had predictably thrown herself into the project with as much pleasure as a child skidding down a water chute. If Ella wanted her, she said, there was nothing she'd like more than to share her daughter's work load. Ella wanted her.

Louis Dettlingen, the night porter from de Trouvère, had star-tled them all by arriving unannounced in New York the day the Bogardes had returned from honeymooning in Hawaii.

"I have resigned," he told Ella.

"But Louis, why?"

"Because I hope to work for you, madame."

"But you can't." She was deeply embarrassed. "I can't take staff away from de Trouvère."

"That is why I resigned," Louis explained simply. "So that no one could accuse you of poaching, madame. I am, after all, a free man." He paused. "Unless, of course, you feel that I am still not ready."

"We both know that you are, Louis—that isn't the problem."

He smiled. "If you reject me, Madame Bogarde, I shall not return to de Trouvère. Does that assist you?"

"But what will you do? The hotel isn't built—it won't be ready for at least two years. You have to work."

Dettlingen nodded. "That is why I wish to ask your father if he can employ me in the meantime, perhaps as a porter." He shrugged. "I'm accustomed to precious objects, as you know, and my hands are strong." He flexed them in evidence.

Ella laughed. "And capable of a smart uppercut, I seem to recall."

"Will you consider me, madame?" His dark eyes were fervent.

"You'll need papers—you'd be an immigrant."

"Mr. Hunter can arrange that, I'm sure."

"You're very confident, Louis."

"My mother taught me to be patient, but to seize opportunity when I recognized it."

"Consider it seized."

Ella received another happy surprise in those early weeks of planning, a telephone call from Alex Monselet, the chef who'd resigned three years before in a fury over Olivier. He, too, expressed a desire to work for Ella again, having heard *"sur la vigne"* about her plans. He, too, was prepared to wait, provided she wanted him.

"He's a superb chef," she told Harry.

"So grab him."

They all came to Southampton in early April, so that Alberto could share with everyone concerned his initial plans. He was seventy-one, and his hair was white, but his eyes and his brain and aesthetic sense were as acute as ever.

It was an ebullient time, a time for dreaming and hoping, with no room for conservatism or thoughts of failure.

"If only the Baronessa were here." Alberto sighed, happily consuming the spaghetti that Krisztina had urged Ella to stock up on for the duration of his stay.

"Grand-maman would have approved, wouldn't she?" Ella had asked her mother anxiously. "I depended on her so much for advice and common sense."

"Approved?" Krisztina chuckled. "She'd probably have insisted on laying the foundation stone herself."

Ella and Harry drove regularly up to Rhinebeck to be nearer the site. Every day, regardless of the weather and the half-hour hike from North Lake (since work had not yet begun on the new road they planned), Ella insisted on spending an hour up at Pine Orchard, though there was still little to be seen, for she was in the throes of a sudden loss of confidence and needed to be there, reaffirming its wonders, in order to reassure herself.

"You're overtaxing yourself, darling," Harry told her, concerned. "You forget you're pregnant."

"Don Kleinman said that walking and fresh air are good for me."

"He never told you to climb a fucking mountain every day!"

"I can't say I asked him." Ella chewed at her lower lip. "Anyway, he's an obstetrician, not a psychiatrist. He wouldn't understand that I need to be up here to convince myself."

"Of what, for Christ's sake?"

"That I did the right thing. That I haven't made a terrible mistake."

"Does that just relate to the hotel, or does it include marrying me?" Harry asked ironically.

"Everything but that," she said.

"So tell me."

"I've left my home, Harry," she said frantically, "my beautiful home, and now we're trying to replace Alsace—lovely, rolling wine country—with a mountain!"

"You'll never replace it, sweetheart," he said gently. "You're starting over—only you're taking all the good points of a house that was never intended to be a hotel, and throwing out all the bad."

"What was bad about de Trouvère?"

"It was too small, for a start. How you ever ran a commercially viable hotel with so few rooms, I'll never know."

"Money," Ella said disgustedly. "There are other, much more important things in life."

"I agree," he nodded amiably, "but if we're going to spend around twenty million dollars, we might as well try to get some of it back."

She was contrite. "I'm sorry, chéri."

Harry put a protective arm around her shoulders. "It's going to be okay, my love. It's going to be wonderful, believe me."

Ella leaned against him. "I think I do."

The contractions began on the night of June 20, almost nine weeks early, while her parents were staying in Manhattan.

Their daughter was born, by cesarean section, ten hours later in Northern Dutchess Hospital.

Ella woke briefly from the anesthetic, and saw a white-coated woman standing beside her.

"You're in Recovery, Mrs. Bogarde, and you have a little girl."

Ella tried to move, but pain swamped her. "Is she all right?" she whispered.

"Just perfect," the woman answered soothingly, and Ella saw a hypodermic syringe in her hand. "This will help the pain, dear, and let you get some more sleep."

"Where is she? I want to see her."

"Soon, Mrs. Bogarde," the woman said.

"But I—"

"Very soon."

She slept.

When she woke again, it was evening, and Harry was sitting on a chair near the bed.

"Hello, darling." He stood up, came over and kissed her. "Do you remember? We have a beautiful daughter."

"Where is she?"

"She's very tiny, so they're keeping an eye on her, but you're not to worry, she has everything she needs, all her fingers and toes, and your hair."

Ella attempted to sit up, but the pain made her whimper and lie back. She noticed a great bowl of red roses on the table near the window. "I want to see her, Harry. Make them bring her to me."

He stroked her cheek tenderly. "She's in an incubator, darling."

"*Why?* You said she's all right!"

"And she is, I swear it. But she only weighs four and a half pounds, so she has some catching up to do."

"Do Maman and Papa know?"

"They're on their way."

With another effort, Ella began to push away the sheet that covered her. "I'm going to see our baby."

"Hold on, darling." Harry restrained her gently. "You shouldn't try to walk yet."

"So get me a wheelchair."

"I'll have to get permission."

"So get permission," she said fretfully. "I'm not going to wait any longer."

Harry rang for a nurse, who looked dubious.

"Your daughter's fine, Mrs. Bogarde," she told Ella. "She's only tiny, as you know, so we're giving her a little help with her breathing—"

"What do you mean?" Ella demanded fearfully.

"She's on a ventilator," the nurse replied calmly, "but that's just so she doesn't have to work too hard. She can breathe, and suck and swallow on her own."

"I want to see her."

"We'll have to check with the doctor, Mrs. Bogarde."

"I'm going to see her now!"

Harry spoke quietly to the nurse. "I don't think my wife's going to get any worthwhile rest until she sees our baby, do you?"

The nurse glanced at Ella, who was sitting bolt upright, quivering with resolve. "I'll find a wheelchair."

Except for one vigilant nurse, they were left alone beside the incubator.

Ella stared through the glass. "My God, she's even smaller than I imagined," she breathed.

Harry stared wordlessly, though he'd seen her before, at the tiny scrap who was his daughter.

Ella, gripping his hand tightly, looked at him. "You okay?"

He nodded, suddenly close to tears. "She's incredible," he whispered.

"I want to hold her."

He swallowed. "Soon, my love, very soon."

"Maybe we should move her?" Ella said in a low, conspiratorial voice. "Fly her to the city?"

Harry shook his head. "I asked Don—he said that this is a fine unit. And anyway, since she's holding her own, we'd do more harm than good."

"Is it normal for her to breathe so fast?" Ella was bending forward, ignoring the pain in her own body, checking every visible centimeter of baby flesh.

"Darling, look at all the others."

But Ella could not look at any other child except her own, refused to be diverted from the creature, the being she had, until a few hours ago, carried inside herself.

"Her name," she murmured. "Are we still agreed?"

"Danielle." Harry stared down at the baby, pondering.

"It'll get shortened to Dani." Ella wrinkled her brow, imagining. "That's nice. I like Dani—it's soft and feminine, but not flowery."

"I'll call her Danielle," Harry said.

Ella smiled. "Papa's prerogative."

"I love you, Ella Bogarde."

"*Je t'aime*, Harry Bogarde," she whispered.

He saw that she was weakening, and put an arm firmly around her, helping her back into the wheelchair. "Let's get you back to bed."

She grasped his wrist. "Harry, she will be all right, won't she?"

"She's going to be perfect."

Ella felt nauseous and shaky, but happier than she had ever been in her life. "Good times ahead," she said softly.

Harry began pushing the chair toward the door.

"The best."

PART FIVE

Ella: New York, 1983–1984

Chapter 33

They had become, in just seven years, something of a legend, and that, in a section of country as steeped in fable as the Hudson River Valley, was an accomplishment in itself.

Château Bogarde, almost three times as big as her Alsatian prototype, had opened her doors in the first week of June 1976, ready to welcome up to two hundred guests at a time in seventy-two double bedrooms and twenty suites. Giordano, working in happy harmony with a firm of New York architects and a hand-picked work force, had built, in just two years, a veritable miracle of modern luxury couched in noblest tradition, yet all softened by the same uniqueness of touch that had made Château de Trou-vère feel to its visitors like a second home.

For the short- or long-stay holidaymaker, the new hotel at Pine Orchard offered everything. The bedrooms were designed with individual personalities to pander to all tastes, from sybaritic to the almost ascetic. Château Bogarde sported an indoor and an outdoor swimming pool, two Jacuzzis and a gymnasium, all-weather tennis courts and an equestrian club. Its huge terrace was furnished with ten barbecues where guests could either be served or could charcoal broil their own private dinner parties without having to light the coals or clean up afterward. There was a cinema, a soundproofed amusement room for youngsters, a chandeliered ballroom, a library, two bars, a beauty salon, and a single restaurant of effortless elegance. Ella, with Alex Monselet's hearty approval, had vetoed the suggestion of two separate "theme" dining rooms and vehemently rejected the idea of a coffee shop—if guests wanted a light, informal meal, they could either enjoy a snack at the poolside or in one of the bars, or order from floor service. Meanwhile, the restaurant that Alberto had created—an all-seasons room with a great glass wall that could be opened electrically during summer so diners could sit out under the stars in a walled garden—would, as was fitting, represent the heart of the hotel.

"It has everything," Ella had said anxiously to Harry prior to opening, "but how can we be sure that it will work?"

Harry smiled. "Think of Danielle. She has a beautiful, brilliant mother and a reasonable-looking, extremely contented father. Look at her and what do you see?"

Ella looked at their flame-haired daughter of nearly two years. "A peach. But what does that have to do with our hotel?"

"With Château de Trouvère for a mother and the old Mountain House for a father—a place they used to call 'the noblest wonder of the valley'—how can she fail?"

Ella was still doubtful.

"I remember you told me once that getting a grand hotel right was like a theatrical production—you needed the right set and the right cast."

"It needs more besides, Harry. It needs a magic ingredient."

"That's you."

"Me?"

"You don't see yourself as others do, Ella. I've watched you in action at de Trouvère, and I saw then that you were the key to its success, the source of it."

"My mother and grandmother were the source."

"But that's your inheritance," he insisted. "You told me that there was hardly a job in the hotel that you hadn't done yourself at some time or other—you knew how to light the furnace, fold perfect corners on the beds, scrub the bathrooms till they shone, and clean the silver. And yet you knew the names and life histories of every customer *and* every bottle of wine in the cellar." He paused. "You are the consummate *hotelière*, Ella Bogarde—*you* are the magic ingredient, and believe me, it's you who'll make this place work."

It had worked, and even Harry had not foreseen the measure of its success, though he had correctly perceived that the hotel's European-American pedigree would lend it a unique appeal. Ella and Krisztina had agreed to keep alive the memory of the old Catskill hotel, not just with paintings and the printed word, but by re-creating one of the rituals that had made the Mountain House famous. Once a week, on a Saturday night, Château Bogarde would sweep the river far below with powerful searchlights, while boats, great and small, would return the favor by focusing their own strong beams on the creamy château, and watching the show from the observation terrace, the hotel guests would sip champagne or hot spiced toddies, according to the season.

"They used to get up before dawn, you know," Ella told Harry, "to watch the sun rise."

"I hope you're not thinking of bringing back that old custom," he said wryly. "I doubt if today's *de luxe* travelers would consider sunrise worth getting up for."

"It was good enough for presidents and generals and the artists and writers of that day," she said loftily.

"Maybe they considered it fashionable fun. We'd be better off, I'd say, making sure the beds stay nice and comfortable. God knows a good mattress is a rare commodity in hotels these days."

"You know you have a one-track mind—you think of almost nothing but bed."

"I just don't think you should take all this red-blooded Yankee energy too far. I'll bet the Europeans at de Trouvère never knew that dawn existed."

"Well . . ."

"And another thing," Harry added, "if you do get them up, you'll have to be up, too, smiling companionably, and I, for one, am selfish enough to want my wife snuggled up beside me at that ungodly hour."

"Bed again."

"Always."

Ella grinned. "I guess sunsets would do almost as well."

"You bet they would."

Harry had transferred his household from Southampton to the new house he'd had Giordano build for them in the grounds of the château. It was quite small, with only five bedrooms and a guest suite often used by Krisztina when she was too tired to drive back down to Rhinebeck. And while it had, of course, every amenity, it was fundamentally basic—a decision arrived at mutually, since both Ella and Harry felt they had more than enough luxury practically force-fed them all day every day. They wanted their house to be, purely and simply, their home.

The Bogarde household itself had also, since their marriage, decreased in size. Harry, at his Long Island residence, had employed a chauffeur, three gardeners, a cook, two maids, and a secretary; now that he was content to spend most of his time in a far smaller property, with his own hotel on the doorstep and with a new Aston Martin, which no one else was encouraged to drive, such a staff was redundant, and so he and Ella kept just a single maid and the secretary.

There was only one person he would not consider parting with, and that was Lin Tsung, who had started life with the Bogarde family as Harry's father's personal valet, and who had chosen, after Joshua Bogarde's death, to stay with Harry because he felt Harry needed him more than his brother, Saul.

From the moment of their first meeting, Ella had been fascinated by Lin Tsung, especially after seeing more than a dozen crates of books unloaded in his new room in their house.

"Shall you be content," she'd asked him, "to sit up on an American mountain with people who are intellectually inferior to you?"

"Superiority and inferiority do not exist for me," Lin Tsung had told her. "A Chinese scholar wishes for nothing more than to be able to converse with others, and should be able to speak about anything. I have had more stimulating conversations with your husband through the years than any man, scholar or otherwise, has the right to hope for. And now that he has brought you and little Dani and, of course, your dear parents, into my world, my life is replete."

They became great friends, and he taught her many things, and though Ella's days and evenings were already full almost to bursting point, it became a habit of hers to set aside at least fifteen minutes each day for conversation with him. Sometimes they sat in their single private acre of walled garden, and Lin Tsung would name insects and flowers and birds and trees, and identify cloud patterns and forecast, with uncanny precision, the weather to come. Sometimes they sat at the big oak table in the kitchen and watched Dani play, and he would tell the small girl stories—sometimes of modern America, sometimes of ancient China. On other occasions, when Ella had more time, she and Harry would go to Lin Tsung's room, and they would drink his special tea. Then they would speak about politics or life or people, about paintings or music or literature, about Danielle, about their individual philosophies, about anything, but never about the hotel or any other business.

Through Lin Tsung, Ella learned about many other things, about Oriental practices and arts, about the use of herbs and natural medicines and acupuncture. And as their friendship developed, as the months and years passed, Lin Tsung tried to teach her patience and forbearance and tranquillity, and as he became aware of how disturbed she and Harry were that no new pregnancy had come to pass, he read to her from his books of philosophy and poetry and showed her the path to relaxation and acceptance of whatever fate had in store for her.

"There is nothing physically wrong, is there?" he asked Ella, being above all a practical man.

"Not a thing."

"In that case," Lin Tsung smiled, "lie back and enjoy yourselves. You have Dani, you have a fruitful, full, enviable life, and one day you may, or may not, bear another child." He scrutinized her. "It is not a source of despair to either of you, is it?"

Ella shook her head. "No. We're disgustingly happy on the whole and, I think, reasonably well adjusted."

"In that case, let the good Lord point the way."

As Danielle walked, ran and grew strong, taught by Lin Tsung, she became an adept pupil at *t'ai chi.*

"He says that Dani has excellent balance and very strong muscles," Ella told her mother.

"He mustn't forget that her bones are still soft," Krisztina said anxiously.

"Maman, no one knows more about such things than Lin Tsung. You have nothing to worry about." Ella smiled. "He also says that she has inherited your talent for dance—he thinks she should begin ballet lessons as soon as possible."

"She's only four."

"When did you begin?"

"At five."

"Could you teach her?"

"Me?"

"Why not?"

"I'm too old, for one thing—"

"Nonsense."

"And I'm not qualified. I gave up ballet when I was twelve."

"But you learned the rudiments?"

"Considerably more than that."

"So you could start her off."

"I suppose so."

"Good."

The two women were sitting companionably side by side on a low stone wall near the vegetable gardens, the setting July sun warming their bare legs and arms.

"What's Harry been up to lately?" Krisztina asked, changing tack.

"Not much. He's enjoying Château Bogarde too much to want to get involved in too many schemes."

Krisztina frowned. "He should keep his own interests. He's always traveled, had fingers in dozens of pies—he'll get stale."

"Between the hotel and our daughter, I think he's pretty absorbed, Maman, and very content."

"He's still collecting art at least, isn't he?"

"Not as much. He's filled the hotel, and our house can't take any more."

"William says he's hardly been to Hunter's for months."

Ella eyed her mother. "Why are you so concerned about Harry?"

Krisztina reflected a moment. "I just don't like seeing anyone, man or woman, too entirely absorbed, as you put it, in an enterprise that isn't his own."

"But it is his, Maman. It was his money that made it possible."

Krisztina shook her head. "He *gave* you Château Bogarde, as a kind of wedding gift. It's your business—you were its creator, you make it function—some people have even begun calling it 'Château Ella.' "

Ella laughed. "Just some of the local people."

"I've heard it's spreading to the guests too."

"But I don't think any of that troubles Harry. Quite the contrary—he's proud of me."

"Nor am I exactly troubled," Krisztina tried to explain. "I just have a faint uneasiness. You've been married nearly five years, and your husband seems to have spun a cocoon around you all."

"But isn't it wonderful to have such a happy man, and to have him around so much of the time? You talk as if I should send him away, which I have not the least desire to do."

"Nor should you, *chérie*."

"Then what are you saying?" Ella asked impatiently.

"That Harry has you and Dani up on a pedestal and that he no longer has anything else to care about. The hotel is just a wondrous plaything, important to him chiefly because it makes you happy."

"And that's not enough," Ella said.

"The Harry you met five years ago was a different man. He kept on going—rushing from home to home, city to city, doing a little business here and there, making deals, collecting his treasures. I think—and your father does too—that he believes that he found his ultimate treasure when he met you, Ella, and that's why he stopped looking. And he's too young to stop, don't you think?"

"If you put it that way," Ella said slowly, "yes, I suppose I do."

"So?"

"So a little push is required."

Krisztina nodded. "I think so."

Ella had pushed, with the result that Harry, rather halfheartedly, had taken up the reins again of some of his concerns, had traveled a little, checking up on properties and visiting the occasional auction in New York or San Francisco, but none of it really stirred his blood. At the end of the day, Château Bogarde and home was where he wanted to be—nothing could change that, neither did Ella wish to change it.

The years rolled pleasantly by, good years. The hotel became *the* place to stay, attracting a wide variety of guests—business people, honeymooners, convention clients, city folk seeking escape, retired couples and single people, young and old. Some came for peace, others for the long-lost, gently gregarious atmosphere of a permanent soirée; some believed Château Bogarde had become the pinnacle of fashionable society, some sought the physical pleasures of the hotel's outdoor challenges, and others—

perhaps the majority—wanted nothing more than to let the château's luxuries wash over them for days and nights on end.

Milestones came and went. Krisztina entered her sixties and William—incredibly to all who knew him—approached his seventies. Ella welcomed her thirtieth birthday and Harry bemoaned the passing of his fortieth. Lin Tsung went to visit relatives in China, stayed three months, and returned restored, as if from some spiritual tune-up. Alberto Giordano died, eating spaghetti at his favorite restaurant in Milan, and Krisztina and Ella attended his funeral in Rome.

Château de Trouvère, as they had all predicted, was in financial difficulties. Ella waited for Olivier to make contact, to seek help, but they remained estranged. They had news of him, of course— they knew that he had entered into and rapidly exited from a marriage with one Marianne Dubois, a young woman who had been his secretary. According to Alex Monselet, who still kept in touch with staff at de Trouvère, Olivier had, as in the past with other women, impregnated Marianne, but she, unlike the others, had not been willing to let him go. Wedded bliss, if it had ever been present, swiftly vanished; the child, a daughter named Claudette, had gone with Marianne to live with her parents, and neither Krisztina nor Ella had ever seen the baby. By the time Ella paid a rare visit to de Trouvère just six months after her birth, it was as if neither Claudette nor her mother had ever existed.

Danielle, meantime, attended a day school in Rhinebeck and went to two ballet classes each week in Woodstock. She practiced almost every day with her grandmother with an unflagging verve and joy that encouraged her family to believe they had a future student for the School for the Performing Arts on their hands, and celebrated a series of birthdays, culminating in her ninth on June 21, 1983.

"I hope you haven't granted late checkout to the Sandersons," Ella said to Chris Logan, her front office manager, at fifteen minutes to ten on the morning of August 6.

"One o'clock as usual. Why, Mrs. Bogarde?"

"Because we have a distinguished guest arriving at around five, and I want the Salle Bleu in the greatest shape possible."

"Who is it?" Logan was unsurprised that the booking had not come through normal channels, for there were a number of regu-

lars who preferred to speak directly to Ella, in the mistaken belief
that this would lend their reservation greater importance; in fact,
it was a house rule that every client be treated like royalty.

"Sandor Janos," Ella replied.

"The conductor? But he stays at the Pierre."

"Yes, when he's rehearsing or performing, but he has four free
days before he starts work at Lincoln Center, and since that's the
end of his U.S. tour, I gather that he's exhausted and looking for
an oasis."

Janos swept into the hotel with the force of a half-spent hurri-
cane.

"What a hunky man!" Lorna Trivett, the head housekeeper,
murmured after she'd made her brief customary welcome visit to
his suite.

"What a dish," breathed Justin Browne, the hotel masseur,
while Janos sampled the Nautilus equipment in the health club,
displaying the impressive leanness and muscularity that were
common to many conductors.

"What a remarkably attractive man," commented Krisztina,
observing him at dinner.

"Is he?" Ella said. "I hadn't noticed."

Harry, sipping vichyssoise, glanced up. "Typical Hungarian."

"Really?" asked Krisztina. "He doesn't look much like me, does
he?"

"Hardly," said William. "Dark hair, darker eyes, aquiline nose,
narrow mouth—"

"Amazing cheekbones," Krisztina added.

"You have those, Maman," Ella joined in.

"The man looks like a gigolo," said Harry.

"Yet he's one of the most accomplished conductors in the world
today." Krisztina smiled. "What a lovely combination."

Janos, aware that he was the object of their scrutiny, raised his
wineglass and gave a tiny bow from the waist.

"Conceited too," Harry said sourly.

"Why are you being so disagreeable, *chéri*?" asked Ella, surprised.

"He's jealous," William replied.

"Jealous?"

"What's Harry got to be jealous of?" enquired Krisztina.

"Of the way Janos is looking at Ella."

"Don't be silly, Papa."

"There's nothing so remarkable about that, darling," William said mildly. "As a matter of fact, he's looking at your mother in much the same way. The man clearly has taste."

"Nerve, more like," Harry retorted.

"Oh, don't be so stuffy." Ella grinned.

Janos proved a difficult customer, complaining at the drop of a hat, and insisting on laying even the most trivial grievance directly at Ella's feet.

"He may be very talented," Ella told Krisztina, "and he may even be considered, by some, to be good-looking . . ."

"Not by you?" Her mother's eyes twinkled.

"Not particularly. But what he is, is a pain in the ass."

"You've become very American." Krisztina sighed.

"I'll be glad when he leaves."

"You are still coming to hear the concert, aren't you?"

"Of course. I love Mahler."

"I like him."

"Mahler?"

"No, Janos."

"Have you talked to him much?"

Krisztina nodded. "We've had a few delightful conversations. He's from Buda, too, you know. His father and grandfather were murdered by the Nyilas—"

"Who?"

"A group of thugs set loose in the streets of Budapest by the Nazis."

"What happened to Janos?"

"He was hidden with his mother by friends. He got out of Hungary at the end of fifty-six."

"Perhaps that explains the chip on his shoulder," Ella said doubtfully.

"He may have several. He began as a violinist, you know, then fell in love with the piano, but during the rioting after the Russians moved into Budapest, the fingers of his left hand were crushed and weren't properly set until he reached a British camp in Austria. He knew he'd never be able to play the piano seriously again, but he started conducting a group of fellow musicians right there in the camp."

"You *have* been talking to him, haven't you?" Ella looked surprised.

"I always talk to people who interest me, *dragam*, you know that."

It was not until she saw him on the podium at Lincoln Center that Ella accepted the fact that Sandor Janos *was* an interesting man.

The audience was capacity, gowns and jewelry glittering, perfume asphyxiating, the atmosphere scintillating, as Ella and Harry sat with Krisztina and William before the concert. Voices chattered, strings, brass, and percussion were plucked, blown, pounded, and rattled, sheet music and libretti rustled by the waiting orchestra and chorus. The leader, golden-haired and bespectacled, entered to polite applause, and a moment later the orchestra rose as Sandor Janos emerged from the depths and stalked, amid tumult, up toward the rostrum to take his place and to welcome the soloists.

At the hotel, Ella really had found Janos quite unimpressive, but now, suddenly, standing in that halo of light, engulfed by expectant silence, baton raised, he appeared to her like some resplendent, raven-haired giant.

For a long moment he remained motionless, suspending all movement, all breath, a larger-than-life puppet master holding violinists, cellists, sopranos et al. in his thrall. Then suddenly, with a devastatingly effective movement, he brought down his right arm like an executing sword, and more than fifty performers were swept headlong and unresisting into the dramatic first movement of Mahler's Resurrection Symphony.

"I've never seen you the way you were tonight at the concert," Harry said later, watching Ella removing the last traces of her mascara.

"What do you mean?"

"I mean that usually when you get involved with the music, you wear a hazy, distant expression."

"And tonight?"

"Tonight, your eyes were fixed—glued—to the conductor."

Ella threw a tissue into the wastebasket. "He's a riveting performer."

"Undoubtedly," Harry agreed. "But so were Mehta and Muti and Bernstein."

"I'm sure I looked at them too."

"Not in the same way. You looked through them—it was still the music that absorbed you."

"It absorbed me tonight too."

"I know. You were immersed—but as much in Janos as in Mahler."

Ella turned in her chair to look at him. "I told you, I found him a very exciting performer. Do you mind that?"

"Frankly, yes."

"Why?"

Harry stepped into his pajama trousers. "Perhaps William was right—maybe I am jealous."

"But of what, for heaven's sake? I don't even like Janos."

"You didn't like me when we first met."

Ella looked exasperated. "You're being a bit of an ass, you know, Harry."

"I know."

"So stop it."

"Okay." He climbed into bed, pulled up the duvet, then shoved it away again disconsolately. Ella slipped off her peignoir and got into bed beside him.

Harry sniffed. "Did you just put on scent?"

"No."

"You smell great."

"Thank you." She paused. "Why do you think you're jealous of Janos?"

He looked awkward. "I am being an ass, you're right."

"I still don't understand why."

"He's Hungarian."

"Yes."

"And Jewish."

"Yes." She waited.

Harry shrugged. "That's it."

"I think I must have missed something."

"No."

"Then forgive me if I say so what."

"Well, so are you."

"What am I?"

"Hungarian and Jewish."

"Let me get this straight," Ella said slowly. "You figure that because of that, I must have a deep-seated passion for Janos." She grinned. "There must be a lot of Hungarian Jews in the world, Harry. I'm going to be pretty busy."

"Not many of them are world-famous conductors," he pointed out, "and not many of them have been staying in your hotel, seizing every possible opportunity to be alone with you."

"He hasn't!"

"You said that he has."

"Well, even if that were true," she said, "he's checked out, so you don't have to worry anymore."

"He'll be back."

"I hope so—he's a valuable customer."

"You told Kriszti he was a pain in the ass."

Ella looked aggrieved. "Do you two still talk about me behind my back?"

"All the time," he said, unabashed.

"Well, don't."

"Your mother's my friend. Would you rather I talked to someone else?"

"Certainly not."

"Then shut up."

"Not unless you shut up about Sandor Janos."

"I'll only do that if you kiss me."

"Is that all it takes?"

Harry stroked her neck, just below her right ear. "For a start."

Chapter 34

In the second week of September, Olivier, who had not made spontaneous contact with either his sister or his mother for more than a year, telephoned Ella.

"Can I come and visit you?"

"Of course you can," she said, audibly surprised.

"Thank you. I'll be there on Friday then."

"This Friday?"

"Is that inconvenient?"

"No, just sooner than I'd expected. Shall you be alone?"

"Yes."

"I'll reserve you a suite, and tell Maman and Papa."

"If you must."

"Ollie, they'll want to see you."

"Will your husband be there?"

"Of course."

"I doubt that he'll be thrilled."

He was only thirty-eight, but he looked at least ten years older, with a now unmistakable beer belly and a generally dissolute appearance to match.

"What does he want?" asked Harry the morning after his brother-in-law's less than welcome arrival.

"I don't know that he wants anything," answered Ella.

"Don't kid yourself. Christ, he looks awful."

"He looks tired," she admitted.

"He used to be handsome. Now he looks like the degenerate he is."

"Don't be unkind."

"I'm sorry, baby, but you know I don't like the man, and I certainly don't trust him."

"He's troubled, Harry. We all know that de Trouvère's in bad shape."

"Obviously, with him at the helm."

"You can't stop my caring about him, you know, whatever mistakes he's made."

"I know," Harry said, a little more gently. "And I understand that you couldn't turn him away. How long's he staying?"

"I'm not sure."

"Let's hope it won't be long."

Ella looked reproachful. "Harry, please try, for my sake."

He sighed. "I will, darling, but I don't honestly know how long I can keep it up."

"Tell me about the marriage," Ella said softly to Olivier as they sat in her private sitting room on the ground floor of the hotel. It was the third night of his stay.

"Nothing to tell."

"Surely there must be. I'm still your sister, Ollie—we used to share all our secrets."

"That was a long time ago."

"The divorce must have been painful for you."

"It was."

She gave up. "Another Armagnac?"

"Please."

She refilled his glass and sat down again. "You do have something you want to discuss, though, don't you?"

Olivier took a drink. "I'm in trouble."

"What kind?"

"Money."

"I'm sorry."

"Don't be patronizing."

"I didn't think I was." Ella paused. "Have you come for advice, Ollie, or for something a little more practical?"

"I've come because I couldn't think of anyone else who might bail me out," he replied candidly.

"What are you up against?"

"I've brought figures and facts. They're downstairs in the vault, but I have the bottom line right here." He withdrew a single folded sheet of paper from his breast pocket and handed it to her.

Ella stared at it. She felt nauseous.

"I'm waiting," he said.

"For what?"

"For you to say something recriminatory—at the very least, 'I told you so.'"

Ella was still staring at the paper in her hand. She looked back at him. "You must know that I can't help you, Olivier. Not with this. It's out of my league." Her mouth twisted wryly. "It's out of most people's league."

"I know that."

"What, then?" A thought struck her. "Were you thinking of Harry?" she asked, openly incredulous.

"Of course not. The man loathes me, and I wouldn't take a franc from him."

"I think that's beside the point. Even if he were to want to help you, he has financial advisers who'd have him committed if he tried. You're hardly a blue-chip investment."

"I wasn't thinking of Harry," Olivier said quietly.

"Who then?"

"William."

"Papa?"

"Why not?"

"For the same reasons."

Olivier drained the rest of his Armagnac. "Will you ask him?"

"Why not ask him yourself?"

"I haven't spoken to him for over a year."

"I'd say that was your problem, wouldn't you?"

A small muscle twitched at the side of Olivier's face. "You've changed, Lalla. You used to be the softest little thing in the world."

"I grew up."

He changed course. "It's de Trouvère that's dying, Ella. Doesn't that mean anything to you?"

"A great deal."

"So help me," he pleaded.

"I don't see how," she said sadly.

"It would kill me to lose it."

"No, it wouldn't."

"Why did you leave me?"

Ella sighed. "You know why."

Olivier took her hand. "Help me, Lalla, please. At least say you'll think about it."

"Even if I do, I don't see a way."

"There's always a way," he said desperately. "That was what Grand-maman said, wasn't it? That there's always a solution to every problem."

Ella thought for a few moments. "I'll need to see the complete figures."

"You'll have them in five minutes." Eagerly, he got up.

"Not tonight. Let me have them in the morning, and Harry and I will go over them when we have time."

"I don't want Bogarde involved."

"Bogarde, as you call him, is my husband and my partner," Ella said coolly. "If you don't wish him to share your problems, then you may as well leave right away."

"All right, I'm sorry. It's just that I'd rather you talked it over with William than Harry."

"I daresay I'll talk to them both." Ella, too, rose. "I'm tired, Ollie, and I still have things to deal with before I can get to bed." She went ahead of him to the door. "And Ollie."

"Yes?"

"If you have any serious drinking to do, please restrict it to your suite. Floor service will bring you anything you need."

"L'hotelière parfaite."

Ella shook her head. "Hardly perfect." It's just that having been given a second opportunity, I won't do anything to jeopardize it."

Olivier looked at her somberly. "I won't do anything to compromise this place, I promise you."

She returned his gaze. "I hope not."

"Do you realize," asked Harry, "that your brother has become a neo-Nazi?"

Ella stared at him, horrified. "What do you mean?"

"Confrères de La Fontaine."

She was relieved. "Fontaine isn't a neo-Nazi group, Harry. It's right-wing, and I detest it, but it's basically just a troop of overgrown students with foul habits."

"I'm not talking about the Fontaine of the past," Harry said grimly. "From what I hear, they're not simply playing pranks anymore."

"How do you know?"

"I've done a little checking."

"And what have you heard?"

"Nothing that would stand up in a court of law—"

"I should hope not!"

"Things have developed on the neo-Nazi front in Europe during the last few years, Ella. In France alone, a whole bunch of groups have sprung up."

"What do they have to do with Olivier's fraternity?"

"Nothing much, except that Fontaine print a newsletter from time to time in which they've condoned the existence of these groups."

"But they're not active themselves?" She looked up, fresh fear chilling her. "They're not, are they?"

"I don't know." He hesitated.

"Harry, tell me."

"There's another group, a fraternity in Germany."

"I know them."

"Do you know that their members sometimes desecrate Jewish graves? They daub messages on stones threatening revenge for Nuremberg and other similar niceties."

Ella shuddered.

"I'm sorry, darling, but I think you have to know."

She nodded, not trusting herself to speak.

"Are you okay?" He put a protective arm around her shoulders.

"No."

"I'm sorry," he said again.

"You—" She swallowed. "You were right to tell me." Ella's mind was spinning. "Do you know if he's given Fontaine money?"

Harry shook his head. "Not that I know of. Though that might be because he doesn't have any."

Her eyes filled with tears. "Sometimes I hate him," she whispered. She shut her eyes. "And yet at the same time I find it impossible to stop loving him, stop caring about what happens to him." She opened them again. "It's crazy, but I feel responsible for Olivier."

"That is crazy. I can comprehend the rest, but you are *not* responsible for anything that your brother—your half brother—does."

"I know. But I don't know what to do."

"I'd suggest that you kick him out, but I guess you won't do that. In any case, you have a large stake in de Trouvère, and you have to take that into account. But—" He broke off.

"What?"

He looked awkward, then shook his head. "There's no easy way to say this." He paused. "Ella, I can't stay while Olivier is here."

Her eyes widened. "What do you mean?"

"What I say. I've tried, really tried, to be civil, but I don't know how much longer I can keep from punching him on the nose."

"I see."

"No, you don't." Harry was distressed. "I can't help it, darling. I don't just dislike the guy, I despise him! I'll keep on trying until I go, for your sake and Kriszti's, but there isn't enough space here for both of us."

Ella looked at him coolly. "Where will you go?"

"I don't know. It doesn't matter. Just off this mountain before I explode."

"And you won't return until he's gone?"

Harry plowed frustrated fingers through his hair. "I can't, Ella. The man incenses me every time I look at him." He tried to reach for her, but she stood her ground stiffly. "Honey, if you need me —if you have any problems with Danielle or anything like that—I'll come running, but . . ."

"I have a problem."

"You mean Olivier."

"I do."

"That's something I can't help you with."

"Or won't." Ella lifted her chin. "When will you go?"

"Tomorrow. If that's okay with you."

"It has nothing to do with me, Harry."

He winced. "Ella, I don't have the right to play the heavy husband and order you to dump your brother. It would be wrong, and it's not in my nature."

"No."

He gazed at her unhappily. "There's one more thing." He paused. "If I've found out this much about Olivier and his friends, how long do you think it'll be before someone else does?"

A new, unpleasant worm of thought buried itself in the pit of Ella's stomach. "The press," she said dully.

"Exactly."

She forced herself to maintain her calm front. "I'll just have to deal with that if it happens. After all," she added coldly, "it's my problem, not yours, isn't it?"

"What are you going to do?" Krisztina asked.

"I'm still thinking it over, Maman." Ella had not told her mother what Harry had learned about Fontaine.

"He's been here nearly three weeks. Apart from the fact that he's driven your husband away, I dread to think what's happening at de Trouvère."

"We knew when I came here that we were abandoning it to Olivier." Ella tried to speak lightly. "Anyway, the staff are probably managing better without him."

Krisztina shook her head sadly. "He still treats me almost as a stranger, you know."

"He's a fool."

"It must be hard to be prejudiced against one's own mother— perhaps even against oneself. He's never really spoken to me normally since the day he found out that I was Jewish." She paused. "It's a terrible thing, knowing that my son is a bigot."

Ella said nothing.

"You still want to help him, don't you, *dragam*?"

"I'm sorry, Maman, but I do."

"Don't be sorry. I feel the same way. I rejected his father when he was at the end of his tether; I shan't do the same to his son."

Ella waited a moment before speaking again. "Actually," she said slowly, "I have thought of a solution, if you agree."

"Go ahead."

Ella took a deep breath. "I see only one way out, for Ollie and de Trouvère. It has to be sold."

Krisztina was silent.

"I'm sorry, Maman."

"You're perfectly right, Ella." Krisztina spoke quietly.

"Olivier holds only half the stock." Ella hesitated. "I want him to have my shares. As a gift." She looked tensely at her mother. "I have more than enough money, Maman. This way, Ollie could save his skin, and at least de Trouvère could pass into responsible, caring hands, rather than crumble into total decay."

Krisztina was pale. "What makes you think he'll agree to sell?"

"He'll have no choice."

"William would help, you know, if I asked him to."

"It would be utter madness."

"It won't be easy to find a buyer."

"Not easy, but not impossible."

Krisztina regarded her daughter. "You haven't asked about my shares."

"I've no right, Maman."

Krisztina sat straighter. "I shall not give them to Olivier." She paused. "I shan't stand in his way if he finds the right buyer, but I'm not going to deprive you of what would one day rightfully have come to you."

"I'm hardly in need."

Krisztina patted her hand. "You looked after de Trouvère for many years, Ella. You kept it beautiful and healthy and strong. Your brother is a wastrel and a fool. I don't want to see him ruined, but I can do no more."

"Do you think I'm wrong?" Ella asked.

Krisztina smiled. "In a way, of course. But you've always protected Olivier—leaving him was one of the hardest things you've ever done." She fell silent again.

"What are you thinking, Maman?"

"About the chapel," Krisztina answered softly. "And the graveyard. About Michael, and Belle-mère, and Mama and the others."

Ella took her mother's hand and squeezed it. "We could still fight to save it all, Maman—go back, challenge him, put it right again."

Krisztina shook her head adamantly. "You can't run two hotels successfully at the same time, chérie—not our kind of hotel, at least. You've brought everything that was glorious about de Trouvère with you, in any case. It won't ever be lost, thanks to you and Harry."

"Harry," Ella said wistfully.

Krisztina patted her hand. "He'll be back soon, don't fret."

"He shouldn't have gone."

"He'll be back when Olivier leaves," Krisztina said simply.

Deliberately, Ella changed the subject. "What do you think Ollie will do? Without de Trouvère."

"Probably buy a flamboyant appartement on the Bois de Boulogne and strut around the casinos making full use of his title."

"Is he really that shallow?" Ella asked sadly.

Krisztina shook her head again. "I don't know."

The first mention appeared as a brief, snide remark in one of the less reputable New York gossip columns two days later, and was instantly picked up by an eager free-lance journalist with an eye for the sordid.

NEW "EAGLE'S NEST" IN CATSKILLS?

"Tell me it isn't true," Krisztina pleaded with Ella after she'd seen the half-page article.

"It's a gross exaggeration."

"But there's a grain of truth?"

"I'm afraid so." Reluctantly, Ella told her mother what Harry had discovered.

Krisztina was ashen-faced. "His father's son." She bit her lip. "William's seen it, too, of course."

"Two couples have already checked out, Maman."

"Didn't you reassure them?"

"Of course I did, but they clearly felt there was no smoke without fire." Ella spoke far more calmly than she felt. "I'm waiting for the cancellations to begin."

"Olivier has to go, Ella," Krisztina said starkly.

"I know."

"You have to speak to him now about selling de Trouvère. Unless you've changed your mind."

"I haven't."

"Then make it clear there's nothing else to discuss, no other alternative. And get him out before he destroys Château Bogarde too."

Olivier was shocked, but Ella was adamant. "It's the only way, Olivier. You're incapable of running either the hotel or the estate, and no one in his right mind is going to provide you with another franc."

"Thank you for your confidence."

"I have no more confidence in you, Ollie."

"And neither has your father, I gather."

"Have you given him cause?"

Olivier said nothing.

"Either way, I'd be grateful if you'd leave as soon as possible."

Olivier flushed. "You don't believe that trash they printed, do you?"

"That you'd like to turn Château Bogarde into Berchtesgaden? No, of course not. You are, after all, half Jewish yourself." She watched his face darken. "But I do know the kind of people you've been associating with, and I can tell you here and now, it has to stop."

"Or what?"

"Or not only will I withdraw my offer of my shares, but Maman and I will not *allow* you to sell. You will be bankrupt and disgraced."

"And you'll go down with me."

"No, we won't. And in any case, we don't bear the heavy weight of your name, do we? Think about it. Think of your father, your grandfather—of all the Barons de Trouvère."

Her words had the desired effect.

"I'll resign from Fontaine," he said.

"You never have before. Are you sure they'll let you?"

"They can't stop me." His words began to tumble wildly. "I swear I'll resign—on all that's sacred."

"And what is sacred to you, I wonder?" Ella asked quietly, then held up her hand. "No, don't tell me any more lies, you'll just make it worse." She felt as if a lead weight were dragging her down. "You've sworn that you'll disassociate yourself from those people, so I suppose I have to try to believe you."

"And you'll help me?"

"If you leave today."

Olivier got slowly to his feet. "You asked me what I hold sacred."

"Is there anything left?"

"You." His dark eyes glistened. "Still you—always you." He paused. "And Danielle, too, now that I've met her."

"Yes, Dani." Ella nodded. "I can understand that, at least."

"She's the image of you, you know, Lalla. As you were at that age—all golden and brave and sweet."

There was a brief silence. A fleeting tenderness had crept into the air.

Ella grew brisk again. "I have various people to consult with. It will take time," she said. "And Maman and I will insist on being party to all negotiations regarding a sale."

"Naturally."

"And you'll leave today?"

"I will."

At the door, he said, painfully, "I know I destroyed it. I wrecked it all."

"Yes, you did." She paused, and added more gently, "Perhaps you couldn't help yourself."

"What will I do when de Trouvère's gone, Lalla?"

"Maman says you'll buy a grand home in Paris and gamble for a living."

His mouth twisted. "Perhaps she's right."

"Do you want to see her? She's gone down to Rhinebeck, but I'm sure she'd be pleased if you'd stop by on your way to the city."

"Maybe I will."

"But you won't, will you?"

Olivier shook his head. "Probably not."

Harry telephoned next morning.

"I'm in Manhattan, with William."

"So you know he's gone?"

"Yes."

"And does that mean you're coming back?"

"If you'll have me."

"Why wouldn't I?"

"Because I pulled a low stroke running out on you."

"I think so."

"Will you ever forgive me, Ella?"

"Don't be dumb, Harry," she said wearily. "Of course I'll forgive you."

"But you haven't yet?"

"Not quite."

"What will it take?"

"I'm not sure."

Chapter 35

Thanksgiving, Danielle complained, was a real drag at Château Bogarde. When most families got to sit down together at home for the turkey, *they* had to share their dinner with two hundred strangers.

"I love the hotel, Mommy," she declared three weeks before the day, "but couldn't we just have a few hours by ourselves?"

"Well, the rest of you could, sweetheart," Ella explained reasonably, "but then I wouldn't get to see any of you until everything was over in the restaurant. This way, it may not be private, but at least we all get to sit together."

"I guess so," Danielle said dubiously.

"You always used to think it was fun having so many people around."

"I was a baby then."

Ella smiled. "I see."

Danielle reflected. "Mommy, could I visit with Janey's family this year?"

"On Thanksgiving? No, darling, that's for families to be together."

"I meant after dinner," the child said eagerly. "Janey's mom said they'd love to have me—and I could stay over."

"That depends."

"On what?"

"On what your father says, for one thing, and on the weather, for another."

"The *weather*?" Danielle echoed in disgust.

"We've had snow at Thanksgiving up here before now, and you know how bad the roads can be."

"But I can go if it's okay?"

"Probably."

"Oh, great! Thanks, Mommy."

The first great winter storm hit three days before the main event, cutting the hotel off; thirty-six hours later, the clouds sank down into the valley and Château Bogarde stood like a floating mirage, bathed in sunlight, while plows and men with snowblowers and shovels set to work. Those lucky enough to be safely ensconced in the hotel sat snugly before roaring fires and slithered merrily down toboggan slopes.

"Are the supplies getting through now?" Krisztina asked Ella anxiously.

"So far, so good."

Harry woke on Thanksgiving morning with a bad head cold and not a trace of festive bonhomie. The traditional fare—turkey, sweet potatoes, corn, cranberry sauce, and pumpkin pie—was enjoyed by guests and family alike, accompanied by champagne and claret and followed by port and cognac. Harry, trying unsuccessfully to bolster himself, drank steadily throughout.

While coffee was being served at their table, Ella was called to the telephone.

"Who was it?" Harry was waiting for her at the restaurant entrance when she returned.

"Olivier."

He scowled. "What the hell did he want?"

"Nothing special."

"You've been gone a half hour—he must have wanted something."

"He wanted to talk," Ella said quietly.

Harry's unreasonable mood heightened. "Doesn't he know you've better things to do than talk to him in the middle of Thanksgiving dinner?"

"As a matter of fact, he wanted me to send his good wishes to everyone, and special love to Dani."

"Just what she needs—special love from a Nazi."

"Harry, for God's sake, what's wrong with you today?"

He flagged down a passing waiter and asked for another cognac.

"Don't you think you've had enough?" Ella said mildly.

"You worry about your goddamned brother, not me! I guess we should be grateful he didn't show up in person and give us some more free publicity."

"That's all blown over, Harry, as you very well know."

Danielle came running over. "When can I go to Janey's, Mommy?"

"I'm afraid you won't be going," Ella said.

"But you said I could!"

"No, I didn't. I said it depended on the weather."

"But it's not snowing now," Danielle pointed out. "Anyway, I packed my bag, all by myself."

"Then you can unpack it just as easily," Ella told her.

"Oh, *Mommy!*"

"Why can't she go?" asked Harry.

"Because the roads are bad."

"But Janey only lives in Palenville, doesn't she? It's hardly far." Harry's voice was loud.

"Mommy, I have to go," Danielle chimed in. "It's rude to say I can't come right at the last moment, you always say so."

"I'll take her," Harry said.

"No, you won't."

"Why the hell not?"

Ella tried to keep her tone soft. "Because you've had too much to drink."

"Just because you can't stand to hear the truth about your lousy brother doesn't mean I'm drunk!"

"Harry, please keep your voice down."

"I'll take you, sweetheart," he told their daughter.

"No, you won't!" Ella compromised swiftly. "Dani, go and get your things. Lin Tsung will drive you to Janey's."

"Oh, great!" Danielle disappeared.

Harry looked at Ella belligerently. "Thank you, dear wife."

"Lin Tsung's only had one glass of wine," she pointed out calmly. "Maybe you should go and lie down. Your cold's obviously making you irrational."

"The hell it is!" He turned on his heel.

"Where are you going?"

"Out." He looked back at her bitterly. "Since you'd rather talk to your brother than your husband, I doubt I'll be missed."

"You're not going with Dani!"

"No, not with Dani—on my own. To get *really* drunk, drunk as a skunk."

Ella put her hand on his arm, suddenly anxious. "Harry, please don't drive when you're like this."

He shook her off. "You go worry about your guests, and leave me the fuck alone!"

When Louis Dettlingen came to find her, two hours later, his face pale, Ella knew immediately.

"*Bon Dieu,*" she whispered. "It's Harry, isn't it."

"No," Louis said.

Relief overwhelmed her. "What, then?"

"It's Dani and Lin Tsung."

Ella stared at him.

"They've had an accident, madame."

When Ella, William, and Krisztina arrived at Memorial Hospital in Catskill, Lin Tsung was standing, unhurt, outside in the snow.

Ella leapt from the still-moving car.

"Where is she?"

"In the emergency room." He had been weeping. "They wouldn't let me stay with her."

Ella ran inside as William and Krisztina hurried up.

"What happened, Lin Tsung?" William asked.

"A truck," he said, his voice dull. "The driver lost control and hit us."

"How's Dani?" Krisztina's voice was choked with fear.

Lin Tsung looked at her in utter misery. "I don't know."

"Head injuries."

The words sounded, like a death knell, in the whitewashed, linoleum-floored corridor.

"How bad?" Ella hardly knew her own voice.

"Impossible to say, until we've carried out a number of tests."

"When?"

"Mrs. Bogarde, I'm afraid you'll have to be patient. There's no more I can tell you now."

"She's doing very well, so far as we can tell."
"But she's still unconscious."
"There's no fracture, and there's been no internal bleeding."
"What about—damage?" Even William could not bring himself to say the word that was knifing through them all.
"Brain damage?" Gently spoken. "That's unlikely. We'll know for sure when she wakes."
"How long?"
"I really cannot tell you. But I think we'll all know soon enough."

Ella, William, Krisztina, and Lin Tsung were in the room when she opened her eyes.
"Mommy?"
Joy, unspeakable and glorious, swelled in their hearts.
"Yes, my darling, I'm here."
A tiny, frail smile curved the child's pale lips.
"Where's Daddy?"
"He'll be here, sweetheart."
A strange, puzzled expression came over Danielle's face. "Where's Daddy?" she asked again.
Ella bent closer. "He'll be here soon—don't worry, Dani."
Confusion turned to fear. *"Where's my Daddy?"*
Ella stroked her forehead, careful of the bandages. "He'll be here as soon as he can, my love."
"Why are you whispering, Mommy?"
"What, darling?"
"I can't hear you, Mommy."
Ella stared.
"Mommy, I can't hear you!"

"She's deaf, Doctor!"
Florence Cain, the specialist swiftly summoned by the resident surgeon, looked calmly at the frantic woman facing her. "Not necessarily, Mrs. Bogarde."
"She can't hear! Not a thing!"
"That doesn't seem to be quite true. Danielle complained that people were whispering, didn't she?"

"Yes," Ella acknowledged wildly, "but she still couldn't make out a word anyone said."

"You understand there's been no brain damage, don't you, Mrs. Bogarde?" Dr. Cain asked.

"Yes, thank God, but what does this mean? Is it just temporary, is that what you're saying?"

"It means that the accident has resulted in a degree of deafness. How profound that deafness is, and whether it's going to be temporary or not, is what we have to find out."

Ella nodded speechlessly.

"Danielle's been asking for her father."

"Yes."

"Has he been told about the accident?"

"I don't know where he is—he went out just before Dani, and . . ."

The doctor looked sympathetic. "Why don't you go check on your daughter, and then you may as well go home and get a good night's sleep."

"I'm going to stay with Dani."

"She'll be sleeping, too, you know."

"I'd prefer not to leave," Ella insisted.

Dr. Cain nodded. "I'll arrange for a cot to be put up in her room."

"Thank you."

Harry arrived, chalky-faced, at six in the morning. For an hour, he cradled Danielle in his arms, wrote her jokey notes, and assured her that no one was angry with her.

"She thought we might blame her because she insisted on going to Janey's," he told Ella in the waiting room.

"Poor baby," Ella said.

He looked at her, then sank onto a wooden chair and buried his face in his hands. "Christ, what a mess."

Ella waited a moment. "Where were you, Harry?"

"In Tannersville," he said. "In a bar."

"All night?"

He shook his head. "I slept in the car."

There was a pause.

"I had to be very strong last night," Ella said, her voice drained, "and I needed, more than anything, to have you with me."

"And I wasn't there."

"No." Ella sighed. "We should get back to her room now. I don't want her to be alone too long."

Harry rose, slowly, shakily. "Of all times for me to pick a fight," he said. There were tears in his eyes. "I'm so sorry."

Ella gave him her hand. "I know."

"We have three separate problems," Florence Cain told Harry and Ella a few days later.

"Three?" echoed Harry.

Ella sat stiffly in a chair, her hands, white-knuckled, in her lap.

"We'll take the worst first." From her open briefcase, Dr. Cain produced a colored, clearly marked illustration, which she set before them. "The auditory pathway in Dani's left ear was badly damaged by the blow to her head."

"Can it be repaired?" Harry asked.

Ella held her breath.

"I'm afraid not."

"Does she have any hearing in that ear?"

"A vestige."

"What about her right ear?"

"The second problem." Dr. Cain took a pencil and pointed to the diagram before them. "These three tiny bones are called ossicles. They form a chain that carries vibrations of sound from the eardrum membrane to the fluid contained in the inner ear." She paused. "In Dani's case, the bones have been separated because of the bang on her head, and the result has been a serious loss of hearing."

"What can be done?" Harry asked.

"We can operate to reposition the ossicles." The doctor smiled. "The operation has a fairly high degree of success."

Ella relaxed a little. "So she will be able to hear again?"

"If the operation is a success."

Harry asked about the third problem.

"I'm afraid that Dani's organs of balance were also damaged in the accident."

Ella and Harry both blanched.

"Now, that doesn't mean that Dani is going to be disabled, unable to walk or anything of that kind, but you will find that when she's allowed out of bed, she'll have an alarming loss of her sense of balance. It's important that we're all prepared for that, most particularly, of course, Dani herself."

Ella's hands were tightly clenched again. "What can be done about that?"

"We can't repair the damage, I'm afraid, but Dani will provide her own best therapy, supported, naturally, by professional help." The doctor sat back in her chair. "If such damage occurs in an adult, they may be in a lot of trouble, but we find that children compensate remarkably swiftly. There are other things that help us to balance—the sensations from the soles of the feet, for example, and obviously the eyes."

"So Dani will be able to manage without these nerves?" Harry said.

"Not for some time, and not in every situation. She'll probably always have difficulty walking on an uneven or soft surface—a thick carpet, for example, or grass. And she'll also have problems in the dark, but even then, she will manage. It will become second nature to Dani to walk more cautiously and to use her hands and arms for support."

There was a sorrow at that moment, Dr. Cain reported to her colleagues later, so deep and intense that she could have sliced it with a knife. She had offered them what was in many ways an optimistic prognosis, but she was aware that she had, in a comparatively few words, destroyed perfection.

"She's a dancer," Ella said, very softly. "A very promising ballet student."

There was a lump in Florence Cain's throat. "I'm sorry."

Harry took his wife's hand. "Dani's tough," he reminded her, his voice husky. "Lin Tsung always says she has the finest natural balance he's come across in a child."

Ella's eyes stung.

"Had," she murmured.

The first time they saw Danielle trying to walk unaided, staggering like a little drunk and managing, somehow, not even to cry or throw a tantrum, Ella wept profusely and Harry escaped into the bathroom, threw up, and sat like a stone for an hour, not saying a word.

Of them all, it was Harry, throughout, who found it hardest to cope. Even after a successful operation on Danielle's right ear, and even after they brought her home, it became no easier for him.

"He thinks the fact she's learning to lip-read is a sign of failure," Ella told Krisztina. "She can hear, he says, so why does she have to be treated like a stone deaf child? And when he forgets, and speaks to her from the wrong side and gets no response, his face is so tormented. I don't know what to do, Maman."

Krisztina shook her head. "I think it's partly related to something I told you a long time ago—when you and Harry married and had Dani, he felt that he'd set up the definitive, permanent idyll. Right now he feels it's crumbling." She paused. "I also think —and I may be wrong—that Harry believes you blame him for the accident."

"Why?"

Krisztina shrugged. "You didn't want Dani to go down to Palenville on Thanksgiving. He pressured you into it and then disappeared and got roaring drunk when he should have been with you."

"But I've never said that I blame him."

"Haven't you thought it?"

"Only that first night—because I was frightened and angry."

"I think he still feels guilty. He sees Dani suffering, and you along with her."

"But Dani's going to be all right! There are bound to be rough times ahead, but she's not suffering."

"You and I know that, Ella."

"But Harry doesn't."

The tensions between Ella and Harry were still too high for comfort when, after Christmas, Olivier arrived at Château Bogarde without warning.

"What the hell's he doing here?" Harry asked Ella.

"He's come to see Dani, brought her belated gifts. I know he's been anxious about her."

"Good old Uncle Ollie," Harry said ironically.

Ella sighed. "Give him a chance, Harry, please, just this once."

A week later, Olivier was still there.

"I want him out," Harry told Ella. "Tell him to go."

Ella shook her head. "Not this time."

"What's different about this time? Aside from my personal feelings, which don't seem to matter to you, if the press realize he's here, they'll have a field day."

"That's yesterday's news," Ella said calmly. "And Olivier's not here to make trouble. He came for Dani, not out of any ulterior motive, and she loves having him here." She paused. "He's even been making an effort with Maman and Papa."

Harry's jaw was rigid. "I don't like Danielle's spending time with him."

"He's her *uncle*—he's doing her no harm."

He shook his head. "How can you be so blind?"

"In this particular instance, I don't think I am being blind."

"Ella, darling, for God's sake!" He took her by the arms, his eyes pleading. "Don't you understand by now? I can't stay in the same house as that man!"

"He's hardly in the house, Harry. He's at the hotel."

He let her go impatiently. "It comes to the same thing, and you damn well know it!"

"And what's that?" Ella asked bitterly. "Your walking out on us again?"

"I don't want to, believe me!" he said desperately.

"Why not? It's becoming quite a regular event—your leaving when things don't go exactly your way."

"Ella, why won't you see that Olivier is dangerous?"

"Only to himself." She paused. "You know what I think? I think that my brother's just an excuse—oh, sure, you hate his guts, and maybe that's fair enough; he's not your brother, after all." Her eyes narrowed. "But there's more to it this time. You've been a mess since Dani's accident, Harry, and Lord knows I've tried to talk to you, but you keep it all bottled up inside, and now you think that walking out is the answer." Her voice trembled. "But you're wrong, terribly wrong."

"I'm not walking out, Ella," he said softly, brokenly. "I just need some time away from here." He hesitated. "Maybe you're right—maybe it isn't just Olivier. But having him here is just too much. He makes me crazy."

Three days later, Harry packed two suitcases and stood them in the front hall of their house while he waited, with Ella and Danielle, for Lin Tsung to bring the car to the door.

Moving slowly but steadily, her bare feet silent on the parquet floor—since the accident, most carpets in the house had been replaced by ceramic tiles or wood block floors—Danielle went to her father and put her hand in his.

"Daddy, why are you going away?"

"I've told you, honey." Harry's face was gaunt. "I'm going to open an art gallery in Zurich."

"But why can't you do that here?" Danielle's face was turned up to his, concentrating hard so as not to miss a syllable of his explanation, though she'd heard it several times before.

"Because Zurich is a better place for the kind of gallery I have in mind, Dani."

"Then why can't we come with you?"

Ella stepped forward so that she was on Danielle's good side. "Because I have to stay and look after the hotel, sweetheart. And you know you have a lot more work to do."

The front door opened, and Lin Tsung appeared, his face somber. "It's time."

Harry nodded. "I'm coming, Lin Tsung."

"Daddy?" Danielle still held firmly on to his hand. "How long will you be gone?"

"I'm not sure," Harry replied truthfully.

"You have two cases." Her voice was accusing. "When you go away usually, you only take one."

Ella helped Harry out. "Daddy has a lot of papers packed this time."

Lin Tsung stooped to pick up the bags, but Harry stopped him. "I'll get them."

"Then I'll wait in the car," Lin Tsung said.

Harry looked at Ella, his eyes desolate. "I'll call you later to let you know I've arrived."

Ella nodded, her mouth taut. "If you like."

He kissed her forehead, his lips cold.

"Daddy?" There were sudden, choking tears in Danielle's voice.

"Yes, my love?" Harry bent and picked her up in his arms.

"Come back quickly."

"Of course I will, Dani." He pressed his face to her warm neck and then, quickly, remembering that she couldn't hear or see his lips, drew back and looked earnestly into her face. "You don't think I could ever stay away for long, do you?"

Danielle's mouth trembled.

"I don't know," she said.

Chapter 36

Olivier left two weeks later.

Harry remained in Zurich.

Sandor Janos came back to Château Bogarde.

"I'm glad to see you again, Mr. Janos."

He looked quizzically at her. "Truly, Mrs. Bogarde?"

"Of course," Ella said steadily. "We're honored to have you here."

"Thank you. Where is your beautiful mother?"

"In New York for a few days with my father."

"And your husband?"

Ella tried to conceal her irritation at being interrogated. "He's away too."

"Ah, yes, in Switzerland."

"If you knew, why did you ask?"

His dark eyes twinkled. "I must have forgotten momentarily."

Ella glanced over at Louis Dettlingen's desk. "Your suite is ready for you, Mr. Janos."

He stooped to pick up a small attaché case. "Are you by any chance free to dine with me this evening, Mrs. Bogarde? I'm anxious to talk to you."

"This evening?" Ella repeated, trying to think of an excuse.

"I can recommend the food here," Janos smiled. "That is, if Monsieur Monselet is still your chef."

"He is."

"Excellent." He gave a small bow. "Eight o'clock?"

"All right," she said bemusedly.

"A drink first in the bar?"

Ella nodded. "In the Kaaterskill Bar."

He arrived, armed, to Ella's astonishment, with his own bottle.

"One of the few things I don't expect to find, even in the best-stocked bar," he explained, and showed her the label.

Ella smiled. *"Barack."*

"For after dinner, of course, if you're still speaking to me."

"Why shouldn't I be?"

"I never make assumptions where ladies are concerned."

Over a dinner of oysters, *loup de mer en croûte*, and *Pêche Bogarde*, a simple confection of fresh peaches with champagne ice cream, Janos became mellow and loquacious. Ella was aware that this was the first evening since Harry's departure that she had not been utterly miserable.

Afterward, companionably silent, they went out onto the observation terrace for a few moments. The moon was almost full and the visibility excellent. The steeply sloping landscape, still draped with early March snow, gleamed softly, every field, forest, and rooftop a natural highlight.

An airplane droned high above them, and Janos looked up. "I don't much care for planes," he said, "but on a night like this, when they become extra, mobile stars, they are almost beautiful."

Ella shivered. "I hate this time of year."

"Really?"

She nodded. "February is worst of all, but March here isn't much better. It should be spring now, with life beginning—but everything's suffocating under that icy blanket."

Janos smiled. "It's wonderful up here. You are depressed because everyone has deserted you."

"No one's deserted me," she said defensively.

"Only temporarily, perhaps, but you are feeling lonely, aren't you?"

"A little," she admitted.

He took her elbow gently. "Let's go inside and drink some *barack.*"

"I think I've drunk enough for one evening."

"Nonsense. Anyway, I have to talk to you."

"We've talked for over three hours."

"But not about this."

"About what?"

"Come inside, and I'll explain."

Janos told her he had come to Château Bogarde this time with an ulterior motive: He wanted Ella to cooperate with him on a new project of his, a series of concerts for handicapped children.

"Why have you come to me?" Ella asked quietly.

"Because I thought you'd want to help. Because you're in a position to help."

"How? With a donation?"

"You have a large ballroom with good acoustics, and you are a fine organizer."

"No other reason?" Ella sounded chilly.

"You mean Danielle's accident?"

"I have no intention of allowing my daughter to be exploited, Mr. Janos."

"Please," he protested, "we were using first names over dinner —must we revert to formality now? I have no desire to exploit anyone, least of all your daughter. I should like to give pleasure to some children in much worse shape than Danielle, and I merely thought you might wish to participate."

"I see." Ella drank a little of the apricot brandy, which was warming and delicious.

"Well?" Janos prodded.

She raised an eyebrow. "I gather patience is not one of your virtues."

"It never has been." He poured more *barack* into her glass.

"Are you trying to get me drunk?" she inquired politely.

"Yes."

"It won't work."

"I didn't think it would."

Her eyes became friendlier. "To what end did you think you might get me drunk?"

"To what end do you think?"

"That's an aggravating habit."

"What is?"

"Answering questions with more questions."

"It's a Jewish trait."

"Is it?"

"Will you help me with my project, Ella?"

"I may."

"Good."

It seemed natural, since they had arrangements to discuss, for them to have dinner together for most of the next week, sometimes eating in the Bogarde house with Danielle and Lin Tsung.

Janos and Danielle seemed enchanted by each other. The Hungarian had a marvelous, easy manner with her, adapting swiftly to her one-sided hearing and not for one moment falling into the trap of pussyfooting around her disability, which Danielle complained many adults did.

"Obviously you haven't danced since the accident," he said to her, over Rocky Road ice cream.

"They told me at the hospital I'd probably never be able to dance again."

"But you don't believe them."

"No." Danielle spooned marshmallow hungrily into her mouth. "But everyone else does, except Lin Tsung."

"I don't rule it out," Ella said. "I'm learning not to rule anything out where you're concerned, miss."

"Mom got mad at me for walking in the snow the other day," Danielle confided to Janos.

"That's not fair, Dani," Ella said. "I got mad, as you very well know, because you went out on your own, and you might easily have fallen and hurt yourself."

"Kids fall down all the time, Mommy."

"I have to admit she did pretty well," Ella confirmed with considerable pride. "She did take a tumble—"

"That was only after you yelled at me."

"You were slipping and sliding long before that."

"Of course I was, Mother," Danielle said disdainfully. "My organs of balance are damaged, you know, and it was my first time out alone."

"And your last till I say so."

"Maybe."

"Dani . . ." Ella warned.

"She'll be sensible," Lin Tsung reassured, "or she knows I will stop teaching her *t'ai chi.*"

"A little Chinese blackmail?" Janos grinned.

"Certainly."

"Never hurts, does it?"

"We can discuss possible dates for the first concert," Ella said later, when she and Janos were alone. "I have three to suggest."

"I don't want to discuss dates."

"Oh? What do you want to discuss?"

"You."

"Me?"

Janos leaned forward, his expression suddenly grave. "Since my arrival at the top of this mountain, I have had a problem."

"What kind of problem?"

"A serious, but delicious problem."

"Oh, yes?" Ella looked suspicious.

"I am longing—yearning—to kiss you, Ella."

Ella grew a little pink. "Are you?"

"Are you offended?"

She smiled. "Should I be?"

"Scandalized?"

"Only a little."

"This is not going well," Janos said, disconcerted. "It's unromantic. I should have taken you outside, under the stars, and swept you into my arms."

"I'd have slapped your face."

"Would you?"

"Probably." Ella was apologetic. "Sandor, I'm a happily married woman."

"Without a husband."

She flushed. "My husband is away on a business trip."

"I know. He's opening an art gallery."

"That's right."

"And you're not angry with him?" Janos asked softly.

Ella looked into his eyes. "I love my husband."

"I'm not asking you to stop loving him—I'm asking you to have a love affair with me. One need not preclude the other."

For an instant, Ella's blush heightened, then she began to relax again. It was hard to be annoyed with this man for long, and after all, this was little more than harmless banter—wasn't it?

She had poured them both some calvados, and now she sniffed it, enjoying its scent even more than its taste. "I've never had an affair," she said lightly.

"I wish I could change that."

Ella felt a pleasant tingling sensation. It was good to be flirted with at a time like this, when she'd cried herself to sleep almost every night for more than five weeks.

"If I were to have a love affair with anyone, Sandor," she said warmly, "it would almost certainly be with you." She sipped her calvados. "But I can't."

"Are you sure?"

"I'm afraid so."

He sighed, then smiled. "I think I'll stay a little longer, in case you change your mind."

"Don't you have work to do?"

"Mayn't I take a vacation?" He considered. "Which reminds me—when did you last have one?"

"Not for a while."

Janos looked disgusted. "What is the point of being rich if all you do is work?"

"I have fun too," Ella defended.

"Not real fun."

Now Ella sighed. "You're right. I could use a break."

"I'm going to St. Moritz when I leave here."

"Lucky you."

"Come with me."

She laughed. "What a lovely thought."

"Then do it."

"Don't be silly. I can't go anywhere. I have a hotel to run, for one thing."

"Your mother is in Manhattan, and I'm sure she'd come back here in a flash if she thought you wanted to go."

"And what about Dani?"

"She can come too."

"To St. Moritz?"

"Why not?" he repeated.

"Because she's at school. And more importantly, because she'd spend most of the time falling over."

"You said she did well in the snow."

"For a few minutes, concentrating hard, but it wouldn't be much of a holiday for either her or me, watching her like a hawk."

"If you rule out snow, you rule out sand too. Are you going to make Danielle take all her vacations on concrete sidewalks?"

"It's still early days. I want her to get her confidence back on familiar territory first."

"Then at least put back a few carpets."

"It's easier for her on hard surfaces."

"She needs challenge."

"She has challenges every day!"

They paused, and Janos smiled at her.

"Come to St. Moritz."

"I can't."

He shrugged. "I suppose we could always start our love affair here." His eyes twinkled.

"No, Sandor, we could not."

He shrugged again. "Perhaps tomorrow."

"Have you been to the Kaaterskill Falls?" Ella asked Janos next morning.

"Not yet."

"Until we opened the château, they were virtually cut off, though in the past, especially when the other hotel on this mountain was open, they were a favorite attraction."

"Do they freeze?"

"They certainly do. Would you like to see them?"

"Will you take me?"

She looked at her watch. "All right."

"What do we wear for this adventure?" he asked.

"Everything."

They were just approaching the falls when Ella's eye was caught by a small splash of red over to the right, about a hundred yards away, quite close to the edge of the frozen waterfall.

"What is—?" Ella shielded her eyes from the sun's strong glare, then blanched. "Oh, dear *God!*"

Danielle, dressed in a scarlet anorak, hair uncovered and flying like a banner in the wind, was walking back and forth, her hands and arms outstretched, her face puckered in intense concentration.

Ella clutched at Janos's arm. "The ledge behind her is just ice!" she hissed frantically. "If she falls—"

"She won't fall," Janos said in a low voice. "Keep calm, and keep your voice down. It'll be all right."

"I'm going to get her."

"No." Janos spoke sharply and grasped her shoulders.

"What are you doing? Let me go! If she slips . . ." Her lips were white.

"You stay here," he said quietly. "I'll go."

"Don't be ridiculous. I'm her mother!"

"And if she sees you, and has a fright because she thinks you may be angry?" He still gripped her firmly. "I won't let her be hurt, I swear it."

Ella nodded, her teeth starting to chatter.

Janos glanced around. "Get back behind those bushes, where she won't see you."

"What are you going to do?"

"I'm going to edge around there out of her line of vision." He pointed. "Then I'll wait till she's facing my way, so she won't be startled."

"All right, but *hurry.*"

"Go on, behind the bushes."

Ella obeyed silently, and watched in terror. Danielle was still doggedly tracing her own frozen bootprints back and forth, still horrifyingly near to the ice ledge. Ella began to pray.

It seemed like an eternity before Janos emerged into the clearing behind Danielle. He waited, motionless, until she completed another straight line and then, as she turned, he began to walk slowly, casually, like a man out for a stroll.

Danielle saw him, stopped in her tracks, and then waved.

"Hi!" she called.

"Hello there!" Janos continued to walk calmly.

"Did you see me?" Danielle shouted excitedly.

"I saw, Dani."

They were still fifty yards apart.

"Look, Sandor! Watch me!" Danielle yelled.

"No, Dani, wait till I get there!"

But Danielle had already turned eagerly away, and failed to hear him.

"Danielle!" Janos quickened his pace.

She took the first three steps with ease, but then, perhaps because she now had an audience, wobbled on the fourth, steadied herself with her arms, then, on the sixth pace, the heel of her boot skidded and she slipped over onto her backside.

"Okay, stay still, Dani!" Sandor shouted.

Danielle began to clamber to her feet, gave a much wilder,

more frantic swoop with her arms and slithered sharply toward the ice ridge—

"*No!*" Ella screamed, and hurtled out from behind the snowy bushes.

Janos launched himself in a flying tackle, seized Danielle by her legs, and brought them both to a halt just inches from the ledge.

"Oh, Dani, Dani!" Ella sobbed over and over again, as they all sprawled, clutched in each other's arms. "Thank God you're okay, thank God!"

Danielle's face was flushed with the sudden shock of being so roughly manhandled. "I don't see why he had to go and do that," she complained. "I was miles from the edge."

"You were two goddamned inches from *that*!" Ella shrieked in outraged, breathless emotion, one shaking gloved finger pointing at the ice.

"Looks solid enough to me," Danielle said mulishly.

Janos, moving gingerly, flexing both arms tentatively and mercifully feeling no pain, climbed to his feet.

"Get up," he told Danielle sternly, helping Ella, who was still trembling like a leaf in a gale.

He steered them all safely away from the ledge, then looked around, found a medium-size rock and threw it, hard and fast, at the ice, which promptly developed a lethal crack and showered fragments down into the crevasse.

"See?" he said curtly.

Danielle's eyes had widened. "Oh."

"Oh?" Ella repeated. "*Oh?* Is that all you can say?"

"I'm sorry."

"I should damn well think you are! You had me scared witless— you had us both terrified!"

Danielle's mouth began to quiver. "I'm really sorry, Mommy," she said, and began to cry.

Janos took pity. "You didn't realize," he comforted her. "She didn't, Ella, or she wouldn't have done anything so stupid."

"He's right, Mommy," Danielle wept, her face tilted up to hear, the tears streaming down her cheeks. "I just come here because it's so pretty, and I didn't—"

"You mean you've been here before?" Ella turned white again. "When? There's always someone with you."

"No, there isn't."

"I should think not," Janos said. "Everyone's entitled to some privacy, right, Dani?"

"Will you mind your own business!" Ella snapped at him, then looked appalled. "I'm sorry, Sandor. Dear God, I'm so sorry—will you ever forgive me?"

"Instantly," he smiled. "On one condition."

"Anything."

"That we get back to your nice warm, safe hotel, and have something to drink."

Ella looked at him. "Is that all you want?" she asked softly, candidly.

"No," he answered, equally softly. "But the rest is up to you."

"You were magnificent," Ella whispered, as she lay in the crook of Sandor's arm in the guest bedroom of her house.

It was three o'clock in the afternoon.

"Was I?" He looked pleased.

"I don't mean just now." She grinned. "Or rather, yes, I do, of course—but I was really talking about what you did this morning."

"Oh." The word was solemn, but his dark eyes danced.

"You could have been killed."

"Definitely. Or worse, I could have injured my arms."

"You *are* all right, aren't you?" Ella sat up. "I couldn't bear it if you'd hurt yourself for us."

"Of course you could, considering the alternative."

Ella shuddered, remembering.

"Don't think about it anymore," Janos said.

"Easier said than done."

"With children, there are always incidents, *edesem.*"

She lay back again. "Perhaps it is my fault, for wrapping her up in cotton wool."

"Perhaps, just a little." He paused. "She'll be wiser after today."

"Will she?"

"She had a bad scare. When I threw the rock and the ice shattered, she realized. Better than a scolding."

They fell silent, the steady tick of the antique clock on the mantelpiece the only sound in the room.

"Are you all right?" Sandor asked her gently, after a few moments.

"I'm not sure."

"Feeling troubled? About this?"

Ella closed her eyes. A picture of Harry bobbed before them. She opened them again.

Sandor stroked her arm. "Don't spoil something beautiful by feeling guilty," he said quietly.

Ella shook her head and swallowed, suddenly close to tears. "I can't help it."

"You have nothing to be guilty about."

"Haven't I?"

For an instant, regret showed in Sandor's face, then he covered it with resignation. "We both know why we made love today."

She said nothing.

"For me," he went on, "it was desire. For you—" He hesitated. "For you, it was half shock, half gratitude."

"It was much more than that," Ella protested.

"A little more, perhaps, but mostly that." He paused, and grinned. "A reward fuck."

"Sandor, don't!"

"Don't look so outraged." He smiled. "It was glorious, at least for me."

"For me too!"

"That's good." He slipped one arm about her shoulders. "I'm just being realistic about you, Mrs. Bogarde, because, like it or not, I see now that that's who you are. You're Harry's wife, and you love him very much. We were attracted to each other, and I saved your daughter's life. That's all."

"That isn't the reason I went to bed with you."

"Yes, it is, and it's nothing to be ashamed of. It's done no one harm. On the contrary, it's sealed the friendship between us."

"Has it?"

He looked at her with undisguised tenderness. "Definitely."

Ella turned her head and kissed him, softly and warmly, on the cheek. "Thank you," she whispered. "For everything."

Very slowly, with another sigh, Sandor slid away from her and got out of bed. He looked down at her. "Probably, Ella, darling, we will never do this again—but we will be friends, won't we? Good friends."

Ella sat up. "I'm glad."

He found his clothes and began to dress. "You know what I think you should do to show Danielle that you do trust her?"

"What?"

"Bring her to St. Moritz."

"Oh, Sandor, she'll fall all the time."

"But everyone falls in the snow, Ella. And think of the fun she could have. She'd be far safer there on the nursery slopes than here on the edge of a mountain."

"I don't know."

"There's another good reason for you to come."

"What's that?"

"Your husband is in Switzerland."

Ella stiffened.

"You want to see him, don't you?"

"I don't know," she said again. "Yes, of course I do, but—"

"It's time he came back, I think." He paused to pull on his sweater. "Separate suites, at the Suvretta House."

Ella began to weaken.

"Come to St. Moritz," Sandor urged again. "You and Dani. Make it a milestone, a flag to mark the end of the bad times, and the start of something better."

Ella got out of bed, covering herself with a corner of the duvet, and crossed the room to him. "If I tell you that I think I love you, will you believe me?"

The regret in his eyes mixed with pleasure. "As a friend, yes." He smiled. "The finest friendships are founded in love, aren't they, *edesem*?"

For the first time, she laughed. "Reward fuck indeed!"

Janos grinned. "And how much better than a medal."

Chapter 37

Ella and Danielle walked, hand in hand, along the Bahnhof-strasse, from the broad, flag-hung Paradeplatz, under the naked linden trees past Café Sprüngli, past the big Grieder department store, past the great stone banking edifices, their small, discreet windows alive with flickering computer screens.

"Mommy, can we have a tram ride?"

"Later, darling."

They strolled on, past Bucherer and Cartier and a wealth of other jewelers, past the Baur en Ville hotel and a big toy store, before turning right into Augustinergasse and going in search, among charming cobbled uphill side streets, of the gallery.

Ella glanced at the directions in her hand. "We go left into Widder-Gasse and then right into Glockengasse."

"There it is!" Danielle cried excitedly.

It was a large, impressive gallery, with two big plate-glass windows—a Miró and a Max Ernst on the right, a Monet, a Pissarro, and a Sisley on the left. The name *Galerie Bogarde* was inscribed in gold italics above the door.

Ella stood still.

"Come on, Mommy!"

Her hands and feet were suddenly warm and tingling, her heart pumping hard. Taking a deep breath and trying to compose herself, she allowed Danielle to tug her to the entrance.

"It won't open." Danielle jerked vainly at the handle.

A low buzz sounded.

"Try it again," Ella said, and the door opened.

A woman in her fifties, with gleaming brown hair fastened off her oval face with combs, greeted them.

"*Gruezi miteinand.*"

"Herr Bogarde, *bitte*," Ella said, smiling back.

"*Ihren Namen, bitte?*"

"Frau Bogarde."

Without a flicker, the woman excused herself and walked away through the long gallery, disappearing through a polished timber door at the back. Ella and Danielle glanced around with interest. A lovely bronze sculpture of a woman by Aleksandr Archipenko stood on a plinth in the center of the outer room, and along one wall was a series of unusual abstract paintings by an artist with an unfamiliar Swiss name.

The door at the back opened again, soundlessly, and Harry appeared.

"*Daddy!*" Danielle squealed, and ran toward him, hardly clumsy at all, even on the plush carpet, almost tripping halfway but making it unscathed into his outstretched arms.

"Oh, Dani, Dani, baby, I've missed you so." Harry picked her up, whirled her around, and then buried his face in her hair.

Ella watched, tears pricking at her eyes, a faint smile on her lips.

The embrace broke, and Harry looked at Ella.

"Hello."

"Hello, Harry."

"Aren't you guys even going to kiss?" Danielle demanded.

Harry flushed, and it was left to Ella to come forward and brush his cheek softly.

She stood back and scrutinized him, looking for changes, even though they'd been apart less than two months. His hair was a little longer, as perhaps became a gallery owner, and there were new lines around his eyes, small wrinkles that cradled them and spread also from his nose to the corners of his mouth.

He's going to be craggy, Ella thought, and felt a distinct pleasure at the idea, for it was good to see a beloved face becoming even more satisfactory with age.

"I know," he said huskily, "I look awful."

She shook her head. "On the contrary, I was just thinking how fine you look."

He was staring at her.

"And me?" she asked. "How do you find me?"

He contemplated her for another moment, and then said, "Awesome."

Ella laughed.

"How else do you describe a beautiful sight that you thought you might never see again?"

"You knew you'd see me again, Harry."

He shook his head.

"Daddy, this place is neat!" Danielle said. Though her father had been a notable collector all through her life, and both Château Bogarde and their home housed a wealth of priceless works, this gallery—this attractive, straightforward *shop*—somehow charmed and impressed her. "Are all these paintings yours?"

"Some of them. Some of them are just borrowed."

"Show us what you like, Dani," Ella suggested.

"Okay." Danielle began to walk around, making up her mind with rapid simplicity. "I like that one—I hate that—those are funny, and that one's gross." She stopped abruptly in front of a small, signed Chagall lithograph. "This is my favorite. Do you own this one, Daddy?"

He nodded.

"Oh, great! Can you bring it home with you?"

Harry couldn't answer, and Ella helped him out. "One day, if the gallery doesn't need it anymore, then maybe Daddy will bring it home."

"Okay."

Harry drew Ella over to one side. "What are you both doing here? Your cable didn't explain—and you didn't tell me your flight, or I'd have met you at Kloten."

"We managed," she said lightly.

"I can see that." He looked at Danielle. "She seems in incredible shape—I can hardly believe it."

"Why not? She was doing pretty well when you left, and she's had six more weeks to improve since then."

"Six weeks and two days."

"You're counting, too, are you?"

"What do you think?"

"So's Dani," Ella said cruelly. "She's made a calendar, and she marks off each day till you get back."

Harry closed his eyes.

"So?" Ella said. "Do you have any plans to return? My brother left over a month ago, but you know that."

He opened his eyes. "I had to get away for a while, Ella."

"I know that." She paused. "I also know that when you leave somewhere, you leave a hole, but a hole has a nasty way of closing up the longer you stay away."

Harry looked at Danielle, who was having a conversation with the brown-haired woman, who had quietly emerged from the back.

"I know you didn't come here just to see me. Where are you going?"

"To St. Moritz."

"Why?"

"For a vacation. We need one."

He frowned. "Surely that's the most unsuitable vacation you could have picked for Dani at this stage."

"I gave it a lot of thought," Ella said quietly. "She's come a long way in the last few weeks. She can walk in snow—slides around a lot, but she copes. You know our daughter."

"Is Lin Tsung with you?"

"No."

"And I guess Kriszti's minding the hotel."

"Of course."

Danielle, growing impatient, came over to join them. "Can we go out somewhere, please?"

"Are you staying over?" Harry asked Ella.

"For one night. At the Dolder Grand."

"Good." The tension eased a little.

"I promised Dani some of the best cake and ice cream in the world at Café Sprüngli, and I also promised her a tram ride."

"So what are we waiting for?" Harry asked.

"You, Daddy."

Since Danielle was thoroughly exhausted by eight o'clock, they put her to bed under a big, soft duvet, called the front desk for a pleasant-faced Swiss sitter, and went out to dinner at the Kronenhalle in Bellevueplatz.

"You know, I can never believe how many truly great restaurants there are in this small city," Harry said later as they sat in the hall at the Dolder, drinking coffee and sipping Napoléon cognac.

"I'm not surprised you love the Kronenhalle," Ella smiled. "All those paintings, aside from the food."

Harry paused. "How's business been at home?"

"Good."

They fell silent again. There had been frequent, awkward gaps in their conversation all evening.

"More coffee?" Harry asked.

"No, thank you." Abruptly, Ella put her cognac glass on the table. "Harry, look, what are we playing at? Haven't we made enough small talk?"

He nodded. "You're right. I'm sorry."

"I haven't come here to play the aggrieved wife, you know." She took a deep breath. "I came because I've missed you—and because I don't believe there's been a moment's doubt on either side that we still love each other." Her voice trembled a little. "Has there?"

"No." Harry reached for her hand and held it, clutching it like a lifeline. "God, no."

"I think you've been in shock ever since the accident," Ella continued gently. "I don't honestly think that Olivier had a lot to do with your leaving this time. And I'm sure that this has been good for you—you should have opened a place like Galerie Bogarde long ago."

"I'm just sorry I had to do it this way."

"And now? What's your plan?"

"Plan?"

"Are you going to come home or do you want to stay in Switzerland?"

He smiled ruefully. "No, I don't want to stay here, though Lord knows it's a wonderful place."

"Do you have someone to manage the gallery?"

"The woman you saw this afternoon, Maria Hämmerli. I think she's more than capable of running things on her own." He paused. "Have you been to Hunter's yet?"

"No. In the morning, if there's time, I thought I might show Dani the lake. We'll drop by then."

Harry stirred sugar into his coffee. "How are you getting up to St. Moritz?"

"By train."

"Dani will enjoy that."

Ella was beginning to feel exasperated. "Harry, you still haven't answered my question. Are you coming home?"

"Do you want me to?"

"What kind of an idiotic question is that? Of course I want you to. I think I've made that painfully clear."

Harry's eyes were somber. "I thought you really must despise me, that you'd never forgive me."

"I think I love you too much not to forgive you," Ella answered frankly. "And you've never been despicable."

"Then I suppose there's just one problem left," he said softly.

"And what's that?" She hardly dared to ask.

"I haven't forgiven myself."

"Then isn't it about time you did?"

His eyes were bright. "I guess so."

He stayed the night with her—and for as long as they made love, skin on skin, arms encircling, mouths thirsting, bodies desperately driving, hearts pounding, all the fears and misgivings were forgotten. But later, when they lay in the silence, still and sleepless, the doubts returned, and they both knew that it would never be the same as it had been, until they were safely back home together again.

"I wish you were coming with us."

"So do I, believe me, but if I'm going to get away soon, I need to sort arrangements with Frau Hämmerli. And I have a whole bunch of buyers and dealers to see in the next two weeks."

"Will you call? I know it will mean a lot to Dani."

"Of course I'll call, but not just for Dani."

They embraced briefly, emotionally, and then Harry lifted Danielle up over the steps and helped Ella up behind her.

"Take care of each other."

"I'll miss you, Daddy," Danielle called past her mother, her voice high and anxious.

"And I'll miss you, honey, like crazy!" Harry looked at Ella. "Are you two going to be okay on your own?"

Ella's eyes were exceptionally bright and clear.

"Who said we're going to be alone?"

It was on the fourth day that Harry appeared in St. Moritz. It was early afternoon, and Sandor, Ella, and Danielle were sliding, in a hand-in-hand threesome, down the gentle nursery slope just outside the Suvretta House.

"There's Daddy!" Danielle shrieked, and promptly fell over, dragging the two adults down with her.

"So it is," said Janos, getting up and brushing snow off his black *salopettes*.

"You stay here with Sandor, Dani," Ella ordered. "Don't try to ski without me."

"Bring Daddy up here!"

Ella skied down to where Harry stood, handsome in his long wolf coat and boots.

"What a lovely surprise!" she said, sliding to a halt and trying to get close enough to kiss him.

"Is it?"

"Yes, of course." She smiled. "Why didn't you tell us you were coming?"

"Why should I have?"

"So we could have met you, why else?"

His face was grim. "Perhaps so you could have gotten rid of him."

"Him?" Ella looked up at the slope. "Why would I want to get rid of Sandor?"

"So now it's *Sandor*," he said, exaggerating her pronunciation derisively. "You conveniently omitted to tell me he'd be here."

"I didn't think it was relevant."

"Didn't you?"

"No."

Danielle, too impatient to wait another second, came sliding haphazardly down the hill, Janos more in tow than leading.

"Daddy, you came!" Encumbered by her short skis, she tried to hug him, failed, and fell flat. Harry bent and picked her up, while Janos released her boots from the skis.

"Thanks, Sandor," she beamed, and lurched into her father's arms. "Daddy, isn't this *great*? And did you see, I can ski!"

"Mr. Bogarde," Janos said, holding out his hand.

"Mr. Janos." Harry shook it curtly. "Having a good time with my family?"

"Superb, thank you."

"Oh, Daddy, he's a wonderful skier, you should see him! He's been teaching me, though of course I'm not too great yet because of my stupid ears, but I am getting better, aren't I, Sandor?"

"You learned to ski when you were five, honey," Harry reminded her.

"Yes, but that was before. Now I have to start all over again, like walking and dancing. Lin Tsung says I'm *bound* to dance again!" she bubbled on gaily, intoxicated by the diamond-sharp air, warm sunshine, and the euphoria of having both her parents at the same time.

"Have you been here long?" Harry asked Janos.

"Five days."

"One day longer than my wife and daughter."

Danielle pulled at Harry's sleeve. "Daddy, we're going to have tea at Hanselmann, which is this really terrific place where everyone meets after skiing."

Sandor glanced at his watch. "As a matter of fact, it's about that time now."

"Sure you won't mind if I tag along?" Harry asked laconically.

"What a silly question." Ella stepped out of her skis, stood them up on end, and shook off the snow.

"Only you seem such a happy little clan."

"Perhaps I'll stay in the hotel," Sandor said diplomatically. "You three should have some time alone together."

"Not at all, Mr. Janos. I wouldn't dream of spoiling your day. If anyone stays behind, it should obviously be me since I'm the latecomer."

"Oh, Daddy, of course you're coming." Danielle put an end to their nonsense. "But let's go quickly, or we'll never get a place by the window."

Somehow, they all got through the rest of the day, although when Harry discovered that Ella and Janos had adjoining suites, it took all his self-control not to explode into violence. "If only he'd just come right out and asked me if Sandor and I were sleeping together," Ella told her mother a few days later, "we might have cleared the air, but he didn't. He just sat like a steaming, molten rock, glaring at us both."

They all slept in separate rooms that night.

Next morning dawned cloudy, with the forecast for fresh snow by lunchtime. Sandor awoke to find a note pushed under his door.

*How about going up to Piz Nair, if you're up to it? I'll be at the
Corviglia cable car at nine.*

Bogarde

Sandor smiled wryly, crumpled the note into a ball, tossed it
into the wastebasket, and started to pull on his clothes.

Just before noon, Ella, who was having a glass of mineral water
in the lounge with Danielle, saw them coming through the automatic doors.

"*Merde,*" she said softly.

"What, Mommy?"

"Nothing, darling." The girl had her back to the hotel entrance. "You stay here for a few minutes—I'll be right back."

It was patently obvious, even from first glance, that they'd
been fighting. Sandor, limping, was leaning on Harry's arm, and
Harry had a large, rapidly darkening bruise under his right eye.

"What happened? Or don't I need to ask?"

"We're okay," Harry said shamefacedly.

"Oh, sure, you look just wonderful. Sandor, what's wrong with
your leg? Do you need a doctor?"

"I've seen one already. It's nothing—I just twisted my ankle. I
fell."

"On my husband's eye, I suppose," she said with heavy sar-
casm. "Where did you punch it out? On a ski slope? Did you have
a good audience?"

"There weren't many people around."

"I seem to recall you disapprove of dueling, Harry." she said.
"Or is that just where others are concerned?"

Sandor tried to calm her. "It was just a misunderstanding, Ella.
We've resolved our differences now, haven't we, Harry?"

"So now you're friends, are you?" Ella glared at them both.

Harry looked around awkwardly. "We're beginning to attract
attention."

"Oh, God, I forgot Dani," Ella said.

"Where is she?"

"Sitting over there." She glanced back. "Have you given any
thought as to what to tell her?"

"I should imagine she'd relish the truth," Sandor said.

"Which is?"

"That her father defended her mother's virtue."

"Danielle's too young to know about virtue," Harry asserted. Ella gave a small smile. "Don't you believe it."

"And what happened after that?" Krisztina asked, the day after Ella and Danielle returned from Switzerland.

"We had a good time—but it was still a strain."

"When will Harry get back?"

"In a week or so."

Krisztina smiled. "Things will improve then, *chérie*, when you get back to normal."

Ella felt like weeping.

She had cause for bleakness.

That morning, while drying herself after her bath, she had discovered a small, soft, but unmistakable lump in her left breast.

"You must tell Harry," Krisztina said immediately.

"Not unless I have to." Ella patted her mother's hand. "Don't you go worrying too much. It could be nothing at all." She grimaced. "But I know what Don will do—he'll pull me in for a biopsy before I have time to blink, and there may be decisions to be made."

"You have to tell Harry," Krisztina insisted. "You have no choice."

"Since he isn't here, Maman, I do have a choice." Ella shook her head. "I don't want to load him with this, just when things are about to get better. If I wait, there may be no need to tell him anything."

"He's your husband, *chérie*. He has a right to know."

"And it's my body," Ella said stubbornly.

Krisztina sighed. "At least call Don right away. Maybe he'll call it a harmless cyst and won't even take you in."

"Maybe," Ella said, unconvinced. "Either way, I'll call him tomorrow, I promise."

"Why not today?"

"Because today I have something else to do."

"There can't be anything more important than your health."

"One more day isn't going to make a difference, Maman."

Ella and Sandor had eaten dinner in Café Pierre. She had told him briefly and succinctly, explaining her doubts and fears starkly and without elaboration.

"Do you understand why I chose to tell you rather than Harry?" she asked him quietly.

"Because you needed to speak to a man who is not the most important person in your life, but who is also deeply aware of your beauty."

Ella flushed.

Sandor grew grave. "You want to know how I feel about the fact that you may have to have your breast removed."

She nodded.

Sandor touched her hand in a gesture of strength and comfort. "Ella, the answer is simple. To any man who loves you—and believe me, you are very easy to love—you will remain just as beautiful without your left breast as you are with it."

"Please, Sandor," Ella stopped him. "No platitudes. Be honest."

Janos smiled. "I have a reputation, as you know, for being something of a womanizer. I admire beauty, it's true. I enjoy beauty. The thought"—he lowered his voice—"that a surgeon may cut even the tiniest morsel from your body, wounds me— angers me. The knowledge that it is a part of you which you regard as crucial to your womanhood distresses me, but not for a moment do I feel what I think you fear I may feel. Repelled?" He shook his head. "Not for a moment."

Ella could not speak.

"Let's get out of here," Sandor said. "I want to take you in my arms, and I can't do that with so many people around, for your sake."

She blinked away tears. "Thank you."

"De rien." He smiled. "Will you tell Harry now?"

"I haven't decided," she evaded.

"You're still afraid."

"I guess so. And I'm still hoping it won't be necessary."

Sandor signed the check. "Are you going back up tonight?"

"There's no point. I'll be calling the doctor in the morning."

"Have I helped you at all, *edesem*?"

She reached across the table and squeezed his hand. "Very much."

He looked directly at her. "You should not be alone tomorrow."

"I won't be—Maman will drive down."

"You should tell him."

"You may be right," she admitted wistfully.

"But you're not going to."

"No."

"She may never forgive me for this," Sandor said to Krisztina a half hour later on the telephone.

"I think she'll thank you for it."

"That depends on Bogarde. She could be in the hospital by midday tomorrow," Sandor pointed out. "He has to get on a flight out of Zurich right now or he won't make it in time."

"I'll talk to Kleinman," Krisztina said. "Try to see that he gives Harry a chance to get there."

Sandor spoke tersely. "If he doesn't come . . . if he betrays her again, I promise you, Krisztina, *I* shall be there after she wakes up, and that'll be the last chance he has with her if I can help it."

Krisztina heard the intensity in his voice. "You really care for her, don't you, Sandor?"

"Who could not?"

"I think Harry will make it."

"I hope, for Ella's sake, that he does."

Harry arrived just as Ella was being wheeled on her way to the operating room.

"Thank God!" He was white-faced and breathless.

Ella, light-headed from premedication, stared up at him, hardly able to comprehend his being there. "How did you get here?" She tried to sit up, but felt dizzy and sank back. "Who told you?"

"Never mind all that." He walked alongside the trolley, holding her hand. "How are you, baby?"

She clung to him. "Harry, you know they may have—" She stopped, unable to say the words.

"To do a mastectomy." His voice was steady. "I know."

Ella began to cry.

"Don't, sweetheart." They stopped outside an elevator, and he stroked her hair and spoke softly. "I talked with Don, and he says that with luck, it may not happen. But even if it does, how could you ever, ever think it would make any difference to the way I feel about you?"

*

"Benign," she said to Krisztina two days later in her office at the hotel. "God Almighty, how is it possible for life to be so good?"

"Just a short while ago you thought it intolerable."

"I know." Ella looked around at the familiar, beloved walls, at the paintings and photographs, at the little rug she'd bought at the Hunter auction more than ten years before, its dreamy clouds and songbirds trodden by the shoes of an endless stream of staff and guests.

She shook her head. "Will I ever learn? When I first realized I might have to leave de Trouvère, I thought I wouldn't survive. I simply could not imagine being happy away from there. And now here I am, quite ludicrously contented to be back home here at Château Bogarde."

Krisztina smiled. "It's because you've made it so very fine, *dragam.* I feel that way, too."

"I could never have done it without you, Maman."

Krisztina paused. "What's Harry going to do now? How much time will he spend in Switzerland? He really does love his gallery, you know."

"Of course he does, it's exactly right for him. That's why I woke up this morning, knowing at long last how I could repay him for the hotel."

"I'm sure he's never wanted to be repaid."

"I know, but nevertheless it's time I got him a little something."

"What do you have in mind?" Krisztina asked curiously.

"A second Galerie Bogarde, but nearer to home. Somewhere like Rhinebeck, probably. He'll give it more than enough prestige and éclat to draw people up from the city, and they'll probably stay here while they're browsing."

Krisztina smiled. "It's a good idea. And your Papa will definitely approve."

Ella watched her for a moment. "Maman, is something wrong?"

"Wrong?"

"You seem preoccupied."

Krisztina waited a moment. "Olivier called, while you were in New York."

Ella knew immediately. "They've found a buyer."

"Yes." Krisztina's face was impassive. "And I have to admit it sounds like the right deal."

"Financially, or for de Trouvère?" Ella asked with suspicion.

"Both, surprisingly."

"Then it's not a group." Ella had long feared that de Trouvère would go to a chain and become depersonalized.

"No, it isn't. That is, they do own two other hotels—one in Aix-en-Provence and one in Annecy—but they're a large family, with four grown-up children, and it does seem that they've fallen in love with de Trouvère."

"What are the other hotels?"

"The one in Aix is classified as *très confortable* by Michelin, with one star for its restaurant; Annecy has had two stars since last year."

"Can they handle *grand luxe,* do you think?"

"Probably far better than Belle-mère and I when we began."

"Times have changed."

Krisztina smiled. "Ella, *chérie,* they're being investigated, of course, as are the other hotels, but if they're half as good as they sound, we've been remarkably fortunate to have found them."

"At least it will remain a hotel," Ella said slowly. "I was afraid we might have to agree to something dreadful, like apartments, or worse."

"Well, the details have yet to be arranged, and we shall have to approve everything, naturally, but so far as I understand it, although they intend to bring the plumbing up to date—"

"About time."

"—and I'm sure Olivier's neglected the annual decorations, too, but apparently they want nothing more than to collect the keys and carry on business as usual."

" 'The old order changeth, yielding place to new,' " Ella quoted softly.

Krisztina smiled again. "It's strange. You're sometimes so uncannily like Belle-mère, and yet you shared not a drop of blood."

"I lived with her for more than twenty years. I'm grateful if I inherited some of her traits." Ella paused. "How did Ollie sound?"

"All right, surprisingly," Krisztina replied. "Quite sensible. Sad, undoubtedly, but resigned." Her eyes darkened, and she looked at Ella anxiously. "What about the other thing? I seldom dare to think about it."

"Fontaine?" Ella sighed. "He swore to me that he had resigned, and I suppose I was glad to believe him. To be honest, I discouraged Harry from probing any further because I truly don't want to know."

"I think, *chérie*, that losing de Trouvère may turn out to be the making of Olivier. Perhaps if he gets right away from the past, from all the late barons, and moves to Paris . . ."

"Has he said he will go to Paris?"

"He's apartment-hunting already."

"Thank God for that."

"Why so relieved?"

"I was afraid he might cross the border," Ella confessed.

"Into Germany?" Krisztina shook her head. "Never. He's too French, *chérie*. And he would not do that to the name of de Trouvère."

The sale of Château de Trouvère was completed three months later, on June 30, 1984.

The night before Olivier was to leave, he sat alone in one of the rooms in the west wing, looking at a small pile of items that he had not yet packed, reluctant to remove them from their rightful place.

Leather albums, gold and silver trophies, medals and photographs. The collection that Ella had thought of as a shrine to his father, Laurent de Trouvère.

Olivier held one photograph in his hand—the picture of Laurent laughing with the Nazis.

"I'm sorry, Father," Olivier said aloud.

Sorry. Was that a word to describe what he felt now—the wretchedness, the degradation, the sense of total failure?

He had done so much to make it his own. Things that no one else knew about. Evil things.

And yet he'd still lost everything.

He had contemplated suicide—the idea of following in his father's footsteps had a sweet irony about it. But then that would have been such an admission of failure, one more public humiliation, and the absolute, irrevocable end of the line of de Trouvère.

But what was left? His family. William, unbearably tolerant, though Olivier knew he'd given up all hope for him long ago. His mother, a constant reminder of the part of himself he found it impossible to think of without revulsion and self-hatred. Ella, shrewder and harder than she had been, but still endlessly forgiving and loving. And Danielle, sweet, tender little Dani, who took him back to childhood and thoughts of what might have been . . .

What was really left?

Olivier looked once more at the photograph in his hand, and then put it back with the others.

Friends.

People who accepted him, understood him.

He rose, walked slowly over to the built-in wardrobe, and opened the door.

It was empty but for one item.

The burgundy velvet ceremonial uniform of the Confrères de La Fontaine.

PART SIX

Ella: New York, 1986

Chapter 38

Suddenly, after months of concentrated, confident strategizing, Ella sank down onto the floor of her dining room, which had been transformed into an operations nerve center, stared up at her husband and her parents, and said, in a voice of utter horror:

"It's going to be a disaster!"

Krisztina paused from her scrutiny of one of the latest seating plans. "What is, *chérie*?"

"The beginning, the middle, *and* the end."

"Is that all?" Harry said easily, getting down on the rug with Ella and Aphrodite, one of her favorite wolfhounds. "For a moment you had us worried."

"You may joke," she said direly, "but you'll grin on the other side of your face when we're the laughingstock of the nation."

"The whole nation?" William inquired placidly. "Surely not?"

"It isn't funny, Papa."

"Of course not, my darling. I just think that there's a very simple, fundamental answer for this attack of anguish."

"Which is?" Ella demanded.

"Panic."

"It's natural, honey," Harry agreed with William, putting an arm around her rigid shoulders. "We've taken on one of the biggest, grandest, most complicated events that any hotel of this kind has ever attempted."

"But that's just it!" Ella clutched at Harry's shirt, wide-eyed.

"I'm right to panic, aren't I? It's the most normal, sensible thing I've done in months!"

It was going to be the greatest event that they'd ever planned, but then, they had never had an excuse before for such a celebration. The month of June that year would see the tenth anniversary of the opening of Château Bogarde, Danielle's twelfth birthday, and—unexpectedly—Olivier's wedding to one Héloïse Lefèvre, a thirty-three-year-old Parisian divorcée with whom he had lived for a year.

"Ella, you're nuts," Harry had said flatly when she first suggested organizing her brother's wedding as a gift. "And your father agrees with me."

Ella had no intention of allowing Olivier to create a rift in their marriage again, since they had never been happier, and so she had calmly explained to Harry that this was the first time in so very many years that her brother had expressed a genuine wish to share his happiness with them. She simply could not bear to slam her door in his face.

"Besides," Krisztina had pointed out, "he does seem to have sobered up since losing the estate, and whoever this Héloïse is, she is apparently making my son a more contented man."

Harry could not bring himself to disappoint them both.

In the last few days of May, when the surrounding trails were already littered with hikers perching on vantage points such as Artist's Rock, Bear's Den, and Inspiration Point, and following the Rip van Winkle Trail, the first hotel guests began arriving at Château Bogarde for the jamboree, much of which had been planned as a giant benefit for several children's charities.

There were to be a number of gastronomic luncheons and dinners, two fashion shows sponsored by a storm of generous couture giants from Maryll Lanvin to Ralph Lauren; a concert for handicapped children and a performance of Aaron Copland's ballet, *Appalachian Spring*, conducted by Sandor Janos and danced by students of Danielle's ballet school. In addition, there would be the security nightmare of an exhibition of jewelery by Van Cleef & Arpels, and all would culminate in a lavish gala ball on the evening of June 7. The concept of interweaving family events with hotel festivities had given Ella and Krisztina several outsized migraines, but at last the plans were impeccably laid.

Olivier and Héloïse would be married at noon on the seventh, and their personal wedding guests would attend the ball that night.

"They've arrived," Harry told Ella late in the afternoon of June first.

"Who? Ollie?" She stood up from her desk and checked her hair and makeup in the small antique mirror behind her. "What's she like?"

"Straight from central casting."

"What does that mean?"

"Tall, Teutonic, charming but chilly."

"Teutonic?"

"If Héloïse Lefèvre is French, then I'm from Fiji."

"She's German?"

"I don't mean normal, healthy German, sweetheart," Harry said regretfully. "In fact, it's not so much the lady as her father."

"Oh, God."

"His name's Franz Winzler, and he's a beauty, a real oil painting. Eyes like weasel's, nasty, fleshy mouth, and the perfect age to have played a prize part in the Holocaust."

Ella had grown pale. "Who else?"

"Héloïse's brother, Gerhard, another likable guy, her two kids by her last marriage, they looked okay, and—" Harry stopped.

"And?"

"Her mother, of course."

"And?" she persisted, knowing there was more.

He looked sympathetic. "A bunch of your brother's friends."

"Fontaine?"

Harry shrugged. "Hard to say for sure, of course, but two of them have dueling scars just like his." He paused. *"Plus ça change."*

Ella felt nauseous. "Oh, Harry."

"William's going to be mad as hell when he claps eyes on them, and your mother . . ." He shook his head. "Poor Kriszti. It'll be toughest on her."

Ella sank back into her chair. "What am I going to do, Harry?"

"Tell them to leave?"

"How can I? Believe me, I'd love to, but I promised my brother a wedding, and besides, it's all hooked up with everything else. If I start playing the heavy sister, I may end up with a real scandal."

"Are you worried about the hotel or Olivier?"

"I'm worried about Maman and Dani," she answered, distressed. "And yes, of course I'm worried about the hotel. My brother's wrecked one place that I loved; I'm not prepared to let him do it again."

"Do you want me to talk to him?"

Ella shook her head. "That would only create a big scene." She sighed. "No, I'll have to speak to him, appeal to whatever decency may be left in him."

She called Olivier's suite, and invited him to the house.

"How could you?"

He looked startled. "How could I what?"

"Don't look so innocent. How could you bring a horde of Nazis into my hotel? Into my home? How could you do that to me? How could you do that to Maman? Or to yourself, for that matter?"

She had expected outrage, defensiveness, and wounded anger. She had not anticipated what appeared to be genuine remorse.

"I didn't want to. Believe me, I never meant it to be this way."

"So you admit they are Nazis?"

Olivier had lost a great deal of weight since she had last seen him, and looked generally fitter, but now there was a gaunt, hunted expression on his face.

"Olivier, are these people Nazis?"

"Héloïse's father was a captain in the SS."

"And the others?"

He was very pale. "Don't ask, Ella. You don't want to know about them."

"Neo-Nazis?" She shook her head. "No, you're right, don't answer, I *don't* want to know." She paused. "You don't seem happy about them."

"Happy?" His mouth twisted ironically.

"Yet you're marrying one of them. . . ."

"Héloïse isn't one of them. She can't help what her father did years ago."

"True," Ella assented quietly. "But you've invited her father and these others to your wedding. Am I allowed to know why?"

"They're my friends," he answered, his voice almost a whisper.

"So why look so miserable about them? If they're your friends, why not be proud of them? Why not at least have the guts to admit that you run with rats, with scum?"

"Can I have a drink, please?"

She poured him a whisky and handed him the glass. "You'd better sit down." She indicated the sofa.

He sat and drank, quickly.

"Well?"

"You should never have done this, Ella."

"Done what?"

"Made this gesture. Arranged the wedding."

"I wanted to trust you," she said simply.

"And I wanted your trust. More than anything."

"So why?"

"I had no choice."

"There's always a choice, Ollie. It's called free will."

"Not always."

"What are you saying? That they wouldn't let you resign from Fontaine?"

"It's not just Fontaine anymore, Lalla."

"Do they have some kind of hold over you?" she asked, growing gentler and more afraid for him by the minute. "What is it? Money? Surely after the sale you must have been able to settle all your debts. Or are you still gambling?"

He hesitated before nodding. "Yes."

"Oh, Ollie. And these people, do you owe them money?"

Another tiny pause. "I owe them, yes."

Ella sat down opposite him. "What about Héloïse?" She paused. "Do you love her?"

He raised his face to meet her gaze. "Yes."

"And she loves you?"

He smiled, distantly, for the first time. "I believe she does."

"That's something at least." She stood up again. "Olivier, I won't embarrass you or the rest of our family by throwing out your guests. But if there's any trouble—even a *hint* of trouble while they're here—"

"They haven't come to cause trouble, Ella, I swear it. They're here because they care for Héloïse."

Her eyes were narrow. "And don't let me catch any one of them anywhere near Dani, or they'll be out of here so fast they won't have time to pack. Is that clear?"

"Of course."

"Then that's all." She looked up at the clock on the mantel-piece. "You'll have to excuse me, I have a great deal to do."

Olivier drank the rest of his whisky and put his hand in his jacket pocket. "I have something for you."

"Oh?"

He stood up. "I thought you or Maman might like to have this."

Ella looked down and saw a large, badly rusted key in the palm of his hand.

"It's to the door of the chapel at de Trouvère," he explained. "It hasn't been a chapel, as such, for years, and the new people agree that it should remain private. They feel we should have access whenever we wish."

Ella stared at him. "You spoke to them about it? Neither Maman nor I did; we assumed it was as lost to us as the rest of the estate."

Olivier grew stiff. "I'm not entirely insensitive, Lalla. The graveyard means something to us all, but I know the chapel has special memories for our mother."

"Why don't you give her the key yourself?"

He shook his head. "I'd rather you did it, if you don't mind."

"I don't mind. Thank you, Ollie." She took it from him, feeling its cool weight. "Maman will be grateful."

"I'm glad," he said, his voice gruff, "to bring you something besides grief."

"Something didn't ring true," Ella told Harry later.

"You said he seemed sincere."

"He did. In fact, for once in his life I'd swear he really was deeply ashamed, but of what?" She tried to remember their conversation exactly. "When I mentioned gambling, his answers came more easily. He wanted me to believe that all his problems stemmed from that, that it was money he owed these people."

"You think he was lying?"

She nodded unhappily.

"And you're scared for him, is that it?"

"I know I shouldn't be. I know by this time I should have learned to let him stew, but—"

"But you can't."

"Can you begin to understand, Harry?" she appealed to him.

"I only understand how lucky a person is to have you to love them, Ella." He paused. "Want me to try and find out what's going on?"

"I think so," she answered slowly, "but let's wait until after the wedding. They do seem to care for each other, and in spite of what her father may have done, Héloïse has been good for Ollie."

"I wonder . . ."

"What?"

"Nothing."

"What?" she insisted.

"I was just wondering whether Olivier had mentioned to his future wife or in-laws the small detail that his mother is Jewish."

A little while later, after Harry had left the room, Ella sat at her dressing table and stared into the mirror.

She had been going to tell him this evening. She'd had the call from Don Kleinman a half hour before Harry had told her about Olivier's arrival, and she'd begun to plan exactly how she would break the news, had pictured the expression on his face.

They'd longed for this baby for more than ten years.

And now the moment was soured. Ella knew that she would not—could not—tell Harry until those terrible people were safely out of the hotel, and out of their lives.

The week coasted gloriously by with scarcely a hiccup. Château Bogarde had never looked more magnificent; it pulsated with vitality, its splendor enhanced by an air of constant feverishness as its happy guests bustled from one glittering event to the next. Krisztina and Ella maintained a calm front, gnawing at their knuckles behind the scenes, hardly daring to admit to raging success, while the staff worked smoothly and vigorously, Alex Monselet in a delirium of joy as he directed each successive feast.

"Neither the Shah of Persia nor Queen Elizabeth herself can have eaten more sumptuously!" he roared in immodest ecstasy at his exhausted workers.

Sandor arrived one day late, complained to Ella endlessly about acoustics, amateurs, and the mysterious absence of his piano tuner, and then, predictably, led his orchestra in two flawless performances. The fashion galas extracted shrieks of rhapsodic delight from both sides of the catwalk erected in the small ballroom, and the security team employed to guard the resplendent

Van Cleef collection began to relax as the last day but one drew to a close.

The morning was warm and sunny, but the atmosphere frosty and highly charged, when families and wedding guests gathered in the private rose garden outside the Bogarde's house shortly before midday on the seventh.

The ceremony went off without a hitch, the bride statuesque in Emanuel silk, her son as pageboy and her daughter and Danielle as bridesmaids, looking on in awe as Olivier and Héloïse knelt to make their vows, exchanged rings, and finally kissed.

"*Merci,* Lalla, *pour tout,*" Olivier thanked Ella later, as they finished luncheon.

"*Merci, ma chère,*" Héloïse echoed politely.

"You're both very welcome," Ella said, despising her own formality and wishing, beyond words, that she could sincerely, lovingly embrace them both.

"I can't bear having that man Winzler around," Ella said to Krisztina after they had both excused themselves to continue their supervision of the evening's arrangements.

"I know just how you feel," Krisztina agreed vehemently, "but there's nothing to be done."

"Aside from everything else, I'm so terrified that any second the press will find out the kind of thugs we've just welcomed into our family."

"We have not welcomed them. We were presented with a fait accompli."

"I know that, Maman," Ella said grimly, "but somehow it doesn't help."

"*Viens, chérie.*" Her mother put an arm around her. "Let's go and look at our ballroom."

Ella threw all the switches, and the enormous room blazed as the great chandeliers bounced fantastic light against the thirty-four antique wall mirrors that surrounded them.

"It always reminds me of our old Mirror Hall, though of course this is somewhat grander." Krisztina paused. "It was the first piece of Château de Trouvère that I made my own. It was very important to me."

Ella walked over to one of the tables, picked up a crystal glass, studied it critically, found it flawless, and replaced it. "It's strange. My brother just got married, for better or worse, and now all I can think about is tonight." A feeling of raw excitement gripped her suddenly, and she turned back to face her mother. "Will it be good, do you think?"

Krisztina smiled. "I think it will be *formidable.*"

Ella took a last look around.

"It had better be."

Chapter 39

"More caviar, *chéri?*"

"God, yes . . ."

Héloïse dipped her long, scarlet-tipped fingers into the silver dish, deposited a tiny mound of beluga onto each of her erect nipples, and, lying back against large satin pillows, languidly stroked a fine line from her navel down to the fringes of her pubic hair. Olivier, already mad with excitement, bent his head over her breasts, his tongue licking at the oiled, delicious flesh, but Héloïse pushed him gently away.

"Greedy boy. I want some too, you know."

Back went her fingers into the dish and carefully, slowly, she began to anoint his penis.

"*Merde,* Héloïse!" Olivier shivered. "We have to dress for dinner. It's a quarter past seven . . ."

The new Baronne de Trouvère smiled her most lascivious smile and pulled her husband's dark head back toward her left breast.

"*Bon appetit, mon amour,*" she murmured.

"Darling, do me a favor—tie my tie."

"All right, but quickly. I have to get back over there."

Ella fixed a perfect bow and Harry kissed her carefully, mindful of her hair and makeup.

"How do I look?" he asked.

She inspected him. "Better than any man I've ever laid eyes on. Positively hunky." *And just like a brand-new Papa, if you only knew.* "How about me?" She gave a swift twirl, the sequins of her black Valentino dress shimmering in the lamplight.

Harry looked at her helplessly. "I'm not the man to ask."

"Of course you are—you have great taste."

"But all I want to do is take your clothes off."

"Sex maniac." Ella grinned, and checked her watch for the umpteenth time. "Seven twenty-five. I've got to run. Wish me luck, and for heaven's sake, hurry up!"

He patted the velvet bow on her backside.

"Break a leg, baby."

"Lin Tsung, aren't you ready yet?"

"Patience, Dani."

"I said aren't you *ready*?"

Lin Tsung appeared in the doorway of Danielle's room. "And I told you to have patience."

"Sorry, I didn't hear."

"You look beautiful, Dani." Lin Tsung looked admiringly at the wondrous spread of her red-gold curls captured by two sapphire-tipped combs that matched her softly billowing satin skirt. Danielle, a year away from her teens, was still a tomboy, but she was unarguably learning a sense of occasion.

"What about Daisy?" she said. "Doesn't she look gorgeous?"

The white Irish wolfhound bitch who had become Danielle's personal pet, had been shampooed, brushed, and combed, and her collar entwined with a lovingly fashioned chain of violets.

"I was going to make her a daisy chain, but then I thought that might be too cute. What do you think, Lin Tsung?"

"What if she has to scratch?"

"So she'll scratch. Come *on*, will you! It's half past seven and I want to see everyone arriving!"

"William, please, you have to drive faster!"

"This is as fast as I go on this road."

"But we're going to be terribly late. I should be there—we should both be there with Ella!"

"You've been with her most of the day, Kriszti." William glanced sideways at her. "You're a bundle of nerves, darling. Try and keep calm."

"We should never have gone home to change. I *knew* we'd be late!"

"Ella won't mind if we're a few minutes late."

"A few minutes? At this rate, we'll be lucky if we make it in time for dinner!"

A champagne reception was scheduled for eight, with dinner at eight-thirty. At a quarter to the hour, of the one hundred and ninety-eight guests staying in the hotel, forty-three were downstairs drinking in the two bars, four were in the anteroom outside the safe deposit waiting for their jewelery, fifteen were on the observation terrace enjoying the soft, early summer view of the valley, and another five were taking a final glimpse of the diamonds, sapphires, rubies, and emeralds in the Van Cleef exhibition. The remaining hundred and thirty-one were still upstairs in their suites and rooms, some zipping up their dresses, some having a private drink, and some, mindless of the time, taking a bath or shower or making love.

At ten minutes to eight, the four elevators were in full swing, stopping at every floor to pick up partygoers and deposit them at lobby level. The entrance hall thronged with life as guests who had ventured up the mountain just for the evening swept through the front doors and lined up at the cloakrooms to hand over their coats.

"Have you seen Maman or Papa?" Ella asked Harry as they passed each other in the salon adjacent to the ballroom.

"Not yet."

"They're late, I can't understand it," she frowned.

"Don't worry about them—you've got enough to think about."

Ella touched his arm. "Harry, will you see to Sandor, please? He's sitting in the Kaaterskill Bar, being morose."

"Why?"

"He says he feels lonely, and that he'll have no one to dance with tonight, since all the most beautiful women are married. I said I'd dance with him."

"So long as you dance with me first." Harry looked at her. "How're you doing?"

"I'm nervous as a kitten." Involuntarily, she touched her stomach.

"Butterflies?" Harry asked.

By ten minutes past eight, more than one hundred and fifty guests were already drinking champagne, while some eighty or so others, including Olivier, Héloïse's father and brother, and their friends, were still packing the bars. Sandor Janos was now thumping out jazz blues in one of the barrooms. Héloïse and her mother were still upstairs, seated at their respective dressing tables. Danielle, Lin Tsung, and Daisy were skirting around the crowds, Dani keen to observe everyone and everything, while trying to protect Daisy from being kicked. Harry was in the men's room, sponging tomato juice off his dinner jacket, and Ella was in her office, taking a transatlantic telephone call.

Still on the road between North Lake and the hotel, Krisztina was in a fever of anxiety. "Why did there have to be an accident tonight of all nights? We've never had a holdup on that road before!"

"At least we weren't in the accident," William pointed out calmly. He steered the Bentley around the final, convoluted bend. "Take a look, darling. Isn't it magnificent?"

Krisztina stared up at the château, all its lights on, gleaming softly into the pale evening sky.

"Kriszti? Are you all right?"

There was a strange tightness in her chest, but she nodded. "I'm fine. But we must get there, *now.*" She looked urgently at him. *"Please."*

William stepped on the gas.

By twenty past eight, most of the latecomers had straggled from the bars into the reception salon, and the entrance hall and main lobby were at last fairly quiet.

Howie Dillman, one of the young bellboys, fetched a dustpan and brushed up every trace of grime that had slipped into the hotel on the arrivals' shoes. Behind the concierge desk, Louis Dettlingen and his assistant, Clayton Taylor, a former Amtrak employee from Poughkeepsie, decided it might be safe for them to sit down for a few moments.

At twenty-three minutes past eight, four men and three women, wearing tuxedos and evening dresses, strolled through the front doors.

The two concierges rose.

"Good evening," Louis said.

In perfect unison, the men slid hands inside their jackets, withdrew four small Uzi submachine guns, and pointed them at Dettlingen and Taylor.

"Holy shit," whispered Howie Dillman, and dropped his dustpan and brush.

In her office, still on the phone to a regular Spanish client who wanted to ensure that his favorite suite was being held for his next visit, Ella was trying for the third time to convince him that she really had to go, when the line went dead.

"Señor Alvarez?"

She put down the receiver, faced the mirror, and checked her reflection.

The door opened.

"Yes?" She turned. "Can I help you?"

Her smile faded as she stared into the dark, deadly barrel of an automatic pistol.

"It's quite impossible. The hotel is laced with alarms; the police will be here in minutes."

"They will not be able to enter, Mrs. Bogarde. There are now twenty-two men and seven women, in addition to myself, in the building." The man, dark-haired, aged around thirty-five, and wearing horn-rimmed spectacles, spoke perfect, though accented, English. "Château Bogarde is secure."

"Secure?" Ella's face was ashen, her voice disbelieving.

He detailed their positions for her. There were, he told her, three people at the main entrance, a woman in the telephone switchboard office, and two men at every one of the hotel's eight other ground-floor exits. A man and a woman were stationed by the elevators on each floor, and three people were in the kitchen area.

"We are armed with Uzi machine guns, Kalashnikov rifles, automatic pistols, and grenades," he told her starkly, "and within a half hour, all entrances and exits on every floor will have been booby-trapped."

Ella stared at him. "What do you want? Is it the jewelery exhibit? The vault?"

His eyes, brown behind the spectacles, were unblinking. "This is not a robbery, madame."

She grew even more terrified. "So what is it?"

He looked grave, more like a doctor bearing bad news than the leader of a gang of criminals.

"For the moment, suffice it to say, Mrs. Bogarde, that your hotel has been, in effect, hijacked."

"*Hijacked?*"

"Regrettably, yes."

Her mind reeled. "Where is my daughter? She's just a child, and disabled! You have to let her go!"

"Danielle is not at risk, madame."

"How do you know her name?" Ella asked sharply.

"She is not at risk," he repeated.

"Then let me go to her!"

"Soon."

"At least tell me what you're going to do."

"You will know at the same time as everyone else, inside and outside."

"This is *my* hotel," she said, for the first time more furious than frightened. "The people within it—the guests and every member of staff—are my responsibility. Their safety is in my hands!"

"Their safety is not in question, Mrs. Bogarde." His quiet courtesy confused and alarmed Ella even more.

"How can you say that, when you've brought an arsenal into the building?"

"Provided we are allowed to fulfill our function, I give you my word that not a single innocent man, woman, or child will be harmed."

"Are you terrorists?" Ella asked, her heart pounding.

"Some will say that we are. I can say, with complete conviction, that we are not."

Ella looked directly into his eyes. "And what is your 'function'? What are you doing here?"

His weapon hand had not faltered once.

"We are going to hold a trial."

"What do you mean you can't get in!"

William was walking from the parking lot toward the hotel, having failed to find the doorman or anyone else to park the Bentley for him, when Krisztina came running, unsteady on high heels, toward him.

"I tell you I can't! The doors are locked and I can't see anyone inside!" She was frantic with worry.

"That's impossible, Kriszti."

"Well, *you* try!"

They hurried together toward the main entrance. The big front doors, which normally slid open automatically when one passed the electronic eyes, stayed firmly closed, and no amount of pushing would shift them.

"This is crazy," William said.

"I'm frightened." Krisztina's face was taut. "Something's happened."

He shook his head. "There must be a simple explanation. Perhaps there was no one in security to stay in reception for a few minutes and so they've locked the doors."

"That's ridiculous—there's always someone on duty."

William peered in through the glass, trying to see past the second set of doors. Reception looked deserted. "There's no one . . . Wait a minute, someone's coming."

"Thank heaven!"

Two men in tuxedos and a woman in a green evening dress walked toward them. William rapped on the glass to attract their attention. The three stopped just inside the inner doors and stood very still.

"Good Christ," William said in a soft, strangled voice.

"What is it?" Krisztina clutched at him.

"They've got guns."

The woman who took over the hotel switchboard, and who identified herself only as Katya, telephoned the local police station in Hunter, demanded to speak to the senior policeman on duty, and told him to listen carefully.

"A *trial*? What kind of a goddamned trial?"

Patrolman Martin Levy looked bemused, the lines around his eyes puckered in confusion. "The Sergeant says they told him they're a group of anti-Fascists dedicated to justice."

"So what are they doing hijacking a five-star joint like Château Bogarde?"

"They claim there's a bunch of Nazis staying there who no one else is ever going to punish for their crimes."

"Fanatics!" Patrolman Joe Petrelli clapped a hand to his head.

"Here in the middle of Greene County where nothing much ever happens, we get fanatics—fucking *terrorists*—hijacking our best hotel." He looked at Levy. "What did this Katya woman say they're going to do to these Nazi creeps?"

"I told you. They're going to put them on trial—a show trial, the Sergeant said she called it. She said they have thirty people up there—"

"Thirty! That's a goddamned army! How did they get them in there, for Christ's sake! I thought they had security in that place."

"They do, but I guess they weren't planning on being invaded by an army of thirty with Kalashnikovs, Uzis, and Lugers, not to mention grenades."

Petrelli whistled. "Holy Mary."

"They're setting up a sound system, and they've already set up links with WTEN 10 and WKNY. They'll keep us posted as soon as they have any more information."

"Big of them," Petrelli said drily. "So what are we doing about it? Getting a little help, I trust?"

"The Sergeant's already talking to Leeds."

The telephone on the desk rang. Levy answered it, spoke for a moment, and put it down.

"What now?" Petrelli asked.

"Seems a man and a woman just came in to report the trouble. Mr. and Mrs. Hunter—Ella Bogarde's parents. The Sergeant wants me to make them some coffee."

By ten o'clock, every guest and member of staff in the hotel had been ushered into the ballroom at gunpoint and were sitting, as ordered, either at their preordained tables or on the floor.

At a family table near the center, with two places empty, sat Ella, Harry, Danielle, Lin Tsung and Sandor Janos. At another, larger, table nearby, were Olivier, Héloïse, her family, and their five friends.

The platform, where until a few minutes earlier the dance band had sat in nervous silence, was in the process of being converted into a trial area, with makeshift stands for witnesses, defendants, and a jury.

Harry nudged Ella. "He's going to speak."

Everyone stared up at the platform, where the same man who had earlier talked to Ella was now standing at a microphone in the center of the stage.

"My name," he began, in his carefully modulated tones, "is Tadeusz." He paused. "You have all heard, by now, that our purpose here tonight is to hold a trial. Before long, you will know who is to be tried, and on what charges. Prior to that, however, since it will unquestionably be a long and unpleasant night, we wish you to have the dinner for which you have so handsomely paid."

The ballroom buzzed with confusion and speculation, and Tadeusz held up his hand for silence.

"Waiters and waitresses, please take orders for food and wine. Chef Monselet and staff, please return to your kitchen and serve us the fine meal you have so painstakingly prepared."

"The man's crazy," Olivier said to Héloïse.

She nodded, tight-lipped. "Perhaps."

Winzler looked at his son. *"Meistens Juden,"* he said quietly.

"Ich habe es schon bemerkt," Gerhard agreed.

"But not all of them," Helga Winzler said. "Over there, look, he's not a Jew, and the woman there, too—see?"

"Enough of them, though," Winzler said.

They fell silent.

The waiters passed among them, and with churning stomachs and quaking voices the guests ordered, were served, and attempted to eat.

"I can't stand much more," Ella muttered to Harry, trembling with rage and apprehension. "Seeing all these people—our *guests*, for God's sake—being put through this . . ."

"Hold on, darling," Harry said. "Keep a calm front, for Dani, if no one else."

Danielle, on his left, heard him. "I'm okay, Daddy," she said bravely. "Don't worry."

"I wish I knew where Maman and Papa were," Ella fretted.

"Not here," Harry answered grimly. "And that has to be one blessing."

"Have they really put bombs at all the doors and windows, Lin Tsung?" Danielle asked.

"I don't think so, Dani."

"Even if they have," Sandor added, "we're all safe in here."

"I wish they didn't have those big guns, Sandor."

"So do I, Dani, believe me."

The "prosecutor," a moon-faced, balding man of about forty, with an accent that might, the Bogardes decided, be Dutch, began the list of accusations.

SS Captain Franz Winzler was charged with kicking to death one Sara Graber at Birkenau concentration camp in September 1943, and ordering the deaths, by whipping, of twenty-one men, women, and children.

Peter Kalasz was charged with ordering thirty-three men, in Budapest in 1944, to be tied together in groups of three, shooting dead the middle one of each group and then throwing them into the Danube River, the two living victims unable to stay afloat because of the weight of the corpse.

Gerhard Winzler, Günther von Edrichstein, and Olivier de Trouvère were charged with conspiracy to murder Helena Freiberg, Jakob Moszkowicz, and Lucien Sagan, respectively, during the period between July 1984, and March 1985.

Danielle burst into tears.

"It's all right, Dani, don't cry." Harry tried in vain to comfort her, looking meanwhile at Ella, sitting motionless, her eyes closed. "Ella? Darling?"

"It can't be," she whispered, and then, opening her eyes, stared pleadingly at him. "Harry, he couldn't—he *couldn't.*"

"Conspiracy to murder," Harry murmured, giving Danielle his handkerchief to wipe her eyes. "What the hell does that mean?"

Lin Tsung noticed that Sandor, too, was sitting rigid and white-faced.

"Are you all right, Mr. Janos?" he asked gently.

Sandor did not answer.

In the small, bare room at the police station, Martin Levy handed William and Krisztina the list of defendants and charges. "The Sergeant asked if you'd take a look, in case any of them mean anything to you."

A moment later, Krisztina gave a low moan.

"Mrs. Hunter?"

William silenced the patrolman with a glance. Firmly, he took Krisztina's icy hand in his. "Maybe it's a mistake," he said softly.

She still stared at the piece of paper. "Do you really think so?"

It was not a question.

"What's going on now?" William asked Levy.

"They're selecting a jury, going through all the motions. Taking guests at random—or it looks that way—asking them a bunch of questions, like they do in a real court. This Tadeusz guy sounds like a lawyer."

"Some lawyer."

Tadeusz and another man, carrying an Uzi, came to the Bogardes' table and looked down at Ella.

"Mrs. Bogarde, would you please come with us."

"What for?"

"I should like to speak to you."

"Why not speak to her here?" Harry asked aggressively.

"She'll come to no harm, I assure you."

Ella touched Harry's arm. "It's all right." She rose.

Outside the ballroom, Tadeusz said: "You have been selected for the jury, madame."

Her head jerked up in disbelief. *No!*

"Yes, madame."

"Are you quite mad?"

"I don't think so."

"I will not serve on your phony jury." Ella's voice trembled, but was clear.

"I'm afraid you have no choice."

"Are you threatening me?"

"Not directly," Tadeusz replied coolly, "but I must remind you that you said that you consider yourself responsible for the safety of your staff and guests."

Ella looked at him. "Aren't you aware how much harm you're doing your people's cause?"

"By my people, do you mean the Jewish people?"

"I suppose so, yes."

"They're your people, too, Mrs. Bogarde."

"I know that perfectly well."

His eyes glinted behind his glasses. "Of the twenty-nine men and women acting with me tonight, madame, I must tell you that there are five Protestants—two of whom are German, incidentally—three Catholics, and eleven Jews. The other ten have been paid to join us and I have no idea what their religion is, or if they have any faith at all, but they were willing to help us."

"At a price."

"Everything has a price." He paused. "The price of bringing

five men to trial who would otherwise, in all likelihood, never face justice under other circumstances, may well be my own life and the lives of some of my dearest friends."

"Not to mention your hostages," Ella said bitterly.

"If they leave us to conduct the trial in peace, no innocent person will be harmed."

"How can you call this farce a trial, when the defendants won't even have a chance to defend themselves!"

"There are four qualified lawyers among us," Tadeusz replied, "who intend to see justice properly upheld."

"Lawyers?" Ella laughed harshly. "After tonight, they'll be branded common criminals, like the rest of you."

"Will you sit on our jury, Mrs. Bogarde?"

"I don't know how you can even suggest it, when you've put my brother on trial."

"Surely this is your best chance to make sure that justice is done."

"You want me to sit in judgment over my own *brother*?"

"Together with nine others."

"But if you know the law, then you must know that I'd never be allowed to sit on this jury in a real trial."

"It is appropriate for you to serve on this jury." Tadeusz paused. "It will also ensure that the media remain properly focused on the trial."

"Extra human interest," Ella said bitterly.

"Exactly."

She clutched at a straw. "If I agree, will you let my daughter leave?"

Tadeusz looked regretful. "Impossible."

"Why?"

"Because she might give the police information that could damage us." He considered for a moment. "I could, however, allow her to leave the ballroom. It would be less distressing for her, perhaps."

"With my husband?"

"She may sit in the Kaaterskill Bar with Lin Tsung."

Ella stared at him. "How long have you been watching my family? How do you know so much about us? What have we *done* to you? It can't just be because of Olivier, surely. He doesn't live with us . . ."

"Circumstances, madame."

"Circumstances?"

Tadeusz nodded. "Your brother, your beautiful château, your fame and success, your family background, these celebrations, this ball itself—"

"We suited your purpose."

"Exactly."

A colonel in the State Police arrived at the station and spoke to William and Krisztina.

"We'd like to set up a local HQ close to the hotel. Any suggestions?"

"Our daughter's house is in the grounds."

"How far away?"

"Quite a way," William answered. "It's a good ten-minutes walk, if you hurry."

"Anything closer? Not so near that Tadeusz and his friends will see us, of course."

"How about the pool house?" Krisztina suggested, grateful for something positive to think about. "It's ideal—you get a pretty good view of the château from one side, but it's shielded by trees."

"Sounds perfect," the colonel said. "Thank you, ma'am."

William rose. "We want to go with you, Colonel."

The other man hesitated. "Generally in situations like these, we don't encourage civilians near the scene—but under the circumstances, it could be useful having you around. You know the hotel building better than anyone, after all."

Krisztina stood up eagerly.

"Not you, Mrs. Hunter, thanks just the same."

"I'm coming," she said resolutely.

The colonel looked at William for support. "We don't want to expose your wife to unnecessary distress, Mr. Hunter."

"My husband is rarely at Château Bogarde, Colonel," Krisztina said, suddenly crisp. "I know every inch almost as well as my daughter does. You need me."

The colonel smiled.

"I guess we do."

Just before two in the morning, the trial began.

First in the dock was Franz Winzler.

Tadeusz's voice was strong. "Mr. Prosecutor, will you call your first witness."

The prosecutor got to his feet and spoke into a microphone. "I call Dora Graber Friedlander to the stand."

From a table in the far right-hand corner of the ballroom, a white-haired woman, elegantly dressed in black silk chiffon, rose and walked, with calm dignity, toward the platform.

"Oh, my God." Ella, now in the jury stand on the platform, stared.

"What is it?" asked the man beside her.

"The witness."

"What about her?"

"She's been here all week—she's eaten here, seen the fashion shows, watched the ballet, slept in our bed." Ella grew even paler, her fists clenched in her lap. "Even our guests are part of it."

The night wore on. Witness after witness was summoned—a man Ella knew as a dentist from Colorado, a woman guest from Vienna, the philanthropist from Chicago who'd checked in only the day before. From candle-lit tables all around the ballroom, diners confounded their companions by rising and going forward without apparent shock or protest. Trapped with the other jurors, Ella sat, increasingly staggered by the meticulousness of Tadeusz's operation. From the very moment she had made the decision to incorporate Olivier's wedding into the anniversary celebrations, she realized, each stage of their own organization must have been studied, their ranks probably infiltrated even to the extent of making reservations for the witnesses.

Dear Lord, what a fool I've been, she cursed herself, only half her mind concentrating on the appalling litany of accusation and remembrance of inconceivable, repugnant crimes against humanity.

She looked up, from time to time at the faces of the accused; Winzler, vacant, almost bemused; Kalasz, flushed with outrage and fear; Winzler's son, Gerhard, and the young aristocrat, von Edrichstein, arrogant, tiny smiles on their lips.

And Olivier . . .

For the thousandth time, Ella tried to read his mind, longed with utter desperation to believe him innocent of whatever crimes they would accuse him of. But she remembered instead his increasing instability over the years . . . the early days with Mischa, and Olivier's sadistic taunting . . . his fury against Gabor and the bizarre blood pact with Ella . . . his growing, irrational grievances against Geneviève . . . and more, so much more . . . the things she'd always done her best not to think about. . . .

Krisztina and William sat waiting in the pool house, where the bar area had been set up as a communications center linking the police from Hunter and Leeds with the SWAT team who'd been assembled to deal with the situation.

"What's happening?" William asked the two local patrolmen, who'd driven them up the mountain road.

Petrelli looked over at the sergeant, who was manning the telephones and radio. "They're still checking the perimeter. Seems the gang are all inside. We're guessing they've planted a handful of explosives at most, but since we don't know where, that doesn't help a whole hell of a lot."

"What's happening inside?" asked Krisztina nervously.

"They've just put Kalasz in the dock," Patrolman Levy said. He looked at his watch. "It's nearly five. The longer this goes on, the better for us."

"I call Sandor Miklos Janos to the stand."

"*What?*" Harry's head jerked up.

Sandor rose.

"Sandor?" Harry's voice was harsh. "Did you know?"

Sandor looked down at him. "Only since they read out the charges."

"Mr. Janos," the prosecutor repeated.

"You know Kalasz?" asked Harry.

A nerve in Sandor's temple throbbed. "No, I don't know him." He paused. "But I think he may have murdered my father and grandfather."

"This guy Tadeusz is a real humanitarian," the radio operator reported wryly to William, Krisztina, and the others at six o'clock. "The conductor just finished his testimony, and Tadeusz ordered up eggs, toast, and coffee for three hundred and fifty people."

"Do you know how *we're* doing?" asked Levy.

"They think the booby traps are a bluff."

"So we're going in?" Petrelli, who'd been suffering from boredom, stirred with new interest.

"Not yet. It's too risky."

"But if they're bluffing?"

"We think they're bluffing. Anyway, there's not much doubt they've got enough firepower to take out at least half the hostages, so don't you think perhaps we'd better be sure?"

William and Krisztina looked at each other, both aware of what the other was thinking. One part of them wanted the SWAT team to go in and end the ordeal, but the other, bigger, part was starkly, blatantly terrified of the consequences for Ella, Harry, Danielle, and all the others if they did so.

Just after seven o'clock, while many of the guests were finishing their breakfasts, amazed at how hungry they'd felt, a man three tables away from where Harry and Sandor were sitting suddenly knocked over his coffee cup and grasped his left arm, an expression of agony and terror on his face.

The woman beside him gasped and clutched at him, but the man, his skin suddenly clammy and gray, slumped back in his chair. She stared at him for one more second, and then she jumped to her feet, and began to scream: "He's having a heart attack! You *bastards*! Do you see what you've done! God help us, my husband's having a heart attack!"

The radio operator listened intently. "They've brought someone out."

"What? Who?" William and Krisztina froze.

"Don't know." He listened. "An old man, name of Chapman. Mean anything?" He looked at the Hunters, who shook their heads. "He's had some kind of heart attack, and Tadeusz let him out for treatment."

"How bad is he?" William asked, leaning toward the radio operator.

"They said he was on his feet, so it may not be too bad. They're talking to him now."

"Poor old guy." Levy was sympathetic. "He should be on his way to Memorial Hospital, not talking to the State Police."

"There are a lot of other lives at stake, Marty," Petrelli pointed out reasonably.

"Anyway," the sergeant manning the radio said, "it's proved one thing. . . . If they got out that easily, we can get in."

Chapter 40

At ten minutes past ten, almost fourteen hours since the siege had begun, the prosecutor got to his feet again. If he felt any weariness, it did not show.

"I call Olivier de Trouvère to the stand."

From the floor, Harry watched Ella intently, longing to be beside her, supporting her, giving her strength. Her eyes were on Olivier, wide and unblinking, her mouth tense, her whole body rigid.

"You are Olivier, twenty-seventh Baron de Trouvère?"

"I am."

"Monsieur le Baron, you stand accused of conspiring to murder Lucien Sagan in April 1985. How do you plead?"

Olivier stared at the prosecutor. "I did not murder Lucien Sagan," he said, his voice tight but clear.

"Do you plead guilty or not guilty to the charge?"

"I do not understand the charge."

The other man's tone hardened. "Then let me clarify it for you. Lucien Sagan was knocked down on Boulevard Saint-Marcel in Paris, on April fourteenth, 1985, by a blue Peugeot 504. You are accused of arranging the rental of this vehicle, and of providing its driver with a safe house after the murder." He paused. "Now how do you plead?"

Olivier's chin jutted. "Where is the driver? Why is *he* not in the dock?"

"I repeat, for the last time, do you plead guilty or not guilty?"

For the first time, a flicker of fear showed in Olivier's expression, though his voice remained steady.

"I do not recognize this *court*." He stressed the word disdainfully.

The prosecutor smiled. "Whether you recognize it or not, Monsieur le Baron, you are still on trial for your crime against Lucien Sagan."

While William and Krisztina pored over an architect's plan of the hotel, answering the colonel's questions, the two patrolmen and the sergeant spoke in low voices.

"Do we know *why* they murdered these people?" Petrelli asked.

"Supposedly, they're involved with a neo-Nazi revenge gang who go around disposing of people who have borne witness against their relatives or friends or heroes," the sergeant answered.

"Witnesses at the war trials, you mean?" Petrelli was incredulous. "But they were forty years ago."

"Most of them," Levy amended. "Quite a few Nazis have come to trial since then, and others are still under investigation."

"According to Tadeusz and his so-called prosecutor," the sergeant went on, "the authorities haven't wanted to accept the fact that the gang exists, because the deaths have all been disguised as accidents." He checked over the notes he'd made while listening to the evidence on his headset. "Helena Freiberg, in Mulhouse, and Lucien Sagan, in Paris, were both hit-and-run victims, and the other man, Moszkowicz, apparently threw himself under a train in Vienna." He glanced quickly over at the Hunters, to make sure they were still fully occupied with the colonel. "The claim is that Winzler the younger and de Trouvère helped set up the two French killings, while von Edrichstein took care of the one in Austria."

"Do you believe it?" Petrelli asked.

The sergeant shrugged. "I only work here."

"Marty?"

"What I think doesn't matter, Joe."

"Sure it does."

Levy sighed. "Why shouldn't it be true? People like to kid themselves there are no more Nazis." He paused, and went on grimly. "If these three *are* neo-Nazis, then sure, I think they probably did what Tadeusz says they did."

William's voice startled them. "I'd say you're forgetting one basic point in all this, gentlemen."

"What's that, Mr. Hunter?" Levy tried to avert his eyes from Krisztina's pale, increasingly strained face.

"This man, Tadeusz, may sound like a lawyer—but what he actually is, is a terrorist."

At half past eleven, while some of the hostages dozed uncomfortably at their tables and the rest sat, still listening and watching, dizzy with exhaustion, the two "defense lawyers" began their closing addresses to the jury. They were, predictably, brief, unimpressive, and unsupported by any hard evidence in their favor. Forty minutes later the prosecutor spoke, also briefly, but with all the power that the defense had lacked, his passion unequivocal, though deliberately restrained, couched beneath and within his words.

It remained for Tadeusz to sum up.

"Two of the accused, men of the *old* brigade, have already enjoyed more than forty years of liberty in luxury. If they do not come to justice today, here, it is safe to assume that they will never be brought to justice at all, for before too long, many of the witnesses who have appeared before you today will be gone forever.

"And the other three—Gerhard Winzler, Günther von Edrichstein, and Olivier de Trouvère—will surely never be accused in the accredited courts of any land, for their victims have not even been acknowledged as *being* victims."

Tadeusz regarded the jury.

"This is your chance—if you find any or all of the accused guilty —your special, historic opportunity, on behalf of millions of victims. And it is not just the Jewish victims, but *all* the victims of Nazism, for even in this small trial, neither Lucien Sagan nor five of Peter Kalasz's alleged victims were Jews."

He removed his glasses, wiped them with a large handkerchief, and replaced them on the bridge of his nose.

"This is your chance," he repeated, "*if* you decide that guilt has been proven, to strike what may be the last possible blow against monsters who have, directly or indirectly, been responsible for the collective slaughter of fifty-eight men, women, and children."

He paused again.

"Ladies and gentlemen of the jury, would you please retire and consider your verdicts."

Ella stared down from the platform and across the ballroom at Harry and Sandor.

Harry was looking directly at her.

Wondering what I'm going to do, she thought.

She smiled bleakly at him and transferred her gaze to Olivier, who sat stiffly, his face bleached of all color.

My brother.

Ella shuddered.

"How long have they been out?" Krisztina asked William.

"Three hours." He looked at the radio operator. "Any news on your action?"

"Still getting ready, sir."

"What the fuck are they waiting for?" hissed Petrelli, the atmosphere making him edgier than the other men.

"For the verdicts," the sergeant replied.

"Why?" asked Krisztina fearfully.

"Because when the verdicts are in, ma'am, there's a pretty fair chance they'll all be in the same room at the same time."

"But they *are* going in?" William said.

"Oh, they'll go in, all right."

Tadeusz came into the library to see the jury.

"You're taking too long."

Ella looked up angrily. "We didn't know there was a time limit."

"Common sense decrees there must be, madame."

"How so?"

His expression was grim. "Please come outside."

"What for?"

"I wish to speak to you."

"Speak to me here."

"Outside." It was a command.

Ella looked at the other weary jurors, all strained almost beyond endurance, and got up.

In the corridor, Tadeusz grew even sterner. "I'm relying upon you, Mrs. Bogarde, to bring this to an end as quickly as possible."

"Then you're relying on the wrong person."

"You're forgetting your responsibilities again, madame."

"Not for a moment," Ella said bitterly.

"Then you must realize, surely, that the longer it goes on, the greater the likelihood that the police, or the military, will lose patience and come busting in."

"I'm depending on it."

"At which point," Tadeusz said sharply, "any number of your family, friends, and guests may be injured."

"Do you really care?"

"I do."

"Then stop now, and let them go."

"I can't do that."

Ella grew softer. "Surely you've proved your point? Isn't it enough?"

"I wish it were."

"But you intend to see it through to the end."

"I have no choice, Mrs. Bogarde."

"And what then?" she asked tentatively.

"That depends upon the verdicts."

"Do you really believe you can squeeze true verdicts out of people you've bludgeoned into being here?" Ella tried to reason with him. "Even if they wanted to cooperate, they're too tired and confused. They can't think straight."

"Then you must help them."

"How?"

"By coming to an honest verdict yourself. You represent leadership in that room—they'll follow you, believe me."

Ella was beginning to feel faint from tension and lack of sleep, and for the first time she wondered anxiously if the baby might be adversely affected. She put out a hand against the wall to steady herself.

"Mrs. Bogarde, are you all right?"

She swallowed down the nausea that had gripped her, and looked at him defiantly. "You'll never get a verdict from me, Tadeusz. I won't pass judgment on my brother or anyone else in your kangaroo court."

Tadeusz's eyes narrowed. "You will have to, sooner or later. I would prefer the former, for reasons I've already made clear."

"And I've made myself clear too."

His face grew stony. "I should prefer not to resort to threats, Mrs. Bogarde."

"What kind of threats?"

"The kind I have avoided making since this began." He waited an instant. "A verdict for a life."

Shock flickered in Ella's eyes.

Tadeusz went on. "For each judgment that this jury is unable to bring in, one hostage will be shot."

"I don't believe you," Ella whispered.

He smiled wryly. "If you had met me before last night, madame, I fancy you would not have believed that I would take hostages in the first place."

For another, long moment, Ella stared at him. Then she said softly: "I'll go and tell them."

"Thank you."

"Please," she said savagely, "don't thank me."

Tadeusz opened the library door for her. "Majority verdicts will be sufficient, Mrs. Bogarde."

Ella went inside.

Harry and Sandor walked, under guard, to the men's room.

"I wonder how she's standing it," Harry said, under his breath.

"She's a strong woman," Sandor muttered.

"It's been over four hours." Harry was distraught. "I don't think Tadeusz will let it go on much longer. He needs to finish it fast."

"And how do you suppose he plans to do that?" Sandor asked.

"I don't know the other jurors, but I'm sure Ella won't give him what he wants."

"Unless he makes it impossible for her to do otherwise."

They splashed their faces with cold water. At the door, their armed guard shifted from foot to foot.

Sandor glanced at Harry. "If the verdicts, rigged or not, are guilty, what do you think they'll do?"

"Shoot the bastards, I guess."

Sandor nodded. "And her brother?"

Harry was poker-faced. "Well, they sure as hell won't be sending him to jail."

At five o'clock, a woman carrying an Uzi entered the library and tossed ten pieces of paper down onto the table before Ella.

"Ballot papers," she said. "You are to complete them. Write the name of each defendant, and beside it, guilty or not guilty."

"It's too soon," Ella said.

"Tadeusz says it's enough time. Complete them."

Within ten minutes of the papers being collected, Tadeusz himself returned and again summoned Ella out into the corridor.

"Yours, I presume?" He threw a single ballot paper at her. *"Mistrial."*

She began to perspire. "Mine."

"You were the only one, Mrs. Bogarde."

"I advised the others of your threat," she said, with false bravura. "You said that I represented leadership—a leader may still choose her own way."

"You will all complete them again."

"Didn't you get your majority?"

"Do them *again!*"

Ella sensed that he was close to striking her. Her fingernails gouged into the palms of her hands. "I will not bow to an illegal court."

"Then we shall shoot our first hostage." He began to turn away. *"No!"*

Tadeusz turned back, and placed ten fresh sheets in her hand. "Again."

"Lin Tsung, what's happening?" Danielle, waking from a fitful doze, sat up fretfully. "Isn't it over yet? When can I see Mommy and Daddy?"

Lin Tsung, red-eyed with fatigue and the strain of remaining calm for Danielle's sake, shook his head. "I don't know, Dani. We must be patient a little longer, I'm afraid."

The wolfhound bitch whined, and Danielle fondled her ears. "Daisy needs to go out. She hates peeing inside."

"We all have to stay here, Daisy too. Try and get some more sleep."

"I'm not tired." She looked exhausted. "What are they going to do to Uncle Olivier?"

"Probably nothing."

"They think he killed those people."

"They are criminals, Dani," Lin Tsung said quietly, mindful of the guard outside the door of the bar. "And I'm sure that the police will be here soon to release us all, including your uncle."

Danielle's eyes were scared.

"I think they'll shoot him," she said.

Tadeusz slapped down the ballot paper wearily. *"Not guilty by mistrial."* He smiled ironically. "At least she changed the wording, if nothing else."

"What do we do?" asked the prosecutor. "Shoot one of them?"

Tadeusz scratched his short dark hair. "No."

"What then?"

"We have majorities. I wanted Ella Bogarde's verdict, but we'll get nowhere with her unless we shoot innocent people." Tadeusz rose and spoke to the woman near him. "Get the jury back into the ballroom."

"They're back!"

In the pool house, the three policemen sat up straight and Krisztina and William stopped pacing.

"Are we going in?" asked Levy.

"I don't know," the sergeant answered. "I guess we're waiting for the verdicts."

Krisztina sank back down onto her chair, suddenly unable to stand. Silently, William sat beside her and took her hand.

Tadeusz spoke loudly into the microphone, waking all those who had managed to fall asleep.

"I shall now read you the verdicts of the jury in the cases of all five defendants."

Harry looked up at Ella and willed her to be strong.

"In the case of Franz Ludwig Winzler, the jury has found him guilty as charged."

Héloïse gasped, her mother began to weep, and up on the platform, in the dock, Winzler's son gave a low moan.

Tadeusz continued relentlessly.

"In the case of Peter Bodog Kalasz, the jury finds him guilty as charged."

Kalasz, his small blue eyes burning with hatred, glared down from the dock at Sandor Janos.

"In the case of Gerhard Winzler . . ."

". . . guilty."

The sergeant, headset over his ears, continued his stark report as Krisztina sat, frozen with fear, her hand still numbly clasped in William's.

"Günther von Edrichstein—guilty." The sergeant paused, his face inscrutable.

"Sergeant." William's voice jarred the silence. "Tell us, please."

"Olivier de Trouvère—guilty."

Krisztina did not flinch. William put his arm around her.

"They got what they wanted," Levy said somberly.

"Think that's all they want?" Petrelli asked.

"Quiet." The sergeant held up his hand. "Tadeusz is about to pass sentence."

"*That's* what they want," Petrelli said cynically.

The sergeant hunched over the radio. Several more seconds passed.

"Well?" Petrelli couldn't stand it.

He looked up, his face disbelieving.

"Death," he said. "By hanging."

"I want to talk to my brother." Ella left the jury box, heedless of the guards, and faced Tadeusz.

"There's no time."

"*Make* time. It's human decency."

"You're in no position to give orders, madame."

She looked into his eyes. "Please," she said softly.

He relented. "A few moments."

Involuntarily, Ella glanced toward the windows.

Tadeusz nodded. "They won't wait much longer."

"You won't really hang them, will you?"

His face was implacable. "We'll hang the SS man if it's the last thing we do," he said quietly. "And Kalasz, too, if we get the chance."

Ella hardly dared to breathe. "And my brother?"

"If there's time."

She stared at him, aware suddenly, chillingly, that she was looking at a man who believed that he was, in all probability, soon going to die.

"Thank you," she said.

"We will hang him, if we can. Your brother is guilty, madame."

Ella's cheeks were hot, the beautiful Valentino dress felt like a dead weight, dragging her down.

"Go," Tadeusz said. "Speak to him, quickly."

"May we be alone?"

"I'm sorry."

"Ollie?"

He sat, flanked by his co-defendants who slumped, numb and disbelieving.

"Ella."

She reached up to the dock, fabricated out of the dance band's deserted brass section, and took his hand. His skin was cold and clammy, and she sensed his silent terror.

"Ollie, try not to be afraid. Help is coming."

His mouth twitched. "Help."

"It's Héloïse's father they really want, and the Hungarian. With luck, it may be over before—"

"My turn?"

She looked up at him. Every trace of condemnation in her vanished and only pity remained.

"They'll hang me," Olivier said, his voice unnatural and flat. "They killed my father, and now they'll hang me."

"Ollie, your father committed suicide."

He shook his head. "Forced into it. As good as murder." He smiled slightly. "The fate of the last two Barons de Trouvère to end their days at the mercy of thugs."

Ella said nothing.

"Ella?"

"Yes?"

"Don't you want to know if it's true? What they accused me of?"

"Only if you want to tell me."

"It is true," he said dully. "I didn't want to do it, but I owed it to them."

"Oh, Ollie." Her eyes were full of tears. "I want so much to help you, but—"

"But you can't save my life." He paused, and then said, distantly: "Knights and Ladies."

"What?"

"Our game. Don't you remember?"

Mischa, in the river, flashed before her eyes.

"I remember."

Olivier's hand, limp in hers, came briefly to life, grasping her tightly. "I always wanted to be the one to save *you*, Lalla," he whispered, chokingly.

With her spare hand, stretching painfully, Ella stroked her half brother's cheek.

"I know you did," she said.

The ballroom was a hub of activity. From various doors, with deadly efficiency, men came with thick ropes, nooses already tied. Five ropes. Two large tables were cleared, one placed on top of the other, and a ladder brought from the hotel stores.

"The scaffold," murmured Sandor.

The first rope was tied to the massive central chandelier, the tables dragged beneath.

"The gallows," Harry said softly.

Every muscle in his body ached. He turned his head to look at where the jury were still being held, bunched together, facing the condemned men.

"Where the *hell* are the police?"

The sergeant slammed his fist hard against the pool house wall. "All *right!*"

"What?" said Levy.

"*What?*" shouted Petrelli.

"We're going in!"

"Now?" said William.

"*Now!*"

Krisztina began to pray.

In the ballroom, three hundred and fifty people watched with incredulous horror as former SS Captain Franz Winzler was removed forcibly from the dock, and pushed to the scaffold by four of Tadeusz's men.

"Climb up," Tadeusz ordered.

Winzler's face was purple with rage and terror. "*Niemals! Ihr Gottverfluchten* Verbrecher!"

"Get him up!"

"*Nein!*" Helga Winzler screamed while Héloïse covered her face, sobbing.

"They're going to do it," Harry breathed. "They're really going to do it!"

Winzler stood on the tabletop, hands tied behind his back, trembling violently.

"*Herrgott, rette mich, rette mich.*" His lips moved in frantic prayer as the noose, heavy and cumbersome, was looped over his head.

Below him, three men stood, hands flat against the tables legs, ready to send the scaffold flying from under him the instant Tadeusz gave the signal.

Tadeusz stared up at the aging Nazi, and felt not a trace of pity. He raised his right arm.

"*For Sara Graber and all the others.*" His voice, sonorous and spellbinding, echoed through the ballroom.

And then he brought his arm down.

They exploded, like a dark, annihilating streak, from every door, every window. Their own faces masked, armed with shotguns, sniper rifles, and .357 Magnums, they fired a cloud of tear gas and then, using the gang's own weapons as badges of identification, began firing.

"Lin Tsung! What's happening?!"

In the Kaaterskill Bar, Danielle, Lin Tsung, and Daisy all leapt to their feet, shocked by the immense clamor.

"What is it!"

"It must be the police," Lin Tsung said.

"Oh, my God, they're *killing* everyone!" Danielle put her hands up to her ears and began to sob in terror.

"No, Dani, I'm sure—"

She ran to the door and saw that their guard had gone.

"He's not there!" she cried. "We can go!" She opened the door.

"*No,* Dani!"

Lin Tsung ran to stop her, but the dog and the girl were too fast for him, bolting from the bar and tearing down the hall toward the ballroom.

"Ella! For God's sake, where *is* she?"

Harry scanned the turmoil, searching frantically for his wife. All around, people were throwing themselves down in a desperate attempt to escape the bullets and fragments of glass and wood that were flying through the air.

In the center of the room, Helga Winzler sat rigid with horror, riveted by the sight of her husband's body hanging limply from the chandelier, while Héloïse de Trouvère screamed hysterically for someone to cut him down.

Eyes searing, throat burning from the tear gas, Harry shouldered a path toward the platform, still hunting for Ella. He saw, instead, Danielle standing just inside the entrance, one hand on Daisy's collar, the other clamped over her good ear, her face glazed with bewilderment and fear, as Lin Tsung came running behind her.

"Dani!" Harry yelled. "Get out of here!"

One of the SWAT men, weaving through the mayhem, shoved him roughly down onto the dance floor. Momentarily disorientated, Harry rose again, and saw that Sandor, too, had spotted Danielle and was hurrying toward her.

Peter Kalasz, freed from the dock, saw Janos. He spun around, seizing a Luger dropped by an injured member of Tadeusz's gang. His face contorted with hatred, he raised the gun and took aim—

"No!"

Ella, coming from behind, saw Danielle in firing range, and flung herself at the Nyila murderer, fighting vainly to wrest the pistol from his hands. Kalasz bellowed and grabbed her, his left arm slamming around her throat, choking off her breath.

"Mommy!"

The gun went off, and Daisy, struck on her right side, dropped to the floor. Danielle sobbed piteously, her face buried in the animal's bloodied white fur, while Lin Tsung tried to cover them both with his body.

"You dirty bastard!"

Enraged, Harry lunged at Kalasz, who swung at his temple with the Luger's butt, stunning him. Ella, half fainting from the pressure on her throat, slumped in Kalasz's arms as he pointed the pistol directly at her head.

The police stopped shooting.

All eyes turned to the small, dramatic tableau near the main doors.

"Let her go," Sandor said quietly. "Nem."

"It's *me* you want, Kalasz. I gave evidence against you, not Mrs. Bogarde."

"She sat on the jury that found me guilty!"

Harry, his head still spinning from the blow, staggered to his feet. "There *was* no trial," he said groggily. "You've been found guilty of nothing. Let her go, and you're as free as you were when you walked into this ballroom."

Kalasz spat. "Don't take me for a fool, Bogarde."

Sandor tried again. "There are at least fifty weapons pointing at you right now, Kalasz."

"If they shoot me, she'll die too."

No one moved.

On the floor, Danielle whimpered.

Kalasz's eyes darted around, and he pulled Ella upright against him, so that she formed a human shield.

"I'm going to leave now," he said. "And if anyone tries to stop me"—he raised his voice threateningly—"as God is my witness, I will kill her."

The sounds of quiet sobbing and moaning and anxious, hushed whispering filled the ballroom.

Olivier crouched behind a table in the middle of the room.

Time had gone back nearly thirty years.

The tables and chairs, the carnage, the SWAT men, and all the people had disappeared, and he was back in the undergrowth near the river at de Trouvère.

The Enemy had his Lady.

The Uzi submachine gun lay on the floor.

His eyes were narrow and burning, the flabbiness of his forty-one years contracted into the leanness of his boyhood. His brain was cool and clear, and his heart pounded. His target stood with his back to him, holding her.

He steeled himself.

I am an athlete—I am a tiger—I am a great White Knight—

"Let her go!"

The roar cut through the air like a scimitar, as Olivier hurtled forward, seized up the gun, and took aim.

"No!" Harry launched himself at Kalasz and grabbed Ella, tore at flesh and hair and wrenched her away and threw her down.

The brief, deafening fusillade of bullets ripped apart Kalasz's skull and neck and shoulders, and pierced mirrors and crystal and Harry's left arm . . .

And Lin Tsung's chest.

Olivier stopped shooting.

He saw Kalasz's raw, gaping body, and saw Ella, alive and watching him, her eyes astounded and shocked and wonderful.

And he felt, rather than saw, the men beginning to move, encircling him, trapping him.

And he raised the gun once more, and turned it around, so that its monstrous round black eye stared into his own.

And Olivier squeezed the trigger.

And the eye exploded.

It was impossible, he thought, that he was still alive.

He felt nothing at all, the agony all dissipated in a strange, whirling red cloud that encased his head and made him dizzy.

"Ollie . . ."

He opened his eyes, and there was Ella, tears streaming down her cheeks and her mouth stretched in pain.

"Don't cry, Lalla," he tried to say. "Not for me." He wanted to console her, to stop her weeping. "It's better for me this way, Lalla. You never knew it, but I've done such terrible, wicked things . . ."

But he knew that Ella did not hear him. And he closed his eyes again and saw, through the mist, the old faces of his nightmares . . . Mischa and Geneviève and the pilot . . .

And the red fog grew denser, and darker, closing in on him, suffocating him, and Olivier knew for certain that he was dying, after all, that maybe, already, he no longer existed. . . .

And it occurred to him at that moment that, perhaps, he was descending into hell.

At one in the morning, five hours after the siege had ended, after the dead and injured had been removed and taken away to morgues and hospitals, Patrolmen Levy and Petrelli walked slowly through the ruined ballroom, while a BCI team of detectives went about their grisly business of cleaning up.

"I've never been in here before," Petrelli said, "but they say this room was gorgeous—better even than anything in New York City."

"Not anymore," Levy said.

Petrelli whistled. "Will you look at that!"

They stared at the shattered remains of the great central chandelier, most of which had crashed to the floor when the SS man had been cut down.

"I guess he got his, all right," Levy said.

Petrelli shook his head. "I still don't know what that guy Tadeusz achieved. He's on a slab, along with most of his buddies."

"He knew what would happen."

"Think so, Marty?"

Levy nodded silently.

"I don't know," Petrelli mused. "Three dead Nazis, and a whole bunch of dead or injured, terrified people who'll probably have bad dreams the rest of their lives."

Levy shrugged. "Justice?"

"Think so?" Petrelli asked again.

Levy looked solemn.

"I think so."

Pine Orchard, New York
June 11, 1986

They came to find her—her mother and father, Danielle, and Harry, his arm in a sling.

Her family. All but one.

Ella got to her feet. "Maman, you shouldn't be out—you're supposed to be resting."

The dogs skittered around, and Krisztina smiled. "I'm all right, *chérie.*"

William kept his arm tucked firmly through his wife's. "She wouldn't rest, darling, not until we'd found you."

Harry was staring at the great wrought-iron gates. "You closed them."

Ella nodded.

"Why?"

"Because we're closed," she answered simply.

"For how long?"

"I don't know."

"We could stay open," Harry said quietly. "The only real damage is to the ballroom."

"No," she said.

"No?" Krisztina looked at her searchingly.

Ella's eyes were still sore from gas and weeping. "It's a battle-field, Maman, not a hotel."

Danielle, pale and emotional from the ordeal of Lin Tsung's funeral the previous day, following so hard on the heels of a nightmare she would never forget, came forward and took Ella's hand. "Daisy's going to be all right, Mommy," she said softly. "They called just a while ago from the animal hospital and told us. She'll maybe always have a limp, but she's going to make it."

Ella bent and hugged her. "That's very good news, Dani."

The child continued in the same hushed, strained voice. "Daddy says that Uncle Olivier couldn't help shooting him and Lin Tsung." Her mouth quivered a little. "He says that Uncle Olivier was a hero because he saved your life."

"Does he?" Ella bit her lip and looked at Harry.

Danielle tugged at her. "Mommy, how long does the hotel have to stay shut?"

"I don't know," Ella said again.

"The ballroom doesn't look so bad now. Louis and Howie and the others have been cleaning it, and almost all the—" She stopped abruptly, flushed.

"It's okay, Dani," Harry said gently.

They were all silent for a moment.

"Daddy, do I have to go back to school tomorrow?"

"No, honey. Not till after your uncle's funeral."

"When's that?"

"Soon."

There was another pause.

Slowly, Ella's right hand moved to her stomach and rested there. *Life and death,* she thought. *New life.*

She took a deep breath of mountain air, and fixed her eyes on her husband's face.

"Harry," she said. "I have something to tell you."

A week later, Ella and Krisztina stood among the graves, after the others had left.

Eight Barons de Trouvère buried there.

"There'll never be a ninth," Ella said.

From the far side of the stone wall came the joyful sound of laughter, of children at play.

"At least the place is still alive," Krisztina said softly, gratefully. "It was kind of them to let us keep the graveyard."

"And the chapel."

Krisztina nodded.

"Do you have the key, Maman?"

"Of course." She felt it, heavy in her pocket.

"Shall we go inside?"

"Later, perhaps." Krisztina sat down, slowly, on the old wooden bench near Geneviève's headstone. "This afternoon is for being outside, in the fresh air."

"With the living," Ella said quietly, sitting beside her.

They were silent for a while, with the droning of bees and the heavy scents of climbing roses and freshly dug soil.

"What will you do?" Krisztina asked at last.

"Do?"

"About Château Bogarde."

Ella could not speak.

Krisztina took her hand. "It has a life of its own, just as de Trouvère has."

"De Trouvère's survived without us, Maman."

"But that's the past, *dragam*. Château Bogarde is the future."

"I know," Ella whispered, her eyes bright.

"So will you let it live again, for Dani and the baby, if not for yourself?"

A breeze stirred the branches of the old silver birch in the corner of the graveyard.

Ella closed her eyes, and took a long, sweet breath, drew it deeply into her lungs.

"Perhaps," she said. "In time."